ROWAN OF RIN

THE JOURNEY

Also by Emily Rodda

Something Special

Pigs Might Fly

The Best-kept Secret

Crumbs!

Finders Keepers

The Timekeeper

Bob the Builder and the Elves

Dog Tales

Raven Hill Mysteries *(series)*

Deltora Quest *(series)*

ROWAN OF RIN

THE JOURNEY

Emily Rodda

An Omnibus Book from SCHOLASTIC Australia

Omnibus Books
335 Unley Road, Malvern, SA 5061
an imprint of Scholastic Australia Pty Ltd (ABN 11 000 614 577)
PO Box 579, Gosford NSW 2250.
www.scholastic.com.au

Part of the Scholastic Group
Sydney · Auckland · New York · Toronto · London · Mexico City ·
New Delhi · Hong Kong · Buenos Aires · Puerto Rico

First published in this edition in 2004.
Reprinted in 2004.
Text copyright © Emily Rodda, 1993, 1994, 1996, 1999, 2003.
Maps copyright © Omnibus Books, 2003
Jacket artwork copyright © Matt Wilson, 2003,
reproduced with the permission of Greenwillow Books,
an imprint of HarperCollins Publishers, New York, USA.

National Library of Australia Cataloguing-in-Publication entry
Rodda, Emily, 1948–   .
Rowan of Rin: the journey.
ISBN 1 86291 474 5.
1. Rowan (Fictitious character: Rodda)—Juvenile fiction.
2. Dragons—Juvenile fiction. 3. Riddles—Juvenile fiction.
4. Courage—Juvenile fiction. I. Title.
A823.3

Typeset in 13/15.5 pt Garamond by Clinton Ellicott, Adelaide.
Printed and bound by Thomson Press (India) Ltd.

10 9 8 7 6 5 4 3 2   4 5 6 7 8 9 / 0

CONTENTS

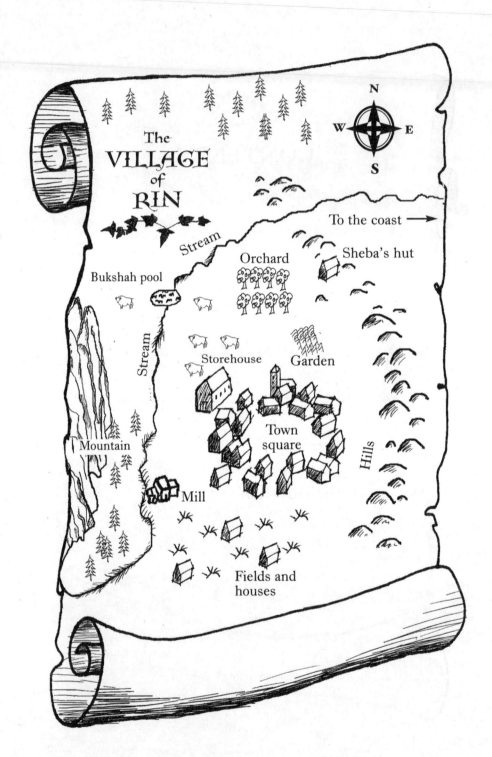

The
VILLAGE
of
RIN

To the coast →

Stream

Orchard

Sheba's hut

Bukshah pool

Stream

Storehouse

Garden

Mountain

Town
square

Hills

Mill

Fields and
houses

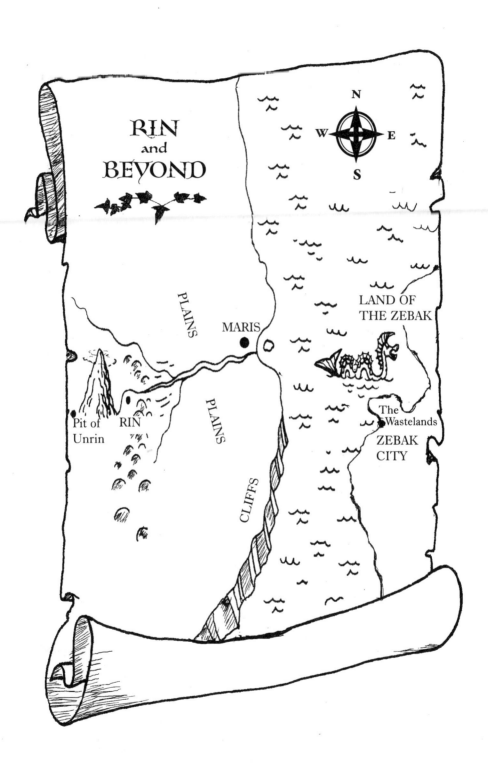

ROWAN OF RIN

1 – The Meeting

One morning the people of Rin woke to find that the stream that flowed down the Mountain and through their village had slowed to a trickle. By nightfall even that small flow had stopped. The mill wheel lay idle. There was no water to turn its heavy blades. The bukshah drinking pool on the other side of the village was still. No bubbling stream was stirring it into life and keeping it topped up to the brim.

There was no change on the second day, or the third. By the fourth day the water in the pool was thick and brown. The bukshah shook their heavy heads and pawed the ground when they went to drink in the morning and the evening.

After five days the pool was so shallow that even little Annad, who was only five years old, could touch the bottom with her hand without getting her sleeve wet. And still the stream failed to flow.

On the evening of the sixth day the worried people met in the market square to talk. "The bukshah could not drink at all today," said Lann, the oldest person in the village, and once the greatest fighter. "If we do not act soon, they will die."

"Not Star," whispered Annad to her brother, who was the keeper of the bukshah. "Star will not die, though, will she, Rowan? Because you will give Star water from our well."

"Bukshah cannot drink from our well, Annad," said Rowan. "It is not sweet enough for them. It makes them ill. They can only drink the water that flows down from the Mountain. It has always been so. If the stream stays dry, Star will die like all the rest."

Annad began to sob quietly. The children of Rin were not supposed to cry, but Annad was very young, and she loved Star. Rowan stared straight ahead. His eyes were tearless, but his chest and throat ached with sadness and fear. The sadness was for Star, his

friend and the strongest and gentlest of all the bukshah. And for all
the other great, humped woolly beasts, each of which he knew by
name. But the fear was for himself. For himself and Annad and their
mother, and indeed for the whole village.

Rowan knew, as Annad did not, that without the bukshah there
would be no rich creamy milk to drink, no cheese, curd and butter to
eat. There would be no thick grey wool for cloth. There would be
no help to plough the fields, or carry in the harvest. There would
be no broad backs to bear the burdens on the long journeys down
to the coast to trade with the clever, silent Maris folk. The life of Rin
depended on the bukshah. Without them, the village too would die.

Annad could not imagine the valley without the village. But
Rowan could. Reading the old stories in the house of books, listening
half-asleep to Timon under the Teaching Tree, and, most of all,
sitting on the grass by the stream while the bukshah grazed around
him in the silence of the morning, he had often imagined this place
as the first settlers must have seen it.

Hundreds of years ago they had climbed through the hills, carrying
the few things they owned on their backs, looking for somewhere in
this strange land that they could claim as their own. They had come
from far away, across the sea. They had fought a terrible enemy. On
the coast they had heard, from the wandering native people they called
the Travellers, of a place at the bottom of a forbidden mountain in the
high country far inland. They had been tramping for many, many
days in search of it. They were very tired. Some had almost given up
hope. Then, one afternoon, they had topped a rise, and looked down.
There below them, nestled between a towering mountain ahead and
the hill on which they stood, was a green, secret valley.

The people stared, speechless. They saw trees loaded with small
blue fruits, and fields of flowers they did not recognise. They saw
a stream, and a pool, and a herd of strange grey beasts lifting their
heads to stare, horns shining in the sun. They saw silence, stillness,
and rich earth, and peace. The people knew then that this was the
place. This would be their home. So they came down and mingled
with the big, gentle animals, who were tame and unafraid. They
called them the bukshah.

"The stream flows down from the Mountain," said Bronden, the furniture-maker, her loud voice breaking into Rowan's thoughts. He watched her stab the air with her stubby finger, pointing. "So the problem must be up there. Up there, something is amiss. Something is stopping the flow."

All eyes turned to the Mountain rising high above the village, its tip shrouded as always in cloud.

"We must climb the Mountain and find out what it is," Bronden went on. "This is our only chance."

"No!" Neel the potter shook his head. "We cannot climb the Mountain. Even the Travellers do not venture there. Terrible dangers await anyone who dares. And at the top—the Dragon."

Bronden sneered at him. "You are talking like a crazy Traveller yourself, Neel! There is no Dragon. The Dragon is a story told to children to make them behave. If there was a Dragon we would have seen it. It would prey on the bukshah—and on us."

"Perhaps it takes its prey elsewhere. We do not know, Bronden." Allun the baker's light, pleasant voice rose above the muttering of the crowd. "But if you will excuse me for talking like a crazy Traveller—remembering that my father was one, and it is only to be expected—let me remind you of what we do know." His usually smiling face was grim as he stared Bronden down. "We do know that we hear it roar almost every morning and every night. And that we see its fire in the cloud."

Bronden rolled her eyes disdainfully, but Rowan shivered. Tending the bukshah in the cold and dark of winter mornings, and in the evenings when the sun had slipped behind the Mountain, he had heard the sound of the Dragon. He had seen its fire too, in the sky above the cloud. The bukshah swayed and grew restless at these times. The calves bellowed, and the bigger beasts pawed the ground, flared their nostrils and huddled together in fear. Even Star moaned when the Dragon roared, and when he stroked her neck to calm her, he would feel the nerves jumping under her long, soft wool.

Suddenly he realised something. Something no one else seemed to have thought of. He must speak. Nervously he rose to his feet.

The villagers stared curiously at him. What could the boy Rowan, the shy, timid herder of the bukshah, have to say?

"The Dragon has not roared since the stream dried up," said Rowan. "Not in the mornings, and not at night." He spoke as loudly as he could, but his voice sounded small in the silence. He sank back to his place.

"Is this so?" Allun looked around the circle. "Is the boy mistaken?"

"No, he is not," said Bronden slowly. "I recall it now. Indeed, there has been no sound from the Mountain for days." She lifted her head. "So I am right. There is something amiss, high above us. I have told you what we must do."

"But we cannot do it," insisted Neel, with dread. "The Mountain is too steep, too dangerous. We cannot climb it."

"Has anyone ever tried?" enquired Allun.

"Yes!" said tall, straight-backed Marlie, the weaver and dyer of cloth. "In times gone by, some people *did* climb the Mountain, to look for new fruits to plant in our orchard. But they never returned. After that, the people of Rin heeded the warning, and left the Mountain alone."

"You see?" Neel burst out. "You see? If we climb the Mountain, we will die."

"But Neel," boomed Bronden. "If we do *not* climb the Mountain, we will die."

"Bronden is right. We must make our choice," said Strong Jonn, who was the keeper of the orchard. "We remain here and hope the stream begins running again of its own accord, or we climb the Mountain and try to remove whatever is stopping the water from flowing down to us. Both ways are dangerous. What is our decision? To go, or to stay?"

"We must go," Marlie replied. "We cannot simply stand by and let death slowly come to our village. I vote to go."

"And I," shouted Bronden.

"I vote yes!" said Strong Jonn.

"I too," added Allun lightly.

"Yes! We agree!" growled mighty Val the miller, who had stood silently listening in the shadows, shoulder to shoulder as always with Ellis, her twin brother. Val and Ellis toiled together in the mill, grinding the grain into flour, endlessly cleaning the great stone building so that not a speck of dirt or the tiniest spiderweb could be seen within its walls. Jiller, Rowan's mother, said that since childhood no one had ever seen them apart.

"Yes!" "Yes!" "Yes!" One by one the villagers stood up. Rowan looked around at the familiar faces, now so serious and so stern. Maise, the keeper of the books, was standing, with her son and daughter. So were Timon the teacher, and Bree and Hanna from the gardens. White-haired Lann leaned on her stick beside them. And even fat, soft Solla, who made sweet toffees and cakes and never could resist his own cooking, had struggled to his feet. Then Rowan saw Jiller rise slowly and join them. His heart thudding with fear, he scrambled to his feet beside her.

Soon Neel the potter and four others were the only ones still seated.

"So it is decided," cried Bronden triumphantly. "We will arm ourselves and set out at dawn."

"Wait!" said Marlie. "We must not go without consulting Sheba."

"That mad old hag? That spinner of children's nightmares and curer of pains in the belly? What has she got to do with this?"

"Sheba is old, Bronden, but she is not mad," said Marlie firmly. "As anyone who has been cured of illness by her remedies will tell you. Sheba knows more than herbs and spells. She understands the Mountain as you and I never will. Sheba knows the way up the Mountain. The secret way she was taught by the Wise Woman before her. We must ask Sheba to help us."

"This is a good idea," agreed Strong Jonn.

The people murmured. Many did not trust the Wise Woman, Sheba. She lived alone beyond the orchard, gathering herbs and other growing things and selling the medicines, ointments and dyes she made from them. She rarely spoke to anyone other than those with whom she traded. And when she did it was seldom pleasant. The children of Rin were a hardy crew, like all of their race. But they were afraid of Sheba, and called her not Wise Woman but Witch.

"Oh, come! What harm can it do?" called Allun, grinning. "If the old one can tell us anything, which I doubt, then all the better. If she cannot, we have lost nothing."

"Travellers' foolishness!" snapped Bronden. "This is not a game, Allun the Baker. Why don't you ...?"

"Enough!" cried old Lann. She glanced at Bronden, who scowled. "We are going into the unknown," she said sternly. "And time is precious. We cannot afford to miss a chance to speed our way. Who knows Sheba best?"

"I know her," said Strong Jonn. "She gathers a herb that grows under the hoopberry trees in the orchard."

"I trade with her," said Marlie. "Her purple and blue dyes, in return for cloth."

"Then you two can go and beg her favour," sniffed Bronden, "since you are so keen to do so." She turned her back on them.

"We will wait here for your return," said Allun. "Be speedy. There is much to plan." He laughed. "And take care not to insult her, now. Like Bronden, she is not a woman to be trifled with."

Strong Jonn looked around at the watching villagers and pointed. Rowan jumped. Jonn's finger was pointing at him!

"Boy Rowan," called Strong Jonn. "Little rabbit, herder of the bukshah! Run and get two cheeses from the coolhouse. The oldest, ripest, strongest cheeses from the topmost shelf. And bring them to us at Sheba's hut. Sheba is very fond of good strong cheese. The gift will sweeten her temper."

Rowan stared, open-mouthed, and did not move. He was terrified of Sheba. His mother nudged him. "I will go," piped up little Annad, beside him. "I am not frightened." Laughter rippled through the crowd.

"Go along, Rowan," Jiller urged in a whisper. "Do as you are bid. At once!"

Rowan scuttled away through the crowd.

"He is scared of his shadow, that boy," he heard Val the miller mutter to her brother, as he passed them. "He will never be the man his father was."

Ellis grunted agreement.

Rowan ran on, his cheeks burning with shame.

2 – Sheba

Rowan was panting when he reached the coolhouse. Trembling, he climbed the ladder and took two of the oldest cheeses from their shelf. The coolhouse was packed with cheeses, vats of smooth white milk curd, churns of butter. Plenty for everyone. But not for long, if new supplies did not replace the old.

He left the coolhouse and hurried towards the orchard beyond which lay Sheba's hut. He could hear the sound of the crowd still assembled in the market square and was glad he didn't have to pass them on his way. As he reached the outskirts of the village he thought about what Val had said. Stumbling slightly in the ragged grass, he began moving through the hoopberry trees, dodging the twisted, hanging branches. He thought about Sefton, his father.

Sefton had come home from the market late one night, just after Annad was born, to find his house burning. A log had rolled from the fire and set the ground floor on fire. Flames were licking the staircase, and the house was filled with smoke. Sefton had shouted for help, then leaped up the burning stairs. He had pulled the unconscious Jiller and the new baby from their beds, and carried them down to safety. Then, as the flames burned higher and hotter, he threw a blanket around his head and went back into the house—for Rowan, in the attic. No one could stop him, they said later, though the heat and smoke beat everyone else back. Even the giant millers, Val and Ellis. Even Strong Jonn, Sefton's friend.

They saw Sefton at the attic window, with Rowan in his arms. They saw him fling the window open, and heard him cry out. They rushed to catch what he threw to them—his son, screaming in terror, wrapped tightly in the rug from his bed. And then they heard a crash, and saw the roof fall in and the flames leap and roar. Strong

Jonn, cradling Rowan in his huge arms, gave a shout of grief. Sefton had saved his family. But he had gone from them, forever.

Rowan grew up knowing that his father had died to save him. He knew too that, although they never said so openly, many people in the village of Rin felt that the exchange had not been a fair one. The villagers were farmers and traders now, but they were descended from great warriors. And in their time, when Rin was threatened, many of the older ones had fought to defend it. The War of the Plains was alive in their memories, and recorded in dozens of volumes in the house of books. The people of Rin were proud of their tradition of courage.

At an early age every village child learned to run, climb, jump, swim—and fight. Rowan had trained with the others, but he had never been good at anything. He had always been small for his age. He had always been shy. And since the night of the fire he had been even quieter and more nervous than before. Val was right, he thought. He would never be the man his father was. And neither would he have the strength of his mother, who since his father's death had worked even harder, ploughing the wheatfields with Star, planting and gathering the crop, taking it to the mill.

Rowan had been given the job of herding the bukshah because it was easy. Tending the big, gentle beasts needed no strong arm or great courage. Only once, years ago, had a keeper of the bukshah come to grief. And the mineshaft into which she had fallen trying to save a wandering calf had been closed in long ago. A much smaller child than Rowan could have done the work. But he was allowed to remain with his beasts, and for this he was grateful.

The bukshah loved him, and knew his voice. They would look at him with their soft brown eyes, and nuzzle his hand when he was sad, as if they knew his troubles. In return he tried to make their lives comfortable, learning to cure their ills, treating their cuts and bruises as his mother treated his, combing burrs and prickles from their woolly coats. When the winter snows blew in the valley, he would bring the old and weak to shelter, for he knew that the freezing winds could kill them, and he could not bear to lose even one. In the spring, when the blossom of the orchard sweetened the air, he would run and play with the calves, and carry them handfuls of new peas he stole from the gardens when no one was looking.

Rowan listened. He could hear the beasts now, in their field nearby, rumbling and snuffling to each other as the sun began to dip behind the Mountain. He wished he was with them, instead of tripping over his own feet in the orchard with his arms full of smelly cheeses and his head full of shameful fears.

He scrambled through the fence that marked the orchard boundary, and his steps slowed as he saw light flickering from Sheba's hut. Despite the coolness of the evening air her door was open, and gigantic shadows wavered and crept on the strange, pale grass that grew before it. He began to tremble again as he approached.

Two of Bree and Hanna's children had once told him that Sheba could turn you into a fat slug if she chose. They pointed to the slugs that they were picking from the cabbage leaves. "These were all people, once," they said. "Look—that's our Uncle Arthal, there. We know him by the spot on his forehead. He gave the Witch a rotten tomato in a bag he traded for belly-ache medicine. One rotten tomato in a bag of twenty. And that's what she did to him. Goodbye Uncle Arthal. Hello Uncle Slug. Want to give him a kiss?" They pushed the writhing creature up to Rowan's mouth, and hooted after him as he ran away.

Rowan knew they had been teasing him. He knew it, really. But sometimes in bed at night, or if a bukshah strayed and he had to go near Sheba's hut to catch it, the children's story would come back to him, and he would remember the slow, fat slug with the spot on its forehead, and shudder.

Voices drifted out to meet him as he trod softly among the shadows on the grass. Strong Jonn and Marlie. And another voice, cracked and low. Sheba.

"The stream flows down from the Mountain top, above the cloud," she was saying. "Under the earth and rock it flows, to Rin. And so you must climb the Mountain, to the very top, my fine friends. And none knows the secret way, but Sheba!" Her mocking laugh rang out.

Rowan thought of putting the cheeses down on the doorstep and running home. But as he stepped forward a twig snapped under the toe of his boot.

"At last!" Strong Jonn's head popped out the door. He put his arm behind Rowan's back and propelled him inside. "The boy with the cheeses. Our gift to you, Sheba," he said heartily. "In trade for your knowledge of the way."

The old woman sitting by the fire sniffed the air and smacked her lips with a greedy sound. "The cheeses!" she gloated. Then she frowned, and her eyes narrowed. "Bring them here," she ordered. "Closer, boy."

Rowan hesitated. Marlie, beside him, gave him a little push. His feet felt like stones. He forced them forward, a step at a time.

"What are you hiding?" snapped Sheba, half rising from her chair. "I said closer, boy! Come here and put these famous cheeses in my lap. For how do I know that I am not being cheated? Fobbed off with second-class goods?"

"They are the best we have, Sheba," said Marlie. "Rowan chose them himself, from the highest shelf in the coolhouse. You will like them."

"So you say," scowled Sheba. She hunched her shoulders and stared at Rowan. In the firelight her eyes looked red. Her forehead was bound with a purple rag, and her hair hung like thin grey tails around her face. She smelt of ash and dust, old cloth and bitter herbs. Rowan reached her chair, placed the round yellow cheeses on her lap and backed swiftly away, holding his breath, trying not to look at her.

But Sheba had lost interest in him. She was prodding the cheeses with her bony fingers, sniffing them one by one. Rowan hugged himself and shuddered, sheltering behind the tall figure of Marlie from those terrible red eyes. What if he had chosen badly? What if the cheeses were no good after all? What if Sheba thought he was trying to trick her?

The old woman looked up. "They are good," she pronounced. "As good as you said they would be, Jonn of the Orchard."

"Naturally." Strong Jonn bowed to her.

"Now, Sheba," said Marlie, firmly. "Will you tell us what we wish to know?"

"Ah, brave Marlie!" Sheba giggled unpleasantly. She took some sticks from a basket beside her and threw them on the fire. It flared up as the sticks caught alight, and shadows danced on her face as she turned back to them. "Brave as you weave your cloth safe at home and dream of glory. But how brave will you be on the Mountain? The Mountain has ways of taming big brave girls like Marlie, if they are so foolish as to try their strength against it. It has ways ... so many ways ... as you will discover."

Rowan felt Marlie stiffen, and saw her cheek begin to burn red. "We do not need your warnings, Sheba," she said in a level voice.

"And Jonn! Strong Jonn, keeper of the trees! Fine, tall man!" jeered the old woman, ignoring her. "Now you come here to ask me favours. But what were you but a raggedy bare-bottomed little boy like all the rest once upon a time, crying for your mamma when Sheba passed by?" She bared her long brown teeth at him in a hideous grin. "The Mountain will not test your strength, Jonn. It will destroy it. As it has destroyed the strength of men with twice your courage. You will twist and blubber like a baby in the grip of the Mountain. But the Mountain will not let you go."

There was a moment's silence. Rowan was rigid with horror.

Strong Jonn laughed. Then he planted his hands on his hips and addressed the old woman sternly. "Quit your tales, Sheba!" he said. "They are wasted on me and Marlie. The boy Rowan is the only one to fear them here. You should not think us so foolish as to follow his example. Look, you have scared him half to death, poor skinny little rabbit. And he picked you such excellent cheeses, too! You should beg his pardon."

Sheba went on grinning, but her eyes shone scarlet. "Laugh, then, Jonn of the Orchard," she sneered. "If the boy is the only one afraid, he is the only one of you with sense. It would do you no harm to be guided by him!" She again reached down into the basket beside her. "And so indeed I must beg his pardon," she cackled. Then, fast as a striking snake, she threw a stick straight at Marlie, who yelled and jumped aside in her fright, leaving Rowan to take the full blow of the flying wood.

Rowan stumbled back and nearly fell, the stick clutched in his hand and blood beginning to drip from a gash in his forehead. Strong Jonn exclaimed in anger and stepped forward with clenched fists.

"A gift from Sheba," snarled the old woman. "And I do beg your pardon, Rowan of the Bukshah."

"Sheba, you go too far!" thundered Strong Jonn.

Her lips curved. "Do I so?" she said. "Well then, perhaps this meeting should be ended."

"Not until you have told us what we came to hear," cried Marlie. She glanced at Rowan, cowering in the shadows. "And quickly! The boy's forehead must be attended to."

"It's only a scratch," said Sheba placidly. "But still, I grow weary. I am tired of your childishness. I will tell you what you need to know. As far as I am able. Wait."

She lay back in her chair and half closed her eyes. Her hands stroked the cheeses in her lap as though they were cats. The fire glowed. She began to drone and mumble to herself. For a long time they could make no sense of her words. And then at last she spoke clearly:

> *"Seven hearts the journey make.*
> *Seven ways the hearts will break.*
> *Bravest heart will carry on*
> *When sleep is death, and hope is gone.*
> *Look in the fiery jaws of fear*
> *And see the answer white and clear,*
> *Then throw away all thoughts of home*
> *For only then your quest is done."*

Sheba's eyelids fluttered and her eyes opened. For a moment she stared blankly at Jonn, Marlie and Rowan, as though wondering why they were there, then her expression sharpened and she waved her hand at them impatiently. She no longer looked like a witch. Just a tired, crabby old woman.

"Go now," she said. "I can tell you no more."

"But the way, Sheba. The way we must go," urged Marlie. "You have told us nothing!"

"Have I not? Well, we will see. Perhaps you will feel differently by and by. Now leave me in peace." Sheba's chin sank to her chest and she was silent. They waited, but she did not raise her head again. After a while she began to snore.

"She is asleep," whispered Rowan.

"Asleep or pretending," said Strong Jonn in disgust. "In any case, there is nothing more for us here. We must go back. The others have waited long enough for us."

They left the hut and began to hurry towards the village.

"And we return empty-handed," exclaimed Marlie. "With Rowan bleeding. Rowan, I cannot forgive myself for stepping aside and leaving you to be struck. I was taken by surprise."

"The old devil intended Rowan to suffer," said Strong Jonn grimly. "She was punishing me for laughing at her and telling her to beg his pardon. The fault is mine."

Rowan, trotting along beside them through the orchard, was feeling dizzy and faint, but whether this was because of the cut on his forehead or simply the terror he had felt in Sheba's cottage, he did not know. Her horrible warnings whirled around in his head, and her strange, droning chant seemed to have been burnt into his brain. He could not forget it. "Seven hearts the journey make ... Seven ways the hearts will break ..." He found himself repeating it under his breath, beating time against his leg with the stick he still held in his hand. "Bravest heart will carry on ... When sleep is death, and hope is gone ..."

"Put it out of your mind, boy Rowan," said Strong Jonn uneasily. "Look ahead—the village lights. You will soon be home with your mother." He exchanged glances with Marlie. "And what she will say to me for bringing him home in this state ..." he added in an undertone.

3 – The Heroes

After inspecting the cut on her son's forehead, however, Jiller simply smiled and shrugged. It was nothing serious, she said, and could be attended to at home later. All children had to put up with such things at one time or another. Rowan knew that her words were for him as much as for Strong Jonn and Marlie. She was reminding him to be brave, as befitted a child of Rin, and not to fuss.

Rowan knew that Jiller worried about his nervousness and frailty. He had overheard her telling Strong Jonn so outside their house, only a month or two ago. She tried to be patient, Jiller had said, but Rowan was so different from herself, and from his father, and even from sturdy little Annad, that it was sometimes very hard. She did not understand him. She wished his father was alive ...

Rowan had crept away and scuttled upstairs to the room he now shared with Annad. He had lain on his bed for quite a time, not really thinking about anything, aware only of a dull ache in his chest.

So now he stood beside his mother with swimming head and burning eyes and said nothing. He longed to throw himself into her arms and cry for comfort, but there would be no comfort there. Only shame.

"I told you Sheba was a waste of time!" Bronden was saying, half in triumph and half in exasperation. "Now she has two of our best cheeses in her grubby paws, and we are none the wiser."

"Never mind," Allun said, shrugging. "We decided to try her, and try we did. Now a new decision must be taken. For we cannot all climb the Mountain. Who is to go?"

"I will go," shouted Bronden. She glared at them all, as though daring someone to oppose her.

"Why not?" Strong Jonn said. "No one doubts your willingness, your courage or your right, Bronden. As, I presume, no one doubts mine. I too will go."

Rowan's heart felt as though it was being gripped by an icy hand. He remembered Sheba's words: *The Mountain will not test your strength, Jonn. It will destroy it.* "No!" he gasped. His mother's hand tightened on his arm.

"And I," said Marlie firmly, her eyes on Bronden.

Val and Ellis had been talking quietly together. Now Val raised her gruff voice. "Until the mill wheel turns again we have no work to do," she said. "So we will join you on the Mountain. Better that than sit idle, waiting."

"You could do a bit of house-cleaning for a change," Allun teased.

Val stared at him coldly, while some of the other villagers exchanged amused glances. Everyone knew that Val and Ellis did not like anyone to make fun of their fussy housekeeping.

"This is madness," cried Neel the potter, unable to keep silent any longer. "This is no laughing matter! Bronden, Jonn, Marlie, Val, Ellis ... the strongest of us all, going into the unknown!" He appealed to the crowd. "If they do not come back, these hot-heads, how are we to survive? What will happen if the Zebak invade once more? Or if some other dreadful danger threatens?"

"Another dreadful danger does threaten, Neel," old Lann said. "Right now, as we stand here. Perhaps the most dreadful we have ever faced. And to save the village from it, some of us must journey into the unknown. That is exactly why the strongest must be the ones to go." She turned to Jonn. "Still, I think the party is too small as yet. You need one more."

Allun stepped forward. "I agree. I will join the company to make the numbers even." He saw Bronden open her mouth to object, and went on quickly, "Ah, Bronden, I know I am only half bred of Rin, and my strength may not match yours. But I am not quite a weakling. I have mastered, I think, all the skills the journey will require. And I have other gifts to offer, thanks to my father's blood. A cool head, for one. A good way with a camp fire for another. And a stock of songs and jokes that will not go astray. Besides, with the millers absent and no flour to be had, how else will a poor baker occupy these next few days?"

"You could come and dig my garden, Allun," piped up Sara, his mother.

There was a shout of laughter from the people around. The old woman smiled. Only Rowan and Allun saw that her hands were gripping her apron, twisting the white cloth, and that her eyes were twinkling not with laughter but with unshed tears. She had lived long enough to have heard the old stories of the Mountain, and to fear its power. And Allun was her only child.

But like a true daughter of Rin, Sara knew how to hide her feelings. Only once, many years ago, had she let down her guard. And that was when she fell in love with the man who would become Allun's father, a laughing brown-eyed singer who came to the village one autumn with a troop of Travellers. Rowan had heard the story many times, though the thing had happened many years before he was born, when his mother and father were children themselves. It was part of the village history, and was repeated every time a tribe of Travellers came to camp nearby.

Rowan could imagine the shock it must have caused when it became known that Sara, the sensible village teacher, would leave Rin to marry a footloose Traveller. Most people were horrified, and tried hard to make her change her mind. But she would not be persuaded, and when the Travellers moved on she went too, leaving the peace and security of her old home to wander with the man she loved and his tribe.

The people of Rin saw Sara a few years after that, when the Travellers chanced to come their way again. The small, cheeky-faced Allun was toddling after her by then, and her happiness was in her face for all to see. Some shook their heads and said her smiles would not last. And they were right, though not for the reasons they thought.

For then came the five-year War of the Plains, when again the people of Rin, the Maris folk and the Travellers themselves were forced to join in battle against invaders from across the sea—their ancient enemy, the Zebak. As their ancestors had done before them, they at last drove the Zebak from their lands. But the battle was long, and cost many brave lives. And one of these was Sara's husband.

Sara brought her young son back to the village, after that. Without her man, the Travelling life had no sweetness for her, and she wanted to settle again with her own people, in her old home. But home for Allun was the coloured tents of the Travellers, the smell of camp fires burning in the night, open plains, forests, and winding roads that seemed to have no ending.

Slender, dark-eyed and curly-haired, Allun was the image of his father, and very different from the tall, strong children of Rin. Under the Teaching Tree with Bronden, Jiller, Val, Ellis and the others of like age in those days, he held up his head and smiled at their glances, nudges and whispers. Outside school, though he worked hard to seem as like them as possible, he soon learned that his strength was no match for theirs, and that his wits were his best weapon.

Rowan had often felt that Allun might be the one person in the village who understood how he felt, as he too was weaker, and different from the others. Not that Allun had ever said so. But when he visited the house with Marlie and Strong Jonn he often joked with Rowan, and took an interest in what he was doing, and made excuses for his mistakes.

And now Allun too was to climb the Mountain. Trying yet again to prove himself a worthy citizen of Rin. Jonn and Marlie were looking pleased, and Bronden was rolling her eyes at Val and Ellis, clearly not liking the sixth member of the party, but unable to think of a good reason to deny him. Funny, easy-going Allun the baker was going to vanish with the others into the secret maze of cliffs and forests that rose above them. Once more Rowan remembered Sheba's mocking face.

"Ah, well, if you must go, you must! My weeds will have to thrive for another few days," old Sara was calling, smiling and flapping her hands in mock despair while her eyes still shone with tears.

"Bless you, Mother," said Allun. His tone was light, but the love and admiration in the words were clear for all to hear.

"Now," said Jonn hastily, for he was a man embarrassed by strong feelings openly expressed, "I suggest we go home and make our preparations for the journey. Then a good night's sleep should be had by all before the dawn is upon us. Agreed?"

The others nodded. The villagers called out their goodnights and began slowly to move homewards. Some felt comforted, because something was being done to solve the problem that had come upon them so unexpectedly to spoil the calm progression of their days. Some felt excited, even envious, at the thought of the great adventure awaiting the chosen ones. But many, like Neel, went to their beds that night with heavy hearts, because the leaders and heroes of the village were going on a dangerous quest for their sakes, and might never return.

When Annad had finally fallen asleep, exhausted by the excitement, Rowan lay awake in his bed, looking out of the window at the huge bulk of the Mountain. The moonlight was very bright, but the Mountain loomed black against the sky, secret and full of mystery. Jiller had cleaned the cut on his forehead, but his head still ached, and Sheba's jeering words of warning tormented him.

He tried every way he could to turn his thoughts to pleasant things. To Star, to the new calf soon to be born in the herd, to the taste of cool blue juice from the hoopberry press. And to memories of the mother of his babyhood, a gentler, happier Jiller, singing to him. But always, just as he was about to fall asleep, the other, darker thoughts came creeping back, and made him afraid to close his eyes.

Finally he did sleep—a shallow doze filled with nightmares. He was back in Sheba's hut. But now its four walls were made of rock, dripping with water and slime. And Sheba was huge, her nose long and pointed, her hair greasy grey tails swinging like thick ropes around her grinning face, her eyes red and piercing. Strong Jonn and his mother stood there with him, but they made no move to help as the Witch bent towards him, closer and closer, till her face was all he could see and her breath scalded his cheeks. "If you are the only one afraid, skinny rabbit, you are the only one with sense," she croaked. And she opened her mouth to scream with laughter, but she had no tongue, and the inside of her mouth was as yellow and smooth as cheese.

4 – Seeing is Believing

Rowan woke, and lay panting and shuddering, soaked in sweat. He had no idea what time it was. The dream had seemed to take hours, but it might only have been seconds. Annad slept peacefully on, her mouth slightly open, one hand curled around her soft bukshah toy. She at least was having no bad dreams. But the thought of going back to sleep was terrifying to Rowan. He threw back the covers and leaped out of bed. It was very cold. The cool night air was blowing in the window, and his sleeping shirt was wet through. He peeled it off and quickly began pulling on the day clothes he had left in a pile on the floor when he changed for bed.

Underneath the clothes was the stick Sheba had hurled at him. He had carried it home, unthinking, and brought it to his room. He picked it up and slid his fingers up and down its length. It was a good stick: straight and thick, and so smooth it might have been polished, except for one little pointed bump in the middle. That was possibly what had cut his forehead, Rowan decided, pushing the soft pad of his thumb against the bump. It was hard and sharp enough.

Then the bump moved! It slid forward under his thumb. And the stick began to peel!

Rowan gasped as the smooth surface beneath his fingers came away in a fine, single sheet. He pulled at the sheet, fascinated, as more and more of it unrolled. Then he realised that the "stick" was not a stick at all. It was a tightly rolled piece of parchment. The little bump in the centre had been the catch that held it closed.

With a glance at the sleeping Annad, he hurried to light the lamp. She would not wake, and he had to look more closely at this strange thing he held in his hand. For, even in the dimness, he could see that the parchment was not blank. There were pictures on it, and lines and words. He had to see what they were.

He spread the parchment out on the wooden floor and weighted it on all four corners with his shoes and Annad's to stop it curling up again. Then he carefully put the lamp beside it, and looked.

It was a map of the Mountain, with a pathway marked in red. Rowan clapped his hand over his mouth to stop himself calling out. Sheba had played a trick on them. She had pretended to let them down, knowing all the time that Rowan was carrying away just what they needed. Knowing that they might never discover what she had given them. How she must have laughed to herself at Strong Jonn's disgust and Marlie's disappointment.

Rowan rolled up the map tightly again, and fastened the clasp. He pulled on his shoes. Then he stood in the middle of the bedroom, his thoughts whirling.

"Rowan! What are you doing?" He spun around to meet his mother's startled eyes. She gaped at him from the doorway. He blinked at her. Like him, Jiller was fully dressed as if ready to go out.

"I ..." Tongue-tied, he held out the rolled-up map. "I had a dream, and ..."

"Oh, Rowan," Jiller sighed in exasperation. "These nightmares! What am I to do with you, my son?" For a moment Rowan thought he saw her lips tremble. "And now, this morning ..." She broke off and put her hands up to her face. When she lowered them, she was calm again. "If we wish to bid the Mountain party farewell with the rest of the village, we must go soon," she said. "They leave at dawn. Put down that stick and gather Annad's clothes. I must wake her." She moved towards the little girl's bed.

"Mamma ..." In his confusion Rowan used the babyish word without thinking. He saw her brow crease, and heard her quick indrawn breath of irritation.

"Mother," he went on quickly, and so loudly that Annad stirred and began waking of her own accord. "Mother, I have the map. The map of the Mountain!"

* * *

"He has the map of the Mountain," Jiller said again to Strong Jonn, ignoring the exclamations of the crowd. Her cheeks were pink with excitement, and her hood flung back over her shoulders. She looked to Rowan very beautiful. And perhaps she did to Strong Jonn too, for he was looking at her admiringly.

"Then quickly, let us see!" demanded Bronden, stamping her tough boots in the cold. "But I cannot believe this! Why would the old woman try such a trick? Are you sure the boy is not playing the fool?"

"Of course not," snapped Jiller, taking the map from Rowan and passing it to her. "See for yourself!"

Bronden unrolled the parchment and stared at it for a moment, her breath making little puffs of mist in the cold morning air. Then her mouth turned down at the corners and she passed the parchment to Jonn and Marlie.

"Well?" Allun, standing beside Rowan and Jiller, was feverish with curiosity. "What is it? What has the boy found?"

Strong Jonn turned the parchment around to face them. It was completely blank.

"But ..." Rowan burst out. "It was there! A drawing of the Mountain. And words, and arrows ... and a track marked in red, leading to the cloud and above it! It was!"

Bronden sniffed, and jerked her head towards the empty sheet still dangling from Jonn's hand. "Seeing is believing," she said, turning away. "Small boys should learn that it is a big mistake to try playing tricks on their betters to gain attention."

"Maybe you were dreaming, Rowan," said Allun, patting him on the shoulder. "Too much cheese at dinner, eh? This happens to me sometimes. Things seem to be real ..."

"This *was* real," Jiller broke in. She was frowning, staring at the parchment as if even now she could not believe her eyes. "Rowan held it up to me. I saw it myself. Am I too playing a trick on my betters, Bronden?"

There was an embarrassed pause. Strong Jonn bit his thumb thoughtfully. Then he passed the parchment back to Rowan. "If Jiller and Rowan say the map was there, I believe them," he said. "But the fact remains that now it is not. Perhaps Sheba wished to build our hopes, then send them crashing down."

Jiller smiled at him gratefully.

"That would be very like her," agreed Marlie. "She ... oh!" Her jaw dropped, and she pointed at Rowan. "Look! Look!" she gasped.

Rowan, red-faced and startled, found the eyes of the villagers upon him. People were exclaiming and staring. What was happening? What had he done now? It took him a moment to realise that they were not looking at him. They were looking at the parchment in his hand. He glanced down at it, and the stab of shock he received was immediately followed by a rush of relief and joy. For the map was slowly reappearing. Shapes, words ... and finally the red dotted path, winding upwards.

Strong Jonn held out his hand. "Rowan, give it to me," he commanded.

Eagerly Rowan surrendered the parchment. Jonn took it and held it up. There was a buzz of excitement, and then a groan of dismay from the villagers. For as they watched, the lines and arrows were fading. In moments the parchment was blank and clean again. Jonn passed it around. The people stared at it as it went from hand to hand, unchanging.

"It is witchcraft!" exploded Neel, thrusting it back to Strong Jonn as if it was poisonous. "Sheba is toying with us."

"I fear she is," said Jonn slowly. "And it is a dangerous game she plays." He looked at Marlie. "I am very much afraid that Sheba's idea is to make me eat my words," he said to her.

He put the parchment back into Rowan's hands and watched gravely as once again marks, shapes and lines appeared on its surface—faint at first, but growing clearer by the second.

"What does this mean?" cried Jiller, clutching her son's shoulder.

Strong Jonn hesitated. "Last night, angered by something I told her, Sheba said of Rowan: 'It would do you no harm to be guided by him'. I believe that out of spite she has bewitched the map so that it only reveals its secrets in Rowan's hands."

"You are right." Marlie was thinking aloud. "She threw it at him last night. She intended him to discover it. She intended that this scene we have just witnessed should be played out." She paused. "Sheba wants the boy to join us on the Mountain."

"No!" The word burst from Jiller before she could stop it. She bit her lip and composed herself. "I mean," she went on carefully, "Rowan is young. Too young to be of use to you. And he has the bukshah to see to. He cannot go."

"Of course he cannot!" agreed the teacher, Timon. He pushed his way to the front of the crowd. "And I have the solution to this little dilemma. Rowan can hold the map while I copy it, with my own ink on my own paper." He spread out his hands. "It may take an hour, and Rowan's arms may tire, but it will be worth it to him. For Rowan can then go home to bed, fortunate boy, while you poor fools go off for your little stroll."

"Yes!" Marlie exclaimed. "We will beat Sheba at her own game. She forgets we are not bukshah, to be led about so easily."

But Sheba had forgotten nothing. For no matter what Timon did, he could not copy the map. Whenever he tried, the pens he used and discarded one after the other skated across the copying paper as if it were greased with butter, though they worked perfectly if he tried to draw anything else. After half an hour he had not succeeded in producing one useful line. Finally he threw away his last pen with a grunt of disgust and sat back on his heels in a mound of screwed-up paper.

"Enough!" said Jonn. "We were going without the map before. Nothing has changed. We go without the map now." He nodded to Rowan, carefully avoiding Jiller's eyes. "We thank you," he said. "For at least we have seen glimpses of the way. We will remember much of it, and this will help us. Go home now, with your mother."

"But this is senseless!" snapped Bronden. "The map will ensure our success and safety. We must take it with us. And if the map and the boy are joined, by whatever trick, we must take the boy with us too. Anyone can take his place with the bukshah. His attachment to them is foolishness, in any case."

"We agree with Bronden," said Val. Her brother, beside her, nodded. "The village depends on this. There is no room for faint-heartedness here."

"The boy cannot come," insisted Strong Jonn. "The danger is too great. And he is too young."

"Or is it that his mother is too beautiful?" remarked Bronden pointedly. "And your heart is ruling your head, Jonn of the Orchard?"

Jonn's face flushed scarlet. Rowan felt Jiller's arm stiffen and saw her lift her chin while two spots of bright colour began to burn in her cheeks.

"Mamma, what's the matter with Jonn?" whispered Annad, pulling at her mother's skirt. "Why is he all red?"

Jiller did not reply. Rowan looked from one face to the other in the crowd, and slowly, with a sinking feeling, the truth came to him. There were other children here of his age. If this had happened to any one of them, there would be no argument. It would be taken for granted by Jonn and Timon, by their parents and by everyone else, that they would go. And they would want to go. It would be the greatest adventure of their lives. Their chance to prove themselves heroes.

It was because he was—like he was, that Strong Jonn was taking this stand. Because—he saw it now—Strong Jonn loved his mother, and was trying to save her from shame and pain.

Rowan began to quiver. Sheba's words rang in his ears. *The Mountain will not test your courage. It will destroy it.* Why had she done this to him? If the Mountain could destroy the courage of one such as Strong Jonn, who feared nothing, what could it do to Rowan of the Bukshah, who feared everything?

He was filled with dread, loneliness and shame in equal parts. He could not bear it. He could not bear the rueful eyes of the villagers upon him. They too must be thinking: Why him? The most disappointing child in the whole of Rin. By what unlucky chance was he their chosen saviour, when all he could do was let them down?

He turned towards his mother, ready to hide his face in her skirt, and just at that moment a picture flashed into his mind. He saw himself standing in the bukshah fields, with Star's warm muzzle bent to his hand and the other beasts grazing around him, huge, calm and trusting.

He had never disappointed the bukshah. He had never let *them* down. In the frosty early mornings or in the heat of the sun, when they were injured, or giving birth to their calves, or when they needed comfort as the Dragon roared, he had been there.

Now they needed water. And they would not expect him to fail them. To them he was not an undersized, scared weakling. To them he was leader, guide and friend. They trusted him absolutely. The thought flowed through him like warm, rich milk.

He raised his head and looked straight at Strong Jonn. "I will go," he said. The map he held fluttered in the little breeze that always came before the dawn. "I will go with you, to the Mountain."

5 – The Mountain

They had been walking beside the dry bed of the stream for hours and had left the village far behind. Looking back, Rowan could no longer even see the tall stone walls of the mill, the highest building, because the trees had screened it from view.

In front of them, like a massive wall, rose the Mountain. In another two hours, the others said, they would reach it. The map showed clearly that they must begin their climb at the place where the water gushed from its underground tunnel to form the stream. There they would rest for a while and consult the map before going on.

Rowan was very tired. The bag he carried was dragging at his shoulders, and his back and legs ached. But he knew he had to keep walking, and not complain. The others were trying to make it easy for him to keep up, but he could tell that the slow pace was irritating Bronden and Val, at least. It was hard to tell how Ellis felt, because he rarely spoke at any time. Even when they had passed the mill, and the great wooden wheel lying motionless in the mill race, its own channel on one side of the dry stream bed, he had said nothing. Only looked, then turned his head back towards the Mountain.

Rowan watched him now, striding at the head of the group. He carried his pack, and the extra weight of a heavy rope, a small axe and their supply of torches, with ease. Close behind him walked his sister.

They were a strange, silent pair. Rowan had heard Jiller say to Strong Jonn that it was as though they lived in a world of their own. A world inhabited by only two people. They seemed as hard and immovable as the stone walls of their own mill. They were about the same age as Jiller, and Rowan had taken them for granted as he grew up. They were just part of the normal day-to-day life of the village for him, like the other adults he had known since babyhood. But lately he had come to realise that Val and Ellis really were unusual. And that his mother, and people like Strong Jonn and Allun, thought so too.

Behind Val, a head shorter but stocky and determined, tramped Bronden. Marlie came next, smiling occasionally at Allun who was swinging along beside her, whistling and singing as if he was on a country jaunt.

They had put Rowan second last, with Strong Jonn bringing up the rear. Every now and then Jonn would speak to him. "All well, Rowan?" he would call heartily. Or: "Nearly there now, my friend." Rowan would nod, and mutter an unwilling answer. He knew Jonn didn't really care how he felt. He just felt responsible for him.

Jonn was good-natured and agreeable to everyone. It was his way. And he had always been pleasant to Rowan. But that was different from liking. He cared for Annad—you could see that. But with Rowan he never really relaxed. He tried too hard to be nice. You don't have to try when you really like someone. Rowan knew that. And sometimes Jonn called him "skinny rabbit", and laughed at him for being afraid of things.

Jonn was talking to him now because of Jiller. Rowan had heard his mother whisper, "Take care of him," as she said goodbye to the big man before they left. And Jonn had taken both her hands in his and said: "I will, Jiller. By my life, I promise I will bring him home to you."

Remembering this, Rowan felt a flash of resentment. What right had Strong Jonn to look at his mother like that? What right had he to hold her hands as if he were more to her than her dead husband's friend? It had been a shock to him, there in the market square, when he realised that Jonn might feel more for his mother than simple friendship. It had been horrible to think that he might even plan on becoming her husband one day. No one could ever take his father's place, thought Rowan bitterly. No one.

He stamped along, staring straight ahead. And Jonn *should* feel responsible for this mess, he thought. It was Jonn's teasing that had angered Sheba so that she had made Rowan the keeper of the map. It was Jonn's fault that Rowan had been forced to become the weak, unwanted seventh member of this party.

At that, Rowan's thoughts changed direction, and his anger cooled. He wondered whether Jonn and Marlie had remembered Sheba's words. *Seven hearts the journey make ... Seven ways the hearts will break.* They said nothing, but surely they must have thought about it, as he had. A shiver ran down his spine. There was no way that Sheba could have known the number of travellers in advance. Unless she really had had a vision of the future as she lay back in her chair, her eyes half closed. And if that part of the prophecy had come true ... what of all the rest? Rowan bent his head to watch the ground under his feet. He did not want to look at the Mountain.

As the last hour's tramping drew to a close and the rocks of the Mountain's foothills loomed large and sharp, the sun was already warm on Rowan's back. For some time now he had managed to stay on his feet only by thinking of the bukshah. While Jiller had been loading his pack for the journey, he had slipped away to the fields to say goodbye. He had found the beasts swaying anxiously in the green grass that still surrounded the muddy drinking pool.

"We are going to help you," Rowan had told them as he moved from one to the other, stroking and patting, drawing in the familiar, warm animal smell of them. "Soon there will be sweet water again. It won't be long."

Last of all he had come to Star. He put his arms as far as they would reach about her neck, and laid his head on her shaggy wool. "Goodbye, Star," he had said. "Wait for me. I will bring back the water. I will not fail you."

He knew Star could not understand his words, but she had grunted and snuffled to him as if comforted just by the tone of his voice.

"Annad and Mother will see to you while I am gone," he had told her. "If Dawn has her calf while I am away, they will help her. They promised me."

One final hug, and he had to go. But Star's trust and strength stayed with him, even when his knees trembled with tiredness, and his breath shuddered in his chest.

"Yo, Ellis!" Strong Jonn's shout broke into Rowan's daydream. Allun and Marlie came to a stop in front of him. He stumbled to a halt and looked up. Before him rose a cliff of rock. Beside him the dry stream bed had become a deep round hole, still puddled with a little muddy water. There was a black opening in the cliff just above the hole. Dying weed and moss crusted its smooth edges. So this was where the water came from.

"The water usually gushes from there," Strong Jonn was saying to Val and Ellis, pointing to the opening. "When it is running as it should, you cannot stand here without being soaked by spray."

Bronden clambered down into the empty pool and walked busily around in it, kicking at the soft mud. Then she bent over the rock to look up into the opening in the cliff face, as though hoping to find an answer there.

"Sheba said the problem was at the top of the Mountain," said Marlie, who did not seem to be able to stop herself from being irritated by Bronden. "There is nothing to see down here."

"There is no harm, I suppose, in looking for myself, Marlie the Weaver," Bronden retorted. She rubbed her hand against the rock, feeling up into the hole in the cliff as far as her arm would reach. "A round tunnel. The bottom, walls and top are polished smooth," she reported, and wiped her slimy hands against her clothes before climbing back on to the bank. "All the sharp edges have been worn away by the running water, no doubt."

"As one would expect," snapped Marlie.

Rowan sank down on the grass. His knees would not hold him any longer. He pulled off his heavy bag and fumbled in it for his drink bottle.

"Drink a little, but not too much," Allun warned, kneeling down beside him. "We do not know how long our supplies may have to last. We may not find water on the Mountain."

Rowan swallowed a mouthful of warm, metal-tasting water. It was delicious! He could have drained the flask easily. But he forced himself to replace the cap, and as he did so tears sprang into his eyes. He was so tired. And the real journey had not even begun.

The other members of the party threw down their bags and stretched. Then, one by one, they too flung themselves down on the grass.

"The map, Rowan," urged Allun. "Let us see it now. But hold on to it all the time, mind you. The coming and going of the figures upsets my stomach."

Rowan took the map from his pack and unrolled it on the grass, weighting the corners down with stones. The others gathered around.

"We are here, you see?" said Strong Jonn, his finger hovering over the surface. "And according to the red markings, we must start climbing at just this point. The track goes up past the cave from which the stream flows and continues until the Mountain levels, and the trees begin. Up there." He pointed to a green, waving mass of leaves high above them.

"A steep climb," grunted Val. "The boy will have trouble."

"Then we will have to help him," said Strong Jonn cheerfully.

Allun was puzzling over the map. "What are these white patches?" he asked, waving a finger over several places on the parchment.

Marlie frowned. "They are all beside the path. Six of them in all. Could it be that Sheba has erased some things of importance, to trick us?"

"I would put nothing past her," said Strong Jonn. "But after all, it is the path that is most important and that at least is clear."

"Quite right," put in Bronden, stretching and yawning. "It is pointless to be concerned with anything other than the task at hand."

But Rowan stared at the white patches on the map with a growing sense of anxiety. Why had he not noticed them before? Now that he had seen them, they jumped out at him. Blank spaces almost evenly spaced along the path, the last at the very top. Blank spaces on a surface otherwise completely covered with colour and line. What did they mean? The first space was at the point where the path entered the trees. They would find out what it meant soon enough.

"We go through the forest at first, it seems," Bronden was continuing. "A flat walk, due west. That should be easy enough—though of course with the boy it will take us longer." She sighed heavily, and returned to the map.

"The directions are clear. Where the forest trees end, we turn north-west, and move across this lower ground. A short distance— it should not take long to cover. And so on, and so on, up to the top. Simple! I have a compass, fortunately. And so, I know, do Marlie and

Jonn, for we traded for them together on our last trip to the coast."
She turned to Val and Ellis. "You really should take your turn on the
market trips, my friends. So many interesting things to see, and
useful things to trade for."

Val shrugged. "The mill must keep working, Bronden. We cannot
close it down to gallivant whenever we please."

"But one of you could go, and one could stay," suggested Allun
lazily, chewing a blade of grass and blinking up at the sky.

Val went very still. "That would not suit us," said Ellis flatly. "It is
not our way."

"You never go to the coast either, Allun," Marlie pointed out.
"You always say you are too busy. You are as bad as Val and Ellis!"

Bronden opened her mouth to say something, then thought better
of it. "In any case," she remarked instead, after a moment, "the
compasses are a marvel. The Maris folk use them when sailing the open
sea. How much easier than that will our task be, for we have land-
marks to follow also. We will be home by tomorrow midday, mark
my words."

"If it were so simple, we would not have needed to bring the map
with us, Bronden." Marlie leaned forward. "The Mountain is a dangerous place. A place to fear. You should take nothing for granted."

"I take nothing for granted, Marlie the Weaver, as you know,
except the evidence of my own eyes," snapped Bronden. "And if
you fear, you should not be of this party. It is bad enough that we
must drag the boy along, quavering in his boots."

"Do not forget, Bronden, that you were the one who insisted
upon that," barked Strong Jonn.

Bronden shrugged and turned away.

"It would be better," said Allun mildly, "if we put aside our
differences." Then he sat up and widened his eyes. He held out his
hands, making them tremble violently. "And if fear is the issue, I, for
one, am terrified!" he squeaked. He threw himself back on to the
grass, wagging his head and chattering his teeth.

Strong Jonn and Marlie laughed, and even Rowan managed a
smile. But Val and Ellis stared silently first at Allun and then at each
other. Bronden snorted.

"Well, if Allun can be revived from his terror, I think we should begin," Marlie said, pulling a thick rope from her pack. "We will climb with ropes, will we not? I may not feel the fear of which I am accused, but I do not fancy a fall on those rocks all the same."

When food was scarce in Rin Rowan had to climb trees, bending the leafy branches down to meet the snuffling, eager mouths of the hungry bukshah. But he clung dizzy and pale to even the lowest boughs. He had no head for heights. The climb that followed was to him like the worst of nightmares.

A rope attached him to Marlie, Allun and the other climbers above, and to Strong Jonn below. When he slipped, as he did over and over again, his light body, weighed down by his pack, swung sickeningly into space, as far as the rope allowed. The sky spun above him, the ground spun below. His own terrified screams echoed in his ears. His ribs were crushed by the rope that saved him. And then his body swung back against the rocks with a bruising thud. And he had to climb again.

This was bad enough. But worse was the fear that one of the others would prove as careless as he. If Jonn slipped, the weight might pull them all to their deaths on the rocks far below. If one of the others slipped, even Jonn might not be able to hold them.

Sore, trembling and aching in every muscle, Rowan struggled on. And when at last they dragged him over the top of the cliff, and he fell to the ground sweating and panting, the world swam red before his eyes for a moment before he fainted.

6 – The Forest

tar was licking Rowan's cheeks and forehead with her rough, cool tongue. Rowan smiled. "Stop it, Star! Leave me be," he mumbled. He rolled his head from side to side on the grass.

"He is babbling," someone said in disgust.

The picture of Star slowly dissolved. Rowan opened his eyes and found himself staring into the serious face of Strong Jonn. For a moment, he hesitated. Then with a wave of bitter disappointment, he realised where he was. Not home in the bukshah fields with Star, who loved him. But on the Mountain with Strong Jonn, who disliked him, Marlie and Allun, who pitied him, and Bronden, Val and Ellis, who despised him. "He is babbling," Val repeated impatiently. "By my life, how we are burdened by this weakling. Look at the sun! It must be nearly eleven."

Jonn threw aside the damp cloth with which he had been bathing Rowan's face. "He is awake now," he said bluntly. "And weakling or not, he fought that cliff gallantly, Val the Miller. He fought it to exhaustion." He stood up and walked away, arching his cramped back.

Rowan lay still, looking up at the sky. His body felt heavy, but his head felt very light. There was a soft ringing in his ears. Val was right. The sun was high. He must have been lying here for a long time. Sleeping. Dreaming of home, like a small child. His face began to burn, and he struggled to sit up.

"Easily, easily, boy Rowan," grinned Allun, kneeling down beside him and supporting his back. "We must crawl before we can walk. Have this." He held a flask to Rowan's lips, and Rowan swallowed gratefully.

"When you are feeling better," Allun went on, glancing meaningfully at the others, "we will move on, into the forest. Here!" He

dragged Rowan's pack towards him. "You can spend your time use-
fully by holding the map for us while we look at it once again."

"We have seen the way we must go," frowned Bronden. "We do
not need the map."

"Ah, youth, youth! You must not forget that I am three years
older than you, Bronden," smiled Allun. "And my poor memory is
failing fast."

Rowan knew that Allun was only giving him something to do
while he rested, but he slid the map from his bag and unrolled it
slowly. It would not hurt to study it again. His eyes travelled along
the red dotted line. Past the sketched-in stream bed, the hole into
which the water usually fell, the opening in the cliff, the cliff itself,
the entrance to the forest beside a high, pointed rock not far from
where they now sat, the path through—

Rowan blinked, and looked, and blinked again. He tried to speak
and almost choked.

Allun looked at him quickly, and then glanced at the parchment.
He exclaimed under his breath. Then, "Jonn!" he shouted.

Jonn spun around and ran back towards them, while the other
members of the party craned their necks to look.

Rowan was pointing wordlessly at the map. At the place beside
the beginning of the forest path, where once there had been a clear,
white space, there were six lines of black writing.

In a low voice Allun read the words aloud:

"Let arms be still and voices low,
A million eyes watch as you go.
The silken door your pathway ends,
There fire and light will be your friends.
Then see yourself as others may,
And catch noon's eye to clear your way."

"What nonsense is this?" demanded Val. "Who has been playing
the fool?"

"No one has touched the map, Val," retorted Marlie. "The words
have appeared since we last looked at it."

"That is impossible!" said Bronden. She bent over the map,

squinting at the words as though to find a clue as to how they had come there.

"It matters not a jot where it came from," cried Allun. "The question is, what does it mean?"

Strong Jonn cleared his throat. "Whatever we are dealing with here," he said, "it is certain that the words have not come to us by chance. They give us instructions, and a warning."

"The words suggest we do not fling our arms about, or speak loudly," Allun remarked. "That is clear enough. I shall follow that advice to the letter."

"That may prove difficult for you, Allun," said Marlie dryly.

"The words also mention noon." Strong Jonn was unsmiling. "I suggest we begin our forest journey as soon as we can. It will be noon in about an hour, by my reckoning."

He held out a hand to Rowan, and hauled him to his feet. "Roll up the map and stick it through your belt for now, boy," he said roughly. "My load is unbalanced, I find, and I need to carry your pack as well as my own to even the weight, if you do not object."

He did not wait for an answer, but swung both bags on to his shoulders and began striding towards the pointed rock. The others hurried after him. Rowan, no longer weighed down by the pack on his back, found he was able to keep up quite easily despite his bruises.

They paused at the pointed rock and peered between the first trees. Sunlight filtered through rustling leaves and lay in pools on the forest floor. There was a rough winding path in front of them, soon lost to view behind the undergrowth.

"This looks pleasant enough," said Allun. "Shall I lead this time? The gravity of the task may help me hold my tongue as the verse commands. Stranger things have happened."

"Then lead by all means," grumbled Bronden. "Any peace from your infernal chatter will be a blessing."

They moved into the forest. Rowan noticed that all of them, whatever their feelings about the map's instructions, kept their arms close to their sides. And no one spoke. In a few minutes the path had twisted and turned so that they could no longer see the clifftop from which they had come.

As they trudged deeper into the forest the trees around them became bigger and closer together, tangled with vines and surrounded by straggling bushes. The light became dim. And the silence! Rowan, keeping close behind Marlie and listening for Strong Jonn's firm step behind him, thought that he had never experienced so silent a place. Where were the birds? And the crickets and lizards, and other small creatures that usually inhabited woods like this?

Then he heard it. A faint twittering sound was floating down the path from somewhere ahead of them. A large colony of small birds, by the sound of it. Rowan was familiar with all the birds of Rin, but this sound was like nothing he had ever heard before. These little creatures must belong to a breed that did not stray into the valley. They would not be nesting at this time of year, but still he looked forward to seeing them fluttering and hopping around. His spirits lifted at the thought of it.

The twittering grew louder and louder. Allun began to walk faster, as if he too was interested in what was ahead. Soon he had left Marlie behind. She clicked her tongue and hurried to join him. Rowan, stretching his legs to keep up, tried to peer around Marlie's shoulder as the path turned once more. And so he stumbled and nearly fell as she gasped and cannoned into Allun, standing still and almost invisible in the dimness. The cheeping sound was deafening now.

Strong Jonn grabbed Rowan's arm and steadied him, frowning as Val, Ellis and Bronden bumped into him in their turn. And still Allun did not move.

"Allun, you blockhead, what game are you playing?" Bronden barked.

The twittering stopped abruptly. And a rustling, creeping, whispering sound took its place.

Allun looked back at them, his face creamy pale in the dim light. But he did not answer. Only moved his head, very carefully, from side to side.

And then they saw what he had seen. On both sides of the narrow pathway. Spiders. Thousands of them. Huge black velvety spiders, as big as Strong Jonn's hand, crawling over vast webs of white silk that draped the trees so thickly that the bark and leaves were hidden. Their eyes were shining. *A million eyes.* Rowan's skin began to creep. They were going to have to walk between these crawling webs, the gigantic spiders listening for them, reaching out for them.

"Ugh!" Rowan heard a strangled gasp from somewhere behind him. The spiders froze, and then began moving again, in the direction of the sound.

Strong Jonn reached over Rowan's shoulder and pushed gently at Marlie, as a signal to move on. She pushed Allun in her turn and he began easing forward, making as little movement as possible. But they had only gone a few steps before again there was a shuddering groan behind them, and Val was pulling at Strong Jonn's sleeve.

"Ellis," she breathed. "He—cannot."

Jonn, Rowan, Marlie and Allun turned incredulously. Beyond Val's worried face they could see the massive form of Ellis, his clenched fists crossed over his chest. His face was gleaming with sweat. He was panting and trembling, and every now and then a low moan slipped from his lips.

"Spiders," breathed his sister. "He cannot abide them. From a child, he could not. At home, not a speck of dust or a dry leaf may lie in a dark corner in case a spider seeks its shelter. The smallest of them is terror to him. And these ... are beyond anything ..."

"Ellis?" whispered Strong Jonn urgently. "Come, man. It is not far. They are not on the path. If we take care ..."

"No-o—" The sound bubbled from the big man's lips. Abruptly he turned and pushed past Bronden, nearly toppling her off the path and into a web. He tottered back the way they had come. Then he rounded the bend and they could see him no more. But they heard the sound of his feet—running. Running out of the forest.

"Go on!" whispered Val, her voice fierce with worry and shame. "Go on! He will not return."

Silently they obeyed. After a few minutes, the twittering sound rose up again. The spiders were communicating once more, slowly rubbing their great ribbed back legs together like poisonous crickets. The noise was strange and horrible to hear now that they knew where it came from. Rowan crept along behind Marlie, breathing in shallow gasps, making himself as thin and small as possible. Trying not to look from side to side. Trying not to think of the sticky white curtains that swathed the trees, the huge, crawling spiders and their million eyes so close.

To allow himself to speak or cry out would be to attract the spiders again. To touch one of the strands of thick white silk would be to call them, running, to him. He had seen enough insects caught in webs to know that. He must go on walking and force down the fear. He must think, remember the last lines of the verse: *The silken door your pathway ends, There fire and light will be your friends. Then see yourself as others may, And catch noon's eye to clear your way.*

The silken door ... noon's eye. It must be nearly noon now.

He jumped nervously as Strong Jonn's hand touched his shoulder. He looked up. They were in a small clearing. Before them was the silken door. It was a huge gleaming white web, so thick that you could not see through it. Its surface was scattered with twigs and leaves caught in its sticky threads. It stretched from one side of the path to the other, blocking it completely. And all around it crouched hundreds of spiders. Waiting.

Allun turned carefully to face his companions. "What now?" he mouthed.

"The verse," breathed Marlie.

"The verse has no meaning," hissed Bronden. "Cut through the web and be done with it, Allun. Or if you do not have the stomach for it, let me through and I will do it myself!"

The spiders rustled and moved in the web.

"No!" whispered Strong Jonn. "Not while the spiders hang about the silk in such numbers. As soon as we touch the web they will be upon us. We cannot risk that."

"They may be quite harmless," said Val.

"Or they may not," answered Marlie. "As Jonn says, we cannot risk it. We have already lost one member of our party."

"What then?" Bronden was angry. Ellis's flight from the forest had been a great shock to her. How could such a big, strong man have such a childish weakness? She was baffled by it. She took care not to look at Val. How shamed she must feel.

The light changed. From directly above them a ray of sun penetrated the gloom of the forest, bathing them in warmth. The spiders around them began to chitter and creep back.

"They do not like the light," Rowan breathed. "The verse said it—'Fire and light will be our friends,' it said."

"Fire!" whispered Bronden. "Throw a torch at the web!"

"Ellis was carrying the torches," said Val dully.

Allun felt in his pockets and pulled out his tinder box. "Who has something that will burn easily?—even for a brief time."

"Do not make any sudden movements," warned Strong Jonn, his eyes on the spiders.

Marlie slipped her hand into her jacket pocket. She pulled out her compass, a comb, a mirror—and a handkerchief. She held the handkerchief out to Allun. He knotted it loosely and struck flame from the tinder box.

"Ready!" he warned. Then he lit the cloth and threw it straight at the centre of the white barrier.

The silk sizzled and shrank as the handkerchief blazed. The spiders shrieked and scattered. But only for a moment. Within seconds, before even one of the party had taken more than a step forward, the flame had died down and the spiders were back. A hole gaped in the web now. But amid the smoke still rising from its blackened edges hundreds of spiders were crawling. And more were on their way.

"They are spinning," gasped Allun. "Already! They are mending the hole."

"We must drive them back!" Strong Jonn looked around desperately. "There must be a way."

"They do not like the light," Rowan said again. "They do not like the sun."

"We have no materials to make a torch here, Rowan," Marlie answered. "We have nothing that will make a light that will burn long enough to hold the creatures at bay."

But Strong Jonn had grasped Rowan's shoulder. "Rowan—the verse. Say the last lines again."

Rowan repeated in a low voice: "'Then see yourself as others may,

And catch noon's eye to clear your way.'" A thought struck him, and he looked quickly at Marlie.

"'Noon's eye'—the sun!" Allun squinted upwards at the glare. "But the sun is falling here, where we stand. The web is in shadow."

"What is it, Rowan?" asked Marlie, staring at him. "Why are you looking at me?"

"The mirror," whispered Rowan. "Your mirror. In a mirror you see yourself as others may. And the sun ..."

"Yes!" Strong Jonn clenched his fists. "But quickly, quickly! Before the light goes. We have been here too long."

Marlie handed over the mirror. John held it in front of him, twisting it until it threw bright reflected sunlight on to the web. The spiders scuttled away from their work around the hole, shrinking back into the shadows.

"Give it to me!" cried Val. She snatched the mirror from Jonn's hand. She jiggled the glass, caught the sun, and dazzling light danced round and round on the silken door. She pushed Bronden ahead of her. "Go!" she shrieked. "Go now!"

Rowan ran with the others, his eyes fixed on the hole in the web, and the glimpses of green beyond. Already the dancing light was fading. He reached the net and leaped through, while a million eyes glowed angrily in the shadows, cheated of their prey.

7 – Dreams

trong Jonn and Bronden hit the ground beside Rowan and rolled to their feet.

"Val!" called Jonn, stumbling back towards the hole in the web. "Val! Now! Before the sun moves on!" He peered through the opening. "She is just standing there!" he muttered in amazement. "She keeps looking back along the path, after Ellis."

"Jonn, make her come!" shouted Allun. "The sun will soon—"

"Val!" roared Strong Jonn, cupping his hands around his mouth. "You are needed. You must come. Quickly!"

There was a cry from the other side of the web, and the sound of running feet. And then Val was hurtling through the black-ringed hole, hitting the ground with a thud, and Strong Jonn, Marlie and Allun were stamping, stamping the grass all around her as crawling spiders fell from her clothes and hair.

Val sat up, brushing feverishly at her face, her shoulders, the back of her neck.

"No, no!" exclaimed Marlie. "All is well, Val. There were only a few of them, and now they are dead."

Val looked around her cautiously, taking in her surroundings. Then she opened her clenched fist and looked at the mirror. Amazingly, it was still in one piece. "It did good service, but I could only keep the light on the web while I remained in the sun," she said. "I leaped from a distance, but some of the creatures had already returned to the hole before I reached it." She passed the mirror to Marlie and sat with slumped shoulders, staring into space.

"We appear to be safe here." Allun waved an arm at the surrounding trees. "From the spiders at least. Their territory seems to end with the silken door. What other surprises this forest has to offer, I cannot guess."

"If I recall the map correctly, we are nearly at its end," Bronden answered. "So I suggest we move on now, and rest and eat when we are free of it. It is an unwholesome place."

In silent agreement, they set off again. Due west, along the path. They were six now, instead of seven, and all felt this keenly. Ellis had barely spoken ten words during the journey, but the absence of his looming figure among them made their group seem very much smaller and weaker. His sister was particularly affected. It was as though half her strength had been drained, and she walked like one who was ill, or exhausted.

In barely five minutes they noticed the trees thinning. In another five they had left them behind, and turned north-west as the map directed. Though the Mountain still rose steeply before them, they were moving down instead of up. The grass grew green and thick now, and the ground softened with every tread.

"Let us stop here," said Strong Jonn. "It seems we are moving into a low area that may be marshland. We will eat in more comfort out of the damp."

Rowan sat down thankfully. Jonn tossed his pack to him, and suddenly he realised just how hungry he was. He pulled out his water flask and bread and cheese, and started eating ravenously. His mother had packed this food for him in their kitchen at home this morning, he thought with wonder. Only this morning! It was hard to believe that he had been away from the village for so short a time. So much had happened to him that it seemed days, not hours, since he had patted Star and murmured to her; since he had hugged Annad, and kissed his mother goodbye.

The walk from the village, when he had felt so strange and shy. The terrible climb up the cliff. And then the forest. The spiders, twittering, crawling ... Ellis's face rigid with fear before he turned and ran. Rowan shuddered. The bread and cheese lay tasteless now in his mouth. He felt like spitting it out, but instead took a sip of water, and forced himself to swallow.

Sheba had said this was how it would be. She had said the Mountain would break their courage, and their hearts. Well, it had broken Ellis's. In a way no one could possibly have predicted. He was gone, leaving six hearts to carry on. Would they break in their turn? Would Rowan's be next? And if the journey was itself so filled with danger, what of the journey's end—and the Dragon?

Rowan shivered again. He must not think of that. One step at a time, or his fears would overwhelm him. One step ...

The map! Rowan pulled it from his belt and unrolled it. Half in excitement, half in dread, he looked at the second blank space.

It was filled.

Nothing here is as it seems;
Dreams are truths and truths are dreams.
Close your ears to loved ones' cries,
Die if you believe your eyes.
Bind with ropes your flesh and blood,
And let your guide be made of wood.

Rowan stared. "The map ..." he began timidly. "A message—"

In a flash Jonn was behind him, looking over his shoulder. Allun and Marlie too came running. Bronden joined them more slowly, grumbling a little. And Val remained where she was, slumped with her back against a rock.

"This verse is more confusing than the last!" exclaimed Allun.

"Yet we know the last was important to us," said Marlie. "And this must be too." She read, and frowned. "'Close your ears to loved ones' cries'." She glanced at Allun. "We are going again into danger, it seems."

"We knew from the start," said Strong Jonn, "that every part of this journey would be so." He rubbed his chin thoughtfully. "'Bind with ropes your flesh and blood, And let your guide be made of wood.' So the party leader is of importance, this time. We had better decide what is to be done about that. What does 'made of wood' mean?"

"Wood is hard," said Marlie. "Hard ... smooth ... cool ..."

"Bloodless," Allun put in helpfully. "Unfeeling. Incapable of pain."

"Strong," added Bronden. "Sturdy. Natural. Of the earth."

"Yes." Strong Jonn rubbed his chin again. "The least emotional of our party, then. The one who can most resist the cries of others. The one with fewest ties to flesh-and-blood things. That person should lead us."

"Well, it is not I," said Allun decidedly. "And of course it is not Rowan. And I would venture to say, Strong Jonn, that it is not you. Not these days, at any rate." He shot a sly look at Rowan, who turned his head away. He did not want to think about Strong Jonn and his mother. Not now. *Not ever.*

"I believe that of the three remaining, I am the most likely," said Bronden. "For I have no family, no loved ones. I work alone with wood day in, day out, and find it pleasing. I believe only what I see with my own eyes. I will lead."

And so it was decided.

Thirty minutes later, fed and rested, they were travelling once more, walking north-west by the compass. There was no obvious path now. Pleased to be leading, Bronden was in a good mood for the first time since the journey began. Val walked behind her, still strangely silent, her feet dragging. Allun and Marlie came next. Then Rowan with Strong Jonn, who was again carrying the boy's pack "to balance the load". All of them stopped obediently when Bronden decreed, to help cut the limp, spiky tips from the pine-smelling trees that were growing along the way. Bronden said that later the stems could be bound together to make long-lasting torches to replace the ones that had been lost when Ellis fled.

They were still walking downhill, and the ground was becoming wetter underfoot. The green grass had disappeared, and their boots were beginning to sink slightly into the mud.

Allun sniffed the air and wrinkled his nose. "Swamp!" he said in disgust.

The trees they pushed through here were different again—dark-leaved and still. Fat white roots slid up from their damp, twisted trunks into the air. Clumps of bright fungus stuck out from their bark like tongues. The mud grew softer. Rowan's boots splashed with every step he took.

And then came the mist. Bronden bent over her compass, frowning in her efforts to guide their way as it swirled, thick and yellow-white, around them. It swirled around the trees, too, and rose like steam from the glossy mud and clumps of reeds that stretched away on all sides. As the minutes passed it grew thicker.

At last it seemed as though they were enclosed in a still, secret world. A world of mist and mud. The only sound was the squelching of their feet as they plodded on. Before them, behind them and around them swirled the mist, changing shape and direction by its own will, it seemed, for not a breath of air stirred the trees.

Then, to his left, Rowan saw something moving. Something large, and dark. He slowed, straining his eyes to see through the mist that twisted and billowed, disguising the shape. The shape of ...

Rowan cried out. It was Star! Star, heaving and panting in a wallow of mud that was sucking her down, down. The mist cleared and he could see her rolling her eyes in panic, thrashing her neck from side to side in the sticky, suffocating swamp.

Without a thought he leaped to her rescue, ignoring Jonn's shout of surprise. He could hear her now, bellowing in fear. Calling to him for help. "I am coming, Star!" he screamed.

But the mud was sucking at him, pulling him down. He could not find a place to put his feet. There was no firm ground. He was sinking, sinking into mud that had no ending. He cried out again, and beat at the mud with his arms. And still Star called to him. And the mud rose to his waist, his chest ...

"I have him! Pull!"

Strong Jonn's voice woke him from his dream of terror. Strong Jonn's arms caught him under the armpits and dragged him, with a horrible sucking sound, from the mud. And Bronden and Val, holding Jonn's ankles, hauled them both back to safety. They fell in a heap on the oozing ground.

"Fool of a boy! What idiocy is this?" roared Bronden.

"Star!" cried Rowan, struggling in Strong Jonn's arms, sobbing and beating at Strong Jonn's wet, muddy chest. "My Star—my bukshah! She is out there. Oh, help me! She is drowning. She is dying! Listen to her!"

"There is nothing there, Rowan." Strong Jonn spoke slowly and loudly. "Nothing! Think, little one, think! How could Star be here? It is impossible."

Rowan's struggles slowed. He fell silent. He looked out to the spot where Star had been. The mud lay still and untroubled. The mist swirled above it as before. He rubbed his eyes. "It ... seemed so real," he faltered.

"You—" Bronden began, leaning over him menacingly. "Real or not, would you endanger our lives and our quest for the sake of a dumb beast? What value is there in a bukshah's life, compared to a human one? What madness—?"

"Leave the boy be, Bronden," Jonn broke in. "You have reasons for what you say, I know. But not all share your views."

"The map," Marlie added quickly, as Bronden drew a sharp breath. "The map warned of this. It spoke of dreams that seemed true, and loved ones who called to you. There are spirits abroad here who do not wish us well."

The map! Rowan felt anxiously at his belt. The map was still there. Covered in sticky mud, but at least not lost forever.

"Spirits!" spat Bronden. "You have been spending too much time with your half-Traveller friend, Marlie the Weaver. Do not listen to his tales. You are a daughter of Rin, and should be a person of sense." Bronden scowled and turned away.

Allun and Jonn exchanged glances. "Let us get on," Allun suggested. "We have lost time. And we will have to lose more in due course, while Rowan and Jonn dry their clothes. Which are"—he held his nose—"rather in need of attention, in my opinion."

"Let us take great care where we tread," warned Strong Jonn. "The mud is a snare. We may not be so lucky next time."

They moved along at a snail's pace, the mud dragging at their boots. The mist thickened around them, filling their mouths and noses with the taste and smell of the bog. Rowan hung his head as he walked. The wet filth sticking to his clothes and filling his shoes weighed him down. And still his head was full of Star. He dared not look up in case he saw her again, struggling hopelessly in the swamp. He wondered why Bronden had been so angry with him. Surely she could understand ...

He felt, rather than saw, Marlie begin to flick her hands and rub at her cheeks and the back of her neck. "I can feel—someone is touching me," she gasped, glancing behind her. "Fingers. Cold fingers, on my face and neck, and ..."

"It is only the mist, Marlie," soothed Allun. "Only—" Suddenly he stopped walking. His neck jerked and he too looked behind, gazing over Strong Jonn's shoulder. The others turned curiously to see what he was staring at. But there was nothing there.

"What ...?" Allun's mouth had dropped open. He began to walk back the way they had come, pushing past Jonn and Rowan, looking into the mist. "How ... Mother? Mother! Wait!" His feet squelched in the soft, sucking mud.

"No, Allun," screamed Marlie. "There's no one there! Jonn, stop him!" Then she shook her head violently. "Oh! Stop it! Stop touching me!" She slapped again at her neck and arms, and rubbed at her face.

Lost in the mist ahead, Bronden cried out, just once.

Jonn caught at Allun's jacket and pulled him back. Allun turned on him angrily. "Leave me be, Jonn," he shouted. "It is my *mother*, you fool! She is calling me. She is lost in the swamp. I must go to her." He began to struggle, trying to wrench away from Strong Jonn's grip, throwing punches at his face.

"No, Allun, no!" shouted Jonn, shaking him. "It is a vision! A vision! Your mother is at home, man!"

"What is happening?" wailed Val from further up the path. "Why don't you come? Oh, my life, help! Ellis! Oh, Ellis! Marlie! Jonn! Help me! Bronden ... Bronden is ... and I can't hold her. Help!"

8 – Flesh and Blood

arlie and Rowan ran towards the sound of Val's voice. Jonn followed, dragging Allun, who was still struggling but starting to look confused instead of angry.

They found Val lying face down in a clump of reeds, her feet on solid ground, her body in the mud, her arms around Bronden's waist. And Bronden was fighting her. Silently and determinedly fighting to be free—stretching her fingers out to something only she could see, while the swamp pulled her down.

"She suddenly called out, and plunged away into the mud," gasped Val. "I cannot pull her back. She will not listen to me. Oh, if only Ellis were here. I—I cannot think without him."

Marlie pulled a coil of rope from her pack. "Hold me, Rowan," she called, and flung herself down to lie beside Val.

Rowan held Marlie's ankles and watched her stretch across the reeds, reaching for Bronden. Marlie was tall, but not as tall as Val. As she crawled further out into the mud, Rowan was pulled forward, until he too was lying on his belly across the pathway. His muscles strained as Marlie pushed her hands under Val's and looped the rope around Bronden's belt. Val, too, groaned. She had been bearing Bronden's weight for so long. She would not be able to hold on much longer.

"Back! Rowan—try to pull me back, now," shouted Marlie. "Can you do it?"

Rowan heaved with all his might, but Marlie was heavy, and her ankles were slippery with mud. To his horror he felt his hands beginning to lose their grip. "Jonn," he shrieked in desperation. "Help Marlie! I can't ..."

"Marlie!" There was a scuffle behind him. Then two slim, strong hands had come down on top of his own, and Allun's voice was calling, "I have you, Marlie," as he heaved her to safety, with the rope that was Bronden's lifeline clutched in her hand.

It took all three of them to haul Bronden back, while Val lay exhausted on the ground and Rowan stood helplessly by. The mud was holding fast to its victim, and Bronden herself was fighting them. Even when they had her safe at their feet she was moaning and crying, trying to crawl back into the ooze that had nearly swallowed her forever.

"Minna," she was weeping. "Minna, Minna, Minna!"

"Who is Minna?" Rowan whispered to Strong Jonn. He had heard the name before, but he could not think where. "Who did Bronden see?"

Jonn was shaking his head sadly, looking down at the crying woman. "I had forgotten little Minna," he said. "I had forgotten all about her, until Bronden became so angry with you for thinking of the bukshah. And I think, except in a secret part of her mind, Bronden had almost forgotten her too. But this place ..."

"When we were all children, Rowan," said Allun, "and I still new to Rin, Bronden had a friend. One friend. Minna, the keeper of the bukshah in those days. A little girl as quiet and gentle and fearful as Bronden was loud and bullying and fearless. They were never apart. For Minna, there was only Bronden and the bukshah. For Bronden, there was only Minna."

"I remember Minna," said Marlie softly. "And so would your mother, Rowan. We all went out looking for her—even the children—the night she disappeared."

Bronden groaned, and looked up at Val, who was bending over her anxiously. "Minna is here, Val," she croaked. "I saw her. I heard her voice. I felt her hand on my face. But Val—" her strong face crumpled, and tears fell from her eyes, "Val, she is still a little girl. She has never grown up. She has been wandering here all these years, all alone. Why did you not let me go to her?"

Strong Jonn knelt down beside her. "Minna died, Bronden," he said gently. "They found her bones, at last, and the bones of the calf she was trying to save, in the old mineshaft. You remember."

Rowan stared. Minna had been quiet and shy, like him. Minna had died, seeking a lost bukshah. Was that why ...?

"We do not know that that was Minna, with the calf," Bronden moaned. "We do not know for sure. I have always wondered ..."

Jonn stroked her forehead. His face was full of pity. "Minna is dead, Bronden. Minna is safe, and resting in the graveyard. The spirits of the swamp played a terrible trick on you, to make you leave the firm ground. As they did with Rowan and his bukshah. And tried to do with Allun and his mother."

"I do not believe in such things." Bronden looked around her with terrified eyes. "And yet you must speak truly, for Minna cannot be ten years old still. But I saw her. I felt her. I heard her." She gripped Strong Jonn's hands. "Jonn! Do not let them touch me again! Do not let me hear them! I could not bear it." She struggled to her feet. The mist billowed around her, and she started like a frightened animal.

"Come along, Bronden," said Strong Jonn, still in that gentle voice. "Come along." He began to lead her on.

"No!" Bronden dug in her toes, her eyes black with fear. "No! I cannot!"

"Bronden, you must come!"

"No!" She tore away from him, panting, then turned and began to run back the way they had come, her thumbs over her ears, her hands blinkering her eyes.

"Bronden," shrieked Val. "Come back!"

But Bronden did not turn or hesitate. Soon she was out of sight.

Now we are five, thought Rowan.

"The spiders!" Val groaned. "She will not be able to go through the forest!"

"She has the branches she cut to make torches," Allun said. "Once she is out of here she will stop and bind them, for the fear will die in her and she will regain her senses. From this side she can burn the silken door to nothing and leap through in safety. She is strong. She will be safe. She will return to the village, like Ellis."

Val began to shiver. She looked shrunken and exhausted. "Ellis has not returned to Rin," she whispered. "He is waiting for me, at the edge of the forest. I feel it. I know it. I have known it all along. Never have we been apart so long. Never in our lives, since we were in the cradle. I have tried so hard not to think of it, but ..."

"Let us go," said Strong Jonn heavily. "We will tie ourselves together. None of us can be trusted not to stray."

Bind with ropes your flesh and blood.

But tears were rolling down Val's plain, muddy face. "I cannot go further," she said. "I knew it when I called to Ellis as Bronden struggled in my arms. I am sorry, so sorry. But I cannot go on with you." She buried her face in her hands. "You will not understand. You will think ill of me. I do not blame you. But I cannot go on alone. Half of me is missing. Ellis is waiting. He needs me, and I must go to him."

She turned away. "I have torches to make also," she said. "I will move fast, and catch up with Bronden. We will go together."

Rowan, Jonn, Allun and Marlie watched silently as she trudged away, shoulders bowed. She did not look back.

"It is true," said Marlie at last. "It was as if half of Val departed when Ellis did. She struggled bravely, but in the end she could not carry on without him. It is strange. They both seemed so strong, as though nothing could touch them."

Four, thought Rowan. There are only four of us now. So soon.

"The Mountain is doing its work well," said Strong Jonn, echoing Rowan's thoughts. "And there is yet far to go."

Allun smiled wearily. "All the better, then, that those who are friends continue together. Come. Let us go."

"And Allun—sing," added Marlie. "For once, I wish to hear nothing else."

They looped Marlie's rope around their waists and bound themselves together in a line. Jonn, Rowan, Allun and Marlie. They trudged on, looking neither left nor right, keeping their eyes to the ground, their ears filled with Allun's singing. His voice was sweet, but it sounded small and sad in the mist, and they took little joy in it.

"It was fortunate that you regained your senses, Allun the Baker, in time to prevent me from sinking in the mud and taking poor Rowan with me," remarked Marlie lightly, after a time.

"I heard Rowan's voice calling your name," said Allun, shaking his head. "And it was as though I was waking from a dream."

There was a shocked yell from Strong Jonn at the head of the line. He staggered backwards, pulling one wet and muddy leg from the treacherous ground into which it had plunged. "The north-west path has failed," he called. "I cannot tell how deep the bog is. We will have to find another way."

He felt cautiously around him. But wherever he turned, the mud sank beneath his feet.

"What are we to do?" cried Rowan.

"The map's warning said 'And let your guide be made of wood'," Marlie began hesitantly. "We believed this to mean that the guide should be a person who would not feel too deeply about others." She thought for a minute. "But perhaps the words have a different meaning altogether. Perhaps they mean exactly what they say. And were intended to help us at just this moment."

And so it was that the map's instructions were finally understood and carried out. They went back and cut the straightest branch they could find from one of the trees. They measured it against Rowan, the smallest of the party, and marked it at his shoulder height. And this branch, this wood, became their guide.

Jonn would plunge the branch into the mud ahead of them. Where it came to rest on firm ground, and the mud reached a point below the mark, they would step forward. Where it sank so deep that the mud rose above the mark, he would try again and again until a safe stepping place was found.

One step at a time they struggled forward, wading often up to their chests, in thick, sticky mud. Progress was painfully slow. And all the time the yellow-white mist floated about them, and sometimes shapes flitted just within their sight, and voices whispered. But they looked only forward, and closed their ears to the moans and cries that tempted them, holding fast to the rope that joined them one to the other.

Finally there came a time when on every side the wood sank so low that the mark was covered. Then Allun and Marlie shouldered Jonn's load, and Jonn took Rowan upon his back. And again they pushed forward, feeling their way, veering always to the north-west, till at last the mud began to firm beneath their feet, and the ground began to rise, and they knew that the dreadful journey was nearly at an end.

Staggering and exhausted, they climbed out of the swamp and mist, past the twisted, dark-leaved trees, on to land where grass grew again. Up and up they crawled, to where the air smelled sweet and the sun shone. And there they fell to the ground at last, and slept.

9 – Moving On

owan woke shivering. The sky was orange and red around the cloud-covered Mountain top, and the air was growing chill. Jonn, Marlie and Allun were still asleep, sprawled around him on the ground. All of them, even Strong Jonn, looked younger and more helpless like this. Their clothes, like Rowan's, were still damp and stinking from the swamp. Their hands and faces were streaked and filthy, their hair was soaked and caked with mud. How different was this small company from the one which had started out so bravely this morning. And how differently did he feel about his place in it.

Rowan watched the three adults sleeping, and wondered at the feeling of affection for them that welled up in him. Before, though he had known them all well from his earliest childhood, he had been afraid of them. Now he trusted them. Not just to look after him, but also—almost—to like him. He thought about this with surprise.

Marlie opened her eyes, blinked sleepily for a moment, and then saw him watching her, and smiled. She sat up and ran her fingers through her sticky hair. "We had better wake the others," she said. "And light a fire. It seems to have been decided that we spend the night here."

Later the four of them sat around the blazing fire, feasting on toasted bread and melted cheese, sun-dried fruits, honey and oat cakes, and Solla's best hard brown toffee. It was dark now, and cold. The moon shone white in the star-filled sky, behind a hazy veil of cloud.

While they ate in the bright circle of light, Allun, Marlie and Jonn talked of the village, and told tales of times gone by, and things that made them laugh. They could have been sitting beside Jiller's hearth in Rin.

Rowan sat and listened to them as he did at home, and wondered why things suddenly seemed so natural and relaxed. Then he realised.

It was because Bronden, Val and Ellis were no longer with them, and Allun had let down his guard. He still chatted and joked as usual, but his mouth had no bitter twist to it, and he was often content simply to sit quietly, poking lazily at the fire.

Rowan had heard Jiller say that when they were all children she had decided that Allun's joking and play-acting formed an armour stronger than Val and Ellis's iron muscles or Bronden's bad temper. And in a way, though Allun was grown up now, Rowan could see that the armour was still kept at the ready. And needed to be, since it was clear that for some villagers—like the three who had left them today—Allun would never be one of them. He would never be quite accepted, however much he wanted to be and however hard he tried, because of his Traveller father.

Rowan, watching Allun's lean brown face in the firelight, saw that in a way he was caught between two peoples. In his own eyes, at least. This knowledge kept him on guard. But here and now, with friends he trusted, he could truly be himself.

Rowan listened as the others talked, feeling comforted by their presence. No one mentioned Bronden, Val or Ellis. No one looked at the map as it lay spread out to dry by the fire. No one talked about the swamp, or the spiders, or the trek still to come.

But when the food had been put away, and they had woven Bronden's green stems into torches for the following day, and the fire had burnt down to glowing embers, the heavy darkness began to press in on them. Gradually they fell silent. Rowan wriggled uncomfortably. They had dried their clothes as best they could, and combed out their filthy hair, but they could not wash. The water in their flasks had to be saved for drinking.

Rowan would have given much for a long, hot bath. Mother would smile at that, he thought. I usually complain about having baths. And at once a pang of loneliness stabbed through him.

By now Ellis, Bronden and Val would be nearly home. They would surely not let darkness stop them. They would stumble into Rin at a time when people were thinking of putting out their lamps and going to sleep. Annad would be sleeping already, in the little room she and Rowan shared. Jiller would be sitting by the fire downstairs.

Reading, maybe, or mending something. Would she be thinking of him? What would she feel, when she heard of the others' return?

Allun glanced at his sad face. "The same moon is shining over Rin, you know," he murmured, pointing to the sky. "Think of that."

"It is not worth packing this last piece of toffee, Rowan," said Marlie, holding out the package. "You could finish it for us, I am sure."

"The map should be dry by now. Do you not think so, Rowan?" asked Jonn casually, at almost exactly the same moment.

Rowan realised that all of them were trying to comfort him in their own way.

He grinned shyly at Allun, took the toffee from Marlie, and nodded at Strong Jonn. "I will look at the map," he said.

He brushed the dried mud from the parchment. With his finger he traced their path, and found the place where they now camped. It seemed that they had completed about a third of their journey. From here they must turn due west again, climbing until they reached what looked like a steep cliff. There the red line rose abruptly. Rowan's heart sank at the thought of another fearful climb.

He looked for the third blank space on the map. There it was. Or rather, there was the spot where it had been. He bent over the parchment and haltingly read the words in the dim light of the fire:

"Look for the hand that points the way,
And take the path where children play.
Then, where the face with breath that sighs
Bends to admire its gleaming eyes,
Your way is marked by lines of light
That mean escape from endless night."

"Children," exclaimed Allun. "Are we to find *people* in this place? Ah, people mean water, Marlie! And hot tubs to wash in. And soft beds. And bowls of soup!"

"Perhaps," said Marlie. "But do not forget that people can also mean weapons, and fear of strangers. They will be many, and we are few."

Strong Jonn looked up at the dark, silent Mountain. "If there is a village so near, it is well hidden," he said. "Still, we shall see. Let us rest now. We will start at first light. It would be well to be early visitors, if visitors we are to be."

Despite his tiredness, Rowan lay unsleeping for some time after goodnights had been said. The others lay quiet, Jonn and Allun rolled up like caterpillars in their blankets, Marlie lying flat with hers flung over her. She would be cold in the night, he thought. He himself was warm, and the fire was banked up and glowing. But the words of the map's verse ran around and around in his head, always ending in the same way. The same frightening way that would jerk him awake and start the process all over again. *Endless night ... endless night ... endless night ...*

* * *

He woke with a heavy head to the sounds of Marlie heaping earth on the fire, and Allun whistling. It was still quite dark, but the sky had lightened and somewhere birds were singing. Rowan thought of Star and the other bukshah, moving to the pool for their morning drink with Jiller and Annad. He imagined their bewildered snuffling sounds as they found the water even lower than before. They would be getting very thirsty now. They would taste the brown muddy stuff that was left, and then they would shake their heavy heads and paw the ground. And they would wonder where he was.

We are going as fast as we can, Star. Rowan closed his eyes and thought the words as hard as he could, as if by doing this his message would reach his friend. *Soon we will be at the top of the Mountain. We will make the water flow again. Soon ...*

Then he remembered, and his eyes flew open again, filled with horror. Tomorrow—or the day after—they would reach the top of the Mountain. And—the Dragon. His heart lurched, and he felt sick. So much had happened to him, he had been so afraid on this journey, that for a while he had actually forgotten about his greatest fear. Until now. And then he thought of something else. Another day. Another dawn. And the Mountain was silent, except for the birds. Again, the Dragon had not roared.

He was still considering this when they set off again, due west, and climbing. "Allun," he said timidly, "do you think that the Dragon could be dead? Or gone to another place?"

"I certainly hope so," replied Allun cheerfully. "After thinking the matter over carefully, I have decided that I would prefer not to meet it."

"There was no sound from the Mountain top this morning," put in Marlie.

"No, nor was there last night," agreed Strong Jonn. He glanced at Rowan. "Many do say, of course," he added, "that there is no Dragon at the top of the Mountain. No one has ever seen it. We have no proof that the old stories about it are true."

"Bronden certainly did not believe in it," said Marlie.

Instantly the same thought entered everyone's mind. Bronden had not believed in anything she had not seen with her own eyes. And Bronden had found that she had been wrong. Very wrong.

Strong Jonn began to walk a little faster. He was carrying Rowan's pack again, but even without the extra weight Rowan had to struggle to keep up. After a while he had no energy to think of anything but the steep way ahead of him. As perhaps Jonn had intended.

They pushed through some ragged bushes clustered at the top of the rise. Then Allun exclaimed, and Marlie muttered under her breath. Rowan looked up. Rising over the tops of the trees directly ahead of them was a sheer cliff of red-gold rock glistening in the first rays of the sun. He gasped for breath and stared at it, fascinated.

He realised that he had seen this place before, many times, while tending the bukshah at sunrise. But then it had been small and far away. Then, gazing up at the Mountain, you would see a mass of green, then a strip of gleaming red-gold, then the cloud that hid the Mountain's tip. But now the cliff rose in front of him, and he could see that it dropped from the cloud like a wall—a wall almost as smooth and straight as the side of the mill of Rin.

He could not climb it. He knew he could not. The very sight of it filled him with terror. He pressed his lips together so that he would not cry out, and despair welled up in him. They had come so far, and fought so hard, only to be defeated by the Mountain at last.

For it was not only he who could not climb this cliff. The closer they came to it, the more he could see that no one could climb it. There were no footholds. There was nothing at all to cling to on that red-gold stone. Not a plant, or a hole, or a sharp piece of rock. Nothing.

"We have a problem," Allun remarked.

"So it seems," Strong Jonn said. He scanned the cliff with narrowed eyes.

"We should not despair," said Marlie, wiping the sweat from her forehead and shivering at the same time. The air was cold now, and a chill wind blew around them. "The way may be clearer to us when we arrive at the spot."

Allun and Jonn looked grim as they began walking once more. Rowan could see that they did not share Marlie's hope.

But when half an hour later they emerged from the trees and saw what lay at the foot of the cliff, they realised the wisdom of her words.

"A cave!" said Jonn. He peered inside the dark opening that was like a door in the rock. "A very deep one, too. Could it be ...? Rowan!"

They clustered around as Rowan unrolled the map. The red line moved upwards quite steeply, that was true. But not as steeply as the cliff rose to the clouds.

"Wonderful!" carolled Allun. "An easy way. And indoors out of the weather, too!" He turned to Marlie. "What a relief!"

She forced a smile. "Indeed," she answered. But Rowan saw that her face had grown pale.

They lit one of the torches they had made the night before. It flared up and then settled to a slow and steady flame. Marlie led the way, holding the torch out stiffly, as they stepped into the cave.

Piercing shrieks greeted them. Shrieks and the flapping of a thousand leathery wings as bats in their hundreds, disturbed from their daytime rest, fell from the roof of the cave and wheeled around them, beating at their faces.

Shouting, they bent their heads and crouched on the sandy ground, their arms protecting their eyes. Rowan could hear himself screaming with the others. It seemed an age before the high-pitched screeching sound had died and the panic-stricken creatures had departed. Only then did Marlie, Strong Jonn, Allun and Rowan rise slowly to their feet, breathing heavily as if they had been running. They looked at each other, and then Allun grinned. "Who was more frightened, do you think? We, or the bats?"

Relieved laughter echoed on the stone walls. The torch flickered, casting high shadows.

"Look!" cried Rowan.

At the far end of the cave, by the side of a wide, arched opening that seemed to lead into yet another chamber, stood a tall, oddly-shaped rock, all by itself. It was narrower at the bottom than at the top, and from it pointed a long, narrow finger of stone.

Look for the hand that points the way ...

Torch held high, they walked forward and through the archway, deeper into the Mountain.

10 – Endless Night

It was dark, so dark. And very cold. Marlie held up the torch, and Rowan drew breath in amazement. Countless rainbow-coloured spears of stone hung glistening from the soaring roof of the chamber. Strange, squat shapes rose from its floor in groups and lines. The cave was huge. You could not see its ending.

Jonn took a step forward, glanced at his compass, then hesitated. "The compass needle is wavering," he said. "Something is interfering with its workings."

"Metal in the rock, perhaps," suggested Marlie. The torchlight flickered yellow on her face. She fidgeted, moving from foot to foot.

"Perhaps. In any case it would be foolish to rely on it too completely. But without it, how can we find the path we are to take? We could so easily become lost in this maze."

"'And take the path where children play'," said Rowan. "This is what the map told us."

"It would be a brave child who would venture here," Allun observed.

Rowan peered around him, standing on his toes and craning his neck until he saw what he had been searching for. "I think, perhaps—" he began, and faltered. Perhaps he was being foolish. He did not want to lead them astray, or be laughed at.

"Speak up, Rowan," urged Strong Jonn. "This is not a time for anyone who has any plan at all to hold his tongue."

"It—it may be the stones," Rowan stammered. He pointed. "Those stones that are smaller than the others. Over there. There is a space between them, like a path. And their shapes ..."

"Of course!" Allun took the torch from Marlie and led them to the spot. Sure enough, two lines of the strange stones, bent and knobbly like children tumbling and crawling, climbed off into the darkness. Between them wound a clear, sandy path.

"So our way is marked for us," said Jonn with satisfaction, putting away his compass. "And now—"

"We look for a face that breathes with sighs, and has gleaming eyes," laughed Allun. "That should be interesting."

He led them up the path, the torch lighting the way in front of him. Looking back, Rowan saw the cavern receding into the darkness. *Endless night.* He shivered.

They moved on. Upwards. Always upwards. They were climbing through the centre of the Mountain. Rowan tried not to think of the tonnes of rock and earth that surrounded them, pressing down, cutting off light and air. If they were lost here, no one would ever find them. They would wander in the endless night until they died, and the Mountain would be their tomb. He pushed the fear down, but it grew and pressed on his belly and his heart, making it hard to breathe.

Higher and higher they climbed, through one chamber to the next. By their sides, the rocky children bent and stretched in a game that had no ending. The climbers said little, for the way was steep. The silence was as thick around them as the darkness. Rowan listened to the hissing of the torch, to his own breath, to the panting of Marlie behind him, and the sounds of Jonn's boots crushing sand and hitting rock in front.

"Another cavern!" Allun's voice bounced back to them from walls they could not see. They heard him scrambling forward, and the torchlight disappeared. "The face!" he exclaimed. "The face is ..." His voice trailed off.

"Allun, what is it?" shouted Marlie, pushing forward. "Allun, answer! Allun, bring back the light. We cannot see!"

"The face," he called. His voice sounded strange, as though he were choking. "It is here. Come. But slowly."

The torchlight reappeared, and cautiously they climbed towards it. Allun was standing by a wide gap in the rock. He did not smile as they reached his side, but thrust the torch through the gap. "See for yourselves," he said. "But again, take care."

They squeezed through the opening, into the cave beyond. Rods of white and yellow stone hung thickly from the roof, but the black and shining floor below the ledge on which they stood was as smooth as glass. Facing them, on the far side, was a wall of rock. A wall, with a bulging lump in the middle. A lump shaped like a face, looking down. They saw the twisted, rocky nose, swollen cheeks, slitted mouth, broad chin. And gleaming eyes that cast beams of light across the floor. *Your way is marked by lines of light.*

There was sound here, too. A sighing, whistling, breathy sound.

"It breathes," whispered Marlie. "The face breathes, as the rhyme foretold."

"A passage on that side must open to the air," exclaimed Jonn. "That is the outside air we hear, Marlie! We have climbed far in these caverns. We must surely be almost at our journey's end."

"I fear," said Allun, still in that strange voice, "that I, at least, am at my journey's end now."

He was standing with his back pressed against the cavern wall, and as they stared at him, he slid down until he was sitting on the ground.

"Allun, get up!" Marlie ordered. "What game are you playing?"

"I would not have come if I had known," Allun said wearily. "But how could I have known? Whoever would have dreamed it possible?" He rubbed at his eyes, shaking his head.

"Allun, we do not know what you mean! Come! We must move on." Strong Jonn frowned and turned away. As he did so, his boot kicked a pebble from the ledge and it fell to the shiny black floor.

There was a splash, and the pebble disappeared. Ripples spread in silent, ever-increasing circles across the smooth surface of what they had all mistaken for solid ground.

"Water," said Allun. He looked haggard. "The cave is half full of water. Deep water, for it is black and cold and you cannot see the bottom."

"So?" Marlie demanded. "So we put up with the cold, and swim."

Allun raised his eyebrows. "But you see, Marlie, my dear, I cannot swim."

"*What?*" They gaped at him, and he stared back defiantly.

"It is not a skill the Travellers teach their young," he said. "The Travellers sensibly leave swimming to the Maris folk. After all, they are the ones who get their living from the sea, and have webbed feet and hands to make the whole miserable business more efficient. The Travellers refuse to have anything to do with water in larger quantities than a tin tub will hold."

"But in Rin we *all* learn to swim," Rowan burst out. "We have to. As soon as we can walk, practically. We have to go to the coast or the river on the plain especially to learn." He winced, remembering those lessons in the river. He had learned to swim, in the end. But he had not enjoyed it.

Allun smiled bitterly. "Ah, yes. In Rin it is different. In Rin you must have every physical skill, of course, or you are regarded as useless. Even if you live far inland. Even if you have to travel a day and a night to practise swimming, and may never swim from one year to the next, or ever again in your life, still you must be able to swim. As you must be able to climb, fight, run, and so on and so on. Such things, in Rin, are thought so important."

"They *are* important," cried Marlie. "A person must be prepared for whatever adventure he or she might meet. As we can see, right now, Allun!" She faced him despairingly. "So you did not learn to swim as a small child. That is unfortunate. But why on earth did you not learn once you arrived in Rin?"

Allun glared at her. "Was I not already a figure of fun and ridicule? I, the strange-looking, skinny Traveller boy who had never worn shoes and knew nothing of your village ways? At ten years old the taunts of other children are very hard to bear. Rowan will tell you that." He glanced at Rowan, who nodded silently. So he had been right. Allun *had* understood how he felt.

Marlie took Allun's arm. "I understand, Allun. But you could have asked about swimming lessons ..."

He rounded on her. "No, you do not understand. Was I to make even more of a clown of myself by letting those bullies under the Teaching Tree know of my weakness? I could not teach myself in secret. There is no water in Rin but the stream and the bukshah pool. I would have had to ask to be taken to the river on the plain for lessons with the three-year-olds! How Ellis would have crowed over that." He shrugged, twisting his face into a comical mask.

"And as you can imagine, the longer I waited, the more impossible it became," he said. "Before I knew it I was that unthinkable thing: an adult of Rin who could not swim." He smiled. "It did not matter, of course," he went on softly. "It did not matter a jot. Until now."

Strong Jonn shook his head. "There must be a way," he began. "If you just—"

"Jonn, you must accept this, as I have. I cannot swim. Not a stroke," said Allun firmly. "So if you are thinking of helping this lame duck along, pulling him by one useless wing, perhaps, think again. The water is icy. You will have enough trouble keeping yourselves afloat, without attempting to stop me from drowning also. The ropes will not stretch across to the other side. So put that out of your minds as well."

"This is why you never take the chance to visit the coast on market days, Allun." Jonn looked at him thoughtfully. "I have often wondered ..."

"Well, now your wonderings are at an end," smiled Allun. But he turned his head away.

Marlie bit her lip. "You cannot return to Rin alone now, Allun," she burst out at last. "The swamp will surely be your death, without a partner."

"I have thought of this." Allun brushed at his coat, as though removing the dried mud that clung there was all that was important to him. "I will make camp beside the cave mouth. I will wait for you there." He laughed bitterly. "I had thought to be a hero of Rin. Show them what the half-Traveller could do. Who would have thought that such a small weakness would be my undoing? And that because of my foolish pride I would let down my friends?" He did not look at Strong Jonn. "I would give much for it not to be so. Forgive me."

Seven hearts the journey make. Seven ways the hearts will break.

But Jonn put out his hand. "There is nothing to forgive, old friend. Wait for our return. Make more torches, if you can find good wood. We will need them." He hesitated, then went on in a lower voice. He had turned his head away from Rowan, but Rowan still heard what he said. "If we do not return in three days, Allun, you must wait no longer. You must find your way back to Rin somehow. To those who love us. Better that they hear the worst than that they do not hear at all. Is this agreed?"

"Agreed." Allun took Jonn's hand and squeezed it warmly.

"Let us go then," said Marlie. Her eyes were full of tears. She threw her arms around Allun. "We will be back," she whispered. "Take care."

"And you, Marlie."

Jonn, Rowan and Marlie stripped off their boots and outer clothes, and stuffed them into their packs. Then, shivering, they entered the water and began swimming.

It was, indeed, bitterly cold. So cold that Rowan's flesh first stung, and then grew numb. The water flooded his mouth, harsh and sour. Across the black pool they crept, sidling like crabs along the lines of light, striking out with their right hands, holding their packs with their left hands so that they dragged along behind them, half in and half out of the water.

Nameless things brushed Rowan's feet and legs as he swam. He clenched his teeth at the thought of them, but kept pulling himself along with an arm that grew heavier and slower with every stroke. Soon he was in agony, but worse than the pain of continuing was the thought of sinking down into this black, still hole, never to see light and air again.

Then his hand struck rock, and with a wave of relief he realised that he could stand. He looked up. The huge stone face was above him. Marlie was already climbing out of the pool, gasping and dripping. Behind him Strong Jonn heaved his pack out of the water as he too reached the shore. All of them turned and called to Allun, who was waiting anxiously on the other side. They were standing in shadow, so he could not see them, but he lifted the torch high in response to their shouts. At least he knew that they were safe.

Marlie bent and offered a hand to haul Rowan up beside her. His teeth were chattering so much that he could not speak. He jumped up and down to warm himself. With cold, clumsy fingers Marlie unbuckled his pack and pulled out the clothes he had stripped off before the swim.

"Take off your wet things and put these on before you freeze to death," she advised. "They are a little damp, but much better than nothing."

Rowan knew he couldn't do that. Not in front of Marlie. He didn't even undress in front of his mother any more. He hesitated.

"By my life, Rowan!" Marlie exclaimed in amused exasperation, her own clothes clutched in her arms. "You have been menaced by giant spiders, nearly smothered in a swamp and now half drowned and frozen, and you are embarrassed about taking your clothes off in front of me! Does that not seem ridiculous?"

"Not at all," grinned Strong Jonn, coming up behind them. "I understand completely. Some things a man simply cannot do. I suggest you turn your back, Marlie. Then modesty can be preserved and we can all get warm without delay."

11 – The Snare

The torches were damp, but at last they managed to light one. The map, tightly rolled and securely wrapped in Rowan's clothes during the swim, had survived. John and Marlie crouched beside Rowan as he unrolled it and spread it out on his knees.

The red lines continued upward, twisting and turning. And in the next blank space, the verse Rowan had come to expect had appeared:

Left or right, which will you take?
For both of them your heart will break.
One is cruel, one is fair,
One a passage, one a snare.
Choose the one that hides the light,
And you will know your path is right.

They all looked up at the huge stone face. The gleaming eyes still cast their reflections over the water, and now that they were directly below them they could see that they were hollow. They were entrances. To what? Which one was the door that led to the Mountain top? Rowan bent his head to the map again. The outline gave no clue. There was no marking showing twin passages. The only clues were in the verse.

"We will look at both, and decide," Jonn said.

But when they had climbed the rocky face and peered into its eyes, they found that both caves looked alike. The walls of both were gleaming with a strange white-blue fungus that shone in the dark. Both were roughly the same size and shape, though the left was slightly higher and wider than the right. And from both came the sighing, breathy sound.

"What does it mean, 'One is cruel, one is fair'?" demanded Marlie. "They are both the same!"

"It says we should choose the one that hides the light," Rowan pointed out. "Perhaps we should try each of them in turn, to see where the torch flickers and dies."

Marlie moved uncomfortably, shaking her damp hair from her eyes.

"Agreed," said Strong Jonn. "We will first try the right-hand side. Who knows but that the last line of the verse is speaking the absolute truth, as it was in the swamp. It says 'your path is right'. Perhaps it means just that."

They held up their torch to Allun, and watched him raise his in answer and turn away to begin his lonely journey back to the cave entrance. Then they crawled up into the right-hand passage. It curved immediately, then curved again, and Rowan soon lost his sense of direction.

He could walk upright, but Marlie and Jonn had to bend their heads slightly, for the roof was low. They crept along, stumbling on the rocky floor, and the flame of the torch burned as brightly as ever. Then abruptly they came to a halt. In front of them the cave-like passage narrowed into a low tunnel, barely large enough to crawl through.

"That settles it," panted Marlie. "A snare if ever I saw one. Now we try the left. It was too much to hope for straight advice from Sheba."

The left-hand passage was easier to walk in. It was straight, at first, and larger than the other, and its sandy floor was smooth. But again the flame of the torch did not flicker. They walked on and on, turning corner after corner, in increasing puzzlement. The map had never failed them before.

The sighing sound was louder now. It filled their ears and whispered around them. And Rowan could smell something. A smell like damp, and mould, and cold, thick darkness.

At first he thought it was his imagination. Or the glowing fungus on the walls. He rubbed his fingers over it and smelt them. No. The fungus smelt of nothing at all as far as he could tell.

Strong Jonn, who was leading, slowed and finally stopped as the tunnel curved yet again.

"Go on, Jonn," called Marlie, impatiently. "The faster we go, the sooner we will be out of here!"

"The tunnel is starting to go down quite steeply now," Jonn said. "The walls are smooth, with no handholds, and the sand will make it difficult for us to keep our feet."

"I do not like this place," Rowan murmured. "It looks fair, as the rhyme said. But it feels like danger."

One is cruel, one is fair, One a passage, one a snare ...

Fear fluttered in his chest.

"Nonsense," Marlie said. "We have no choice. The other way is blocked."

"Not quite blocked," said Jonn, turning to face her. "There is room to crawl. It would be a cruel journey, but perhaps it is the way after all. The verse, remember, rhymes 'fair' with 'snare'. And I agree with Rowan. This place smells of death."

"You are both absurd!" Breathing in short, shallow gasps, Marlie pushed past Rowan. She grabbed the flaming torch from Jonn, darted around him, took two steps and slipped. She scrabbled in the shifting sand, trying to rise, while the torch tumbled away from her down the slope, bouncing and turning.

Then it fell. Fell over the terrible drop that lay at the end of the tunnel. Fell and fell, while Marlie screamed. It hit bottom, finally, with a sickening crack.

They pulled Marlie up after them as they scrambled out of the tunnel, almost running, their hearts beating wildly at the thought of the fate they had escaped. One more minute—half a minute—and they too would have tumbled helplessly to their deaths over that underground cliff. Stumbling around the last bend, they fell on their knees at the tunnel entrance.

Marlie was shaking. "I am sorry. I am sorry," she said over and over.

Rowan too was trembling. Strong Jonn's weatherbeaten face was drawn, but he roused himself with an effort. "Looking on the bright side, as Allun would say," he said, trying to smile, "at least we now know that the right-hand passage must indeed be the way. The tunnel is narrow, but if we leave our packs behind, and take only what we can carry in our pockets, we can do it. We will have to crawl. And pray that it is not too long."

Rowan swallowed, thinking of that cramped, dark hole they had seen in the right-hand cave. The idea of creeping into it, without any idea of where he was going or when the ordeal would end, was frightful. The red line on the map had been long. Very long. But he said nothing. The other way had been a snare indeed. It had nearly killed them. If they were to reach the Mountain top, they were going to have to crawl. So be it.

They lit another torch and edged across the right-hand passage. They entered it and followed its sharp bend as before, cutting them- selves off immediately from the sight of the gleaming pool. Rowan drew a breath as he realised the truth. *Choose the one that hides the light.* This was the light the verse had meant. Not the torchlight, as they had thought, but the reflected light on the pool, cut off from their view by the turning of the right-hand tunnel, but clearly visible for minutes in the straight, fair left. They had misunderstood the words again. *Choose the one that hides the light, And you will know your path is right.* The answer had been there, twice, clear for all of them to see. And still they had blundered.

When they reached the place where the passage narrowed, Jonn, Marlie and Rowan opened their packs and began transferring the most important of their possessions to their pockets, and winding rope around their waists. It was clear that no baggage would fit through that tiny hole. As it was, Strong Jonn and Marlie would almost totally fill the space, and crawling would be slow and uncom- fortable, with no turning back.

"Before we begin, we will eat," said Jonn, pointing at the food they had discarded. "We do not know when we will have another chance."

Rowan squatted on the ground and began to nibble at some bread and cheese. His stomach was empty, but it was churning too, from fear, and the bitter water he had swallowed in the black pool. He thought he had never enjoyed a meal less.

Marlie crouched over her pack, breathing hard. She ignored the food Jonn offered her. Rowan wondered whether she was ill. She had not seemed herself since they entered the caverns, except for the brief time when they were swimming. And now she was obviously in distress. Sweat was breaking out on her forehead, and she bit her lips as she pulled out her sleeping blanket and cast it aside with shaking fingers.

"Marlie." Strong Jonn's voice was low. She stiffened, but did not raise her head. "Marlie," he said again. "It is the tunnel, is it not? It is the smallness of the tunnel that worries you."

"I am not afraid," Marlie said loudly. But still she did not look up.

"Once we begin, Marlie, there will be no turning back," Jonn said. "If you feel you cannot do this, you should say so now. You have been uneasy ever since we entered the caverns. We have all seen that. You fear enclosed spaces."

"I do not! I am not afraid," Marlie said again. But her voice was thick. She threw back her head and looked Jonn in the eye. She was quivering with fear and tension. "I am ready," she said. "Let us begin."

She walked to the narrow opening and threw herself to the ground. Slowly she began to wriggle into the tunnel. They watched her head and shoulders disappear into the gloom, then her body, then her legs and feet. They felt her agony of mind as if it were a living thing. But they could do nothing but wait. Only when at last her strength broke, and she began to scream and gasp, to cry out to them and beat on the rocky walls, could they act. Only then could they pull her from the suffocating prison her fear had made, and help her to breathe again, and still her cries.

"I thought I could defeat it," she sobbed. "I was sure that this time, for such an important task, I could do it. But it overwhelms me, Jonn. As it always has." She buried her face in her hands.

"It is all right, Marlie. Marlie—be still," soothed Jonn.

"I do not like any shut-in place," Marlie whispered. "But when I cannot lift my head and shoulders, when I cannot move my arms freely, it is as if I cannot breathe. I cannot even wrap myself tightly in a blanket, for fear of it." She lifted her head and gulped at the air.

"So I saw, last night," said Jonn, smiling. "I thought perhaps you did not feel the cold."

"I nearly froze!" Marlie managed to answer his smile. "Jonn, I am so sorry. And Rowan ... What will we do now?"

"We will do what must be done," said Jonn simply. "I will continue. You have a compass. Rowan has the map. You two will join Allun, and together make your way back to Rin. If you follow the way we came with every care, and remember ..."

Marlie stared at him in horror. "But you cannot go on alone! Jonn, you cannot!"

"Marlie, I must. You know I must."

"No!" Rowan heard his own voice, loud in the echoing space of the cave. He could feel his face burning. "You cannot send me home. I have the map. You need the map. There are two blank spaces left. Two verses of warning still to come. You need to know what they are, Strong Jonn. You must take me with you."

"I cannot do that, Rowan." Jonn shook his head.

"I will not go back," cried Rowan. "You cannot make me." He ran over to the narrow passage entrance and sat down in front of it. "I must hold the map for you," he said. "I must find the water for the bukshah. I promised them." He set his chin.

Jonn stared back at him in helpless silence.

Marlie half smiled. "It seems you have met your match, Strong Jonn. With the son as well as the mother." She regarded Rowan curiously. "Who would have thought it?"

Jonn hesitated, then gave in. "Very well," he sighed. "So, what will be, will be, and Sheba is to have her way." He put a big hand on Marlie's shoulder. "Goodbye, Marlie. And good luck on your journey home. Remember all we have learned. This time you will face the dangers well prepared. You will survive. Tell Allun that we four will meet again, in Rin." In two strides he was at Rowan's side. "Come then, before either of us changes his mind, skinny rabbit. You first."

"Take care," called Marlie as they disappeared into the tunnel. "Take care, Strong Jonn and Rowan of the Bukshah."

Her voice echoed in the cave behind them, then faded into the silence.

Now, thought Rowan in the darkness, we are two.

12 – Bravest Heart

owan was crawling with his eyes shut tight. He had found that this was better than facing the sighing blackness ahead. His hands were bleeding—grazed and cut by the rock. His legs ached with weariness. He could hear Strong Jonn pulling himself along behind, groaning with the effort as he struggled against the walls that pressed against his broad shoulders. They had stopped speaking long ago.

The passage had circled and turned back on itself many times. They crawled and rested, crawled and rested, in a nightmarish pattern that repeated itself over and over again. Twice they had fallen asleep, and woken in the darkness, crying out to each other in panic. Now they did not know how long they had been in the tunnel. They did not know whether it was day or night. All they knew was that they were climbing. Upwards, always upwards.

Seven hearts the journey make. Seven ways the hearts will break. Sheba's words spun around in Rowan's exhausted brain. The Mountain had struck five times. In five different ways five brave hearts had been forced to retreat in shame from their quest. Ellis, Bronden, Val, Allun, Marlie. All gone. Now only he and Jonn remained. The last two hearts for the Mountain to break.

The tunnel narrowed, and he reached yet another turning. With despair he heard the scraping of Strong Jonn's boots and clothes against the rock, the struggling gasps as Jonn heaved himself forward and then lay still. Jonn's every move was hampered by the tunnel walls that gripped him. In all this time he had not been able to reach his flask, or Rowan's, to drink. He was nearing exhaustion. And so was Rowan. If they should come upon a blockage—a fallen rock—anything—they were doomed. Rowan knew that he would not have the strength to move it. And Jonn was tightly wedged behind him.

Panic rose in him, as it had so many times since this terrible journey began. He screwed up his eyes more tightly, and breathed deeply. He had discovered that this helped.

Star helped, too. Rowan crawled on around the bend, thinking of Star, the most peaceful and loving thing he knew. He imagined himself walking beside her to the bukshah pool in the evening, his hand on her mane, the cool breeze blowing in his face. The fear died in him. The picture in his mind grew stronger. Now he could almost see the bukshah pool, and Star bending her head to drink. He could almost smell the trodden grass, the blossom from the orchard. And he could almost feel the cool breeze on his face. He smiled in the darkness. It was extraordinary. He really could feel that breeze. Just as if ...

Rowan's eyes flew open. He stared, licked his lips, and shouted as the cool breeze, the cold breeze, the icy-cold breeze, blew full in his face.

"Jonn," he screamed. "Come on! We are there! We are there!" He pulled himself along, faster and faster, careless of his bleeding hands and aching legs, towards the source of that icy wind, and the glimmer of white that beckoned him. And behind him, with a last, desperate effort, crawled Jonn.

Agonising minutes later, they were lying together on the floor of a shallow cave that opened to the air. It was freezing. Outside, there was howling wind, and the whiteness of moonlit snow.

"Water," croaked Strong Jonn through cracked lips.

Holding the flask to Jonn's mouth, Rowan looked down at him in fright. Jonn's clothing had been torn away by the rock in many places, and the skin beneath was grazed and bleeding. His face was grey. His eyes were closed. The water bubbled from his mouth and dripped to the ground. He shivered without stopping.

Some sticks and dried leaves were heaped in the corner of the cave, blown in by the wind. Rowan gathered them together, found Jonn's tinder box, and managed to light a fire. It smoked and spluttered, but at least it gave out a little warmth.

Strong Jonn lay still. Rowan waited, his hands clasped anxiously. After a time, a little colour began to creep back into the man's face. He stirred and opened his eyes.

"We are above the cloud, Rowan," he muttered. "I believe we have been underground for a night and a day and part of yet another night. By this time, if they are safe, Allun and Marlie will be back in Rin. And we are nearly at our journey's end. The map ..."

Rowan unrolled the map. He followed with his fingers the path they had taken, traced the way above the cloud. "We are almost at the top of the Mountain," he said slowly. "And close to us—very close—there must be another cave, or something like it. Very large. Very deep. The red line ends there ..." He swallowed. His eyes had moved to the second-last blank space.

"And the verse?" Jonn's voice was very weak. "Read the verse."

Rowan read it aloud, the map shaking in his trembling hands.

"Fire, water, earth and air
All meet in the Dragon's lair.
Six brave hearts have failed the test,
One continues in the quest.
Remember well the words you know,
When on to find your fate you go."

"So," said Jonn, and closed his eyes again.
Bravest heart will carry on ...

"But Jonn, the verse does not speak truly!" cried Rowan. "There are two of us. Two!"

Jonn moistened his lips with his tongue. "No, Rowan. I am finished. You must leave me here and at dawn go on alone. As Sheba foretold." He turned his head away.

When sleep is death, and hope is gone.

The fire gave a final flicker and went out.

Sleep is death ...

"Jonn!" Rowan screamed, in terror. He shook Jonn's shoulder savagely, so that the big man stirred and groaned. "Jonn, do not go to sleep! It is too cold. You are too weak! You will freeze! You will die! Jonn, get up!" Jonn did not move. Rowan sobbed, beating at the ground. "Jonn, I cannot go on alone! You know I cannot! Sheba did not foretell this! Sheba said the bravest heart would carry on. That is what she said. And I am not the bravest heart. I fear everything! Everything!"

Jonn's pale lips curved. "Yes, skinny rabbit. So you do," he murmured. "Fearing, you climbed the Mountain. Fearing, you faced its dangers. And fearing, you went on. That is real bravery, Rowan. Only fools do not fear. Sheba knew that. Sheba knew everything, all along."

Rowan stared. And slowly an icy calm settled on him. He knew what he must do. "Sleep now," he whispered. "I will look after you."

Rowan crept to the entrance of the cave. He took off his jacket and wrapped it around his hands. Then he plunged them into the snow and began to build a wall of snow up around the entrance, filling the gaping space till only a small hole was left for the wind to penetrate. It took a long time, and despite the jacket his hands were throbbing with cold when at last he was satisfied.

Strong Jonn lay curled up by the ashes of the fire. It was already warmer in the cave, but still not warm enough for safety. Rowan pulled on his jacket. Staggering now with weariness, he collected some stones and put them in the ashes, then laid over them the two torches he and Jonn had carried through the Mountain. He lit the torches, and watched them flare up, then settle down to burn slowly. He lay down beside Jonn, cuddling close and warming him with his body.

The torches would heat the air. They would heat the stones. The stones would hold the heat after the fire had died. *And hope is gone ...* No, the verse had reckoned without him. He still had heart, and hope. Now, with luck, the dawn would find both him and Jonn alive. Then they would see.

Rowan closed his eyes at last, and slept.

His sleep was deep and dreamless, and when he woke he thought at first that no time had passed. But then he saw the pale light that streamed into the cave through the hole in the snow wall, and became aware of the silence. It was dawn, and the wind had dropped.

Rowan sat up and with beating heart peered at Jonn. He was warm—and breathing.

Gently Rowan shook his shoulder. "Jonn," he whispered. "Jonn! Wake up. It is morning. And we must go. Together."

* * *

They pushed their way through the snow, Strong Jonn leaning on Rowan's shoulder. Their boots sank into the soft whiteness as they walked, squeaking and crunching it into holes that shone icy blue. The tracks of animals that had hunted for food in the night criss-crossed their path, but the animals themselves were not to be seen. Once Rowan thought he saw a sharp nose twitching in a burrow, but in the blink of an eye, whatever it was had disappeared.

Thick cloud floated around them. Above them it cleared to a light haze, and through it they could see the sky. It was a clear, pale pink. A fine day in Rin, thought Rowan, glancing behind him, though he knew he would see nothing. Rin was somewhere there below, but the cloud hid it from view. He felt Jonn's compass in his pocket, the map in his belt. With these, I will find the way back, he promised himself. However long it takes, I will bring Strong Jonn back to Rin. I will see Mother again, and Star, and the bukshah pool in the dawn. I will!

He faced ahead and squinted into the cloud, trying to see. Jonn was struggling beside him, his breath coming hard and fast. Now he was leaning more heavily on Rowan's shoulder, but still he moved on without complaint. Rowan was filled with pity for his suffering and wonder at his courage.

"All well, Jonn?" he asked, as cheerfully as he could. "Nearly there now." And was struck by a sudden memory. An echo of Strong Jonn's voice, saying those very words to him. In just the same way, on that first morning, as they walked away from Rin. Rowan caught his breath. Had Jonn's heart been aching for him then as his ached for Jonn now? And for the same reasons? Had he then been wrong, quite wrong, about Jonn all along?

"Rowan!" Jonn clutched his shoulder. "I think I see something."

A shape rose within the cloud, behind a natural wall of snow-covered rocks. It was white on the edges, and pale, shining blue in the middle. It was huge, high and wide. Above it, there was only sky.

"We are at the top," breathed Rowan. His heart began to race. "But ...?"

Slowly they moved closer. And as they did so, they understood. The whole tip of the Mountain was hollow, making a vast cavern of rock, snow and ice. The cavern's walls soared to the heavens, flashing in the rising sun like white fire. *Fire, water, earth and air ...* A thick carpet of powdery snow covered the ground from its entrance to the wall of rock where they stood.

Rowan stared. There was no sound. No tracks marked that flat carpet of snow. Nothing at all had crossed this place for a day at least. Perhaps many days.

He helped Jonn over the rocks and they walked to the cavern entrance and cautiously peered inside. White. Nothing but blinding white and shadowy blue. Huge icicles fringed the entrance and the roof. Weird ice shapes covered the walls, rose from the floor. And everywhere there was snow. Their eyes dazzled. They moved forward, blinking, climbing over the ridges and drifts that covered the floor, gazing in wonder.

Rowan turned to Jonn to speak. Saw his face change. The look of horror—

And then the ground erupted beneath their feet. Snow scattered, and a mighty tail lashed, hurling Rowan on to his back, throwing Strong Jonn crashing to the wall. And Rowan, screaming, watched as the back of the cave came to life, opened its blood-red eyes and lunged for him, shaking snow and ice from its shining white scales, baring its dripping teeth. Huge. Ancient. Terrible. The Dragon of the Mountain.

13 – The Answer

Rowan screamed, waiting for the hot breath, the tearing fangs and claws that would mean death. But they did not come. He uncovered his eyes fearfully. The Dragon was very near. It was watching him. Its flat, snake-like eyes stared into his, compelling him.

"Jonn," called Rowan in a low voice, without looking away. "Strong Jonn?"

"I am here," came the answer. "The creature's tail has me pinned to the wall. I cannot move. Rowan, save yourself if you can."

The Dragon growled. It turned its head towards Jonn's voice, then looked back to Rowan. It swayed its huge body and clawed at the soft place in its neck, where dried blood crusted wounds made over many days. Its eyes were red pools of anger and—something else. Rowan saw it, and in amazement recognised it for what it was: dumb animal pain.

He slowly got to his feet, never breaking his gaze. "What ails you?" he said quietly, in the voice he used for the bukshah.

The Dragon lowered its head and opened its jaws. It moaned, deep in its throat. Needle-sharp teeth dripped watery blood on the snow at Rowan's feet. Hot, stinking breath beat in his face. Rowan shrank back, but again the Dragon did not strike.

"Rowan!" hissed Strong Jonn. "Back away slowly, and go. You have the map and the compass. You can get home. You have a chance. Take it!"

Rowan barely heard him. He was looking at the claw marks around the Dragon's neck. An idea forming in his mind suddenly became crystal clear. He glanced around the cave. No bones, or flesh. Just fresh white snow.

"You have not been eating," he crooned to the Dragon, as if he were talking to Star. "You have not been hunting. Yet your jaws drip blood." He met the Dragon's eyes. Long ago, in a very different place, and in a pair of very different eyes, he had seen that look before. If he could earn the beast's trust ... He made his decision, and took a deep breath. "I think I know what is wrong. And I can help you," he said. "I am a friend. A friend."

The Dragon stared at him, unblinking.

"Be still," said Rowan.

He moved closer. He looked into the red and dripping mouth, then leaned inside, further and further, till he found what he sought.

Look in the fiery jaws of fear, And see the answer white and clear.

The bone was sharp and white. It had jammed between a tooth and the back of the Dragon's throat, as a twig had once caught in Star's throat. Rowan had removed that twig. He could remove this bone.

He worked gently, knowing the agony the creature was feeling. The Dragon growled. One wrong move, and those terrible jaws would snap closed. Little by little, Rowan eased the bone loose. At last, with a delicate twist, he pulled it free. He backed out of the Dragon's mouth and towards Strong Jonn, holding the bone in his hand.

"Now," he said softly. "Now let us go. You are well. You can hunt. Let us ..."

The Dragon's eyes flashed. It rose up on its hind legs. It beat its scaly white wings. At last it was free of the terrible pain that had stilled its roar and quenched its fire for so many days. The pain that had stopped it from hunting, wheeling through the skies above its cloudy kingdom. It was free—and hungry.

It roared, and the sound was like thunder, beating and echoing around the walls of the lair. Icicles fell from the cave roof, smashing and splintering on the ground, and the ground itself shook. It roared again, and sheets of fire belched from its mouth and nostrils, melting the snow and ice so that steam billowed into the air to mix with flame and choking smoke.

Then it turned to Jonn. Hunger burned in its red eyes. It would not yet attack the boy who had healed it with his gentle hands. But the man was a different story.

"No!" shouted Rowan. He ran to Jonn's side, slipping and sliding on the now icy floor of the lair. He threw himself down by the help-less man and shielded him with his body.

The Dragon twisted and roared, and Jonn cried out in agony as the movement crushed him even more firmly against the cavern wall. Rowan pulled out his knife and stabbed desperately at the Dragon's tail, but the knife blade bent and broke against the shiny white scales. It was useless. The Dragon howled with rage and spat a wall of flame that singed Rowan's hair and eyebrows. Again and again the roaring flame came at them. They huddled together.

"Rowan," groaned Jonn. "Rowan, it is trying to scare you off. It only wants me now. Get out while you can, for Jiller's sake if not for your own. Rowan, I promised her. I beg of you. Go!"

But Rowan would not give in. He had to make the Dragon move its tail so that Jonn would be free to run. He had to do it before the Dragon lost patience, and killed them both. But he had no weapons. "What will I do?" he cried out. "I don't know what to do!"

Remember well the words you know ...

"What words? What words?" Rowan whimpered. "Oh please ..."

"The map." Strong Jonn's voice was faint beside him. "Rowan ..."

Crouching low, Rowan pulled the map from his belt and unrolled it.

Remember well the words you know.

The last blank space was filled. The words swam before his eyes. The words he knew indeed. The words that he had heard for the first time with a thrill of dread, the words that had filled his dreams and haunted his thoughts in the long days since:

Seven hearts the journey make.
Seven ways the hearts will break.
Bravest heart will carry on
When sleep is death, and hope is gone.
Look in the fiery jaws of fear
And see the answer white and clear,
Then throw away all thoughts of home
For only then your quest is done.

All the prophecies had come to pass, except the last. The last, and the most terrible. And now it was time.

Rowan rolled up the map, and drew Jonn's compass from his pocket. He waited his moment.

Throw away all thoughts of home ...

The Dragon threw back its head and again roared its anger. Its soft neck, scratched and torn by its own claws in its efforts to dislodge the choking bone and end the pain, gleamed pale and exposed.

And with all the strength and desperation of his fear, Rowan hurled the compass at that white, tender target. It struck, like a hard, sharp stone, and the Dragon cried and thrashed in pain and fury, tossing its head from side to side, lifting its tail from Strong Jonn's body.

Just for a moment. Just long enough for Rowan to pull Jonn free, to drag him, sliding, over the icy ground, towards the entrance of the lair. Just long enough for him to turn and throw the rolled map hard, straight and spinning, to strike the exposed neck again, so that again the Dragon roared and for precious seconds turned its head away from them.

Throw away all thoughts of home ...

Then they were running. Running from the lair. To find a place to hide, to burrow like the night animals, away from the Dragon's rage.

For only then your quest is done. Yes, the quest was done. Done, and lost. As they were. "Mother ... Star ..." Rowan sobbed. His heart was breaking. Yet still he ran.

But the snow before the lair had melted in the Dragon's fire, and now the flat surface was a sheet of swimming ice. Rowan and Jonn slipped and fell, their hands flailing helplessly, their feet sliding from beneath them as they struggled to rise and run again.

The Dragon's red eyes burned. It raised itself in anger. Sheets of fire, hot as a hundred furnaces, burst from its mouth and nose, scorching their feet, boiling the ice to a hissing mass of water and steam. Rowan and Jonn rolled, crawled, beating at the melting ice, twisting their bodies to save themselves.

Then, with a screeching crack, the ice split beneath them, the ice that had formed and lain unmelted all the long days of the Dragon's pain, but now at last was feeling the heat of its flames, and giving way. The cold, sweet water from the melted snow poured through the ice and into the underground channel that was its old escape from the Mountain top. And with it fell Jonn and Rowan, gasping and shocked, tossed like corks in the bubbling rush. Rowan drew breath, struggled to regain his feet. They were beneath the earth. Beneath the ice. He could no longer see the Dragon. He could no longer see the sky. The water was pushing him. He could not resist it.

All was darkness and glassy-smooth rock, freezing water and rushing sound. Rowan called for Jonn, and grabbed for his hand. All at once, he knew what had happened. They had found out the secret of the stream. Sweet water foamed around them, pushing them along. They had released it from its icy prison. Now it was free to flow. And flow it would, down through the long, steep tunnel that was its track through the Mountain's core. And it was taking them with it. Down, down, to the village of Rin.

* * *

Val and Ellis had been woken before daybreak by a feeble tapping on the mill-house door. They had opened it to find a nightmare—Allun and Marlie, filthy and ragged, nearly fainting from exhaustion and thirst. They had taken them into the mill, bathed their wounds and given them food and drink. Then they had heard something of the fearful journey the two had shared as they retraced their steps through the swamp and forest to the clifftop and down to the Mountain's foot. They exchanged grave looks as they learned what had happened in the caves.

"Strong Jonn was a brave man," Val said at last.

"You speak as though he were dead!" Allun cried, pushing his cup away.

"If he is not," Val replied stolidly, "he soon will be. And Rin with him. He is on the Mountain, alone. He cannot succeed now. And he cannot survive."

"He is not alone," Marlie objected. "Rowan is with him."

Val and Ellis stared at her as though she were mad.

"Of what use to Jonn is a scared weakling like Rowan?" Val demanded. "He needs a strong, courageous companion to—"

"He had five strong, courageous companions." Allun lifted his head and looked her straight in the eye. "They all ran away."

Marlie buried her face in her hands.

Ellis finally spoke. "Dawn is breaking. We must go to Jiller," he muttered. "She will be in the bukshah fields, seeing to the beasts. We must tell her what has happened."

With heavy hearts the four left the mill. The sky was golden-pink by the time they reached the dried-up pool. They saw Jiller standing there with Annad, her shawl pulled tightly around her head. She was looking up at the Mountain, shivering in the cool wind. Then she turned, and saw them. The sadness on her face became terror. She screamed. "Allun! Marlie! What has happened? Where is Rowan? Where is Rowan?"

At that moment the roaring from the Mountain top had begun. And it had gone on, and on, and on.

* * *

Star raised her head, and called to Annad and Jiller. Annad did not hear. She had her arms around Dawn's new calf, comforting it as it trembled at the sound of the Dragon. And Jiller, deep shadows under her red-rimmed eyes, was standing rigidly between Allun and Marlie. She heard nothing but the thundering sound high above them on the Mountain, saw nothing but the flashing fire that lit the sky above the cloud.

Val and Ellis stood silently by. With them were Bronden, and every other member of the village. All had come running when they heard the sound. Now they stood, looking up, their faces masks of dread and fear. None of them paid attention to Star's call.

Star moved away from the empty drinking pool and began to walk upstream, along the dry stream bed. She did not know why she was drawn this way. She only knew that she must go. And quickly.

A fence blocked her way. She nudged it aside with her shoulder, trampled over it without a glance, and moved on.

She heard Jiller's shout behind her, and other voices, but she did not look back. The silent call was stronger now. She broke into a lumbering run.

"Star! What is it?" They were chasing her. She could hear Jiller's sobbing voice, and the sounds of many feet. She ran faster.

The stream bed gaped brown and empty beside her. Earth, grass and flowers scattered beneath her hoofs.

The mill was ahead, on the other side. The tall stone mill, with its huge wooden wheel that had stood silent for so many days.

And yet ... Star's ears pricked. There was a sound. A creaking sound. And a rippling, rushing sound. Water! Her parched throat ached for water. But there was another sound too. A voice. A voice she knew.

"Star! Star! Star!"

Star answered the call. She plunged into the dry stream bed. She thundered to the place where the sound came from: the mill channel up ahead, where the great wheel creaked and strained. Sweet water! Her nostrils were full of the smell of it now. For the water was coming, in a wave that rose higher and higher every second, tumbling between the banks of the stream, pushing at the mill wheel's wooden paddles, pouring through it and past it, down to Rin.

Star met and breasted the wave head on. She tossed her head and heaved herself through the foam, ignoring the sticks and rocks that beat against her legs, ignoring the urge to stop and fill her parched mouth. She forced her way across the earth bank to the mill channel that lay beside the stream. And with a groan of love, relief and pleasure, she reached the mill wheel and thrust her muzzle into the reaching hand of the boy who clung there.

She dipped her head to take the burden he guided on to her broad back and felt clutching hands on her mane. Slowly and carefully she waded into the foaming stream and through it to the opposite bank, not looking back as the great wheel finally gave way to the pressure of the water and began to turn, crushing the branches and sticks caught between its blades. She clambered from the water. She felt Rowan's hands gripping her wool as he stumbled beside her. Heard Rowan's voice in her ear.

He was talking to her, as he had always done. And he was talking to the man lying on her back. Telling them both: "It is all right. We are safe ... We are home ..."

* * *

Rowan threaded his fingers more tightly through Star's soft, damp coat. "Home," he said again, tasting the word on his tongue. His mind whirled. Everything had happened so quickly. Their journey from Rin to the Dragon's lair had taken long days and nights. Their return, that terrifying downward slide through the underground stream, had taken minutes.

It seemed unbelievable that he was here, safe in the valley, with the grass beneath his feet and the morning breeze in his face. He screwed his eyes shut, suddenly afraid that this was a dream, and he was still on the Mountain top with the fire, the ice, the terror and despair. But when he opened them again, the green fields of Rin were still there, and Star, and the stream bubbling beside him. It was true. They were home. They were safe. The water had come back to Rin. And they had come with it.

"Rowan! Rowan!" A cry shrilled in the distance. Rowan looked up. A figure was running towards them, along the stream bank. It was Jiller, calling to him, her arms spread wide. Annad ran a little behind her, and far behind them both surged a crowd. It seemed as if the whole village was there, racing towards him. As the people drew closer Rowan could hear that they were cheering, shouting, laughing with joy. But his eyes were swimming and he could not see their faces clearly. He could see only Jiller's as she reached him at last, swept him into her arms and hugged him as though she would never let him go.

Rowan clung to her, listening to the words she crooned to him over and over again, feeling her overwhelming relief and thankfulness for the return of the child she thought she had lost, and her love, which at last he understood. And in that moment the old, cold ache in his heart melted away like snow before the fire, leaving no trace behind.

Together they lifted Jonn from Star's back and knelt beside him. "I think his leg is broken," said Rowan in a low voice. "He is in pain. But he is alive."

Jonn's eyes opened, and he looked up at the two worried faces bending over him. So unalike, yet so alike. He tried to say something, struggled to rise, then fell back with a groan.

"Jonn, lie still," begged Jiller. "Do not try to speak. There is no need."

The injured man wet his cracked lips with his tongue. "There is a need," he said. Rowan could see that every word was an effort for him, but he was determined to continue. "There is something I must tell you, Jiller. I promised—I promised that I would bring your son home to you. But it is Rowan who has brought *me* home. He made me go on when I would gladly have fallen and died. He fought cold and fire for me, when he could have saved himself. He faced the Dragon alone."

Rowan crouched on the grass, one hand in Jiller's, the other resting on Jonn's chest. He had not heard the crowd gathering behind him. He did not see the looks of wonder on their faces as they listened to Jonn's words. But Jonn saw. With a great effort he raised his voice.

"It is thanks to Rowan that the stream flows again," he said. "He never gave up. He would not give up. The smallest and weakest among us proved the strongest and bravest, in the end. Rin owes him a great debt."

There was silence. A tiny bird chirped in a nearby tree. And then a tremendous sound rose up. Rowan spun around, startled. He saw cheering people all around him. There were Allun and Marlie, their faces still streaked with mud, shouting and laughing, and pounding each other on the back. There was Bronden, clapping her hands, and the millers, Val and Ellis, staring at each other in amazement. There was Neel the potter, his mouth stretched into a vast grin, the people from the gardens, and Timon the teacher. And all the others. "Rowan! Rowan!" they were chanting. "Rowan of the Bukshah! Rowan of Rin!"

Jonn smiled. "Skinny rabbit," he whispered and, well satisfied, saw Rowan begin to laugh.

Star rumbled to herself. Quietly she moved away and lumbered to the edge of the stream, filled now to the brim with clear, sweet, running water. She listened. Low, joyful bellows from the village reached her ears. The water had reached the bukshah pool.

The herd was safe. Rowan was safe. The stream ran again.

All was as it should be. Star lowered her head at last, to drink.

ROWAN

AND THE

TRAVELLERS

1 – Good News, Bad News

The Travellers are coming. The Travellers are coming!"

The news spread quickly through the village of Rin. The children shouted it in excitement, their voices ringing through the valley and echoing back from the great Mountain that rose above the town. They shouted it running, running madly down from the hills, past the bukshah fields and the orchard, beside the gardens and all the way to the village square.

They had seen the three Forerunners flying over the hills, the silken kites to which they clung brilliant against the sky. They knew the carts, the horses and the chattering, singing people were not far behind.

The Travellers were coming, bringing games and stories, dancing and music, wonderful things to trade. Soon their bright tents would spread, fluttering like huge butterflies, among the yellow slip-daisies on the hills above the village. At night their bonfires would brighten the darkness, and their music would ring through the valley. They would stay a week, or two, or three, and for the children every day would be like a holiday.

* * *

"The Travellers are coming!"

Standing by the bukshah pool, watching a butterfly struggle from its cocoon on the branch of a tree, the boy Rowan, keeper of the bukshah, heard the cry. But he had already guessed the news.

Long before the other children spied the Forerunners, he had seen the bukshah raise their heads and look across the valley, to the hills. The big animals were listening to something he could not hear.

"So the Travellers *are* coming?" he said to Star, his favourite of all the great beasts. "You heard their pipes, before, didn't you?"

Star stood swaying, looking out to the hills.

"We did not expect to see them this year," Rowan went on, "but it is the season for them. The tadpoles in the stream are growing legs and changing into frogs. The caterpillars are becoming butterflies. And the slip-daisies are in bloom." He sniffled. "As well I know. The pollen makes my nose run."

Star rumbled deep in her throat and shifted her feet restlessly.

"What ails you, Star?" Rowan asked her, scratching her neck under the thick wool. "Be still. All is well."

He looked at Star in puzzlement. All the bukshah had been unsettled lately. And he could not understand why. He had checked them over very carefully. There was no sign of sickness. And yet for days they had seemed nervous and unhappy.

"All is well, Star," he said again.

But Star pawed the ground, pushed at his hand with her heavy head, and refused to be comforted.

* * *

"The Travellers are coming!"

Strong Jonn, working in the orchard, heard the cry with surprise, then smiled. The Travellers had come in Rin's direction only twelve months before. He had not expected them again so soon. But he welcomed them. For with the Travellers came their bees.

Soon the bees would be busy in the sweet white blossom of his hoopberry trees. Their hives would begin to overflow with rich, golden hoopberry honey for the Travellers to gather, to eat and to sell.

But while the bees worked for the Travellers, they would be working for Jonn too. Bumbling from flower to flower, they would spread the sticky yellow pollen, making sure that fruit would form when the flowers fell. Thanks to the Travellers' bees, Jonn would have a very good harvest in the autumn.

So Jonn was pleased when he heard the children's voices. But he knew others would not be so pleased. For others, the news would be bad.

* * *

"The Travellers are coming!"

Bronden the furniture-maker heard the cry and frowned, drumming her stubby fingers on the smooth wood of the half-finished table under her hand.

"Slips," she grumbled, kicking her feet in the sawdust on the floor. "Time-wasting, idle, useless Slips!"

She ran her hand over her forehead. She was tired. Tired out. And this—this was the last straw.

The Travellers turned the settled life of the village upside down. They cared nothing for rules, or order, or hard work. They had no settled homes, or proper jobs, and wanted none. That was why she, and others who thought like her, called the Travellers Slips, after the wild slip-daisies on the hills. They made her uncomfortable. They made her angry.

* * *

"The Travellers are coming!"

In his little house Timon the teacher heard the cry, and sighed over his books. While the Travellers were camping near, the Rin children would fidget and whisper under the Teaching Tree.

Their pockets would bulge with the toys and tricks they had begged or bought from the camp on the hill. Their mouths would be full of honey sweets and chews. Their heads would be buzzing with Travellers' tales and legends.

But still, thought Timon, leaning back in his chair and putting his hands behind his head, this visit might be a blessing. It has been a long, hard winter. The children have been tired and out of sorts lately. The Travellers will cheer them up.

He smiled. By my life, I loved Travellers' tales myself, as a boy, he thought. And if stories of the Valley of Gold, the Giants of Inspray, the Misty Crystal, the Pit of Unrin and all the rest did not hurt me, then why should they hurt the children now?

Timon considered. Perhaps he could visit the Travellers' camp himself this year. Listen once again to the stories. And perhaps buy a handful of honey chews. It was a long time since he had tasted one of those.

Timon closed his eyes and chuckled sleepily to himself at the thought. His mouth was already watering.

* * *

"The Travellers are coming!"

Allun the baker heard the cry as he kneaded dough in his warm kitchen. "Do you hear that, Mother? My father's people are on their way," he called over his shoulder. "You had better stop all that talk of growing old, and get your dancing shoes out."

Sara came slowly in from the shop, wiping her hands on her apron.

"I think my dancing days are over, Allun," she said, with a tired smile. "But you had better get your voice in order. For once, we of Rin have a tale to tell the Travellers. As good as any they have ever told us. Our friends will want to hear of your quest to the Mountain. Yours, and Jonn's, and ..."

"And young Rowan's most of all," laughed Allun. "But Rowan is much too shy to tell the story himself. So, yes, I will. Who better to surprise the Travellers—since I am half a Traveller myself!"

Sara fingered the thin string of plaited silk that hung around her throat. It was a Traveller wedding necklace.

Long ago, when she was young, Sara had left Rin with a Traveller husband. But her perfect happiness had ended when her man was killed by the invading Zebak during the great War of the Plains. When the land was at peace once more, she had returned to the village with Allun, her only son, then just a boy.

Sara had been glad to see her home again. But she knew that times had often been hard for her half-Traveller child as he grew up in Rin.

It was as though he was caught between two worlds: the free-ranging life of the Travellers, and the peaceful, settled life of his mother's people. Sara's heart had sometimes bled as she saw him struggling to be accepted by those Rin folk who despised and distrusted the Travellers, and who therefore were ready to despise and distrust him, too.

She had not wanted Allun to join the group that had climbed the forbidden Mountain in the autumn. She had feared for him. But now she was glad that he had gone. For on that terrible journey he had found that he had no more weaknesses than the others, the heroes of the village. And those who scorned him had realised it too.

And more: Allun had brought back from his quest a special gift. A gift that looked as though it would bring riches to the town. So at last he felt he had proved that he was a worthy citizen of Rin. And because of that, he had found a new peace. Surely nothing could destroy it now.

"Why, I wonder, have they returned so soon?" Allun murmured. His merry face had grown thoughtful. "Many in the village will not be pleased to see them here again."

Sara watched her son as he turned back to his work. She listened to the children's voices ringing through the valley. And for the first time a shadow of fear fluttered through her mind. Why *had* the Travellers come again so soon?

Why?

2 – Darkness Gathers

In the gardens, Bree and Hanna heard the children's cry, and put down their hoes. For them this news was very bad indeed.

"How can this be?" exclaimed Hanna, turning to her husband and wiping the sweat from her forehead. "They *never* come two years in a row."

Bree and Hanna, and the keepers of the Rin gardens before them, had always hated the Travellers' visits. Travellers could move silently, like shadows in the night. New peas, tender herbs—all the best things in the gardens—had a habit of disappearing like magic overnight when Travellers were about.

Others in the village, people like Jonn of the Orchard and Allun the baker, always laughed when the gardeners raged. Even if a few vegetables *had* somehow found their way into Travellers' cooking pots over the years, what did that matter, when the Travellers brought the village so much useful trade, and so much pleasure?

Bree spat on the ground in disgust. Perhaps such people would sing a different tune this year. Even the half-Traveller Allun. For after all, it was he who had brought the seed for the new crop to the valley.

He looked at the young Mountain berry plants that now filled a quarter of the garden. They were thriving, holding their small, glossy leaves up to the sun and stretching delicate new tendrils out across the brown soil. Perfumed red flowers bloomed along their tiny branches, already weighed down with luscious little red fruits.

A sturdy, fast-growing plant that bloomed and fruited at the same time! Truly the Mountain berry was miraculous, and a precious new crop. A crop that Bree was determined to keep for Rin alone. He thought of Travellers slipping into the gardens by night, plundering his precious bushes, gathering the fruit ...

"Thieving Slips!" he burst out. "They must not hear of the Mountain berries, Hanna. They must not!"

She nodded. "We will call a meeting," she said. "We will tell the others of our fears. Then no one will breathe a word. And we will guard the gardens well."

"I stood guard last year," Bree muttered. "And what good did it do?"

"Last year you fell asleep, Bree."

"They put a sleep spell on me! I know it!" Red-faced, Bree scowled in the direction of the hills.

"Nonsense!" snapped Hanna. "Sleep spells! I never heard such rubbish. You sound like Neel the potter, talking childish nonsense like that."

Bree turned away, hunching his shoulders. "We will call a meeting," he mumbled. "Come and wash, Hanna. We do not have much time."

Hanna said nothing. After a moment, Bree picked up the hoes and trudged to the toolshed.

Hanna rubbed her eyes. A great wave of tiredness was suddenly rolling over her. She would have given anything to lie down and rest—just for a minute. I am tired out, she thought. I am so tired of working day in, day out. And now this.

She glanced at her husband. He was wearily putting the hoes away, and closing the shed door. Poor Bree. What had she been thinking of? She had to keep going, just as he did. Now there was a new problem to be faced. Well, they would face it together.

If all went well, next season there would be Mountain berries in plenty. Then they could rest, and Rin could feast. Trade, too, for no one on the coast had ever tasted this new, delicious fruit. Wealth would be theirs at last.

If all went well.

* * *

The bell sounded in the village square. Rowan heard it from the bukshah fields.

"There is a meeting, Star," he said. "I must go. You take care of the herd while I am away."

Star rumbled in her throat and looked out towards the hills.

"The meeting will be about the Travellers, I am sure," Rowan told her. "Jonn will be pleased to see them again. And so will Allun. And Marlie the weaver will be glad, because the Travellers will trade their silk for her warm cloth. But Bronden will be angry. And Bree and Hanna will be *furious*, because the Travellers steal from the gardens."

He smiled guiltily. If Bree and Hanna were not looking, he himself sometimes grabbed a handful of new peas through the fence on his way to the bukshah fields. His animals were very fond of new peas.

Then Rowan remembered the Mountain berries, and the brightness of the afternoon seemed to dim. If the Travellers interfered with the Mountain berries ...

Star swayed and pawed the ground restlessly. Rowan forgot his own problems and gripped her rough mane in concern.

"Be calm," he soothed. "You have nothing to fear."

Star fixed him with her small black eyes, and nudged him with her shoulder. It was as though she was trying to tell him something. He felt her skin quiver under the thick wool.

Rowan sighed. Behind him, the butterfly finished stretching its new wings and flew away, leaving its hard cocoon hanging empty in the tree. A light, cool breeze ruffled his hair, carrying with it the scent of slip-daisies from the hills. His nose began to run again, and his eyes prickled.

In the village, the bell went on ringing.

* * *

Crouched by the fire in her tiny hut, Sheba the Wise Woman heard the bell through a dream. She jerked awake, and bent to throw sticks on the blaze. The fire leapt.

"A meeting, is it? You fools!" she croaked, watching the pictures in the flames. "You fools, to chatter on while darkness gathers."

She pressed her hands to her head. The terrifying words that had cried in her mind for so many days circled there, endlessly and without meaning. And with the words, over and over again, were the pictures ...

Three kites: yellow, red and white, against a blue sky. The pale face of a boy she knew—Rowan of the Bukshah. And a golden owl, with glittering green eyes that stared at her, full of knowledge. Commanding her to understand.

There were other pictures, too, lit by flashes of golden light, then shut off by inky blackness. The bukshah fields empty. The village of Rin still and silent. And, most terrifying of all, a heaped bundle of old rags and straggled hair, lying by a dead fire. She herself, in this very room. Helpless. While the enemy ...

Sheba struggled to her feet. Waking or sleeping, there was no escape. The fire spat and crackled. She backed away from it.

Suddenly she knew what she must do. She must go about her work. She must escape from this place of nightmares. She must go collecting roots on the hills, where the sweet slip-daisies bloomed, and the air was clear. There, perhaps, she could think.

As she shuffled from the hut, the bell stopped ringing. The people of Rin were gathered. They were meeting in the square.

"Fools!" spat Sheba. And staggered on her way.

3 – The Forerunners

Welcome, friends!"

Jonn's voice sounded loudly on the hills. He, Marlie the weaver and Allun the baker shaded their eyes against the sun as they watched the three approaching Forerunners raise their arms in answer to the call. Rowan, standing behind them, saw the one in the centre put something to her lips.

Wherever the Travellers went, the Forerunners flew before, warning of dangers ahead, signalling with their tiny reed pipes to tell if the tribe should halt, or go forward. The pipes' sound was pitched too high for ordinary people to hear. Only the Travellers, their ears trained over centuries, heard their messages. The Travellers, and, as Rowan had discovered, the bukshah.

Perhaps other animals heard the pipes too. Rowan did not know. In fact, the older he grew, the more he realised just how little he did know about the land beyond the valley of Rin.

The Travellers had ranged far and wide over the land for ages past. They knew it as they knew themselves. They were part of it, as were the trees, the rocks, the birds, and the bukshah. Some of the tales told by Ogden, their storyteller and the leader of the tribe, were thousands of years old.

But the people of Rin were newcomers. Barely three hundred years had passed since their ancestors were brought to the coast as warrior slaves of the invading Zebak. It was then that they turned against their masters, joined with the Maris folk and the Travellers to defeat them, and finally travelled inland to find the valley that was now their home.

Three hundred years was as nothing to the Maris folk—and less than nothing to the Travellers, who believed that their tribe had roamed this land since time began.

Yet I do not feel like a newcomer, Rowan thought now, looking down to Rin, with its neat lanes and houses, its bubbling stream, the green-and-brown patchwork of its fields, the hoopberry orchard, and the bukshah straying up towards the hills. This is the only home I know.

"It will not be long now," murmured Jonn to Allun and Marlie. "Let us hope that what we hear will satisfy the worriers below."

He bent and picked the leaf of a slip-daisy, twisting it between his fingers. Rowan knew that the leaf was part of the Welcoming. Slip-daisy leaves were made of three round lobes joined together, as clover leaves were. They were used as a sign of the friendship between the Travellers, the Maris folk and the people of Rin.

The Forerunners had begun flying low, their bare toes lightly skimming the tips of the grass and flowers. Their kites—one yellow, one red, one white—rippled and flapped in the breeze as the ropes of plaited silk that guided them were pulled tight in agile brown hands.

Rowan drank in the sight greedily. He had never seen the Forerunners so closely before. Three adult Rin Welcomers usually met them alone.

But this time the villagers wanted news quickly. They had decided at their meeting to find out the reason for the Travellers' unexpected visit before discussing the Mountain berry problem further. Rowan was to run to the village with the news as soon as it was given.

"It is my one regret," said Allun, watching the bright kites, "that my mother took me from the Travellers before I was old enough to train as a Forerunner."

"Would you have wished that, Allun?" asked Jonn, in some surprise. "It is a rank of honour, I know. But great dangers go with it, surely."

Allun smiled wryly. "You are right, of course," he admitted. "If the Forerunners meet trouble, they meet it alone, while the tribe stays back in safety. That is their duty. But the kites, Jonn! The kites! To fly on the wind is every Traveller child's dearest wish."

As he spoke, the Forerunners' flight slowed to walking pace. Then, with one movement, the three put their feet to the ground. Their kites billowed behind them for a moment, then folded gracefully into thin, trailing sacks of silk. The Forerunners gathered them up unhurriedly, draping the silk over their shoulders as they moved forward to greet the Welcomers.

Jonn held out the slip-daisy leaf. "Welcome, friends," he said again.

Rowan stared at the Forerunners with fascination. They wore clothes of bright silk. Their feet were bare. Their brown hair, threaded with flowers, feathers and ribbons, fell in tangled curls over their shoulders. They were two boys and a girl, all a little older than he was.

The boys were small-boned and slim, like Allun. They looked up at Jonn with dark eyes that danced under slanting brows. The girl was sterner. She was tall—almost as tall as Marlie. Her brows were straight, her eyes a strange, light blue. She stepped forward and took the leaf from Jonn.

"I am Zeel, adopted daughter of Ogden the storyteller. The Travellers thank you for your welcome, friends," she said formally. "We will make camp here while it suits your pleasure, and will welcome your visits each night after sunset."

These, Rowan knew, were the words that were always said. They meant little. The Travellers made camp anywhere they liked. No one but the Zebak had ever tried to interfere with them. And the Zebak, according to the tales, had regretted it.

He waited for what would come next.

"May we know what brings you here again so soon?" Jonn asked. "Never before have the Travellers visited Rin two years in a row."

The pale eyes never moved from his face. "The idea took our fancy," said Zeel the Forerunner. "We felt the need, and so we came."

"We thought you may need food, or other trade," Jonn persisted. "The winter has been long and hard."

"It has," said the girl smoothly. "And we are always pleased to trade with you, our friends. But our need is no greater than it is in any spring."

"We thought you may have news from the coast," Marlie put in. "News of our enemy stirring, perhaps. We thought you may have come to warn us."

Rowan watched Zeel carefully. Had he seen a flicker deep in those pale eyes?

But she shook her head. "We have no news to tell you," she said.

She is lying, thought Rowan. I can feel it. She is lying. Or, at least, not telling the whole truth.

There was silence on the hill. The Forerunners faced Jonn, Marlie and Allun calmly. Plainly they had nothing more to say.

"So be it," said Jonn at last. He stepped aside, so that the Forerunners could see Rowan clearly, and turned to him. "Run to the village, then, Rowan, and tell the people what our friends have said. There is no special reason for their visit. The idea simply took their fancy."

Rowan could tell by the way Jonn spoke that he too felt that Zeel was holding something back. And he was sure that the three Forerunners were quite aware that the Welcomers had not been fooled. They looked a little startled as they stared at him with unblinking eyes, then looked at one another as though passing an unspoken message.

Rowan wasted no more time, but nodded, turned, and ran straight back down the hills towards the village. He knew the people in the square would be anxiously awaiting him. He had no comfort to give them. But there was no point in keeping them waiting. And, besides, he wanted to get back to the bukshah.

From the hilltop he could see that the herd was still moving along the stream, every moment straying further and further from the village. A fence must have been trodden down. He did not want the beasts to get too far away. Even now it would take him a long time to coax them back to their fields.

He began to pant with the effort of running. Angrily he rubbed at his blocked-up nose and puffy eyes, and wished for the millionth time that he was as strong as other boys his age.

He wished it every time he saw Jiller, his mother, trudging behind the plough that turned the soil in their fields. He wished it every time he saw her back bend under a load of grain. At his age he should be able to take his dead father's place to help her—at least in part.

But when he ventured to say this to her, she only smiled. "Strength I have for myself, Rowan," she would say. "And one day you will be big enough to help me more in the fields. For now, you help me in every other way. Let that be enough for you, as it is for me."

The cheeky-faced yellow daisies bowed their heads under his flying feet, and then sprang up again behind him. Pollen filled the air in a pale golden cloud. Rowan sneezed as he ran. His eyes watered so that he could hardly see.

Wrinkling his nose, he reached into his pocket and pulled out a small green bottle. He held his breath and took a sip. The strong, horrible-tasting medicine flooded his mouth. He coughed and gasped, forcing himself to swallow.

The medicine was vile. And worse, to him, because it came from Sheba. He shuddered to think that her bony hands had gathered the slip-daisy roots from which the brew was made, and stirred the pot in which it simmered.

He was sure the old woman cackled with laughter as she poured the potion into bottles. He was the only person in the village who had to take it, and he had long ago decided that Sheba made it especially foul-tasting for him on purpose. That was the sort of cruel joke she enjoyed.

With relief he saw the shadows of a grove of trees ahead. Soon he would be out of the slip-daisies, and the medicine would start doing its work in a few moments. With luck, then, the sneezes and sniffles would leave him in peace for a while.

He slowed to a walk and began threading through the trees. His streaming eyes, used to the bright sunlight, blinked blindly in the shady dimness. He had to feel his way.

And so it was that at first he did not see the humped shape rising in front of him. He did not shrink back in time to avoid the bony arm that shot out to bar his way. He did not twist quickly enough to stop the iron-hard fingers gripping his shoulder, forcing him to stop.

Rowan shrieked in shock and fear. The figure before him began to laugh. It was a frightful, jeering laugh. All too familiar.

It was Sheba.

4 – The Rhyme

"So, Rowan of the Bukshah," the old woman said, tightening her grip on Rowan's shoulder. "Where are you going in such a hurry?"

"To the village," Rowan answered timidly. He felt his nose start to run again, and sniffed.

"You need another dose of my spring potion, boy," Sheba said softly. "Your nose is running like the stream."

She pointed to the bulging bag at her feet. "I have the slip-daisy roots here. I have walked all the way to the hills to pull them. It is hard on my poor old bones. Tonight I will brew the potion. Is that not good? Are you not grateful to old Sheba?"

Rowan scowled. The taste of the medicine was still foul in his mouth. He looked at Sheba's bag. It was stuffed to overflowing. Enough for a cauldron of the hideous stuff.

Sheba's fingers pinched his shoulder. "Are you not grateful?" she repeated.

Rowan nodded dumbly. What does she want of me? he thought.

Sheba pushed her face close to his. Her skin was grey. She smelt of ashes and bitter herbs. Her hair swung like greasy ropes around her shoulders.

"Why have the Travellers come to the valley, Rowan of the Bukshah?" Her voice was urgent and low. "You must know. In the vision your face is clear when all else is a mystery. Why have they come again so soon? Tell me! Tell me! It may be the key."

"They—they say they have no special reason," stammered Rowan, trying to pull back. The vision? The key? What did she mean?

Her lips drew back from her long brown teeth in a snarl. "Lies!" Her eyes searched his. They were like black holes in her face. They seemed to burn into him. He felt his head beginning to spin. But he could not turn away.

Finally she nodded. Her eyelids drooped. "So," she mumbled. "Not your lies, but theirs, then, Rowan of the Bukshah." She pushed him roughly aside. "So I was wrong. You are of no use to me. Get out of my sight!"

"What is the matter?" Rowan burst out. Sheba terrified him, but he had to know what all this meant.

She picked up her heavy sack, and began to shuffle away.

"Do not go!" Rowan called. "Sheba! How do you know the Forerunners lied? Is there some danger threatening us? Please tell me. You *must* tell me!"

She spun round, baring her teeth at him. "I *must* do nothing, boy," she cried, her voice cracking with sudden fury. "Who are you to order me? Do you think that because the foolish villagers think you are a hero you can tell me what to do? Pah!"

Her eyes narrowed. She seemed filled with a rage that Rowan could not understand. "I know you for what you are, Rowan of the Bukshah," she sneered. "Skinny rabbit! Weakling, runny-nosed child, scared of your own shadow! No use to your mother in her need. No use to me. No use to anyone. Run away and snivel in the bukshah fields. It is all you are good for!"

Rowan shrank back as if he had been struck. Her words echoed his inmost thoughts. She was right. He was no use to anyone, whatever people said. His face burned. He turned to run. To run away from her hateful voice and spiteful face.

But as he turned, he saw the Mountain, rising dark and secret above the trees. And he remembered the great lesson he had learned there. The lesson the six heroes with him had learned too. The lesson none of them would ever forget.

He swung around again.

"Only fools do not fear, Sheba. You said that once, and it is true. I know I am not a hero. But I know I can face fear if I must. And now I can face you, and ask again, what ails you? What trouble do you feel, for Rin?"

She stared at him. "The Mountain has taught you well," she said slowly. She looked up at the jagged rocks, the icy tip where snow gleamed in the slowly sinking sun. The jeering look that had veiled her face had dropped away. And underneath it there was something else. Fear!

Rowan's heart leapt in terror. What thing could be so dreadful that it would bring fear to Sheba's face?

"What is it?" he cried.

She shook her head. "I do not know," she said hopelessly. "I do not know. I only know my dreams. The pictures. The words that haunt me, night and day. The enemy is coming again. The wheel is turning. And this time—this time—"

"What pictures? What words?" Rowan demanded. "Tell me!"

Suddenly, Sheba's hands began to quiver. Then the shuddering spread until her whole body was trembling as though with a terrible fever. Her eyes rolled back in her head. The whites gleamed horribly in the shadows of the trees. Her mouth gaped open.

Rowan sprang forward and grabbed her arm. He shook it violently. "Speak!" he shouted. "Sheba!"

The gaping mouth began to move. The croaking chant began.

"Beneath soft looks the evil burns,
And slowly round the old wheel turns.
The same mistakes, the same old pride,
The priceless armour cast aside.
The secret enemy is here.
It hides in darkness, fools beware!
For day by day its power grows,
And when at last its face it shows,
Then past and present tales will meet—
The evil circle is complete ..."

The voice trailed off in a bubbling groan. The old woman swayed. Rowan staggered as he tried to hold her, to stop her crumpling to the ground. His throat felt as though it was being gripped by an icy hand.

What did this mean? Sheba's words ran round and round in his mind as he searched for an answer.

The rhyme was about treachery. Betrayal. And it was not a warning for the future. Or not all. Rowan's breath caught in his chest.

The secret enemy is here. The secret enemy ... is here.

5 – Disagreement

ross faces turned to Rowan as he stumbled at last into the village square.

"Where have you *been*, Rowan?" asked his mother. "We have been waiting so long!"

"So *long*!" repeated his little sister Annad. She put her small hands on her hips and glared at him, waiting for his explanation.

"I—met Sheba in the trees," Rowan said hesitantly. "She—hindered me."

There was a murmur from the crowd. Sheba was necessary to the village, because she made potions that healed all manner of ills. But she was feared by many as a witch, and disliked by others because of her bad temper and wicked tongue.

"What did she want?" quavered Neel the potter.

"Forget her!" ordered old Lann. "Tell us the news from the hills. Tell us now, quickly!" She banged her stick on the ground.

The oldest person in the village, Lann had once also been its greatest fighter. Now she needed her cane to walk, but her mind and her voice were as strong as ever. And she did not like to be kept waiting.

Rowan did not know what to do. Should he tell what Sheba had said? Should he say that he thought the Forerunners had been lying to Jonn?

He looked around the ring of faces in the square. Some people, like Neel the potter, were anxious. Some, like Bronden, Bree and Hanna, were suspicious. Some, like Solla the sweet-maker, were excited. Some, like Val and Ellis from the mill, were merely curious.

Rowan knew how those faces would change if he repeated the rhyme he had heard in the trees. He did not feel certain that he could deal with the fear, anger and panic that would sweep through the crowd.

"Well?" Bronden's voice rang through the silence.

Rowan made his decision. He would wait until he had had a chance to talk this over with his mother and Strong Jonn, in private. They would know what was best to do. Sheba's words sounded terrifying, but it was possible that she had been playing a trick on him, for spite. For now, he would just repeat the message he had been given on the hill.

"The Forerunners said that the Travellers have no special reason for this visit," he sniffled. "They said that the idea simply took their fancy."

Lann's eyes narrowed, but she said nothing.

Bronden snorted in disgust. "It took their *fancy* to waste our time and eat our food!" she said. "How excellent it must be to be able to have such fancies!"

"They invite us to their camp tonight, and every night they are here, should we care to join them," Rowan went on.

Several adults, and all the children, cheered.

Bronden scowled. "Well I, for one, certainly do not care to join them," she said.

"Nor we," said Bree, glowering at Rowan as if he was at fault. "And all who *do* want to waste their precious time visiting that nest of thieves should remember what we have decided. Not a word of the Mountain berries must be breathed in a Traveller's hearing."

"For certain they know of them already, Bree," growled mighty Val the miller. "For why else have they come? This talk of fancies makes no sense." Her twin brother Ellis nodded slowly in agreement.

Again there was a murmuring in the crowd. And this time it was an angry sound.

"Nevertheless," said old Lann, "we will hold our tongues. If we are shutting the gate after the bukshah has already strayed, so be it. It is better to be careful than to be sorry. And as well as keeping our mouths shut, we must keep the Travellers out of the gardens at all costs."

"The gardens are not the only places where the berry bushes can be found," Timon reminded her. "Allun and the rest of the Seven who climbed the Mountain have bushes of their own. The birds have feasted on their berries, and have spread the seed. New plants are popping up everywhere. More every day. The village is already sweet with their scent." He waved his hand around the square.

"Then we must tell the Slips they are not welcome in the village," said Bree. "They must stay in their camp on the hills."

"We cannot do that, Bree," Timon objected. "The Travellers are our friends, and our allies in time of trouble."

"I agree. We cannot afford to anger the Travellers," Jiller said quietly. "We have fought the Zebak together in the past, and may need to do so again one day. We need their friendship."

"And they need ours." Old Lann held her head high. "So they will have to abide by what we say, Jiller. For good or ill. This matter is too important for us to let weakness guide us."

Bree, Hanna and Bronden nodded in agreement. So did many others.

"So it is decided," said Lann curtly. "It will be done."

Jiller made a small sound of irritation and dismay. Timon looked very grave.

They were not the only ones who would think the decision a foolish one. Rowan could imagine what Allun, Marlie and Jonn would say when they heard that the Travellers were to be barred from the village.

He turned and began to walk away from the square. The meeting was making him uncomfortable. And he had to see to the bukshah. Soon the sun would slip behind the Mountain and the valley would begin to grow dark and chill. It was important that he return them to their fields before then.

"Rowan, where are you going?" called Annad. She ran up to him and tugged at his hand. "We must go home, so we can be ready for dinner early. Jonn is coming to eat with us. Then afterwards we can all go to the Travellers' camp together. Mother says."

"I have to go to the bukshah fields first, Annad," Rowan told her. "Star and the others strayed while I was on the hills."

"Why?" the little girl asked.

Rowan tried to smile. "Maybe, like the Travellers, the idea just took their fancy," he joked weakly. "But don't worry, Annad. If bringing the beasts home takes too long, I will miss dinner and meet you and Mother and Jonn at the camp. You tell Mother for me. All right?"

She nodded, and ran back to the crowd.

Rowan began walking towards the fields. He turned once, and saw Annad waving to him. He waved back, then went on his way. What a funny little girl she is, he thought. Always asking why.

Why is the sky blue? Why can't I stay up all night? Why do tadpoles eat weed, and frogs eat insects? Why don't the clouds fall down? Why have the bukshah strayed?

Rowan reached the bukshah pool. There were no beasts in sight at all. With a sigh he began to trudge along the stream.

Why *had* the bukshah strayed, today of all days? There was plenty of new grass in the fields. There was plenty of water. The bukshah never moved far from their pool. But today they had. Just when Rowan wanted to get home with all speed. Sheba's terrible chant was weighing him down. Cruel joke or not, he wanted to share it with his mother and Jonn, and relieve himself of the burden of carrying it alone.

He squinted ahead and saw the bukshah in the far distance. They were still moving down the stream. He quickened his steps.

Life in Rin goes on day by day, unchanging, he thought. And then three strange, worrying things happen all at once. The Travellers arrive, Sheba becomes afraid—or pretends to—and now the bukshah stray. It is bad luck.

Then he frowned.

Was it just bad luck? Or were all three things somehow related?

The sun dipped behind the Mountain. The light dimmed. Rowan shivered. Again Sheba's words were ringing in his brain.

The enemy is here ... The enemy is—HERE.

6 – The Valley of Gold

And so the Giants of Inspray fought on the Mountain side, to see which one of them would have the fabled Valley of Gold for himself. For six long days and six long nights they fought. The sound of their shouting was like a furious hurricane, and the clash of their weapons was like a thousand cymbals, and the stamping of their feet was like thunder. And still neither would give in ..."

Ogden the storyteller sat by his fire telling his story. Around him clustered many children—children of Rin, and Traveller children too. For though the Traveller children had heard Ogden's stories time and again, they never tired of them.

Behind them, in the shadows, stood taller figures. These were the Rin adults who had been drawn to Ogden's campfire. Rowan could see Timon the teacher there, among the rest. Maise, the keeper of the books, stood with him. And there was Allun, too, with Sara, and Marlie, and Solla the sweet-maker.

The adults might laugh afterwards at the Travellers' tales. They might say the stories Ogden told were not truth, but legend, cleverly brought to life. Still, now they would be listening as carefully as anyone else.

Rowan knew that his mother and Strong Jonn of the Orchard were in the crowd as well, for Annad sat beside him now, at the fire. He had not had time to see or speak to them. He had come straight to the camp from the bukshah field.

It had taken hours to see the beasts safely home. When he had finally caught up with the herd he had needed to speak softly to Star for a long time before she had obeyed him and led the others back to Rin. Then he had mended as best he could the gate they had pushed open to start their wanderings.

He hoped they would settle to sleep now. They could easily break the gate down again if they chose. Star had still seemed restless, but surely she would not try to roam again, in the dark.

Ogden's voice rose, breaking into Rowan's thoughts. The storyteller's tale was reaching its climax.

"For six days and nights the earth of the Mountain side was trampled and blood-stained. For six days and nights the grass was torn, the trees were battered. For six days and nights the air was filled with the terrible sounds of the giants' fury and the foul smells of the giants' sweat and hatred. And then, as the seventh day dawned, and the battle still raged, it was as though the Mountain cried, 'No more!'.

"The ground trembled. Great cracks and pits opened in the land, and smoke and flame rose up to cloud the sky.

"Huge rocks fell crashing from the Mountain top, beating at the giants, tearing down the trees, tumbling down to pile one upon the other around the Valley of Gold. And the people in the Valley were terrified. They cried and clung to one another, thinking that now indeed their last hours had come."

Ogden looked around at the wide eyes of the children sitting at his feet. The wood of his campfire popped and spat. Under his beaky nose his lips curved into a smile. His voice dropped to a murmur.

"And then, at last, the fighting stopped. The smoke and dust cleared. The giants lay dying on the Mountain side, their bodies broken by the rocks the Mountain had flung at them in its anger. They looked down with glazed eyes, seeking one last glimpse of the beautiful place each had wanted for his own.

"And then they groaned. They howled. They shook their battered fists in helpless rage and pain. For all they could see below were great piles of stones, and yawning pits that scarred the earth. The golden prize over which they had fought, in a fury that had been their deaths, was gone from their sight. Gone from the sight of all who would threaten it. Gone forever. Gone, gone, gone ..."

Ogden's voice dropped away to nothing.

"Oh, no!" whispered Annad, who had not heard the story before. She clenched her fists. "Those wicked giants destroyed the Valley of Gold. The falling rocks covered it. They crashed down and killed all the good, wise people. They buried the jewelled paths, and the silver spring, and the fruits and birds and little white horses and ..."

Rowan took her hand. "Sshh, Annad. Listen," he said softly.

Ogden nodded, his black eyes gleaming in the firelight.

"The giants died cursing and weeping. They cursed each other, and they cursed the Mountain. They wept for the loss of the brightest treasure in the land. But they did not know the Mountain's secret."

He paused. "Do you?" he asked.

The children around him, even those who had heard the story over and over again, shook their heads wordlessly. They wanted Ogden to tell the end.

He leaned forward. His voice was as gentle as the evening breeze now.

"Then I will tell you," he said. "The Valley of Gold was *not* destroyed by the rain of stones. Even as its people clung together, terrified and fearing death, they saw that a miracle was taking place. No rocks were falling into the Valley."

Rowan felt Annad's hand tighten in his. Ogden's soft voice went on.

"While all around it the earth cracked open and huge rocks piled up in heaps, the Valley of Gold remained secure and protected. And when the fall had ended, great new hills of Mountain stone had risen up around it, and the hideous Pit of Unrin, crawling with evil and death, barred the way to its entrance. So the people knew that now their home was safe forever from prying eyes and greedy hands. And they could live on in peace and happiness, without fear."

Annad could not contain herself. "So the Valley of Gold is still there, beyond the Mountain?" she squeaked. "And the people, and the white horses, and the painted houses, and the silver spring, and ..."

Ogden smiled at her. "As I told you, young one," he said. "But from that day to this, no outsider has ever seen it. Even the Travellers, the great friends of the Valley's people in ages past, do not know where it lies. For the Travellers were doing battle with the Zebak on the coast when the Giants of Inspray fought and died.

"Many foolish souls, those who only believe what they can see, say it exists no more," he went on. "Some say, indeed, that the Valley of

Gold never existed at all! But I know it did, and does. And so, now, do you."

Ogden leaned back and folded his hands. Annad relaxed, breathing a sigh of pleasure and contentment.

Rowan wondered yet again about the power of Ogden the story-teller. His words could hold you in a spell, a spell as powerful as any spun with special herbs picked in moonlight, or read from an ancient book. Rowan had heard the story of the Valley of Gold several times before. But every time was like the first.

Even now, with all the other things that were filling his mind, the spell had worked on him. Again his mind was filled with wonder. Again he almost believed in the fabled Valley of Gold.

He closed his eyes as Ogden's voice whispered in his memory. "The Valley of Gold ... A wondrous place, filled with light, and life, and laughter ... The silver spring, bubbling cool and fresh from beneath the earth ... Bright coloured lanterns in the trees ... Beautiful people, tall and strong, wise and good ... Flowers and fruits of every kind, spilling across the paths of gleaming gems that wound between the gardens ... Small white horses, saddled with silk ... Houses painted with beautiful patterns, each one different ... Before each house, a golden bird—an owl with emerald eyes ..."

Almost, Rowan believed. Almost, he believed that out there, beyond Rin, beyond the Mountain, lay a place of peace and beauty, lost and hidden from prying eyes. Waiting, just waiting ...

"The Valley of Gold," Annad breathed, her face radiant. "The Valley of Gold."

7 – Allun Tells a Tale

There was a stir in the crowd, and Rowan looked up, his dream interrupted. Allun was stepping forward.

"And now, Ogden," he was saying with a smile. "We of Rin have a story for *you*, if you will listen. It is a new story. A story of great courage."

Rowan's heart thudded. He hadn't known this was going to happen. He felt his face beginning to grow hot. Annad nudged him proudly.

The storyteller looked up in mild surprise. The firelight danced upon his hair. "I will listen with pleasure, Allun," he said mockingly.

He winked at the Traveller children at his feet. "Now what great story do the Rin folk have for us, do you suppose?" he cried. "Did a hero save Allun's bread from burning, perhaps? Did the fearless Rin gardeners fight a plague of slugs with their bare hands? Who knows what terrors await us in this tale? I shudder to think of them."

The Traveller children shouted with laughter.

Annad jumped up. "Stop laughing!" she shrilled. "Our story is just as good as one of yours."

Rowan pulled at her dress. "Hush, Annad," he whispered. "Ogden is only teasing us." But as she sank back to the ground he knew that his little sister was not the only one to be infuriated by Ogden's words.

Many of the Rin children, and the adults too, were frowning. Already some of them distrusted the Travellers. And they did not like to be teased.

But Allun had not lost his smile. "You may mock, Ogden," he said, in his light, clear voice. "But remember that the people of Rin were not always simple farmers. Our ancestors were warriors. Remember that in the past our two peoples have fought side by side to defeat the enemy that would invade our land."

"Yes!" growled a familiar voice. The crowd stirred. People turned to look at the white-haired woman leaning heavily on her cane in the shadows. Rowan's heart sank as he recognised old Lann.

"You were happy enough to stand behind our strength when the Zebak came, Traveller!" she called. "Remember their iron cages. Remember the War of the Plains. Remember our many dead. Remember these before you make jokes at our expense."

The Rin crowd muttered agreement.

"We remember, respected old one," said Ogden peacefully, holding out his hands to the fire. "We Travellers do not forget. We do not forget, for example, that your warriors depended on the Travellers' cunning and knowledge to make their plans and set their traps."

His voice dropped. "We do not forget how Travellers fed and sheltered them when they would have starved on the wild plains, far from their little fields and cosy homes and well-stocked storehouses. And we do not forget how Travellers fought beside them and died, too, in their hundreds, when they could have slipped away to safety and left them to perish alone."

He half smiled. "No," he murmured. "We forget nothing. Though others seem to—all too easily." He picked a slip-daisy leaf from the ground, and looked at it thoughtfully.

There was silence around the campfire. An uncomfortable silence. Then Ogden looked up. His eyes glinted, dancing like the flames, and his smile broadened.

"But still you speak truly, Lann of Rin," he purred. "Your short history is a history of heroes, as well we Travellers know. We know how highly you value courage."

His wide lips twitched. "You value it as highly as you value hard work, solid houses, full bellies and settled ways. And that means you value it very highly indeed. We know this, though we do not pretend to understand it. And if sometimes we useless Slips mock, it is only because of our ignorance, people of Rin. We would sooner enter the Pit of Unrin than knowingly offend you. We beg that you will forgive us." He bowed his head.

Many of the Rin people nodded solemnly. But the Traveller children smothered giggles in the palms of their hands. Rowan knew that Ogden was making fun again. And he knew, too, that underneath the joke was something darker. Lann's words had cut into old wounds. They had cut deeply.

Allun felt it, too. Rowan could tell by the nervousness in his eyes and the tightness of his mouth. But he simply nodded to Ogden and smiled at the crowd. "Well, now that that is settled," he said, "may I tell my story?"

Ogden spread out his hands. "Tell on, Allun, son of Sara of Rin and Forley of the Travellers," he said coolly. "The blood of both our peoples runs in your veins. Our ears are open to your words."

"Tell well, Allun the Baker," called old Lann. "But guard your rattling tongue. We want no long-winded ramblings. Take care you add nothing that is not needed to the tale."

Ogden raised his slanted eyebrows, and shot a curious glance in her direction.

But Rowan knew her meaning. Lann feared that as part of his story Allun would tell how he had found sweet red berries growing by the Mountain caves. She feared that he would boast of how he had eaten some of them, given some to Marlie, and then filled his pockets with others, to bring them home to Rin. She feared he would tell their secret.

"Do not be alarmed, Lann," Allun said lightly. "I will not fail you."

He fixed his eyes on Ogden, and raised his voice.

"One morning," he began, "the people of Rin woke to find that the stream that flowed down the Mountain and through their village had slowed to a trickle. By nightfall, even that small flow had stopped ..."

A hush fell over the crowd around the campfire. Rowan saw Traveller adults stopping to listen, moving closer. He recognised Zeel, the chief Forerunner, as she slipped into the circle. The Travellers knew that the stream meant life to Rin and to its bukshah herd. Even Ogden's eyes had lost their spark of mockery.

Rowan closed his eyes as Allun spoke on. He did not need to hear this story. He had lived it, with Strong Jonn of the orchard, Allun the baker, Marlie the weaver, Bronden the furniture-maker and Val and Ellis from the mill.

Six months ago the seven of them had climbed the forbidden

Mountain to find the source of their dried-up stream, and try to bring its sweet water back to Rin. And in the end, as Sheba had foretold, it was Rowan, the smallest, weakest member of the party, who had succeeded in the quest.

But Rowan knew he wasn't a hero, really. Just as Sheba had said, he was still the same boy he had always been—shy and full of fears.

It was just that now he understood that there were different kinds of courage. He knew now that if those he loved needed help, he could feel terror, face it, and do what he had to do.

That knowledge warmed him. The cold, lonely feeling that had ached in his chest ever since his father died years ago had disappeared. He was happier now, by far, than he had been before he climbed the Mountain. As Sheba had said, it had taught him well.

But he did not *feel* a hero. Not at all. And when people called him one, he was uncomfortable. He fidgeted now in his place on the grass. He wished with all his heart that he could slip away, find Jonn and his mother, and talk to them. But it was impossible. It would be seen as great discourtesy for him to leave the campfire now. He would have to wait.

Annad's small hand tugged at his shirt sleeve. "They are listening," she whispered. "Look at them. Wait till they hear what you did, Rowan. Wait till they know the dangers you faced to save the village."

She puffed out her chest. "I hope they know *I'm* your sister!" she added.

Her eyes darted around, watching the Traveller children as they crouched, wide-eyed, by the fire. "They will not dare make fun of us after this." She nodded with satisfaction.

Rowan patted the hand that clung to him. "I would not be too sure of that, Annad," he whispered back. "Travellers like to laugh. They take nothing seriously for long."

* * *

Allun's tale was ended. There was silence around the dying embers of the campfire. Then the Travellers, and the people of Rin alike, clapped and cheered.

Allun grinned at them, and held out his hand to Rowan, crouched in the shadows. Rowan knew he wanted him to stand. But he could not do it. He shrank back, not wanting the curious eyes of the Travellers to find him.

"So!" said Ogden, stirring his fire thoughtfully. "So, Allun. Now I have another tale to tell through the land. The tale of Rowan of Rin."

He nodded. "It is a fine story," he said. "You told it well." Then he smiled. "But I will tell it better."

Everyone laughed, Allun loudest of all.

Ogden dropped the stick he was holding and leaned forward. "And now, Allun, we must talk, in private," he said.

Allun hesitated, and Ogden frowned slightly. "There are questions I must ask you." He paused. "The Mountain is a great mystery. It is said that the people of the Valley of Gold climbed it, before the Giants of Inspray fought and hid them from our sight. But I have waited long to meet a witness who can tell me of its wonders. Please do not disappoint me, Allun."

A small silence fell on the group around the fire. Rowan could feel that the people of Rin were holding their breaths.

"I fear I must disappoint you, Ogden," said Allun. "I cannot stay. My mother is tired and I need to return to the village with her."

"Then I will come with you," Ogden answered pleasantly. "The three of us will share a cup of soup in your warm kitchen, as we so often have before."

Again Allun hesitated. Rowan could almost feel the pain behind his smile. And pain was easy to see on Sara's face, as she stood clutching her son's arm.

"We prefer, this season, that none of your tribe come to the village, Ogden of the Travellers." Lann had stepped forward. Her voice was firm and strong, and she looked Ogden straight in the eye. "We find that your visits excite the children. And they are tired after the long winter. We ask, therefore, that you respect our wishes, and keep to your camp."

Not a muscle in Ogden's face moved. It was impossible to tell what he was thinking. But Rowan could see the darkening faces of Zeel and the other Travellers around the fire. They were not taking this refusal well.

"Perhaps you could talk to another member of the Mountain party, Ogden," Sara broke in, desperate to make peace. "Strong Jonn of the Orchard is here. And Marlie the weaver, too."

Ogden stared at her for a moment. He seemed to be thinking.

"Another time I would very much like to speak with every one of the Seven," he said politely at last. "But for now ..." His piercing eyes searched the faces round the campfire. "Let me meet the boy Rowan. He, in particular, is of interest to me."

Rowan shuffled his feet and felt his ears grow hot. He felt Annad pushing at him excitedly. He knew that he was going to have to stand and go forward to meet the man by the fire. But he did not want to do it. He did not want to do it at all.

He forced himself to his feet and stumbled forward. He felt the eyes of the crowd upon him. But the only eyes he saw were Ogden's: deep, dark, drawing him in.

8 – The Storyteller

o, Rowan of the Bukshah," said Ogden, putting out a thin brown hand to beckon him closer. "We have much to talk about. This is the second time I have heard of you this day. You were on the hill with the Welcomers, I am told."

Rowan nodded. He remembered the curious looks the Forerunners had given him. So they had remembered his name, and reported it to Ogden. Why? he wondered. Why had they been interested in a messenger boy?

Ogden put his head on one side. "You think and wonder much, do you not?" he said in a low voice. "More, perhaps, than most of your people. And perhaps you sometimes feel apart from them, because of this. Perhaps you feel most quietly content tending the great beasts you serve. Would that be so, Rowan of the Bukshah?"

Rowan stood motionless, not knowing what to do. Was this man able to see into his mind? Into his soul? He looked nervously behind him. Where were his mother and Annad? Where was Jonn?

He saw that they were standing watching a Traveller magician make a small silver bell appear and disappear. The magician's hands moved like fluttering birds, throwing the bell this way and that, so that it shone in the firelight, winking in and out of sight. Annad's mouth hung open in wonder.

"Do not fear me," said Ogden, still in that quiet, gentle voice. "I mean you no harm. I merely wish to ask you some questions. Simple questions. I wish to understand you better."

Rowan felt his cheeks grow even hotter. He made himself stand straighter, and prepared himself to meet whatever was coming. He knew it would be difficult to lie to this man, with his all-seeing eyes. Rowan did not know what he would do if Ogden the storyteller asked him directly if anyone had brought anything with them down from the Mountain.

But to his puzzlement and relief, Ogden did not. He asked instead about Rowan's mother, and his father. He asked about the bukshah, and the life Rowan led. And at the end of the questioning he took the boy's chin in his hand and looked deep into his eyes.

"Honest as the day is long," he said, and dropped his hand. He glanced at Rowan's bewildered face, and his lips curved briefly.

"Your ordeal is ended, Rowan of the Bukshah," he sighed. "You are free to go, with my blessing."

Rowan ducked his head, and carefully moved back from the fire. When he dared to glance up, Ogden had put his hands behind his head and was gazing up at the starry sky. His brow was deeply furrowed, as if the worries of the world had settled on his shoulders.

Rowan turned, and scuttled away.

* * *

Soon afterwards, Rowan walked home with Annad, Jiller and Strong Jonn. It was past Annad's usual bedtime, and she was sleepy. But she was still chattering about Allun's story as she trotted along, bubbling with pride and excitement.

Rowan looked at his mother, striding tall and strong beside him. Despite her anger over the decision to forbid the Travellers entering the village, she looked livelier than she had for many days. The visit to the hills had done her good.

Should he tell her and Jonn about Sheba now? He did not really want to do it in front of Annad. Perhaps he should wait until they were home, and Annad had gone to bed. A few minutes' more delay would not matter one way or another.

Besides, under this starry sky, with his family around him, his fear was starting to seem childish. The more he thought about the scene under the trees, the less certain he was that Sheba had not been tricking and teasing him.

Jiller turned and saw him looking at her. "You did well, Rowan," she said quietly. "I watched you talking to Ogden the storyteller. You were calm and stood straight. I was proud of you."

Rowan said nothing. He still felt shaken after his time with Ogden. He was sure that the man's questions, which had seemed on the surface so simple, had had some meaning that he had not understood. But still his heart was warmed by his mother's words. She did not often say such things. She thought it better to teach him to be strong and not to look for praise for doing what he should.

"Rowan showed them," yawned Annad happily. "He showed those Slips a thing or two."

"Annad!" exclaimed Jiller, half-shocked, half laughing. "Do not call the Travellers by that name."

Annad yawned again. "Why not?" she asked. "Everyone else does. Everyone calls them 'Slips'."

"Everyone else does *not*, little one," Jonn put in firmly. "Your mother does not. I do not. Marlie and Allun do not. Only those who wish to insult the Travellers use the word."

"Oh." Annad thought about that. "Why?"

"Such people think the Travellers serve no useful purpose," Jiller explained. "So they call them Slips, after the wild slip-daisies."

"Why?" Annad asked again. Her eyes were nearly closing with weariness, but she stumbled on determinedly beside them. "Why?" she repeated.

Rowan saw Jiller and Jonn smile at each other over Annad's head.

Then Jonn swung the little girl up into his arms.

"Because the slip-daisies have no use or purpose," he told her, as he strode along. "When our people first came to Rin, slip-daisies grew wild all over the valley, as they do still on the hills and beyond. But as useful crops were sown, and houses and lanes were built, the daisies were weeded out. Other plants, it seems, do not thrive where slip-daisies grow. So good farmers do not like them. As some do not like the Travellers."

Annad thought about this. "Slip-daisies are not *completely* useless," she argued. "Their roots make the medicine that Sheba sells us, for Rowan's nose."

Jonn laughed. "Their pollen makes skinny rabbit's nose run, and then their roots make it stop," he said, glancing at Rowan. "The disease, and the cure, in one small plant. Truly nature is very strange and wonderful."

They reached Bree and Hanna's gardens, and Jonn stopped. Rowan sniffed. Even his blocked-up nose could sense the sweet scent of the Mountain berry flowers drifting deliciously on the cool air.

"I must leave you here," Jonn said, swinging Annad to the ground. "I am to stand guard with Bree and Hanna this night."

Rowan felt a stab of disappointment. He had been sure that Jonn would come home with them, to sit by the fire for a while. He had done it so often before! What bad luck that on the very night that Rowan needed him he was staying away.

Jiller pulled her shawl more tightly around her shoulders. "Watch well," she said. "I am afraid, as others are, that Allun will tell Ogden of the Mountain berries. He has not so far. And he and Sara left the gathering early tonight. But they may go back later, alone, and then who knows …?"

"Allun is not a fool. He will keep his mouth shut, as will his mother," said Jonn firmly. "Why do you think they left the camp early? They want it to be clear to everyone that should the Travellers find out about the berries, it was not Allun or Sara who told them."

"Yet Allun is half-Traveller himself," Jiller argued. "And he thinks the fuss about the Mountain berries is foolish."

"Mother!" protested Rowan, shocked by her words. "Allun would *never* betray us!"

Jiller said nothing.

"I thought you were his friend!" Rowan accused.

"I am Allun's friend indeed, Rowan," Jiller said gravely. "But this does not mean that I cannot see his faults. I agree, he would never betray us knowingly. But he may not agree that telling of the Mountain berries would *be* betrayal."

She bit her lip. "Traveller blood runs strongly in Allun's veins. He believes that growing things belong to all. He cannot understand why the Rin people wish to keep his gift a secret. I know this, because he has told me. He has told Marlie, too."

Rowan started to speak again, but Jonn held up his hand to quiet him.

"Whatever Allun does or does not do, both he and I are fairly sure that the Travellers know of the new crop already, Jiller," he said. "And if they do not, they soon will."

"But how?" cried Jiller. "Lann told Ogden that—"

"Lann's insulting order will not stop the Travellers from visiting the village in the night, if they so choose," said Jonn quietly. "And then they will have only to use their eyes and noses to find the Mountain berry bushes. They are everywhere!"

Jiller sighed.

"I do not think we need to fear, Jiller," Jonn told her gently. "There will be Mountain berries in plenty in Rin next year. More than enough to ensure good trade, and feasting, too."

He smiled. "Soon the Mountain berries will be so many, they will be as thick as the slip-daisies used to be," he said. "People will start complaining about them, and calling them wild and useless, and pulling them out."

"I doubt that," Jiller laughed. "The flowers are beautiful. The scent is wondrous. And never have I tasted such sweet, rich berries. Good for eating, cooking, making into juice ..."

"Will no one want my hoopberries then, when the Mountain berries thrive?" Jonn asked, hanging his head and pretending to mourn. "Will my trees disappear from the valley like the slip-daisies have? Then I will have to trudge up to the hills, like Sheba does, to harvest my crop."

"That will never happen. I like hoopberries *much* better than Mountain berries," Rowan said stoutly.

"So do I," shrilled Annad. She loved the Mountain berry fruit. But she loved Jonn more.

Jonn stretched wearily. "Well, I must bid you all good-night and let you go to your warm fire," he yawned. He began moving towards the garden gate.

"Ho!" Rowan heard him call, as he rattled the gate. "Hanna! Bree! Open!"

There was silence from the gardens.

"Bree! Hanna!" roared Jonn good-humouredly. "Are you deaf, or asleep? Let me in!"

Silence. Deep, dark silence.

Rowan shivered. Far away he could hear low, restless bellows from the bukshah fields. And from the hills, faint music.

There was an exasperated grunt, and then a clattering sound as Jonn heaved himself up onto the locked gate, and jumped down to the ground on the other side.

"What do you think you're playing at, you two?" Rowan heard him shout. "Where are you? If I find you're snoring in your bed while I—"

There was a gasp. A silence. Then there was the sound of running feet, and the gate being unbolted from the inside. Jonn's voice came again, sharp and urgent.

"Rowan! Jiller! Come quickly!"

9 – Trouble

They bent over the two shapes huddled face-down on the ground beside the Mountain berry garden. Stakes lay scattered on the grass around them.

"They are breathing!" exclaimed Jiller. "Oh, they are so still that at first I thought—"

"So did I," Jonn said grimly. "But they are alive, all right. And yet they will not wake."

He shook Bree's shoulder. The man did not stir. "You see?" he said.

"The children!" gasped Jiller. Without another word she sprang up and ran to the darkened house that stood nearby, behind some fruit trees.

Rowan waited nervously for her return. Bree and Hanna's three children were not particular friends of his. They were too scornful of his shyness, and teased him too much, for that. But he hated to think of them in danger, or crouching terrified in that dark house, with their parents lying so still outside.

In a moment Jiller had returned. "Sleeping, tucked up in their beds," she panted. "They seem safe enough. But I did not try to wake them. For all I know they have the same illness as their parents."

She put her hand to Bree's cheek, gleaming white in the deep shadows. "He has no fever," she said. "But this is not a natural sleep, Jonn."

She looked around, shivering, as though on guard for watching eyes. "I feared something like this would happen," she said, putting her arm around Annad's shoulders. "I feared it as soon as I heard the children shouting this afternoon."

Quickly she glanced at the bushes in the garden beside them. "I do not know if they have been disturbed, or if any fruits are missing," she muttered. "I cannot tell, in the darkness."

Jonn stared at her, his mouth tight. Then he shook his head, as though to clear it. "We will talk of this later," he said. "Now we must tend to Bree and Hanna. We must move them to shelter, Jiller. They are heavy, but between us I think we can manage it."

"Do you want me to go for help?" asked Rowan. "Bronden's house is near. And Marlie's."

Jonn hesitated. "No," he said finally. "I think for now we would be better dealing with this on our own, Rowan. We do not want news of it to travel too quickly. Until we know ..."

He looked straight into Rowan's eyes. "You understand?" he asked.

Rowan nodded. He knew as well as Jonn what would happen if rumour spread that Bree and Hanna had been struck down. He knew that some villagers would not hesitate to storm up to the Travellers' camp with lanterns and torches, to accuse and threaten.

And that would be dangerous. Dangerous to the whole of Rin.

It would be much better if Jonn and Jiller could wake Bree and Hanna and get the real story of what had happened to them. Something simple could be at the heart of this. Something that had nothing to do with the Travellers at all.

"You can help by staying here and keeping watch, skinny rabbit," Jonn said. "No task is more important now than keeping intruders from the gardens."

"I will help!" Annad insisted sleepily. "I will keep watch too."

Jonn smiled at her, his teeth white in the dimness. "I am depending upon it, Annad," he told her.

"Call us if there is the faintest sound to alarm you, Rowan," warned Jiller.

Rowan nodded. He watched his mother and Strong Jonn bend to lift Bree's limp body, then begin to carry it towards the cottage that stood just beyond the gardens.

Jiller and Jonn, staggering slightly under their burden, disappeared into the shadows of the house. Left alone with Annad and the sleeping Hanna, Rowan strained his eyes in the darkness. Shafts of moonlight stretched in bands across the gardens.

It was quiet now. So quiet that Hanna's deep breaths sounded loud. There was no sound from the bukshah fields. No sound from the camp on the hill. And yet the silence was not peaceful. It was like the silence of waiting: heavy, and full of secrets.

The secret enemy is here.
It hides in darkness, fools beware!

Rowan felt his sister's weight grow heavy on his shoulder. He looked down and saw that her eyes were closed.

"Annad," he said. "Do you want to go inside the house, to sleep there?"

She forced her heavy eyelids open. "I don't want to sleep," she murmured. "I am keeping watch."

"So you are," he agreed. "Watch, then."

She nodded happily. Her eyelids fluttered closed again.

Rowan put his arm around her to keep her warm. He watched, peering into the darkness beyond the gardens, searching the shadows for the tiniest, stealthiest movement. He listened, in the deep silence, for the slightest sound. He waited for the smallest sign that someone or something was lurking near, watching and listening as he was.

But there was nothing. Only a droning, chanting voice in his head. And to go with the voice, a picture. Sheba, with fear on her face.

He heard his mother and Jonn moving out of the house and towards the gardens. They were coming back for Hanna.

He glanced at Annad. She was sleeping heavily. She would not wake. He knew the time had come.

"Jonn, Mother," he whispered piercingly. "I have something I have to tell you. Now!"

* * *

Jiller's eyes were dark with fear.

"What does this mean?" she breathed. "What does it mean, 'the old wheel turns'?"

Rowan looked at her in surprise. He had not thought much about this part of the rhyme.

"I don't know," he said. "I don't know what *any* of it means. And neither does Sheba. But she is afraid."

They stared at him. A cloud glided over the moon, and the

gardens darkened. A bird rustled in a nearby tree. Annad muttered in her sleep, and stirred against Rowan's shoulder.

Jonn stood up. "We need help, I think," he said. "We cannot keep this matter a secret any longer."

Jiller nodded. "It is late. We cannot rouse the whole village at this hour."

"Nor do we want to," Jonn said grimly. "Rowan must go and wake only those who can be of real help."

"Timon," Rowan suggested. To him, Timon the teacher was the one most likely to be able to think clearly about Sheba's rhyme. And one of the villagers least likely to panic.

"Yes," Jiller agreed. "Timon. And Marlie."

"And Allun," added Jonn.

"I do not think it would be wise to bring Allun into this," Jiller said. "For plainly the Travellers have something to do with it."

"Then who better than Allun to help us?" asked Jonn. "We are fortunate to have a friend who knows the Travellers' ways."

Jiller said nothing, but Rowan could see that she was troubled.

"I will go and get Timon, Marlie and Allun, then," he broke in quickly.

It worried him to see Jonn and his mother disagree. There was a time when he had hated the idea that one day Strong Jonn of the Orchard might marry Jiller, and become his stepfather. But now he felt differently. Jonn would never take his father's place in his heart. But he had made his own place—the place of a good and special friend, to be depended on and loved in his own way.

"Yes Rowan," Jiller said quietly. "And also bring Lann."

Rowan and Jonn stared at her in surprise. She returned their looks gravely.

"I have been thinking of the rhyme," she said. "'The old wheel turns', it says. And it talks of 'the same mistakes, the same old pride'. It seems to me that it is telling us that whatever trouble we are facing has been faced before."

Rowan's heart thudded. He had suddenly remembered what Sheba had said, before the chant began. *"The enemy is coming again,"* she had said. *"The wheel is turning. And this time—this time—"*

He repeated the last lines of Sheba's chant aloud.

"For day by day its power grows,
And when at last its face it shows,
Then past and present tales will meet—
The evil circle is complete."

He shuddered. He knew his mother was right. Something dreadful was going to happen. And it had happened before. Slowly the wheel of time and fate was turning. Some evil circle was forming. And when it made a perfect whole

Jiller looked at Jonn. "The answer to this lies in our past," she said. "I am sure of it."

He nodded slowly.

"Lann is the oldest person in the village," Jiller went on. "She remembers much that even the books do not tell us. If the trouble we face now has happened before, Lann will know of it. She may be able to help us stop it, before the wheel turns any further."

"You are right," exclaimed Jonn. He spun around to Rowan. "Go then," he ordered. "Go quickly."

10 – The Secret Enemy

imon stroked his chin. "The books tell us that hunger has always been an enemy for Rin to fear," he suggested. "We have faced it several times when crops have failed or the winter snows have cut the village off from the coast for too long."

"I doubt it is the enemy of the rhyme, though," said Jiller. "The rhyme says the enemy is here already. In hiding, perhaps, so we do not recognise it. But here."

"I believe we should go to Sheba," Marlie said. "We should ask her what the rhyme means."

"She does not know!" Rowan exclaimed. "I told you."

"She did not know when you spoke to her, Rowan," Jonn answered. "But by now her knowledge may have grown. We should try."

Lann nodded. "True enough," she said. She pointed her stick at Rowan. "The boy should go. And Jiller and Jonn with him. The rest of us will stay here with the sleepers. Timon will be company for me, Marlie can guard the Mountain berries ..."

"And I?" asked Allun with a twisted smile.

"I want you here under my eye, Allun the Baker," said Lann calmly. "In case you decide to take a walk to the hills."

Allun's face darkened with anger, but he kept silent.

* * *

The orchard was dimly lit by moonlight. Rowan, Jonn and Jiller did not speak as they moved through the hoopberry trees, treading carefully so as not to crush the sweet herbs and tender Mountain berry bushes that clustered underfoot. It was very quiet. No birds rustled in the trees. There was no sound from the bukshah fields.

They climbed through the fence that marked the end of the

orchard, and began walking quickly over the pale grass that grew in front of Sheba's hut.

The door stood open, and light streamed, flickering, from the room beyond. Light, and the long shadow of someone moving around inside. Rowan felt his heart begin to beat faster. He glanced at his mother. Her face was set and determined, but he could tell by her rapid breathing that she, too, was afraid.

They reached the door and looked inside. Sheba was there, bent over the great iron pot that hung over the glowing fire. She was muttering to herself, stirring the brew.

"Sheba!" Jiller said softly.

The old woman turned slowly. She stared blankly at Jiller and Jonn. And then she saw Rowan. Her glazed eyes widened and she threw up her hands with a cry of fear, as if to protect herself.

"Leave me!" she gasped. "Leave me be! Take your nightmare face away!"

Rowan stepped back in shock.

"We need to talk to you, Sheba," said Jonn urgently. "The rhyme you gave to Rowan. What is its meaning?"

She shook her head, shutting her eyes. "Leave me," she moaned. "Leave me to do my work. There is no time. No time left."

The firelight leapt behind her. The evil-smelling brew in the cauldron bubbled.

"The work does not matter now," Jiller exclaimed. "The rhyme is what matters, Sheba. You must tell us what you know."

"I know nothing," the old woman droned. "Nothing but my nightmares. And all of it—all—is coming true. I feel it. Even now the wheel is turning. And soon the enemy will be upon us. Soon, soon—"

"Sheba, help us!" Jonn begged.

But Sheba's face was empty. "I must make the brew. This I can do. This is what I know. The boy—take him away. His face haunts my dreams. The face ... the kites ... the golden owl with green eyes ..."

Rowan heard his own strangled gasp, and his mother's sharp cry.

"All of them—torment me!" Sheba thrust her fingers into her hair and swayed. "And I do not know why. I only know that I must work. I must go on. And I am tired, so tired …"

She took a staggering step towards them. "Leave me, tormentor!" she screeched, looking directly at Rowan. "*Leave me!*"

Jiller put an arm around her son and held him tightly.

"Let us go," said Jonn. "There is nothing more for us here."

* * *

Old Lann hobbled to the partly open window. For a moment she stared out at the tall figure of Marlie still standing on guard by the Mountain berries. Then she turned to face the others.

"Three kites—what can this mean but the Travellers? And the golden owl with green eyes is a symbol of that Travellers' tale—the Valley of Gold. We must take good note of these visions. Sheba may not know what they mean. But they are warnings. Of that there is no doubt."

"She said the wheel was turning," said Jiller fearfully. "She said that soon the enemy would be upon us."

"But what enemy?" Timon frowned.

"Why look for secret meanings to the word?" Lann answered, in a tired voice quite unlike her usual fierce tones. "Rin has only ever had one real enemy. The Zebak. We must arm ourselves and prepare for war."

There was silence in the cheery, well-lit living room. Rowan looked up at his mother. She had been to the bedroom to check on Bree and Hanna, still sleeping their strange, unnatural sleep.

She had returned just in time to hear Lann's words. Now she stood by the door, her hands pressed tightly together. Her eyes flickered to Annad, curled up on the couch in the corner, then to Jonn, sitting at the big table, and finally to him.

She is afraid for us, thought Rowan. He watched her move swiftly to the table and take her seat again. She looked exhausted. Grey shadows marked the skin underneath her eyes. Her face was pale.

"There has been no word of the Zebak coming again, Lann," she argued, leaning across the table. "No news from the Maris folk of strange ships near the coast, or rumour on the seas."

"It has been a long, hard winter, girl," said Lann. "No one from Rin has been to the coast since autumn. How do we know what is happening there? The Maris folk could be defeated and enslaved, even now."

"The Travellers would know," Timon put in. "And the Forerunners said they had no news."

"They said they had no news *to tell us*, Timon," Jonn corrected. "That is a different thing from having no news at all." He looked at Allun. "The Forerunners were keeping something back. I could feel it. It could be that the Travellers know something that they cannot or *will* not tell, for reasons of their own."

"Nonsense," said Allun, looking away.

Lann glared at him. "Is it?" she demanded.

Allun met her stern look with a calm one of his own. "Yes," he said quietly. "The Travellers would not keep news of a Zebak invasion from us. Not only because they are our friends, but because, as you pointed out at the camp this very night, Lann, because they *need* us."

"This is true, Lann," nodded Jonn. "The Travellers do not wish to be enslaved to the Zebak, any more than we do. As Ogden told us this night, they well remember the War of the Plains. And they remember, too, the great battle before that, when our ancestors came to this place, and were freed."

"Not just these, either," Timon's soft voice put in. "There are Travellers' tales of Zebak invasions going back for ages past. According to legend, their people were fighting a great battle against the Zebak on the coast at the same time as the Giants of Inspray were fighting on the Mountain for the Valley of Gold."

Lann scowled. "The Giants of Inspray—the Valley of Gold! Children's stories!"

Timon cleared his throat. "Perhaps," he said. "Fact and fantasy often mingle when a history is passed down only in pictures and the spoken word, as the Travellers' history is. But it seems true enough that the Zebak have always wanted to take this land. They tried many, many times before we came here."

"And they always failed," Jiller reminded him.

"Yes," Timon agreed. "Their might has never been a match for the

Maris folk's wits and the Travellers' knowledge of the land. In the end, they were always forced back and driven away."

"And then they brought our race to these shores. And this was a fatal error," added Lann with satisfaction. "They thought to add to their strength with an army of warrior slaves. But instead the slaves rose up and turned against them, joining with those they wished to conquer. For the past three hundred years, instead of two peoples defending this land, there have been three."

She paused, and a shadow crossed her wrinkled face. "But we must consider whether there are three still, my friends. Or whether—as the witch's rhyme warns us—treachery is in the air."

"What do you mean?" cried Allun angrily.

Timon rubbed his hand across his tired eyes. "We must not let our feelings guide us, Allun," he said. "We must consider everything. What if—" He hesitated, glanced at Jonn and Jiller, and then went on. "What if the Zebak, realising they cannot win this land by strength alone, have grown cunning? What if they have made promises to the Travellers—promises to give them something they dearly want, perhaps—in return for help?"

"The Travellers want for nothing. What could the Zebak promise them?" Allun demanded.

"Something they could get from no one else," Timon said simply. "The Zebak could promise to use their might to help the Travellers brave the Pit of Unrin, and find the Valley of Gold."

11 – Betrayal

The room fell silent. In everyone's mind, Rowan knew, was a single thought. Timon was right. The one thing that could tempt the Travellers was the chance to find the legendary place of all goodness that was at the heart of their tales. To re-discover, after thousands of years, the great, wise race of people who had been Traveller friends and allies.

"Think what it would mean to Ogden, to be the leader who gained for his people such happiness," said Timon. "The Pit of Unrin has always been a forbidden place to the Travellers. They cannot enter it, any more than they can climb the Mountain. If it is to be defeated, others must do the deed. And Ogden knows that neither we nor the Maris folk would offer help to find the Valley."

"Why would we waste our time and endanger lives in such a quest?" Lann said at last. "The Valley of Gold is a legend. It does not exist."

"The Travellers believe it does." Allun's voice was flat and cold. "They believe it as they believe the sun rises in the east and sets in the west. They have no doubt." Suddenly he pushed back his chair and half-stood. He was shaking his head violently.

"No!" he shouted. "No! The Travellers would never be taken in by Zebak promises! *Never!* Not even for this. Not even for the Valley of Gold. They are our friends. They would never betray us!"

Timon bowed his head. "The Zebak may at last have learned a lesson from the Travellers," he said. "They may have learned that you catch more bees with honey than with black looks and fighting words. They might, by trickery and lies, have turned the Travellers against us, Allun. Who knows?"

Rowan stared. *Beneath soft looks the evil burns.* He looked quickly at his mother and at Jonn. Had they realised how closely Timon's words matched the rhyme?

By their faces, he could see they had. And more. They were remembering Sheba's visions. Three kites. The Travellers' kites. And a golden owl with green eyes.

He heard again Ogden's voice. "The Valley of Gold ... Houses painted with beautiful patterns, each one different ... Before each house, a golden bird—an owl with emerald eyes ..."

Before he could say anything, there was a groan from the room beyond. Jiller sprang to her feet and ran to where Bree and Hanna lay. Everyone else quickly followed.

Bree was stirring, tossing his head on the pillow.

It was stuffy in the little room. Timon turned and threw open the window. The cool night air streamed in, bringing with it the scent of the Mountain berries and new grass, but no sound. No sound at all.

"Bree, what happened?" asked Lann sharply. "Tell us! Come on, man! Make an effort!"

Bree's eyes slowly opened. He gazed in bewilderment at all the people crowded into his small bedroom. Then he turned his head and saw his wife, still unconscious on the bed beside him.

"Hanna!" he groaned, and reached out for her.

"She is asleep, Bree, as you have been," Jiller told him. "Bree, we need to know what happened."

"We were building a fence," Bree mumbled. "Around the Mountain berry plants. To protect them from thieving Slips who may come in the night."

Allun made a sharp sound of disgust and protest. Jiller shook her head at him. She wanted Bree to go on.

"I was pounding stakes into the ground," said Bree. "Pounding them in, then sharpening the tips. But the ground was hard—like iron, it seemed. The stakes would not go in very far, however hard I hammered them. I got so tired. Then Hanna tried, while I rested. But in the end she had to give up, too."

Rowan saw the adults around the bed look at each other over Bree's head. This was very strange. The soil in the gardens was rich and moist. Stakes should have entered it as easily as a knife enters soft butter.

"I was so tired," Bree sighed. "So tired. I had to lie down. To rest. So tired." His eyelids drooped. His mouth fell open.

"Bree!" cried Jonn, shaking him. But Bree did not answer. He was asleep again, and this time he would not wake.

"He is enchanted," growled Lann, angrily beating her stick on the ground. "He, and Hanna too. Not content with betraying us to our enemy, the Slips are after the Mountain berries. They hardened the ground to prevent the fence being built. They put the gardeners to sleep. And—"

"Perhaps they did put the gardeners to sleep!" hissed Allun. "But *if* they did—*if*, Lann, what of it? It is a harmless enough trick. It has nothing to do with the Zebak, or Sheba's rhyme. You lurch from one thing to the next, you people, without thought, guided only by your dislike of the Travellers."

"That is not so, Allun." Jiller put her hand on his arm.

"It is!" he shouted, shaking it off.

"It is *not*," roared Lann, banging her stick. "Be still, Allun the Baker!"

Jiller slipped quietly from the room. Rowan followed.

He found her bending over Annad, still lying on the couch. She straightened up to face him, her forehead creased with worry.

"I do not like this, Rowan," she said. "Already I feel the trouble coming upon us. We are arguing and fighting among ourselves, when we should be banding together to face whatever is coming. Only that way can we be strong."

Rowan nodded. He felt close to despair. Sheba's words drifted into his mind.

The same mistakes, the same old pride,
The priceless armour cast aside.

Was this what the rhyme had meant? If so, then Sheba was right, and the evil circle was already nearing completion. The wheel was turning, every moment bringing the enemy closer and closer. He shuddered.

"Do you think Timon could be right?" Jiller murmured. "Could the Travellers have turned against us?"

"But why then would they have *come* here?" Rowan said.

"To spy!" said Lann from the bedroom door. Rowan watched her hobble to the fire. Her face looked withered and exhausted as she lowered herself painfully into an armchair.

"They have come here to spy on us," she said. "To report to their new friends on our food supplies and arms." Her head drooped, and she struggled to raise it. "I am tired," she mumbled. "So tired."

Jonn quickly crossed the room to kneel beside her.

The old warrior feebly waved him away. "The Slips have come to spy on us," she repeated.

Then Rowan saw her eyes widen. "Or something worse," she muttered.

She twisted in her chair to stare at them wildly. "Oh, we have been blind!" she shrieked. "Bree—Hanna—" She tried to get to her feet, but fell back with a groan.

"Lann, what is wrong?" cried Jiller in fear. She put her hand to her mouth and looked down at Annad, but her voice had not disturbed the little girl. She did not stir. A shadow of puzzlement passed over Jiller's face.

"Marlie," groaned Lann. "Quickly!"

Allun looked at her sharply and went to the door. He pulled it open and called to Marlie. But the tall figure standing in the garden did not turn or reply.

Jonn and Timon stepped forward, but Allun was already running. They heard his voice calling, more and more urgently in the silence of the night. "Marlie! Marlie! Answer me!"

"He will rouse the village," worried Timon.

But nothing stirred. Least of all Marlie. For when, in answer to Allun's despairing cries, Rowan, Jonn and the others rushed out to his side, they found him clutching and shaking her in terror, while she stood as still as a statue, her eyes fixed and staring.

* * *

"She breathes," Jiller said, bending over Marlie's rigid body lying by the fire. "But—"

"She will not wake," mumbled Lann. "One by one we are falling prey to this—this witchery. And this is the plan. We sleep—and then ..." Her voice trailed off. She fell back in her chair.

It hides in darkness, fools beware!

With a cry Jiller jumped up and put a hand on the old woman's forehead. But she did not move. Jiller turned away, tight-lipped, and went to the couch where Annad lay.

"Why has no one come to find out what is happening here?" asked Timon suddenly. "Allun's shouts should have brought a dozen people running. Bronden's house is just nearby. And there are others. Many others."

"Perhaps they did not hear," said Jonn gravely. "Perhaps they are sleeping too deeply. Like Bree and Hanna's children. Like Bree and Hanna themselves. Like Marlie. And now, it seems, Lann."

Jiller made a small, anguished sound from her place on the couch. As they looked at her she licked her dry lips. "And Annad, Jonn," she whispered. "Annad—she—is like the others."

Rowan felt his stomach turn over. He ran over to the couch and shook Annad violently. But the little girl did not move. He spun round to Allun, his eyes stinging.

"Allun!" he shrieked. "Allun, you have to tell the Travellers— to stop it!"

Allun stepped back. His face was white. "It cannot be," he said. "It cannot ..."

Then he looked at Marlie on the floor, Lann slumped in her chair, Jiller crouched over the small bundle on the couch.

"I will go," he said softly. "And if this is my people's doing I will have it stopped. I will, I swear it!" He gripped Jonn's arm. "Ring the bell in the square," he gabbled. "Ring it loud and long until some people come. We cannot be the only souls still in our senses this night."

"I will go," said Timon. "Jiller and Jonn can stay here with the sleepers, to see that no harm comes to them. You, Allun, go to the camp on the hill. Go quickly, and do not go alone. Take Rowan with you."

"No!" cried Jiller. "Why Rowan?"

"Ogden knows Rowan now, and respects him as the hero of the Mountain," said Timon. "He seemed to recognise something in the boy tonight. Something he found interesting, and that he liked. Next to Allun, Rowan is our best messenger."

"Yes," agreed Jonn. "Rowan should go. Sheba said she keeps seeing his face in her dreams. Perhaps he is to play his part in this mystery now."

Jiller nodded and slumped wearily back on the couch, with Annad's head on her lap. She looked exhausted. The grey smudges under her eyes had darkened to black.

"Mother! Don't go to sleep!" warned Rowan anxiously.

Allun pulled at his arm. "Come now," he urged. "Let us hurry!"

They left the house and began running through the village. Already the first pale signs of dawn were streaking the sky. As they reached the trees where Rowan had met Sheba they heard the bell begin its warning, clanging sound.

Rowan imagined Timon standing alone in the square, his long fingers grasping the bell rope, pulling it over and over again. His ears would be deafened by the bell. His eyes would be searching the darkness for people starting half-awake from their beds in answer to his call.

Rowan and Allun burst from the trees and began racing up the hill. Rowan ran with his head down, panting and gasping.

He heard Allun curse, felt him falter and slow.

"What is it?" he choked. "Allun?"

Allun stopped.

"Look," he said, and pointed.

The hill where the Travellers had camped was bare and empty. They had gone.

12 – The Wheel Turns

Allun bent to feel the ashes of Ogden's fire.

"Still warm," he said. "They moved out only a few hours ago."

"Why did they go?" exclaimed Rowan. "So silently, without saying goodbye?"

Allun's mouth tightened. "Perhaps they were hurt and angry because the village of their so-called friends had been forbidden to them."

Rowan looked at his lean face, outlined against the lightening sky. At this moment, with his hair ruffled and his dark eyes secret, Allun looked very little like a man of Rin, and very much like a Traveller.

"Or perhaps," the man went on in a hard voice, "they left because they had done what they came to do. Perhaps old Lann is right."

Rowan caught his breath.

"We must go back to the village," Allun said abruptly. He started down the hill.

"Allun!" Rowan cried. "What are we going to do?"

"We are going to visit my mother, and yours," said Allun, quickening his pace. "We are going to get water and food. And then we are going to find the Travellers, and get to the heart of this matter, for good or ill, before it is too late. If the Zebak are coming—"

"But Allun …" Rowan panted, struggling to keep up with him. "How …? Where …?"

Allun glanced at the boy beside him. His voice softened. "Rowan, do not ask questions. Save your breath. We must hurry."

* * *

The village was quiet as they entered it. The ringing of the bell had stopped. But Rowan's heart leapt with relief as he heard low voices coming from the square. People were awake and gathered there, then.

And they were not shouting in fear and panic. They were talking quietly to each other.

"It's all right," he said to Allun eagerly. "People are there. Maybe Annad has woken too—and Marlie and the others."

But Allun's face looked set and grave.

"Wait," he said.

They turned a corner and reached the square. Timon was still standing by the bell. A dozen people were gathered around him. Others were moving into the square from laneways all around. Still others were walking quietly away.

Rowan blinked at the scene before him. And in that blink, his hope vanished. The gathering was all wrong. He had been pleased that there were no shouts of panic. But there should have been much more noise than this!

There should have been far more movement, too. There should have been children running, excited by the unexpected call. There should have been people walking briskly around, wanting to hear the news, wanting to know why they had been so rudely wakened.

But there was none of that. There were no children in the gathering. And the adults who were there seemed to be wandering in a daze. Their faces were dreamy and their voices low. Some had not even troubled to pull a coat on over their nightclothes, but trailed around in white gowns and shirts, shivering, barefoot and tousled, like ghosts.

They were awake, yet not awake. It was as though they had simply stirred in the middle of sleep, and would at any moment turn to sleep again. Even as Rowan watched, he saw Neel the potter sigh and sink slowly to the ground. The paving stones must have been very cold, but he curled up on them as though they were his own soft mattress, and closed his eyes.

Rowan clapped his hand over his mouth to stop himself from crying out.

Allun crossed the square in three strides and grabbed Timon's arm. The teacher slowly turned, and to his horror Rowan saw that his face, too, was blank and empty.

Allun shook his arm. "Timon!" he called. "Timon, wake! Ring the bell again!"

He caught at the bell rope himself, and pulled at it furiously. The sound of the bell rang out, shockingly loud, in the square. The people turned to look, and blinked, then turned away again.

"Timon!" shouted Allun. Timon's face cleared for a moment. He licked his lips.

"It is too strong, Allun," he mumbled. "It is growing. I cannot fight it any more. And the others ..." He shook his head.

Allun spun round to face Rowan. "Come with me," he said. He began to push his way through the people milling in the square. They barely looked at him, or at Rowan. They just moved aside gently as he passed, like grass bending in the wind.

The bakery door was closed. Allun pushed it open and walked through the cool, dark kitchen to the back of the house. "Mother!" he cried sharply.

But there was no answer.

"Mother!" Allun called again. "Answer me!"

But still no sound disturbed the silence.

Rowan watched helplessly as Allun darted from room to room, shouting, banging doors. He saw that the back door was open and went outside. The neat back garden lay spread out before him, dim and sweetly perfumed. And there ...

"Allun," he gasped.

Sara was lying back in an old wooden chair on the grass, an over-turned cup by her limp, hanging hand.

Allun bent over her. He touched her with trembling hands. "She was here, drinking soup, when you came for me last night. She must have been overtaken after I left. She has been here ever since. In the dark and the cold. Her clothes are wet with dew."

He buried his face in his hands. "What is happening here?" he groaned. "By my life, Rowan, what is happening? How could the Travellers do this? To Sara, who loved them? Last night she was laughing with Ogden himself. And now ..."

He gathered the limp body of his mother into his arms, and staggered with her towards the house.

"Go to the kitchen and get bread and water," he barked over his shoulder. "And quickly, Rowan. Quickly! We must get to Jonn and the others as soon as we can, and go for the Travellers. Before we too are overtaken and there is no one left standing in the whole of Rin. The sun is coming up. And the enemy—"

But Rowan was already hurrying to the bakery kitchen, stuffing rolls into a bag, and filling a flask with water from the great jug that stood beside the door. In a moment he was back at Allun's side. He watched as Allun covered his mother with a rug and leaned over her, fumbling with something at the back of her neck.

"Allun, come on!" he urged.

Allun straightened, pushed his hand deep into his pocket, and nodded. With a shock Rowan saw the paleness of his face, his hollow eyes.

"Allun!" he cried in fear. "You—"

Allun nodded. "I feel it," he murmured. "It is—a heaviness. Growing. I—"

Rowan tugged at his arm. "Come quickly," he said. "Come to the gardens. Do not stand still. Perhaps it is our movement that is keeping the illness from us. Come!"

He tugged Allun out of the living room and through the kitchen to the front door. Then he pushed him out into the street and took his hand.

"Run!" he whispered. "Run, Allun!"

They ran. Rowan could hear Allun gasping by his side. All around them in the street people lay sleeping on the hard stones. And now that it was lighter, Rowan could see that there were others.

Some were slumped in chairs in their gardens, like Sara had been. Some were lying by wells, with overturned buckets by their sides. Solla the sweet-maker hung half in, half out of his window. A group of children who had been chattering around Ogden's fire only hours before were sprawled together under the Teaching Tree, still in the clothes they had worn to the storytelling.

Rowan pulled Allun through the square. They had to step over the bodies of people who lay there. Timon stood by the bell, his hand still on the rope, his eyes unseeing. Rowan called to him, but not a flicker crossed the teacher's face.

They began to run for the gardens. And it was then that Rowan noticed the birds.

Birds of every kind lay scattered under the trees beside the path. Like small bundles of feathers they lay motionless among the Mountain berry flowers and the grass, as if they had fallen from their nests and perches in the night. Their eyes were closed. Their beaks gaped. Their legs were like tiny, stiff twigs.

Rowan's throat ached. It was as though every living thing in Rin had been captured by the spell that had overtaken the village.

"Star!" he whispered. His stomach lurched as he realised that the great beast must have known some trouble was coming. That was why she had been restless. That was why she had led the other bukshah away.

And he had made her return! If only he had seen that she would not have strayed without a cause. She had obeyed him at last, trusting him. But in his blindness he had made her bring her herd back into danger.

Sobbing, he pulled Allun on. They reached Bronden's workshop. Almost Rowan stopped, thinking to find help. But then he saw Bronden's stocky body, crumpled against her own front door. Her brow was creased, and her strong arms were flung out as though she had fought to the last against whatever power was clouding her brain, and forcing her eyes closed.

"Rowan," mumbled Allun, dragging on his hand. "I cannot—"

"Yes you can!" cried Rowan, panic-stricken. "Allun, look, Bree and Hanna's house is near. Do not stop. We have to find Jonn, and Mother. They will help us."

He pushed through the gate that led into the gardens. He pulled Allun, stumbling, to the house behind the trees. And then he knew that there was no help to be found here either. For the door hung open, and Jonn lay face-down on the grass at the bottom of the steps, with Jiller at his side. They were still as death.

13 – The Call

Rowan ran away from Rin with tears streaming from his eyes. He and Allun had not been able to lift Jonn and Jiller into the house. Neither of them had had the strength. So they had had to leave them where they had fallen.

Never had Rowan done such a difficult thing. None of the horrors he had ever faced had matched that of turning his back on his mother lying helpless on the grass, and running away.

Now he stumbled forward, his heart as cold and empty as a grate in which the fire had burned out. He barely saw the ground under his feet. He barely felt the dawn breeze against his face.

At the top of the hill he paused, and looked down into the valley. Only yesterday he had done this, he thought. Then he had looked at those patchwork fields, and those tidy lanes and houses, and his heart had been warm. But that was before he had met Sheba under the trees. That was when the village had been full of life.

Without surprise he saw that the bukshah fields were still. He could see the bodies of some of the calves lying in the grass. But further on—he bit back a gasp of relief—far away along the stream, other beasts were moving. And ahead of them all was Star.

In the night she must have decided to move the herd on after all. And she had done it. She, at least, had not made the old mistake. The mistake of trusting someone who did not know how wise she was to fear.

"Rowan," murmured Allun, by his side. "Rowan, we must go on. This—this thing—you are right—grows more strong when I am still."

Rowan nodded, and turned his back on the village. The thought crossed his mind that he might never see it again, and he shook his head. He would not think of that. He began walking.

The daisies under his feet were already doing their work. His eyes were puffing up, and his nose was running. Stop it! he told himself. He dug in his pocket for the hated medicine, and took a sip. The disgusting, sour taste burned on his tongue. The memory of Sheba's cackle filled his mind.

But Sheba, perhaps, was not cackling now. Was she, too, hunched by her fire in a sleep-like trance, while the evil she had so feared made ready to show its face?

Then past and present tales will meet—
The evil circle is complete ...

With a sinking heart Rowan faced the only possible meaning of those words. In the past, in a land far away, the people of Rin had been slaves to the Zebak. Now, after three hundred years of trying, the Zebak were about to swoop on them again. They were going to take them back into slavery. The evil circle would be complete.

And it would be soon. Very soon. Unless ...

Rowan dug his fingernails into his palms. Unless he and Allun could find the Travellers, beg them to undo the mischief they had done, and stop the wheel from turning.

They moved on in silence. Rowan's legs were already tired, and he had been up all night. But his brain was working feverishly. They were following the tracks of the Travellers' carts. But the tribe had passed this way hours ago, and already the grass and slip-daisies were springing back into shape, softening their traces.

Soon they would disappear altogether. Then what would he and Allun do? And even if they *could* go on following the tracks, how could they possibly catch up, walking at this speed?

He looked up at Allun. The man's lean face was set, but his eyes were clearer now than they had been.

"You feel better, Allun," he ventured.

Allun nodded. "The movement helps," he said. "And you?"

"I never felt the tiredness," Rowan said. The thought had been troubling him. "I cannot understand it. Everyone else in Rin—even Bronden, even Jonn—was struck down. You are half-Traveller, so it makes sense that you might escape. But why me?"

Allun shook his head. "Ogden took a fancy to you," he said

lightly. "Perhaps he decided that you should be spared the sleep—and whatever evil is to follow it."

Rowan stared at him in horror. Somehow, despite everything, part of him had never quite believed that the Travellers had lulled Rin to sleep for a truly evil purpose. He had, he realised, clung to the hope that they had simply enchanted the village as a lesson. A strong lesson, perhaps, but a lesson that could be delivered, understood, and then undone.

But Allun's words filled him with dread. He bit his lip to stop himself from crying out, and stumbled on.

Then Allun stopped, looked behind him, and dug in his pocket.

"We are far enough away now, I think," he said. "Now, Rowan. We will see what we will see."

He held out his hand. Cupped in it was a long, thin ribbon of faded, plaited silk. Sara's wedding necklace. Rowan had seen it a thousand times, around her neck. But he had never before noticed the small brown object that hung from it. It had always been hidden under Sara's clothes, he supposed.

He watched in amazement as Allun raised the tiny thing to his lips, and blew.

No sound reached Rowan's ears. But he knew at once what was happening. The object was a reed pipe. Allun was signalling. He was calling the Travellers.

"I did not know Sara had a reed pipe," he whispered.

Allun brought the pipe down from his lips. "It has been a secret, until now. Mother was given it when she left the Travellers many years ago. She was told that she only had to call in time of trouble, and they would come. From anywhere. At any time. But it has never been used, till this day."

"And *will* they come?" asked Rowan. "Even ...?"

Allun knew what he was thinking. Even though Sara's trouble was *caused* by the Travellers themselves?

"It was a solemn promise," Allun said gravely. "And if they fail to keep it ..."

Rowan scanned the horizon, slowly turning to look in all directions. To the east and to the north, pale blue morning sky shimmered over hills golden with flowers. Behind them, to the west, the great Mountain rose, white-tipped. Beside it, a little to the south, brooded the jagged rocks and caverns of—

He exclaimed, and pointed.

Three spots of colour dipped and swayed against grey-brown distance. Moving closer.

"The Forerunners!" Allun breathed. Rowan saw him close his eyes for a moment, as if giving thanks. "They have heard me. They are coming."

* * *

The Forerunners slowed, skimmed the grass, lightly came to earth.

"Greetings, Allun, son of Forley of the Travellers," said Zeel. "Greetings, Rowan of the Bukshah." She walked forward, folding her kite behind her with one hand. The two boys stayed where they had landed. Watching.

"Greetings," said Allun, after a moment. "We thank you for hearing our call."

"Where is Sara? Why have you summoned us?" Zeel asked.

"Sara is ill. I must speak with Ogden," Allun replied.

The Forerunner shook her head. "Ogden is with the tribe," she said coldly. "He cannot come."

Allun stepped forward. "I must speak with him, Zeel," he insisted. "I claim my right to a hearing. By my Traveller blood. By my father's name. And by ancient treaty." He bent and snatched up a slip-daisy leaf, holding it out to her.

Zeel regarded him suspiciously. Then she took the small, three-lobed leaf from his hand, raised her pipe to her lips, and blew. She waited. A moment later she frowned, and shook back her tangled curls. She had sent a message, and received one, Rowan thought in wonder. And he had heard nothing. Nothing at all.

"Ogden will grant a meeting," the girl said unwillingly. "But he cannot come to you. Will you journey to him?"

"How long will it take?" Rowan burst out.

"Not long," Zeel said. Her eyes were pale and cold. "You will fly, with the Forerunners. The Travellers will call the wind." She turned and walked back to where her friends were waiting, already spreading out their kites.

Rowan and Allun stared after her. She looked back. "Come!" she ordered. "Already the wind is changing. It is time to go. Ogden waits for you."

She paused, and over her smooth, suntanned face crept a shadow. A shadow of dread. "He waits," she said, "by the Pit of Unrin."

14 – Shocks

The wind flowed past Rowan's ears, and tugged at his hair. The strong leather belt that bound him to Zeel and her kite cut into his ribs. Below him the ground slipped away. Fast. So fast. In moments they were far away from the hillside where they had met the Forerunners. In minutes the grey-brown distance was rushing to meet them.

So this was what it was to fly, to soar, like a bird on the wind. Rowan could not take it in. He was dizzy with a hundred different thoughts. His mother. Annad. Sheba. The Zebak. The Travellers. Ogden. Secrets. The Valley of Gold. The Pit of Unrin …

Round and round his mind raced, while the kite sped on. The Pit of Unrin was not a legend. Not just a tale. It was a real place. And Ogden had taken the Travellers there. Why? Except that Timon's idea was right. The Zebak had promised the Travellers safe passage through the evil place, and entry to the Valley of Gold.

Were the Zebak even now camped with their new friends? Were their savage faces, that Rowan had seen so often in books, showing false smiles as they whispered lies in Ogden's ear?

Were he and Allun flying with the wind into terrible danger? So they would die, and the last hope of help for Rin would disappear?

The Pit of Unrin. A legend of darkness, to balance the legend of light that was the Valley of Gold. Or so Rowan had always thought.

He had heard of it, often, in Ogden's tales. He could hear Ogden's low voice in his mind even now, whispering while the fire crackled and the children listened. "… And guarding the Valley of Gold, the hideous Pit of Unrin. It is a place of evil and darkness, a place of death. It is a place to fear. A place to dread. Hope, children, that you never, never see it."

The first time Rowan had heard of the Pit of Unrin, he had woken in the night, screaming with nightmares. That was when he was little, and his father was alive. His father had come into the room, bringing with him the smell of soap, and clean towels, and the warm fire. He had gathered Rowan up in a hug, listened to his frightened babblings, smoothed his pillow, and laid him down again.

"Do not fear, small Rowan," he had said gently. "There is no such thing as the Pit of Unrin. It is only a story."

"But what if it is true?" Rowan remembered crying. "What if it is? And what if one day I have to go there?"

His father had smiled. "You will never have to go there, Rowan," he had said. "I promise."

He had thought he was speaking the truth. How was he to know otherwise? For the hardworking people of Rin never wasted time journeying to the barren lands beyond the Mountain. When they travelled, they travelled east, to the coast, to trade. The west was a mystery to them. A mystery they rarely wondered about, and never tried to solve.

You could not know I would come here at last, Father, Rowan thought now, peering fearfully down as the kite began to glide lower and lower. No one could know. For even without the terrifying vision of the Pit of Unrin, why would anyone journey to this barren place?

The hard earth, softened only by a few scrubby bushes, a sprinkling of slip-daisies and tufts of spiky grass, rose up to meet his dangling feet.

He saw the tents of the Travellers pitched ahead, in the shadow of the Mountain, and the people themselves gathered together, watching silently. He saw the figure of Ogden standing alone near a steep hillock of cruel-looking rocks.

Were the Zebak there also? Rowan searched the ground desperately, looking for a sign. No. There were no helmeted figures, no weapons, no great machines of war. Were the Zebak hiding somewhere near? Or were they even now marching into Rin, while the Travellers waited here to collect their reward for treachery?

There was no room in his mind for fear as his feet touched ground with a dragging thud that jarred his teeth and sent pains shooting up his legs. Suddenly, he felt numb.

What was awaiting him in this terrible place?

He stood still as Zeel unbuckled the strap that had held him to the kite. He became aware that he was shuddering all over. He felt Allun's hand on his shoulder, and his knees nearly gave way.

"Allun—" he choked.

"Wait," said Allun, his face pale.

Zeel left them and went forward to Ogden. She handed him something. It was the slip-daisy leaf that Allun had given her.

Ogden took the leaf, and raised his head to look at Allun. Then, slowly, he walked towards them.

"Greetings, Allun, son of Forley of the Travellers," he said. "What do you want of me?"

"I will not waste words, Ogden," replied Allun. "Time may be very short."

Ogden raised his slanted eyebrows. His dark eyes were unreadable. "Explain," he commanded.

Allun stared pointedly at the three-lobed leaf in Ogden's hand.

"Our peoples have been allies for three hundred years," he said. "For three hundred years our fortunes have been linked, so that we have been separate, but one."

Ogden said nothing. He rolled the stalk of the slip-daisy leaf around and around in his thin brown fingers.

Allun took a deep breath. "In the name of that old friendship, Ogden of the Travellers, I ask you to release the people of Rin from the curse you have placed on them," he said. "If we have been at fault, then we beg your forgiveness. We will do what we can to—"

"Wait!" Ogden ordered loudly, holding up his hand. His eyes flashed. Zeel and the other Forerunners ran to his side.

Allun had drawn back, and was standing rigidly silent. Rowan moved closer to him and held on to his arm. His heart was thudding. Never had he seen Ogden, the mysterious, smiling storyteller, look like this. Frowning, fierce, and very angry.

"What do you mean by talking of curses to me?" Ogden demanded. "What lies are you trying to tell? What plans are you hatching? And by whose orders?"

Allun gaped at him in shock. He tried to speak, but no words came.

The same mistakes, the same old pride,
The precious armour cast aside ...

"We aren't telling lies!" Rowan burst out. He knew it was not his place to speak. But he could not bear to stand helplessly by while fear and anger got in the way of help for his home.

Ogden's black eyes turned on him. Rowan forced himself to speak on.

"Everyone in Rin is—is ill, because of what you did," he stammered. "Allun and I got away—to find you. To ask you to stop it." The hot tears stung in his eyes. He struggled to hold them back, but they spilled over and started rolling down his cheeks.

"The bukshah knew there was danger," he sobbed. "They heard your pipes—they must have understood what you were planning. Star tried to tell me, but I wouldn't listen. She took the herd away, away from the village and out along the stream. She kept them safe, all but a few little calves. But the people—my mother, my sister ... They're lying helpless. And when the Zebak come—"

His throat closed up. He could hardly breathe. "Oh, please, please help them," he begged. "Don't make the rhyme come true. Don't!"

Ogden's face had changed. Now, mixed with the fierceness, there was bewilderment. He glanced at the three Forerunners by his side.

The two boys looked uncertain. But Zeel frowned and shook her head.

"It is a trick," she said. "Do not listen to the boy. They are using him because they know you liked him, when you met last night. As they are using the other because he has the reed pipe and is half-Traveller."

Her voice rose. "Why should these two be the only ones to escape this so-called illness? Why, except that there *is* no illness, and they have been chosen to track us down?"

"That is not true!" breathed Rowan, looking wildly at Allun and back to Ogden. What was happening here? The Travellers seemed to think that the people of Rin were the betrayers.

Ogden said nothing.

"It was a grave mistake to answer the call," Zeel cried passionately. "The enemy doubtless tracked our kites. And you are letting these spies delay our escape. As they hoped. We are wasting precious minutes. Let us go! Into the Pit of Unrin and on to the Valley of Gold, as we planned. It is our only chance!"

Rowan's stomach turned over. He looked closely at Zeel, the adopted daughter of Ogden the Traveller. He looked at her strong, straight black brows and her pale eyes. He looked at her height, and her broad shoulders. Now that she was angry it was as though a mask had dropped from her face.

Take away the feathers, the flowers, the long hair, the bare brown feet, the loose, bright silk. Put on close-fitting clothes of steel grey, hard boots, a black streak from hair to nose, and Zeel would be a picture from the house of books. A picture of a Zebak.

He pointed at her. "It is you!" he gasped. "*You* are the enemy! *You* are the spy! You have whispered poison to the Travellers, and betrayed us all. You have done this to us! You!"

15 – Darkness and Light

He leapt at Zeel, catching a glimpse of her startled face as he sprang forward. He beat at her with his fists. She stood unresisting, making no move to defend herself.

It was Ogden's hands that caught at him and pulled him back. Ogden's voice that commanded him to be still.

He struggled against the grip that held him, panting and choking still with the anger that had swept over him. His ears roared, and at first he could hardly hear what Ogden was saying to him.

"You are wrong, Rowan," Ogden was shouting. "Listen to me! Listen!"

Rowan finally quietened. Gradually his rage died in him. He stopped struggling, and stood shuddering under Ogden's hands.

"That is better," said Ogden. He glanced at Allun, and for the first time, his face was open.

"This child of Rin is far more fierce than he looks," he said, smiling faintly. "I see now why he conquered the Mountain."

"He is right to be fierce," Allun murmured, without returning the smile. "I have been blind. The Forerunner Zeel is a Zebak. And you must know it."

"There is nothing about my tribe I do not know," Ogden said quietly. "Zeel was a foundling, washed up by the sea, on the coast. We took her with us. She was born a Zebak, that is true. We knew it from her earliest days, though we did not speak of it to others. We feared they would react in the same way as our young friend Rowan has just done."

He squeezed Rowan's shoulders. His voice was sad.

Rowan looked at Zeel. She returned his look proudly, yet he could see the hurt in her eyes. He struggled to stay suspicious and angry. But he could not.

"Zeel was born a Zebak, but she has been raised a Traveller, from babyhood," Ogden went on. "She is one of us. She would die for us. If we have an enemy, it is not Zeel. Be assured of this. Zeel has said nothing to me that she did not truly believe. And she has said nothing that I did not fear myself."

He pressed his lips together. "Be assured of this also, people of Rin. The Travellers have done nothing to harm your friends."

"Why then did you come to us unexpectedly, and then leave so quickly, without warning?" asked Allun.

"We came because we felt a wrongness in the land," said Ogden simply. "We felt a danger. We came to you, as friends, to see if the trouble lay with you. And when we had come we felt hardness. We felt secrets, and anger, under the smiling faces. We were forbidden the village, and ordered to keep to the hills."

"But that was just because of the Mountain berries!" Rowan exclaimed.

Ogden paused. "The new *fruit*?" he said. "But why should that cause your people to close their hearts to us?" He frowned. "Rowan of the Bukshah, I fear you are mistaken. There must be something you do not know. Something far more—"

Allun was shaking his head. "No, Ogden," he sighed. "There is nothing else. The people of Rin—it is hard to understand, I know— but they wanted to keep the fruit a secret. So as to breed a great crop that would be theirs alone, to sell on the coast next year."

Ogden stared in amazement. "But there was no secret, Allun," he said. "We knew about the new crop when we were still a day's journey away from Rin. We smelt its scent. We saw the stains of its fruit upon the birds. And why would anyone want to keep a source of food secret, just for gain? Are you *sure* ...?"

"Quite sure," said Allun firmly. "If you sensed secrets and suspicion in the people of Rin, that was the cause, Ogden. There is no other."

Ogden glanced at the three Forerunners, who were looking even more surprised and disbelieving than he was.

"It is incredible," he muttered. "I will never understand your mother's people, Allun. Never as long as I live."

He spread out his hands. "We thought you must have made an

alliance with the Zebak against us. We decided to move on, to escape their coming. And it came to me that we should journey here. The place called me. And when the land calls, I listen."

He looked around him at the dry, rocky land. "I did not know the reason. But the Valley of Gold has been much in my thoughts of late. Visions of it keep rising in my mind unbidden. I thought perhaps I was drawn here because it was time at last for the Travellers to find again their ancient friends. They, then, could join us to fight the enemy, since you had deserted us."

"You think to find the people of the Valley of Gold?" whispered Rowan. "But is the Valley of Gold really true? I thought—"

Ogden smiled. "You thought it was but a legend? You of all people, Rowan of the Bukshah! Surely you know by now that all legends are silken threads woven around a gem of truth. And the Pit of Unrin is real enough." His face darkened, and he glanced behind him.

Rowan looked, but could see nothing but the jagged pile of rocks he had noticed before, and, far beyond, a golden cliff-face rising steeply towards the sky.

"The Pit of Unrin lies there, behind the stony hill," Ogden said. "And our tales tell us that it guards the Valley of Gold. This we believe. This we have always believed. Forerunners have flown across the Pit, many times. But nothing can be seen from the air. Therefore, we must enter the place of evil, to discover the secret way to our goal."

"But the Pit of Unrin is forbidden," Allun burst out. "Travellers cannot go there. It is their law."

Ogden nodded, his face grim. "Travellers born cannot. But—" He glanced at Zeel. "Zebak may do as they please. It has come to me that perhaps this is why Zeel was given to us. Perhaps it was always intended that she—and we—should finally come to this moment."

Zeel lifted her chin proudly.

Rowan struggled to put his thoughts into words. "But does all this mean that you—that the Travellers—did *not* enchant the village?"

"Of course we did not!" snapped Zeel, looking like a true Zebak again in her irritation. "Ogden has told you!"

Rowan felt himself blushing, but made himself go on.

"Then how has it happened?" he pleaded. "And why?"

Ogden rubbed his thin hand over his mouth. "I do not understand," he said. Then his eyes narrowed. "You spoke of a rhyme," he went on. "What rhyme is this?"

"Our Wise Woman, Sheba, told it to Rowan, the day you came to Rin," Allun explained. "It was one of the reasons I—we—thought that you had betrayed us to the Zebak. It—fitted."

Ogden scowled. "Did it indeed? Well, perhaps you had better let me hear it, since it has done us such harm."

Rowan felt his face growing hot again. But he did as he was told, and spoke the words that he had grown to dread:

"Beneath soft looks the evil burns,
And slowly round the old wheel turns.
The same mistakes, the same old pride,
The priceless armour cast aside.
The secret enemy is here.
It hides in darkness, fools beware!
For day by day its power grows,
And when at last its face it shows,
Then past and present tales will meet—
The evil circle is complete ..."

Rowan's voice died away. Ogden was silent for a moment. Then he turned to Allun.

"I see why you were deceived," he said. He paused. "It is a puzzle," he went on. "And from it I draw one thing only. The answer to this trouble lies somewhere in the past."

"That is what my mother thought," Rowan broke in. "And Lann said the rhyme spoke of our enslavement to the Zebak, and warned that it was going to happen again, if we forgot old lessons."

Ogden nodded. "It could have been that," he said, "but I think that it is not. Both our peoples fear the Zebak. But perhaps there is another enemy for us both to fear."

"But how can that be?" cried Rowan. "We have known no other enemy, since we came to Rin."

Ogden regarded him thoughtfully. "Ah yes," he said. "But what of secret enemies, here before you came and after, but never revealed to you, or even to us, till now? Ancient enemies of the land and its people. Enemies who can wait a thousand years, two thousand, ten thousand, for the chance to strike again. What of those?"

He bent his head and closed his eyes. They waited. Rowan held his breath. Zeel's face was so still that it looked as though it was a moulded mask.

Finally Ogden looked up. "I have thought," he said. "I followed my heart in coming here to this place, where it is said the Giants of Inspray fought and a wondrous valley was lost. I was called here, and the feeling is still strong in me. I cannot deny it. I know that here lies the answer that we seek."

He turned to Zeel. "Make ready, Forerunner," he said gravely. "You are, after all, to have your wish. You will go to seek the Valley of Gold. Are you still willing?"

She nodded, her face paling.

"The Pit of Unrin guards it," Ogden went on. "And the Pit of Unrin is a place of evil. Are you still willing?"

"Yes," she said in a low voice.

Ogden stared at the slip-daisy leaf, twirling it in his hand.

"You are Zebak born, and brave to your bones, my adopted daughter Zeel," he said. "You are a Travellers' Forerunner, bred to face the unknown to protect and lead the tribe. But—" He glanced up at the two boy Forerunners, standing motionless beside him. "But on this journey Tor and Mithren, your usual companions, cannot go with you."

"I understand," said Zeel.

"Yet I am unwilling for you to face this evil alone. So I choose another to go with you. One whose help will prove that the old friendship between our two peoples is indeed unshaken. One who also follows his heart, and who has proved that he can face fear and danger in the quest."

He turned, and handed the leaf to Rowan.

16 – The Nightmare

They climbed the hill of rocks without speaking. When they reached the top, Zeel embraced Tor, Mithren and Ogden.

"I will see you again," she said to each of them in turn. And they repeated the words, looking into her eyes.

Allun gripped Rowan's hands. "Take care," he said. Then he caught Rowan in his arms and hugged him. "Take care," he repeated.

"Go now," said Ogden softly. "Listen to your hearts. They will guide you. We will await your call that all is well."

Rowan and Zeel turned, and began to pick their way downwards to the valley floor.

Rowan looked down, and his head began to swim. Not because the drop was very steep, or the way too hard. Behind the hill of rocks the land sloped away quite gently, and tufts of grass and slip-daisies softened the ground underfoot.

His dizziness was caused by fear. Terrible fear. Because at the foot of the slope crouched a place that he would have known was evil even if he had never heard its name spoken. The very sight of it chilled him to the heart.

He could see only a mass of short, stubby trees. But they were hideous, not beautiful. Thick black trunks writhed up from the grey, dead-looking ground in a twisted mass. Dull purple-coloured leaves clumped at the tips of the branches.

Here and there puddles of yellow fog crawled and clung around their roots. And there was a vile smell, like nothing he had ever smelt in his life. It filled his nose and clung to his clothes, making him sick with disgust and terror.

He looked across at Zeel, determinedly scrambling down the slope beside him. Her feet, covered now with soft shoes, did not skid on the loose, pebbly ground the way his did. The grass and daisies seemed to welcome her tread, and cushion her every step.

She did not speak to him. She did not smile. She had not wanted his company. She had wanted to go on this great adventure alone.

And Allun had not wanted Rowan to go either. "Rowan is just a boy, Ogden," he had objected. "Surely I would do as well. I too am a citizen of Rin. If I accompany Zeel in Rowan's place, that will surely prove to you that the friendship between our peoples is as strong as ever."

But Ogden had shaken his head.

"Rowan of the Bukshah is almost the same age as Zeel, Allun," he said. "And Rowan was the only one of you to conquer the Mountain. I have great trust in him, and his feeling for the land. And I feel a rightness in my choice. It is he I want to accompany Zeel."

Rowan slithered on the loose ground, trying to stay on his feet, knowing that Ogden and Allun, and the two other Forerunners, Tor and Mithren, were watching him.

He felt his breath coming faster as the twisted trees of Unrin loomed larger and larger, and the foul smell of the place rose up to meet him. He skidded the last few metres to the bottom of the slope, and wished with all his heart that Zeel would talk to him. Say *something*. Just to keep his mind from his fear.

As if she had heard his thoughts, she turned to him. "Are you afraid?" she asked coldly.

He thought of lying, but dismissed the idea. She could obviously see how terrified he was.

"Yes," he answered. And asked, just for the sake of it: "Are you?"

She looked at him proudly. "Remember, I am a Zebak," she said. "Zebak never admit to fear." Then suddenly she smiled, and for a moment she reminded him of Allun. "But I am a Traveller, too," she laughed. "And as a Traveller, I say, yes, yes, yes! I am scared to death." She paused. "Travellers do not believe in lying, when there is no point," she added.

Rowan felt a wave of thankfulness wash over him. At least he was not alone. He grinned back at Zeel, ignoring the pounding of his heart.

They began to walk across the small strip of flat land that separated the rocky slope from the trees. The cheerful yellow daisies in their path seemed to mock them. Trodden underfoot, they sprang back to face the sun as soon as Rowan and Zeel had passed. They were not made sad and fearful by the Pit of Unrin. They grew just as carelessly as ever up to the very rim of the trees.

But, as Rowan saw, they grew no further. Once the trees began, there were no more clumps of grass, no more daisies. It was as though every scrap of normal life ended where Unrin began.

It was all ugliness, and silence. Absolute silence. No butterflies flitted among those squat, twisted trees. No birds rustled in their branches, looking for seeds and tiny caterpillars. No lizards skittered around their roots, hunting insects. No frogs croaked amid that poisonous yellow fog.

"It is all—dead," whispered Zeel, pointing to the grey earth. "Not the trees, but everything else. And the smell!" She wrinkled her nose.

"Zeel—" Rowan hesitated. "Zeel, do we know what dangers we might face here?"

She shook her head. "Our stories do not tell us that." She bit her lip. "All they tell us is that it is a place of monsters. No living thing has ever entered Unrin, and returned. It is forbidden."

It is forbidden.

"That's what they said about the Mountain," Rowan said. "And yet seven of us climbed it, and seven of us returned."

Zeel straightened her shoulders. "Then maybe it will be the same with Unrin," she said, forcing a smile. "And why not? Who knows, in these tales, what is truth and what is just imagination? And it may have suited the people of the Valley of Gold to let outsiders think Unrin is deadly."

She nodded briskly, as if to assure herself that what she had said was true. "Come on!" she said. "We have wasted too much time already."

They turned and waved to the watching figures above them. And then they bent and moved forward, Zeel first, Rowan second, into the twisting maze that was Unrin.

Shuffling slowly along, his eyes darting everywhere, the hair prickling on the back of his neck, Rowan held his hand over his nose to try to keep back the odious smell. Fine grey dust puffed out under his feet. But underneath the dust the ground felt as hard as stone.

Within seconds they could no longer see the slope down which they had scrambled. They could no longer see the sky. The twisting trunks and branches closed in behind and above them, locking them into a dim, evil-smelling world of grey-black silence.

"Should we mark the trees?" Rowan whispered nervously. "So we know the way back?"

"We will be able to follow our footprints in the dust," murmured Zeel. "Be still. Listen to your heart. Trust it." Her voice was tight with tension.

They walked on. For five minutes. Ten. Nothing happened. But Rowan did not relax. He kept finding that he was holding his breath. And in his mind there were pictures. Growing brighter. Growing stronger.

"It is near." Zeel's pale eyes were glowing. Her steps quickened. "The Valley of Gold. I feel it."

"I, too," said Rowan.

The silver spring, bubbling cool and fresh from beneath the earth … Beautiful people, tall and strong, wise and good … Flowers and fruits of every kind, spilling across the paths of gleaming gems that wound between the gardens … Small white horses, saddled with silk … Houses painted with beautiful patterns, each one different … Before each house, a golden bird— an owl with emerald eyes …

A fabled place of good. Guarded by a place of evil.

Voices whispered to him from the past, clouding the bright pictures, piercing him with dread.

… a place of evil and darkness … a place of death … a place to fear. A place to dread …

"Do not fear, small Rowan …"

"But what if it is true? What if it is? And what if one day I have to go there?"

"You will never have to go there, Rowan. I promise."

Something was watching them. Rowan could feel it. Something knew they were here. Something was waiting. Waiting …

His whole body shuddered with the knowledge, as his eyes desperately searched the dark shadows between the trees, the twisted branches over his head, the crawling yellow fog on the ground. But there was nothing. Nothing.

Yet he knew. "Zeel!" he hissed to the hurrying figure in front of him. "Zeel—"

And then the ground shifted under his feet. The dust flew high. And he shrieked as something grabbed at his ankles, wrapping around them, pulling his feet out from under him.

He fell heavily, screaming, hearing Zeel's screams. He stared with unbelieving horror at the thrashing grey-white thing that had risen up like a great blind worm from the earth and was binding him with terrible strength in loop after loop of its whipping tail.

"Snake!" shouted Zeel, throwing herself on the creature, stabbing at it with her knife, tearing at it with her fingers.

Bands like iron tightened on Rowan's legs, his stomach, his chest. He could feel his strength leaving him as the breath was squeezed from his lungs. He was being crushed. He was being dragged towards the swollen, twisted base of a tree, where more of the great grey-white worms were rising from the dry earth, reaching for him like the tentacles of some sea-monster in Ogden's tales.

A red mist of horror swept across his eyes as he realised the truth. The monsters of Unrin were not hiding in the trees. The monsters were the trees themselves. Trees that fed on living creatures. It was the roots of a tree that were dragging him in. And the tree itself seemed to be quivering, bending towards him. Wanting. Hungry.

He tried to scream in terror, but no voice came from his mouth. He felt Zeel pulling at him, trying to tear him free. And then he thought he could hear a sound. A creaking, groaning sound. The sound of something that had waited long, and was going to feed at last.

His head was pressed against the base of the tree now, crushed into the dusty mass of tiny bones and the dried, shrunken bodies of birds, lizards and other creatures that the tree had fed on while it waited for bigger game. He saw a grey-white tentacle rise up beside him, and felt a hideous, evil-smelling smoothness slither over his face and mouth.

Filled with horror, hardly knowing what he was doing, he bit at the root with all his strength. It quivered, and he bit harder.

The root thrashed and struggled, pulling roughly away from him. There was a deep, growling noise from deep within the tree. Was it pain? How could it be, when Zeel's sharp knife had torn at his attacker in vain?

But the tentacle was whipping back, away from him. And with disbelief he felt and saw the others pulling away also, freeing his hands, his chest, his legs, and being sucked back into the earth. And then Zeel was hauling him to his feet, screaming at him.

"Run!" she was shrieking. "They are all around us. Run, run run!"

17 – Escape

They ran, leaping and stumbling through the dust. Roots broke through the earth ahead of them, beside them, twisting and reaching for them, till the ground seemed to writhe with grey-white snakes.

Rowan ran blindly, every breath sending shooting pains through his bruised chest. "Come *on*!" begged Zeel. "Rowan, do not give up!"

She caught at his hand, grasping it tightly. She dragged him on with her. The air was filled with dust and the slithering, thrashing sounds of the seeking trees. Roots coiled in a mass under their feet, whipping upwards, snatching at their ankles, but never quite taking hold.

Rowan knew he could not go on like this much longer. Soon he would stumble and fall. And then ...

"Look ahead!" cried Zeel. "There is an opening here. This may be it—the way. Oh hurry!"

They burst through the trees into a small clearing—a patch of wet, marshy ground quite different from the rest. The trees grew closely around the edges of the marsh, bending forward, locking their branches overhead.

Rowan and Zeel waded into the sticky grey mud. Pebbles and larger stones held in the ooze bruised their feet and knocked against their bodies as they struggled to the centre.

They stood there together, panting and clinging to each other.

"We cannot stay here," gasped Rowan. "They know where we are. They are coming for us." He shivered all over. The mud was heaving and alive. The tree roots were slithering through it like white eels, searching for them.

"Rowan, I can see light!" Zeel screamed suddenly, and pointed.

Rowan looked up, but could see nothing. Nothing but mud, and trees, and wriggling, seeking tentacles nosing towards them.

Zeel began struggling forward. "Rowan, look ahead! Can't you see? We are nearly there! We are nearly at the end of the trees! We are nearly—" Her words were cut off by a choking scream as she was pulled down.

Rowan lunged for her. He pulled her head and shoulders out of the suffocating mud. He struggled desperately to free her from the strangling tentacle that bound her around the chest. He felt a big stone against his leg. He pulled it, dripping, out of the marsh and beat at the tentacle with it, battering it, clawing and biting it at the same time, refusing to give in.

It jerked, and let go. Sobbing and choking, Zeel and Rowan flung themselves forward. Rowan looked up again. Now he too could see what the Forerunner's sharp eyes had seen before him. Light, glimmering faintly, ahead.

He felt the ground begin to harden under his feet. The marsh was ending. And the trees were ending too. He could see the towering cliff-face. It was shining golden in the sunlight.

"Zeel! A few more steps!" he shrieked. "Zeel, come on!"

They ran forward, leaping clear of the last of the grasping tree roots, clambering up the jagged golden rocks while the roots writhed up after them, lashing and twisting. Rowan turned and beat uselessly at them with the stone he still held in his hand.

"Don't try!" gasped Zeel. "Climb! There is a ledge higher up. We should be safe there. Don't look down. Don't look down!"

Rowan pushed his aching body on, every moment expecting to feel a lashing tug on his ankle that would send him crashing to the ground below. He saw Zeel reach the ledge and turn to him, stretching out her arm.

With the last of his strength he held up his hand, and felt her pull him to safety. Then he fell back on the hard rock, and blackness closed over him.

* * *

Rowan opened his eyes and saw blue sky. He heard the sound of birds. He took a deep breath of sweet air, and winced with pain. Every bone and muscle in his body seemed bruised.

"Are you all right?" Zeel's voice was as brisk as ever, but when he looked at her, he could see that her eyes were warm.

He nodded, then shook his head. "I don't know," he said finally. He sat up, groaning, brushing pebbles and wet filth from his arms. The big muddy stone that had been his weapon against the trees lay beside him. He picked it up and put it on his lap, patting it thankfully.

The girl watched him, her face serious. "You saved my life," she said. "My people owe you a debt."

"No they don't," said Rowan. "You saved my life too. We are even."

She peered over the ledge to the trees of Unrin crouched below them. "No," she answered. "You saved yourself. Nothing I did helped. It was when you bit at the tree root that it let you go."

Her pale eyes turned to him. "You are stronger than you look," she said thoughtfully. "Ogden was right to send you with me." Frowning, she began scraping pebbles from her soft shoes, black and soaked from the marsh.

Rowan rubbed the stone. It felt cool, smooth and comforting under his fingers. He blinked at a small blue bird fluttering behind Zeel's head, picking at some berries on a bush growing from a crack in the cliff-face. The bird was strange to him.

He leaned over a little to see it more clearly. And then he saw what it was feasting on. A Mountain berry bush. Now he realised what the sweet smell was.

Rin! An agonising jab of fear ran through his whole body. The danger he had just faced had driven everything else from his mind, but suddenly he remembered why they were here. Why they had faced the terrors of Unrin in the first place.

"Zeel," he exclaimed, trying to get up, and falling back. "Zeel, how long have we been here? We have to move on. We have to find the Valley of Gold. We have to—"

Zeel shook her head. Her mud-streaked face was grim. "I am sorry, Rowan," she said gently.

"What do you mean?"

"I have called the others to come for us. I have told them we have failed."

"No!" Rowan looked around him wildly. "No! Listen! Ogden

said it was here. Beyond Unrin. And a Mountain berry bush grows there, behind you. How could it have come here unless the people of the Valley of Gold brought fruit down from the Mountain long ago? Ogden said they climbed it."

"Ogden does not know everything, it seems," said Zeel.

Rowan would not give in so easily. "But we felt it was near, Zeel. You felt it, and so did I. The entrance to the Valley could be down there, anywhere along the base of this cliff! It could be—"

Zeel shook her head again. "Our visions were but dreams made by hope and fear. The Valley of Gold is not here."

There was terrible sorrow in her face now.

"How often we have looked down from the cliff-top, believing. But we were foolish to believe. From this ledge you can see the whole of the cliff-face, as you cannot see it from the top. Look and see for yourself. There are no caves, no tunnels in the rock. Nothing."

Rowan hung his head so she would not see the desperation on his face. He could not believe this was happening.

Zeel's voice went on. "So the Valley of Gold was a legend all along," she said bitterly. "It never did exist. It was never going to help us. It was all a lie—a tale to amuse children around the fire."

Rowan gripped the stone, rubbing it, looking for an answer.

"Maybe it is somewhere else," he muttered. "Maybe, if we try—" He broke off, staring at the stone beneath his muddy fingers. His heart pounded, and he gave a strangled cry.

"What is wrong?" barked Zeel, dropping her shoes and starting to her feet.

Rowan looked at the cliff-face, glimmering gold. He looked down at the evil trees of Unrin, and the stone in his lap. He reached out with trembling fingers and took a handful of muddy pebbles from the ledge, picked others from his own clothes, rubbed them between his hands. And as he saw bright, flashing colour shine through the black coating, a wave of pain washed over him, and he bent double, hunching over on the ground.

"Rowan, what *is* it?" the girl shrieked. "Have you gone mad? All right, so we have not found the Valley of Gold. So Ogden was wrong about everything. So it was a legend after all. And this is sad for all of us." Her voice began to tremble. "But we must face it, as the others must. And we can still try to help your people—"

"Ogden was not wrong about everything," Rowan breathed. "*You* are wrong, Zeel. The Valley of Gold is not a legend. We have found it."

Zeel stared at him, shaking her head in disbelief and fear.

"We have found it," Rowan repeated, staring down at the twisted mass of black trees below. "We have seen its golden wall. We huddle on it now. We have walked its jewelled paths. Their gems are sticking to our shoes and clothes. We have crossed its silver spring. Its mud and ooze still cling to us."

He held up the big stone. Cleaned of the sticky mud, its shape was clear, and streaks of its true colour glinted in the sun. It was a golden owl with emerald eyes.

Rowan took a deep, shuddering breath. "The Pit of Unrin does not guard the Valley of Gold, Zeel," he said. "The two are one and the same."

18 – "And when at last its face it shows …"

I do not understand!" Zeel shook her head over and over again, looking at the gems slipping through her fingers, and then staring down at the dark mass of Unrin. "How could this have happened? Why did no one know of it?"

"It happened long ago," said Rowan, remembering the stories. "The Travellers were on the coast, fighting the Zebak. They returned after years away. The new place they called the Pit of Unrin was here. The Valley they knew had disappeared. And by chance rocks had fallen from the Mountain to make everything look different. Perhaps they made up the story of the Giants of Inspray to explain it. Who knows?"

"But the people of the Valley!" exclaimed Zeel. "They were supposed to be so clever, and so wise. How could they let their home be overtaken by such an enemy? How could they? How did the trees come here and take hold in so short a time?"

She paced along the ledge, putting up her hand to feel the wind. "It is changing," she said abruptly, stuffing the shining gems into her pockets. "Come. We must climb to the top of the cliff to await the Forerunners."

Rowan picked up the golden owl and tucked it into his shirt. As he clambered to his feet he caught sight of a patch of blue beneath the Mountain berry bush. He moved closer to investigate.

It was the bird. It was lying very still, its eyes closed, its tiny beak open. The feathers on its chest fluffed softly as it breathed. It was fast asleep.

The rich perfume of the Mountain berry flowers drifted sweetly on the air. The luscious red berries winked temptingly.

"The Mountain berries," whispered Rowan. In his mind he saw

the birds of Rin, lying still, like this, on the grass. He saw the people huddled on streets and in gardens. The people who had breathed in the scent of those sweet red flowers as they bloomed everywhere in Rin, more every day. More and more ...

"Zeel!" he gasped, spinning round to face her. "My people—it is the Mountain berry flowers that are putting them to sleep. The scent of the flowers! Look at that bird."

She looked curiously at the sleeping bird, then moved closer, touching it with a gentle finger.

"Who would have thought it?" she murmured, shaking her head. She glanced up at Rowan's anxious face, and grinned.

"Rowan, don't look so worried," she said. "Do you not realise what this means? It means that our journey through Unrin was not wasted. It means that the answer *did* lie here, after all!"

She jumped up, and clasped his hand. "Do not fear!" she cried. "The bird is sleeping, not dead. And your people are sleeping too. All we have to do is go back to Rin and pull out the Mountain berry bushes, or at least, most of them. And then the sleeping sickness will be gone."

Rowan frowned doubtfully.

Zeel put her hands on her hips and stared at him in irritation. "I do not understand you!" she shouted. "You should be rejoicing! Your problem is solved! And no wonder the Mountain berries were the cause of your trouble. The Mountain is forbidden. It is full of strange, monstrous things we cannot even imagine."

"I am just not sure, Zeel," mumbled Rowan, watching the sleeping bird. "I am not sure we have the whole answer. It is the rhyme. Sheba's rhyme. It doesn't fit. She spoke of a great evil, a secret enemy, whose power grows in darkness. It cannot be these little bushes. Or a sleeping sickness so easily cured. There must be something else."

He repeated the chant under his breath.

"The secret enemy is here.
It hides in darkness, fools beware!
For day by day its power grows,

And when at last its face it shows,
Then past and present tales will meet—
The evil circle is complete ..."

Beneath soft looks the evil burns ... It hides in darkness ... Day by day its power grows, And when at last its face it shows ...

Something stirred in Rowan's mind. An idea, fluttering just where he could not see it clearly. He blinked, trying to catch at it. And then he saw himself, standing in the bukshah fields with Star, thinking about the Travellers and the changes of spring, watching the butterfly crawl from its cocoon.

He heard Annad's voice. "Why? Why do tadpoles eat weed, but frogs eat insects? Why ...?"

Tired of waiting, Zeel sighed with impatience. Then she pointed at the sky. Two kites, one white, one red, were wheeling against the blue.

"Tor and Mithren are coming," she cried. "We must go. Wait— I will get the bird. It will starve if we leave it sleeping here."

Things change, Annad, thought Rowan. Nature is strange and wonderful. One sort of creature can become another, in a season. Adult creatures can be quite different from their children—with different looks, different appetites, different ...

His eyes widened. Tadpoles and frogs. Caterpillars and butterflies.

Zeel bent to pick up the small bundle of feathers beneath the Mountain berry bush.

"Zeel!" shouted Rowan. "Come away!"

And at that moment the ground beneath their feet began to rumble and shudder. Zeel cried out in shock, falling back with the bird in her hand and nearly knocking Rowan off the ledge.

"What is happening?" she screamed, clutching Rowan in terror.

Pieces of golden rock began to crack from the cliff-face below the Mountain berry bush, falling and smashing to the ground far below. The cliff was cracking open. The Mountain berry bush was thrashing wildly, its berries and flowers tumbling from its branches as it was pushed up and up out of the rock by something huge and powerful beneath.

"Climb!" shouted Rowan. "Climb!"

And when at last its face it shows ...

Zeel thrust the bird inside her jacket and they began to scramble upwards, their fingers straining, their feet scrabbling on the rock.

"What *is* it?" panted Zeel, looking backwards.

"It is the enemy," gasped Rowan. "The enemy! Showing its face. Zeel—it is one of them. One of the Unrin trees. The Mountain berry bushes—they are just the young form of those trees down there. The adults grow underneath them. The bushes collect the trees' first food, with their scent. They—"

With a hideous sound of splitting rock, a squat black shape rose up beneath the tiny bush that crowned it. Its grey-white roots, like thick, twisting worms, slithered around the ground, looking for food—the food they expected to find.

Zeel clutched her jacket. "I have the bird," she hissed at the tree. "I have it! You will have to go hungry!"

The roots began to feel their way up the cliff-face. Reaching for them.

"Climb!" cried Rowan desperately.

They heaved their way up the cliff. Rowan looked up, trying to forget the tearing pains in his legs and chest, trying to forget the awful drop below. He saw Tor and Mithren looking down, helplessly holding out their arms. He could hear the roots of the Unrin tree slapping the rock behind him, and the grating sound of more stone splitting away as the adult tree reached up and out, released at last from the darkness of the earth.

Gasping and panting he climbed, and in his mind was only one horrible vision. The valley of Rin, changed utterly to a hideous maze of twisted trees and dried grey earth. Its houses and lanes crushed under reaching black branches and tentacle-like roots. Its sleeping people locked to the bases of the feeding trees, their lives slowly ebbing away.

Then past and present tales will meet—
The evil circle is complete ...

No! He would not let the circle be completed. He would not let Rin be destroyed as the Valley of Gold had been. He would not let its people, *his* people, disappear, as so long ago another race had vanished. This time it would be stopped. This time ...

Tor's hand grasped his wrist, and pulled him over the cliff edge. Rowan saw gentle hills and plains, with grass and slip-daisies stretching to the horizon. The golden owl fell from his shirt and tumbled onto the ground. He stood, swaying, watching Zeel crumpling beside him.

She lay still, panting and exhausted. Then she thrust her hand inside her jacket and brought out the bird. It had woken. It sat on her palm for a moment, and then, in a flash of blue, it was fluttering free.

"Good," Zeel groaned, with a spark of her old fierceness. "Fly away. And let the devil tree go hungry."

"Zeel, get up," Rowan urged her. "We must go! We must go to Rin!"

19 – Hurry!

They flew. Rowan with Zeel, Allun with Tor, and with Mithren—Ogden.

It had taken only moments to glide back to the waiting Travellers. Only moments to tell the tale. Only moments for Ogden to give his orders, and for the third kite to be made ready.

But every second was agony to Rowan. In his mind he saw his mother and Jonn lying helpless on the grass outside Bree and Hanna's house. He saw Annad asleep inside. And Lann. And, sprawled on lanes, in gardens, on their own doorsteps, the other people he had known all his life. While all the time the enemy grew in darkness, and the Mountain berries bloomed.

How long did it take for the adult tree to grow strong enough to emerge? With a shudder he remembered Bree's voice. "But the ground was hard—like iron, it seemed." Hard, so hard—not because of magic, as they had thought, but because the adult tree was growing there, secret and safe, making itself ready …

Faster, faster, he thought, willing the wind to speed the kite on. And yet, he realised, with a feeling of panic that trembled on the edge of despair, he did not know what he would find when he got to Rin.

"Nearly there," cried Zeel, her voice almost lost in the wind. "We will land on the hills, where it is clear."

Rowan looked down, and saw golden hills, and ahead, the valley. Gone was the brown-and-green patchwork. Now Rin was a carpet of red blossom.

The Mountain berries had spread—astonishingly fast. They were everywhere: in the gardens, the lanes, the fields, the orchard. The great stone mill stood alone in a sea of red, the bukshah pool was surrounded by a scarlet band that spread right to the orchard.

"Zeel, what will we do?" he shouted in despair.

Her fierce black-browed face turned to him, and in her pale eyes he saw the remorseless rage of a Zebak warrior. "Thank the stars that they have not yet spread out of the valley," she shouted. "Now it will be easy to do what we decided. We will burn them, Rowan. Burn them! Burn them!"

* * *

They ran down the hill together. Pollen from the slip-daisies blew into Rowan's face, and he sneezed, tears running down his cheeks. But never again would he curse the daisies, he promised himself. Sweet, happy, wild things, they had been weeded out in Rin, because they were useless. But the Mountain berries had been welcomed, because they were a source of pride and riches. The people of the Valley of Gold had probably felt the same way when they had brought their own handfuls of Mountain berries down from the Mountain in triumph.

The same mistakes, the same old pride.

The rhyme made sense now. All but one line. Rowan thought about that as they reached the grove of trees where he had met Sheba. The memory of her words rang in his ears. Still one mystery. Still—

"There!" shouted Zeel savagely, pointing at a froth of red shining under one of the trees. She picked up a stick covered in dead leaves and lit it.

"No, not here, not yet," cried Allun, racing past her. "The people. We have to get the people out first! My mother, Marlie, Jiller, Jonn … oh, so many. We must hurry! Hurry!"

"It will only take a moment," Zeel shouted after him, throwing the flaming leaves into the centre of the Mountain berry bushes. "A moment to get these devils and … Oh!"

Her scream stopped them in their tracks, made them turn, and look. They saw flames, leaping among the berry plants. Then they saw the flames hissing and dying. They saw the ground breaking and cracking, clods of earth and clumps of grass falling.

And they saw the trees rising—huge, swollen, black as night. Their roots, as thick as giant snakes, thrashed out, whipping through the air towards Zeel, towards them, towards any living creature they could snare and drag in.

"Run! Run!" Rowan heard his own voice screaming, as in horror he saw Zeel leaping for her life—away from the trees, away from the writhing tentacles that were hunting her.

She reached his side, her face white. "The fire," she gasped. "As soon as it hit the plants, the adults broke out. It must anger them. And they are huge, Rowan. So much bigger than the trees of Unrin."

"The ground is far richer here," said Ogden grimly.

Allun was trembling. "Marlie and I saw nothing like that on the Mountain," he said. "Nothing at all. There were some small, twisted trees behind the bushes where I picked the berries, but ..."

Ogden rubbed his chin. "On the Mountain, rock lies just beneath the soil, and cold winds blow. There this cursed plant must remain stunted, preying on insects and other crawling creatures. But here— as in the Valley of Gold—there will be no stopping it."

Rowan stood frozen. The flames in which they had placed such hope were useless. And there was no other way he could think of to save the valley.

Allun grabbed his arm. "We must get our people out," he said urgently. "It is our only chance now. We will have to get them out—as many as we can. Before—before—"

He could not go on.

Ogden's brow was deeply creased. "There must be a way," he muttered. "There is always a way. The land knows. It protects its creatures. It keeps the balance."

"Not this time," cried Allun. "Because these *things* are from the Mountain. Thanks to me, they are here!" Tears sprang into his eyes. "I cannot wait for you!" he shouted.

He ran towards the village. Zeel, Tor and Mithren ran with him.

But Rowan stayed where he was, with Ogden.

"The Mountain is also part of the land," Ogden said to him. "And there must be a way."

They heard distant shouting, but they did not move.

"Say the rhyme, Rowan," Ogden commanded.

Rowan swallowed, and began.

"Beneath soft looks the evil burns,
And slowly round the old wheel turns.
The same mistakes, the same old pride,
The priceless armour cast aside—"

"Stop!" Ogden held up his hand. "'The priceless armour cast aside,'" he repeated. "What does that mean?"

"I don't know," Rowan whispered desperately. "I have been trying and *trying* to understand it. But it doesn't mean anything to me. It seems a nonsense. Yet everything else in the rhyme is important. Everything!"

"And so must this be," said Ogden. "Rowan, think! Somewhere in you is the clue to this. It is buried deep, perhaps, but it is there. Because you are special. Something about you is special. *You* escaped the sleeping sickness and saved Allun from it. *You* saved yourself, and Zeel, in the Pit of Unrin. You alone have done these things. How? Why?"

"I don't know! I don't know!" cried Rowan, burying his face in his hands. Like a mocking echo he heard Sheba's sneering voice. "Skinny rabbit! Weakling, runny-nosed child, scared of your own shadow! No use to your mother in her need ... No use to anyone ... weakling, runny-nosed child, weakling, runny-nosed ..."

He gasped. He saw himself dragging Allun out of Rin, out into the hills. He remembered biting and tearing at the strangling roots of the Unrin trees. He remembered something Jonn had said. He remembered Zeel: "Thank the stars that they have not yet spread out of the valley." He remembered Sheba, eyes glazed: "I only know that I must work."

He spun round to Ogden. "The plants *couldn't* get out of the valley!" he shouted. "Because the hills still have their armour on. Their golden armour. Their priceless armour. Like me. Don't you see?"

Ogden stared at him.

"Call the others!" Rowan cried. "I know what we need. And I know where to get it. It is ready. It is waiting for us. Ogden, please!"

Ogden wasted no time with questions. He put his reed pipe to his lips, and blew.

20 – An End, and a Beginning

But Rowan was already running. "Here, here!" he shouted as he ran. He went the shortest way he knew, brushing through trees and ducking through bushes, calling, calling so they could follow.

Dozens of Mountain berry bushes clustered around the low door of Sheba's hut. They were big. They were ready. Mice, lizards and birds lay waiting to be devoured. And inside, something bigger.

Rowan burst into the hut. Like a bundle of old rags and straggled hair, Sheba lay huddled by the cold fire. He leaped past her, to the great iron pot that hung over the dead coals. It was filled to the brim with oily, foul-smelling liquid. Rowan took a ladleful and sipped. Yes!

"Rowan! Are you there? Rowan!"

He ran to the doorway. Ogden and the Forerunners were standing there.

"Look!" shouted Rowan. He tipped a few drops of liquid from his ladle over the plants at his feet. They quivered, and drooped. The ground heaved. And then, as Zeel, Tor and Mithren screamed, the hideous, familiar black trunks appeared, pushing, twisting, reaching out.

The Forerunners fell back. But Rowan did not move. He let a few more drops of the brew of the slip-daisy roots fall onto the writhing things. And then they shuddered and turned back on themselves, and finally, with a horrible seething sigh, split from end to end, and lay still.

"The slip-daisies," Rowan choked. "They are the armour. Jonn told Annad that other plants don't thrive where slip-daisies grow. So we weeded them out. Every one. And the people of the Valley of Gold—they would have done it too. To make their orchards, and build their houses, and pave their jewelled paths. So when the Mountain berries came they were defenceless. Just like us."

He held up the ladle. "But this—this potion is made from slip-daisy roots. I have been drinking it, all along. I am the only one who has. I am full of it, so the trees could not take me. It kills them. It kills them!"

The Forerunners ran towards him.

"There is lots more," he gabbled. "Sheba made it. She knew. She knew she had to. But she didn't know why. Inside! Quickly!"

"Fill the bottles with it," ordered Ogden. "Take the kites. Drop the liquid on the village first, then on the fields. Be sparing. Do not waste any. Rowan, take jugs, bowls, anything! We will go on foot."

"My mother!" gasped Rowan. "My sister! At the gardens!"

* * *

The gardens seethed with grey-white snakes. They crept across the grass, coiled in Jiller's hair, felt for Jonn. The trees leaned forward, breaking through the fencing, reaching for the house where other flesh lay sleeping.

Rowan ran among them, shouting, hurling the precious liquid at them, watching with savage pleasure as they split and withered, and their roots fell lifeless on the grass.

Ogden let him go, and went on his way, quietly pouring the liquid from his jug here and there, wherever it was needed, watching the kites dipping and wheeling, and his young people doing their work over the town.

He understood how the boy felt. He knew what it meant to defend a home. The whole land was his home. And he had fought for it, in his time. But never quite like this, he thought. There has never been an enemy quite like this.

Then he corrected himself. But, of course, there had. He was forgetting the circle. Long, long ago, the same ancient enemy had come down from the Mountain. And then it had won.

"But not this time," he said aloud, tipping his jug. He watched three drops fall, and the pretty, sweet-smelling little plant at his feet droop and die. "This time, a boy with the sniffles beat you."

He paused. He watched a sleeping mouse by his foot stir, sit up, clean its whiskers in surprise, then scuttle away. He smiled as he saw it go. He was thinking of the story he would tell.

* * *

The flames of the fire leaped high. The children listened, wide-eyed.

Ogden the storyteller leaned forward, his lean face ghostly and shadowed. "And Rowan took the liquid from the witch's cauldron, and he ran, shouting like a wild man, shouting with a hundred voices, right into the midst of the ravenous trees that writhed and spat at him."

Jiller squeezed Rowan's arm. Jonn put his hand on his shoulder. Annad nestled closer to him. "Was that how it was, Rowan?" she breathed.

He shrugged. It was not *quite* as he remembered it. But he was not going to spoil a good story. Not yet, anyway. He was too happy. Too relieved. Too filled with joy.

He grinned at Allun, standing near Ogden with his arms around Sara and Marlie. He knew no one blamed Allun for what had happened. Everyone took the blame equally. They had said so. And Allun had been greeted as a hero, for joining with him in finding the Travellers, and fighting the enemy.

He grinned at Zeel, smiling at him over the leaping flames. He saw Neel the potter, and Bree and Hanna with Maise and all their children. He saw Bronden, Val and Ellis, Timon, Lann. And all the others. Everyone was there. Everyone but Sheba, who cursed them all as fools, and stumped back to her hut.

The months ahead would be hard. There would be much work to do, repairing the damage done to the village by the trees of Unrin. Food would be scarce. New crops would have to be planted. But everyone was rejoicing. Just to be alive.

Ogden's voice was rising.

"And Rowan spattered them with the brew once, twice, three times," he shouted. "They screamed, and twisted, and split open—and died." He paused, looking around him. His voice dropped to a low murmur. "And their coiling roots, tangled still in his mother's hair, just withered and crumbled away. Useless. Helpless. Dead."

There was a breathless hush.

"And all around the village Allun and the Travellers were doing their work, and the other plants of evil were dying. So by sunset, the village was safe. The bukshah had returned. The people had woken. And so had the birds, and the bukshah calves, and all the other creatures that had so nearly been swallowed up and destroyed by the trees of Unrin. The valley was alive again. The wheel had been stopped. The old story had a new ending. The circle had been broken.

"And the people of Rin rejoiced, and sang, and were happy. For a while, they cared nothing for riches. For once, they were like the Travellers. Just happy to breathe the air. To look at the sky. And that night, when the moon was full, Ogden the storyteller told a tale. A tale he would tell over and over again, across the land, for many years to come."

He leaned back. "It was a tale of courage and fear; of legend and truth; of a puzzle and an answer; of suspicion and friendship; of a treasure lost, and another treasure saved; of a terrible enemy who came not from outside, but from within."

He smiled. "And most of all it was the tale of a skinny rabbit with a runny nose and a great heart, who came back to save his home, and would not stop until it was done."

The people started to cheer and clap. The sound went on for minutes. It roared through the valley. It echoed from the Mountain. It floated across the hills to where the Travellers' carts trundled quietly back to Rin.

And when the sound had finally died, Ogden stood up.

"There is one more thing," he said.

He took a silk bag from Zeel. He walked slowly around the fire, to Rowan.

"Your people owe you a debt," he said. "But so do we. You saved the life of our beloved adopted daughter Zeel, and for that you only have to call on us, and we will come to you. From anywhere. At any time. This is our solemn promise."

He handed Rowan a reed pipe.

Rowan stammered his thanks. "And," added Ogden casually, putting his hand back into the bag, "you left these behind, at our camp. We return them to you now. The village may find a use for them, in the months to come."

The precious gems fell from his fingers into Rowan's lap like many-coloured raindrops. There was a gasp from the crowd. Ogden's black eyes glittered. His arm dipped back into the bag. And into Rowan's hands he put the golden owl. It had been cleaned and polished. It shone like the sun. Its eyes were green fire.

"Sell the rest, but keep this," he said. "Like me, it is very old, very precious, and has many stories to tell. Keep this, Rowan of the Bukshah, as a sign of our friendship. It is the only one of its kind now. For we will not seek to clear the Pit of Unrin, and uncover the sad bones and lost glories of the Valley of Gold. The time of that golden place has ended. As the time of Rin has just begun."

Amid a stunned silence he walked back to the fire, and sat down. "Now!" he said, looking around and plumping his hands on his knees. "Could anyone spare a poor, useless Slip some dinner?"

And there wasn't a person there who didn't run to do his bidding.

ROWAN

AND THE

KEEPER OF THE CRYSTAL

1 – The Message

even words, written in dull black ink on a thin parchment that smelt of oil and fish.

The Crystal dims. The Chooser is summoned . . .

The sun was gentle on the valley of Rin, the day the message came. A faint breeze ruffled the blossoms of the hoopberry trees in the orchard.

Rowan stood by the bukshah pool, breathing in the sweet scent carried to him by the breeze. As the great beasts he tended drank, he gazed up at the snow-capped Mountain that overlooked the valley. He could hear the sounds of the birds, the insects chirruping in the grass, the people working in the vegetable gardens and the fields. He could hear the bubbling of the stream as it rippled through the village and wound away through the dreaming green hills behind him, on its journey to the sea.

For Rowan, this seemed a day like any other. And yet the messenger was already very near. He was no longer just a flicker of shining blue in the distance. Already he was almost in sight of the village as he half ran, half stumbled through the hills, following the stream like a lifeline. Already his small webbed hands were feeling inside his cloak for the parchment he carried.

In just a few moments the bell in the village square would ring, to signal his arrival, to call a meeting.

And after this day, for Rowan, nothing would ever be the same again.

* * *

Rowan joined the crowd in the square, standing on tiptoe the better to see the messenger. He had come running, like the others, when he heard the bell ring. Now he watched as Lann, the oldest person in the village, took the parchment from the fainting Maris man and read it aloud.

Seven words.

The Crystal dims. The Chooser is summoned.

Afterwards, Rowan remembered it all as though it was a dream. Lann's voice, loud in the square. Her wrinkled hand holding out the parchment. The midday sunlight filtering through the trees. The surprised, murmuring crowd.

The soft breezes and sweet scents of the valley of Rin moved about him. He was surrounded by people he had known all his life. Familiar birds sang in the trees above his head. He felt no prickle of fear, or inner warning. All he felt was interest, and pleasure, because something unexpected had happened to interrupt the routine of the day. A strange visitor, all the way from the coast, from the home of the Maris. And an even stranger message.

The Crystal dims ...

"What do you think it means?" Rowan whispered to Jiller, his mother, standing tall and straight beside him.

She didn't answer. But when he looked up at her, to ask her again, the words died on his lips. Jiller's face was drained of colour, and her eyes were fixed on the parchment in Lann's hand. Behind her, Strong Jonn of the Orchard moved to put an arm around her shoulders. His mouth was grim.

Rowan realised then that the message was of great importance. But still, he had no idea that it was something that was going to affect him.

Feeling a rising thrill of excited curiosity, he looked again at the figure crouching in exhaustion on the hard stones of the village square. It was his first glimpse of a Maris man. And none of the stories told by villagers coming home from journeys to the coast, none of the pictures he had seen in the house of books, had prepared him for the reality. He knew he shouldn't stare, but it was hard to tear his eyes away.

The man was clothed from wrist to ankle in tight-fitting blue garments that glimmered in the sunlight. Light boots covered his feet. He had cast aside the hood and gloves he had been wearing when he first staggered into the village. Now everyone could see the glistening, hairless, blue-white skin of his head, face and neck, his flat, glassy-looking eyes, his wide mouth and his small webbed hands.

He huddled, panting, at Lann's feet. She looked down at him, leaning heavily on her stick.

"What is your name, Maris man?" she asked abruptly.

"Perlain, of the clan Pandellis."

"How long since you left the coast, Perlain?"

"Four suns," gasped the man. His voice was dull and rasping, and he raised his webbed hand to his throat as he spoke, as if the words hurt him.

A murmur of surprise rose from the crowd. It took the people of Rin at least a week to travel between their valley and the coast. This man must have run much of the way, and barely slept. No wonder he was exhausted. They looked at him with new respect.

"You have made good time," said Lann. "You have done well, Perlain of Pandellis."

"There is great danger," croaked the Maris man. "The Chooser ..."

"The Chooser of Rin has heard the summons, and will obey it," Lann said calmly. "There has always been danger. But never in three hundred years have we failed to answer the call. The Chooser and the First-born will leave for the coast with you at sunset."

Rowan's heart leaped. Danger! Someone was about to go into great danger. Someone from Rin. But what was the danger? What did all this mean? Who was the Chooser? Chooser of what?

Perlain was shaking his head. "No. Not—so long. Every hour—every minute—is precious!" His throat moved as he swallowed painfully.

"You have been travelling in the sun, as well as under the moon, for too long. You must rest. You must soak. Or you will die, Perlain," said Lann.

"It does not matter." The Maris man wet his dry lips. "The death of one is—of no account."

"This is your belief, but not ours," Lann answered firmly. "And besides, our people must prepare for the journey. The Chooser will leave at sunset." She raised her voice. "Is it agreed?"

There was a moment's silence. Rowan looked up curiously into Lann's face. She was frowning, staring at someone in the crowd. Someone very near to Rowan.

He turned his head to see who it was. All around him, other children and most of the adults were doing the same thing. But a few of the adults' faces were serious and intent.

They know, he thought. *They know.*

"Is it agreed?" Lann repeated. "Does the Chooser agree?"

Rowan felt a movement as someone stepped forward to stand alone in the centre of the square.

"Yes," said a quiet voice. "I agree. We leave at sunset."

The Maris man looked eagerly towards the sound, then bowed his head, touching his forehead to the ground.

"Chooser of Rin, who holds the fate of Maris in your hands, I greet you in the name of the Keeper of the Crystal," he breathed. "I am your servant. I am the sand beneath your feet. My life is yours."

Rowan blinked, and gasped. He couldn't believe what was happening. He couldn't understand it.

This can't be right! I would have known of it. There must be some mistake, he thought wildly.

But there was no mistake.

The person accepting the reverence of the crouching Maris man, the person the message had called the Chooser, the person who was about to go into unknown peril, was Jiller, his mother.

2 – The Crystal of Maris

What is happening? Mother, tell me!"

Rowan clutched at Jiller's arm as they hurried home from the square. But she strode on, frowning and silent.

"Wait, skinny rabbit," Strong Jonn muttered to him. He jerked his head at the chattering crowd behind them. "Your mother will not speak till we are alone. Be patient." His voice was as confident as always, but Rowan could tell by his face that he was worried and shaken.

Jonn and Jiller walked quickly on. Rowan's young sister, Annad, skipped along in front of them. Annad understood little of what had happened in the square. She and her friends had been far too busy whispering to each other and peeping at the strange-looking Maris man to pay attention to anything else.

Rowan stumbled behind, his mind whirling with questions, thoughts and fears.

All he understood so far was that his mother had to go to Maris. That he, her first-born child, had to go with her. And that some terrible danger awaited them at the end of the journey.

But what danger? And why did they have to go at all?

Maris. Rowan tried to remember all he knew about it. Timon the teacher had told the children many tales of the land on the coast. Tales of serpents of the sea, of battles and storms—and some of the history of the strange Maris folk.

But suddenly Rowan remembered one special day under the Teaching Tree. A warm summer's day.

Timon had been showing them pictures from a book. Pictures of Maris folk. They all looked alike to Rowan, except that some wore silver, some blue, and some green.

"The Maris are a secret people," Timon had said, pointing to the pictures one by one. "Though they trade freely with us and others from across the sea, they do not open their hearts to strangers, and little is known of them.

"But some things we do know. The Maris are divided into three tribes, or clans: the silver clan of Umbray, the green clan of Fisk, the blue clan of Pandellis. In ancient times the clans fought bitterly. Every night, it is said, the sea ran with blood, and the serpents feasted on Maris flesh.

"But for a thousand years the clans have been united under one all-powerful leader—the Keeper of the Crystal. The first Keeper was a man called Orin the Wise. It was he who found the Crystal, a treasure of great power and mystery, in a cave beneath the Maris sea ..."

Rowan was tired, that day. He had been woken in the night by a bad dream, and it had taken him a long time to fall back to sleep.

So he was half drowsing under the Teaching Tree, listening to Timon with only part of his mind.

"Rowan of the Bukshah! What did I just say?"

Timon's voice jerked him wide awake.

"Ah—ah—there are three clans ..." he stammered, feeling himself blush. "Their leader is—the Keeper of the Crystal."

The other children giggled and nudged one another. They knew how shy Rowan was. And usually he was quiet and good in lessons. They thought it was funny to see him caught out.

Timon frowned warningly at them, and went on. "Very well. Once there was a fourth clan, the clan of Mirril. They were experts in poison. They created a thousand and one deadly poisons, and for every poison, an antidote. But the Mirril were all destroyed when the Zebak invaded the coast three hundred years ago."

Again he looked at Rowan, his grey eyes piercing.

"What else happened three hundred years ago, Rowan?"

"That was when our ancestors came here, and Rin began," Rowan said in a low voice.

Timon nodded.

"Correct. The Zebak have tried to invade the coast of this land many times. But three hundred years ago they came with an army of warrior slaves chained to the oars of their ships. Those slaves were our ancestors."

Timon's face was grave as he continued.

"The morning the Zebak landed, all the Maris clans were meeting in their separate meeting houses. No one had been left outside on guard. No one knew the enemy had come. The Zebak crept up to the Mirril house and threw an exploding fire inside. There was a great roar. Sheets of flame shot up to the sky. The building fell, and burned. Everyone died. Not a single member of the Mirril clan was left alive. No man, no woman, no child."

Timon had everyone's attention now. The children under the Teaching Tree were silent. All well knew the terror of fire.

"Our ancestors saw this happen," Timon went on. "They saw the Zebak laugh as the fire raged. The horror of that moment was one of the reasons they were roused to turn against the Zebak at last. They broke their chains and joined the people of this land to fight and defeat their enemy. It was the most important day in our history."

Then Timon did a strange thing. He closed the book, and leaned forward. And suddenly it seemed to Rowan that Timon was speaking to him alone.

"We must never forget," Timon said slowly, his eyes fixed on Rowan's, "that the Maris folk have been vital to our safety ever since. For the Maris guard the coast. Without them, the Zebak would have come and claimed us again, long ago. The Zebak plot ceaselessly against this land, and they grow more cunning with every year that passes. We must never lose the trust of the Maris, whatever the cost."

Soon afterwards, the lesson had ended. Thinking about it later, Rowan decided that he had been foolish to think that Timon was speaking particularly to him. For why should this story be more special to Rowan than it was to any of the other Rin children?

But now, the message from Maris still ringing in his ears, he felt differently.

Timon *was* speaking especially to me that day, he thought, his heart beginning to thud. Timon knew that some day the message from Maris would come. He was warning me that I must not fight it. That I must do my duty.

What duty?

It was something to do with the Crystal. The fabled Crystal of Maris.

The Crystal dims. The Chooser is summoned.

"Few outside Maris understand just how powerful and mysterious the Crystal is. Very few," Timon had said once.

And again, his grey eyes had seemed to flick in Rowan's direction.

Rowan's steps slowed. Yes. The Crystal was at the heart of this. Had Timon said anything more about it?

Just one thing. And he had said it gravely, as though it was very important.

"The Maris live long. Far longer than we of Rin. And the Keepers reach a greater age than any of them, because of the power of the Crystal. But still there comes a time when each Keeper knows death is near. At this time the Crystal begins to lose its fire and its strength. Then a new Keeper must be chosen, to take the old one's place. The new Keeper must join with the Crystal before the old Keeper dies, so that its power is not lost."

The Crystal dims ...

Rowan's throat tightened. Suddenly he saw what the message meant. Far away in Maris, the Keeper of the Crystal was dying. A new Keeper had to be chosen.

But why had the message come to Jiller? Why had the messenger called her the Chooser? What did she, a woman of Rin, have to do with the Keeper of the Crystal?

Rowan looked up and saw that Jiller and Jonn had stopped, and were waiting for him. They had reached the pathway that led into their garden and the fields beyond. Annad had run through the gate already, leaving it gaping wide.

He hurried to join them.

"Go into the house, now, Rowan," Jiller said in a low voice. "Pack clothes for the journey. Warm clothes, for it will be cold in Maris. Then go to the bukshah fields and make Star ready. She will have to come with us to carry our supplies."

She waited for him to go, to do as she had asked, but he hesitated.

"Make haste now," she said sharply. "We leave at sunset."

Rowan stood where he was. "Please, Mother," he said. "Why do we have to go? How can you be this—this Chooser?"

"Jiller—you must tell him," Strong Jonn urged her. "You can delay no longer."

Jiller sighed. She closed the gate and gazed out over the crops that rippled like a green sea before her. "I am the Chooser because I was born to the task, Rowan," she said finally. "It is a duty that has been handed down through our family for hundreds of years."

"*Our* family?" Rowan could hardly believe what he was hearing. "But—why? And why did I not know of it before? Lann knew it. Jonn knew it. Timon knew it. Many must have known of it." He felt a quick rush of baffled anger. "Why did no one *tell* me?" he demanded.

"It is a thing known to few in Rin, by the wish of the Maris," said Jonn, putting a steadying hand on Rowan's shoulder.

"Perhaps I should have told you before now. But I did not want to trouble you until it was necessary," Jiller said, still looking straight ahead. "You have always been—one who worries about things, Rowan."

Rowan flinched. He knew very well that had he been a stronger, braver person, his mother would have shared the secret with him long ago.

She seemed to understand what he was feeling, for she glanced at him quickly, and touched his hand. "I wanted to protect you for as long as I could," she whispered. "That is all."

"Well, the time to tell the truth has come," said Strong Jonn. "Now Rowan must hear the whole story."

3 – The Chooser

And so at last, pacing beneath the trees in the garden, Rowan heard the secret that his mother had kept from him for so long.

When the Zebak had invaded the coast, on the day Timon had called the most important in Rin's history, they had timed their arrival carefully. Their spies had told them that the Crystal of Maris was fading. The Keeper was dying. The Choosing of a new Keeper was about to begin.

The Zebak were sure that this was the perfect time to attack. Not only because the jealous Maris clans were busy plotting so that one of their own would be chosen as the new Keeper. But also because the Crystal itself was weak, and would not grow strong again until the Choosing was over.

The Zebak knew that the Choosing was governed by special rules, set down by Orin the Wise. Orin had realised that when he died, each clan would demand that one of its own must be Keeper. He did not want the power of the Crystal to be lost while the clans fought over it.

Orin's rules were simple. The Candidates for Keeper would go together to the Island in the Maris harbour. Not to fight, because the Maris did not greatly prize physical strength, but to take special tests of cleverness and cunning. The Candidates would be judged by a single Chooser. Whichever Candidate was chosen at the end of the tests would be the new Keeper of the Crystal.

Orin was clever, and he understood his people well. He knew that the Chooser had to be someone everyone could trust. So he decreed that the Chooser would always come from his own clan, the clan of Mirril. But in return for this honour no Mirril could ever again be Keeper of the Crystal.

The Mirril Chooser would select from only three Candidates—one from Fisk, one from Umbray, one from Pandellis. In this way the Chooser's clan would have nothing to lose or gain. The choice would always be fair.

The people accepted Orin's decree. It held for centuries—until something happened which even Orin himself could not have foreseen.

The Zebak attacked, while the old Keeper lay dying. And their very first act was to destroy the Mirril.

Not by chance. Not because the Mirril house was closest to the shore. But because they wanted to destroy the Chooser clan. They wanted to stop a new Keeper from being chosen. Then the Crystal would fade for ever, and victory would be theirs.

Their plan nearly succeeded. There were Candidates for Keeper, but with the Mirril all dead, there was no Chooser. And even in this crisis, with a battle raging on Maris shores, the Fisk, Pandellis and Umbray clans would not agree to leave the choice to one of their own. Nor would they leave it to the Keeper himself, who was in any case dying, and unable to move from the Cavern of the Crystal where he lay.

But the Zebak had forgotten one thing: the Crystal, even dim, carried within it the wisdom of the ages. And the old Keeper, even dying, had the cunning of Orin himself.

The old Keeper knew where he could find a Chooser his people would accept. He turned to the strangers—the warrior slaves who had risen up against their Zebak masters and were fighting beside his own people. With the help of the Crystal, he selected a man to be the Chooser. That man was Jiller's ancestor, and Rowan's. His name was Lieth.

"So while the battle raged, Lieth went to the Island and chose the new Keeper," Jiller said. "The Crystal began to shine with new, radiant life. My father told me that its power is at its strongest when a new Keeper is chosen. And so it proved that day.

"Immediately, the tide of the battle turned. The Zebak were beaten and driven away. This land was saved. And our ancestors were freed from slavery, to start a new life."

"That was hundreds of years ago," said Rowan.

Jiller nodded. "It was. But the duty Lieth accepted at Maris that day has been passed down through our family ever since."

"It is a great honour," said Jonn quietly.

"A great honour, and at the same time, a curse." Jiller's face was set and pale.

"Why?" begged Rowan. "Why a curse?"

Jiller put out her hand, and grasped the latch of the door.

"Because to be a Chooser in Maris is to be in terrible danger," she whispered. "It is to risk death."

Suddenly she spun around, and took Rowan's face in her hands. "I would give anything to spare you, Rowan. Anything. And yet I cannot spare you. I must take you with me, to take my place as Chooser should I die. And each of us must face whatever comes with courage. Each of us. Alone."

She dropped her hands from Rowan's cheeks, turned, and hurried into the house.

Rowan followed her inside. His mind was filled with confusion and fear. "Why, Mother? Why should we be in danger?" he cried. "Because of the Zebak? Because they know the time to attack the coast is when the Crystal is dim?"

"No!" Jiller cried sharply. Her eyes were fierce.

Rowan shrank back. It frightened him to see his mother like this. She was usually so calm and unafraid.

"Jiller!" Strong Jonn stepped forward. "Let us sit down. We will sit, eat and drink. And you can answer Rowan's questions as they should be answered. In peace."

"There is no time—" began Jiller, wringing her hands. And then, quite suddenly, she gave in. Her shoulders slumped. She pulled out a chair and sat down at the table.

"You are right," she said softly. "I am at fault. I have carried this burden alone for so long that it is hard for me to share it, now that the moment has come." She shook her head. "My father said the same thing to me, in his time."

"Did Grandfather choose a Keeper?" asked Rowan, sitting down timidly beside her. His grandfather had died when he was a small child. Rowan mainly remembered a wide, gentle smile, blue eyes, and hands, hard and rough from work in the fields, carving animals from wood with a small, sharp knife.

Jiller shook her head. "No, my father was never summoned," she said. "The present Keeper was chosen by his mother, my grandmother. But Father knew the Crystal would almost certainly dim in my lifetime. And it grieved him, very much."

Jonn put bread, cheese and milk on the table. "Eat, Jiller," he said. "And Rowan, you eat, too. You will need all your strength in the days to come. Missing meals will help nothing."

They began to eat the food. And Jonn was right, Rowan thought. Eating did help. He had not realised he was so hungry.

"So to be the Chooser is dangerous," he said, as calmly as he could. "Why is that?"

"It is because the Maris have not changed," growled Jonn. "The jealousy between the clans is like a madness." He put his hand on Jiller's arm. "Tell him the rest, Jiller."

Rowan's mother nodded reluctantly, and began to speak again.

"As each Keeper grows old, the Maris clans prepare for the Choosing. Each clan has at least one Candidate, trained from his or her earliest years for the tests to come. The people of each clan will do anything, anything at all, to make sure their Candidate will win. They will steal, spy, cheat and lie. They will even kill, if they suspect that the Chooser is favouring another."

She crumbled the bread on her plate, staring at it with unseeing eyes. "Many in our family have died in Maris. My great-grandfather was the last. Grieving and in fear, my grandmother, his first-born child, had to take his place as Chooser while he lay dead in the Cavern of the Crystal. She did it bravely, it is said, though she was only fifteen."

Rowan felt his stomach turn over. But he forced himself to keep silent.

Jiller went on. "She had always known the danger. Many others in our family had died in the centuries before that, killed by jealous Candidates, or clan spies. Very, very often, the Choosing has brought death to the Chooser. Poison. Sharp blades in the dead of night. Bodies bound with nets and thrown into the hungry sea."

Rowan looked at his mother in horror. "But—that is madness."

Jonn nodded. "As I told you. Madness," he echoed. "A madness that has been going on for a thousand years."

"It is the Maris way," sighed Jiller. "There is no point in raging against it. Now, at least, the clans savage one another only when the Crystal dims. Once a new Keeper has been chosen, the Maris will come together again, swearing loyalty, and obeying their leader without question. So it has always been."

So it has always been ...

Rowan took a deep breath. "If both of us are killed," he said, in a level voice, "does that mean that Annad—?"

"No." Jiller smiled tiredly. "My one happiness is that Annad is too young to be summoned. If you and I should die, Rowan, the duty passes to another. To Timon. For his family is the next in line."

Timon. So that was why Timon's eyes had been so grave as he spoke of the Crystal of Maris.

Jonn pushed his plate away and stood up. "Well," he said, "we have talked, we have eaten, and now we must work. If we are to leave at sunset there is much to do."

Jiller looked up, startled. "*We?*" she asked. "You are not coming with us, are you, Jonn?"

"Of course," he said. "Do you think I would let you and Rowan go alone?"

She shook her head. "Jonn, this is my duty, and Rowan's. But there is no need for you to put yourself into danger also. No need."

"There is every need," Jonn said gently. "You know it. You know, too, that if Rowan's father were alive he would have gone with you to the coast. To be with Rowan while you are at the Choosing, if for nothing else. You must allow me the same right."

"We are betrothed, not married yet. And now, perhaps ..." Jiller's voice trembled, and she turned her face away.

Rowan felt his breath catch in his throat.

Jonn gripped the edge of the table, his eyes hard. "Do not say such things," he said loudly. "All will be well. You will be safe, and so will Rowan. I will see to it."

The words were brave. But Rowan knew that Jonn, for all his strength, could not protect them against what they were about to face. No one could protect them.

His mother's voice echoed in his mind.

Each of us must face whatever comes with courage. Each of us. Alone.

4 – The Journey

hey left at sunset. Few saw them go. Only Timon and old Lann came to the edge of the village to say farewell.

Annad was to stay with Marlie the weaver while Jiller and Rowan were away. She would be safe there, and happy. And she would feel important, too, for she was to care for the bukshah in Rowan's place.

"And if—" Jiller had whispered to Marlie. "If Rowan and I do not return ..."

"I will care for Annad as if she were my own," Marlie said quickly. "Do not fear. But, Jiller—you will return. You will."

Old Lann echoed those words, as she farewelled them.

"You will return," she said, her strong, wrinkled face showing none of the fear that perhaps she felt. "One of you at least will return. The summons has come late. The Maris man has told me that the Keeper is weakening very quickly. There will be no time to send to Rin for another Chooser. For which Timon, no doubt, is grateful."

Timon bowed his head. "That is not so. I would take Jiller's place willingly, if I could. But the Maris folk will not accept me as Chooser while she and Rowan live."

Lann glanced at Perlain, who was waiting impatiently by the stream. "Maris is not what it was," she mumbled. "Bound hand and foot by rules, and following old ways, the people learn nothing. The Keepers guard the Crystal, but do not use it as once they did. They fear new ideas. They will not change. They will not grow. Yet the Zebak become more cunning with every year."

She frowned fiercely. "I beg you, Jiller, and you, Rowan of the Bukshah, if the duty comes to you, to choose wisely and well."

"I will try," Jiller murmured. Rowan swallowed, and nodded.

Lann bent forward. "And take care," she added in a harsh whisper. "Those slippery Maris devils will be watching you every moment. Now go. Our thoughts and our trust go with you."

* * *

For years, like every other child in Rin, Rowan had wanted to visit the coast. He had longed to gaze at the great ocean, sparkling, moving, blue as far as the eye could see.

He had imagined himself watching the mysterious, pale-skinned Maris folk sailing their boats into the sunrise, gliding like fish through the waves in the midday heat, mending nets at dusk. Safe at home in his green valley, he had shivered with pleasant fear at the thought of the huge, glistening coils and dripping jaws of the sea serpents, hunting their prey under the moon.

Rowan had seen so many pictures and heard so many stories about this place. He longed to see it all for himself.

He had thought he would travel to the home of the Maris on one of the Rin trading trips. Every year a group of villagers set out, excited and full of talk. Four or five great beasts from the bukshah herd went with them, pulling wagons loaded with cheese, fruit, vegetables, woven bukshah wool and other goods.

Rowan always ran from his work in the bukshah fields to watch them go. And three or four weeks later he stood with the crowd to welcome them home again.

If trade had gone well, the Rin goods would be gone from the wagons. In their place would be bundles of dried fish, jars of oil, packages of salt and sponges.

The returning villagers would show the small things they had bought for themselves and their friends: strange, beautiful ornaments carved from driftwood and pearlshell, tiny, hard, speckled biscuits that tasted of the sea, glittering fish-skin belts, necklaces bright with tiny crystals. Rowan listened to their tales with excitement and envy.

One day, he told himself, I will be old enough and strong enough to go to the coast. One day ...

But that day had arrived far sooner than he had expected. And it had come in a way that had shocked him. For a reason he had never dreamed of.

* * *

The days and nights passed. It was a long journey. A hard journey, too, for they travelled by night, and in haste. Stumbling along the rough ground in the dark, following first the stream and then the river that led to the sea, all of them had grown very weary. Although they took what rest they could during the day, it was difficult to sleep deeply and long with the sun bright in the sky.

They travelled by night for the sake of Perlain, the Maris man. Away from the sea spray his soft skin dried and cracked. The sun of the inland, even at this gentle season, burned him.

He did not thank them for their care. He told them not to spare him. He said that time was too precious to waste. But after three nights of walking, he was too tired to argue further. He simply retreated into silence.

At night he flitted ahead of them, his feet soft on the grass, his blue clothes shining in the moonlight. During the day he soaked in the river while they slept on the bank.

One afternoon, when they were nearly at their journey's end, Rowan woke from an uneasy doze to see Perlain step dripping from the water, and sit down on the grass.

The shadows were long. Rowan knew that soon it would be time for them to eat and be on their way once more. But Jiller and Jonn were still asleep. Even Star was dozing. On an impulse, Rowan got up and went over to the Maris man.

Perlain watched him approach. His flat eyes showed neither surprise nor welcome.

Rowan had thought he might try to talk to Perlain, ask him questions about Maris. But now he found he did not know how to begin. He stared at him dumbly, very aware of the Maris man's odd appearance, his strange, fishy smell.

"Did you sleep well, First-born of the Chooser?" Perlain asked politely.

"Yes, thank you," lied Rowan. "Did you?"

Perlain shrugged, and his thin lips curved into a smile. "I will be home by morning," he said simply.

He looked at the sky. "It is time for the Chooser to awake," he said. Obviously he wanted Rowan to leave him.

Rowan bit his lip. "Perlain," he said, in a rush. "The Crystal of Maris. Could you tell me about it?"

Perlain stared. "I am only the Keeper's Messenger. I do not know all the secrets of the Crystal."

"I do not want to know the secrets," Rowan pleaded. "Just the things everyone in Maris must know. Even we in Rin know a little. The Crystal was found long ago by a man called Orin the Wise. I know that. But I do not know where it was found, or how. Could you not tell me that, at least?"

Perlain seemed to consider for a moment. Then, slowly, he nodded. "I will tell you what I know," he said.

He looked out across the river.

"Orin was fishing, unwisely, as the sun went down," he began. "The full moon had risen. The Great Serpent, the mother of all the other serpents of the sea, rose from the dark water, upset Orin's boat, and hunted him to the Island in the harbour."

Rowan shuddered. In the house of books there was a picture of the Great Serpent of Maris. It had always filled him with true fear. A huge, twisting, scaly beast, with the head of a dragon and the body of a giantic snake, rose from the sea. A boat filled with screaming Maris folk, their hands pressed to their ears, was crushed in its terrible, dripping jaws.

Perlain smiled slightly, and went on. "In his terror, Orin fled into a cave, and from there he plunged through a dark tunnel that led deep below the sea.

"In a small, rocky cavern, he found the Crystal. When he touched it, it began to glow—as though a hundred rainbow fires were trapped inside it. He stayed in the cavern all night, and the next morning he carried the Crystal to the shore.

"The people knew at once that the Crystal was a great wonder, though in those days no one realised just how powerful it was. They soon found that it shone only for Orin. And they saw that he had been changed by it. Suddenly he could see things they could not. Feel fish below the surface of the sea. Sense serpents lurking. Taste the wind and say when storms were coming. Even see into other people's hearts.

"And Orin was changed in other ways. Before he found the Crystal he had been filled with hatred for clans not his own. Yet now, though his clan urged him to use his new power to destroy its rivals, he would not. He shared with everyone the knowledge and wisdom of the Crystal."

"So he became the Maris leader," Rowan put in. "The first Keeper."

"Yes. By the power of the Crystal," said Perlain. "And then everything happened as he had said it would. Once the people put their minds to building, and planning, and gathering food, instead of warring with one another, our nation prospered. Other Keepers followed Orin, each chosen according to the rules he laid down. And the Crystal—"

"Yes," Rowan prompted him eagerly. "What of the Crystal?"

"As the years went on, it was found that the Crystal was more, much more, than even Orin had thought."

Perlain hesitated, then continued, choosing his words carefully. "The Crystal does not just give. It takes and keeps, also. It now contains all the knowledge of Maris. When an old Keeper dies, all his learning and experience passes into the Crystal. And from there it passes into the new Keeper. So nothing is lost. Everything is remembered."

"So each Keeper is wiser than the Keepers of the past!" breathed Rowan. "Wiser and more powerful."

"So it is said."

"No wonder, then, that to be Keeper is a great prize," said Rowan. "Everyone in Maris must long to be chosen as a Candidate."

"Oh, no," Perlain answered softly. "Not everyone. I for one cannot think of anything I would care for less."

And then, suddenly seeming to feel he had said too much, he jumped lightly to his feet and moved away.

Rowan looked out over the river. The water ran swiftly, carrying sticks and leaves with it, moving endlessly towards the ocean.

Tomorrow, Rowan thought, we will be where that water is going. We will be at the place where the river meets the sea.

Tomorrow, we will be in Maris.

5 – Danger

ootsore, cold, and tired to his bones, Rowan felt the stinging wind in his face, tasted salt on his lips, and stared with watering eyes at the endless, wave-capped sea. His hand reached for the comforting warmth of Star's rough mane.

Star rumbled deep in her throat and swayed against him. Like Rowan, she was far from home. She longed for the sweet air of the valley of Rin, and the soft grass of the bukshah fields.

She did not like the chill wind that blew the salt spray into her small black eyes and the sharp, fishy scent into her tender nose. She did not like the sand and pebbles under her hoofs. She did not like the dim stable where she was tethered, or the strange, silent people who stared at her as they passed.

"You will feel better when you have rested, Star," Rowan murmured to her, rubbing her nose. "We will all feel better then."

He knew he was talking to himself as much as to her.

The wind blew harder. Star pawed the ground, turning her head away from the stable door, away from the noise of the wind, and the stinging sand.

"I must go now," said Rowan. "Jonn will be waiting for me. But I will be back to see you soon."

Star rumbled unhappily.

"Your water is here, and your food. Eat and drink, now, then sleep," Rowan urged her. "Sleeping will make the time pass more quickly."

He patted Star's humped neck one more time, then turned away. He hoped his comforting words were true. He hated leaving Star alone, locked up like this. But the Maris had nowhere else to keep her.

At least here she will be safe, Rowan thought, as he barred the stable door behind him and began trudging along the pebbled street to the place where he and Jonn were to stay. The stable was strong, built of the rock-like bricks the Maris made and used for their own houses. The fearsome creatures that slithered from the sea to hunt in the darkness of the night could not break those strong walls down.

Perlain had told him this, smiling slightly, with his head on one side. It was not the way of the Maris people to bond closely with animals. Perlain was amused that Rowan cared so much for Star, but he was far too polite to say so.

Rowan looked out again into the harbour, where the Island hunched, dark and covered with thick forest, beaten by waves and wind. He could see no movement on its rocky shore, but his mother might already be there, hidden among the trees. She had been taken away as soon as they arrived in Maris. And that was a couple of hours ago at least.

Rowan and Jonn had been told that she would go first to the Cavern of the Crystal and then to the Island. There she would stay until the Choosing was complete.

Rowan gazed at the glittering sea and the black shape of the Island, but he did not really see them. He no longer saw the shore of Maris, or the hard, pebbled street on which he stood, or the rounded houses that crowded one against the other behind him. He no longer noticed the curious glances of the passing Maris folk.

In his mind, he was back in Rin, standing by the bukshah pool. The bukshah rumbled and snorted around him. His mother was working in the fields. Strong Jonn was in the orchard. All was quiet. All was safe ...

Rowan felt a hand on his shoulder, and jumped. He spun around to see Perlain looking at him enquiringly.

"What are you doing here, alone, First-born of the Chooser?" the Maris man asked. "Why are you not in the safe house, with Jonn of the Orchard, where I left you?"

"I—I was seeing to Star, my bukshah," stammered Rowan.

A weary smile crossed Perlain's face. "You people of Rin are very strange," he sighed. "Do you want to be found tomorrow morning in a ditch, stabbed to the heart, my friend? Is this beast, this bukshah, so important that you would risk that?"

"There is no reason why anyone should wish to kill me, Perlain," said Rowan stoutly. "I have done no harm to anyone. And I do not know anything about the Choosing, as yet. I have not even seen the Candidates. No one could know how I would vote, should it be left to me."

A cloud seemed to veil Perlain's pale eyes for a moment, then once more his mouth curved in a smile. "You are wiser than you seem, Rowan of Rin," he murmured. "And yet not as wise as you believe. The Candidates study the ways of Rin, and your family more than any. Their trainers know how you think. They have collected news of you since the day you were born."

Rowan's cheeks grew hot, despite the icy wind. He did not like to think of his life being spied on from a distance by cold, pale-eyed strangers. He glanced at Perlain, and his face showed clearly how he felt.

The Maris man spread his small webbed hands.

"That is how it has always been," he said. "It is best that you understand. Come with me now, to the safe house. And I would suggest that from now on you wait there, and that you do not go into the streets alone."

He took Rowan by the arm and drew him on down the pebbled street.

"I have to visit Star at least twice a day," said Rowan stubbornly. "To fill her water bowl, and give her food. She is lonely, and perhaps afraid."

"And you are not afraid?" Perlain stared at him. His flat eyes seemed to pierce Rowan's soul. Then he nodded. "Oh, yes. I see it now. You are afraid, but you are trying not to show that you are. This is the way of Rin, is it not?"

Rowan said nothing. He walked on, feeling Perlain's cool breath on his cheek. He saw the other Maris people, especially those who wore the silver and green of the Umbray and Fisk clans, staring and whispering as they passed. Perhaps they were wondering what Perlain was saying to him. Wondering if Perlain was taking advantage of his place as the Keeper's Messenger. If he was singing the praises of the Candidate from the clan of Pandellis. Just in case the First-born should become the Chooser.

The low voice went on, close to his ear. "Yet you are different from others I have met. Different from the loud, large people who come to trade with us each year. Different from your tall, brave mother, the Chooser. Your eyes have the look of one who has seen the Great Serpent, and lived. Deep, and full of knowledge. Strange in a boy so young. I have known only one other."

Rowan stumbled, and looked down at his feet, not knowing what to say.

"You keep silence," said Perlain. "This is good. In silence, you are safe." He stopped, and pointed. "There is your safe house," he said. "I will go with you no further. Food will be brought to you soon. Our finest fish. The eggs of the Kirrian Worm, gathered fresh from the sands this morning. But I suggest you keep to your own supplies."

"Why?" asked Rowan.

Perlain shrugged. "You may find that something in a Maris dish does not agree with you," he said calmly. "Tell your friend Jonn, if you wish. If you value his life as much as you value your own."

He bowed and moved away, slipping like a blue shadow down a narrow lane between two houses and disappearing from sight.

Rowan paced the last few steps to the small building where he was to stay with Jonn.

Perlain was warning him of poison. Poisoned food, poisoned drink.

Jiller had taken her own food and drink with her to the Island. She, Rowan and Jonn had all agreed on this. But they had not thought that Jonn and Rowan would have to take similar care. Not so soon. Not unless the worst happened, and Jiller was killed.

The people of each clan will do anything, anything at all, to make sure their Candidate will win. They will steal, spy, cheat and lie. They will even kill, if they suspect that the Chooser is favouring another.

Take care, Mother, thought Rowan, pressing his hands together. Do not let anyone know how you are feeling. Do not even hint at which Candidate you think the best. Guard your words, and your face, and even your thoughts ...

For perhaps, after a thousand years of the Crystal, the Keeper was not the only one in Maris who could read thoughts. Rowan remembered how Perlain's pale eyes had searched his. Perlain had seemed to know what he was thinking. Could it be? If so, then Jiller could not be safe, however careful she was.

She would not be safe until she was back in the Cavern of the Crystal, until she had put a hand on the shoulder of one of the Candidates and had said the words she had whispered to Rowan on the journey to this place. The words every Chooser had said since the time of Orin.

The Chooser has made the Choice. Let the other Candidates leave this place.

Rowan found that he was panting with fear. Deliberately, he slowed his breath. He rubbed his sweating hands on his shirt. He knew he had to keep calm. As calm as his mother would want him to be. But it was hard. So hard.

He wondered for the thousandth time whether Jiller had been right to keep their family's secret from him all these years. Would it have been better to have been prepared?

Or would the story have burdened his childhood, as it was burdening him now? Would he have worried about it, and feared every day the coming of the Maris messenger? Would his dreams have been haunted by pale, watchful people with cold eyes and webbed hands, a rocky black island circled by foam, a crystal burning like fire?

Rowan heard a sound and looked up. The people on the street were parting to let a hurrying group through. A group of three, two men and a woman, wearing capes that flapped and snapped in the wind.

One man wore the silver of Umbray, the other the blue of Pandellis. The woman wore the green of Fisk. Their faces were serious. They were coming straight towards him. Something had happened. Something terrible.

Rowan's whole body began to shake. His heart felt as though it was bursting. He heard muttering around him as a crowd gathered to watch. The three Maris stopped in front of him, and bowed low. The man in blue glanced at the others and began to speak.

"Chooser of Rin, who holds the fate of Maris in your hands, I greet you in the name of the Keeper of the Crystal ..." he began.

As his voice droned on, whispers rose from the crowd on the

street, filling Rowan's ears, rising and falling, hissing like wave-foam on the sand. Chooser ... Chooser ... the mother ... Poison ... Poison ... Poison ...

And as the red tide of horror rose and flooded Rowan's mind, a single thought floated to the surface. Jiller had been right to keep him in ignorance for as long as she could. For nothing she could have told him would have prepared him for this agony. Nothing at all.

6 – Poison

W ho has done this?" Rowan heard his own voice speaking as though from far away.

"There is no way of telling," said the taller of the men, the man of Umbray. "Your mother fell ill on the Island. She was there alone with the Candidates. The Choosing had just begun." His face showed no expression at all. His flat eyes were cold.

One of the Candidates, thought Rowan. Someone who thought they were going to lose. His head swam.

There is no way of telling.

But there had to be.

The green-clad woman looked at the sun. "We must hurry," she said. "The Crystal dims. The Choosing must go on. Time flows away from us like the tide." She began to move away.

Blindly, Rowan caught at her arm to hold her back. His fingers slipped on the smooth surface of the garment she wore. Beneath the fabric the flesh felt cool and slightly damp.

"Jonn! Does Jonn know?" he burst out, glancing at the closed door of the safe house just ahead.

"Not yet," she said.

"He must be told!"

"He will be. And would know already, had you been with him as expected," she said. "We were surprised to see you on the street alone." Her voice was icy: her disapproval was very clear.

"I wasn't—" Rowan broke off, biting back the words. He had been going to say that he hadn't been alone. That Perlain had been with him. But with a stab of fear that had pierced even the pain and confusion he was feeling, he realised that to admit this would be dangerous now.

Perlain was of the Pandellis clan. If the Fisk and Umbray people thought the Chooser was becoming too friendly with a Pandellis man, even the Keeper's Messenger, they might be jealous. They might decide that Rowan would be sure to choose the Pandellis Candidate for Keeper. They might—

"Come," said a quiet voice beside him. It was the Umbray man. His face was so close that Rowan could see his own reflection in the colourless eyes.

"Come," the man repeated. "We must delay no longer. You are the Chooser now. The fate of Maris is in your hands."

"I want to see my mother," Rowan managed to say.

The man nodded. "Of course. That is why she has been carried to the Cavern of the Crystal, by order of the Keeper. You must bid her farewell before you take her place on the Island, Chooser of Rin. She will no longer be alive by the time you return."

Rowan's heart gave an enormous leap. "You mean she still—*lives?*" he gasped. "I thought ..."

"She breathes," murmured the Umbray man, turning his face towards the crashing sea. "But her heart beats ever more slowly as the poison spreads within her. Soon she will breathe no more."

"She does not suffer," the Pandellis man added quickly, glancing at Rowan's stricken face. "She sleeps, and dreams, and with every dream she slips further away from the shore of life. That is all."

The Umbray man smiled, thin-lipped. "Do not pretend to the Chooser that you are soft-hearted like him and his people, Pandellis. The whole of Maris knows that the Pandellis are born with chips of ice floating in their veins. That they are cold and feel nothing. Whereas the Umbray—"

The Fisk woman whirled around to face him. "The Umbray are as bad as the Pandellis. They are simply better at deceiving, slippery as the eels that coil in the river slime," she spat. "My clan, however—"

"Shut your serpent's mouth, Fisk!" growled the Umbray man, raising a shimmering silver arm.

The three stepped closer to one another, crowding Rowan between them. Their voices rose, loud and bitter. Around them the crowd muttered, drawing into separate groups. Pandellis. Umbray. Fisk.

Webbed hands felt for knives, long and narrow. Blades flashed and glittered in the sun.

Rowan's head was spinning. He looked around at the strange pale faces, twisted with fury, the thin wide lips, open, shouting, the flat eyes glazed with anger.

Hot rage rose within him. He hated these people. He hated them all. Their stupid, murderous rivalry had killed his mother.

He gritted his teeth. "Stop it!" he shouted, clapping his hands to his ears. *"Stop it!"*

With quick, hissing breaths, the Maris stiffened, fell silent and drew back. Their faces grew watchful.

The wind wailed, the waves crashed on the shore.

A lump rose in Rowan's throat. He felt as though he was choking. His eyes burned with tears. He swallowed and blinked to hold them back.

At last he found his voice.

"Take me to the Cavern of the Crystal," he said. "Take me to my mother! Now!"

* * *

As Rowan walked, he stared straight ahead at the slim back of the Umbray man who led the way. Dimly he was aware of the Fisk woman gliding along on his left, the Pandellis man on his right. They weren't very much taller than he was, yet now that his sudden rage had died, leaving numbness behind, he felt trapped by them. Hemmed in, surrounded, helpless.

Swiftly the group moved through the streets, cutting through the green, blue and silver of the milling crowd like a great fish through water.

"The Chooser ... the Chooser ..." Rowan heard the voices as he passed. The people were talking about him. They knew. They knew what had happened to his mother. Perhaps some of them even knew who had poisoned her, and why.

Soon she will breathe no more.

The words were so final. And yet ... Rowan quickened his pace until he was almost treading on the Umbray man's heels. How did the Maris know this for sure? They did not know his mother. They did not know her strength. Perhaps even now something could be done to help her.

"How much further?" he demanded aloud. Suddenly he was terrified that Jiller would die before he reached her.

"No further," said the Pandellis man briefly. "We have arrived." His shoulder touched Rowan's as they made a sharp turn to the right, towards the sea.

Waves crashed and pounded. Rowan felt spray on his face. He looked up and around.

They were standing in front of a rounded, sand-coloured building with huge doors covered in gleaming pearlshell. On the roof was a cupped shape where a flame would burn to tell the whole of Maris that the Choosing was completed and that the Chooser was about to name the new Keeper. Now it was cold and empty.

In front of the building was a courtyard of pale green stones. Behind it was the sea, dashing itself against the rocks. And across the water, ringed with white foam, was the darkness of the Island.

The Umbray man stopped, and stood aside. "You must enter alone, Chooser of Rin," he said with careful respect.

The woman of Fisk made a quick movement, as though she was about to speak. But then she appeared to change her mind. She looked down at her hands, and kept silence.

Rowan felt, rather than saw, the three Maris people watching him as he walked towards the building. He no longer cared what they did, or what they thought. As he pushed open the shining doors and entered the strange round room beyond, he did not even feel afraid. It was as though he was beyond feeling anything. As though he was watching himself in a dream.

The doors swung closed behind him and he found that he was alone.

The room was large. Its walls and ceiling were curved. They, and the floor, were made of polished stone, hard, smooth and shining. Candles burning in holders fixed to the floor gave the only light.

A stairway in one corner led downwards.

Rowan went to the head of the stairway. Below, he could see

light glimmering. He put his hand on the railing, and his foot on the first stair.

Welcome, Chooser of Rin.

The voice echoed in Rowan's brain. His head jerked up. Shocked, he looked around.

I am below. Come to me.

The voice was soft, beckoning. Rowan obeyed it.

He knew that he was about to meet the Keeper of the Crystal.

7 – The Keeper

he stairs wound down, down. Rowan lost count of them. He realised that he was under the earth, under the sea. A soft, blue-green glow lit his way.

The walls on either side of him were stone, and the steps themselves were stone, hard and cold under his feet. There was the sound of dripping water and the smell of salt and sea plants.

With every step he took, the more his feeling grew that something was drawing him in. His legs seemed to be moving without his willing it. It was as though he was being pulled down through water by an invisible net.

Fear rose in him, overwhelming every other feeling, every thought.

He shivered, and gripped the railing till his knuckles turned white. He wanted to sink down to the cold stone. He wanted to claw his way back up to the surface. But still he moved down, down.

Do not be afraid. It is the Crystal's power you feel. It will not harm you. And your mother is here with me.

The voice filled his mind, lapping over his fear, washing it away, leaving sorrow and shame in its place.

Mother, Rowan thought. Mother is there. How could I have forgotten? How could I have hesitated? Even for a minute?

Now his fear seemed like madness. Holding tightly to the railing to stop himself from stumbling, he moved on. The blue-green light grew brighter. The sound of dripping water grew louder.

At last he saw that he was nearly at the bottom of the stairs. Ahead, there was a wall of shining rock. And cut into it was an archway, curtained by falling drops of water that glittered like tiny crystals in the light that flooded from the Cavern beyond.

We are here.

Rowan no longer needed the voice to lead him. He could feel the power of the Crystal, beaming out from the Cavern as strongly as the light.

He stepped from the last stair and in two strides had plunged through the watery veil. Chill, salty droplets pattered softly on his face, filled his eyes and clung to his hair. Then he felt sand beneath his feet. He looked up. Through a blur he saw gleaming rock walls, running with water, and light.

"Again, welcome, Chooser of Rin."

This time the voice had spoken aloud. Whispering, husky, ancient, it echoed from the dripping walls over and over again till every corner of the Cavern seemed filled with the sound. There was no way of telling where the speaker was. Rowan rubbed at his eyes, looked wildly around.

Blue-green light flooded the space, so that the air was like deep, clear water lit by the sun. The source of the light was somewhere in the centre of the room, but Rowan did not even glance at it. For to one side, on a couch draped with silken cloth, was Jiller.

He ran to her, dropping onto his knees beside the couch. She was very still. Her eyes were closed. The hand he touched was cool. But when he put his face close to hers he could feel her soft breath. It was as though she was simply asleep.

She sleeps. She dreams. And with every dream she slips further away from the shore of life.

"Mother," he whispered. "Mother, it's me. It's Rowan." Drops of water from his face and hair fell on her cheek. He brushed them away.

The pale lips slowly curved into a faint smile. Rowan's heart thumped. She could hear him! He gripped her hand tightly.

"Mother, wake up," he begged. "You must fight the dreams. Fight the poison. You are strong. You must not die! You must live! For Annad. For Jonn. For me!"

A tiny line appeared between Jiller's eyebrows, and her eyelids flickered.

"Do not disturb her peace, Rowan," whispered a voice. "She cannot wake. Say farewell, and let her rest. You are the Chooser now."

Rowan spun around. But the words of anger he had been about to utter died on his lips when he met the eyes of the being who had spoken.

The Keeper of the Crystal was sitting motionless in the centre of the room, bathed in light.

She did not look old as the people of Rin looked old. She was not wrinkled like Lann. But Rowan knew at once that never had he seen a living creature so ancient. She seemed almost transparent. She was so faded, so thin and shrunken, and her delicate skin was so fine and pale, that it was difficult to see her clearly against the background of her chair.

And her eyes! They were huge in her tiny face. They seemed to speak of the wisdom and the knowledge of ages, and, above all, of a terrible yearning for rest. Such things I have seen, the eyes seemed to say. Such things I have known. But now I am tired. So tired.

Her tiny hands, the webs between the fingers almost transparent, spread lovingly over the source of the light—a huge, glowing crystal she held on her lap. Now she bent slowly towards it. The light flooded her face, and she shut her eyes, as if basking in warmth.

"The Candidates are waiting for you, Rowan of Rin," she said. "The Choosing must go on without delay. My time draws near."

Rowan felt himself begin to shiver all over. "One of the Candidates gave my mother poison," he said.

"It may be," answered the Keeper.

"Which one?"

"I cannot tell. The Crystal is dim. I no longer see as far as the Island. And I cannot read the thoughts of those trained to veil their minds, as the Candidates have been from earliest childhood. The poison is an ancient Mirril brew called Death Sleep. It has not been seen in Maris for centuries. It kills slowly, but surely. That is all I can tell you."

The Mirril. Experts in poison. Suddenly Rowan was back in Rin, under the Teaching Tree, listening to Timon's tales of the clans of Maris. The Mirril. Experts in poison. And for every poison ...

The whispering voice went on, breaking into his memories. "Rowan! Attend to me! Time is short. You must continue the Choosing."

"How can I continue?" Rowan demanded. "How can I, knowing that one of the Candidates is a murderer? While my mother lies here, slipping away from life?"

"You can because you must. As your ancestors have done before you," said the Keeper. "And the Mirril Choosers before them. So it has always been." She hunched over the Crystal. Waiting.

"Just because a thing has always been, that does not mean it must always be." The words burst from Rowan before he thought about them.

The Keeper breathed a long sigh. Slowly she opened her eyes.

Rowan glanced behind him, at his mother lying on the couch. He knew what she would say to this. She would urge him to be strong. To accept the pain, and do his duty. As her grandmother did. As she would have done. As the people of their family had done for centuries.

"Yes," said the Keeper, as he turned back to face her. "You must be strong."

She had read his mind.

Rowan looked straight into her face. "I will be strong, Keeper of Maris," he said. "I will be strong in my own way."

In the Keeper's eyes he thought he saw a spark, like an ember flaring suddenly in a dying fire. Perhaps it was anger. Perhaps it was surprise. Or—something else. It was impossible to tell. No movement disturbed the smoothness of her face.

"There must be an antidote for Death Sleep," Rowan said.

She shook her head. "Nothing can be done." She bent her head to the Crystal once more.

Rowan clenched his fists. She was lying to him. He knew it. Again he remembered Timon's words.

The Mirril. Experts in poison. A thousand and one deadly poisons. And for every poison, an antidote.

For every problem, a solution. For every poison, an antidote.

But there was no way that he could make the Keeper tell what she must know. Her mind was fixed on the Choosing. On the need for haste. She was not willing to spend precious time searching for a cure for Jiller. Old and wise and rich in knowledge she might be, but she was still a Maris.

"The death of one is of no account," Perlain had gasped in the Rin village square.

That was the Maris way.

But old Lann had answered, "This is your belief, but not ours."

"Not ours," Rowan said under his breath.

The Crystal glowed. Somewhere beyond the Cavern he heard a grating sound, as of a door sliding open.

"I have summoned the Candidates," said the Keeper. She raised herself from the Crystal and leaned back in her chair.

Again the Crystal glowed. Still the Keeper's face did not change. Yet Rowan had the feeling that her mind was fixed on something outside the room.

"Your friend Jonn of the Orchard approaches," she said. "But I must deny him entry to the Cavern. Jonn is full of sorrow and anger. He wishes to avenge your mother's death."

"My mother is not dead," said Rowan loudly. His voice echoed. *Not dead. Not dead.*

On the silk-covered couch, Jiller stirred.

There was a sound from the back of the room.

"Enter," said the Keeper.

Three figures stood framed in the doorway. One wore silver, one blue, one green.

Rowan stared at them. He had expected the Candidates to be at least as old as his mother, or Jonn. But these people were much younger. For a moment this surprised him. Then he remembered that the Crystal brought with it the knowledge and memories of a thousand years of Maris history. Age and experience of life were not important qualities for the Candidates: just the tests of brainpower, set down by Orin the Wise, for which they had studied all their lives. Intelligence was important. Determination was important.

And a will to win is important, thought Rowan savagely. And, it seems, a murderous heart. He went on watching the figures by the door. His mind was cold with loathing.

One of you had a reason to cheat my mother of life, he thought. And you think you have succeeded. But somehow I am going to defeat you. And no one, not even the Keeper of the Crystal, is going to stop me.

8 – The Candidates

Asha of Umbray," said the Keeper.

The silver-clad figure stepped forward and bowed. She was tall, for a Maris, and looked down at Rowan, meeting his gaze without flinching.

"I greet you, Chooser of Rin," she said in a level voice. "The fate of Maris is in your hands."

Are you the one? Rowan thought, staring deep into her steady, pale grey eyes. Could you look at me like this if you had poisoned my mother, Asha? Perhaps you could, for the Umbray are skilled at deceiving, I am told. Slippery, like the eels that coil in the river slime. Did you find my strong, practical mother difficult to twine around your finger? Did you think it would be easier to impress a younger, more timid Chooser? A boy? Like me?

"Seaborn of Fisk," droned the Keeper's voice.

The green figure bowed and repeated Asha's words. He was even taller than she was, and looked stronger. He stood straight, and held his arms rigidly by his sides. But he spoke softly, and as he spoke his eyes kept drifting to the still figure on the couch, and back to the Keeper's chair.

Or is it you who is guilty, Seaborn of Fisk? thought Rowan. Is that why you cannot look at me? Was it you who slipped the poison into the Chooser's food or drink, thinking that as a woman she might favour the girl Asha instead of you? Or do your eyes slide away from mine because you are disappointed, brave, strong Fisk? Did you think my mother was going to choose you? Are you sorry that now you must face me in her place?

"Doss of Pandellis," said the Keeper.

The blue figure stepped forward, and again the bow, and the words, were repeated.

Doss was younger than the other Candidates. He was slighter and smaller, too, and his eyes seemed darker, deeper and more mysterious.

A memory floated into Rowan's mind. Perlain, looking at him curiously. Perlain's words: *Your eyes have the look of one who has seen the Great Serpent, and lived. Deep, and full of knowledge. Strange in a boy so young. I have known only one other.*

Are you Perlain's "other", Doss? thought Rowan. You are of the Pandellis clan, like him. Did Perlain see in me something that reminded him of you? Did others see it? Others in your clan? Did they tell you? Did they think that I would feel closer to you than my mother would? That I would be more likely to choose you? Is that why …?

"The Chooser is ready, Candidates," said the Keeper. "He has only to join with the Crystal, in place of his mother. Then you can return to the Island, and the Choosing can once again begin."

The three bowed their heads.

Join with the Crystal? thought Rowan. What does that mean? Could this be my chance? He felt a small flutter of fearful hope.

"I tell you all," the Keeper warned. "If anything should happen to this boy, as happened to his mother, there will be no time to begin the Choosing for a third time."

She twisted her chair around to face them.

"The Crystal dims," she croaked, looking at them one by one. "Soon I shall die. And if no new Keeper stands beside me at my death, to take the Crystal's knowledge from me and renew its power, the Crystal too will die. Then the Maris clans will be divided once more, and with the Crystal dimmed for ever there will be no protection when the Zebak come again to our shores, as certainly they will. For us, and for this land, all will be lost."

Lost, lost, lost, whispered the echoes.

The Candidates lifted their heads and stood silent.

"Give me your hand, Chooser of Rin," said the Keeper.

Rowan hesitated. His heart was hammering in his chest. He forced himself to be calm. "Please explain to me why I must do this," he said quietly.

Again, something flickered in the Keeper's eyes. Anger? thought Rowan. Amusement?

"The Crystal must know you, through me," she said. "Once this has happened, it will recognise you as the only Chooser. Please hurry. Jonn of the Orchard is very near. I would have this finished before he arrives demanding entry."

Rowan stepped forward. With his whole being he concentrated, hiding his thoughts, waiting for the moment.

I will be strong in my own way.

He stretched out his hand. The Keeper's webbed fingers touched his. Soft, cool, damp. Rowan felt a tingling running up his arm.

Now, he thought. He shut his eyes and gripped the fingers tightly. Then he toppled, fell, plunged into the deep, deep water of the Keeper's mind, the Keeper's memories.

Pictures.

Beauty, and light. Waves curling, blue-green, breaking to hissing white foam on golden sand. A child, laughing, free, ducking, diving, playing, with friends. Long, long ago ...

Study, teachers, advisors, candles burning far into the night. The Crystal, bright as the sun, beckoning. A world shrunk to a cavern beneath the earth ...

Panicking, Rowan struggled, falling deeper. Into older minds, older memories.

Ancient seas. Creatures twisting, hunting, hidden under glittering water ... the Great Serpent towering above me, fangs dripping poison ...

Poison. Rowan caught the word, and held it like a lifeline. He shut out the swirling pictures. Made his own picture.

Jiller, my mother. Poisoned. Lying so still. Dreaming while her life slips away.

He fixed his mind on the picture, and the words Death Sleep. *Tell me*, he demanded. *Tell me, Keeper.*

The Crystal dims ... I am so tired ... there is no time ...

Tell me!

And then, suddenly, something gave way, and the answer was there before his eyes. He saw a jar, held in small webbed hands. The jar was half filled with silvery liquid. As Rowan watched, the liquid

changed colour, becoming as blue as the sky. The blue changed to
green. Then the liquid changed again, losing all colour, becoming
crystal clear. And a voice spoke.

> *"To mix the brew that wakes Death Sleep*
> *Fill one spread hand with silver deep.*
> *In hungry pool moons raise their heads:*
> *Pluck one and add the tears it sheds.*
> *Stir slowly with new fighter's quill,*
> *Three times, no more, and let it still.*
> *Add venom from your greatest fear—*
> *One drop—and then the truth is clear."*

With a gasp of triumph, Rowan broke free. He staggered back
from the Keeper's chair. His mind was spinning. His hand was
burning.

Slowly he opened his eyes. He saw darkness, shot with darts and
swirls of colour. Then, at last, his sight cleared.

The Keeper was slumped back in her chair. Her eyes were closed.
The Crystal pulsed dimly under her limp hands. Behind the chair
stood Asha, Seaborn and Doss, staring at him as though he were
some demon from the deep.

"What have you done?" breathed Seaborn.

"What I had to do," said Rowan. The words sounded strong, but
he was not feeling strong at all. His legs wobbled like the legs of a
new-born bukshah calf. The hand with which he had gripped the
Keeper's fingers still throbbed and burned.

The Keeper's eyelids fluttered and opened.

"Keeper—" Asha began. But the ancient woman did not even
glance at her. Her whole attention was fixed on Rowan.

"What do you want?" she asked bluntly.

Rowan did not have the chance to answer, for at that moment
there was the sound of thudding feet on stone steps, and Strong
Jonn burst through the curtain of dripping water, into the Cavern.

He looked around rapidly, taking in everything in a single glance.
Then he strode to Jiller's side and bent over her. He gathered her in
his arms, lifting her to his chest, calling her name. She did not stir.

He turned to Rowan, grim-faced. "She spoke of danger, but I did not really believe," he said. "I thought, no, not Jiller. Nothing could happen to Jiller. Rowan—"

"It will be all right, Jonn," said Rowan quietly. "There is an antidote for the poison Mother has been given. The Keeper has just shown it to me."

There was a gasp from behind the Keeper's chair. Rowan looked up quickly. Asha? Seaborn? Doss? He could not tell.

"I will not let Mother die," he said. And he was telling himself, and everyone in the room, as well as Jonn.

"The Choosing must continue," said the Keeper urgently.

Rowan turned to face her.

"No," he said. He heard his own voice shaking as the word echoed around the Cavern walls. "I am sorry, but the Choosing must wait."

He felt Jonn's eyes fixed on him. He knew that Asha, Seaborn and Doss were staring, too. But he could see only the Keeper.

"I know that time is short," he said. "But before anything else can be done my mother must have the antidote to Death Sleep. You must give it to me, Keeper. Or tell me where to find it. I must help my mother. Nothing is more important than that."

9 – The Rhyme

ou said you would be strong, Rowan of Rin," the Keeper accused him. "You let me join you to the Crystal, confirm you as Chooser. You deceived me."

"I said I would be strong in my own way," said Rowan, trying desperately to sound calm and firm while his legs trembled beneath him. "You must tell me what I must do to save my mother."

"It is impossible!" the Keeper said. She clawed at the Crystal with her tiny hands as though willing it to save her from what was happening. But it only glowed feebly.

"Speak to him!" she ordered the Candidates. But they stood silent, wondering.

The Keeper took a deep breath. "I told you. Death Sleep has not been used in Maris since the time of the Mirril."

Rowan glanced at Jonn. He had put Jiller down and was standing beside her couch, his fists clenched. Rowan knew what he was thinking. If the poison was so rare it should not be too difficult to find out where it had come from. To find out which clan had discovered the Mirril secret, and used it.

But Rowan was not interested in revenge. Not now.

"There is an antidote," he repeated. "I saw it, Keeper. A silver liquid, changing to blue, then green, then becoming clear. I saw it, held in Maris hands."

The Keeper's steady gaze did not waver. "The hands were Orin's," she said.

"Orin," whispered Asha. Seaborn raised his hand to his mouth. Doss remained expressionless.

"Orin was making the antidote to Death Sleep on the Island, the day he found the Crystal," the Keeper said. "That is what you saw in my mind, Chooser of Rin. You saw Orin's memories. The last drop of the mixture in that jar was used five hundred years ago. There is no more."

No more, no more, whispered the echoes.

"Then the mixture must be made again," said Rowan, lifting his chin. "If they were Orin's hands I saw, the words I heard were his also."

"What words, Rowan?" urged Jonn.

The three Candidates leaned forward as one. Even cold Asha. Even withdrawn Doss.

"The recipe for the antidote," said Rowan.

He said the words aloud. He had no trouble remembering them. He felt as though they had been burnt into his brain.

"To mix the brew that wakes Death Sleep
Fill one spread hand with silver deep.
In hungry pool moons raise their heads:
Pluck one and add the tears it sheds.
Stir slowly with new fighter's quill,
Three times, no more, and let it still.
Add venom from your greatest fear—
One drop—and then the truth is clear."

Asha snorted.

"What ingredients are these?" muttered Seaborn.

Doss's eyes gleamed with interest. "Orin made a secret of his recipe," he said.

"Yes," said the Keeper. "And his secrets are mine." She turned to Rowan. "By Orin's will I cannot tell you how to read the rhyme," she said coldly. "But, believe me, even if I could tell you what the ingredients were, you would fail to obtain them. The antidote cannot be made."

"It can," said Rowan. "It must."

The Crystal glowed. Rowan felt a tug—a pulling at his mind. He fought it desperately.

"You cannot make me do your will, Keeper," he gasped. "You cannot change my mind. You are too weak."

"There is no time!" hissed the Keeper. "And what you plan is foolish, boy of Rin. If preparing the antidote was as simple a matter as you seem to think, I would have it here already, and your mother would be healing now. I am not a monster. I would cure her if I could. But the antidote to Death Sleep is made of things rare and almost impossible to obtain. You alone could never gain them, never—"

"He would not be alone," Strong Jonn broke in. "I would be with him."

He left Jiller's side and strode to the centre of the Cavern to stand beside Rowan. He towered over the Keeper. Compared with him she seemed as small and fragile as a child. But she shook her head, quite unafraid.

"By Orin's decree the Island is forbidden to all except the Keeper," she said. "And, at the time of the Choosing, the Chooser and the Candidates, who must be alone. You cannot go there, Jonn of the Orchard, on pain of death."

Jonn's mouth tightened. He turned to look at Jiller, still and pale, scarcely breathing. "There are things I fear more than my own death," he said.

"I, too," said the Keeper. "And one of them is breaking my trust. You cannot go to the Island, Jonn. I will prevent you. I still have power enough for that."

"So Rowan goes alone, by your will." Jonn's eyes were hard. "He goes alone, and we wait here. And you say he cannot succeed alone. So he does not succeed. Neither does he return to choose a new Keeper. So Jiller dies. And you die. And the Crystal dims, for ever. Is that not breaking your trust also?"

The Keeper smiled faintly. "You argue well, man of Rin. But you cannot go to the Island."

There was silence, broken only by the soft pattering of endlessly falling water.

Rowan saw what he must do. He needed help. He knew where he must take it. There was no choice. He looked at the three figures still standing behind the Keeper's chair. Masking the distrust and fear in his eyes, he spoke to them directly, for the first time.

"Asha of Umbray, Seaborn of Fisk, Doss of Pandellis. The Island is not forbidden to you. Will you help me?"

He had thought they would agree readily. After all, he was the

Chooser. They would want to impress and please him. Each would want to convince him that it had not been they who had poisoned his mother.

But they hesitated, their eyes on the Keeper. They would not help him against her will.

She sat motionless, bent over the Crystal. Then, finally, she nodded.

"Very well," she said, her voice flat, expressionless. "What must be, must be. But I warn you. At sunrise, my life will end. And the Crystal will die with me, if the Choosing is not complete by then."

"I will return in time to finish the Choosing," whispered Rowan. "I promise."

"No doubt you mean what you say," said the Keeper. "You will return—if it is within your power. But the course you have decided to take is a dangerous one, Chooser. Dangerous for you, and for Maris, and for the whole of this land. Even now, perhaps, Zebak ships speed towards our shores. They will have had word of the dimming of the Crystal. They have spies everywhere."

"This is always a danger at the time of the Choosing," said Rowan through lips that suddenly seemed dry and stiff.

The Keeper looked at her hands, the webs transparent in the Crystal-light. "But only once before has the power of the Crystal itself been in such danger. Once before, three hundred years ago, when the Mirril perished. And then your ancestor, Lieth, accepted for your people the burden of the Choosing, and let the Crystal live for the good of all."

She raised her eyes. "You look very like Lieth, Rowan of Rin," she said. "Very, very like. It is strange to think that as he saved the Crystal's power, you may be the one who destroys it."

Rowan went cold. He glanced at Jonn, who was watching him gravely. Just for a moment his determination weakened. Then he looked at his mother, and knew that he was right.

Seaborn had been fidgeting restlessly. "Let us go," he urged. "Already the sun is on its downward path to the west. We should take advantage of the light."

Rowan turned to Jonn. "Will you see to Star while I am gone?" he asked.

Jonn nodded. Then he dug in his pocket and brought out a soft leather pouch. He tipped what it contained into his hand. It was a small, shining glass jar, with a gleaming silver top shaped like a flying fish skimming the waves.

"This was for Jiller," he said. "I had just bought it at the market when Perlain ran to me with the news of her illness. I thought it— beautiful. And therefore fit for her. Take it now, Rowan, and fill it with what will save her life. I can think of no better use for it."

His voice was strong and calm. But his work-hardened finger quivered as he gently touched the tiny silver fish before slipping the jar into its pouch once again, and handing it to Rowan.

Rowan put the pouch carefully into his own pocket.

He wanted to say something that would comfort Jonn, but he knew that anything he said would sound false. He could not promise that he would succeed in his quest. And he knew that whatever troubles and dangers he was about to face, they would be nothing to the pain Strong Jonn would suffer, waiting helplessly here.

"I will do my best, Jonn," he murmured. "My very best."

Jonn put a heavy hand on his shoulder. "I know you will," he said. "And my thoughts and hopes go with you."

Rowan turned away and walked to where the Candidates stood waiting for him.

"Are you not going to farewell your mother, Chooser of Rin?" croaked the Keeper, watching him through slitted eyes as he passed her chair.

Rowan felt a surge of anger. And the anger gave him the courage to say the words he had not been able to say to Jonn. "No. I do not need to farewell my mother," he said, loudly enough for all to hear. "She will still be here, and alive, when I return with the antidote."

"We shall see," said the Keeper. "We shall see."

10 – The Island

They walked through the tunnel to the Island in silence and in single file. Rowan was leading. Asha, Doss and Seaborn had all stood back respectfully, waiting for him to enter the dark and dripping passage first.

Now they walked behind him, measuring their steps to his. Their soft shoes made no sound on the smooth, damp stones. Several times already Rowan had looked back, not sure that they were still following. But always they were there, three paces behind him, their eyes watchful.

They carried flaming torches to light their way. Shadows flickered eerily on the roof and walls of rock. Water gleamed where it seeped through cracks and trickled to the floor.

We are walking under the sea, Rowan kept thinking. The idea of that vast, moving weight of water above and around them made him shiver.

He turned his thoughts to the task ahead. In the Cavern of the Crystal he had been so intent on forcing the Keeper to open the way for him that he had not really had time to think. And since then, the strangeness of his journey under the sea had driven everything from his mind.

He had not yet tried to guess what Orin's riddling list of ingredients might mean. He had not really considered the Keeper's warning that he had no hope of obtaining the ingredients, even if he knew what they were.

But now he thought of both these things. He wondered if the three Maris padding behind him were thinking of them too. Or were they too worried about the Crystal, and the Keeper, and themselves, and the delay they were all being forced to suffer, to think at all?

He saw a dim light ahead. The tunnel was ending. He realised that he could hear the sound of waves, too. A dull, distant crashing of water on the jagged rocks and cliffs of the Island.

"At the end of the tunnel there is a stair, Chooser of Rin."

It was Asha's voice, flat and cold.

Rowan turned to look at her. "Perhaps it would be better if you called me by my name," he said, trying to smile.

She did not smile back. "As you wish," she answered.

Rowan turned back towards the light at the end of the tunnel. Asha, at least, was not trying hard to please him, he thought. She was not pretending to be anything other than she was.

Perhaps that is what her trainers have told her to do, a voice in his head told him. Remember what Perlain said. The Candidates study the ways of Rin, so they will know how to please the Chooser. Perhaps Asha's trainers have told her that we of Rin despise pretence. So she plays the game of seeming to be honest with me while she schemes in secret. Who knows what she is really thinking?

He shook his head to drive the uncomfortable thought out. He wished he could trust the three people with him. It would be hard enough for him to do what he had to do, without wondering all the time who was speaking the truth, and who was lying. Let alone who was a poisoner, and who was innocent.

At the end of the tunnel rose steep stone stairs, just as Asha had said. Daylight glimmered at the top.

Rowan began to climb. The sound of waves became louder with every step he took. The light grew stronger, streaming down through the bars of what seemed to be a gate.

He began to move faster, though by now he was panting, and his legs were aching. Whatever dangers the Island might hold for him, he was eager to breathe fresh air again, and see the sky above his head.

With relief he climbed the last few stairs, pushed open the rusting iron gate, and stumbled through it. His legs were trembling after the climb. He stood gasping, trying to catch his breath.

He had been so long underground that the daylight seemed blinding. His dazzled eyes watered so much that he could hardly see. He blinked furiously, wiping at them with the back of his hand. As his sight slowly returned to normal, he saw that he was standing on the Island's rocky shore. In front of him was thick forest, hung with vines.

He turned around to see Asha, Seaborn and Doss following him out into the open. The iron gate clanged shut behind them, screening off the stairs that seemed to fall away into darkness. Beyond, waves dashed themselves into foam on the rocks. And far away, across the choppy water, stretched the golden sand and rounded buildings of Maris.

Narrowing his eyes against the spray, Rowan searched the buildings, trying to pick out Star's stable. He knew Star would wonder where he was, when Jonn came in his place to fill her water bowl. She would miss him, and be unhappy.

On the beach children darted in and out of the waves, uncaring of the chill wind. Here and there men and women sat mending nets. A lone hooded figure, a woman dressed in the green of the Fisk clan, paced the shore.

For some reason she looked familiar. It was something about the way she was walking. Her arms were folded under her cape, and her back was very straight. Ah, of course. It was the stern Fisk woman who had been one of his guides to the Cavern of the Crystal.

Rowan became aware that someone was standing beside him, and slowly turned his head.

It was Seaborn. He did not know he was being observed. His face was grave, and his eyes were fixed on the beach.

What was he looking at? The children? The buildings? The people mending nets? Or was it the woman of Fisk he watched?

The woman on the beach stopped, turned, and faced the sea. She stood motionless. Her green cape whipped around her in the wind, the hood blowing back from her face.

She is looking at us, thought Rowan. He glanced again at Seaborn. He too was standing perfectly still, as though concentrating with all his strength. The salt spray beat against his face like rain, but he did not turn away or narrow his eyes against it as Rowan had had to do.

They do not move, or wave, or make any sign, thought Rowan. But still she is sending him some sort of message from the Fisk. If they cannot read each other's thoughts, then the message is in how she stands. Or even that she has appeared on the beach at all. The plots and plans of these people are never-ending.

A fresh wave of anger rose in him, sticking in his throat. He felt as though he was choking with it.

He must have made some small sound, because Seaborn looked at him quickly, his face surprised and guilty.

"Does your clan know already that the Choosing has been delayed?" Rowan asked bluntly. "Is that what her message is about?"

"Whose message? There is no message," said Seaborn, turning away.

But Rowan knew he was lying.

It's nothing but lies in this place, he thought bitterly. Lies twist in these people's minds like the serpents that coil under the surface of their sea.

Anger still boiled within him. He did not regret letting Seaborn know that he had not been fooled.

I do not have to watch my words, or pretend, with these people, he thought. Whatever else I have to fear, I do not have to fear death at their hands. The Keeper has told them that there is no time to send for another Chooser. None of the Candidates would risk the loss of the Crystal by killing me now.

And yet ... another thought suddenly rose and brushed against Rowan's mind like a slimy thing in the dark. Yet time had always been very short. The Keeper had called for the Choosing when it was already almost too late. The Candidates had known that from the start.

But Jiller had been poisoned. Delay in the Choosing was dangerous for Maris, yet delay had been caused.

The thought grew larger, stronger, and twisted itself into a question.

Why? Why would anyone with the fortunes of Maris at heart have done such a thing? What value would there be to a clan in winning the Choosing, if the Crystal was no more?

Rowan turned to look at the Candidates.

Seaborn had crouched to pull his shoe more tightly around his foot. Or so he pretended. His face was conveniently hidden. Asha and Doss stood apart from each other in the mist of spray—a tall silver figure, cape streaming back in the wind, a smaller figure in blue.

Rowan remembered Perlain's words.

The Candidates study the ways of Rin ... Their trainers know how you think. They have collected news of you since the day you were born.

If these strangers know me, know me truly, they could have guessed that I would not let my mother die without seeking help for her, thought Rowan. They could have guessed that I would delay the Choosing even further. Just as I have done.

His heart thudded. The thought was filling his mind now. He could see it face to face. And it was ugly and terrifying.

He had behaved just as someone had expected he would. He had been trapped into being part of someone's plan.

Someone wanted the Choosing to fail.

Someone wanted the Crystal's power to fade.

And they were using Rowan to help them do it.

11 – The Beginning

We have rested enough. We should delay no longer."

It was Asha's voice, stern and cold.

Rowan swallowed. He did not trust himself to speak. He pressed his hands together, trying to stop them from shaking.

"What is the matter?" asked Seaborn sharply. "Are you ill?"

Rowan felt, rather than saw, the Candidates exchange quick, suspicious glances.

"I am not ill," he forced himself to say.

He drew a shuddering breath, and tried to calm his mind. He thought of Star, of Jonn, of Annad at home in Rin. Of his mother lying dreaming in the Cavern of the Crystal.

Nothing has really changed, he said to himself. Whoever is behind this wickedness, and whatever their reasons are, I must do what I came to do. I must follow Orin's directions. I must make the antidote to Death Sleep. And quickly.

In his pocket was the glass jar Jonn had given him, nestled in its soft leather pouch. He pulled the jar out and looked at it. A beautiful, shining thing, but empty. Waiting to be filled with what would save his mother's life.

He held the jar in his hand and repeated Orin's verse in a low voice.

"To mix the brew that wakes Death Sleep
Fill one spread hand with silver deep.
In hungry pool moons raise their heads:
Pluck one and add the tears it sheds.
Stir slowly with new fighter's quill,
Three times, no more, and let it still.
Add venom from your greatest fear—
One drop—and then the truth is clear."

"These words make no sense to me," said Seaborn.

"They are Orin's words," said Asha harshly. "They are secret words, not intended to be understood by others. For a thousand years they have been hidden. It is wrong to go against Orin's will. So it has always been."

Doss hesitated. "The first line is simple," he began finally. "But the second ... 'silver deep' ..."

"The second is simple also," said Seaborn impatiently. "To begin the brew we must take a handful of water from the deep. From the sea."

Asha looked scornful. "The first two lines a child could under-stand," she said. "It is not they that are the problem."

Rowan unscrewed the lid of the jar. His fingers shook. Do not listen to their squabbling, he said to himself. Think only about what you are doing. Get the water. The first ingredient. Make a start.

He moved away from the Candidates, and walked quickly through the mist of spray towards the rocky edge of the Island.

"Wait, Chooser of Rin," he heard Asha call.

Rowan kept walking. He was angry. You want me to fail in this, Asha, he raged at her in his mind. You have tried to discourage me. But you will not.

He reached the rocks and began to clamber from one to the other, down towards the sea.

It was then, as his anger died, that he saw his danger. The waves flung themselves against the Island, breaking into clouds of spray and sheets of hissing foam. His heavy shoes slipped on the wet, glass-smooth rocks. It was like walking on ice. As he edged closer to the water, chill spray rained on his head and beat into his face, stinging his eyes, blinding him.

His stomach lurched as a wave struck and his right foot slipped from under him. He cried out, struggling desperately to regain his balance. Before his streaming eyes the world tilted crazily ...

Then three pairs of hands were catching at his arms, pulling him back, steadying him. He turned, gasping, to see the faces of Seaborn, Asha and Doss looking at him gravely.

Rowan felt sick. He had so nearly fallen. His head would have struck the iron-hard rocks. The waves would have sucked him into the cold, churning sea.

The Candidates had all moved to save him. Could it be, then, that he had been wrong? That he did not have an enemy among them?

Or was it just that it was not yet time for him to die? Did some- one need him alive, and wasting precious moments, till the Keeper finally slid away from the shores of life and the Crystal dimmed for ever?

Rowan blinked at the three faces before him, and wiped his eyes. "Thank you," he said dully.

Seaborn smiled. "Your shoes are not made for rock-walking, Rowan."

"I told you to wait," said Asha severely. "You must let us swim the dangerous waters, if they are to be swum at all."

"I asked you to help me," Rowan mumbled. "But I do not expect you to risk your lives."

Asha's lips made a straight, hard line. "The death of one of us is of no account," she said. "But if you are lost, the whole of Maris is lost also."

Seaborn nodded. "Give me the jar, and I will fetch the water," he said. "We should waste no more time."

Doss opened his mouth as if to say something, then seemed to change his mind. His eyes, so strangely dreamy for a Maris, slid from Rowan's face to the boiling sea.

"What is it?" Rowan asked him.

"I—I do not believe this water fits the words of the rhyme," said Doss. "I think we must look in another place."

The others stared.

"The sea is the deep," said Asha.

"And all shines silver in the sun," said Seaborn.

Doss shook his head. "The words 'silver deep' are still, and quiet, and full of mystery," he said. "But in this place the sea is wild. It fights the land. It churns itself into foam. I do not think Orin would have called it the silver deep."

"Who are you to know the mind of Orin?" snapped Asha.

Doss looked at the ground and did not answer.

Rowan bit his lip. Slowly he screwed the silver top back on the jar. Now that he thought about it, he could see that Doss was right.

He felt sick with disgust at his own foolishness. He had let anger and fear drive him. He had forgotten how cunning were the Maris folk—and the great Orin more than any. He had been desperate, and far too willing to believe that Orin's first ingredient could be so simple to find.

He had been so unthinking, indeed, that he had nearly lost his life by rushing to collect something which would have proved useless.

I must be more careful, he thought. I must panic no more. I must be as cold as these Maris, if I am to outwit them.

He took a deep breath.

"What do you think the silver deep is, Doss?" he asked quietly.

"I do not know," murmured Doss. "But it must be here. On or around the Island. Because it is here that Orin made his brew."

"We will search, then. Search until we find it." Rowan stuffed the jar back into his pocket, and looked around him. Rocky shore, crashing waves, tufted grass, wild, tangled forest ... Where should they begin?

He repeated the question aloud. "Where should we begin?"

Seaborn's voice rose above the sound of the waves. "The Island is like unknown waters, to us," he said. "None but the Keeper may visit here, except at the time of the Choosing. But often I have sailed around it. And on the other side, the side you cannot see from Maris, there are quiet, sandy bays and sheltered places. Perhaps there ..."

Rowan considered this, then nodded. "We will try," he said. "We will go around the shore. It will not take long. Better that than try to break through the forest."

"If we go to the other side of the Island we will be hidden from Maris," murmured Asha. "And the Crystal is too dim for the Keeper's mind to follow us. If any danger befalls us on the secret side, there will be no help."

"We will have to depend on each other for help," said Rowan.

As the words left his lips he saw the three Candidates again exchange suspicious looks, frown, and touch the knives at their belts.

Despair settled over him. There was little chance that the

Candidates of Fisk, Pandellis and Umbray would depend on one another. For them, at this time, no enemy was more dangerous than one of their own kind.

He began to pick his way along the shore, keeping close to the trees, and as far away as possible from the treacherous rocks.

Asha's words came back to him. Whatever happened on the other side of the Island would not be seen from Maris. He would be quite unprotected. There would be nothing to stop one of the three Candidates from killing him. Whoever it was could kill the others too, then return to the Keeper with the story that they had all fallen by accident into the sea.

Was this journey, too, part of someone's plan?

12 – Out of Sight

Rowan felt lonely and afraid. If only I could talk to someone I know I can trust, he thought.

He glanced behind him. The Candidates were following in single file. Asha, her silver cape reflecting the trees and the sea in turn, was first, gliding along very close to him.

Rowan suddenly realised why she seemed so familiar. Despite her strange looks and clothes, Asha reminded him of Jiller, his mother. She seemed strictly honest, stern, straightforward, determined to do what was right, whatever the cost.

He faced forward again, and moved on. They were rounding the Island now. Soon the Maris shore would be lost to sight.

His thoughts ran on. Yes, Asha reminded him of his mother. Despite his anger at her lack of encouragement, it made him want to trust her. He remembered that Asha was the one who had sounded the warning about the Island's secret side.

But she knew I would not hesitate because of that, he thought. Knew, perhaps, that it would make me all the more determined.

Their trainers know how you think.

I must not forget that, Rowan told himself. I must never forget it.

He turned his thoughts to Seaborn, who was striding behind Asha, tall and solid in green. Seaborn was energetic, confident and strong. A man who could be depended upon. He reminded Rowan of Jonn—Strong Jonn, who had so often helped him and stood beside him in times of danger.

It was Seaborn who had suggested going to the secret side of the Island. He had seemed to suggest it only because he was eager to help. Keen for action, as Jonn would have been.

But was he? Or was he simply carrying out the next step in a plot? Rowan shook his head. He could not be sure of Seaborn either.

So—Doss. Doss was last in the line. He was so much smaller than the others that all Rowan had been able to see of him was a flickering blue shape appearing briefly and then disappearing behind Seaborn's green.

Doss was quiet and dreamy, and more uncertain than the others. Did Doss remind Rowan of anyone?

Yes, of course he did. Doss was like Rowan himself. Surely, then, he was the one to trust.

Yet it was Doss who had raised doubts about the silver deep. It was his seemingly hesitant words that had led finally to this journey, though Doss himself had not suggested it.

Was Doss in fact the cleverest and most dangerous of all?

Rowan's mind spun. Nothing was certain. He was drifting help-lessly in swirling tides of questions and confusion. He slid his hand into his pocket and gripped the silver-topped jar, drawing comfort from its solid hardness.

I can trust none of them, he thought. I can trust only myself.

Suddenly he became aware that he was walking on sand, instead of rock. He looked up and discovered that while he had been thinking, he had rounded the Island's curve without noticing it.

As Seaborn had said, the other side of the Island was a sheltered bay. The trees beside him were no longer a solid mass. Instead, dim, ferny trails wound away into the forest depths, and he could see grassy clearings through the vines and trunks.

Gentler waves broke and foamed on this softer, curving shore. At the other end of the beach a high, jagged cliff rose from the sea like a barrier. Around it, two large birds swooped and called harshly. They were the only sign of life.

Beyond the waves, as far as the eye could see, there was nothing but sea and sky.

Now, thought Rowan, I am truly alone. He forced his mind away from his fear.

Silver deep ...

Rowan looked along the line of waves rolling into the shore. They were smaller than the waves on the other side of the Island, certainly. But still they did not seem to match the words.

He felt a prickling at the back of his neck, and spun around to see Asha, Seaborn and Doss standing close behind him. They had caught up to him and were waiting. How long had they been there? He couldn't say. They moved so silently.

I must tell them what we are going to do next, thought Rowan. And again despair swept over him.

I am not a leader, he thought. I do not know where to turn next. I am a stranger here. I am afraid. I have insisted on doing this thing, and now I do not know where to go or what to do.

He looked again at the three Candidates. And slowly he realised that they seemed different.

Just a couple of hours ago, he would not have seen it. But since then he had become used to seeing Maris faces. They had stopped looking alike to him. He had started to notice expressions and changes of mood in those he spoke to.

Now he saw that Asha, Seaborn and Doss were afraid. Their eyes were wary. They were standing stiffly, holding themselves ready for danger. Their hands hovered close to the knives on their belts.

On this side of the Island they are as much strangers as I am, he thought. They have not studied this place. They cannot see their home. They have never set foot on this sand before. They do not know what they will find here.

For some reason, the thought helped him.

"I think we should start by walking along the sand," he said aloud. "Look left and right, for anything that fits the words."

"The deep is the sea," said Asha, behind him. "We will not find it among trees, Chooser of Rin."

"Deep has more meanings than one," said Doss in a low voice. "The rhyme does not say '*the* silver deep', but 'silver deep' only."

"What difference does that make?" the woman retorted. "It is clear what Orin meant."

Seaborn laughed. "Who are *you*, Asha of Umbray, to know the mind of Orin?" he jeered.

"Watch your slimy tongue, Fisk!" spat Asha.

"Watch your own," said Seaborn.

Rowan said nothing. He felt like shouting at them. He felt like begging them to work together, to help him. But he knew it would be no use.

He trudged along, knowing that they would follow. The sand squeaked under his feet. As he walked, he looked from sea to forest and back again.

His heart sank as the minutes passed.

Nothing. He could see nothing.

Not too far ahead, the sand ended at the foot of the high, rocky cliff that stretched across the beach and jutted far into the sea. Once they reached that, they could go no further. The only place left to search would be the forest itself. And though the Island was small, with no clues to guide them such a search could take days.

If only I knew what I was looking for, Rowan thought desperately. He passed yet another gap in the trees, peered into it, saw waving plumes of tall, spiky grass, and moved on.

One of the birds he had heard before screeched from the forest depths. He glanced towards the sound. And then, as he began to turn his head back to the sea, he saw something. Just a flash, glimpsed from the corner of his eye.

He stopped dead, and took a pace back. He peered through the trees. Yes, there it was again. Somewhere in the green depths there was a glint of silver. Like still, secret water, touched briefly by the sun.

"I think—there's something in there," he said, pointing. He tried to speak calmly, but his heart was thudding with excitement.

Somehow he knew without doubt that he had at last found Orin's silver deep.

13 – Silver Deep

They pushed through the tall grass, and crept cautiously into the forest. For a moment they hesitated, wondering and silent.

The trees rose high on either side of them. Leafy branches, locked together, made a roof over their heads, blocking out the sun. And now that they were beyond the tall grass, they could see that they were standing on a wide path that wound deep into the forest.

Rowan saw Doss shiver as he looked around.

"Who has made this?" Seaborn wondered aloud.

For it was certain that the path had not come about by chance. It was flat and wide—wide enough for the four of them to walk easily side by side. It was edged by high banks of earth that had been pushed aside and then completely overgrown by bushes, moss and ferns.

"It must be the Keeper," said Asha. "For only the Keeper is permitted on the Island. But clearly the path has not been used for a long time."

She pointed at the thick layer of rotting leaves that covered the trail, and the clusters of ferns that uncurled tender fronds here and there.

Rowan nodded. "At least a year," he said. "If these plants grow as they do in Rin."

"Nevertheless," Seaborn said grimly, "we should be on the watch for danger."

They moved forward, their feet sinking into the brown, leafy carpet. Fat grey moths fluttered blindly into their path, brushing their faces with soft wings.

Rowan strained his eyes in the dimness, searching the way ahead for another glint of silver.

Through the trees he saw a flash of brighter green, and heard again the fierce squawking of one of the birds he had seen swooping near the cliff.

It doesn't sound too friendly, he thought. An idea stirred in his mind, but immediately excitement swept it aside. For suddenly, just ahead, while the bird call was still dying away, the silver he was seeking gleamed again.

"There," he gasped. He began to run.

He could hear Asha, Seaborn and Doss hurrying behind him. For once they were having more trouble than he. Their light shoes sank into the softness of the path, slowing them down.

A smell of damp and earth rose from the leaves as they were trampled beneath his feet. It mixed with the other scents of the forest. Fresh leaves, bruised ferns, mould ... and something else.

Rowan's nose twitched as he tried to make out what the something else was. It was a heavy, sweet perfume. Some forest flower, perhaps, but like nothing he had ever smelt in Rin. And it was growing stronger.

The path curved slightly, then opened out into what seemed to be a natural clearing, ringed by trees. Leaves and grass covered the earth around the edge of the clearing, but in the centre rose a smooth, bare brown rock, folded and curved, like a huge, huddled animal sleeping.

The sky made a pale circle overhead, lighting the clearing. The rough cliff towered grey above the treetops on one side.

There was no wind. No noise, except the distant sound of the sea. It was a still, secret place. On the rock, puddles of water gleamed.

"There must be a pool up there," Rowan whispered. "A spring, fed from a stream under the rock."

There was no reason to whisper. But Rowan's skin was prickling. He sensed danger.

Perhaps it was the light, after the dimness of the forest. Perhaps it was the strange, sweet smell that was suddenly all around him. Or perhaps it was the silence of the place, and the strangeness of it.

Asha, Seaborn and Doss, too, seemed to have been struck dumb. Rowan only knew they were behind him because he could hear them breathing.

He stepped on to the rock. They followed as he slowly climbed to the top.

And there, just as he had hoped, was a deep pool of crystal-clear water, cupped in the rock. It was almost perfectly round, and so small that two people could touch hands across it.

Far below the surface, silver gleamed. The bottom of the pool was covered in some sort of shining mud or sand.

But this was not what made Rowan gasp, and his heart fill with hope. There was something else under that clear, rippling surface. Something round and white, shining through the water like a full moon floating in the sky.

It was a flower. Its face was turned to the sky, the petals fanning out to make a perfect circle. Rowan could smell its perfume rising from the water. The heavy, sweet scent he had noticed before.

In hungry pool moons raise their heads ...

"Flowers cannot grow under water," exclaimed Asha, shocked out of her silence.

She sounded almost angry, because the laws she had thought to be fixed had been overturned. For Asha, flowers grew in the air and sun. That was how it had always been. That was how it always must be.

But Seaborn's face was alive with curiosity and excitement. "This one does," he said. "And it is the second ingredient. We have found two in one place! Quickly, Rowan. The water, and then the flower."

Rowan pulled the glass jar from his pocket and unscrewed the lid.

Fill one spread hand with silver deep ...

He spread his hand, bent to the water, looked at his fingers, hesitated ...

"Wait," breathed Doss, touching his arm. "Remember—"

Rowan barely heard him. He was staring, fascinated, at the water. For suddenly the moon flower was disappearing from sight. The pool was no longer clear. It was turning silver as he watched.

He turned to Seaborn, to tell him. And in that instant he saw the man's face change, felt himself being roughly pulled to the ground.

"Beware!" yelled Seaborn.

A terrible, piercing cry split the air. Great wings beat above their heads. There was a splash. Water flowed out onto the rock.

And then a huge green bird was flying away, soaring back to its cliff-top, several small, wriggling fish clutched in its claws. Rowan had never seen such a bird. It was as big as he was.

Seaborn snorted with shaken laughter. "I thought it was attacking us. But it was only intent on filling its belly! And the bellies of its young. No wonder Orin called this 'hungry pool'."

Doss began to speak, but his voice was drowned out by Asha. She had scrambled to her feet, and was pointing fearfully at the pool.

"That light!" she called. "What is it?"

Rowan crawled back to the edge of the pool. The perfume of the flower was very strong. And the water looked like melted silver. Silver as Asha's cloak. Silver as sunlight striking water. Silver as a fish. He could hardly look at it, so brightly was it flashing in the sun.

In an instant he realised what had happened. The fish, diving for safety from the bird, had stirred up the shining sand at the bottom of the pool.

Fill one spread hand with silver deep ...

"Seaborn!" he yelled. "Quickly! Before the silver sinks again. Take a handful of the water!"

Seaborn hesitated, puzzled.

"My hand will not do," shouted Rowan. "I realised it just before the bird struck. Spread, my hand is useless. The rhyme means a Maris hand. With webbed fingers, like Orin's."

Seaborn nodded, and sprang to Rowan's side.

"*No!*" cried Doss.

But already Seaborn had scooped his spread hand through the water.

He began to lift it out again. Rowan readied the jar to collect the water. Then suddenly Seaborn screamed in agony.

He jerked his hand into the air. Silver liquid brimmed from the wide cup made by his spread fingers. But the whole of the back of his hand and his wrist were covered by dozens of wriggling fish. Even out of the water they were still biting into the flesh, then dropping back into the pool covered in pale Maris blood.

Asha shrieked with disgust and horror.

"Hungry pool ..." murmured Doss.

"Rowan, the jar," shouted Seaborn, shuddering with pain. "Oh, quickly, for Orin's sake! They are eating me alive!"

Wordlessly Rowan thrust the container towards him. With his free hand Seaborn gripped his injured wrist, steadying it, and tipped the precious silver liquid into the jar.

Fish were still falling from his flesh. His blood was dripping freely into the pool. And the pool was swarming, seething, as the fish feasted.

Groaning, Seaborn staggered back. He plucked the last of the squirming creatures from his hand and threw it to the rock. He swayed. His face was as pale as the underbelly of a fish.

Rowan ran to his side, and helped him to sit, and then to lie back on the ground. Gently he turned over the small webbed hand. Only then was the full horror of the injuries revealed.

The fish had truly been trying to strip the flesh from Seaborn's bones. The wounds were terrible.

"In my supplies," gasped Seaborn. "Healing cream. Bandages."

Asha and Doss came closer as Rowan pulled a jar of sticky brown ointment and a roll of soft, silky bandage from a pouch sewn into Seaborn's cape.

"I will help you," said Asha, reaching for the bandage.

"No!" Seaborn cried feebly, clutching with his good hand at Rowan's jacket. "Rowan! Do not let them touch me! Do not let them near my supplies!"

Asha drew back. "I would not try to harm you, man of Fisk," she frowned. "It is forbidden. And in any case, there is no need. You have done enough harm to yourself, without my doing more."

Rowan began to smear the brown ointment on Seaborn's hand. He was as gentle as he could be, but Seaborn closed his eyes, his face twisted in pain.

"If Seaborn is injured, it is my fault," Rowan muttered. "The pool was rippling, yet there was no wind. I took no note of that. And even when I saw the bird take the fish from the water, I did not think of danger. I did not heed the warning in Orin's rhyme."

He looked up at Doss. "You did," he added. "You tried to tell me. I wish that I had listened to you."

"I wish that I had spoken more firmly," said Doss. "But I was not certain. It was an idea only." He gazed thoughtfully down at Seaborn's white face.

Now that the crisis had passed, Doss was as calm as ever. He did not seem particularly upset by Seaborn's distress. Even for a Maris, he was strangely unmoved.

Rowan wondered about this as he bent to bandage the groaning man's quivering hand. Was Doss secretly glad that Seaborn had been injured? Had he deliberately held his tongue until his warning was too late?

Or was it just that Doss had seen so much pain and death in his life that he was no longer moved by it?

There is so much about these people I do not know, thought Rowan. When it comes to the Choosing, how will I decide which of these Candidates will best rule Maris?

He tried to turn his mind away from the question. The important thing now was the cure for Jiller. That came first.

One ingredient for the antidote had been found. Now the second had to be added.

In hungry pool moons raise their heads:
Pluck one and add the tears it sheds.

Just a few minutes ago, that task had seemed easy. Plunge an arm into that clear, rippling water. Pick the flower growing deep within it.

But now ... who would risk such a thing?

No one.

14 – Hungry Pool

Rowan finished bandaging Seaborn's hand, and helped him to sit upright while he bound his arm into a sling. He saw the man gaze with loathing at the fish, now lying still on the rock where it had fallen.

Now they could all see clearly its transparent, worm-like body, and the swollen head that seemed just big enough to hold its double row of needle-sharp teeth.

"Never have I seen such a thing!" breathed Asha. "And there are thousands of them."

She climbed the rock and stood staring down at the pool.

"It is clear again," she said.

Rowan went to look.

Sure enough, the pool shone clean and clear. The silver sand had sunk once again to the bottom. There was no trace of Seaborn's blood, either. The fish, it seemed, had made short work of that.

The moon-flower floated temptingly in the rippling depths. It looked as though you could reach down and pick it—easily, easily. And just a few minutes ago, Rowan had thought he could.

"We will have to break the flower's stem with two sticks and lift it from the water," Asha suggested.

Rowan shook his head. "I do not think we can do that," he said. "The rhyme says we must add the tears the flower sheds. I think the tears must be the juice that drips from the broken stem. If we simply break the stem from above, it will flow to waste in the water. The flower must be picked by hand, and the stem pinched hard to hold the juice in place."

One of the grey moths from the forest bumbled over the pool, attracted by the scent of the flower. The water rippled. Perfume rose from its surface in waves of sweetness. The moth flew lower. Its wing just touched the water …

In a blink, it had disappeared below the surface. The water seethed and swirled as though it was boiling. And then there was nothing.

Rowan shuddered. He fought down the sickness that churned his stomach.

It is the way of the world, he told himself. The fish eat the moths. The bird eats the fish. So it goes.

But still, the death of the helpless moth had upset him.

"If a few moths are all those creatures have to eat, it is a wonder they are so many," Asha commented, unmoved.

Rowan swallowed, and nodded. "Somehow, we have to find a way to deal with them," he said. "Somehow, we have to pick the moon-flower."

"There is only one way to deal with fish," said Asha firmly. "Even fish as extraordinary as these. We will catch them. Net them, every one."

"I do not think we have a net that will hold them," called Doss, overhearing.

Asha faced him, wrapping her silver cape around her. "We do not have a single net fine enough, it's true," she retorted. "But if we lay all our nets together, so that the lines of the mesh cross one another, the web will do. I am sure of it."

Doss glanced at the sky. "You had better move away from the pool," he said urgently. "The bird is coming back."

Remembering what had happened last time, Rowan and Asha hastily moved further down the rock.

Rowan turned to look. The bird swooped down towards the pool at enormous speed. It was huge. Its beak was cruel and curved. Its claws were stretched out, glinting, ready to grasp its prey.

As Rowan watched, the bird hovered for a moment over the pool. The water began to turn silver as the fish scurried to safety.

And then, suddenly, the bird swerved in the air, and with a harsh cry headed straight for Rowan and Asha.

"Down!" shrieked Rowan, pushing Asha to the ground.

Just in time. The snapping beak, the beating wings and razor-sharp claws missed them both by the tiniest space.

Rowan stared in amazement as the bird wheeled away.

"What—what is it doing?" cried Seaborn.

"I don't know," panted Rowan. "It seems to have decided that we are its enemies."

Asha climbed to her feet, pale and shaken.

"I will be glad to leave this place," she said. She pulled a fine net from the pouch in her cape. "And to this end," she added, "I would ask the Candidates of Pandellis and of Fisk to give me their nets, so I can clear the pool."

Without a word, Seaborn plucked at his own cape with his uninjured hand, and brought out a net even finer than Asha's. He held it out.

Doss hesitated, then did the same.

Asha spread all three nets out on the rock, one on top of the other, and tied the edges in many places. Rowan could see that, joined together, the nets made a fine web. There were very few spaces through which fish might escape, even fish as small as those in the pool.

Asha stood up with the three nets made one in her hand. She glanced at the cliff-top beyond the trees. The green bird was shrieking there, beating its wings at one of its own kind which had dared to enter its territory.

"Our friend is busy for the moment," she said. "Now is our chance."

She carried the net to the moon-flower pool, and knelt beside it. Rowan and Doss ran to help her. They crouched around the pool, holding the net between them.

"We must dip the net, lift the fish out, tip them onto the rock where they cannot harm us, and dip again as quickly as we can," Asha said. "It will take time to empty the pool completely."

She looked behind her at Seaborn, who was watching helplessly, nursing his injured hand. "Warn us if the bird approaches," she ordered. "No doubt you will be pleased to have something useful to do."

She turned back to Rowan and Doss. It suits her to be the one in charge, thought Rowan.

"Ready?" said Asha. "Now!"

They dipped the net into the pool. The water seethed. Rowan felt a slight tug at his hands. He tensed his muscles, ready to lift ...

"Out!" called Asha.

They lifted together. Rowan had expected a small weight—but there was no weight at all.

He rocked back on his heels, staring stupidly at the ragged piece of net he held. He looked up at the others. They, too, were blinking, as though they couldn't take in what had happened.

The entire centre of the net had disappeared. And in the pool, the fish feasted.

"Never—" Asha was trembling with shock and anger. "Never have I seen anything like this. What devils are these?"

The water was calming. Soon it was gently rippling once more, and they could again see the moon-flower blooming. There was no sign of the net, or any part of it. It had been completely consumed.

"I do not believe it!" Asha shouted. "They eat our net, yet they do not eat the flower!"

"I think I see why," said Doss. "It is because they need the flower. Its perfume attracts the moths that they often use for food." He smiled. "And of course," he added, "the flower needs the fish also. They eat whatever falls into the pool, so the water stays clear and clean, and the flower can always see the sun."

"Beware!" cried Seaborn.

They scrambled away from the pool, staying low.

The green-feathered bird swooped down. The pool began to turn silver. The bird plunged, then rose, screeching, clutching wriggling prey.

"The bird can take the fish," said Doss slowly.

"It has been fitted by nature to do so!" snapped Asha. "And we cannot wait for it to empty the pool for us."

"Do we have a container with which we can take the water out?" asked Seaborn.

No one did. And after what had happened to the net, they all knew that a container made of leaves, cloth or bark would be useless.

"I have it! We will fill the pool with sand and rocks," said Asha, jumping up. "Then the water will overflow and run away, and the devil-fish will die."

"We have no time to waste. It would take many, many hours to fill that pool," murmured Seaborn. "And I—" He winced, nursing his injured hand. "I will be able to help you little."

"It does not matter!" Asha's pale eyes were burning with anger. "Those creatures must be destroyed. They must!"

Rowan shook his head. "You are forgetting," he said gently. "Our aim is not to destroy the fish. Our aim is to pluck the moon-flower. If we fill the pool, the flower will be buried deep. It will be damaged, perhaps broken. Then it will be useless."

Asha threw up her hands. "We must destroy the fish before we can pick the flower!" she raged. "If we cannot destroy them, the thing cannot be done!"

"Yes, it can," cried Rowan. "It must."

"It can be done," said Doss. "Because Orin did it. There is a way. We have only to find it."

There was silence. They crouched on the rock, watching as the great green bird once more swooped to the pool, hovered for a second while the water silvered under its shadow, then plunged.

"The fish are afraid of the bird," said Doss suddenly. "They rush to bury themselves beneath the silver sand just before it swoops. And there they stay until the danger has passed."

"You are thinking that at that moment we could pluck the flower in safety," Rowan murmured.

Seaborn looked doubtful. "It all happens in the blink of an eye," he said. "And there are still fish in the water, for the bird always catches some. But we could try, and hope that there are too few to do too much damage."

Asha snorted. "You dream, you three, if you think of standing in the way of that bird as it attacks. It would be madness. You would be cut to pieces."

She looked up to the cliff-top, where the bird was again fighting with one of its own kind. Green feathers fell to the sea below as it beat its wings in fury, its curved claws slashing at the intruder.

Rowan nodded. The bird was in its way as dangerous as the

ravenous fish. And in any case, Seaborn's objection, too, was serious. The moment of safety, while the bird hovered, was too fleeting. Even the fish did not all have time to scatter and bury themselves in the silver sand.

But they all tried. Because they knew they were in danger. Like the cornbirds that scattered from the grain fields in Rin when someone approached. Or when Jiller placed a ...

Rowan caught his breath.

"What is it?" asked Doss.

"I know what to do," said Rowan. "I need a knife. And Seaborn's cloak. And some long, straight sticks."

15 – The Plan

The green bird had plunged to the pool many times before Rowan's work was finished.

"In Orin's name, please hurry," Seaborn urged him, glancing restlessly at the sun.

Rowan bit his lip, forcing himself to concentrate on what he was doing. He knew only too well that time was precious. And yet the work had to be done properly, or it would fail.

Finally he tied the last knots, and stood back.

Asha, Doss and Seaborn stared silently at the thing Rowan had made. It was a bird shape, cut roughly from part of Seaborn's green cloak, and stiffened with sticks like a kite.

Seaborn frowned. "It is a curious idea," he said. "How did you think of it?"

"My mother makes a figure from wood and dresses it in her clothes, to scare the cornbirds from our fields," said Rowan, lifting the shape in his arms.

"But it will not fool the devil-fish, surely," said Asha.

"I hope it might," said Rowan. "In Rin, the trick does not work for cornbirds that are old and wise. But it scares away those that have not yet learned how to tell real danger from false. And I believe these fish are like those young cornbirds. For if I am right, no one has tried this trick here since Orin's time."

He carried the shape to the pool, and scanned the skies. The green bird was nowhere to be seen.

"Now is the time," he said, beckoning. "Quickly, before the real bird returns, or the sun sets. It is important that the shadow of the bird shape falls on the surface of the water."

Doss and Asha stood back from the pool and took the shape between them, holding it by the edges of its wings.

Rowan lay down beside the pool, his eyes fixed on the moon-flower. Seaborn, wincing with pain as he moved, crouched beside him, holding the glass jar.

In hungry pool moons raise their heads:
Pluck one ...

"Now," Rowan murmured.

Asha and Doss moved forward, one on either side of the pool. The shadow of the bird shape they held between them fell over the water.

Immediately, the pool began to cloud, and then to shine. The fish were burrowing for their lives beneath the silver sand.

"Wait ... wait," Doss whispered. "Let them all go."

Rowan's hand tingled. He counted to five, slowly. And then he knew he could wait no longer. Gritting his teeth, he plunged his arm into the cold, silvery depths. Down, down ... every second expecting the piercing pain that would signal that the ravenous fish had emerged from hiding, realising they had been tricked.

The stem of the moon-flower was between his fingers, smooth and hard. He bent it, but it did not break.

"Make haste!" Seaborn begged.

Desperately Rowan leaned further over the pool and plunged his other arm into the water, tearing at the moon-flower stem with his nails. The silver water lapped at his chest, his neck, his chin. If the fish were to attack now ...

He felt the stem break. Pinching the end with the fingers of one hand, holding the flower with the other, he wriggled backwards, grazing himself on the rocks. And just as the white flower broke the surface of the water, blazing pain shot through his forearms and wrists.

He heard Asha and Seaborn shouting in horror. He smelled the heavy, overwhelming scent of the already wilting flower. He looked down at his arms, where a dozen transparent, biting creatures hung, wriggling.

His mind was clouded by pain that was like a thousand needles. But Seaborn was holding out the glass jar, calling to him.

Pluck one and add the tears it sheds ...

Rowan thrust the stem of the flower over the jar, and loosened his pinching fingers.

... add the tears it sheds.

And precious drops were falling into the jar. Mixing with the silver liquid. Turning it blue. Blue as the shining cloth of Doss's cloak. Blue as the sea. Blue as the sky.

* * *

"There. It is done," said Doss, fastening the last bandage.

Rowan thanked him. His arms still throbbed and ached. But the sticky brown ointment and the bandages were comforting.

He looked over to the rock where the moon-flower lay broken and already yellowing. He felt sorry that it had to die.

Doss followed his glance, and gave one of his rare smiles. "Come," he said, beckoning. Rowan stood up and followed him.

The pool was rippling and clear. And far below its surface glimmered the perfect white face of another moon-flower.

"There was a bud beneath the bloom you picked," Doss said, as Rowan gasped. "It opened the moment the pool cleared. I saw it happen. It was like a miracle."

"A miracle!" exclaimed Asha, coming up beside them. "How can you call a thing so evil a miracle?"

Doss turned serious eyes towards her. "The flower is not evil because it blooms where it does," he said. "It simply exists. As do the fish in this pool, and the bird on the cliff, and you, and I."

Asha returned his look coldly. "You never forget that you are the Candidate, do you, Doss of Pandellis?" she sneered. "And how well you have studied this Chooser! You say exactly what will please him."

Doss frowned. "I do not," he said. "I say what I think."

She laughed disbelievingly, and went to sit by herself at the edge of the rock.

Rowan looked quickly at Doss, then away again. He was thrilling with shock. He had suddenly realised he had let down his guard.

For a while he had actually forgotten that his companions were not his friends, or even his willing helpers. He had forgotten what Perlain had told him: that they had been trained from earliest childhood to be cunning, and to please the Chooser, whatever their true thoughts.

He had forgotten that one of them had poisoned his mother.

But now he remembered, and his anger returned. He lifted his head, ignoring the throbbing pain of his arms, and the even greater ache in his heart.

"We must find the third ingredient," he said loudly, avoiding all their eyes.

"Stir slowly with new fighter's quill,
Three times, no more, and let it still."

The calm, strong voice that said the words was Seaborn's.

"I believe I have the third ingredient already, Rowan," he said. He held up a long green feather. "The bird plucked this from its own wing, in rage, when it was attacking Asha."

Rowan thought quickly. A quill was a feather. That was true. The bird could be called a fighter. That was true. The other two ingredients had been found here, in this place. It was very likely that the third would be also.

And the fourth?

Rowan shut his eyes. He would not think of the fourth. He had never wanted to think of the fourth.

He held out his hand, and Seaborn put the feather into it. They saw the bird coming towards them again, and jumped aside. But the bird paid no attention to them. It simply splashed into the pool as before, and flew away.

Rowan unscrewed the lid of the jar. He put the sharp end of the green feather into the blue liquid and stirred. Once, twice, three times.

Nothing happened.

The rhyme says, "let it still", he thought. He set the jar upon the rock and watched its contents carefully.

Slowly the liquid settled, and became still. But the colour remained unchanged.

Rowan willed himself to say nothing. He turned the feather around, forced its broad end into the neck of the jar, and stirred the mixture again. Then once more he moved back, to watch and wait.

After two long minutes, he knew he could wait no longer. Slowly he screwed the top back on the jar.

All three Candidates were watching him curiously. They could see that something was wrong, but they did not understand what the problem was.

"The mixture should have turned green," Rowan told them. He tried to speak strongly, like a leader. But he could hear that his voice was thick with disappointment.

"Then the feather was not what the rhyme meant at all," said Seaborn. He shook his head. "I am sorry," he said. "I was sure it was."

"I, too," Doss put in. He met Rowan's eyes briefly, saw the unfriendliness there, and looked down again.

"I do not agree," said Asha firmly. "I never did see how a simple feather could add anything to the brew. Feathers are used for decoration, and sometimes as a pen for writing. That is all they are ever used for."

Rowan rolled the pointed end of the feather between his fingers. Despite what Asha said, he was sure that Orin's rhyme *had* meant the feather of the green bird. Again he repeated the instructions to himself. Had he done exactly what they said?

Stir slowly with new fighter's quill,
Three times, no more, and let it still.

He had stirred the mixture with the feather. He had stirred three times, no more. He had let it still. There was nothing more. Nothing ...

And then he saw it. The one word he had not considered.

He sighed. At last he knew what he had to do.

16 – The Fighter

ew. That was the word that counted.

"A feather *could* add something to the brew," Rowan said to Asha. "It could add a trace of the oil it draws from the bird's body to make it waterproof. But only if it is freshly plucked. The oil must dry up and vanish into the air very quickly."

The Candidates looked up, as one, to the dimming sky above the cliff-top, where the bird shrieked and plunged, flapping and clawing at another invader. As they watched, a feather fell from the bird's wing and drifted down towards the sea far below.

"It is when the birds fight that the feathers fall," said Doss.

"We cannot climb that cliff, Doss of Pandellis," scoffed Asha. "Maris hands are not made for climbing. And the Chooser cannot go alone into such danger."

"I would be a fool to try," Rowan said unwillingly. "I am not strong enough for the climb. My arms are injured. Besides, I have no head for heights, and would probably fall."

None of the Candidates seemed to find this surprising. Of course they wouldn't, Rowan realised. Unlike Perlain, who had been surprised at how different he was from the Rin people who came to Maris on market visits, they knew all about him. Their trainers would have told them that he was unlike most of his people, who were strong and brave by nature.

He felt his cheeks redden. Sometimes it was still hard to face this difference. Not for the first time, he wished with all his heart that Strong Jonn was with him. Jonn would not have stood here talking and being afraid. Jonn would have been half way to the cliff by now.

"The birds fight over the sea," Doss said. "The feathers fall into the water. I do not believe it would be possible to catch one from the cliff-top, even if we could reach it."

"So?" Seaborn waited impatiently. "What then are you suggesting?"

Doss looked at him, unblinking. "We wait for the bird to come to us. It will be here soon enough, when it wants more fish."

Asha nodded. "Yes. And then we trap it," she said fiercely. "And take the feather by force."

Rowan half smiled. "And with what do we trap it?" he asked.

"With our nets, of course," she answered. "What else should—? Oh!" Her mouth closed into a rigid line as she realised the problem.

Seaborn laughed. "Sadly, we have not one net between us. Thanks to your experiment in fishing, Asha!"

She turned away, furious, feeling she had been tricked.

Seaborn nodded to Rowan. "It is simple. We wait till the bird comes to the pool. But this time, we do not run from it. We face it. Make it fight us."

Rowan's heart swelled with gratitude. If Jonn could not be with him, at least Seaborn was.

Asha spun back to face them. "Are you mad, Seaborn of Fisk?" she spat. "Have you started to *believe* yourself to be the part your trainers have taught you to play? The fearless hero, so beloved of the farmers of Rin?"

Again, Rowan felt a jolt.

Seaborn is not Jonn, he reminded himself. Seaborn is a Maris. The Maris value cunning, not strength. He must be playing a part, just as Asha says.

But Seaborn was staring Asha down. "It is you who are mad, Asha of Umbray," he said coldly. "I am what I am. And if a feather freshly plucked from the bird is what we need, I am willing to fight for it."

"One of your hands is already useless," she retorted.

Seaborn drew his knife. "Then I will use the other," he said.

"The bird is coming," warned Doss.

Trying to ignore the aching pain in his bandaged arms, Rowan picked up a stick and ran to the pool. Seaborn went with him, his knife held in his good hand. After a moment's hesitation, Doss drew out his blade and followed. But Asha gathered her silver cape around her and turned her back again.

The bird hurtled towards them. They could hear the beating of its wings. Rowan, Seaborn and Doss stood waiting, shoulder to shoulder.

It is huge, thought Rowan. Its claws are like knives. He braced himself.

"Leave the fight to us, Rowan," shouted Seaborn. "You try for the feather while we——"

His voice was drowned out by the angry screeching of the bird. It was upon them! Rowan saw the wicked gleam of its black eyes. He staggered back as its giant wings beat the air above his head.

And then, dazed, he realised that the bird had swooped past him, past them all. It was heading straight for Asha, who was still standing stubbornly with her back to them.

"Asha!" he screamed.

She half turned, saw what was happening, and flung herself to the rocky ground. The bird skimmed over her, its beak snapping, then swooped away into the sky.

Rowan ran to her. Already she was crawling to her feet, bruised, scratched and shuddering with shock. "What happened? Why did it do that?" she gasped.

"It took no notice of us at all!" shouted Seaborn, as he and Doss ran to join them. "Yet we were at its feeding pool."

"It attacked Asha once before, and ignored the rest of us," muttered Rowan.

"But why? Why?" Asha glanced up fearfully. She raised her hand to her mouth. "It is turning!" she hissed. "It is coming for me again!"

Rowan looked up. Sure enough, high in the sky, the green bird was wheeling in a circle, preparing to attack once more.

"Hide in the forest," said Rowan urgently. "We will try to stop it."

Asha began to limp down the rock towards the trees. Her silver cloak flared and billowed behind her. Over its shining surface moved a wavering confusion of pictures: the rock, the sky, the small shape of the approaching bird, the larger shapes of Rowan, Doss and Seaborn.

Rowan's eyes widened.

"Asha!" he screamed. "Your cloak! Take it off! Take it off!"

The woman hesitated.

But Rowan was already running towards her, calling back over his shoulder for the others.

"Don't you see? Your cloak is a mirror!" Rowan gabbled as he reached Asha's side. He began tearing at the strings that held the silver cloak around her shoulders. "When you turn your back the creature sees its own reflection. So it attacks. It thinks it is fighting another of its kind."

Now Asha could not get the cloak off fast enough. It dropped to the ground, and she backed away.

Just in time. The bird had almost reached them.

"Do not waste the chance," shouted Doss, darting for the cloak and picking up one side of it. "Asha, stand back! Seaborn—hold it up with me."

Seaborn did as he was told, asking no questions. They stretched the cloak out between them. The giant bird shrieked a furious warning. Its reflection on the cloak grew larger and larger, filling the silver surface with moving, wavering green.

The bird stretched out its claws and flapped its wings in a frenzied display of anger. A rival had dared to invade its territory! It was like the one who sometimes appeared in the silver pool. But this rival was bigger. It was flapping its own wings, and stretching out its claws. It was refusing to fly away. Refusing to surrender!

Screeching, the bird beat at the cloak with its huge wings, ripped it with razor-sharp claws. Doss and Seaborn lurched and staggered, trying to keep their grip.

Again the bird threw itself at its imagined enemy. Rowan's heart leaped as a feather fell, gleaming, to the ground.

"Drop the cloak!" he screamed. "Throw it away!"

Doss and Seaborn hurled the cloak aside. It fell in a tangled, tattered heap on the rock. The bird swooped on it, tearing at it with its beak and crying out its triumph.

Rowan dived for the feather, tears springing into his eyes as pain shot through his injured arms. He pulled the precious crystal jar from his pocket. Trying to stop his fingers from shaking, he unscrewed the lid.

Stir slowly with new fighter's quill,
Three times, no more, and let it still ...

The feather was still warm in his hand. The smooth, pointed end gleamed with oil. Rowan plunged it into the blue mixture. Holding his breath, he stirred slowly. Once, twice, three times.

He set the mixture on the rock in front of him and closed his eyes. He could not bear to look.

Then he heard three voices crying out. His eyes flew open.

The liquid in the jar was shining brilliant green. Green as the trees. Green as the feathers of the fighter bird. Green as the grass in the valley of Rin.

17 – The Greatest Fear

Now it was Asha's turn to be bandaged. Her hands had been grazed on the rock, her back and shoulders scratched and beaten by the bird's wings and claws.

She would not let anyone touch her wounds except Rowan. She sat rigidly as he smeared on the ointment through the tears in her clothing. It must have hurt her, but she gave not a single whimper of pain.

Doss and Seaborn stood watching from a distance. Seaborn kept looking at the sky. Finally he spoke.

"We must move quickly to find the last ingredient," he said. "Already it is dark. Night is upon us."

Rowan knew Seaborn was thinking of the Keeper's failing strength. But all Rowan could think of was his mother. How much time did she have left?

"The Choosing should be completed by now," muttered Asha. "By now the Chooser should be naming the Choice."

"How can the Keeper be so sure she will die at sunrise?" Rowan asked.

"So it has always been," said Asha. "It is part of the mystery of the Crystal. This night, of all in the year, is always the night of the Choosing. The night of the full moon. Orin found the Crystal in this month, on the night of the full moon. But always, before, the flame above the Cavern of the Crystal has been lit by sunset."

She looked at Rowan accusingly.

"It is not my fault that time is so short," Rowan exclaimed. "We came from Rin as soon as we were summoned. And I did not ask for my mother to be struck down."

The last lines of Orin's verse were ringing in his mind.

Add venom from your greatest fear—
One drop—and then the truth is clear.

What was his greatest fear? It was that he would fail to do all he had to do. That his mother would die. That a new Keeper would not be chosen in time to keep the Crystal alive. That, because of him, his land would be threatened by a last and terrible Zebak invasion. That he and Jonn, Annad, and all their friends would be taken back into slavery, and their beautiful valley destroyed.

And yet this could not be what Orin's rhyme had meant. Orin was talking about a different kind of fear. Orin was a Maris. His recipe was meant to be understood by Maris minds.

He looked at Doss, Seaborn and Asha, one by one. Pale, tense faces. Expressionless eyes.

"What is your greatest fear?" he asked.

There was only a second's hesitation. Then they all said the words together.

"The Great Serpent."

Rowan drew a deep breath. He had suspected this. But he had not wanted to think of it.

"The Great Serpent's fangs drip poison," said Doss. "I believe that is what Orin's rhyme means. We must obtain a drop of the poison, to complete the antidote."

The other two nodded.

The silence hung heavy between them. It was quiet and dark in the clearing. The fighter bird no longer shrieked at rivals on the cliff-top. And it had not returned to the pool. Perhaps it had gone to its nest for the night.

"How do we find the Great Serpent?" Rowan asked at last.

In his mind was the picture he had seen in the house of books at home in Rin. It had frightened him then. The thought of facing the real beast filled him with terror.

"The sea is full of serpents," said Seaborn. "And they are not hard to find. Venture onto the shore after the sun has gone down, and they will find you."

"But the Great Serpent?" Rowan persisted.

Asha and Seaborn glanced at Doss. And Rowan remembered what Perlain had said.

"Your eyes have the look of one who has seen the Great Serpent, and lived. Deep, and full of knowledge. Strange in a boy so young. I have known only one other."

He turned to Doss. "You have seen it," he said quietly.

Doss nodded. "I have." He did not look at Rowan as he spoke.

Rowan waited. He knew that if he waited long enough, Doss would speak again.

"It was at exactly this time, a year ago," Doss murmured finally. "That day I was with my family, in our boat. There was to be a full moon that night, as there would be at the Choosing. It was my Day of Farewell."

"Each Candidate has a Day of Farewell," Seaborn said, in reply to Rowan's enquiring look. "It is the day we say goodbye to our families. After that we live apart from the rest of Maris. We retire to our clan's Candidate house, with only our trainers and our books for company, to prepare in earnest for the Choosing."

"That must be hard," said Rowan, thinking how he would feel to be separated from everyone and everything he knew and loved.

"It is necessary," said Seaborn.

"And it is preparation, too," Asha added. "For a new Keeper is taken to the surface and shown to the people only once. After that he or she returns to the Cavern of the Crystal, for ever."

Rowan felt a cold thrill of horror.

"You mean—Keepers never again leave the Cavern?" he stammered. "Never see their homes and friends, or breathe the open air, or see the sky?"

Doss smiled. "They do not need to do so, Rowan. The Crystal is all to them."

"They are there to serve," said Seaborn.

Rowan closed his eyes. To him, this sounded like a living death. Now he realised what Perlain had meant when he said that to be Keeper was not a thing everyone desired.

"You do not understand," Doss said. "It is not pain, but joy."

"It is a glorious duty," said Asha. "So it has always been." Her eyes glowed.

Rowan told himself that this was not his business. It was not for him to judge the ways of the Maris.

"Tell me about the Great Serpent, Doss," he said abruptly.

"We had sailed far," said Doss. "We were thinking of turning for home, when our boat began to take in water. Not just from one place, but from many. The wood had been pierced, and then the holes had been filled cleverly with something that fell away only after a long time, when the boat was out of sight of land."

He was staring straight ahead. He accused no one. But Seaborn and Asha frowned.

"My clan did not touch your boat!" snapped Asha.

"Nor mine," said Seaborn.

Still Doss did not look at them. "However it happened, the boat sank," he said. "We swam, but the tide was strong." He was speaking so softly that Rowan had to lean forward to hear him.

"Soon I lost sight of my mother and father, and my brothers," the quiet voice went on. "I fought the tide. I was exhausted. The sun began to set. And then I heard a sound. A high, ringing sound. It seemed to come from all around me. From the sky above, and the sea beneath. It grew louder. It went on and on. It filled my ears, and seemed to enter my brain and fill it too, so that I could think of nothing else. It was the singing of the Great Serpent."

Again the picture that Rowan had seen rose up in his mind. The boat, and the people screaming, with their hands over their ears. He shuddered.

Doss's voice had become flat and lifeless, a chant, as if he were reciting a lesson repeated many times. "The Great Serpent came up from the depths. It towered above me. Its eyes were golden, and full of ancient secrets. Its scales glittered like fire in the setting sun. It looked at me. I knew that I was going to die."

"But you didn't," Rowan breathed. His own heart was beating rapidly. He knew what it was to face nightmares.

"No," Doss said simply. "Blackness closed in on me. I know nothing of what happened after that. I remember nothing of the night. But when I awoke, the sun was rising, and I was lying on part of my family's boat, drifting in sight of the shore. My clan saw me, and brought me in. They searched for the others, too. But no one was ever found."

He turned his dreamy eyes on Rowan. "I alone of my family was spared. And I—was changed. I could feel it. Everyone around me could see it. It was as though something had been lost—or added. I do not know which."

"It is a wonder," said Asha harshly, "that your clan allowed you to remain their Candidate. Were there not others, undamaged, who could have taken your place?"

"Of course," Doss replied. "And I expected this. But then I realised that my trainers believed the change was for the good. It had not affected my wits. But it separated me from others. Made me different. And, they thought, special."

Again, a strange smile hovered on his lips. "For, of course, to see the Great Serpent, and live, is a powerful charm. No one is known to have done it since Orin the Wise."

Seaborn, who had been listening in silence, finally spoke. "There are some who say the whole story is a lie," he growled. "A lie invented by your trainers, to impress the people, and, one day, the Chooser. As perhaps it is doing at this moment."

Doss met his cold gaze calmly. "I wish it was a lie," he said. "For then that sound, and those yellow eyes, would not haunt my dreams … as after this night they may haunt yours."

… as after this night they may haunt yours.

Rowan straightened his shoulders. Whatever his fears, whatever his doubts, he knew that the only way for him to go was forward.

"The sun has set," he said. "Time is short. And we must find the Great Serpent. How do you think we should begin?"

18 – The Moon of
the Choosing

I do not see how it is possible," said Asha. "Only fools venture on to the deep by night, even in a boat. And we have no boat. If we swim, we will surely be taken by the smaller serpents without ever sighting the great one we seek."

The sky was dark, and filled with stars. The moon-flower showed white in the dark pool. Waves crashed on the shore beyond the forest.

"There must be a way," said Rowan, watching Doss. "Because Orin did it. The answer lies with him."

To see the Great Serpent, and live, is a powerful charm. No one is known to have done it since Orin the Wise.

Orin the Wise …

A thousand years ago, on the day he found the Crystal, Orin met the Great Serpent, thought Rowan. It was just at this time of year. That is why this is always the time of the Choosing.

He went over the story in his mind. The story Perlain had told him. Orin was fishing. He started for home in his boat, after sunset. The Great Serpent rose from the sea. It upset his boat, and chased him. He fled to the Island. He found the Crystal.

And that is how all this began, Rowan thought. Then he frowned. There was something odd about the story. Some detail that was wrong. At first Rowan could not think what it was. And then he remembered.

Orin had not been fishing on the day he found the Crystal. The Keeper had let slip that Orin was actually on the Island that day, making the antidote for Death Sleep.

Rowan thought it through. Orin must have just said he was fishing, to hide his real purpose. He did not want others to know he was making the secret Death Sleep antidote. And no one then, or since, had questioned his story.

No one had questioned it because Orin had brought the Crystal back with him, and all interest was focused on its wonder. And after that, no one questioned the story because Orin had become Orin the Wise. Someone extraordinary. The first Keeper of the Crystal.

But on the day Orin found the Crystal he was still just an ordinary Maris man. And when you thought about it like that, the story of his meeting with the Great Serpent was even more unlikely.

Would Orin's fear of staying on the Island overnight have been greater than his fear of taking a boat into dark water? Almost certainly not.

And even if he had braved the water, could Orin really have out-swum the Great Serpent if it was chasing him? Again, almost certainly not.

Rowan's thoughts ran on.

That part of the story too, then, was a lie. Orin had not left the Island after sunset. He had not met the beast in the sea.

Had he really seen it at all?

Yes, because its poison was the fourth ingredient in the antidote.

So ... The back of Rowan's neck prickled. So that meant something very strange indeed. It meant that somehow Orin and the Great Serpent had met on land. On the Island. Perhaps even ...

"Look at the moon," murmured Doss, pointing.

A great full moon had risen over the treetops. Still, cold and white, it floated in the grey sky like the flower in the depths of the dark pool.

"The Moon of the Choosing," whispered Asha.

And then they heard it. A heavy, slithering sound, coming from the path through the forest. Coming closer.

"What is it?" panted Seaborn.

Doss stood, his eyes wide. "Quickly," he hissed. "Away from here! Away!"

They ran from the rock, and crouched among the trees.

The sound grew louder. The sound of leaves being crushed and swept aside. The sound of ferns being bent and broken under a giant weight.

Into the clearing writhed the Great Serpent, leaving behind it a cleared path, as it had done so many times before. The water of the deep still dripped from its dragon head. Its yellow eyes were glazed. Its drying golden scales shone under the Moon of the Choosing. Its huge, swollen body thrashed and curled.

Waves of terror flowed over Rowan. He heard the soft whimpering of Doss, the heavy breathing of Asha and Seaborn, close beside him. He slipped his hand into his pocket and gripped the small, hard jar, the jar that contained the mixture that would save his mother's life. If one small thing was added. One drop ...

"Why is it here?" whispered Asha, in dread. "Why does it invade the land? The deep—the deep is the Great Serpent's kingdom. So it has always been."

But Rowan had guessed. "Once a year it comes here," he whispered back. "*This* is how it has always been. But you did not know it, for it happens on this side of the Island. The side you in Maris never see, once the sun has set."

The scent of the moon-flower was strong in the air. It billowed from the pool. The serpent writhed towards it, slowly, painfully, climbing the rock.

"It is looking for us," hissed Seaborn, in an agony of fear.

"No," Rowan said. "It does not even know we are here. There is something else it seeks. A place. Watch. Wait."

The serpent reached the pool at the top of the rock. It stared with its yellow eyes at the moon-flower, floating white in the rippling water. Then it looked up at the moon in the sky. It opened its massive jaws, and cried out. A weird, ringing sound that pierced the ears, and filled the mind.

Doss wrapped his arms around his head and moaned softly.

Asha, too, hid her eyes.

But Seaborn watched, fascinated, as the monster coiled its enormous body around the pool.

"It is laying eggs," he breathed.

"Yes," said Rowan. "It is like the giant turtles that swim in your seas. Like the Kirrian Worm, whose eggs you collect every spring morning. It lives in the deep, but it lays its eggs on land. And this is its place. This is where Orin found it."

The serpent was laying eggs indeed. They shone silver in the moonlight. As each was laid, the tip of the great tail swept it into the moon-flower pool, where it sank through the water to rest on the bed of silver sand.

"What better place to hide the eggs." Rowan was filled with wonder. "No creature could dare to touch them there. The shells must be hard as stone, so that the fish cannot harm them."

By now, Doss and Asha were looking too. "But when they hatch—" Asha began.

"By the time they hatch, the fish will not be so many," Rowan said quietly. "The fighter bird will have taken a great number of them."

"The fish that are left will attack the new-born serpents," nodded Doss. "And many will be killed. But some will survive, swimming to the surface, crawling out of the pool, wriggling down the path to the shore, and into the sea."

"And the broken shells will remain, gradually to be ground down by the moving water to make more of the silver sand," said Seaborn. "By Orin, it is incredible." His face was alive with interest. He was so entranced that he had forgotten his fear.

"If it were not for the fighter bird, the pool would be thick with fish, and the baby serpents would all die when they hatched," Rowan whispered. "If the fighter bird did not defend the pool against all its neighbours, the pool would be emptied of every last fish. Then all the eggs would hatch safely, and the sea would be thick with serpents, but empty of every other living thing."

"No fish," said Doss. "No food for Maris, oil for our lamps, fish skin for our shoes and clothing. No safety, even in daylight, for the ships that come to trade, because the serpents would be hungry, and desperate. And so the Maris would die. And the serpents, too, in the end. It is all a great whole."

"It is meaningless!" Seaborn was scowling now. "The birds eat the fish. The fish eat the serpents. Why need the cycle exist at all? If we were to come to the Island each year and destroy the Great Serpent's eggs, using the way Rowan has taught us, our seas would soon be completely free of danger. We could fish at night as well as by day, and so double our catch, or triple it. We could sell to the traders, and feed multitudes."

"The Island is forbidden by Orin, Seaborn of Fisk," said Asha sternly. "And the serpents have always existed in our seas. That is the way it has always been."

For Asha, that was enough.

But not for Seaborn.

"Why should we not destroy the serpents?" he demanded. "Of what use are they? All they do is stop us fishing when we wish."

Do you not see it, Seaborn? Rowan thought. Do you not see the use? You yourself have just explained it.

But he said nothing. Instead, he stood up. He was trembling all over, but he knew what he had to do. He unscrewed the lid of the silver-topped jar, and stepped towards the rock.

19 – One Drop

he Great Serpent turned its head. Its yellow eyes were fixed on Rowan.

"Do not look at it," Doss cried.

But it was too late. Already Rowan was staring into those glazed eyes. And he couldn't look away. It was as though his body had gone numb.

Hands tugged at his sleeve. "Rowan!" came a choking voice. "Remember! Your mother! The poison!"

Rowan tore his eyes away from that cold, golden stare. Doss, Asha and Seaborn were behind him. Their faces shone ghastly white in the moonlight.

It was Asha who had spoken. Dimly Rowan realised that she had at last used his name. She grabbed his arm fiercely.

"You are the Chooser. You must not do this. I will go in your place. My death would be of no account. Yours will mean the end of Maris. Give me the jar."

He looked into her pale eyes. They were full of fear, but met his own steadily. She *is* like my mother, he thought. She will always do what she feels is right. Even to her death.

Seaborn shook his head. "I am stronger, and taller," he said in a low voice. "It is for me to face the beast. Give me the jar."

On the rock, the serpent waited.

Rowan hesitated, then turned to Doss, a small blue shadow in the dim light.

"No," Doss said quietly. "None of us can do this thing in Rowan's place."

Asha and Seaborn broke out in angry argument, but Doss held up his hand.

"From birth we have feared this creature and its kind. And it knows us, and our kind. It knows our smell. It knows our pale skin. It knows how we move. We are its natural prey. It will strike out at us without thinking. The only one of us with any chance of creeping close to it is the one who is the stranger."

Rowan took a deep breath. "Yes," he said.

He turned back and faced the beast again. This time he did not meet its eyes. He took a step forward. And another.

The serpent did not move, but its huge jaws opened, a black, forked tongue flickered out, and it hissed. The inside of its mouth was smooth and yellow. Its fangs were white, tipped with black. Poison dripped from the black needlepoints like drops of steaming liquid gold and fell, sizzling, to the ground.

Rowan climbed. He could feel the rock smooth under his feet. He could hear himself panting. He clutched the jar tightly.

His foot brushed against something on the ground. It was the dead moon-flower. Already brown and dried-out, its petals were curled like shallow cups of leather. He knelt, and tore one away.

The serpent was still laying eggs. Still pushing them one by one into the pool. The moon above it shone huge and white. But its yellow eyes were fixed on Rowan.

Doss was right, Rowan thought. It does not quite know what I am. And it wants to finish laying its eggs. It will threaten, but it will not stir unless I make a sudden movement. There is a chance.

He crept up towards the pool. Nearer, nearer ... till he could see the moon-flower shining beneath the dark water, like a reflection of the moon above. He began to edge around the vast coils that encircled the pool, moving towards the head.

The Great Serpent's eyes blazed. It arched its neck, and its eerie, ringing cry split the air.

The sound was so piercing that tears sprang into Rowan's eyes. He longed to cover his ears. But he had the flower petal in one hand, and the precious jar in the other. He could do nothing.

And then the serpent hissed again. Its jaws, which could crush a Maris boat to splinters, gaped wide. Its tongue flickered, tasting the air. Its fangs glinted in the moonlight, white tipped with black, dripping deadly liquid gold.

Now! Rowan darted forward, holding out the moon-flower petal, catching the venom in the leathery dish it had become.

The serpent struck at him, screaming its anger. Rowan lurched backwards and fell, the sound tearing into his brain. Pain shot through his bandaged arms. The venom smoked and sizzled in the moon-flower petal. The jar tilted dangerously.

Add venom from your greatest fear—
One drop—

In panic, Rowan looked at the jar. The green liquid was still safe. Then he turned his eyes to the petal, and to his horror saw that the venom was burning through it. The precious golden liquid was trickling away through black, scorched holes, and falling to waste on the rock. It was falling in a fine, smoking stream. Almost gone.

"No!" He was hardly aware that he had screamed.

"Rowan, get away! Oh—oh, in the name of Orin, run! Run! It is stirring! It is going to—"

The shrieking of the three Maris sounded dimly in his ears. He was aware of a monstrous shape rising above him, blocking out the moon. Of great slithering coils unwinding from around the pool. Of dripping jaws opening to strike again.

But the antidote ...

One drop ...

With trembling hands he tipped the petal over the jar.

And one last golden drop fell, hissing, into the darkness of the shadowed green liquid. Turning it clear. Clear as the water in the pool. Clear as the glass of the jar. Clear as truth.

"Rowan!"

He clapped the silver lid on the jar. He stumbled to his feet. He leaped for his life, tumbling down the smooth brown surface of the rock, his prize clutched in his throbbing hands.

But the beast was roaring its rage, thrashing and twisting after him with terrifying speed. He could hear it behind him—close, and closer every second. Dazed with pain and terror, he plunged forward. Where should he go? Which way should he run?

"Here!"

The three Maris were calling him. Through a blur he saw them running to meet him, their own faces twisted with fear.

Blindly Rowan held out his hands. Asha and Seaborn caught hold of him and swung him down from the rock and into the trees. Half dragging him, they began to struggle away through the trackless wood.

Thickets of bush and fern choked their way on every side. Vines hung thickly from the trees, twisting and tangling, catching at their hands, feet and clothes, holding them back. Leaves formed a roof over their heads, cutting out the light of the moon. Seaborn and Asha pulled Rowan between them. Doss struggled on behind.

The monster bellowed. Trees cracked and fell as, shrieking and hissing, it writhed after them. It did not need light. It was following their sound, and their scent. Every second it drew closer. They tore their way through the undergrowth, sobbing and gasping, blind in the darkness, the terrible cries ringing in their ears. So Orin must have run, in terror for his life.

"Which way?" Rowan heard Asha wailing. "I cannot see!"

And then there was a terrified, choking yell from behind them.

At first, straining his eyes against the blackness, Rowan could not see what had happened. Then he saw. Doss was caught in a looping vine. It had twisted around his neck, and his struggles to free himself had tightened it. He was choking, and trapped.

The beast was almost upon them. They could see the trees shaking and falling in its path. It howled as it smelled their terror. Doss hung, helpless, the tips of his toes kicking uselessly at the soft ground.

"Leave him!" shrieked Asha.

But Rowan could not. He twisted from her grasp, and from Seaborn's clutching hands, and darted back to where Doss hung.

He clawed at the choking vine with his fingers, ignoring his wounds. Agonising pain shot through his bandaged arms.

Doss gave a strangled scream. Then a knife cut cleanly through the vine, and he fell to the ground. He lay there, fainting.

"Get up!" hissed Asha, kicking at him. The knife that had freed him glinted dully in her hand.

Seaborn bent and swept Doss into his arms.

"Quickly!" he gasped. And staggering with his burden he lunged away once more, with Rowan and Asha close behind him.

They blundered on through inky blackness.

"Leave me," rasped Doss, stirring. "Put me down. Leave me. The Chooser must live … The Crystal must live …"

"Be still. The Chooser will not leave you," panted Seaborn.

"There!" shrieked Asha. "Oh, there!"

She was pointing at a winking light. So faint, so small, it shone through the black trees like a star.

"Maris!" cried Seaborn.

They struggled on, towards the light. It grew larger and brighter. They began to hear the crashing of waves. Never could they have found their way so quickly in the daylight. But in the night the Maris lights gleamed across the water, piercing the darkness, guiding them.

Hissing, writhing, the serpent plunged behind them. The land was not its place. But it was angry. It was hungry. It was hunting.

Struggling for breath, crying with fear, they burst out of the forest and onto the shore. Huge waves beat upon the rocks. Salt spray tingled on their faces. Across the water, every house in Maris blazed with light.

"They have lit every lamp for us," gasped Seaborn, letting Doss slip to the ground at last. "They must—they must all be—waiting."

"Hurry!" urged Asha.

There, in front of them, was the iron gate.

Dragging Doss between them, they ran to it and wrenched it open. Together they tumbled into the darkness of the stairs, and just as the great beast tore its way through the last ring of trees, the gate clanged shut behind them.

They heard the creature's tail thrashing in fury. They saw its huge head darting this way and that as it looked for them.

They clung together, trembling and exhausted. But they knew they were safe. The beast could not follow them into this small space. Like Orin before them, they had escaped.

Rowan touched the jar in his pocket. And like Orin, he thought, we are bringing back something precious.

Precious, if it was not too late.

His shaking voice echoed against the rock walls of the tunnel. "Come," he said. "We must hurry."

20 – The Deceiver

They half limped, half ran through the tunnel. It seemed endless. Ahead was only darkness.

"Where is the light of the Crystal?" panted Asha. "We must be nearly at the Cavern, and yet I cannot see it. What if ..."

"The Keeper is alive," said Seaborn firmly. "Or the people would not have been in their houses, burning lights for us."

"There!" called Rowan.

He pointed at a dim glow just colouring the blackness ahead.

They hurried towards it. Rowan's head was pounding in time with his heart. His throat felt closed and tight.

They were nearly at the Cavern, and yet he felt nothing. No unseen pull of the Crystal, drawing him. No voice whispering in his mind like his own thoughts.

They were at the entrance. Within, all was silent except for the ceaseless dripping of water. Seaborn, Doss and Asha fell back. Rowan took a breath, and crept in, afraid of what he might find.

The Keeper was huddled in her chair in the centre of the Cavern. The Crystal glowed feebly under her hands, spreading a circle of green light around her chair, and leaving the rest of the room in dimness.

In the shadows Jonn knelt by Jiller's couch, his head bowed. Rowan's heart gave a great thud.

"So, Chooser of Rin. You have returned."

The Keeper had not moved, or looked up. But her low voice filled the room.

Jonn's head jerked up. He leaped to his feet. And by the look of wild, unbelieving hope on his face Rowan knew that, after all, he was not too late.

He ran across the room and knelt down beside his mother. Yes. She still breathed. But faintly. So faintly.

His teeth were chattering. He was shaking all over. His fingers were stiff and clumsy as he pulled the jar from his pocket, and unscrewed the lid.

"I have the antidote, Keeper," he said, looking back over his shoulder. "How much should I use?"

Still the Keeper did not move. But he thought he saw her thin mouth curve into a smile.

"It seems you are everything they say, Rowan of Rin," she said. "Dip your finger into the brew, just once, and smear it on her lips. That will be enough."

The liquid in the jar was cold. It tingled on his finger as he rubbed it onto his mother's mouth.

Jiller frowned slightly in her sleep. Then, sighing, she licked her lips.

Jonn's strong hand gripped Rowan's shoulder.

"When—?" Rowan began.

"Soon." The Keeper's voice was dry and hushed, like the rustling of dead leaves. "Death Sleep takes two full hours to show itself. You cannot expect it to be undone in moments. But we cannot wait. I cannot wait. The Crystal dims. My time comes soon. Very soon. Step into the light."

"The Choosing ..." Rowan began, staggering to his feet.

The Keeper looked up. Behind her stood Doss, Seaborn and Asha, but she paid no attention to them. Her huge, pale eyes, dimming like the Crystal, sought Rowan in the darkness.

"Step into the light, Chooser of Rin," she repeated.

Rowan did as she asked.

She gazed into his face. "The flame is alight. The Choosing is completed," she said.

Rowan's mouth fell open. He glanced up and past the Keeper to the silent figures of the Candidates. Their eyes were wide with shock and disbelief.

"Keeper, the Choosing has not yet begun," he stammered. "The tests—"

"The trials you have just completed *were* the tests," she said.

Rowan stared at her.

Wearily she closed her eyes. "The old tests are no longer of use. More and more, the Candidates study for them. And study the people of Rin, too, so they may win their Chooser's favour. They are locked away from their fellows. From life itself. This is no way to choose a Maris leader. Long ago, I realised it was a mistake. I realised it when I saw that I myself could never do more than guard the Crystal. That I could not lead the Maris, or change their ways."

"You—" Rowan caught his breath. He looked wildly back at the watchful Jonn, at Jiller, lying still and silent on the couch.

He swung back to face the Keeper. Understanding flooded through him on a red tide of anger that washed away fear and doubt.

"It was you!" he hissed. "*You* planned all this. *You* gave my mother Death Sleep."

"You dare to accuse *me* ..." The voice was low, and full of warning. But Rowan cared nothing for that.

"Yes, I accuse you," he shouted. "You just admitted that the poison took two full hours to work. That means Mother took the poison when she first came to this Cavern. Before she even met the Candidates. Before she set foot on the Island."

He pointed at the Keeper with one bandaged hand. "You did it. You planned it all. You tricked me, and the Candidates, and you risked my mother's life! Just because you wanted to set tests for which no one was prepared!"

The Keeper opened her eyes, and for a moment the Crystal glowed with its old green fire.

"The Choosing must reveal the truth," she said. "The Crystal provides the knowledge, the experience, and the power. But the Keeper provides the care and cunning. The Keeper must be able to solve new problems, as well as old ones. The Keeper must be able to change as the sea changes, dare to try ways that have not been tried. Only then will Maris survive."

"You nearly killed my mother," Rowan panted.

"The death of one is of no account."

"And you risked so much else."

"Not so much, perhaps. For I trusted the Crystal, as I always have, and it told me all would be well. That you would succeed, and return in time. I had to break the chains that bind us. I did it in the only way I could. I used you. The one person I knew was not like the others of Rin."

They have collected news of you since the day you were born ...

Rowan stared at her. He should have realised that if the Candidates knew him, so did the Keeper. She, more than any.

"The Choosing is completed," droned the Keeper. "Name your Choice."

Rowan raised his eyes to the three Candidates standing behind the Keeper's chair.

Asha. Seaborn. Doss. He had grown to admire all of them. They had all stood by him when he faced the Great Serpent. And he knew now that none of them had been playing a part.

Seaborn really was brave and strong, and loved life, like Jonn. He had been chosen as Candidate by the clan of Fisk because of that. He was unusual for a Maris, but they thought he would please the Chooser of Rin.

Asha really was dutiful, honest and plain-speaking, like Jiller. She had been chosen by the clan of Umbray because of that. She was unusual for a Maris, but they thought she would please the Chooser of Rin.

And Doss. Doss really was dreamy. He cared for living things, and he had faced death, like Rowan himself. He had been chosen by the clan of Pandellis because of that. He was unusual for a Maris, but they thought he would please the Chooser of Rin.

All three Candidates had helped Rowan to solve the riddle of the antidote to Death Sleep. Each in their own way. But which one had shown the most care and cunning, the willingness to try new ways, that the Keeper had said the Maris needed?

"Name your Choice," said the Keeper weakly. "You—must— name it. Speak!"

The Crystal flickered.

Hurrying footsteps sounded on the stairs. Through the veil of water burst Perlain.

"Sails. We have seen sails," he gasped. "The horizon is filled with them. And they are moving in. It is the Zebak!"

21 – The Choice

Why do they come now?" Asha cried. "It is senseless! They can surely see the flame of the Choosing. The time to attack would have been before, when the Crystal was weak, and the Choosing had not been completed."

"We have heard they have grown cunning. Perhaps they have a plan we know nothing about," said Seaborn grimly. "Or perhaps they hope the Crystal may yet fail before the new Keeper is joined to it."

"Rowan!" cried Perlain. "Name your Choice. The Crystal dims."

Rowan heard an exclamation behind him, and turned. Jonn was bending over Jiller. Her eyes were open. She was smiling at him.

"I have been asleep," she murmured. "And Jonn, I had such wonderful dreams." Then a slight frown creased her forehead. "But where am I? Where is Rowan?"

Pure joy filled Rowan's heart. But it lasted only an instant. His mother lived. She was awake, and happy. But the Zebak were coming. He had to act. He had to name the new Keeper and renew the Crystal's life, or they were all lost.

He turned again to the Candidates.

"The Keeper has told me to look for care, and cunning, and the willingness to try new ways," he said rapidly. "She has said that the Crystal will supply everything else."

He looked into Asha's burning eyes. "You—you are good, and you will always do what you think is right," he stammered. "But your mind is not open. You cling to the rules and the old ways, and live only by those. So while I admire you, I cannot choose you."

Her expression did not change, but she bowed her head.

Rowan turned to Seaborn. "You are brave, and strong," he said. "And you are willing to try new ways. But you often act in haste, without the care and cunning the Keeper seeks. So while I hope we will always be friends, I cannot choose you."

Seaborn, too, bowed his head. But as he did, his eyes seemed to flash with something—something almost like relief. Rowan wondered about it only for a second. There was no time now for anything except the Choice.

He moved to Doss, and put his hand on his shoulder. They looked at one another. A long, searching look.

I pray I am right, thought Rowan.

"You must say the words," Perlain reminded him softly.

Rowan swallowed. "The Chooser has made the Choice," he said. He felt Doss's shoulder stiffen suddenly under his fingers. "Let the other Candidates leave this place."

Doss stood rigidly still. His eyes were blank, as though he saw nothing.

His usually calm face tense, Perlain took Asha and Seaborn through the veil of water, and then returned.

The Crystal glowed feebly. Once, twice, three times. The Keeper stirred. "The doors are locked and will not open again until the new Keeper wills," she breathed. "Make haste. Soon the sun will rise."

"Doss of Pandellis," said Perlain quickly. "The Crystal."

Doss moved to the Keeper's chair like one in a dream. Stiffly he stretched out his hand towards the Crystal's soft glow. Rowan looked curiously at his blank, unseeing eyes.

The eyes of one who has seen the Great Serpent, and lived.

It is right, Rowan told himself. My Choice is right. Doss has everything the Keeper asked for. And he was meant for this task. Like Orin, he saw the Great Serpent. And after that, he was changed.

Yet there was something wrong. Rowan could feel it.

Doss's hand hovered over the Crystal.

"Join with the Crystal, and with me," murmured the Keeper.

I saw the Great Serpent, too, Rowan thought suddenly. And so did Asha and Seaborn. But we are not changed. Why then was Doss? What happened to him, a year ago?

I remember nothing of the night ... I was changed ... Something was lost—or added. I do not know which.

What had happened to Doss during that long night, under the full moon, out of sight of land?

Under the full moon ...

"Wait!" Rowan burst out. He grabbed Doss's hand. His voice echoed, shockingly loud, around the Cavern. Jonn and Jiller looked up, startled, and Perlain gripped the back of the Keeper's chair.

Slowly Doss turned. He stared blankly, first at Rowan, then at the hand that gripped his own.

"Doss, you could not have seen the Great Serpent a year ago," gabbled Rowan.

"Rowan, this does not matter now," shouted Perlain. "For Orin's sake, do you not see? The Keeper is dying. Letting go of her life. The ceremony has begun. It must continue. The Zebak ..."

Doss's mouth opened. "The Chooser has made the Choice," he said flatly. "Let the other Candidates depart this place."

Rowan was shivering, but still he held fast to the cold, webbed hand. "In this month, at the full moon, the Great Serpent is on the Island laying its eggs. We know that now. Doss, you could not have seen it far out to sea."

"Rowan!" cried Jiller. "Let him go!"

Jonn sprang up and in two strides was by Rowan's side. "Rowan, let his hand go," he whispered urgently. "Nothing matters now. All questions can be answered later."

But Rowan knew the questions couldn't wait.

"Doss, speak to me!" he begged. "What is wrong with you? Tell me what happened to you that night. What changed you? It was not the Great Serpent. What was it?"

"The Great Serpent came up from the depths," droned Doss. "It towered above me. Its eyes were golden, and full of ancient secrets."

Rowan listened in horror. Doss was using the same words exactly as the ones he had used on the Island. Even his voice was the same. He was chanting, as though repeating a lesson learned by heart.

And he believes it, thought Rowan. He believes it. But it is not true!

"Its scales glittered like fire in the setting sun," chanted Doss. "It looked at me. I knew that I was going to die."

"This is not something you have seen in truth!" Rowan exclaimed. "This is something put into your mind by someone else!"

A terrible fear seized him. "Doss, who arranged for your boat to be damaged?" he cried. "Who was waiting for you out there, beyond the horizon? Who picked you up from the dark sea and kept you all night, then sent you back with only a false memory of what had happened to you?"

But he knew the answer. And by the terrified look on Perlain's face, he could see that the Maris man knew, too. There was only one possible explanation.

They have grown cunning …

"A Zebak boat picked you up!" he breathed. "By some means, the Zebak bent you to their will that night, Doss. They buried secret orders deep within your mind, and covered them with the false memory of the Great Serpent. When you came back to Maris, people saw you were changed, but they did not know the real reason. And why should they? Because even you did not."

"It is impossible," Rowan heard Jonn muttering to Jiller. "The boy's trainers would have seen it. The Keeper would have seen it."

"No!" Rowan exclaimed, without looking around. "A year ago, the Keeper's power had already dimmed. And no one else could have seen it, because part of the plan must have been that the secret orders would only come to the surface of Doss's mind when certain words were said."

He looked straight into Doss's blank eyes. "I said those words just a few moments ago, didn't I? They are always said when a Keeper is chosen. 'The Chooser has made the Choice.'"

Doss quivered, staring.

Rowan's stomach churned. It was horrible to see the familiar face so changed. "I saw and felt it happen, Doss. I wondered what was wrong then, and now I know. At that moment, you lost your own will. You became the servant of the Zebak. That is why their ships have come now. They saw the flame, and knew their time had come. They are waiting for your signal that the Crystal, and this land, are theirs."

Perlain groaned. He had covered his face with his hands and was rocking slowly backwards and forwards.

"Perlain!" said Rowan sharply. "Do not waste time despairing! Bring Seaborn and Asha back!"

Perlain shook his head.

"Quickly!" shouted Rowan. "Do you not understand? Doss cannot be Keeper. He will betray Maris. He will betray us all!"

"Look out!" shrieked Jiller.

Before all of them, she had seen the knife flashing in Doss's free hand.

With a cry, Jonn leaped forward and gripped the knife as it plunged towards the dying Keeper's heart. He wrestled Doss aside, and held him. Doss struggled wildly for a moment, then suddenly gave in. He hung in Jonn's grip, limp and still.

"The Chooser has made the Choice," he mumbled. "If the Choice is not Doss of Pandellis, the Keeper must die. The Crystal must die."

"Perlain!" Rowan screamed. "Why are you waiting? Bring—"

"The doors are locked," said Perlain. His voice was filled with despair. "They will open for none but the Keeper. And the Keeper cannot be roused. She is beyond our reach."

"Then you!" said Jonn roughly. "You, Perlain. You must join with the Crystal yourself. It may not be what you would wish. But better you as Keeper than none."

Perlain shook his head again. "I cannot," he said. "I am not known by the Crystal. If I touch it, I will die."

"Then what are we going to do?" Rowan cried out in desperation. "Perlain, what are we going to do?"

Perlain looked at him. "There is only one thing we can do," he said. "Apart from Doss of Pandellis, there is only one person here now who can touch the Crystal and live. Only one person who can join with it, to become Keeper of Maris. And that is you."

22 – Terror

o!” The word burst from Rowan’s lips and echoed around the Cavern. He backed away from the Keeper’s chair, the dying Crystal, shaking his head over and over again.

Never to see home again. Never to see the sky, the green hills, the stream, the snow on the Mountain. Never to feel the fresh, sweet air on his face, or hear the sounds of birds. Never. To spend the rest of his life below the earth, swallowed up, dissolved, in the great mystery of the Crystal.

“No,” he repeated. “No!”

“You must do it,” said Perlain.

“I am not of Maris,” cried Rowan. “I cannot—”

“You can,” said Perlain. “And if you do not, we are lost.” He held out his hands to Jiller. “Tell him,” he shouted.

Rowan spun round to face his mother. Tears were rolling down her cheeks. “You must do it. You are the only one,” she whispered. “The Crystal does not know me now. Only you. Only you …”

“Quickly!” hissed Perlain. “There is no time.”

Rowan turned to Jonn, who still held the silent Doss. Jonn’s mouth was grim and set. His eyes were full of pain as he nodded.

There was nowhere left for Rowan to turn, except to his own heart. And he knew that he had no choice. By giving up the things he loved, he might be able to save them. By refusing to give them up, he would almost certainly destroy them.

He straightened his shoulders, and walked to the Keeper. The Crystal lay like a stone in her lap. Only a tiny spark in its heart remained, lighting her hands with its dull green glow.

Rowan put his hands on hers. She opened her eyes.

“You …” she sighed. “Why?”

"There is no one else," said Rowan softly. Behind him he heard Jiller's low sobbing.

The Keeper closed her eyes again. She was beyond wonder, and questions. But her lips moved. Rowan bent down to hear what she was saying.

"I say the words, but no one believes. Nothing can stand against the power of the Crystal," breathed the voice in his ear. "Feel ... and ... understand."

And it was as though Rowan was falling—slowly, slowly, drifting through swirling ages of time and memory. He could no longer see the Cavern. No longer hear his mother's voice. He felt himself letting go. Giving himself up to the power, not with sadness, but with deep joy.

And as he sank deeper ... deeper, he knew that he was becoming part of something greater than himself. It was like a sea that was deep, broad, and as old as time.

Nothing could stand against it. No love of clan, of family. No ties, or claims of others. All was washing away. His very self—his loves, fears, hopes, mistakes—everything that bound him to his life was slipping from him. He struggled a little, not wanting to let them go.

Feel ... and ... understand.

Had the Keeper spoken again? Or was it a memory?

The hands beneath his stirred.

Nothing can stand against the power of the Crystal ...

Then Rowan understood. At last, he understood.

Help me, Keeper, he called in his mind. *Help me to do as I must.*

He felt a surge of power. And then he was crying out aloud. He was pulling one hand from the Crystal, bending backwards, and reaching out for the still, pale figure of Doss.

"Rowan!" Dimly he heard his mother scream. But he knew what he had to do.

He gripped Doss's hand, and dragged him away from Jonn. He felt the great healing power rushing through him into Doss like a river flowing into the sea.

Then, using the last of his strength, he pulled Doss forward. He guided Doss's small webbed hands over the Keeper's hands, and took his own away.

The separation hit him like a blow. He staggered back from the chair, and fell to his knees on the ground. His chest was filled with the sudden pain of loneliness and loss. Tears blinded him.

He became aware that the Cavern was echoing with sound.

"What have you done?" Perlain was shouting in panic.

"Rowan! Rowan!" Jiller was crying.

He tried to speak, but the words choked in his throat. He crawled backwards, away from the dazzling light. The Crystal was shining, brighter and brighter. It was alive with fire, sparkling with every colour of the earth, sea and sky. Colour and light filled the air, lit the streaming Cavern walls like rainbows ...

And then it was finished. The tiny, wizened body of the old Keeper lay like an empty shell on the chair. A new Keeper stood looking at them. His eyes were the deep, grave eyes of Doss of Pandellis. But he stood straighter and taller than Doss ever had. His clothes were no longer blue, but of no colour and all colours at once, like shining water. And in his hands the Crystal flashed and burned like a star.

Perlain fell back, and bowed. "I greet you, Keeper of the Crystal," he murmured. His face was stiff with terror.

"The sun is rising," said the Keeper. He turned to Rowan. "Come with me, up to the light."

Rowan and the others followed silently as he moved through the veil of water, up the stairs, and across the great empty room above. Without a sound, the doors swung open.

The space outside was crowded with people. Pandellis in blue. Umbray in silver. Fisk in green. All in their separate clans. They were staring out to sea, towards the rising sun.

The Keeper stepped out into the open air, the Crystal bright in his hands. A great cry went up. A cry of welcome, relief, and joy, as the people greeted him, and pointed to the sea.

Slowly the Keeper turned, and looked. The horizon was brown with Zebak sails. Rowan felt a chill of dread.

The Keeper held the Crystal high. It flashed like a beacon in the rising sun. The people's cries of joy became groans of fear as the brown sails leaped forward, as if in answer to a signal.

"He has called them in. We are lost," whispered Perlain.

The Keeper stood watching as the Zebak fleet flew towards them, swept before the wind. He made no move or sign.

Rowan felt a touch on his arm. "Take your mother," Jonn murmured in his ear. "Slip away through the crowd. Go as fast as you can, to Rin."

"I will not leave you, Jonn," said Jiller, overhearing.

"You must," he said grimly. "Someone must warn the people at home, so they are not taken by surprise."

"Then Rowan must go alone," she said. "I am still too weak to travel far. I would hold him back."

"Jiller, you must go!"

"I will not."

The people of Maris were deathly silent. All eyes were fixed on the Keeper. Waiting for his signal. Waiting for the order that would lead them to battle.

But the Keeper did not move.

I have done this, thought Rowan. And in the midst of his despair, he thought of Star, locked in her stable. Unable to run or defend herself. Waiting for slaughter at cruel hands.

He ran to the Keeper's side. "Doss—" he began. But the words died in his mouth as the Keeper turned to him.

"Doss of Pandellis is no more, Rowan of Rin," the Keeper said. "I am the Keeper of the Crystal."

"I thought—" Rowan began again. And again he broke off.

"You were right," said the Keeper softly, as if Rowan had spoken his thought aloud. "Only wait."

The first Zebak ships were so close now that Rowan could see the cruel, triumphant faces of the warriors who lined the decks. He could see the black line that marked each forehead from nose to hairline. He could see the gleaming metal of their weapons.

The Keeper raised his arms. "Now!" he said quietly. The Crystal flashed, blinding.

And at that instant, great black clouds swept across the horizon. They tumbled thick and dark across the sky, driven before an ice-cold wind, smothering the sun, smothering the pale sky. The whole world dimmed, and became dark as night.

"What is happening?" cried Jonn. He grabbed Rowan's arm. "Rowan—"

The Keeper held the Crystal higher. There was a crash of thunder, and lightning split the sky, spearing into the white-capped water.

The people screamed. And on the sea the ships of the Zebak, trapped close together, spun and floundered. Masts broke and sails ripped as wind roared and lightning cracked around them.

Then there was a writhing and bubbling from the sea, and the water foamed as the twisting, coiling serpents of the deep rose to the surface, angered at their waking.

They hissed and snatched at the great fighting ships that in the face of their rage were as frail as leaves in a running stream. Wood tore and splintered, useless weapons clashed and fell into the foam, and the doomed Zebak's terrified cries were lost in the roaring of the wind.

Rowan turned away. He tried to remember that these were the enemies of his people. That they had been coming to bring pain and death to those he loved. Still, he could not watch their destruction.

But the Keeper of the Crystal stood and saw it all. And only when it had finished did he calm the storm.

23 – Farewells

They were going home. Going with the blessings of the Maris, with many gifts, with promises to return soon. They had stayed two more days in Maris, to allow Jiller and Rowan time to rest. But now all of them longed to be gone.

When all was ready for the journey, Rowan left the safe house, and walked alone to the Cavern of the Crystal. The doors opened for him. He walked slowly across the empty, circular upper room, and down the stairs.

Welcome.

The Cavern was bathed in glorious light. The Keeper sat in his chair, surrounded by rainbows.

"I have come to say goodbye," said Rowan.

"It is not goodbye. You know that I will always be with you, Rowan of Rin," said the Keeper. "As you will always be with me."

Rowan nodded. He had not talked about this to anyone, even Jiller. But over the past days he had slowly realised the truth. That moment when the power of the Crystal had flowed through him to Doss of Pandellis had changed him for ever.

The Keeper smiled. "I have memories of Rin, though I have never seen it," he said. "I see the slip-daisies blooming yellow on the hills. I hear the bukshah lowing in the fields. I feel soft earth under my hands, and take pleasure in the small things growing."

"And I feel myself slipping through water like a fish," said Rowan. "I feel cool, wet sand under my feet. I mend nets by oil-fires at night. I hear sea-birds shrieking and see flying fish skimming the waves under a dark blue sky."

"So we understand one another, as no two people of Maris and of Rin ever have," said the Keeper. "And when I tell you that because of what happened on the morning you named your Choice your family will never again suffer at the hands of the Maris, you will believe me."

"Yes," said Rowan. "I will."

"On my orders Perlain of Pandellis has told the people what happened between us," the Keeper said. "He told them that I was a secret enemy of Maris, a tool of the Zebak, before I joined with the Crystal. But they saw with their own eyes what happened when the Zebak came."

He smiled. "And so at last they understand. It does not matter which clan brings forth the Keeper. Nothing can stand against the power of the Crystal. Not love of family, or friends, or home. Not loyalty to a clan or a country. Not even the mind games of an enemy."

"I only understood it when I felt the power for myself," Rowan whispered. "Only then did I realise that no Keeper could ever betray the people of Maris."

He turned to go. "Farewell, Doss," he said.

"Farewell, my friend," said the Keeper of the Crystal.

* * *

Many people stood at the outskirts of Maris to speed them on their way. Asha, Seaborn and Perlain were among them.

"Goodbye, Chooser of Rin." Asha shook Rowan's hand gravely. "I—am grateful to you."

Rowan blinked, unsure of what to say.

"If I had been Keeper, I would have ordered out the boats when the Zebak attacked. Because that is what has always been done. We would have fought, as we have always done. We might have won, by the power of the Crystal, but many of us would have died. You made the right choice in Doss of Pandellis. His mind is new and fresh. He will be like the Keepers of old. Using the Crystal, adding to its power, instead of only taking from it. And so I thank you."

She stepped back, stern and calm as always.

Seaborn came next. With him was a tall woman in the green of Fisk, her face no longer tight and serious, but full of light and joy. Rowan recognised her as one of the three who had escorted him to the Cavern. The woman who had watched them from the shore, when they were on the Island.

"This is Imlay. We are to marry in the summer, when my wounds have healed," Seaborn told him. "Perhaps you will come to our wedding. We would like to see you there, friend. You, more than any."

Rowan nodded, smiling. At last he understood the look of relief he had seen on Seaborn's face when he was told that he would not be Keeper of the Crystal. Seaborn was a strong, brave man. He had bent his will to his duty. He had tried his best to be what his clan wanted. But, having failed, he was free to live his life as he had longed to do. He was free to breathe the fresh air, to see the sky, to marry the woman he loved.

Perlain was last to bid them farewell. He shook hands with Jiller, with Jonn, and with Rowan. But Rowan noticed with a secret smile that he kept well away from Star.

"You may have no wish to visit the shores of Maris again, Rowan," Perlain said, in his formal way. "But should you come, my home will always be yours."

"I will be back," said Rowan. He glanced at Seaborn and Imlay, who stood watching from a distance. "If only for a wedding in the summer," he added.

Perlain smiled, and bowed.

And then Rowan, Jonn, Jiller and Star turned away from the sea, and began to walk. They walked for many minutes without speaking.

The river wound off into the distance, losing itself in the soft green hills. There was a long journey ahead, but none of them regretted it.

They were safe. They were together. And every step was taking them closer to home.

ROWAN AND THE ZEBAK

1 – The Warning

The grach flew west, following the scent. It had flown for a long time and it was tired and hungry, but it did not think of feeding or stopping to rest. There was no thought at all behind its flat yellow eyes. Just one fixed idea. To follow the scent, reach the place it had been told to reach, and take back to its masters what it had been told to take.

The grach was called Bara, and it was a hundred and twenty years old. It had been trained well. Not kindly, perhaps, but cleverly, and for many, many years. The idea that now, far away from the whips and shouts of its masters, it had the freedom to choose what it did, never entered its mind.

The sea had been left behind long ago, and dimly the grach was aware that below it now were rolling green hills and a winding stream glinting bright in the sunlight. It was aware that a mountain, its peak hidden in cloud, rose in the blue distance ahead.

But its eyes were not important now. Its ears, closed against the rushing of the wind and the beating of its own wings, were not important either. All that was important was its forked tongue, flickering in and out, tasting the air, tasting the scent.

It knew it was close to its goal. The scent was stronger—the warm animal scent that made its jaws drip with hunger. Bukshah. It even knew the name.

"Bukshah," its masters had said, so many times, flourishing the grey woolly hide in front of its face, feeding it bloody pieces of meat so that the delicious taste mingled with the hide-smell. When they had sent it away on this quest they had said it again. "Bukshah. Seek." And then they had loosed its chain.

The bukshah scent was strong, but there were other scents, too. Some the grach had tasted before, one it had not. The one it had not tasted was full of danger. It was fire, snow and ice. It was hot breath, dripping fangs and ancient, jealous power.

The leathery spines on the grach's back prickled with warning. But its yellow lizard eyes did not flicker, and the beating of its scaly mottled wings did not falter as it flew on, to Rin.

* * *

Rowan scanned the blue, blue sky above the village. It was still clear, except for the cloud that always shrouded the tip of the forbidden Mountain. And yet—surely a summer storm was brewing. How else could he explain his strange, nagging feeling that something unexpected and fearful was about to happen? The sense of dread had begun at mid-morning, and had grown stronger every moment since.

It is nothing, he told himself firmly. He fought away the fear, and did not speak of it to Jiller, his mother. Why worry her needlessly, today of all days?

Today Jiller should be as light-hearted as his little sister Annad, who was already dancing around the cottage garden, thinking herself very fine in a new pink dress. She should be as plainly joyful as Strong Jonn, even now coming through the gate, swinging Annad into his arms and striding towards the house, splendid in his wedding finery.

Rowan made himself wave to Jonn, shout a greeting. And when the dark, fearful feeling stabbed at him yet again, he forced it down.

* * *

The hard-working people of Rin did not often lay aside their everyday cares for festivals and holidays. But even in Rin a wedding was a cause for celebration, and *this* wedding—the marriage of Strong Jonn of the Orchard to Jiller of the Field—was a greater occasion than most.

Jonn and Jiller were well-loved, and Jiller's son, Rowan of the Bukshah, was Rin's greatest hero, if its most unlikely one. Shy, dreamy and timid though he was, he had conquered the forbidden Mountain and faced the Dragon that reigned at its peak. He had allied himself with the wandering Travellers to save Rin from a terrible fate. And it was whispered that he was joined to the fishlike Maris people on the coast by his strange bond with their mysterious leader, the Keeper of the Crystal.

Once the most disappointing child in the village, Rowan was now respected. No one teased or criticised him these days. No one told him he was too old to be the keeper of the gentle bukshah.

He was even feared by some, who thought he had unnatural powers. Such people stopped speaking when Rowan came into the storehouse or passed by a meeting place, and warned their children not to annoy him. When a black bukshah calf was born in spring— black, instead of the usual soft grey—such people whispered that it was an omen, a sign of Rowan's power.

If anyone had told them that Rowan wanted nothing more than to be accepted as one of them, that this was all he had ever wanted, they would have laughed.

It was largely because of Rowan that this marriage was more than a simple village celebration. Yesterday the three great Traveller kites, their riders dangling beneath them, had appeared in the sky above the valley. Since then, the tribe that always followed them had made camp on the hills, ready to join the party and make music. Perlain of Pandellis had come from Maris to represent his people and bring gifts. He had left the sea and the salt spray of his home gladly, though Maris skin dried and cracked quickly inland, and the journey had not been comfortable for him.

This day was important enough to tempt the stolid millers, Val and Ellis, from their mill. It had even caused gruff, solitary Bronden the furniture-maker to shut her work shed for the day. No one wanted to miss the celebration, or fail to pay their respects.

So at noon, when Jiller and Jonn walked with Rowan and Annad to the great tree above the bukshah field, a crowd was waiting. Only Sheba, the village Wise Woman, had kept away, and stayed crouching alone in her hut beyond the orchard. No one was surprised at that, and everyone was secretly glad. For Sheba, though sought out by many in times of sickness or danger, would have been an uncomfortable wedding guest.

As he entered the tree's welcome shade, Rowan was only half-aware of Annad dancing excitedly beside him, of Jonn and Jiller walking ahead, and of the crowd staring. The feeling of dread was growing stronger, clouding his mind, darkening his thoughts, making him silent and watchful.

He gritted his teeth, trying to make sure the darkness did not show. Everyone in Rin is happy, ready to celebrate, he told himself. Why should I be different?

You have always been different, a voice at the back of his mind said. *And now more than ever.*

Angrily he pushed the voice away. He turned his head and caught sight of Ogden the storyteller, the leader of the Travellers, standing with his adopted daughter, Zeel, and the rest of the tribe at one side of the crowd.

Beside the people of Rin, sober even when dressed in their best, the Travellers looked as bright as birds in their vivid silks, their long, curling hair threaded with ribbons, beads and feathers. But with a stab of fear Rowan saw that their faces were watchful. They were standing very still, as though every muscle in their lean brown bodies was poised for flight. And Ogden's deep-set eyes were grave.

Jonn and Jiller noticed nothing. They smiled and bowed to the Travellers, and Ogden bowed low in return. But his dark gaze looked beyond them to Rowan, and in his eyes was a question. Rowan knew what it was.

Something is wrong in the land. We feel it. You feel it, too. I can see you do. What is it?

Rowan shook his head slightly. *I do not know.*

Ogden's eyes flicked to the front of the crowd where Perlain, the Maris man, stood with Allun the baker and Marlie the weaver, Jonn and Jiller's great friends.

Marlie and Allun were smiling, handing flowers to Jiller. But Perlain, small and glistening in his closely fitting blue garments, stood stiffly, his webbed hands pressed tightly to his sides. The hood that helped to protect him from the drying sun had been pushed back as a sign of respect, so Rowan could see that his flat, glassy eyes were fixed and staring.

Perlain was afraid. But what was there to be afraid of, here under this green shade, in this protected valley?

There is danger, Rowan. Danger in the land.

The message suddenly rang clearly in Rowan's mind. It was the Keeper of the Crystal in Maris, warning him, as he had warned Perlain.

But already Jonn and Jiller were standing before old Lann, and the ceremony had begun.

I cannot say anything now, Rowan thought desperately. If I even try, no one will listen, however much they say I am a hero. They will think I am trying to stop the marriage. Mother and Jonn will think so, too. I cannot do it.

There was a time when he had hated the thought that Jonn might take the place of Sefton, his father. But now he knew that no one would ever take Sefton's place—in Jiller's heart, or his. It was just that hearts were big enough to accept more loves than one. And Strong Jonn of the Orchard, his father's friend, was his friend, too.

He had never said this to Jiller or to Jonn. In Rin it was thought a sign of weakness to discuss feelings openly. Only by appearing happy at this wedding could Rowan show how glad he was that it was taking place.

There was someone else to consider, as well. Rowan glanced at his little sister, standing wide-eyed beside him. Annad had never known their father, who had died when she was just a baby. She adored Jonn. She had looked forward so much to this day. She had loved the idea of dressing up and parading in front of the village.

I cannot do it, he thought again. I cannot break this moment. Perlain and Ogden are content to wait. So I will be content, also. What harm can there be in waiting just a little?

Bitterly, bitterly, in the days that followed, did Rowan wish he had decided differently.

2 – The Attack

here was silence under the great tree as Jonn and Jiller made their final vows. Then, as Lann pronounced them husband and wife, there was a loud burst of clapping, cheering and congratulations.

The Rin adults clustered around and took Jonn and Jiller off to the feast that had been set up nearby, courteously making sure that Perlain and the Travellers were swept along with the tide. Annad leaped to join her friends as though a spring had been released inside her. Rowan stayed where he was, watching.

Jonn and Jiller sat down at the head of the main feasting table, laughing and talking. All the tables were loaded with the best the village could provide. Platters were piled high with fruits and salad vegetables, the best bukshah cheese, the softest bread rolls that Allun and his mother, Sara, could fashion and toffees, jellies and cakes of every kind from Solla the sweet-maker. Great cool jugs of hoopberry juice and slip-daisy wine stood here and there.

The Travellers' music began. Ogden must have decided that it was best to continue with the festivities as though nothing was wrong. Rowan leaned against the smooth trunk of the great tree, trying to order his thoughts. Sunlight sparkled through the leaves, flecking the ground with spots of gold.

Under this green canopy the people of Rin had married, named their children and farewelled their dead since they had first arrived in the valley three hundred years ago. The tree had been large then. Now it was a giant.

"Rowan! Look!" Annad's piercing voice rose above the music, the talk of the adults and the giggling of her friends.

Rowan glanced around. Annad was standing by the fence, looking down at the bukshah field. She beckoned to him excitedly. "Come and see!" she called.

He walked down to join her. Her friends grew silent and moved back shyly as he approached, but Annad ran to him, seized his arm and pulled him towards the fence.

"They are dancing!" she laughed, pointing.

Rowan caught his breath in surprise. The humped grey beasts had arranged themselves, side by side, shoulder to shoulder, into a tight circle. Their heavy heads all faced outwards. Their bodies were pressed together so closely that their manes seemed joined. Many were pawing the ground. At first glance it really did look as though they were doing some sort of dance.

Annad was jumping up and down. "Rowan, come on!" she squealed, tugging at his hand. "Come down and see them with me!"

"No, Annad," Rowan smiled. Much as he would have liked to leave the gathering for the bukshah field, he knew that it would seem odd and impolite if he did.

Annad exclaimed impatiently and pulled her hand away from his. She shook off her soft shoes and, heedless of her fine clothes, clambered through the fence and began running across the field beyond.

"Annad!" called Rowan. But the little girl took no notice. He smiled and shook his head as he watched her jump the stream and run towards the bukshah, calling to Star, their leader. Her hair flew like spun gold around her head. Her pink dress billowed in the faint breeze. She looked like a huge butterfly fluttering across the grass.

Rowan expected the bukshah to break out of their strange formation when Annad disturbed them, but to his surprise there was no movement from the herd at all. They stood like rocks, their noses up, sniffing the air.

Rowan stared in puzzlement. And then something else struck him. Where were the young bukshah—the calves that had been born in the spring? He could not see them anywhere. Even the black one, the smallest of all, was missing.

Annad was dancing towards Star now, chattering to her, stretching out her hand. Rowan jumped with shock as Star rumbled warningly and roughly jerked her head, pushing Annad away.

Star was always so gentle. The smallest child in Rin could lead her. She loved Annad almost as much as she loved Rowan himself. Yet she seemed to be trying to keep Annad away from the herd.

Rowan frowned, gripping the fence. Or—was Star trying to make Annad run back to where she had come from? To shelter. To safety ...

"Annad!" he called urgently. But his voice was drowned by the music and laughter around the feasting tables, and Annad did not hear.

He saw her hesitate for a moment, then take a step forward and again stretch out her hand. This time the jerk of Star's head was hard enough to send her tumbling onto the grass. The huge beasts on Star's left and right pawed the ground, but did not leave their places.

They will not break the circle, thought Rowan. And suddenly he understood why. The calves were inside, enclosed and hidden by a wall of strong adult bodies.

A terrible fear gripped him. He scrambled awkwardly through the fence and started to run towards the stream. "Annad!" he shouted. "Annad! Beware!"

But already it was too late. What happened next took only moments, but afterwards, to the end of his life, Rowan would always remember it as though it had taken long, long minutes.

He was running, running, his chest aching with breathless fear, but he could not run fast enough. He saw Annad turning towards him as she clambered to her feet, brushing at her dress. He saw her pink, annoyed face, her spun-gold hair, suddenly darkened by a rushing shadow that blocked the sun.

He heard a terrible wakening roar from the peak of the Mountain, and an answering defiant, rasping hiss from the sky above. He heard the rush of wings, and the bellowing of the bukshah as a huge shape plummeted towards them—a creature mottled green, yellow and grey, spiked and hideous, with three lashing tails. He heard his own cry of warning, and Annad's high-pitched scream as she realised her danger and began to run, her dress whipping and tangling in the wind created by the mighty wings.

Rowan leaped the stream, shouting in terror, shouting to Annad to drop to the ground, hide herself in the long grass. But he knew, even as he called, that Annad was hearing and understanding nothing but her own need to escape.

With horror he saw the beast's flat yellow eyes slide to one side and fix themselves on the small, fluttering, running figure, bright pink and gold against the green field. For an instant the creature hovered, and around its neck Rowan caught a glimpse of something that astonished and bewildered him.

Then his mind was wiped clear by panic. The creature was turning in the air, wheeling away from the bukshah and plunging instead towards Annad, its huge red talons reaching for her.

"No!" Rowan hurled himself forward, waving his arms, shrieking at the beast, trying to distract it, to make it turn again. But in an instant it had swooped, and then, its great wings beating with a noise like thunder, it was hissing in triumph, speeding away.

Its burden was light and slowed it not at all. In seconds it was a dark spot above the distant hills. In minutes it had disappeared from sight.

And Annad had gone with it.

3 – The Decision

We must go after the beast. Attack it where it lands."

"We cannot leave the village undefended. It may come again."

"But Annad—"

"The child is gone. Gone. There is nothing to be done."

Huddled on the ground, numb with misery, Rowan heard the voices around him. Familiar voices. Sara. Old Lann. Marlie. Bronden.

He clambered to his feet and stared around, dazed. People had come running from the feast tables. Now they clustered together, shocked and bewildered, their festival clothes rumpled, their good shoes sinking into the long, rich grass of the field. There was no sign of the Travellers or of Perlain.

Jiller, all the colour drained from her face, was standing very straight. Jonn was close beside her but she did not lean on him. That was not her way.

Old Lann turned to her. "What do you want of us, Jiller of the Field?" she asked formally.

"Nothing." Jiller spoke through lips that barely moved. "There is nothing to be done. Annad is gone."

"No!" The word burst from Rowan before he could stop it.

His mother turned to him. Her eyes were black with grief.

"She is gone, Rowan," she repeated. "You saw the creature take her. By now she is dead."

Rowan shook his head. "We—we do not know that," he stammered. "The beast—was not wild, but tame."

There was a moment's shocked silence, then Lann hobbled up to him. "What do you mean?" she demanded.

"It—it was wearing a collar. I saw. A metal collar, with a fastening for a chain," Rowan said.

Lann stared at him. Her face was creased into a thousand lines that showed her pain. She, too, had loved little Annad.

Rowan took a deep breath. "I believe—it came from over the sea," he said. He felt the eyes of all the villagers upon him, and his mother's eyes most of all. His face burned, but he made himself go on. "On the coast, the Keeper of the Crystal felt danger come. The Travellers, too, felt a strangeness in the land."

There was a whispering in the crowd.

"And you, Rowan?" Jiller's voice sounded flat and dead.

Rowan swallowed. This was the question he had been dreading. He bent his head and forced himself to speak. "I felt—something. A warning. But I thought—there was time ..." His voice trailed away miserably. He looked up.

His mother's face had gone blank. "You said nothing to me of this," she said.

"I—felt I could not. I did not wish to spoil this day," Rowan mumbled.

Slowly Jiller nodded. Then she turned and walked away.

Marlie hurried after her, but Jonn lingered to put his hand on Rowan's shoulder. His face was furrowed with grief, but his voice was steady. "You could not have known, Rowan," he said. "Do not blame yourself. Come home with us now."

Rowan shook his head. He could not go home. He knew he would be no comfort to his mother. In her heart she must hate him for what he had done. For what he had *not* done.

Jonn hesitated. Then he squeezed Rowan's shoulder, and left him.

The crowd moved restlessly. Rowan caught sight of Allun standing to one side, his usually good-humoured face tight and pale.

"If one creature has come here from across the sea, who is to say when more may follow?" someone called. "We must arm ourselves and prepare."

Timon the teacher took Jonn's place at Rowan's side. "Is there anything more that you can tell us, Rowan?" he asked urgently.

"We need to know nothing more," snapped Val the miller, towering shoulder to shoulder with her brother in the centre of the crowd. "Who would tame such a beast to do their will? Who would collar it with metal rather than cloth or leather? Who would send it across the sea to attack us? It is the Zebak."

The hated name fell into the crowd like a stone into a still pond. A low muttering began, rippling outwards.

"The Zebak were defeated in Maris, not long ago," Bree of the Garden protested. "They suffered heavy losses. Would they try again so soon?"

"It could be that their leaders have at last decided that invasion by sea is too dangerous," Timon said. "So they are testing a new way of attacking us—from the air."

The muttering rose to an angry babble, and many fists were clenched. Only the oldest of the people now living in Rin had battled the Zebak hand to hand. But all had seen pictures of cruel Zebak faces, brows marked with a black line running from hairline to nose. All knew that their ancestors had first come to this land as Zebak warrior slaves. All were ready to fight to keep their freedom.

As the noise around him increased, Rowan looked over to where Allun was standing. But Allun had gone.

Old Lann banged her stick on a rock and silence fell. "We will talk more of this," she said firmly. "But first we must clear the feasting tables, and take what food remains to the coolhouse. Nothing must be wasted. There may be hard times ahead."

Rowan stood silently as the crowd melted away to do her bidding.

"No doubt you did what you thought best, Rowan of the Bukshah," snorted Bronden as she passed him. "You, and your Maris and Traveller friends—who, I notice, have fled at the first sign of danger. But perhaps another time you will think better of keeping special knowledge to yourself."

She was gone before he could answer.

"Your people do not understand how it is with you," a quiet voice said in his ear.

Rowan swung around to see Perlain standing beside him. The Maris man was dripping wet. "I did not want to intrude on your meeting," he explained. "And I was dry. So I soaked in the stream and listened. The man with clever eyes—he spoke wisely, I think."

"Timon. Yes," Rowan murmured.

"This episode may have been only a test," Perlain said calmly. "But, if so, the test has been successful. Soon the Zebak will have proof that their beast has been to Rin, and back."

Rowan's mouth felt as dry as dust. He licked his lips. "Do you think it will deliver Annad to the Zebak—alive?" he asked finally. His heart had begun thudding like the pounding of a Traveller drum.

"Yes," said Perlain simply. "The Zebak have always preferred to take their captives alive."

Rowan shuddered in the warm sun as though chilled to the bone. His mind was a whirlwind of shock and grief, but at the centre of the whirlwind was one clear thought. Annad was a captive because of him. Because he had not sounded a warning when first he sensed danger. Because he had let her go to the bukshah field alone. Because he had been too slow to reach her side before she was snatched away.

Perlain was regarding him thoughtfully. "You are very grieved," he said. "What can I give to help you?"

And suddenly Rowan knew.

"You can give me a boat, Perlain," he said. "I am returning to Maris with you. Then I am going to the place of the Zebak, to find my sister and bring her home."

Perlain shook his head. "You cannot do it, my friend. Such a journey would be filled with peril. And at its end you would only join your sister in her fate, without hope of escape."

He heard a sound behind him and jumped as he saw Star standing there. "Your bukshah wants your attention," he said nervously, moving aside.

Rowan rubbed Star's soft nose, taking comfort in her massive, woolly strength. She pushed against him and rumbled deep in her throat.

"Do not mourn," he whispered to her. "You did your best to warn Annad away from the field. And you protected the calves bravely. They were safe inside your circle."

"Does the creature understand your words?" asked Perlain curiously.

"She understands what I mean by them," said Rowan. He saw Star's nose twitch, and whirled around to search the sky. But no dark shape loomed there—only a bright splash of yellow against the blue.

It swooped lower and lower until the figure of the girl who swung from the great kite was clear. Zeel.

Star huffed gently in Rowan's ear. Turning, he saw Ogden the storyteller approaching across the field.

"The creature was far distant before we could reach our camp and launch the kite," Ogden called. "I fear Zeel lost sight of it. Her signal was of disappointment."

Rowan had heard no signal. But he would not have expected to. The Travellers' reed pipes made sounds that were too high for others to hear.

Zeel's feet touched the ground lightly. The kite billowed behind her, then fell into soft, bright folds. She gathered it up and strode towards them. Her hair had blown back from her face. Her straight brows were drawn together and her pale eyes were angry.

Rowan felt Perlain stiffen beside him. "Rowan! She is not a Traveller!" the Maris man hissed in his ear. "She does not have the black line tattoo on her brow—but still, she is Zebak! I see it, now." His hand moved, feeling for the knife at his belt.

"Peace, Perlain," Rowan hastily whispered back. "Zeel is Zebak born, but she was washed up by the sea as a tiny child, and Ogden took her in. She can be trusted. She is as much a Traveller as any of her people. Believe me."

Perlain lowered his hand, but he remained watchful as Zeel joined them.

"I am sorry, Rowan of the Bukshah," she said. "The beast far out-paced me." She turned to Ogden. "It was as you thought. It turned and took the most direct way to the coast. It will be over the cliffs by now."

Rowan wet his dry lips.

"Will you go after it?" Zeel asked him almost casually, throwing the kite silk over her shoulder.

He nodded.

"This is foolishness," Perlain said coldly. "However brave a fish may be, it is doomed if it ventures into a serpent's lair."

"It will not be just one fish," snapped Zeel. "Rowan will have many companions. The people of Rin are—"

"No," Rowan interrupted hurriedly, feeling his face begin to burn. "I will be going alone."

Zeel looked startled and unbelieving.

"Perlain will arrange a boat for me," Rowan rushed on, in case Zeel, too, should begin to argue with him. "And if the Travellers could spare two kites and their riders to speed us to Maris, we will save much time."

He saw Perlain open his mouth in alarmed protest, but Ogden was already nodding agreement. "Tor may go to Maris," he said. "Tor and—"

"And me," Zeel broke in.

Ogden smiled slightly. "So—it is settled."

"It is madness!" snorted Perlain. "The seas between here and the land of the Zebak are treacherous. And even if by a miracle Rowan survives to reach the shore, what will he do then? Where will he go? No one can know."

Rowan thought about that, and his stomach seemed to turn over. "There is someone who might know," he said reluctantly.

How foolish, he thought, meeting Ogden's amused eyes, to be afraid of *this*, when the journey ahead is so perilous.

"Not so foolish," smiled Ogden, and Rowan realised with a shock that the storyteller had read his thoughts. "But you are wise to face your fear. The time the meeting may take will be well spent." He thought for a moment, stroking his chin, then looked up. "I must leave you," he said. "Zeel will accompany you to our camp, when you are ready."

He bowed, and left them.

Star nuzzled Rowan's neck, and he stroked her gently. "I am going far away, Star," he said in a low voice. "If I do not return, the people will appoint another keeper of the bukshah. Someone kind— do not fear. And in the meantime Mother will see to you—for my sake, and for Annad's."

Star's small, wise eyes regarded him gravely, as though she understood, and was unhappy.

Rowan gave her a final pat, then turned quickly and walked with Zeel and the silent Perlain up to the orchard. They threaded their way through the whispering trees towards the small hut beyond. Rowan did not know what awaited him there. He only knew that if he was to find Annad, he needed help. And his only hope of help lay with Sheba.

The strange pale grass that grew outside the hut was unmarked except for a single set of footprints that led to the door.

"Your Wise Woman already has a visitor," Zeel said. "A man, I think, who treads fast and lightly, like a Traveller, but with heavier shoes, like those of Rin."

Rowan thought that Sheba's visitor might be the only person in Rin, apart from Sheba herself, who would let him go his own way without hindrance. Leaving Zeel and Perlain, he tiptoed across the grass, crept to the door of the hut and pressed his ear against it. A loud cackle of laughter rang out inside and he leaped back, shivering with fright, feeling six years old again.

"Come in, skinny rabbit," growled Sheba. "I have been waiting for you."

4 – The Gift

owan entered the hut, straining his eyes to see in the gloom, choking a little at the thick smell of smoke, ash, dust and bitter herbs that filled the room.

Sheba sat with her back to the door. She was holding her hands out to the fire, rubbing them as if to wash them in the dull red glow. On the other side of the fireplace stood her visitor. As Rowan had hoped, it was Allun. His face was pale with anger.

"The entertainment here has been poor," Sheba rasped, without turning around. "This half-Traveller clown has not amused me with his whining tale. A brat lost through her own foolishness and her brother's weakness—pah! And now he has grown silent, sulking like a child himself. You will provide better sport, skinny rabbit."

She chuckled to herself and spread her bony fingers, admiring the long yellow nails that curved at the tips like claws.

Rowan struggled to keep calm, though her words hurt and angered him. He knew that it was part of Sheba's game to find her visitors' weakest points and prod at them. She liked to watch them first writhe, then give way to fear or fury.

"It seems that your tricks do not work with everyone, old woman," jeered Allun. "The boy is too strong for you."

Oh, Allun, be still, Rowan thought desperately. You do not understand how spiteful she is. But he did not dare to say a word.

"Leave me, Allun the baker," hissed Sheba. "I am sick of your foolish face."

"I have also seen enough of yours," answered Allun, with a grim smile. "But I do not choose to leave my friend Rowan alone with you."

Sheba sneered at him, and turned in her chair to face Rowan. "So— we are to have a gathering," she said, baring her long brown teeth in a horrible grin. "Your companions—those who lurk outside—must join us, then. I have a fancy to see them face to face."

Rowan hesitated.

Sheba's grin disappeared. "Fetch them!" she thundered.

Rowan went back outside and beckoned to Zeel and Perlain. "She wants you, and I am sure she will not speak to me unless you come," he whispered to them. "But once you are inside, say nothing. Do not be tempted to—"

"Wise advice," croaked Sheba's voice from inside the hut. "Do not be tempted to match wits with me. Show yourselves!"

Zeel, brows drawn together in a frown, and Perlain, expressionless as only a Maris could be, followed Rowan into the dim little room.

"Ah! Now the gathering is complete," said Sheba, looking her new visitors up and down. "I had a half-breed clown and a Rin weakling turned hero. Now, to join them, a fish-man out of water and a Zebak who pretends to be a Traveller. What a fine collection of oddities." She laughed heartily, slapping at her knees so that dust and ash flew into the thick air around her chair.

Rowan heard Zeel draw a quick breath of anger, and saw Perlain glance at her and then veil his eyes. But they both kept silence. Allun, unfortunately, could not.

"You are forgetting to include yourself, good lady," he said loudly. "The greatest oddity of all."

Sheba abruptly stopped laughing. "I forget nothing, clown," she growled warningly. "And you would be wise to remember it."

There was a short, unpleasant silence. Then Sheba turned again to Rowan.

"Now, what gift have you brought for old Sheba, Rowan of the Bukshah?" she croaked. "What do you have to trade for the knowledge you seek? The knowledge only I can give you? Come closer." She smiled horribly.

"Beware, Rowan," muttered Allun. "She spits like a cat, but more unpleasantly."

Rowan moved further into the room, his heart sinking. He had completely forgotten that Sheba would expect a gift. Allun had brought her honey cakes, sweet buns and a bowl of fruits from the abandoned feast. Rowan could see them in a basket by the chair. Desperately he felt in his pockets, hoping to find something, anything, he could offer her.

She watched him in silence, waiting.

"I—I am sorry," he said at last. "I have nothing to trade just now. But what I ask is—is very important. I beg you to help me. If you do, I will make sure you are repaid."

"So," grinned Sheba, her eyes shining red in the firelight. "You will make sure, will you? And how, my little hero, will you do that, when you are in chains in the land of the Zebak?"

Rowan heard Allun's muffled gasp beside him, but he did not turn to him, or look at Perlain and Zeel standing by the door. He concentrated all his will on Sheba.

"I will write a note, asking my mother to make my promise good," he said. "She will do it."

"And will you give me whatever I ask?" demanded Sheba.

Rowan thought quickly. He knew she was trying to trap him. "I will give you what you ask if it is within my power to give," he said at last. "And if the giving hurts no other person."

He watched Sheba closely, but the old woman showed neither disappointment nor triumph. She just nodded. "Write, then," she said. "The pen is beside you."

Rowan looked, and saw a pen, some ink and a sheet of paper lying on a small table at Sheba's elbow. Realising at once that she had planned this from the beginning, he knelt beside the table and picked up the pen with a feeling of dread.

"Rowan, do not trust her," Perlain warned.

Sheba darted him a black look. "Silence, fish-man!" she ordered.

But Rowan had put the pen down. "Before I write, give me the help you have promised, Sheba," he said, trying to keep his voice steady.

She grinned at him. "You have grown crafty and bold, skinny rabbit. Crafty like your fishy friend. Bold like the pale-eyed Zebak girl. But what is to stop you running away, once I have given what I have to give, and told what I have to tell?"

Rowan kept silence and looked down at the paper. He felt Sheba's eyes burning into his head, but he did not look up. He knew that if he did he would not be able to hold firm.

A long minute passed. Then Rowan heard a sigh and a rustling sound, as though the old woman was moving in her chair.

"Very well," Sheba said.

Rowan looked up and saw that she was holding something out to him. It was a small, thin package, wrapped in oiled cloth and tied with a cord of faded, plaited silk. He took it, his heart thudding with excitement. The wrapping cloth was thick, and smelt strongly of the fire, of ash and of bitter herbs. He could not guess what might be inside. He began to pull at the cord, but the knots would not loosen.

"Only when you reach the land you seek will it open," muttered Sheba. "Its contents are for use when you really need them. When you have no hope. Till then, keep it well, for it is precious."

Rowan slipped the package inside his shirt, his fingers trembling.

"I have given what I have to give," said Sheba sullenly. "What I have to tell will be told after you have done your part. Now, write."

Rowan dipped the pen in the ink and wrote. *Mother, I owe the Wise Woman Sheba a debt. She is to have ...*

He stopped and looked up, the pen still poised over the paper. Sheba's eyes were gleaming. Her hands rubbed together, making a dry, rasping sound.

"What is it you want?" Rowan whispered.

"My price is small," said Sheba. "It is the black calf, born to the bukshah herd in spring."

Rowan went cold. The bukshah were loving, and took comfort in each other's company. The thought of the little black calf being made to spend its life here alone, away from the open fields, away from its mother and its friends, was heart-breaking.

"The calf is too—too young to leave its mother," he stammered.

A slow grin spread over Sheba's face once more. "I will wait. For a while, as it happens, I will be much occupied, with no time for it."

"Why do you want it?" Rowan managed to ask.

"Because it takes my fancy." Sheba swung round to face him, and her grin broadened. "Because it is an oddity. Apart from the herd.

Like me." She leaned forward, her greasy hair swinging around her face. "Like your friends here. And like you, Rowan of the Bukshah."

The words struck the most tender place in Rowan's mind and clung there, stinging like fiery sparks. He looked down again at the pen.

"Perhaps you care more for the beast's freedom than for your sister's," sneered Sheba. "If so, give me back my gift, and stop wasting my time."

Rowan knew he had to do what she asked. He wrote with a heavy heart, then stood up and held out the note. Sheba snatched it, studied it carefully with narrowed eyes, then nodded, satisfied.

"Good," she said, folding the paper and stuffing it under the cushion of her chair. "So—the time has come." She turned to Perlain, Allun and Zeel. "Leave us," she said abruptly.

"I am comfortable here," Allun smiled.

Sheba's eyes glittered red.

"Please go," Rowan begged.

Zeel and Perlain exchanged glances. Zeel nodded, took Allun's arm and tugged at it. Perlain pushed the door open, and together he and Zeel managed to persuade Allun outside. The door closed behind them and the latch fell with a click.

The little room seemed empty without them. Rowan stood by Sheba's chair, feeling very alone.

5 – The Rhyme

aking no notice of Rowan, Sheba bent, picked up a handful of tiny sticks from the box beside her chair, and threw them onto the fire. They blazed up instantly, red and green flames dancing on the blackened wood. Misshapen shadows leaped like evil spirits about the room. Rowan's skin began to prickle with fear.

"Hold out your hand!" Sheba ordered suddenly.

Hesitantly, Rowan stretched out his right hand and the old woman seized his wrist. She gripped it tightly, her pointed nails digging into his flesh. He took a sharp breath and looked up. His eyes were caught and held by hers. They were strangely mocking, and deep, so deep. He could not look away.

"Now we will see which of us is stronger," Sheba droned, in an altered voice. Her eyes grew deeper still, drawing him in. It was as though he was falling into them, plunging down, down …

Then, dimly, as if from far away, he heard Sheba cackling. He struggled, blinked, and the spell was broken. She was laughing in his face, still gripping his wrist.

"So," she grinned. With astonishing strength, she dragged his hand towards the fire. The flames flickered higher, licking at Rowan's fingers like greedy tongues, scorching and burning.

With a cry he struggled to pull away, but Sheba's grip was as hard as stone and she was no longer listening to him. Her head was flung back, her eyes were closed, and she was mumbling to herself, swaying slightly from side to side. The fire burned higher, higher—she began to speak. The words came to Rowan through a haze of searing pain:

Five strange fingers form fate's hand,
Each plays its part at fate's command.
The fiery blaze the answer keeps,

And till its time each secret sleeps.
When pain is truth and truth is pain,
The painted shadows live again.
Five leave, but five do not return.
Vain hope and pride in terror burn.

Sheba's eyes opened and Rowan felt her grip loosen. He wrenched himself away from her and stumbled back from the fire, cradling his injured hand against his chest, sobbing with pain and shock. He could hear banging on the door, and Allun and Zeel shouting. But the door was sealed against them.

Sheba was lying back in her chair as if exhausted, but still she found the strength to laugh. "Oh, my little hero," she jeered, "did you not like old Sheba's lesson? Here is another."

The pain rose in a great wave, unbearable. And then, suddenly, it disappeared as if it had never been.

Bewildered and shaking, Rowan looked down. Instead of being burned and blistered as he had expected, his hand was smooth and unmarked. He stared at it, astounded.

"Not all is as it seems," croaked Sheba. "Now—be off with you, before your foolish friends injure themselves by beating at my door."

Rowan felt anger rise in him. It burned in his chest, searing hot, like the fire that had burned his hand. He fought it down with all his strength.

"Allun, Zeel," he shouted towards the door. "Wait!"

The banging stopped, and he faced Sheba once more. "You have not yet told me what I need to know," he said, and wondered at the calmness of his voice.

She shrugged. "I have told you what I can, which is all I promised. You have the words. Remember them."

"They are not enough!" Rowan exclaimed. "You have not told me where I must go in the land of the Zebak, and what I must do, to save Annad."

"How could I tell you that, Rowan of the Bukshah?" Sheba yawned. "How could I know? The land of the Zebak is far away. Too far—even for me." Her eyes closed.

"But—you did not tell me this before!" Angry tears stung Rowan's eyes. He dashed them away furiously.

Sheba's thin mouth curved into a smile. "You ... did not ask," she murmured.

"You tricked me!" Rowan started towards her, his hands reaching out to shake her, make her speak to him further. But the fire blazed up with a fierce crackling as he took the first step, and his right hand began to sting and burn.

He jumped back with a gasp, cradling his hand as the pain rose to an agonising peak, and then faded away. He did not dare approach Sheba again. He stood helplessly in the centre of the room, staring at her with loathing. She lay motionless in her chair, breathing deeply. She was asleep, and he knew she would not wake.

* * *

When Rowan stepped outside the hut, he was first amazed, then horrified, to see that it was nearly dark. He looked wildly around, hardly able to believe his eyes. The sun had been high in the sky when first he crossed the clearing to listen at Sheba's door. How could so much time have passed?

Then he remembered the fire flickering red and green, and Sheba's fingers tightening on his wrist. And her eyes—deep, mocking ...

The clearing was deserted. He jumped as two shadows moved under the orchard trees, then relaxed when he saw it was only Allun and Zeel, coming to meet him.

"What did the witch do to you?" Zeel demanded furiously.

Allun's face was drawn. "You were in the hut for so long! Then we heard you cry out in pain—great pain."

"It was nothing," Rowan said. But he could not stop himself from shuddering at the memory of what had happened.

"It was because I teased her that she turned on you," muttered Allun. "Because I could not keep my idiot tongue safely behind my teeth."

Rowan shook his head. "It is not your fault. She tormented you, angered you, to make you do it. I should not have stayed. She tricked me. She enchanted me, to make me stay far longer than I intended. And then she told me little."

And what she told me, I would rather not have known, he thought.

"Tell us," Allun urged.

Reluctantly, Rowan repeated the rhyme. With every word his hand throbbed with remembered pain.

Allun and Zeel listened intently, but when Rowan's voice trailed off, they looked at each other in bewilderment.

"All this talk of fire and burning is not pleasant," said Allun. "And these 'painted shadows' that are going to live again—what are they?"

"I do not know," Rowan sighed. "I do not understand any of it."

He rubbed his eyes, trying to clear his mind, then suddenly realised that someone was missing. "Where is Perlain?" he asked urgently. "We must go."

"Perlain left for Maris, with Tor, long ago," said Allun. He smiled tiredly and held up his hand as Rowan's eyes filled with panic. "No, do not fear. He has not abandoned you."

"Ogden was here, waiting for us, when we came out of the hut," Zeel explained. "He said he believed that you would be with Sheba for some time, and that Perlain should not wait."

Rowan shook his head desperately.

Zeel touched his shoulder with cool fingers, calming him. "Ogden's plan will save much time," she told him. "I am to take you directly to the coast from here, following the way the creature flew. Meanwhile, Perlain will be bringing the boat from Maris."

"But—the cliffs—the rocks!" exclaimed Rowan, confused. "Maris is the only safe landing place on the coast. That is why the Zebak have never come—"

"All that has been thought of, Rowan," said Allun gently. "Ogden has power over the wind, remember. Perlain's boat will wait out at sea, in the calmer water. Zeel and Mithren, who has the white kite, will fly us there from the land."

Rowan nodded, taking it in. Much had happened, it seemed, while he was with Sheba. His friends had been thinking and planning for him.

He blinked, suddenly focusing on something Allun had said. "*Us?*" he exclaimed. "Allun, you said, 'fly *us*'."

"Oh, yes," Allun said carelessly. "I am curious to see what is inside Sheba's little package. Sadly, it cannot be opened until you reach the land of the Zebak. So I have decided that I simply must go with you."

6 – Into the Dark

All the way to the Travellers' camp, Rowan tried to persuade Allun to change his mind. But Allun would not listen. He swung along, laughing and joking, as though he really *was* happy to go into terrible danger just to find out what was in Sheba's package.

"I have inherited my father's Traveller curiosity, Rowan," he said. "Travellers feel they must know everything. And half-Travellers are no different, it seems. What is more, I cannot resist the chance to soar the wind with a kite once again."

He laughed slyly. "Perlain felt differently," he said. "'I cannot understand it,' I said to him. 'There is nothing I love better than flying.' But he was green and shaking at the very thought."

Zeel strode beside them, saying nothing. Finally, when they had reached the camp and were moving to where Ogden waited for them, she spoke.

"Do you not *want* company on this quest, Rowan of the Bukshah?" she asked bluntly. "Did the witch tell you that you must go to the land of the Zebak alone, if you are to succeed?"

Rowan swallowed, looking down at his feet. "No," he said reluctantly. "But—it was *my* fault that my sister was lost. To try to find her is *my* idea—an idea that all in Rin will think is folly. I—do not wish any other person to be in danger because of me."

Zeel nodded, and stopped. She turned to Allun. "So," she said. "Stop your foolishness. Stop hiding your softness like a snail hiding in its shell. Explain your real reason for going on this quest."

Allun's easy smile wavered, then disappeared, leaving his lean face sad and serious. "I will not be in danger because of you, Rowan," he said quietly. "I *always* intended to go after the beast. Why do you imagine I visited Sheba's hut? For the same reason as you did—to try to gain advice and guidance for the journey."

He saw Rowan stare at him in amazement, and shrugged. "I was only partly joking about the Traveller's need to know. I have it, strongly. But in me it joins with the Rin love of home, and a safe, settled life. I cannot simply wait here, preparing to defend the valley. I must know what the Zebak are planning. How can we raise children if we are always in fear that they will be snatched away from us? Come—Ogden is waiting."

He began to walk again, moving very quickly towards the place where Ogden stood. Mithren was there, too, Rowan noticed now. His white kite was over his shoulder. He was ready.

With Zeel by his side, Rowan hurried after Allun. "He is thinking of his own children," Zeel murmured. "The children he will have one day, if he marries Marlie the weaver."

Rowan nodded slowly. Shocked, guilty and grieved, focused on Annad, he had not thought of the future. But now he saw that Allun was right. After this day, the Rin valley could no longer be thought of as a safe, protected place. The arching sky itself was now an open gate through which, at any time, terror might come.

* * *

They flew into the dark, sped by the wind that Ogden had summoned, and it seemed to Rowan, as the lights of Rin winked and faded away beneath him, that the dark was swallowing them up.

He had left carrying nothing but Sheba's small package, the burning memory of her mysterious words and a bitter knowledge of the price he had paid for them. The only farewell he had given was to Star. The only word he had left for his mother was a scribbled note, which Ogden had promised to deliver.

It was as though he had cut himself adrift from everything he knew and loved and was lost in a rushing black sea that had no ending.

Every now and then, out of the corner of his eye, he caught sight of a glimmer of white. He knew it was the Traveller Mithren's kite, and that Allun was flying with it, bound to Mithren by cords of silk, as Rowan was bound to Zeel. But Mithren and Allun were hidden by the dark. Only the kite sail, wheeling and dipping in and out of view, was proof that Rowan and Zeel were not alone.

They flew for hours, and Rowan could only trust that Zeel knew where they were, and was steering in the right direction. The stars were guiding her, he knew that. But to him the stars were just chilly white points in the sky, and all of them looked the same.

He found himself drifting to sleep, then waking with a start. Each time he woke, he thought for an instant that he had been living in a nightmare, and that now he was safe in his bed at home. Then he would open his eyes to the black sky, and feel the cool wind beating against his face, and realise that this was no dream.

Finally, confused and fearful, he would remember Sheba's words. He had tried not to think of them, but could not forget them. They seemed to flame red in his mind, coloured by the memory of burning pain.

> *Five strange fingers form fate's hand,*
> *Each plays its part at fate's command.*
> *The fiery blaze the answer keeps,*
> *And till its time each secret sleeps.*
> *When pain is truth and truth is pain,*
> *The painted shadows live again.*
> *Five leave, but five do not return.*
> *Vain hope and pride in terror burn.*

What could the rhyme mean? He knew from experience that Sheba's prophecies were to be taken seriously, however mysterious they seemed. But this ...

Five strange fingers ...

"Rowan, we are passing the coast," Zeel shouted to him above the wind. "Look down."

Rowan looked, and saw. He saw the still blackness of earth disappear, and the moving blackness of water take its place. He saw white foam flying upward as dark water dashed against darker cliffs. Here, in this place he had never seen before, his land ended, and strangeness began.

Now they were leaving the cliffs behind and flying over the sea.

At first the water below them boiled and frothed around huge hidden rocks, surging angrily in many different directions. Gradually, though, it deepened and calmed as they flew on, on, far out of sight of land.

And only then did Rowan feel a pang of fear. Soon, surely, Ogden's power over the wind would falter. If the wind was to drop, if the kite was to fall, he and Zeel would plunge together into that dark, mysterious water where serpents coiled, hunting for prey. Tied together, the silk of the kite swirling and twisting around them, how could they keep afloat? He was a weak swimmer in any case, and—his stomach tightened as he remembered—Travellers did not swim at all. That was why Allun—

Allun! Rowan realised that he had not seen the white glimmer of Mithren's kite since they crossed the coastline. In panic he twisted left and right, desperately searching the darkness. The kite slowed and swayed.

"Rowan! They are safe behind us. Be still!" Zeel shouted, her voice thin and torn by the wind. "Look ahead!"

She shifted her weight, steadied the kite and steered it on, towards the tiny light that her sharp eyes had seen long ago, and that now even Rowan saw for himself. It was the light of Perlain's boat riding the dark sea, waiting for them.

* * *

Alone, Zeel would have settled on the boat's rocking deck as easily and lightly as she would have landed on the grass of a green field. But Rowan, stiff and clumsy from the long flight, stumbled as his feet touched the smooth boards. He fell heavily, dragging Zeel down with him.

"I—I am sorry," he stammered. He tried to rise, found that his legs would not support him, and fell back. The boat tilted and rolled.

Perlain, sure-footed, padded towards them. He crouched to steady Rowan as Zeel unclipped the ties that bound them together.

Zeel laughed as finally she stood up, gathering the folds of the yellow kite from behind her and tossing them over her shoulder. She looked up into the blackness of the sky. Her eyes were shining with excitement.

"Back," she ordered. "Mithren is coming in with Allun. Give him room."

With Perlain's help, Rowan scrambled awkwardly away from the landing place, finally reaching the mast of the boat. He clung to it gratefully, and at last managed to haul himself to his feet. He heard Zeel give a shout, and quickly turned to look.

She was standing in the middle of the deck, staring upward. The white sail of Mithren's kite hovered high above her, hardly moving. Rowan caught his breath. What was wrong?

"Why is Mithren not landing?" he asked Perlain anxiously. "Why—?"

At that moment there was a call from the kite. Zeel raised her arms and with a shock Rowan saw a body falling from below the white sail. Or—not falling, but drifting downward through the darkness. He watched, open-mouthed, as the figure sank further and at last moved into the light that streamed upward from the boat.

It was Allun, white-faced but determined. He was suspended on a thin cord, swinging from it like a spider on a strand of silk. Zeel was waiting for him, arms still upraised. She caught him around the waist as soon as he was within reach, and held him fast.

"It is well!" she called, looking up at the hovering kite. Immediately the tightly stretched cord slackened as, far above, Mithren cut it free. It dropped lightly to the deck and Zeel staggered as she took Allun's full weight. He slipped from her grasp and fell, stumbling and rolling as Rowan had done, as soon as his feet touched the boards.

Perlain rushed to help him but Zeel paid no attention. She was still looking up.

"Mithren, I will see you again!" she shouted, waving.

"I will see you again, Zeel," came the faint answering cry. The white sail billowed, dipped, and began moving away, turning in a great circle and then speeding off into the darkness.

Still clinging to the mast, Rowan stared at Zeel, his eyes full of questions. She returned his gaze without speaking.

"Does Mithren not want to rest here before returning?" he asked.

She shook her head. "He must get back within the circle of Ogden's power as soon as he can," she said. "The wind out here is changeable and dangerous."

"But you—what of you?" demanded Rowan. He turned to Perlain, standing silent behind him. "And what of Perlain?"

"We are where we want to be," said Perlain quietly.

"We have decided that this quest is not yours or Allun's alone," Zeel added. "It is ours also. We are coming with you."

Rowan's heart gave a great leap.

Allun smiled brightly, though his face was still as pale as death. "A collection of oddities we may be," he said. "But it seems that fate has decided that we are to do its work."

Five strange fingers form fate's hand ...

Rowan made a small sound and clutched his right hand. It was throbbing and burning as the words echoed in his mind.

Zeel glanced at him and lifted her chin. "Fate has decided nothing. We have decided for ourselves. And we are four, not five. Do not fear, Rowan. The rhyme cannot mean us."

"Unless"—Rowan wet his dry lips—"there is another."

The boat rocked dangerously, and he clung to the mast to stop himself from falling.

"The tide is turning," he heard Perlain's flat voice say. "And the wind is rising. We must put up the sails and move from here. Even now we could be swept into shore and smashed on the rocks. There is no time to lose."

7 – The Tempest

Perlain had brought three vests made of cork. One for Allun, one for Zeel and one for Rowan.

"They float in the sea. Our people use them when they have been injured," he explained. "When they have lost the use of their arms or legs, and cannot swim safely in rough water."

"I have perfect use of my arms and legs. And I can swim!" snapped Zeel, looking at the thick, clumsy brown garment in disgust. "The Zebak learn to swim before they learn to walk. How else do you think I survived long enough to be washed up alive on the coast, where Ogden found me?"

Perlain smiled slightly. "Perhaps you can swim," he said. "But not like a Maris. And by the appearance of the waves and the smell of the wind, I fear you may need to swim like a Maris before our journey is over."

Allun and Rowan were already tying on their vests gratefully. After a moment's hesitation, Zeel did the same. Perlain nodded with satisfaction, then turned his attention to the sails.

* * *

The wind rose higher and the sails filled. For many hours the boat seemed to fly over the tops of the waves, speeding as fast and as easily as a Traveller's kite through the air. They took it in turns to rest, though only Perlain seemed actually to sleep. The others lay awake, turning uncomfortably in the hard cork vests, disturbed instead of lulled by the endless movement of the boat.

Dawn came at last, but cloud veiled the sun and the sea was grey, with swelling waves. Perlain, Rowan and Zeel nibbled dried fish and drank water. Allun took only water. His face was greenish-white. Plainly he felt very ill, and as the morning wore on he became worse and worse. Finally he could do nothing but lie, groaning, at the bottom of the boat, covered in a blanket.

Rowan bent over him, his face creased in concern.

"I am dying, Rowan," moaned Allun.

"No, you are not, my friend," said Perlain calmly, looking down from his place at the helm. "As I have told you many times, land-bound creatures often suffer this sickness at sea. It is the movement of the boat, they say."

He allowed himself a small smile as he turned away to check one of the ropes. "I cannot understand it," Rowan heard him murmur. "There is nothing I love better than sailing."

As morning became afternoon, Allun slowly began to feel better. By evening he was able to get up, and even eat a little.

"Never again will I make fun of you for being afraid of flying," he promised Perlain. "If you will swear never to bring me to sea again."

But by this time Perlain was not in the mood for smiling. The bad weather he had felt brewing was almost upon them. The clouds, dark grey and angry-looking, tumbled and raced low above their heads. The wind was blowing harder. The dark, heaving water was being whipped into sharp points tipped with white foam.

And at last the full force of the storm struck them. Rain pelted down, the boat heaved and tossed in the great waves, and the sails were torn by wind that seemed to have no ending, and no mercy.

As they plunged on into the black night, the wind howling around them and the waves beating against the frail sides of the boat, Rowan realised that his plan to make this journey alone had been more than foolishness. It had been insanity.

He could never have kept the boat afloat in this raging sea. Nor could Allun have helped him—or Zeel, whatever her determination and courage. It was Perlain, and Perlain only, who could do it.

Perlain had been born to the sea, and he knew it as none of his companions could ever do. Without Perlain's small webbed hand on the tiller, and Perlain's urgent voice telling them which rope to pull, which way to put their weight, which sail to raise or lower, they would all have perished within hours.

But it was Perlain, the only one of them who truly understood the sea's power, who was most afraid. And it was he who warned them, after hours of fighting the storm, that they were in terrible danger.

"The mast—will not hold," he shouted above the roaring of the wind. "It is strained beyond bearing. We are taking in water. And the gale—is growing stronger. We must prepare ..."

"For a swim?" Allun's lean face tightened. He was wet through. The muscles of his arms strained against the ropes he held as he and Zeel leaned back over the side of the boat, using their weight to keep it upright.

"Yes," shouted Perlain. "But do not despair. The sea is shallower here than before—I can feel it. The wind has driven us fast and hard. I believe we are not far from shore—though not where I intended."

"Where then?" panted Zeel.

Before Perlain could answer there was a huge gust of wind and a terrible, groaning crack as the mast snapped. With a cry he leaped clear as the wooden pole tilted and crashed down, crushing the tiller and smashing the side of the boat. Then a great wave swept over the deck, and where Perlain had stood there was nothing but hissing, swirling water.

"Perlain!" Rowan screamed. But even as he shouted he felt the boat rolling and tilting, the deck sliding out from under his feet. And before he could think or cry out again, he was gasping and struggling in the cold, black sea.

Waves crashed around him. Blinded and deafened by the pounding water, he tossed helplessly, one minute overwhelmed by the tide, the next minute forced to the surface again by the cork vest, choking and fighting for air.

"Allun!" he called. "Zeel! Perlain!" But he could hear nothing. Nothing but the roaring of the gale and the crashing of the waves and the awful splintering, smashing sound of the boat breaking up.

Something reared out of the blackness beside him. Serpent! In his terror and confusion Rowan lashed out, shouting, choking as salt water rushed into his mouth and nose. He struggled blindly, his mind filled with the terrible picture of a slimy, twisting body, dripping jaws, needle-sharp teeth.

Then his hand hit rough hardness, and he realised that the object beside him was not a serpent at all. It was a large piece of wood that had floated clear of the smashed boat. He clutched at it, using his last strength to haul himself partly onto it so that his head and chest rested on its hard surface.

He could do no more. Clinging to the wood, panting and trembling, tossed and blown like a piece of wreckage himself, he screwed his eyes shut. "Annad, I am sorry," he thought. Then he let the waves take him where they would.

* * *

"Rowan! Rowan!"

The voice was calling from a long way off. Rowan did not want to answer it. He wanted to stay where he was, lulled by soft hissing and rippling sounds, dozing in this pleasant half-sleep where nothing was real and there was nothing to be feared. But now a hand was shaking his shoulder and the voice was louder, louder ...

He frowned, mumbled, and opened his eyes. They stung and watered, and at first he could see nothing but darkness.

"Take heart! He is with us!" the voice called.

There were faint, hoarse cheers from somewhere nearby.

Gradually Rowan's vision cleared, and through the watery dimness he saw a face he knew, bending close to his.

Perlain.

Rowan tried to speak but his throat was dry and felt scratched and torn. He pressed his hand to his neck, swallowed, and tried again. "Perlain!" he croaked. "I thought you were drowned."

Perlain smiled and shook his head. "I am not so easily disposed of, my friend," he said. "But I have thought *you* were drowned for the past hour. And now, like a miracle, the tide has brought you in, draped like a piece of draggled weed over some planks of my poor boat."

"Allun?" croaked Rowan. "Zeel?"

"They are both here," Perlain said. "They are resting, feeling sorry for themselves. Like you, they have swallowed a lot of salt water, and it has not agreed with them." He looked around, a little uneasily.

"Do you feel strong enough to move now?" he asked politely. "Serpents often choose to hunt close to shore. Especially after a storm, when there may be injured prey floundering in the shallows."

Only then did Rowan realise that he was lying in shallow water and that Perlain was holding his head up and away from the small waves that were bubbling and hissing around him. Painfully, he managed to stand up. Then, leaning on the Maris man's shoulder, he waded with him to the shore.

Allun and Zeel were sprawled against a small hillock of sand not far away. Both were pale, wet and shivering, but both grinned with pleasure when they saw Rowan.

"We are a fine party of heroes," Allun joked, through chattering teeth. "Half-drowned, half-frozen, half-dead with tiredness and sick to our stomachs through drinking half the ocean. Not to mention that all our supplies are feeding the fish."

"At least we are alive," said Zeel, as Rowan slumped down beside her. "The storm is over. I still have my flint, to start a fire. I have rope, and my kite, too. Perlain has his knife, and has saved one water bag. And"—she looked hopefully at the Maris man—"surely we are somewhere *near* where we had intended to be?"

Perlain returned her gaze, hesitating. The corners of his mouth were tight, and when he spoke his voice sounded strained and odd. "Not so near. But we are in the territory of the Zebak, certainly. I think—this is a place I have seen from far offshore in the past. If it is, we are safe for now, but ..." His voice trailed away.

"But what, Perlain?" asked Rowan.

Perlain shook his head, turned away, and started picking up sticks of driftwood from the sand. "It is nothing. And in any case I cannot tell if I am right until dawn."

For a few moments he remained silent, then he cleared his throat and turned back to them, smiling. "For now, the most urgent task is to light a fire. You are all very cold and wet, and if you rest like this you will be ill. I know how weak and tender you warm-blooded creatures are."

At that, Zeel and Allun laughed, and staggered to their feet to help him. They told Rowan to lie where he was, and indeed he had little choice. He was still dizzy and sick, and his chest ached every time he drew breath.

Zeel started a tiny blaze with dried grass and a spark struck from the flint she carried, then fed small twigs into the flames. The fire grew brighter, then stronger still as heavier pieces of wood were added.

The flickering light, the warmth and the pleasant crackling were comforting, and Rowan began to feel more himself. But as his mind cleared, grim thoughts began to torment him.

The boat was wrecked. None of his companions had spoken of what this meant, but it must be in all their minds. Whatever the result of their quest, there was no easy way home for them now.

And what of Annad? While they lay here on this strange shore, she was at the mercy of the Zebak. Alone, imprisoned, perhaps injured and in pain ...

He pushed the thoughts away and sat up. He realised he was still wearing the cork vest. It had saved his life, but it was uncomfortable now. He fumbled at its ties, managed to undo them, and began to pull the vest off.

As he did so, he felt Sheba's package beneath his shirt. His heart thudded. He had completely forgotten about it. The storm, the wreck of the boat, his fear for his companions and his own fight for life had driven it from his mind.

With trembling fingers he pulled it from its hiding place.

8 – The Hand of Fate

The bundle was sodden—the oilcloth had not been able to withstand its long soaking in the sea.

"Rowan! Sheba's gift—how could I have forgotten?" exclaimed Allun, sitting down beside him. "Quickly, open it! It may be the only thing that will help us now."

"It is wet through," Zeel frowned. "Whatever is inside may be spoiled."

Rowan fumbled with the plaited cord that tied the package. This time the knots loosened easily. He pulled away the cord and slowly began to unwrap the oilcloth. He was afraid of what he might find inside. If the contents were ruined, he could not bear it. He had promised Sheba the black bukshah calf in return for this package, and on it he had pinned all his hopes.

The cloth was folded and rolled over many, many times. Most of the thickness of the package was due to that. There was plainly much less inside it than Rowan had believed.

"Whatever she has given us, she has protected it well," said Allun doubtfully.

"Almost too well for sense, one might think," added Perlain, his face expressionless.

His heart beating fast, Rowan pulled away the last of the wrapping cloth, finally revealing what was inside.

A piece of grimy metal. A small bundle of the pale grass that grew outside Sheba's hut. And a few twigs.

He stared in disbelief. The disappointment was so bitter that it brought stinging tears to his eyes.

"What is this?" hissed Zeel.

Perlain's face was stern. "What I have feared. The witch has played a trick—to repay me for warning Rowan not to trust her, and to repay him for listening to me. He told her he would not write down his promise to her until she had passed over her part of the bargain."

"She gave you some sticks from her fire-basket, Rowan. With some grass and a piece of old iron added for weight," muttered Allun in disgust. "All nicely wrapped in cloth that would disguise them. No wonder she insisted you did not unwrap the package until you were far from home."

Zeel gritted her teeth. "No doubt she believes we will not return, and so she is safe."

"I am sorry," said Rowan in a low voice.

"Do not be," said Allun. "Sheba must have planned to deceive you all along. The package was ready and waiting for her to pass to you, remember. This is not your fault, or Perlain's—or even mine, for once."

He looked down at his hands. Plainly, despite his light-hearted words, he was dismayed by what had happened. Zeel and Perlain, too, were silent, staring into the fire. Rowan knew that the same thoughts were in all their minds. *One flint. One water bag. A piece of rope. A knife. No way to return home. And soon it will be dawn. Where are we to go? What are we to do?*

"There is still the rhyme," he murmured.

"But what does it mean?" Zeel demanded bitterly. "It is impossible to understand."

"Not at all. Sheba simply failed to count us properly," Allun joked. "I have been thinking about it, and I am certain that we are the fingers of fate's hand, even though we are only four. Zeel is the tall, straight middle finger. Perlain is the small, wriggling one at the end. I am the ring finger, good for nothing but decoration. And Rowan is the strong little thumb that makes us all behave as we should."

Even Perlain smiled at this, but his smile quickly faded. "Perhaps you are right," he said quietly. "And perhaps, then, this is another of Sheba's jokes, for the finger that is missing is the first finger. The pointer. The one that shows the way. And it is certain that this is the very one we need."

Zeel moved restlessly, then pulled a piece of burning wood from the fire and stood up. Soon she was climbing the sand-dunes behind them, using the wood as a torch. After a moment Allun joined her. They were quickly swallowed by the darkness, but Rowan saw the flickering light climb to the top of the dunes and then move around as Zeel turned in all directions to peer at the land beyond.

"Do not go out of sight," Perlain called. "Do not leave the shore!"

"Perlain," said Rowan in a low voice, "what is this place? Why are you afraid of it? Tell me."

Perlain shifted uncomfortably. "I think—that we are at the edge of what I have heard called The Wastelands," he said at last. "About it I know nothing, except that it is said to be vast and barren. It is Zebak territory, but no Zebak ventures into The Wastelands. It is a forbidden place."

"Why?" Rowan asked.

Perlain turned his head away. "I do not know," he mumbled.

He looked up and saw Zeel and Allun returning. Their torch had burned down to a dull glow. "Say nothing to them yet, Rowan," he whispered. "Perhaps I am wrong about where we are. I hope that I am."

Zeel and Allun flung themselves down in front of the fire again.

"There is a glow, very faint and far away, on what may be the horizon," Zeel reported, throwing her smouldering torch back into the fire. "We could hear some shrieks and scratching noises. But that is all. The blackness is almost complete. Even the trees do not show against the sky. I had hoped to launch the kite and mark out our course, but we will have to wait till dawn."

"As you say," murmured Perlain. "Sunrise will be the test."

There was an uncomfortable silence, broken only by the sound of the waves breaking on the sand and the crackling of the fire.

Rowan tossed one of the sticks from the unwrapped package into the flames, but it was still too wet to burn. It steamed sulkily and he stared at it, shaking his head. Sheba's gift, on which he had so foolishly depended, was not useful even for burning. How could he have been taken in by her tricks? How could he have trusted her?

Because she has always, in the end, proved worthy of trust.

The thought drifted into his mind, and clung there.

He looked at the piece of metal, still lying with the four remaining twigs on the oilcloth in his lap. He picked it up and held it to the light. It was not just scrap metal, or part of the old fire grate, as he had first thought. It was dirty and dull, and it was heavy, but it was—a medallion of some sort.

Hope flickered in his heart. He rubbed at the medallion with his shirt. As dirt and soot came away from the dull surface he could see that it was decorated, and that a small metal loop was fixed to one end. It was meant to be worn on a chain—around the neck, no doubt.

"It could be that this is more useful than it appears," he said hesitantly, holding it up so that the others could see it.

Allun held out his hand, and Rowan gave the medallion to him. But he did it reluctantly. Suddenly he had become aware that he did not want to let it go. He watched jealously as it was passed around.

"Perhaps it is a charm," said Zeel, looking at it curiously. "Perhaps it will bring us good fortune." She passed it to Perlain and went back to staring into the fire, her brow furrowed in thought.

"It has not been particularly lucky for us up till now," said Perlain, handing the medallion back to Rowan. "But we shall see."

Rowan held the smooth piece of metal tightly for a moment, weighing it in his hand. Was it something? Or nothing? He could not tell. But Sheba had said the package was precious. And the medallion was the only possibly precious thing in it.

On a sudden impulse, he picked up the plaited silk cord which had fastened the package and threaded it through the small metal loop. Working quickly, he tied the ends of the cord together and slipped it around his neck so that the medallion hung low on his chest, hidden by his shirt.

When this had been done he felt strangely relieved. Now that the medallion was safe, protected and hidden from sight once more, it was as though a great weight had been taken from his mind.

But why? he asked himself. Even if it is some magic charm, why keep it a secret? And if it is just an ornament, with no meaning ... He smiled at himself, shaking his head at his own foolishness.

"Rowan!"

At first he did not recognise the voice as Zeel's. It was so low, so choked. He looked up, startled. Zeel was moving back from the fire, pointing into the flames. Her eyes were wide and frightened.

Rowan looked into the blaze. The damp stick he had thrown there had dried out and caught alight. Green flames were dancing along its length. The whole fire was alive with green light, darting here and there, mixing with the orange and red.

He stared, fascinated. He heard the exclamations of Allun and Perlain as they, too, saw what was happening, but he could not look away. There was a shape growing in the midst of the flames. A face. A face with red eyes, staring at him.

And there was a voice. It hissed in his brain like fire itself, and his right hand began to throb with pain as the words came to him:

The light that gleams at their back door
Will guide you from the lonely shore,
But dangers seek you as you go,
One from above, one from below.
One hides by night, one hides by day,
And hard and stony is your way.

The voice faded. The face disappeared. The green light began to die away. Rowan blinked, and took a deep, shuddering breath. When he looked again the fire was glowing red and orange. The stick was just a thin tube of fine white ash that crumbled as he watched.

He looked up and met the startled eyes of Perlain, Zeel and Allun.

"What devilry is this?" whispered Zeel.

"It seems," Rowan said, trying to keep his voice steady, "that we have found the fifth member of our party. The pointing finger, the one who is to show us the way—is Sheba herself."

9 – The Wastelands

After Rowan had repeated the words that had come to him from the fire, the four companions sat for a moment in silence.

"This rhyme is clearer than the other," said Allun at last. "But I cannot say it is any more pleasing."

Zeel frowned. "The light we are to follow must be the glow we saw on the horizon. A light from the Zebak city, no doubt, for the rhyme speaks of 'their back door'. But the glow will not be visible to guide us by day."

"Then we should move on without losing further time," Allun suggested eagerly. He jumped to his feet, but Perlain and Zeel both shook their heads.

"We cannot risk further disaster by plunging into the unknown with no supplies and no knowledge of what is ahead," said Zeel firmly. "There could be cliffs, deep holes, even water into which we could stumble. It is only a few hours till dawn. We should wait till then."

"It will help no one if we all perish because we are unprepared," agreed Perlain. "The rhyme says clearly that our way from here is to be hard. It also says that we are to face dangers both day and night, and they are to come from all around us, including the sky."

"The creature that carried Annad away attacked by day," Allun said. "And it came from the sky. It dropped like a thunderbolt. If there are more—if they patrol this place ..."

Their voices seemed distant and echoing to Rowan. He still felt stunned by what he had seen in the fire, and Sheba's words had filled him with foreboding. But an overwhelming tiredness had settled over him like a heavy mist. It was pressing him down, down into sleep.

Struggling against it, he wrapped the remaining four sticks in the oilcloth and put the package away inside his shirt. But he yawned as he did so, and his eyes kept closing.

Perlain stood up. "The sky will soon lighten," he said. "I cannot soak because of the serpents, but I will lie on the wet sand for a time."

He stalked away, towards the sea.

Allun stared after him, frowning. "Something is worrying Perlain," he murmured.

"It would be strange if that were not so!" exclaimed Zeel. "We have much to think about."

"Well, if we are to stay here till dawn, I, for one, am going to think with my eyes closed, like Rowan," Allun said.

"You sleep," answered Zeel. "I will keep watch."

And Rowan heard no more.

* * *

It was bright day and already very warm when Rowan woke. He opened his eyes with a guilty start and sat up so quickly that his head swam.

He was alone by the cold ashes of the fire. There was the sound of waves softly breaking on the shore. The sky was a perfect blue bowl above his head.

He heard voices and looked around. Perlain, Allun and Zeel were walking up from the sea. All of them were wet, and all were carrying dripping objects in their hands.

"Some of our supplies were washed to the shore during the night," Allun called as they grew nearer. "We have collected what we could."

Perlain reached Rowan first. "Do you feel refreshed?" he asked, bending to place a fish-skin bag and a sodden blanket on the sand.

Rowan nodded, deeply ashamed that he had slept so long—slept for even an hour while Annad was in such peril. He was ashamed, too, that he had slept while the others worked. And ashamed that they had let him do it, out of their kindness.

How tired I am of always being a burden, he thought suddenly. Others of my age in Rin are strong and can face any task. Why was I born such a weakling?

He turned away from Perlain, fighting down the pain he felt. Sheba was right. He was an oddity—a stranger in his herd like the black bukshah calf. He was prized by his people now for what he had done. But he would never be prized for what he *was*. His qualities were not those valued in Rin.

He knew that there had been other shy, gentle children born in the village over the past three hundred years. He had heard tales of them, which only showed how rare they were. Many had been keepers of the bukshah before him, because the great beasts were so easy to manage. Most had never married or had children of their own. They had spent their lives very much alone, with only the animals for company. Oddities. Never really understood or accepted.

"Are you unwell, my friend?"

Rowan looked up and found that Perlain was gazing at him in concern. He shook his head and managed to smile just as Allun and Zeel reached them.

"Two packets of dried fish," announced Allun, as he and Zeel threw their wet burdens down beside Perlain's. "Another water bag. Some sort of speckled biscuit that seems to be so hard that even the sea has not melted it—or is it a piece of cork?"

"It is seaweed cake," Perlain answered calmly. "My people use it on long voyages. It is nourishing, and light to carry. It is fortunate you found it. It will be useful—in The Wastelands."

With a sinking heart, Rowan realised that Perlain, Allun and Zeel had already investigated the land beyond the shore. That was why they seemed so joking and so full of energy. They were keeping up their spirits, taking their minds off what was before them.

"You were right, then," he said to Perlain in a low voice.

Perlain nodded, avoiding his eyes.

Rowan saw Zeel and Allun glance at one another. There was something they were not telling him.

He stood up unsteadily and without looking back trudged up the hills of sand to the place where Zeel and Allun had stood the night before. Then at last the land beyond the dunes lay spread out before him, and dread filled his heart.

The sun glared down on a vast plain that stretched away on all sides as far as the eye could see. Rowan remembered Zeel complaining in the night that it was so dark that she could not even see the trees outlined against the sky. It was no wonder. There were no trees at all.

No bushes. No shade or shelter anywhere. Just mats of tiny plants that clung to the baked earth here and there, making a patchwork of pink, gold and dull green.

Between the plant mats there was smooth, bone-dry clay scattered with lumpy, mottled rocks. The plain shimmered with waves of heat that rose from its dried-up surface like hot breath. And something flashed on the horizon, a blinding glare, as though another sun burned there.

Rowan looked up, squinting. Not the tiniest speck marred the clear, hot blue of the sky. There were no fearsome creatures circling for prey. Just a ball of white heat beating down on the shrinking land, heating it as flame heats an oven.

But dangers seek you as you go,
One from above ...

He felt a hand on his shoulder. Allun was standing beside him, staring at him gravely.

Rowan swallowed. "The danger of the rhyme—the danger that threatens by day and hides by night. It is the sun," he said.

Allun nodded briefly. "So it seems. This is why we did not wake you. We realised as soon as we saw this accursed plain that we could not cross it by day. The delay is unfortunate, but our only chance of surviving is to travel by night. If we begin at sunset and do not spare ourselves we may reach the city before the sun rises again."

"The danger of the night—" Rowan began.

"Whatever danger the darkness holds for us," Allun interrupted, "it can be no worse than being baked alive." He pressed his lips together. "As would be happening at this moment, in the midst of the plain, if I had had my way. Perlain would be dried and dead and we would be about to join him. When will I learn sense?"

He turned and stumbled back down the sand-dunes. Rowan followed, shaken by the bitterness of his words. Allun pretended so well to be an uncaring joker that sometimes it was hard to remember that he was not nearly as confident as he seemed.

While they had been gone Perlain and Zeel had made a tent, using long sticks, the wet blanket and Zeel's kite. They were sitting huddled underneath it, sheltering from the sun and talking in low voices.

Allun and Rowan crawled under the shelter with them. Perlain took his knife from his belt and carefully cut four small, equal slices from the hard brown seaweed cake. He gave one slice to each of them and took the last for himself.

Rowan chewed the tough food gratefully. It seemed a long time since he had eaten, and though the cake's seaweed taste was very strong he did not find it too unpleasing. Zeel sniffed her portion suspiciously, then began to nibble at it without appetite. Allun looked at his with pretended disdain.

"As a baker of some renown, I must protest that you call this 'cake', Perlain," he said. "If we are to live on this, we will have turned into very thin fish before a week is out."

"Better to be a live thin fish than dead of hunger," Perlain remarked, unconcerned. "But as you wish." He finished his own cake with relish, licked the last crumbs from his fingers, then took a drink from the water bag.

"A little water to follow," he said. "But a little only. Supplies are short."

Allun nodded gloomily and began to eat, wrinkling his nose as he did so. Perlain smiled slightly and crawled out from under the shelter.

"While you are resting here, I will soak," he announced, peering back in at them. "Then I will be ready when the sun begins to set. Sleep well."

Rowan waited until Zeel and Allun had settled themselves to rest, then crept out of the tent. He found the Maris man standing at the edge of the water, looking out at the glittering sea.

"Perlain, you cannot come with us into The Wastelands," he said abruptly. "What if we are still travelling when morning comes? There is no shade. There will be little water to drink, or to wet your skin. You will die, Perlain."

"I am in danger whether I go or stay," answered Perlain. "There is no fresh water on the shore, and if I try to escape by swimming, the night and the serpents will come before I reach land. I have considered this well, and I have decided that if I am to die, I prefer to do it with my friends than to do it alone. A fish-man out of water I began, and so I will end."

Rowan tried to speak, but his throat was tight and he could not.

Perlain's thin lips curved in a smile. "I do not regret that I joined you, Rowan," he murmured. "Without me you would certainly have perished in the sea long before we were in sight of land. So I have played my part. As Allun and Zeel, and you yourself, will no doubt play yours, before the quest is done."

He walked into the water and lay down in the shallows. "But I will not die before my time," he said, closing his eyes. "Now go and rest, Rowan. You must gather all your strength. For who knows what the evening will bring?"

10 – The Danger of the Night

They set off just before sunset, when the sun was scarlet fire burning low on the horizon ahead. The sky was stained red. Even the air seemed red as they left the sand of the dunes and began to move across the expanse of flat rocks, still hot underfoot.

They walked quickly, heads bowed so that the sun would not burn their eyes, watching their feet so they would not stumble.

"The rhyme said our way would be hard and stony," complained Allun. "But it did not warn us of cooked feet. These rocks are like baking trays just out of the oven."

"They will cool soon enough," said Zeel. "Later, it will be cold, I think. It is always so in large, empty spaces such as this."

"I am pleased to hear it," Perlain called back over his shoulder. He was well ahead, almost running over the stones, eager to reach the softer, cooler ground beyond. He wore the dampened blanket around his head and shoulders to protect him from the last of the drying heat.

"Perhaps if the sun above is the danger by day, cold is the danger that will threaten us from below, in the night," Allun suggested.

"We can deal with cold," said Zeel crisply. "We will huddle together and wrap ourselves in the silk of the kite for warmth. Tor, Mithren and I have done this often—in the past."

Her voice changed as she said the last words. Her usually strong, eager face was downcast. It looked softened and lost.

She misses her people, Rowan thought. She wonders if she will ever again fly with Tor and Mithren over the green fields or walk with Ogden, barefoot upon the grass. She wonders if she will ever again see her home.

He saw Zeel look up, frowning, into the blazing distance where still the flashes of silver that marked the Zebak city mingled with the scarlet of the sky.

That city was once her home. The thought came to him suddenly, with a small shock. How easy it was to forget that Zeel was not a Traveller born, but a Zebak. Did she remember anything of her past life? Were any memories, good or bad, stirring within her at this moment?

"At last! We are coming to the end of these accursed rocks!" Allun's exclamation broke into Rowan's thoughts and he turned his eyes to the way ahead.

Sure enough, the tightly packed rocks were at last giving way to the smooth, cracked clay and the plant mats that they had seen from the sand-dunes. There were mottled, lumpy stones scattered about as well, certainly, but these could be avoided with ease.

Perlain had already reached the edge of the rocks. He glanced behind him, smiling at his companions with relief, and stepped onto the clay.

And then, with a cry of shock, he threw up his hands, and disappeared from sight.

"Perlain!" shrieked Rowan. But he could hardly hear his own voice—or the voices of Allun and Zeel. For as they shouted, it was as if the whole plain cried out with them and began to move.

The mottled lumps were alive. They were heaving themselves up, spreading scaly wings, leaving the flat rocks on which they had squatted and scrambling into the air. Like a vast flock of hideous, swollen, featherless birds the creatures fought for space, hissing and screeching in their fright. And from beneath the earth there came another sound—an evil scratching, clicking sound that chilled the blood.

Zeel had reached the edge of the rocks and was already scrambling down into the hole in the earth where Perlain had disappeared.

"Perlain, here!" she cried, stretching out her hand. And then the scratching sound came again, louder this time, and her voice rose to a shrill scream. "Oh, by my life! Allun! Help me!"

The flying, swooping creatures filled the air in their thousands, hiding the edge of the rocks from Rowan's sight. Desperately he pushed forward, holding up his arms to protect his eyes. The scaly things dashed against his back, head and shoulders, clinging to his

clothes and hair with their small claws, flapping their wings frantically. Shuddering, he plucked at them, trying to tear them off.

"Rowan!" he heard Allun calling. "Here! Here!" And Zeel was
screaming, "Oh, I cannot hold him. It has him! Oh, help me!"

Rowan turned and ran blindly towards the sound.

And finally he was at the edge of the rocks, where Allun was
stretched out face down, his arms around Zeel's waist, pulling, pulling
with all his strength.

Zeel was lying half in and half out of a shallow hole with her arms
stretched out towards a yawning pit of blackness at one side. In an
instant, Rowan understood. Perlain had fallen into a tunnel that ran
beneath the plain. The thin layer of clay that had formed the tunnel's
roof had collapsed under his weight.

At first Rowan could not see Perlain at all. Then he realised that
Zeel's thin brown hands were clutching Perlain's ankles. The rest of
his body was hidden in the darkness of the tunnel. Zeel was trying
to pull Perlain back, but something was pulling against her with
enormous strength.

"I cannot hold him!" she cried again.

"Rowan, help me!" shouted Allun.

Rowan stood, frozen. A dozen thoughts were clamouring in his
terrified mind. He could take hold of Allun and help him pull. He
could leap down into the hole with Zeel and try to help her free
Perlain from whatever had attacked him.

But he knew he was not strong enough for his efforts to make
more than a tiny difference. His fear might give him strength for one
great effort, but the strength would not last. Not for long enough.

With a sudden jerk Zeel was pulled forward, and Allun with her.

"Rowan!" Allun shouted. He fought to keep his grip, desperately
trying to drag Zeel back towards the rocks.

The ground beyond the hole shifted as whatever was beneath the
earth, whatever had seen Perlain as its prey, thrashed in fury. Clay
cracked and crumbled in a long, crooked line, showing clearly the
path of the tunnel that ran just below its surface, and the long,
twisting shape of the beast within it.

There was a low and terrible growling sound. The clay cracked further. The mottled creatures shrieked and scattered in terror, their wings buffeting Rowan's face, forcing him to duck his head so that he stared at the stones beneath his feet.

The stones ...

"Rowan!"

One great effort ...

Barely thinking what he was doing, Rowan bent and wrestled a great stone from the ground. Muscles straining, he lifted the stone above his head and pitched it with all his strength down onto the line of cracking clay.

"Now!" he yelled, at the same moment. "Allun! Zeel! Pull now!"

The stone smashed through the clay and thudded onto whatever was underneath.

There was a rasping cry, the earth heaved, and suddenly Allun was staggering backwards, pulling Zeel back onto the rocks, and Perlain's limp body was coming with her, sliding out of the earth like a cork pulled from a bottle.

"Get him back!" shrieked Rowan, rushing to help as they lifted the Maris man onto the stones. "Back!"

But they had only managed to take a few paces when the rock Rowan had thrown was heaved to one side in a shower of clay and the growling beast beneath the earth was twisting forward in pursuit of them.

It burst through the hole in its ruined tunnel, rearing up, lunging at them, its huge, curved pincers opening and closing, tearing at the air, the shining red-brown segments of its huge body rippling as it moved, its thousand tiny legs wriggling like horned worms.

Zeel screamed—a high-pitched, terrified scream that was even more horrible to Rowan than the beast's own growling cry.

Holding Perlain between them, they turned and ran for their lives, stumbling back over the stones, expecting every moment to hear the sound of the beast at their heels.

But there was no sound. And when finally they looked behind them, there was nothing to be seen but the red sky and the plain and the small, lumpy flying creatures circling uncertainly above it.

With a sobbing cry Zeel collapsed onto the rocks with her head in her hands. Allun and Rowan lowered Perlain gently till he lay beside her. The Maris man was covered in clay from head to foot. His eyes seemed sealed shut.

Allun knelt and pressed his ear to Perlain's chest. Rowan watched, holding his breath, giving a long sigh of relief when Allun raised his head and nodded.

He took the water bag and moistened Perlain's lips. "You are safe, Perlain," he whispered. "The blanket must have protected you from harm. And the creature has gone. Perlain, wake."

At last Perlain's eyes opened. They were glazed with fear.

"Serpent!" he hissed.

"No," shuddered Zeel, beside him. "Ishkin."

Allun and Rowan looked at her in astonishment. Her face was white under the film of clay, and her mouth was trembling. Never had Rowan expected to see strong Zeel look like this.

"Zeel, you remember," he breathed, suddenly understanding.

She moistened her lips, and nodded. "I—remember a picture," she said huskily. "A picture—horrible, frightening. They used to show it to me, when I was bad. When I—disobeyed. I had forgotten it. Till just then, when I saw—"

She broke off, then forced herself to go on. "There were words, too. They would all point at me, and they would chant a rhyme. I remember it. I remember being so afraid. It went:

"Bad child, wicked child, push you in the bin,
Out with the rubbish on your chin, chin, chin.
Up pops an ishkin, then it pulls you in,
Makes you cry and sucks you dry and throws away the skin."

Her voice trailed off. She was shaking all over.

Rowan felt his own skin crawling. What sort of people would terrify a tiny child like this? Zeel had been only two, at the most, when she was found by the Travellers.

Zeel pressed her hands together to stop them shaking, and tried to laugh. "Just a children's rhyme," she muttered. "It is foolish of me to fear it now." But still she shuddered as though she would never stop.

Rowan and Allun exchanged glances. "Not so foolish, my friend," said Allun lightly. "Now I have seen this ishkin for myself, the idea of meeting it again is not at all to my liking."

"There is not just one," said Zeel. She closed her eyes. "There are many. Many, many. The ground is full of them."

* * *

Leaving Perlain and Zeel to rest, Allun and Rowan walked back to the edge of the rocks. The sun had dipped below the horizon and the moon had risen. The plain was still. The mottled flying creatures were clustered on the flat rocks once more.

"The ishkin, it seems, do not normally attack on the surface," Allun said. "They wait for prey to fall through the clay. The lumpy flying lizard things are safe upon the rocks."

"I cannot understand why there are so many flying lizards." Rowan scanned the strange scene before him. "I have seen no insects or small creatures that could be their prey. And they do not graze upon the plants. How do they feed?"

As he spoke, there was a quarrel among one group of the creatures, and two were pushed aside. One flapped clumsily into the air. The other, less fortunate, fell, scrabbling, onto the clay.

Instantly, the ground collapsed beneath its body, there was a rushing, scratching sound, and the creature was dragged, shrieking, into darkness. Its companions chattered for a moment, then went back to their rest.

Rowan turned his head away, sickened.

"We know how the ishkin feed, in any case," said Allun grimly. "No doubt the whole plain is undermined by their tunnels. Look there."

He pointed to the place where only half an hour earlier they had struggled so desperately to save Perlain. Already the tunnel had been repaired. The earth that formed its roof was as smooth as it had ever been.

"Sheba's rhyme said, 'hard and stony is your way'." Rowan looked again out at the plain—at the treacherously smooth clay, at the mats of small prickly plants, and finally at the flat stones where the flying creatures clustered. "Perhaps the stones ..."

Allun nodded. "Yes," he said. "If the stones are the only places where the lumpy lizards are safe, it seems that we will have to be lumpies ourselves. Lumpies without wings. We will have to leap from one stone to the next to cross these accursed Wastelands."

He took a deep breath. "Very well, Rowan. What must be, must be. We will rouse Perlain and Zeel and begin at once. If we are to reach the city by sunrise there is no time to lose."

11 – Against the Wall

Rowan was silent. The thought of the perilous journey ahead filled him with dread. If anyone should fail to make a jump successfully they would stumble onto the treacherous clay. Then, in the blink of an eye, they would be caught and dragged away by one of the beasts that waited below.

Words from the children's rhyme that Zeel had repeated went round and round in his head. Foolish, horrible words.

Up pops an ishkin, then it pulls you in,
Makes you cry and sucks you dry and throws away the skin.

His stomach churned when he remembered the shriek of the flying creature as it was dragged under the earth, remembered the sight of the ishkin as it reared up, its great curved pincers snapping, its tiny hooked legs clawing.

Yet he knew Allun was right. They had to cross the plain somehow, and there was no other way.

"Perlain is weak with shock," he managed to say at last. "And Zeel—is afraid."

Allun swung round to face him. "And you and I are not afraid, I suppose?" he demanded fiercely.

Rowan stared, unable to find an answer. Allun returned his gaze. "Fear will make us stumble, Rowan," he said, more gently. "So we must pretend confidence even if we do not feel it. We must pretend so well that we begin to believe."

His lean face broke into its familiar clown's grin, and he clapped Rowan on the shoulder. "I, for one, am used to pretending. I have done it all my life. Playing the fool to hide my real feelings is my one great talent. Now is my chance to use it."

* * *

For many hours, in single file, they leaped from one stone to the next, zigzagging across the plain as the moon shone cold above them. Allun led the way, moving quickly, taking the easiest path, but one that led as directly as possible towards the small glow on the horizon.

The plain seemed to boil with movement as all around them the ishkin took their prey. The mottled flying creatures that Allun called "lumpies" were many, and fought together often, so that time and again the horrible scene that he and Rowan had witnessed was repeated.

But never did Allun look down or aside. He looked only forward. His pockets were filled with pebbles, and these he threw to startle the creatures clustered on the stone ahead. "Move aside, lumpies," he would shout. "Make room!"

The lumpies would flap into the air, shrieking and hissing crossly. Allun would leap at once, while the stone was clear. Then he would choose his next landing place, toss another pebble, and leap again.

All the time he called back to Perlain, Zeel and Rowan, who were following him. His voice drowned the scratching, rushing sounds of the ishkin attacks, the despairing shrieks of the victims. He was never silent, never still. He encouraged, joked, whistled—even sang.

"I have always fancied myself as a dancer," he would call. "What an excellent way this is to practise my art." And the next time he leaped he would spread his arms wide, making himself look as ridiculous as possible. Then he would make up a rhyme about a frog or a jumping insect, and leap on, croaking or chirruping to make them smile.

He asked them riddles, made fun of wise sayings, invented insulting stories about everyone they knew. His voice grew hoarse with shouting.

When he stopped for a few minutes to rest he sang long, loud songs and insisted they join in. If they failed to answer him he teased them. He would taunt Perlain about his flat feet, call Rowan "skinny rabbit" or wonder aloud at the uselessness of Zeel's fine yellow kite when there was no wind to drive it.

It was foolish. It was annoying. But Rowan knew that it was saving their lives. It was taking their minds from their fear, forcing them to look ahead, and drowning the terrifying sounds of the plain. It was helping them to leap cleanly, saving them from the faltering clumsiness that would come if they remembered the fate that awaited them should they fall.

So he did his best to shout back at Allun's insults, groan at his jokes and join his singing, though his legs were trembling with weariness and with every jump he felt that he could jump no more. Zeel and Perlain, beating back their own suffering, did the same.

And so, hour after painful hour, as the moon sank lower in the sky and the glow on the horizon grew larger and brighter, they went on.

* * *

In the darkness just before dawn, Rowan realised that the way had suddenly become easier. The flat stones were more numerous, dotting the clay everywhere, even touching one another in places. It was no longer necessary to jump. He could step from one stone to the next in safety.

The lumpies had become more numerous too. They were flocking so thickly that they had become a nuisance. They filled the air, crowded every stone, and quarrelled loudly as they jostled for space. More and more arrived every moment.

Are they following us? Rowan thought, puzzled. They certainly seem to be. And yet they did not follow us before. Can it be because we are nearing the city?

He looked ahead at the glow, which he had at last realised was flame gushing from the top of a tall tower or chimney that rose high above the city. Other, smaller, lights were now visible, too. They were few, but they stretched away on both sides of the tower as far as he could see, shining above a layer of darkness that he guessed was a high wall. The city was huge and seemed to be totally encircled.

He had been concentrating so hard on reaching the city that he had given no real thought to what they were to do when they arrived. But now that the goal was so near and he could see its vastness, questions began rushing into his mind.

How were they going to find Annad in a place so large, let alone free her? How were they going to remain hidden while they searched?

"We should stop for a moment and talk, I think," called Allun quietly. For some time now his voice had been lower. They were very near the city. There could be patrols on the watch, though it was hard to believe that the Zebak could expect invasion from the direction of this desolate plain. It was the city's "back door" indeed.

Weary but relieved, they crouched in a circle, each safely upon a rock. They passed around the food and the water bags, and each of them drank deeply. They felt they could afford to do so, now that The Wastelands had been safely crossed.

Lumpies squabbled and flapped around them.

"Why are they gathering here?" whispered Zeel, batting them away from her impatiently. "They are coming from all over the plain, as if on purpose to annoy us."

"They are useful to us, in fact," Allun said. "No one could see us in this crowd, even if they looked over the wall. Or hear us, either."

Perlain was gazing up at the sky, wetting his face and hands with water. Rowan glanced at him, worried. The Maris man seemed very ill. He needed to soak. He needed rest. And sunrise was not far away. Soon that glaring ball would climb above the horizon at their backs, heating the earth and the air—hotter, hotter ...

"What is our plan? Are we to climb the wall? Or walk along it to try to find a gate?" he urged.

"A gate may be hours away, and we do not know which direction to try. Also, gates mean guards. It will be far safer and quicker to climb," said Zeel firmly.

Allun shook his head. "It will not be safer or quicker for Perlain— or for Rowan."

"Or for you, Allun the baker, I have no doubt," grinned Zeel, taking her revenge for the way Allun had teased her during the long night. "But you have done your part. You brought us through The Wastelands with your clowning. Now it is my turn to—what did you say?—'practise my art'. I will climb the wall, find a place to fasten the rope, and pull you up after me, one by one. But it must be done in darkness."

They hurried forward, almost running in their haste, but soon they had to slow again. They had left the clay behind completely, and reached the solid rock on which the city was built. There they found themselves wading through a thick layer of sticks and stones that threatened to trip them at every step. The lumpies, too, were so many that it was almost impossible to walk between them or to see the way ahead.

There are thousands of them, thought Rowan, stopping for a moment. They could overwhelm us if they chose.

He shivered nervously. Yet surely there was no reason to fear the creatures. Despite their ugly appearance, the spines on their backs and their sharp little claws and teeth, they had not seemed dangerous—except, occasionally, to each other.

Suddenly he realised that he had lost sight of Allun, Zeel and Perlain. "Allun!" he whispered urgently. "I cannot see you. Where are you?"

"Here. Straight ahead of you. We have reached the wall, Rowan." But instead of sounding triumphant, Allun's voice was strained and odd. Rowan headed blindly towards the sound and almost bumped into Perlain, who was standing motionless while lumpies swarmed around him.

"What is it?" Rowan hissed.

Perlain pointed.

Allun and Zeel were together just ahead of them, facing the wall. Allun was staring at it in despair. Zeel was running her hands over its surface as though she had to touch it to believe the evidence of her own eyes.

For the wall was not made of brick, stone or wood, full of joins and toe-holds that could be used by a climber. It was made of metal—polished sheet metal that rose smooth and slippery to a sharp edge high above their heads.

Rowan stared at it, dumbfounded, realising several things at once.

He realised that here was the source of the distant flash he had seen when first he looked over the plain. It had been the glinting of this metal as it was caught by the newly risen sun.

He realised that though the metal was cold now, by mid-morning it would be too hot to touch. It would radiate heat over the plain and everything in it. To stand beside it as he was doing now would be like standing in a fire.

He realised that no one could climb this wall unaided and that the sharp edge at the top would slice Zeel's rope through in a moment.

Could we tunnel under the wall instead? he thought wildly. He crouched, and scrabbled at the ground. And then he cried out as he realised the last and most horrifying thing of all.

He and his friends were not the first to have stood, despairing, in this place.

For the pale-coloured sticks and stones through which he had been wading so awkwardly for the last few minutes were not sticks and stones at all.

They were bleached white bones.

12 – The Mirror Cracks

ow many poor wretches have been thrown into The Wastelands to die?" muttered Allun. "How many thousands, over the centuries, to create this—this horror."

He stared with loathing at the lumpies, whose reason for massing in such numbers, and at this place, now seemed horribly clear.

"Look at them—waiting for us to die in our turn, so they can pick our bones," he growled. "You asked how they fed, Rowan. Now you have your answer."

"It may not be," Rowan said in a low voice. But the lumpies were crowding in, pressing them to the wall, hissing in their eagerness. They were so close that he could see their forked tongues flicking in and out, and their small, hungry eyes.

Now he could see how much they resembled the creature which had snatched Annad. They were its smaller relations, and what they lacked in size and strength they made up in numbers.

"Get away!" Zeel stepped forward threateningly and the lumpies scattered. But only for a moment. Soon they were creeping back, pressing in once more.

The four companions stood staring at the wall.

At their backs the sky was lightening, turning pink. The wall had begun to reflect the colour. It had also begun dimly to reflect their tired, pale faces, and the lumpies crowding around them like creatures from a nightmare.

On both sides the wall stretched into the distance—endless shining metal plates, fused together. There was no hole or gap. No knob or catch. No sign of a gate. No possibility of escape from the heat to come. And bones glimmered on the ground as far as the eye could see.

"Have we come so far, and suffered so much, only to die within sight of this accursed city?" cried Allun.

Suddenly Sheba's words came into Rowan's mind.

When you really need them ...

He pulled the oilcloth package from his shirt and took out one of the four remaining sticks. "Zeel—we must start a fire," he said urgently. "We must see if Sheba can help us."

Zeel pressed her lips together. "The witch lured us to this place of death with her instruction to follow the light. She has betrayed us."

"It is true." Allun's face was grim. "For her own reasons, or for pure wickedness, Sheba wishes us never to return to Rin."

Rowan could not believe it. He *would* not. He glanced at Perlain. The Maris man was leaning against the wall. His eyes were closed.

"Zeel, please! The flint!" he begged. "Give it to me. I must try. The sun is about to rise. The heat will soon begin. And Perlain ..." He broke off, unable to finish.

He threw himself to his knees and scrabbled among the bones, collecting dead leaves and twigs blown from the desert plants. When he had enough to make a tiny blaze, he heaped them up in front of him, with the stick balanced on top. Then he held out his hand.

Grudgingly, Zeel gave him the flint. Rowan struck a spark and the dry leaves and twigs on their bed of bones caught immediately, first smoking and then bursting into flames.

The stick flickered green, then flared up strongly. Sheba's face appeared, wavering, in the blaze. Rowan stared, caught and held by the image—by its growing strength, its deep red eyes. His right hand began to burn so that he almost cried out in pain. And then the voice came to him:

At dawn the enemy attacks,
As hunger howls, the mirror cracks.
Then, pressed against that shining wall,
Like worms among the bones you'll crawl.
It's useless now to fight or plead—
Squirm softly, while the creatures feed.

Horrified, Rowan jumped up and kicked at the fire, stamping it out, crushing the ashes to powder. The throbbing pain in his hand slowly died, but Sheba's terrible words still burned in his mind.

"What did she say?" asked Perlain faintly. He was still leaning against the wall. His face looked shrivelled and white.

The terrible tiredness that had gripped Rowan when he burned the first of Sheba's sticks was sweeping over him again. He could not bring himself to repeat the rhyme, but he knew he had to tell the truth.

"She jeered at us," he mumbled. "Zeel was right. Sheba led us here to die."

Perlain closed his eyes. "So be it," he said calmly.

"Do not say that, Perlain!" Zeel's eyes snapped with fury. "Are we to wait tamely to bake?"

"The sun is rising," warned Allun.

At dawn the enemy attacks ...

The wall flashed blindingly, catching the sun's first rays. The lumpies surged forward, crying out hungrily.

As hunger howls ...

And then there was another sound. It came from the wall. Rowan spun to face it. His eyes watering in the glare, he saw his own reflection. He saw the reflections of his friends and the lumpies flocking, fighting one another for space. And he saw something else—something that at first he could not believe.

A crack was appearing in the wall, right beside Perlain. The crack ran down one of the seams from the top to the bottom. It was as though the seam was splitting.

... the mirror cracks ...

Rowan shouted, pointing. His voice was drowned by the lumpies' screeching, but Zeel and Allun had already seen what was happening. They stood open-mouthed.

The crack grew wider, wider. One whole section of the wall was swinging outwards, like a door. It was being pushed open from the other side. Something was coming through. Something big, making a heavy, rumbling sound.

Then, pressed against that shining wall,
Like worms among the bones you'll crawl ...

"Quickly! Move hard against the wall! Hide!" Rowan shouted, struggling to Perlain's side. He dragged the almost unconscious Maris man to the ground.

Zeel and Allun lunged forward, throwing themselves down beside the wall with Rowan and Perlain, burying themselves as deeply as possible in the bleached white bones.

Just in time. For the next moment the wall was fully open, and a huge covered cart was lumbering through. Four Zebak were pushing the cart, grunting with the effort.

"What sort of job is this for trained guards?" the man nearest to Rowan growled. "One urk with a grach could do it."

His heavy boots crunched on the bones beside Rowan's head. As he passed, Rowan peered up at him cautiously. He was very tall and broad-shouldered in his steel-grey uniform. His pale eyes were angry. The black streak that ran down his forehead from hair to nose made him look cruel and stern.

"The grach have more important duties," snapped the guard next to him. "You have your orders, Zanel. Do not question them, or you will find yourself locked out in The Wastelands, as many have been before you!"

"Choosing between the ishkin and the wall," added another of the guards, sniggering.

Zanel kicked angrily at the lumpies flocking around his feet, but he said nothing more.

Rowan lay motionless beside Perlain, his heart pounding. The guards had passed. The door into the city was wide open. But he did not dare move. The guards had not noticed them yet, but one of them could turn and do so at any moment. And then there would be no escape and no mercy.

It's useless now to fight or plead—

The guards began to work two levers, one on each side of the cart. With a grinding sound, the back of the cart began to tip. At the same time the cover wound back.

A stinking flood of vegetable and meat scraps began pouring onto the ground. The lumpies screeched with one voice and fell on the food. In their thousands they fought and flapped around the cart and the guards in a hideous confusion of scaly wings, mottled bodies and grasping claws. The guards, scraping out the last of the rubbish, yelled and beat at them angrily. The creatures' noise was deafening.

Squirm softly, while the creatures feed.

The moment had come. Rowan wriggled forward, dragging Perlain with him, keeping his head down. He felt Allun and Zeel helping from behind as he crawled through the gap in the wall and into the city beyond.

* * *

They lay in the shadow of the wall, panting with fear, looking quickly around them. They were in a large square paved with red bricks. The square was littered with scraps of food that had fallen from the cart, and was deserted. It was too early for anyone but the guards on duty to be awake, it seemed.

A narrow road ahead led to a tall building topped by the flaming chimney they had seen from the plain. Other lower, longer buildings squatted on either side of the square, their doors firmly closed. The place smelt sourly of smoke and garbage.

Where should they go? Where could they hide? Soon the guards would be trundling the empty cart back into the square. There was no time to lose.

Bells began to ring somewhere in the centre of the city. They clanged on and on. Waking the sleeping people. Stirring the city into life.

"Water ..." groaned Perlain. He waved his hand to their left.

Zeel tugged at Rowan's arm. He saw that she was also looking to the left. To a place beside one of the buildings, where a flight of metal steps led down into the ground.

Rowan hesitated, but not for long. The cart was coming back. Already he could see its front wheels rolling through the gap in the wall.

He nodded, and together he, Zeel and Allun, with Perlain held between them, ran for the steps. The mingled sounds of cart wheels on bricks and the screeching of the feeding lumpies floated after them as they hurried down, down into darkness.

At the bottom of the steps was a door. Allun turned the handle carefully. The door opened and they slipped inside.

They found themselves in a brightly lit passage. It was lined with metal, like the metal of the wall. There was a distant thumping, roaring sound.

"There is a creature here," hissed Zeel, putting her hand to the knife at her belt.

Rowan shook his head, puzzled. "It does not sound like an animal. It is—regular. Like millstones grinding."

"A machine, then," whispered Allun. "Do not worry about it. We must find Perlain some water, and quickly. If he does not soak soon he will die."

His forehead was creased in a worried frown as he glanced at Perlain's closed eyes and pale face.

They went on along the corridor. It was eerie to see their own reflections moving along with them on both sides.

"It is like walking in a crowd," joked Allun. "A foolish crowd of oddities in a corridor under an enemy city, without an idea of where they are going."

They reached a point where the corridor branched into two, and stopped, wondering whether to go left or right.

"There," a voice croaked.

It was Perlain who had spoken. He pointed feebly to the right.

They took the right-hand passage, hurrying as fast as they dared. The sound of the machinery grew louder.

The corridor branched again, and again. Many other smaller passages ran from each main way. All were deserted. All were brightly lit and lined with the same shining metal. None had any doors that they could see. But each time there was a choice to make, Perlain pointed and they obeyed.

13 – The Maze

At first Rowan tried to keep their path fixed in his mind, but he soon gave up. There were too many turns, and every passage looked the same. As well, now that the immediate danger of discovery by the guards had passed, the terrible tiredness he had felt by the wall was sweeping over him again. It was an effort to put one foot after the other. All he wanted to do was lie down and sleep.

"This is folly," muttered Allun, as they turned for the tenth or twelfth time. "We will never find our way out of this maze."

Rowan could hardly hear him. The thumping, roaring noise was very loud now, and he was almost asleep on his feet.

"If this is a maze, I think we have reached the centre," he heard Zeel say.

He looked up wearily and saw what Zeel meant. At the end of the passage they had just entered was a shining metal door. A small black-and-white picture was fixed to it, but he could not see what it was.

With every step they took the roaring noise became louder. But still Rowan could hear Perlain gasping painfully as he struggled on between Allun and Zeel, trying to hurry.

At last they were close enough to see the picture on the door clearly. It was a grinning white skull in a black square.

They halted abruptly.

"This does not look promising," Allun frowned.

"It does not mean that there is danger for all inside the door. It means that the place is forbidden, and the penalty for entering is death," Zeel said slowly.

She saw them looking at her in surprise, and shrugged. "I remember," she said. "It must be one of the first things we are taught."

We, thought Rowan through his haze of tiredness. This is the first time I have heard Zeel say *we* when talking of the Zebak. He glanced at her troubled face and an uncomfortable feeling stirred in his chest.

Perlain struggled weakly, trying to make Zeel and Allun move on. They supported him as he staggered to the door. It was fastened with a padlock. He plucked helplessly at the lock with his webbed hands, and moaned.

"Perlain, how could there be water in there?" Allun asked gently.

"There is—water," croaked Perlain, clawing at the door. "I—must ..."

Zeel, her face stern and set, pulled her knife from her belt. Rowan felt a pang of fear. But then she knelt, took the padlock in her sun-browned hands, and began working away at it with the sharp point. "This, I learned from the Travellers," she muttered. "The Travellers do not care for locks. Or penalties."

After a few agonising minutes the padlock clicked and came loose. Zeel stood back, biting her lip. Rowan realised immediately that though she had broken the lock she could not make herself push the door open.

He stepped forward to do it for her, but Perlain was there before him. The door swung open, and an almost deafening roar came from the dark, echoing space beyond. Perlain took no notice. Before anyone could stop him, he had plunged through the doorway.

Rowan and Allun started after him. Zeel followed reluctantly. Plainly, she was afraid. Rowan wondered again at the strength of her early training. Like her fear of the ishkin, her fear of the sign was something she could not control.

Light from the corridor streamed into the room beyond the door, shining on a metal floor. But as soon as they were inside Zeel pushed the door shut and stood against it.

Then the blackness was complete. The space pulsed with sound—roaring, rushing sound. Rowan could see nothing. He reached out blindly. "Allun! Perlain!" he shouted, in panic.

"I am here," called Perlain's voice. "But do not move. It is not safe for you."

There was a clatter from somewhere to Rowan's right, and Allun bellowed in pain.

Rowan began to edge towards the sound, his heart beating wildly.

"It is all right. I hit my head on something, clumsy fool that I am!" Allun shouted. "What was it? Wait! I think … yes!" There was a scratching noise, and a small light appeared. It glowed, then brightened. At last Rowan could see Allun's face, smeared with a streak of sooty oil, and his hand holding up a grimy oil lamp.

Allun grinned. "If it was necessary to hit something, I am glad it was this," he said. "It was hanging just beside me, here, with striking matches on a shelf beside it, all complete. Now we shall see where we are."

He held the lamp high and moved it slowly around. Rowan gasped.

They were standing on a metal platform that hung over the edge of a vast underground lake—a lake as large as the bukshah field in Rin. Beside them, taking up most of the platform's space, squatted a monstrous machine that chugged and throbbed unceasingly. The lamp had hung from a shelf at its side. On the shelf were some gloves, a few tools and a can of oil.

Allun pointed at the silver pipes that snaked up from the water, climbed the walls and disappeared into holes in the roof.

"They pump water up to the city from here," he exclaimed in amazement. "The lake is like a huge well. This machine must be a great pump that works by itself. Who could believe such a thing?"

Rowan glanced at the door. Zeel was standing there, utterly still and silent. Her face was pale and tense.

He turned back to Allun and together they crept cautiously to the edge of the platform, knelt, and peered over the edge. In the black water below them floated Perlain. His eyes were closed, but they could see that he had come to no harm. He was regaining his strength, slowly but surely. Already he was not so pale and he was breathing steadily.

Looking down, Allun shuddered. Rowan knew what he was thinking. If they had stumbled over the edge of the platform in the dark and fallen into that dark, deep water, they would certainly have drowned. Perlain would have been too weak to save them.

As if he felt their gaze, Perlain's eyes opened. He looked up at them and smiled peacefully.

"You were right, Perlain," Allun called to him.

"Of course. A Maris can smell water wherever it lies," Perlain answered drowsily.

"Rest and soak, Perlain," Rowan called. "We will be back soon."

"One hour," said Perlain, and his eyes closed once more. Rowan's own eyelids drooped as he watched. He was so tired. So tired ...

He shook himself. There was no time for sleep. He turned away from the lake, and followed Allun and his light to the door where Zeel still waited.

"This place is probably as safe as any for us to rest," Allun said, above the roaring of the pump. "A little noisy, perhaps, but one cannot ask for everything."

Wordlessly, Zeel held out her hand for the lamp. Allun looked surprised, but gave it to her. She looked at it carefully, turning it round and round, careless of the black grease it left on her fingers.

She remembers lamps like this, guessed Rowan, watching her fascinated eyes. She was probably warned not to touch them. Yet she was attracted by the flame, as young children are. So she remembers.

Zeel put the lamp on the floor and looked up at Rowan. "Before we rest you must burn another of the witch's sticks," she said abruptly. "I must know what is to befall us."

Rowan hesitated. His hand throbbed as if it already felt the pain that would come when another stick was burned. And he had only three sticks left. Was their need great enough for him to use one now? He turned uncertainly to Allun.

Allun nodded. "If Sheba has advice to give, we should have it. Then we will be prepared should the owners of this lamp pay us a visit in the next hour."

Reluctantly, Rowan brought out the package from his shirt, unwrapped the oilcloth and took out a stick. Before doing anything else, he carefully re-wrapped the last two sticks and put them away. As he did, he felt the medallion, warm against his hand. What part does it play in all this? he asked himself. Is it the medallion that helps me hear Sheba's words, perhaps?

"Burn the stick, Rowan!" cried Zeel impatiently. "Why do you wait? Thrust it into the lamp's flame."

Before he could think about it further, Rowan did as she asked. Green fire ran up and down the stick's length, flickering higher, higher, till shadows leaped on all their faces and on the door behind them.

This time the pain in Rowan's hand was so great and came so suddenly that tears sprang into his eyes. Blinking through a watery haze, he saw Sheba's face appear in the flame. It seemed to grin at him, its red eyes blazing. And then came the words:

The one who first heard Zebak bells
Must use the truth the mirror tells.
The hand must bleed to reach the end,
One finger stands, the others bend.
With chains and sorrow you must pay
For other hands to guide your way.

The green fire wavered and died. The ashes of the stick fell to the ground. The oil lamp flickered and went out, as though its strength had been completely consumed. They were in darkness again.

Trying to keep his voice steady, Rowan repeated the rhyme. He could not see the others, but he had no doubt that their faces were dismayed.

The rhyme did not help. It did not tell them what to do if they were caught in this place. It did not tell them how to get out of the maze, or where to find Annad. It warned of bleeding, chains and sorrow, without hope of escape.

Exhaustion mingled with despair flooded over Rowan like a wave. He bowed his head.

As sleep closed around him he heard Allun's voice, tired and angry. "We heard bells when first we came through the door from The Wastelands. But which of us heard them first? The mirror could be the metal walls of this maze. But what is the truth it tells?"

"No doubt we will discover these things in time." Zeel sounded very cold, as though all warm life had been drained out of her. "It has been so with the other prophecies, and so it will be with this."

Allun groaned with weariness. "I am sick of thinking of it. Sleep now, Zeel," he said. "I will wake you in—"

"No," Zeel broke in. "I will take first watch."

Allun yawned. "As you like," Rowan heard him say.

Then there was no sound but the roaring of the pump and the rushing of the water in the pipes. And at last Rowan slept.

* * *

He woke, startled, with Perlain's voice in his ear and Perlain's cool hand on his shoulder. He sat up with a jerk, shaking his head, trying to clear his mind.

As his confusion passed, he realised that there was light on his face. The door into the passage was open! He scrambled to his feet as Allun, looking very troubled, came back through the door and closed it behind him.

"No sign?" asked Perlain.

Allun shook his head.

"What is it?" Rowan demanded, bewildered and afraid. "How long have I slept? Why did you not wake me before?"

"I have only just woken myself," said Allun. "Perlain found us both here, sound asleep. But Zeel was not with us, Rowan. She is not outside in the corridor, either. She has gone."

14 – The Hand Must Bleed

Perhaps Zeel heard something and went to see what it was," Rowan suggested weakly.

A feeling of dread was rising in him. Ever since they entered the Zebak city Zeel had been quiet and strange. Long-buried memories were stirring in her. But it was hard to believe that Zeel—so strong, so long raised in Traveller ways—would be unable to face her past, and defeat it.

Unwilling to stand longer in the dark, they opened the door again and cautiously moved out into the bright light. The corridor stretched before them, shining and empty.

Allun shook his head. "What will we do now?" he exclaimed. "If she has ventured alone into this maze of corridors she will be hopelessly lost by now."

He caught sight of his reflection in the metal wall. His cheek was still streaked with black from the lamp. He rubbed at it crossly, smearing it even more. Then he gave an exclamation and moved closer to the wall.

"There is a smear of black grease on the wall here. And look—there is another, further along. And another!" He moved along the corridor, pointing out small marks on its shining surface as he went.

Perlain and Rowan hurried after him.

"Zeel had oily soot from the lamp all over her hands," Allun said excitedly. "She used it to leave a trail behind her so that she could find her way back."

"Or so that we could follow," Perlain suggested quietly.

When they reached a place where the corridor was crossed by another, the small black marks continued to the left. They turned the corner and went on.

"This is what Sheba's rhyme meant," Allun gabbled over his

shoulder as he led the way. "Though we all heard the bells, I must have been the one who heard them first. So it was I who saw the marks on the mirror, and realised that they were signs for us. It is wonderful."

"There has been another prophecy?" asked Perlain. "Tell me."

Rowan repeated the rhyme as they followed Allun around another corner and found themselves in a much broader, longer passage that stretched away on both sides, straight and unbroken.

The Maris man listened intently. "I do not like this talk of chains and sorrow," he said, when Rowan had finished. "And the hand that must bleed—I do not like that either. For all of us are the fingers on fate's hand, according to the rhyme Sheba gave you in her hut."

Allun had stopped. When they caught up to him they saw that all the eagerness had drained from his face. "I am a fool to have rejoiced," he muttered. "For if the first two lines of the verse are true, the rest will be also. Zeel may be in terrible danger now. Why else has she not returned?"

Just then, from somewhere ahead, they heard the sound of many marching feet. They were still distant, but fast coming closer. In seconds the corridor where they stood was echoing with sound.

"They are coming this way!" warned Perlain.

They turned and ran back the way they had come—around the corner where Rowan had told Perlain the rhyme, around the corner before that. There they stopped and listened.

The marching sound was thunderous now.

"Why are we waiting?" hissed Allun. "What if they turn the corner?"

"That is in fate's hands. But judging by the sound, there are many of them," Perlain whispered back. "So with luck they will continue along the broad passage, and we will be safe. We will watch and see. There will still be time to run if they turn."

They peered cautiously around the corner until they could see the place where the broad passage crossed the narrower one.

Left, right, left, right. The pounding came closer, closer. The metal of the wall beside Rowan's face began to tremble.

Then, suddenly, marching Zebak guards came into view. They

were four abreast, their grey-clad arms and shining black boots moving in perfect time, their eyes fixed to the front.

Rowan held his breath, poised to run, waiting for them to turn. But they did not turn. They marched straight ahead, as Perlain had predicted they would. Line after line of four passed by as Rowan counted. Six lines ... eight ... ten ... twelve. Then there were no more, and at last the sound faded into the distance.

"Plainly, that broad passage is dangerous," said Allun. "But we must use it if we are to find Zeel. Let us put it behind us as soon as we can."

They went back to the broad passage and began following Zeel's trail once more, half-running in their haste, their ears straining for the sound of marching feet. The passage stretched ahead, wide and straight, with no sign of a break until it ended at a sharp turn. If another group of guards appeared there would be nowhere to hide. They would be seen and captured, as perhaps Zeel had been before them.

But the marks on the wall continued, if less often, and the passage remained empty and silent. They turned the final corner to find themselves in an even broader space that ended in two huge doors with curved metal handles.

They crept up to the doors and listened carefully, but could hear no sound.

"Shall we risk it?" whispered Allun.

Perlain shrugged. "We have little choice," he said calmly. He reached for one of the door handles, then hesitated, pointing. Rowan saw that the handle bore a small black smudge, showing that Zeel had touched it.

Perlain pulled the handle, the door swung soundlessly open, and they entered the room beyond.

It was very large, and lined with metal cupboards and pegs on which hung Zebak uniforms and caps. A huge table stood in the middle of the room, with benches on either side. There was a great brown flag on the wall, bearing in its centre an emblem of black wings like those of the creature that had taken Annad.

"This is where the guards take their rest, if I am not mistaken," said Allun nervously. "It is not a healthy place for us to be."

Across the room was another door. It was partly open, and through the gap they could see a stone wall and the bars of an iron cage.

"Zeel," breathed Rowan. "Perhaps ...?"

They stole across the room and paused at the open door. Again, they could hear nothing. But Rowan thought he could feel something. A stirring in the air. A slight, warm breeze that meant that the outside world was near.

They slipped into the stone-walled space beyond the door. Its floor was paved with bricks. Two more doors took up most of one wall, and it was from under those doors that the fresh air came.

Two wheeled cages stood in the centre of the space. One, they could see, was empty. The other was partly covered by a cloth. They tiptoed towards it. Allun stretched out his hand to pull away the covering. Cautiously, Rowan bent to see ...

And then there was a pounding rush behind him, a heavy weight crashing into his back, a harsh voice ringing in his ears. He yelled and struggled. A powerful hand gripped the back of his neck and drove his head forward into the iron bars of the cage. The world seemed to explode in a blinding flash of light and pain.

"Enough!" thundered a voice. "We want them alive!"

"Yes, sir," growled Rowan's captor.

Rowan was dragged around to face the voice. He could hardly see. His head was spinning, throbbing with pain. He could feel blood trickling down his face. If he had not been held upright, he would have fallen to the ground.

The hand must bleed to reach the end ...

He became aware that Perlain and Allun were beside him, being held by other rough hands. He could hear Allun groaning. Or was it his own voice he could hear?

Sick and dizzy, he blinked at the tall, grey-uniformed figure striding towards them, heavy black boots ringing on the bricks. By her rigidly straight back and impatient tread he knew that this was a Zebak officer of high rank, without fear or pity. The black line from forehead to nose gave her face a cruel, stern look. Her mouth was set in a harsh line. Her pale eyes were cold under the shining brim of the stiff grey cap with its crest of black wings.

"Silence them, chain them, and put them in the cage," she snapped.

And it was only then, with a shock of horrified disbelief, that Rowan recognised her.

It was Zeel.

15 – Chains and Sorrow

Afterwards, Rowan realised that he must have fainted as the guard roughly gagged his mouth. When he woke, with a pounding head and a dry throat, he had no idea of how much time had passed. All he knew was that he was lying on the hard floor of the iron cage, chained hand and foot. He could hear Perlain groaning beside him. Probably Allun was on Perlain's other side.

They were prisoners. Prisoners of the Zebak. Zeel had gone to the side of the enemy. Or had she always been there, in her heart? The thought made him feel sick.

Slowly he became aware that the cage was jolting and rocking and that there was a rasping sound of metal wheels rolling over bricks. The cage was being pulled along a road.

The cloth that had been thrown over the cage did not cover it completely. By turning his head a little Rowan could see glimpses of the street through which they were passing.

He saw houses, and a baker's wagon. He saw stalls piled with fruit, vegetables and bags of grain. He saw children playing. He saw adults working or simply walking along carrying baskets, tools, leather bags, babies. All glanced curiously or in a frightened way at the cage, then turned away.

He was surprised to see that they were wearing ordinary clothes, not uniforms. Except for the black stripe from hairline to nose, which all but the very youngest children bore, they did not look very unlike the people at home.

"The cage cover has slipped. Put it right," barked a voice. Rowan's stomach turned over. The voice was Zeel's, but so changed, so cold.

He twisted his head a little more, wincing at the pain, and saw a straight grey back, a swinging arm, and then the side of a stern face, eyes staring straight ahead. Zeel was striding beside the cage.

Zeel, the betrayer. Zeel, who had used their trust in her to trap them.

One finger stands, the others bend.

"If urks see the prisoners, what does it matter?" growled another voice that Rowan seemed to recognise. "If they know the guards have captured spies inside the city walls they will understand how dangerous our enemies are. Their discontent will cease. They will understand that the war is necessary for their protection."

"How dare you question my orders?" snapped Zeel. "I told you. This affair is deadly secret! Do as I say!"

"Yes, sir," said the other voice hurriedly.

Rowan suddenly realised that the second speaker was the guard who had complained about having to push the garbage cart. He searched his memory for the name. Zanel. That was it.

The cover was pulled more closely around the cage and Rowan could see no more. But he could hear. And as he listened, doubt began to stir in his mind. Was it possible that there was something he had not understood? Was it possible ...?

"If you and your fellow buffoons had not blundered into this business you would know nothing about it!" Zeel was saying sternly. "As it happens, I had use for you and decided against reporting you. But beware. I can change my mind at any time, and then it will be the worse for you."

"We were only taking our break, sir," whined Zanel, thoroughly frightened now. "And only early because we had finished our work before time. We did not know the spies were under your guard. They seemed alone and were not chained. What else were we to think but—?"

"Silence!" Zeel shouted. "It is not your business to think. Go to the front and urge the beast on. We are moving too slowly."

"I fear this grach cannot move any faster, excuse me, sir," Zanel whimpered. "I had to fetch it from the compound, where it pulls the slaves' plough. Being from Central Control, sir, you are perhaps used to the fighting grach, the ones being trained for the invasion. They are young and strong—and fed on meat from The Wastelands lizards, it is said. But this grach feeds only on grass and scraps. And the compound gate is just ahead."

"These prisoners are to be taken to join the other *without delay*." Zeel's voice was loud and icy cold. "Those are the orders. Do you choose to disobey?"

Plainly, Zanel did not. After a moment Rowan heard his voice at the front of the cage. "Hup! Hup!" he was shouting. The cage lurched as the beast pulling it made a greater effort.

"That is better," Zeel's voice said loudly—so loudly that Rowan was sure she intended the prisoners in the cage to hear. "So, very soon our captives will meet their small countrywoman again. How grateful they must be to have a pleasant ride, with us to guide their way. Perhaps they feel that chains and sorrow are not too high a price to pay. What think you, Zanel?"

> With chains and sorrow you must pay
> For other hands to guide your way.

The guard walking at the front guffawed at what he thought was a cruel joke. But Rowan knew that Zeel's words had been a message. She wanted them to know that she was having them taken to where Annad was being kept. And she had used as much as she dared of Sheba's rhyme to tell them so.

Rowan heard a muffled sound beside him. With difficulty he turned his head. Perlain's eyes were wide and excited. He could not speak because of the gag in his mouth, but Rowan knew that he, too, had heard Zeel's message, and understood.

"Open the gate!" shouted Zeel. "Be quick!"

Rowan felt the cage turn off the brick road and onto another that seemed to be made of earth. A gate crashed shut behind them. His body rolled painfully on the lurching iron floor as the cage rumbled on, but he hardly noticed it. His mind was racing as he tried to work out what must have happened.

While they slept by the underground lake, Zeel had gone exploring. Somehow, perhaps by following the troop of guards they had seen returning, she had found the place where the uniforms were kept and taken one for herself. She had put it on and used the grease on her fingers to mark her forehead.

Then, perhaps, Zanel and his fellow guards had come in. She hid from them, only showing herself when Rowan, Allun and Perlain were attacked. She saved her friends from death or capture in the only way she could—by pretending they were already her prisoners.

Now she was continuing to play her part. She was playing it well. And, thanks to her, the problem of how they were going to find Annad had been solved.

There was a shout from the front of the cage, and it stopped with a jolt. "Very well!" Rowan heard Zeel say. "Get them out."

The cover was pulled from the cage. Rowan squinted against the sudden glare of light as slowly, slowly, the world outside the cage came into focus.

He stared, astonished. He had expected to see a prison, with stone or metal walls, iron bars, rows of prisoners in chains. But what he saw were trees, green fields, a stream, small cottages, people harvesting grain. They were so familiar ...

A tide of homesickness rose in him, and he wondered wildly if he was dreaming. If a great mountain had towered above the village, if the animals grazing in the fields had been bukshah instead of the huge creatures the Zebak called grach, he would have thought that he was in Rin.

One thing was clear: Annad could not be here. There had been some sort of mistake. Zeel had tried her best, and at least they were out of the maze. But Zanel had brought them to the wrong place. Perhaps by accident, perhaps not.

The side of the cage opened with a clang. Zanel reached in and pulled Rowan out like a sack of grain, then threw him to the ground.

"Take more care," barked Zeel. "They are not to be injured. Those are the orders."

Zanel grunted angrily, but heaved Perlain and Allun out of the cage with more care. They lay on the ground next to Rowan, unmoving. Rowan stole a glance at the grach which had pulled the cage. It had lowered its head and was tearing eagerly at the grass. It was glad the journey had ended, and it was home.

"You may go now," Zeel told Zanel severely. "And remember, you are forbidden to speak of this matter. If I hear that you have done so you will find yourself outside the wall with the ishkin."

"Yes, sir," mumbled Zanel. He turned to go.

"Wait!" Zeel commanded. "Give me the key to the prisoners' chains. I may need it."

A strange expression crossed Zanel's face. It was surprise, quickly followed by suspicion. "But Central Control guards like yourself have keys to open any lock, sir," he said.

Rowan held his breath. Zeel had made a mistake.

Zeel straightened her shoulders. "I choose to have *your* key, Zanel," she snapped. "Give it to me!"

Zanel stared, then he took a key from his pocket and walked towards Zeel. She waited, unmoving.

She does not want to seem too eager, Rowan thought. She knows he is suspicious. He strained his wrists against his chains, but he was held fast. There was nothing he could do.

Zanel was very near to Zeel now. He peered at her and his eyes narrowed. She held out her hand for the key.

He took another step and then pretended to trip. His hand flew up, grazed Zeel's forehead and knocked off her cap. The black line that ran between her nose and hairline smeared into a black smudge. Her long hair fell to her shoulders.

For a single moment Zanel goggled at her, and at his own hand, which was marked with black grease. Then he gave a roar, drew his dagger and sprang.

Zeel tried to leap away from him, but the heavy boots and stiff uniform hampered her and she tripped and fell. Watching helplessly, unable even to cry out, Rowan moaned with horror as Zanel lunged for her again, grinning with triumphant rage.

And then, as though by magic, the tall figure of a stranger suddenly plunged towards Zanel from behind the empty cage. He seemed to have appeared from nowhere. He must have crept up on them unseen, and stayed hidden till now.

He had fair hair touched with ginger, and he was young—not much more than a boy. He was wearing rough working clothes and carried a homely garden spade. But his face was full of a hero's determination, his shoulders were broad and his arms were powerful.

With a shout he raised the spade and brought it crashing down. The next moment, Zanel was lying unconscious on the ground.

His attacker stood panting above him, kicked him gently to see if he would stir, and then seemed satisfied. He picked up the dagger and looked at Rowan, Perlain and Allun lying helpless on the grass. And at Zeel, scrambling to her feet.

"I am Norris," he said soberly. He leaned on the spade as his eyes scanned them one by one, lingering with curiosity on Perlain. Then he turned his gaze back to Rowan, and his face broke into a smile.

"You are welcome, Rowan," he said. "We have been waiting for you."

16 – Surprises

umbfounded, Rowan stared at Zeel's rescuer. His first thought was that Norris looked very like Strong Jonn, though he was much younger—still under twenty years, by his broad, smooth face.

Keeping her eyes on Norris, still not sure of him, Zeel bent to unlock Rowan's chains. As she moved on to Allun and Perlain, Rowan sat up and with relief tore the stifling gag from his mouth.

"How do you know my name?" he asked huskily.

Just then the grach, which had quietly gone back to eating grass, raised its head and gave a grunt of pleasure. Rowan looked behind him and saw that an old man with long white hair and beard was hobbling towards them from one of the cottages. He was small and thin, and looked very worried.

"Oh, Norris!" he sighed as he reached them. "Again you have acted without thinking and used your strength instead of your wits. My poor boy, what am I to do with you?" As he spoke he fondled the grach, which had lumbered up to him, dragging the empty cage.

Norris's face flushed and he hung his head. It was clear that he felt clumsy and shamed. Rowan was sorry for him. He well understood what it was to be a disappointment to others. How often had he felt it himself? But for entirely the opposite reason.

Zeel stepped forward. "Norris saved my life, old one," she said firmly. "He had no choice but to attack. What else was he to do?"

The old man shook his head. Plainly he could think of nothing, but he stared at Zanel's unconscious body with dismay.

"They will come looking for the poor creature," he said at last in his gentle, hesitating voice. "We must hide him—and the cage, too. Under the haystack behind the cottage, perhaps. And then we will think what we should do."

He sighed again as Norris roughly dumped the guard into the cage and crashed the door shut. Then he seemed to remember the watching strangers. He turned to Rowan and bowed.

"Greetings, Rowan," he said. "Forgive our squabbling. Poor Norris is a good-hearted boy, but his hasty ways drive me to despair. I am Thiery of the Silk. My home is yours."

Before Rowan could answer, Thiery had turned to Allun, Zeel and Perlain. "I am pleased and interested to meet you," he said. "We were expecting Rowan, but no others."

He turned and began to walk slowly back to his cottage. With Norris at its side, the grach followed, pulling the cage behind it.

"Why were you expecting me?" Rowan burst out, stumbling after them.

"Your sister told us you would come," Thiery said simply.

"Annad!" Rowan's heart leaped. "She *is* here!"

Thiery looked mildly surprised. "Of course. Where else would they put a new slave?"

"We thought she would be in a prison," said Perlain. By his polite voice and veiled eyes Rowan could see that he thought the old man was either simple-minded or not to be trusted.

Thiery stopped. "This *is* a prison, my friend," he said. "In the compound we are prisoners of the Zebak as surely as if we were in iron cages." He lifted his stick and swung it so that its tip pointed out for them the high wire fence that stretched around the green fields.

Zeel turned to look at the distant workers and frowned. "But those people are Zebak," she said sharply. "I see their brow-marks."

"Oh, yes," agreed Thiery. "Ordinary Zebak folk—those the guards call 'urks'—come to the compound each day to join us in the fields. It has been many years since there have been enough slaves to do the work alone."

He glanced at Zeel. "You, too, are Zebak," he said. "But where is *your* brow-mark?"

Zeel lifted her chin proudly. "I became the daughter of another land when I was very young," she answered. "These clothes I put on only to deceive the guards."

Rowan felt a snuffling at his shoulder and without thinking he put up his hand. When his fingers felt scaly skin instead of warm wool he jerked his hand away. But then the grach moaned in disappointment, so he put his hand back. If any creature wanted comfort he could not deny it, however fearsome its appearance.

"The prophecy we were given said that the one who first heard Zebak bells should use the truth the mirror told," Zeel was explaining. "I heard the bells long ago, as a tiny child. And my reflection in the walls had made me face the truth that I was Zebak, however much I pretended I was not. Suddenly I saw how I, and I alone, could take us forward. It was my turn to play my part. As Perlain played his on the sea, and Allun in The Wastelands."

"The Wastelands!" gasped Norris, eyeing them with new respect.

"And what will Rowan's part be, I wonder?" asked Thiery.

His voice was very quiet. Rowan looked away from the grach and met his eyes. He thought he saw great sadness there, and wondered. But the old man quickly turned to Zeel again.

"Coming to the city must have been painful for you," he said gently.

"Yes," Zeel admitted in a low voice. "I felt that my friends must hate me for my birth. I hated myself."

So *that* was why Zeel had seemed so cold and withdrawn in the maze, thought Rowan, putting his hand on her arm.

"*Hate* you, Zeel?" Allun was exclaiming at the same time.

"It is not your fault that this land is at war with ours, and its people are cruel," added Perlain quietly.

As Zeel's troubled face warmed, Norris shuffled his feet. "We should move on," he warned. He was clearly embarrassed by this show of feeling. Again he reminded Rowan vividly of Jonn. And of Jiller, too, and even of little Annad. All of them would understand Norris's nature in a way that Thiery could not.

Norris is a stranger to his own people, as I am to mine, Rowan thought, as they began to walk again, matching their strides to the old man's slow steps.

The cottages were now not far ahead, and Rowan noticed for the first time that all but the one from which Thiery had come were in ruins. Their roofs were full of holes, their doors sagged open, and their windows were broken.

He wanted to ask Thiery about this, but the old man had been thinking about Perlain's last words and was speaking again.

"The Zebak people are not cruel by nature," he said, shaking his head. "Most are a little stern, but that is all. The guards are the cruel ones. They use their whips and their boots freely to show their power. Many ordinary folk would escape the land if they could. But the sea, their path to freedom, has been forbidden to them for many years now."

He turned to Zeel. "Your parents must have been among the last to attempt to flee by boat," he said gently. "If they paid for it with their lives, their action gave you, at least, a chance for a new life."

Zeel lowered her head.

"The people are prisoners in their city, as we are in the compound," Thiery went on. "The city walls are high, and the wings of the working grach are clipped each year so they cannot fly." He pressed his lips together. "It gives the beasts great pain," he added, as if this hurt him almost more than anything.

"The guards are all-powerful," Norris growled, glaring at the still figure inside the cage with hatred. "The people are helpless against them."

"But this is changing," Thiery said. "I feel it. The tide is turning."

He threw open the cottage door, ignoring Norris's snort of disbelief. Rowan walked from the hot sun into the pleasant coolness within and stopped short.

Despite his eagerness to see Annad, for a moment all he could do was look around, wondering why he felt so instantly at home. In size and shape, it was true, the room was like the living rooms in Rin. But instead of being plain and containing only those things that were useful, this room was full of light and bright colours.

Long blue curtains were pulled back from the large windows. There was a beautiful patterned rug on the floor and paintings on the walls. The couch was heaped with embroidered cushions. On the shelf above the fireplace stood a yellow jug of flowers.

"My granddaughter's work, and mine," Thiery's gentle voice murmured. "I am glad you find it pleasing. But you will want to see your sister ...?"

With a guilty start Rowan turned and followed him up the narrow stairs to the attic. Perlain, Allun and Zeel crowded behind.

* * *

"All is well, Shaaran," Thiery called as he entered a small bedroom.

There, on a narrow bed under a spread embroidered with leaves and flowers, lay Annad, fast asleep. The fragrant scent of sweet herbs drifted on the air.

A slim, dark-haired girl was standing beside the bed with her hand on the back of a chair. Her soft eyes were startled. She still clutched an open book, as if she had jumped up in fright on hearing their footsteps.

"The child's brother has come," Thiery told her, ushering Rowan into the room. "Rowan, this is my granddaughter, Shaaran."

The girl was about Rowan's age, but no taller than he was. She smiled shyly in greeting and to his astonishment Rowan was filled with the feeling that he had met her before. That is impossible, he told himself. But the feeling was strong and would not leave him.

"I am glad you are here," Shaaran was saying. "Annad has slept for almost all the time she has been with us, but whenever she stirred she said your name."

While his friends waited at the door, Rowan tiptoed to the bed. Annad was pale and there were some scratches on her face, but she was breathing peacefully. His heart swelled with relief.

As he looked down at her, her eyes flickered, then opened. She stared up at him without the least surprise, and smiled. "I knew you would come for me, Rowan," she sighed. "I was not afraid."

Rowan smiled back at her. "You are never afraid," he said. He bent over her, and the medallion hanging around his neck swung free. He heard a gasp from behind him but he could not turn to look because Annad's fingers had caught the medallion and held it fast.

"Pretty," she said, and yawned widely.

"Sleep again now, Annad," Rowan said. "I will be here when you wake."

Annad nodded drowsily. "And you will take me home," she said. Her eyelids were already growing heavy again. She blinked at

Shaaran. "My brother is a great hero, you know," she murmured. Then her eyes closed, the fingers clutching the medallion loosened, and she fell back to sleep.

Rowan straightened and stepped away from the bed. His heart was very full. Home? Would any of them ever see home again? He turned, anxious to know what had caused the gasp he had heard.

Shaaran had put her arm around her grandfather's shoulders. To his surprise, Rowan saw that the old man's faded eyes were glistening with tears.

"I knew you would come one day," he quavered. "I believed, as my father before me. As our family has always believed. And so we went on, painting the silks for you, as slowly we faded away ..."

Rowan stared at him, confused and a little afraid. Was Thiery mad? He looked helplessly at Shaaran and saw that she was trembling.

"Grandfather, Rowan does not understand," she whispered to the old man. She looked back at Rowan. "When Annad came we wondered if at last the time had come," she breathed. "Her face—her strength—"

She broke off, swallowing desperately to hold back her tears. "We hoped—but could not be certain," she went on. "And then—just now—to see the medallion, and know ... It is a great happiness for grandfather, and for me. But a great shock, also."

Rowan shook his head. He felt dazed. "What—what is this place?" he stammered. "Who are you?"

"We are your people, Rowan," Shaaran said softly. "All that are left. And this is your place. This is Rin."

17 – Painted Shadows

"You are not my people! I have never seen you before this day. And this is not Rin! Rin is far away, across the sea!" The words burst from Rowan almost angrily. Shaaran shrank back, looking to her grandfather for help, very aware of Allun, Perlain and Zeel clustered just inside the door, their faces startled.

"They called their new home after their old, Shaaran," the old man murmured. "Their memories had been taken from them, but the name came to them and they used it, without knowing why."

"Who?" Rowan demanded. "Who are you talking about?" He found that he was shaking.

"Your ancestors," Thiery said. "The strong ones who left us over three hundred years ago and never returned."

Rowan stared, open-mouthed.

Thiery smiled wearily and slumped down on the chair beside Annad's bed. "I am very tired," he sighed. "You must show him, Shaaran, my dear. I will watch over the child."

Shaaran was plainly worried about him, but obediently she beckoned to Rowan and together they followed Zeel, Allun and Perlain down the narrow stairs. Shaaran took a folded sheet from a cupboard. Then she led them out the back door of the cottage and into the open air.

Beyond the vegetable garden a large haystack stood. Norris was forking hay over the iron cage, which was already almost completely covered.

The grach grazed peacefully nearby. It looked up as they came out, but when it saw that Thiery was not with them it lost interest and went back to its feeding.

The friends followed Shaaran down some stone steps that led to a cellar below the cottage. Inside, it was as dark and cold as the grave, but the girl lit a candle. Bundles of root vegetables and a stack of fire-wood came into view. The light flickered eerily on walls and floor. Shadows were flat black monsters crawling on the stones.

Shaaran took a pointed iron bar from its place against the wall, carried it to the room's darkest corner and stuck it into a gap between the cornerstone and the wall. Seeing what she was trying to do, Zeel and Allun went to her aid, adding their weight to the bar so that the stone was raised.

Beneath it was a dark hole.

Shaaran thrust her arm inside it and drew out a chain that was attached to a hook somewhere near the top. She pulled, and soon a large box swung into view, dangling from the end of the chain like a fish on a line.

She placed the box on the floor and opened it. Inside were dozens of thin rolls of silk. Each roll was as wide as Rowan's arm was long, and each was tied with a plaited cord like the one he now wore around his neck. Some of the rolls looked newer than others. Some were very old indeed.

"What are they?" Allun burst out, craning his neck to see.

"Our story," Shaaran said. "I will show you."

She spread the sheet on the dusty floor. Then she unrolled the long pieces of silk upon it, one by one, starting with the oldest.

In the flickering candlelight, painted figures and scenes seemed to leap up at them from the silken backgrounds. Clear, bright colours brought to glowing life a time long gone. This village, full of people and sturdy cottages. Men, women and children working in the fields. Mottled grach pulling ploughs and carts. Zebak guards, chains, iron cages ...

Rowan's hand burned.

The painted shadows live again ...

Each silk told a different story. And all the stories put together made a longer tale—a sad and terrible tale that had been three hundred years in the telling.

"Long ago, Rowan, our people were one," Shaaran said, her hand moving over the oldest silks. "We had been slaves of the Zebak so long that our old history had been lost, for the Zebak had killed anyone who mentioned times past. We worked in the fields, growing food for the city. There were many of us—brave and timid, strong and weak, those who could paint and sew and heal the sick—and those who could climb and run and fight."

She was repeating a lesson she had learned long ago, and the words came easily. But her eyes were sad, as though for the moment she was living in the past, and grieved.

"Three hundred years ago the Zebak leaders made a great plan to invade a land across the sea," she went on. "They had fought the people of that land before, and knew they would defend themselves with all their strength. Many Zebak would die. So they decided to add to their forces. They took the strongest and bravest of us away to be trained as warriors and sacrificed to the cause ..."

Such was the roaring in his ears that Rowan could hardly hear her voice as it continued. And he did not need to. One painting showed the story all too clearly.

It showed guards rounding up people from the village and putting them into iron cages to which grach were harnessed. It showed the weeping and pain as sons and daughters were torn away from their mothers, brother was separated from brother, husband from wife.

The ones who were being taken were tall and strong. They reminded him of his family, the people he knew at home, and Norris. The ones who were being left behind were smaller and weaker-looking—of no use as warriors. They were like Shaaran. Like Thiery. Like himself.

Shaaran's slim finger pointed to a bent old woman standing close to one of the iron cages. She carried a bundle of herbs, to show that she was a Wise Woman and a healer. She was secretly passing something through the bars of the cage to another, much younger, woman inside.

Rowan bent closer to see what the object was and when he saw, he gasped. It was a medallion on a plaited silk cord.

"It is the same," Shaaran said. "You are wearing it now. It has been passed down through the generations for three hundred years, and now it has returned. We have always believed that one day it would."

"So you knew that the warrior slaves did not die," Rowan said slowly. "You knew they turned against the Zebak and helped to defeat them."

Shaaran nodded, pointing to the next piece of silk which showed vivid scenes of battle. The Zebak were being driven back into the sea by their own strong slaves. With the slaves were the Maris, who had been painted with fish tails, and the Travellers, wild with feathers and fierce, laughing faces.

Perlain snorted. "The Maris do not have tails," he said stiffly.

"Neither do the Travellers look quite so much like devils as this, I hope," Zeel smiled.

"My ancestors could not paint truly what they had never seen," said Shaaran apologetically. "They had to rely upon the tales they heard when the Zebak who had survived came limping home. That is how they heard that their lost people had remained in the new land."

"And happily forgotten the loved ones they had left behind in slavery!" Allun's voice was harsh.

"Do not judge them, Allun," said Rowan quietly. "The Zebak have ways of controlling minds, and plainly it has always been so. They washed their warrior slaves' memories clean, so that they would fight well and not pine for their loved ones."

Shaaran nodded. "That is why my ancestors took a great risk and began painting the silks. So that if ever the lost ones returned to this land they might find them and learn their story—even if there was no one left to tell it."

Her voice was very quiet as she said these last words. Rowan looked at the remaining silk strips. They showed the people working as before, but even harder, and in greater sadness. They showed guards taking young ones who showed any sign of rebellion, and throwing them into The Wastelands. They showed overgrown fields, and houses gradually falling down. They showed adults growing older and dying, but fewer and fewer children being born to take their places. They showed Zebak people being brought in to do their work, so that there would still be food for the city. The very last showed three figures only. Two children and an old man, standing alone by a grave.

When pain is truth and truth is pain ...

"My parents had children only because our family had always painted the silks, and they wished the work to go on for as long as possible," Shaaran said. "They could see from the first that Norris— was not suitable. So they had me. But we are the last."

So Thiery, Norris and Shaaran were all that were left of these quiet, gentle people. They had preferred to waste away than to go on bearing children in slavery.

Rowan understood. He would have felt the same way. He understood, too, at last, why he was different from others in his village, and why there had been others like him in the past.

The people of Rin had forgotten the loved ones they had left behind, but nature had not. Now and again, like black bukshah calves, oddities were born. Oddities like him, who took after a side of the Rin family that none of them had known existed.

"Grandfather painted this silk after our parents died of fever, seven years ago," Shaaran was saying. "He has painted no more since. He has not had the heart, and there has been nothing to tell."

"Well, there is something now," said Zeel fiercely.

"There is," Allun agreed. "But I do not think we can wait for painting. This place is dangerous for us. Perlain is already impatient. I can see it by the way he lashes his tail."

Shaaran laughed out loud, then bit her lip and glanced at Perlain to see if he was insulted. But Perlain simply smiled coolly.

"I am indeed impatient," he said. "And if I *did* have a tail, it would be lashing like a serpent. We must find a way of leaving here as soon as we can. But we will need help."

"Norris and I will help you," Shaaran offered eagerly. "We have trusted friends among the people who work in the fields. And when the guards come we can delay them while you—"

"No, Shaaran!" Rowan broke in. "We are not going alone. You are coming with us."

She stared at him, astounded. "We cannot go," she whispered. "The guards will not let us go."

"They will not let *us* go, either, if they can help it," Rowan said, as cheerfully as he could. "Pack away the silks. We will not leave them behind."

Shaaran turned away and began to roll the silk strips, her fingers trembling.

"Rowan!" Perlain's face was very grave, and Rowan knew what he was thinking. They had survived so far by a miracle. Their way from here would be doubly hard. Hampered by four more people, including a small child, a timid girl and a frail old man, how could they survive?

But Rowan knew he could not leave them. He fumbled in his shirt for Sheba's oilcloth package, drew out a stick and plunged it into the candle flame.

Green light leaping on the stone walls, on the motionless figures of his friends, on Shaaran's startled face, on the rolls of silk. Burning pain. Sheba's face, grinning at him ...

When evil strikes and fury wakes,
Then love will face the choice it makes.
Death will free the loyal friend.
As it began, so will it end.
Bound to the beast, you play your part—
The comfort of the aching heart.

Struggling against the wave of tiredness and despair that was engulfing him, Rowan repeated the words. His friends said nothing, for what was there to say?

Yet surely the rhyme's meaning could not be what it seemed.

"It does not mean that we have only death and slavery before us," he muttered at last. "It *cannot* mean that."

"Sheba did warn us," said Allun, his lips twisted in a bitter smile.

Rowan knew that he was thinking of the words that had haunted them all from the beginning, though they had never spoken of them.

Five leave, but five do not return ...

Shaaran looked down at the evil-smelling oilcloth lying tangled on the cellar floor. All that remained of its contents were a sorry handful of limp, pale grass and a single stick.

"There—there is one stick left," she stammered. "Does this not mean that it is too soon to give up hope?"

Rowan glanced at her quickly. Her pale face showed her fear, but she was fighting the fear with all her strength. She would not give way to it.

And neither would he.

"You are right," he said, folding up the cloth and putting it back inside his shirt. "The story is not yet finished."

Heavy feet thumped on the cellar steps. Then Norris swung through the door, carrying Annad, sleepy and blinking, in his arms. "Guards are marching towards the compound," he called urgently. "The people will delay them at the gate, but you must make haste. If they find you here they will kill us all!"

18 – As It Began …

Outside, Thiery was waiting for them, his face filled with alarm. The grach hissed anxiously beside him and he stroked its neck, trying to soothe it, as the friends quickly discussed what they should do.

"We cannot face The Wastelands again," Allun said firmly. "That is certain."

"The prophecy said 'As it began, so will it end'," said Perlain. "Our journey began on the sea. We must try to get to the shore and steal a boat."

"If only I had not been forced to leave my kite behind when I changed my clothes!" Zeel shook her head angrily, then swung round to Norris. "Can you show us the quickest way to the shore?"

"I could," said Norris grimly, "but it would not help you. The wall circles the city. The Wastelands is the one place where the doors are not heavily guarded day and night. And in any case, the shore is ringed by spiked wire that cannot be crossed."

"But surely—" Allun began.

Norris's face flushed with anger. "If escape was as easy as you seem to suppose, we ourselves would have done it," he shouted. He looked around at them, his fists clenched. "I am not a coward or a fool. Do you think I wish to remain here in slavery?"

Thiery sighed at his grandson's anger. But the visitors well understood it. It was the anger that any ordinary citizen of Rin would have showed in Norris's shoes.

"No one doubts your courage, or your sense, friend," Perlain said calmly. "But we are with you now. This makes a difference."

"Oh?" jeered Norris. "And why is that?"

"Because if we *can* escape the city, we at least know where we can sail to reach safety," Rowan said.

"Safety?" Norris scowled. "There is no safety in your land. Do you not understand? The test which brought your sister here proved to the Zebak that an attack from the air will succeed. They are wasting no more time. Even now, it is said, the grach fleet is massing in the great square, preparing to leave. Soon your land will be invaded and overcome."

"Our land will *not* be overcome," said Zeel firmly. "Our people will fight."

Norris shook his head. "Nothing can defeat the fighting grach. Their skins are as tough as iron, and their claws, teeth and tails can kill with ease."

"And yet your grach is so gentle." Rowan looked at the huge creature snuffling lovingly at Thiery's hand.

Norris shrugged impatiently. "Unos is a working grach. The fighting grach have been especially bred for war. They learn to seek the scent of a beast that lives only in your land. The trainers have the hide of one such beast, brought back by the survivors of what they call the War of the Plains."

"But the War of the Plains was long ago!" Allun exclaimed.

"Invasion by air has been Central Control's treasured plan for many years," Norris said. "It has cost much in supplies and labour. The people do not like it, but they are told it must be done for their own safety."

"That is a lie," said Perlain flatly. "We fight only to defend ourselves."

"Already the people know this, in their hearts," Thiery nodded, gazing over the fields. "For long ages their labour and their lives have been wasted in making useless war. Their anger is growing strong enough to overcome their fear of disobedience. They whisper of rebellion."

"But that is why Central Control is determined that this invasion will succeed, Grandfather," growled Norris. "The leaders believe that new land to settle and fresh slaves to work in the fields will stop the protest."

Rowan felt a chill of fear, then jumped as he heard distant shouts. The guards had reached the compound gates.

"We must leave at once," said Allun abruptly. "Norris—will you lead us to the shore, or not?"

Norris hesitated.

"If Norris will not do it, I will."

Everyone turned in surprise, for it was Shaaran who had spoken. She had been so quiet that they had almost forgotten about her. Her face burned, but she met their eyes determinedly.

"I, too, know the way," she said.

"No, Shaaran!" wailed the old man, and Unos the grach moaned softly, feeling her master's fear.

"It would be a useless waste of life. There is no escape by sea," Norris said stubbornly.

"This is our one chance at freedom, Norris!" cried Shaaran. "Let us take it!"

The old man paused, looking from one to the other. Then, strangely, he smiled. He bent to kiss Shaaran's brow, and put a gentle hand on Norris's shoulder. "You are both right, my dears," he murmured. "Forgive me. For a moment I wavered. Fear has always been my enemy. You have both taught me to be strong."

He raised his hand to stroke Unos again, then turned away and began hurrying towards the haystack. "Before anything can be done, I must see to the injured guard," he called back over his shoulder. "He will by now have woken."

"The old fool is mad!" exploded Zeel.

"We cannot wait," muttered Perlain. "We will have to leave him."

"No!" Norris exclaimed.

"Grandfather," called Shaaran, thrusting the box of silks into Rowan's arms and running after the old man. "Grandfather, we must go!"

"Stay back, Shaaran," shouted Thiery, tearing at the hay, strewing it everywhere. "This is my task!"

Unos had spread her wings and was half-lumbering, half-flapping after her master like some great bird trying to protect its chick.

Suddenly Rowan realised something. He spun around to Norris.

"Your grach's wings—they have not been clipped!" he exclaimed.

"No. For many years Grandfather has bribed our guards to spare

Unos, by giving them extra food," Norris answered gruffly. "He gave his word that while he lived he would not let her fly, so that Central Command would never know."

Rowan's thoughts were racing. A grach had stolen Annad, flown away with her. *That* was the beginning. And a grach's flight could be the end.

"Unos is big enough to take all of us," he cried. "We could—"

Norris shook his head, watching the old man. "Grandfather gave his word," he said sulkily. "He will never break it. Not even—"

Then, suddenly, his eyes widened, and at the same moment Rowan heard Shaaran cry out.

A dark figure was leaping from within the haystack. Zanel had freed himself from the cage. He had been hiding, waiting …

"Slave! Traitor!" he shouted, his face twisted with rage. "Do you dare to imprison *me*!" He seized Thiery, shaking him like a child's cloth doll. Then the blade of a dagger flashed in the sunlight as he raised it and plunged it into the old man's heart.

Shaaran screamed, running forward as Thiery crumpled and fell. Zanel seized her in her turn and she screamed again. Rowan, Norris, Allun, Perlain and Zeel were shouting as they leaped to help her. But their cries were drowned by another sound—a terrible, animal wail of pain as Unos mourned her master.

"Stay back!" Zanel shouted, the dagger held high in his hand. "I will kill the girl if you move."

They stopped, eyeing him warily.

"Fools!" he snarled. "Did you think I would carry just one weapon? Did you think a lock would keep me in a cage when the dagger in my boot could break it? Lie down. Now! Flat on your bellies in the dust where you belong. Or the girl will suffer for it."

Grimly, the friends glanced at one another.

"Go! Run!" sobbed Shaaran, as she struggled against the guard's strong arm. Tears were streaming down her face, but she shook her head violently. "Please! It does not matter about me! Go now!"

Zanel tightened his grip around her neck, strangling her cries. Lifting her off her feet with ease, he dragged her forward, stepping over Thiery's body, kicking at it carelessly.

The grach looked up from her grieving. Her flat yellow eyes burned and she hissed deep in her throat as she looked at the man who had killed her master.

Zanel looked around in surprise. To him, grach had always been simple beasts of burden, to be used, like slaves, without respect and certainly without fear. But never had he seen animal eyes so full of hatred.

Fear flickered across his face. "Down, grach!" he said uncertainly.

Unos bared her teeth. Her forked tongue flickered out, tasting her enemy's fear. The spines on her neck rose and stood upright. Her whole body seemed swollen as she moved slowly towards Zanel, spreading her huge wings.

"Down!" shrieked Zanel, backing away. He slashed at her pointlessly with the dagger that had killed an old man but which against this terrible foe was as useless as a toy. Then suddenly he turned, cast Shaaran aside and began to run.

The grach paused in mid-step. At first, hardly daring to watch, Rowan thought she was going to let the guard go. Then, as he was almost away, the divided tail flicked. Like three whips spiked with thorns, it struck with casual, deadly force. Zanel screamed once. But by the time he hit the ground, he breathed no more.

Rowan was shaking with the horror of what he had seen. He could hear Shaaran weeping, Allun cursing, and Annad calling to him. But as he watched Unos lumbering back to them, her strong, leathery wings trailing in the dust behind her, the fire of anger in her eyes dying back to dull sadness, he remembered Sheba's words.

When evil strikes and fury wakes,
Then love will face the choice it makes.
Death will free the loyal friend.
As it began, so will it end.

With a heavy heart he moved to Shaaran's side. "Do not weep," he said gently. "Your grandfather died as he wished. He made his choice. His oath died with him, so his loyal friend is free to fly again. And as he planned, she will take us home."

19 – ... So Will It End

The grach flew west, following the scent. She had flown for a long time and she was tired and hungry, but the boy's gentle voice and stroking hands gave her the strength to go on. There was little thought behind her flat yellow eyes. Just one fixed idea. She must follow the scent, reach the place she had been told to reach, and deliver her riders to the place they wanted to go.

The sea had been left behind long ago, and dimly the grach was aware that below her now were rolling green hills and a winding stream of water, glinting bright in the sunlight. She was aware that a mountain, its peak hidden in cloud, rose in the blue distance ahead.

But her eyes were not important. Her ears, closed against the rushing of the wind, the beating of her aching wings, were not important either. All that was important was her forked tongue, flickering in and out, tasting the cold air, tasting the scent.

She knew she was close to her goal. The scent was stronger—the good smell of dust, fire, ash and bitter herbs that made her jaws drip with hunger. Sheba. She even knew the name.

"Sheba," the gentle boy had said, flourishing the small oilcloth bundle in front of her face, feeding her the limp stems of pale grass from inside it so that their delicious sweet-sour taste mingled with the smell. When her riders had climbed upon her back and tied themselves in place the boy had said it again. "Sheba. Seek."

And then the grach had spread her wings, and flown. Over the empty, ruined cottages and the fields where workers looked up, waving and cheering, and a troop of guards shouted. Over the city with its flaming tower, its gathered army of fighting grach, its grey-clad figures pointing, running. Then on over the gleaming wall, over the burning Wastelands, over churning sea, over jagged cliffs and on to this green land.

The Sheba scent was strong. The scents of grach and Zebak were strong, too, and growing stronger. But there were other scents. Some of these Unos had tasted before. Two she had not. One of those she had not tasted was a warm, animal smell. There was no threat in it. But the other was full of danger. It was fire, snow and ice. It was hot breath, dripping fangs and ancient, jealous power.

The leathery spines on the grach's back prickled with warning. But the boy's soothing voice was soft in her ear, so her yellow lizard eyes did not flicker and the beating of her scaly mottled wings did not falter as she flew on, to Rin.

* * *

Star scanned the blue, blue sky above the village. It was still clear, except for the cloud that always shrouded the tip of the forbidden Mountain, and two kites, one white, one red, riding the wind. And yet—surely there was something in the sky to fear. Something to fear—but something to welcome, also. The scents were mixed. Good and evil. Coming closer.

She had already taken the herd to the lowest part of the field, beyond the drinking pool. Now she began to lead them into a circle. It was time. The birds had hidden long ago. She could hear shouting in the village. She could see people with weapons and flaming torches. Beyond the village she could see Ogden the Traveller standing on a hill like a tree against the sky, watching the kites and listening, listening.

But her duty was to the herd. To protect the calves, to hold the circle. She stood as still as a statue in her place, sniffing the air. She was ready. She had done what she could.

* * *

"We cannot be sure where the creatures will land!" Solla the sweet-maker, plump and soft, waddled, panting, towards the bukshah field. He clutched his quickly sharpened spear tightly while his eyes darted to and fro.

"We cannot be sure," snapped old Lann, hobbling beside him. "That is why the Travellers guard the hills, and why I have left some forces in the square. But if the beasts have been trained to follow the bukshah scent, as Timon believes, they will land at the field."

She was leaning heavily on her stick, but in her other hand she, too, carried a spear. It was her own, and she had sharpened it with her own hands. Once she had been Rin's greatest fighter, and she was determined that age would not prevent her from again defending her home—with her life, if fate so willed.

She stopped to rest, her keen old eyes searching the sky. She made out the tiny figures of Tor and Mithren dangling unprotected beneath their kites, watching for the first sight of the enemy. Her warrior's heart thrilled at their courage. She wondered at how often she had jibed at the Travellers for their light-hearted, wandering ways.

I had forgotten, she thought. I fought beside Travellers, and Maris, too, in the War of the Plains. I of all here should have remembered their worth. But time passed, and I forgot.

She glanced at Bronden the furniture-maker, who had stopped beside her. Bronden, too, was looking up, her face haggard. Lann knew that she had not slept since the day Annad was taken and Rowan of the Bukshah, Perlain of Pandellis, Allun the baker and Zeel of the Travellers had left in pursuit.

It had not been what Bronden expected—that the despised ones, the oddities, should do what she herself would never dare. It had shaken her to her core.

Lann saw Bronden's eyes widen, and she looked upward. The kites were dipping, plunging, like waterbirds ducking for fish. And on the silent hill Ogden was raising his arms.

The enemy was coming.

Lann's mouth set into a firm, hard line. She grasped her spear more tightly and set off for the bukshah field once more.

Bronden strode beside her, stocky and strong. When she spoke, her voice was harsh and grating.

"They will not take us," she said. "Our people will not be slaves again. We will die first."

"Let us not think of dying," Lann answered coolly. "Only of winning."

Her words were the words of a leader, but her heart was heavy as she reached the field and saw her people gathered, waiting. They were brave and determined, but they were few. And of what use were their weapons against the creatures they were about to face?

At the front, towering above the rest, stood Strong Jonn. Beside him were Jiller and Marlie the weaver, both holding bows and arrows.

These three seemed apart from the crowd. They were pale, and their faces bore the marks of great grief. But grimly they stood together, shoulder to shoulder. For them, this battle would be for revenge as well as for freedom.

Lann pushed her way through the people until she reached them.

"Did you see Sheba?" she barked. "Did she speak?"

Jiller shook her head. "It was as before," she said evenly. "She has not moved. Specks of ash have settled on her face and a spider has spun a web across her chair. The fire was burning green and would not let us near her."

Lann frowned. "Is it illness? Trance?"

"Whatever it may be, she did not stir, however loudly we called," said Jiller. "Her eyes are closed. Yet she breathes. It is as though her spirit has left her body."

"There!" Jonn shouted, pointing upward. "Look there!"

A black speck could be seen against the pale blue of the horizon. It was growing larger by the second. The kites wheeled and sped towards it.

"Only one!" someone in the crowd called in relief.

"The same, perhaps, come for another child," cried another voice. "Well, we are ready for it this time."

Jonn shook his head. "Ogden said he felt a great menace," he muttered. "Far greater than before. If there is only one, it must be the first of many."

They watched, transfixed, as the black shape grew larger, larger. Now they could see its great wings beating the air. The kites swooped and darted around it, and it seemed to fall lower in the sky.

"They are worrying it," said Jonn with grim satisfaction.

Marlie spoke for the first time. "I see shapes upon its back," she said. "It has riders."

Jiller raised her pale face and squared her shoulders, slowly fitting an arrow to her bow.

* * *

"Kites!" Annad squealed to Rowan over the sound of the rushing wind. She wriggled impatiently, trying to wave to Tor and Mithren, straining at the rope that tied her to the grach's back.

Rowan felt Unos falter. "Annad, be still!" he shouted. Pulling his own bonds, he reached down and rubbed the scaly neck, in the place he had learned the beast liked best. He knew she was very tired. He could almost feel the pain of her exhausted wings and the dryness of her throat. He could almost see the fear lurking behind her fixed eyes.

Bound to the beast, you play your part—
The comfort of the aching heart.

"Good Unos," he crooned in her ear, as he had done so many times before on this long journey. "You will have food soon. More of that pale grass, if Sheba will give it. And cool water, and rest. Do not fear. Just a little further."

"He is as soft as Grandfather! Does he think the beast understands his words?" Norris's voice floated loud on the wind.

"She understands what he means by them, Norris." Shaaran's voice was far quieter, but Rowan could still hear it.

"Without Rowan's coaxing and his comfort, the beast would have given in and fallen from the sky long ago." That was Allun. "She has not been trained for such a journey. She has not flown at all for many years. She has brought us so far only because Rowan is with us."

So, Sheba, this is my part, Rowan thought hazily. But there is one stick left in the package you gave me. What will it tell me when it burns?

"The people have gathered in the bukshah field," shouted Zeel. "They have weapons. They cannot see us! They think—"

The wind whipped away her last words.

Rowan saw Mithren's kite wheel past him. He saw Mithren's eyes, startled, staring into his. He saw the reed pipe raised to Mithren's lips, and a message sent. He wondered if it would be in time.

20 – Terror

o not waste arrows, archers," old Lann was calling. "Aim carefully! Wait for a clear sight!"

For the first time in minutes, Jonn looked up at the hill. Ogden was there no longer. Jonn wondered why.

Jiller and Marlie were in front of him now. All the archers were in front. They were the ones who would try to unseat the riders. The swordsmen, like Jonn, and those with spears were behind. The beast was their target, as were the beasts to come.

The sword was heavy in Jonn's hand. It had been his father's, and had lain idle since the War of the Plains. But now it was to taste Zebak blood again. One last time, perhaps.

The beast was coming. Not like a bolt of lightning, as the first had done, but slowly, as if it was labouring under the weight it carried. Its huge, hideous shape was clear now. Its riders were dark shapes against the sky. There were seven.

"Seven targets," growled Lann. "Seven easy targets."

The kites were still swooping and hovering between the creature and the ground. Why do they not move away? thought Jonn impatiently. They will spoil the archers' aim. Ogden should signal them to retire. Again he glanced up at the hill, but the storyteller had not returned.

From the cloud at the top of the Mountain there was a low grumbling. The Dragon was stirring in its icy palace.

The crowd turned to look, but the archers did not take their eyes from the sky.

"Ready!" called Lann. "When the white kite passes ..."

The archers raised their drawn bows.

Star was calling from her place in the bukshah circle. Jonn swung around to look at her, puzzled because the sound was not a bellow of fear but a sound of greeting. She was pawing the ground and nodding her head. Again she called. But she did not break the circle.

Jonn heard Lann click her tongue in irritation as the white kite swooped aside and the red kite immediately took its place between the archers and the beast. Faintly now he could hear Tor and Mithren shouting. And there were other shouts, too, floating thinly in the air. With a shock he realised that the sounds came from the riders. Why would they call out? Unless ...

"Lann—" he began.

The red kite was caught by a gust of wind and blown upwards. At last the target was clear.

"Ready ..." shouted Lann.

"Stop!"

It was Ogden, waving, running towards them, his high forehead gleaming with sweat. "Put down—your weapons!" he panted, as he ran. "I had—a message. The riders—are friends."

Frowning, Lann hesitated. Then—"Wait," she growled to the archers. They froze in position, keeping aim.

"What is this?" she snapped to Ogden. "Friends? How could this be?"

"I do not know." The storyteller gestured at the sky, shaking his head. "The signal was 'Friends! Do not fear.' I ran, to tell you. I knew—you would listen to no one else. Lay down your weapons. Let them land."

"The beast—" Lann began.

But at the same moment Jiller cried out and cast down her bow. Then she was stumbling forward into the shadow of the beast, lifting her arms. "Rowan!" she was crying. "Annad!"

"Allun!" Marlie just whispered the name. She seemed frozen to the spot, her hands still clutching the bow. Her pale face was even whiter than before.

Jonn looked up. And at last he saw what they had seen.

It was beyond his wildest dreams. Roped to the beast's back, bouncing and sliding as it landed on the grass of the bukshah field, were Rowan, Annad, Zeel, Perlain and Allun.

And between them, already sliding to the ground with the others as their ropes were untied, were two strangers. A fine, strong young man and a delicate-looking girl who looked more like Rowan's sister than fiery little Annad would ever do.

Thunderstruck, Jonn watched as Jiller swept her children into her arms and Marlie flew to Allun's side. He heard cool, quiet Perlain shouting like a madman: "We are all alive! Yet Sheba was right! Five did *not* return. Eight returned. Eight!" He felt the people around him surging forward and heard them marvelling, cheering. He saw the huge mottled beast lumber to the stream to drink, as the bukshah rumbled warningly. He saw old Lann, as bewildered by joy and astonishment as he, staring at the strangers.

"So," murmured Ogden, beside him. "Rowan has brought them home. I should have trusted in him. In them all. But even I feared." He drew a long breath. "And so, indeed, it was time. But are there only two?"

Jonn swung around, his eyes full of questions. But Ogden had already moved forward, opening his arms to Zeel, clapping Perlain on the back, then courteously drawing Lann towards the strangers.

"These are your people," Jonn heard him say to the old woman. "Pray welcome them, but save all questions for later. Our trial is still to come, I fear."

"Yes!" exclaimed the boy. "The Zebak cannot be far behind us. And there are many."

"How many?" demanded Lann, putting all surprise and questions aside like the old warrior she was.

But as Norris began to answer her there was a scream from the crowd, and then everyone was pointing.

The horizon was black with flying shapes. Like swarming bees at first, they grew larger and nearer with every blink—a vast army borne on beating, armoured wings.

The bukshah bellowed, pawing the ground. The grach by the stream hissed a warning. And the Mountain seemed to tremble with the Dragon's roars. Its fire burned in the cloud, staining the misty white with crimson.

"Positions, archers!" ordered Lann. "Others, get behind!"

"Rowan, look after her!" Jiller cried, thrusting Annad into his arms. "The children are all in the mill. Take her there!"

Then she was gone, running to her place.

The people were lighting new torches, straightening their backs, throwing back their shoulders and raising their weapons. Allun, Perlain, Zeel and Norris were joining their ranks with whatever weapons they could find. But Shaaran had backed away to the edge of the field where a pile of unlit torches lay beside a leaping fire. Her eyes were wide with fear as she stared at the sky, and she clutched the box of silks to her as though somehow it could protect her from harm.

Rowan, too, looked at the sky. It was darkening as the enemy rushed towards them, faster than the wind. There are too many, he thought. Too many.

He pulled Annad over to where Shaaran stood. "You must take Shaaran to the mill, Annad," he urged. "Make haste."

Annad shook her head. "You take her, Rowan," she cried. "I will fight!" Tearing herself away from his grasp, she seized a torch and lit it, brandishing it above her head fiercely.

"Let her do what she wills," said Shaaran. Rowan saw to his amazement that her pale lips were curving into a smile as she watched Annad run back to the field. She glanced at him. "She is so strong and fierce," she explained. "She is like Norris. They all are. It is so strange."

"Not strange here," said Rowan grimly. "Here it is you and I who are the oddities."

Shaaran laughed, turning to him. "Not so odd, if there are two of us," she said.

Rowan felt a terrible ache in his heart. "Shaaran, go to the mill," he begged. "You can find the way—" But even as he spoke, he knew that it was already too late. For now the Zebak army had swept over the hills, and the valley itself was darkening under its shadow.

Shaaran put the box down behind her and lit a torch as Annad had done. "There is no hope, is there, Rowan?" she said sadly.

No hope.

The words rang in Rowan's mind as he fumbled for the oilcloth package inside his shirt, and pulled out the last stick.

"Shaaran, hold the torch straight, whatever happens," he said, and he thrust the stick into the flame she held. Pain shot through his arm, and he groaned, but held his hand steady. Shaaran drew a sharp breath as flickering green took the place of red and Sheba's face appeared in the flame. But she braced one slim arm with the other, so the torch would not tremble as the words came.

As fear approaches like the night,
Flee from the field and hide from sight.
The power stirs, the anger wakes,
The rage upon the darkness breaks.
A fearful lesson, learned full well,
A tale that they alone can tell.

The words ended with a sigh, the flame died. Gasping, Rowan shook his head to clear it, and looked behind him.

The Rin army was still standing fast. Not one person had moved. The roaring from the Mountain was like thunder. The bukshah stood like grey rocks beyond their pool. And it was growing dark. Dark as night. The shadow of the enemy was almost upon them.

Flee from the field and hide from sight ...

This time Rowan did not think, did not question. "Take the silks and go into the orchard! Hide in the trees. Make haste!" he called to Shaaran over the noise. Then, shouting at the top of his voice, he ran to the front of the crowd. "Move from here!" he cried, waving his arms. "Run to the orchard!"

The crowd wavered, swaying like grain in a field brushed by the wind.

"Hold your positions!" thundered Lann, scowling in fury.

Rowan spun round to her. "I cannot explain, but I know this is right!" he shouted. "Do not delay! Tell them! *Tell them!*"

As Lann hesitated, Rowan heard a movement behind him. Jiller and Jonn had stepped from their places and were striding towards the orchard. Marlie, Allun, Perlain, Zeel and Norris were pushing through the crowd to join them, with Timon close behind. And when Bronden, too, began to move, beckoning Val and Ellis to follow, the rest of the crowd wavered no longer but ran for their lives.

In moments the centre of the field was empty except for Rowan and Lann, standing face to face.

"We have never run from an enemy till this day, Rowan of the Bukshah," the old woman hissed.

"We are not running from an enemy," Rowan said quietly. "We are clearing the way for—a lesson."

She stared at him.

"Come with me, Lann," he begged. "Come with me, under cover, and you will see."

21 – The Lesson

The slaves are scattering! Hiding their snivelling heads!" The commanding officer of the Zebak fleet looked down at the empty field below, smiling with satisfaction. Then he shouted angrily as his grach rolled in the air, nearly unseating him.

"It is the roaring sound and the flashing light from the mountain ahead, sir," shouted the beast's handler. "Bara fears it."

"You fool! What could be in any mountain for a fighting grach to fear?" spat the officer. "Give it a taste of the whip!"

But the handler had no chance to raise the whip, or even to answer. Suddenly there was a roar louder than anything he had ever heard, and the next moment he was clinging to the grach's neck, in fear for his life. And he was shrieking, as the proud man behind him, and the grach itself, were shrieking. In terror.

For the cloud that shrouded the tip of the mountain was swirling aside. And soaring towards them, roaring fire, was something only hinted at in their worst nightmare—a huge, awesome, ice-white, ancient thing of gaping jaws, needle-sharp teeth and terrible, jealous anger.

Compared with this, the ishkin were like writhing worms. The grach were garbage-eating desert lizards. This was a ruler. It was mighty. The earth below was of no interest to it. But the sky was its domain. They had dared to invade its place.

Bara was crying, twisting, plunging, as were all the other grach in that great close-knit fleet. The bonds that held the riders to their seats were breaking like twine. Guards were falling, howling, to the earth below.

And the Dragon roared in savage fury, its breath scorching the earth and the air with tongues of flame.

"Help me!" The handler heard the long scream as his chief

plummeted to the shadowed ground he had planned to own. But he could not turn. He could do nothing but cling to Bara's scaly neck as the creature wheeled, hissing, and sped away, back the way it had come. Away from the red eyes and the fire. Away from the burning, jealous anger. Away from the place its masters had thought so easy to conquer, but which had proved to have a guardian that would haunt their dreams forever.

* * *

When it was over, the people of Rin crept from their hiding places. All were well. All were safe.

"They will never come again," said Timon. "They have learned a lesson even we did not know. The survivors will spread the word. Our skies are even better protected than our seas."

A fearful lesson, learned full well,
A tale that they alone can tell.

"The Dragon of the Mountain," Lann breathed. "I never thought to see it in my lifetime." She was clinging to Rowan's arm. Her hands were trembling.

The ground where they had stood was scorched black. The bukshah pool still steamed. But the herd was already moving quietly to the stream to drink, the calves were investigating the strange, mottled, but apparently friendly creature that wallowed by the grassy banks, and Star was looking for Rowan.

She saw him, huffed gladly and broke into a run, blackened earth flying from under her hoofs.

"If we had stayed in the field ..." The whispered words passed from one to the other till the whole crowd was murmuring. "If it had not been for Rowan ..."

"That you fools were saved was not due to Rowan of the Bukshah, but to me." The rasping voice sawed through the air like a rusty knife.

Unos the grach looked up from her place in the stream. Hissing eagerly, she began to clamber up the bank.

Sheba stalked from the shade of the orchard trees. Her oily hair swung around her face like rat's tails. Her ragged clothes smelt of ash and dust and bitter herbs.

"Come here, skinny rabbit!" she commanded.

Rowan left Star with Lann and walked slowly towards the old woman. He felt Unos lumber up behind him, snuffling the air with pleasure. People drew back on all sides, shuddering at the sight of her.

"And so you have come back, Rowan of the Bukshah," Sheba screeched. "You and your foolish company of oddities, with two more oddities towed along behind."

She cast a mocking glance at Norris and Shaaran. Norris scowled, and Shaaran shrank back. Sheba cackled with laughter.

"You were with us, Sheba," said Allun quietly.

"And a fine dance you led me," she mumbled. "Days and nights of watching. Days and nights without food or drink or sleep ..."

"We owe you a great debt," said Rowan.

"Yes!" Sheba jeered. "And I have come to claim it!" She held up a crumpled note. "Written in your own hand!" she crowed. "Your promised gift!"

Rowan looked down to the stream where the black bukshah calf played and bounded with its friends, and it was as if bony fingers clutched at his heart. But he had promised.

He turned back to Sheba. "I had not forgotten," he said.

She grinned, showing all her long brown teeth. "But as it happens I have changed my mind about the companion I prefer," she said. "I find the idea of the calf bores me. There have been other black calves in the herd. I have a fancy for—this."

She pointed to the grach.

Rowan glanced at Shaaran and Norris. Norris shrugged. Shaaran watched as Unos lowered her lumpy head and rubbed the old woman's hand, and then she nodded. "Her name is Unos," she said.

"Very good. She will be a proper companion for me." Sheba stroked the grach's mottled neck with strange gentleness. "She is a true oddity."

"Not where I have come from," Norris said loudly.

"Here Unos is rare," Ogden said. "And what is rare is always precious." He put his hand on Zeel's shoulder as he spoke, but his dark gaze moved over the faces of Perlain, Allun, Shaaran and Rowan, and he smiled.

Sheba sniffed and hobbled away, clicking her tongue to Unos as she went. The grach plodded after her, hissing contentedly.

"It is good. Unos will be happy with her," Shaaran sighed, looking after them. But her eyes had filled with tears. Rowan knew that she was thinking of her grandfather, feeling lost. He felt Star's nose nudging his shoulder and turned to pat her. Star, at least, was relieved to see the grach go out of her sight. But Shaaran …

"So we have found a home for one of our new citizens," said Allun from his place in the crowd. "What of the others?"

He and Marlie came forward with his mother, Sara, beaming between them.

"My mother is not much of an oddity," Allun said to Norris and Shaaran. "The only odd thing she ever did in her life was marry a Traveller, and she paid dearly for that by having me for a son. But soon she will be like a bird who has lost her only chick, for Marlie has foolishly agreed to marry me."

He looked around, grinning at the murmur of surprise and congratulation that rose from the crowd and ignoring Marlie's kick on his ankle. Then he turned again to Shaaran and Norris.

"The wedding will be very soon. Before Marlie can come to her senses and change her mind," he went on. "So mother begs you both to come and fill her nest. After all, *someone* must weed her garden. And she is an excellent cook."

Sara smiled comfortably at Norris and Shaaran, who were both looking stunned. "Take no notice of my son's foolishness!" she said. "But I would very much like to have you, if you would like to come."

Shaaran glanced at Norris and saw his face break into a broad grin. She turned to Sara. "Thank you," she said shyly. "We would like it, very much."

Allun rubbed his hands. "So it is settled," he said gleefully. "And now, food! Dried fish and seaweed biscuit are all very well, but bread, cheese and cakes are better."

"That is a matter of taste," Perlain said, moving quietly up beside him with Zeel. "But I will make do with cheese for now. Indeed, I could eat a whole serpent at a gulp, if it was offered."

The people standing nearby snorted with surprised laughter as they began to move towards the village. It was a small joke, but they had not realised that a Maris could joke at all.

Carrying the box of silks, Rowan walked behind with Jonn, Jiller, Annad and Shaaran. Annad was dancing impatiently, chattering, pulling on Shaaran's hand to make her move faster. Jiller was laughing, glowing with happiness.

But Jonn was looking in puzzlement from Shaaran's face to Rowan's.

"You have much to tell us, I think, Rowan of Rin," he murmured.

Rowan looked down at the box of silks in his arms and was filled with quiet contentment.

"Yes," he said. "We have much to tell you."

ROWAN OF THE BUKSHAH

1 – "It is a curse!"

The village of Rin huddled, freezing, in a silent world of white. Deep snow blanketed the valley. The Mountain brooded against the grey sky like a vast ice sculpture capped with cloud.

Never had there been a winter like this. Never had the snow fallen so thickly. Never had the cold been so bitter.

And never had it lasted so long. By the calendar, it was spring— the time for planting, and for blossom, bees and nesting birds. But still the air was deadly chill, fields and gardens lay buried, and snow weighed down the bare branches of the trees in Strong Jonn's orchard.

A meeting was called, but it was too cold for the people to gather in the village square. They crowded instead in the house of books, shivering and murmuring amid the smell of oil lamps, parchment and old paper. Deep shadows flickered on worried faces, gesturing hands. The lamps were turned low, for oil, like everything else, was in short supply.

Rowan, who had been in the bukshah field when the meeting bell sounded, arrived last of all.

For a time he stood outside the door, stamping the snow from his boots. Despite the cold, he was in no hurry to enter. He knew what old Lann, the village leader, was going to say to the people, and he had made his own decision on what he was going to do about it. For now, his mind was still with the bukshah.

The great, gentle beasts he tended had strayed again during the night. They tried it every winter, but this year they had broken out of their field over and over again.

This time they had wandered past the silent mill, its huge wheel stuck fast in the ice of the stream, and moved on till they had almost reached the base of the Mountain. It had taken hours to tempt them back to their field—hours, and the last few handfuls of oats from the storehouse.

There will be trouble when it is discovered those oats are gone, Rowan thought ruefully. But what else could I do? Let the bukshah wander off to die?

He did not blame the beasts for breaking down their fence. They were hungry. The bales of hay on which they fed in winter were almost gone, and in a desperate attempt to make the food last, Rowan had been forced to cut their daily ration by half. Several of the oldest and frailest members of the herd had already weakened and died.

But Rowan knew that if food was scarce in the valley, it did not exist at all outside it. Except where sheer rocky cliffs showed as brutal gashes on the shimmering whiteness of the Mountain, the land was snow-covered on every side, as far as the eye could see.

"You must stop trying to stray, Star," Rowan had said to his favourite, the leader of the herd, when at last all the beasts were back in their field. "You must stay here, where I can care for you."

Star had turned her great head to look at him and rumbled deep in her throat. Her small dark eyes were troubled. She wanted to please Rowan and obey him. But all her instincts were telling her that he was wrong.

Dimly understanding, Rowan had patted her, feeling with dismay the jutting ribs beneath her shaggy coat. "Spring will surely come soon, Star," he had whispered. "The snow will melt and there will be grass for you to eat once more. Just a little longer ..."

But how *much* longer? Rowan thought now. How long can this go on?

Gritting his teeth, he pushed open the door and slipped into the crowded room. Shaaran and Norris, the two young people he had rescued from the enemy land of the Zebak, moved quickly to his side. They had clearly been watching for him. Shaaran's soft eyes were anxious, but her brother's face was alive with curiosity.

"Where have you been hiding yourself, Rowan?" Norris whispered. "We have not seen you for days!" He grinned and glanced at his sister teasingly. "Shaaran thinks you have been avoiding us. She fears we have done something to offend you. Please put her out of her misery and tell her it is not so."

"Norris!" Shaaran hissed, blushing scarlet.

Rowan forced a smile. "Of course you have not offended me," he murmured. That at least he could say truly, though he could not deny the rest. How could he have been with his friends and not told them what was going to happen? So he had avoided them.

But now they were about to hear everything. His heart ached at the thought of their dismay.

Norris would have pressed him further, but at that moment there was movement at the front of the room. Lann, the village leader, was preparing to speak. She was standing in the place of honour, in front of the hanging strips of painted silk which told in pictures the ancient story of the Rin people's slavery in the land of the Zebak. The bright paintings, glimmering in the lamplight, made a strange background to her sober figure.

For over three hundred years the Rin people had lived in freedom in their green valley, with no memory of their past and no idea that many of their own had been left behind in the dreaded place across the sea. Then, just over a year ago, Rowan's little sister Annad had been snatched away and carried to the land of the Zebak. Determined to save her, Rowan had followed. He had found her, against all odds. And at the same time he had found Shaaran and Norris, the last of the lost ones.

Shaaran had brought the box of silks with her when they escaped, and ever since that time the silks had hung in the house of books, to be marvelled over and discussed endlessly by the people of the village.

Lann called for silence. Everyone turned to face her, and a tense hush fell.

"Friends," Lann said. "I ask you to listen carefully to what I have to say."

She spoke firmly, taking charge as she had done so often before. But it seemed to Rowan that her face had grown more haggard overnight, and that she leaned more heavily on her stick. Rowan's stepfather, Jonn of the Orchard, stood at her right hand, and Timon the teacher at her left. She looked very frail between them.

"Our situation is grave," Lann said. "The storehouse is almost empty, and the snow shows no sign of melting. Why this should be so—"

"It is a curse!" cried a voice from the centre of the room. People turned, craning their necks to see who had spoken.

It was Neel the potter. His narrow face was pale and pinched. "A curse!" he repeated shrilly. "We have offended the Mountain, and now the Mountain has turned against us."

Rowan felt a chill that had nothing to do with his soaked boots or frozen fingers.

"That is foolish talk, Neel," said Jonn quietly.

"It is not!" cried Neel. "There has never been a winter such as this one. It is unnatural! Ask Timon if you do not believe me. Timon has examined the weather records. He knows I speak the truth."

All eyes now turned to Timon, who smoothed his grey beard nervously.

"This winter is certainly harsher than any we have had before," he said, in his quiet, hesitating voice. "But there is no need to talk of curses. Our winters have been growing harder and longer for many years. And we must remember that we have lived in this valley for only three centuries. In a land as ancient as this, three hundred years are but the blink of an eye. Who can say what is natural and what is not? There is a Travellers' tale that tells of—"

Lann nudged him and he broke off, but it was too late. Neel was already nodding violently, his reddened eyes gleaming in the lamplight.

"Exactly!" Neel cried. "The tale of the Cold Time, when winter held the land in thrall, and ice creepers came down from the Mountain seeking warm flesh to devour!"

A chorus of jeers, led by Bronden the furniture-maker, echoed through the room.

"Oh, I remember that one!" called Allun the baker. "My grandmother told it by the fire one winter's night when I was six years old. As I recall, I took my wooden sword to bed with me, and lay awake for hours waiting for the ice creepers to attack."

There was a ripple of laughter.

Neel bared his teeth. "You mock me, and ignore the message of the tale, at your peril!" he shouted. "Allun the baker is half-Traveller himself, and should know better! Is he not always telling us that Travellers have roamed this land for almost as long as bukshah have grazed below the Mountain? And that Travellers' tales seem fanciful, but most are woven around a grain of truth?"

The laughter faltered and died.

"Neel is right!" quavered Solla the sweet-maker, his soft chins wobbling as he spoke. "Remember the Valley of Gold! We thought *it* was just a Travellers' legend. Then its ruins were found on the other side of the Mountain. It was real enough once, and so were the people who lived in it, though they are long dead and gone."

The villagers murmured uncomfortably. The noise grew louder, quieting only when Lann held up her hand.

"The Travellers' Cold Time tale simply proves my point," said Timon firmly. "It proves that there is nothing unnatural about this cold. There has clearly been at least one long and terrible winter in the land before this—a season hard enough to have passed into legend. Now—"

"You are deliberately ignoring the most important thing, Timon!" Neel broke in shrilly. "In the tale, the Cold Time came because the people of the Valley of Gold turned their backs on the Mountain and failed to honour it. And we—we have done the same!"

He stabbed a trembling finger at the lengths of painted silk hanging behind Lann. "These images of another land and a time long gone have no place in our valley. They offend the Mountain. They must be burned!"

Rowan's stomach lurched. The room rang with shouts of shock and protest. Norris was red-faced, his fists clenched. Even Shaaran had forgotten her shyness, and was crying out. Norris and Shaaran had spent their lives guarding the silks in the land of the Zebak. The thought of the precious old paintings being destroyed was horrifying to them both.

"The silks are our history, Neel," said Lann, her gnarled hands tightening on her stick.

"No!" exclaimed Neel angrily. "Rin's story, the only story that matters, began the day our ancestors rose against their Zebak masters on this land's shore, and began a new life."

He whirled around, appealing to his neighbours. "Our ancestors were brought to this land to help the Zebak conquer it, but, instead, the land gave them their freedom, and this valley became their home," he cried. "Once, that history was all we knew, and it was enough for us!"

He turned and stared at Norris and Shaaran, his face sharp with dislike. "But ever since the silks and their guardians were brought here, all this has changed. Suddenly our minds are filled with questions about times long past and best forgotten. How long did our ancestors live as slaves in the land of the Zebak? Where did they come from at first? Is there another land, an even better land than this, which was once our own and perhaps could be so again?"

"It is natural for us to wonder, Neel," said Jonn. "There is no harm in it."

"There *is* harm!" Neel gestured wildly, his voice rising to a shriek. "Do you not see? By looking back, by questioning, we have rejected the Mountain's gift of life! And now the Mountain is offended, and is taking its revenge!"

Jonn made a disgusted sound, and Timon shook his head.

"Never have I heard such foolishness!" snapped Lann, her faded eyes flashing with some of their old fire. "Be quiet, Neel, and let others with stronger heads than yours go on with the business for which this meeting was intended!"

Neel flushed and without another word pushed his way through the crowd and out of the room, slamming the door behind him. But Rowan could see that not everyone in the room agreed with Lann. Several people were glancing sympathetically after Neel. And Solla the sweet-maker, for one, looked very nervous.

Perhaps Lann could see this too, and was angered, for when she spoke again her voice was even harsher than it had been before.

"As I was saying, our situation is grave," she rasped. "By my calculation, the food remaining in the storehouse will feed us all for only twelve days more. And then only if we are very careful. The time has come to take action—action that I fear you will not like."

2 – The Decision

The eyes of the crowd were fixed on Lann. She raised her chin. "It is my opinion that we should abandon the village and travel to the coast, where the Maris people and the Travellers will shelter and feed us until we can return," she said.

The room exploded in uproar.

"What?" shouted Bronden, her voice rising above the rest. "Are the people of Rin to become wandering beggars? And what do you think will happen to the village if we leave it now? If wind breaks windows that are not repaired? If snow buries the houses, and roofs crack and fall in?"

Lann's wrinkled face tightened. "It is that or starve, Bronden," she said stiffly.

"Then I would rather starve!" snapped Bronden.

"Well, I would not!" called Marlie the weaver. She drew closer to Allun, her husband since the summer.

Allun took Marlie's hand in both his own and met Bronden's angry gaze. "You may think it foolish, Bronden, but Marlie and I are more interested in living than dying," he said lightly. "Our child will be born before the month is out. We do not choose that it should come into the world only to perish."

Many people nodded, murmuring agreement. Others began exclaiming and arguing.

Lann watched them with hooded eyes. Her shoulders had slumped and her knuckles were white as she gripped her stick.

Rowan's heart went out to her. She had done what she saw as her duty—what he, Jonn and Timon had encouraged her to do—but it had cost her dearly.

"I urge you all to consider this plan with your minds rather than with your hearts," called Jonn, raising his voice to be heard over the tumult in the room. "We need only stay away until the danger is past. The Maris people and the Travellers are our friends and allies. They will help us gladly, as we would help them."

"Perhaps," said Bronden, her broad face creased in a frown. "But why must we go to the coast and leave our homes to be ruined by the snow and the wind? There must be another way. Where is Rowan of the Bukshah?" Her eyes raked the room.

Rowan shrank back into the shadows, but it was no use. "Ah, Rowan, there you are!" cried Bronden, as she sighted him. "Why are you hiding there at the back of the room? You of all people—you who have saved Rin from disaster more than once—should be involved in this!"

Everyone turned to look as she pointed at Rowan.

Rowan felt his face grow warm. His confidence had grown greatly over the past few years, but he still did not enjoy being singled out. And the fact that some people in Rin believed that he had special, even magical, powers made him very uncomfortable. It was true that he had been able to save the village from danger in the past, but there had been nothing magic about what he had done. Magic of a kind had aided him, certainly—but not his own.

"Rowan, it is rumoured that you have some strange bond—some linking of minds—with the Maris people's leader, the Keeper of the Crystal," growled Bronden. "If that is true, surely you could tell the Keeper of our trouble, and ask him to send help?"

"And what of the Travellers, Rowan?" Solla called out. "You are respected by their chief, Ogden, are you not? And firm friends with Ogden's daughter, Zeel, who helped you save Annad from the Zebak? Why do you not use the reed pipe they gave you to call for aid? The Travellers could carry supplies to the valley. We have shared our food with *them* often enough, when they have been camped here!"

Rowan wet his lips. "I fear that neither the Maris nor the Travellers can help us now, however much they might wish to," he said in a low voice.

"Of course they cannot!" snapped Lann. "*We* are the only people in this land who can survive the inland winter. You all know that! Or should. The Maris people and the Travellers always cling to the warmer coast, even in a normal cold season. This bitter chill would kill them long before they reached us."

Solla's face fell amid groans of disappointment from others in the room. Bronden simply folded her arms and exchanged sombre glances with her neighbours.

"Very well," Lann said. "Now. I cannot force any person to leave. The journey to the coast will be long and filled with peril. The snow is deep, the cold is bitter, and the white wolves will be hungry on the plains. The protection and courage of every strong man and woman of Rin will be needed on the march if our weakest and youngest are to survive. But any journey, however perilous, is surely better than a slow and lingering death from starvation here."

The room was utterly silent. Lann's eyes swept over the crowd. Then she took a deep breath. "We will take a vote," she said. "Raise your hands if you agree with my plan."

Faces were grim, but a forest of hands went up. Only Bronden and a few very young children who did not understand what was happening remained still.

Rowan breathed a silent sigh of relief.

"Then it is decided," said Lann soberly. "The march to the coast will begin at first light tomorrow. I myself will divide the food remaining in the storehouse, so that everyone will have a fair share. As for the rest, pack only what you can carry on your backs, my friends, for the way will be hard and long."

"Surely the bukshah can carry—" Norris began, but Lann shook her head and glanced at Rowan.

This was the moment Rowan had been dreading. Feeling the eyes of the crowd upon him once more, he swallowed and forced himself to speak.

"The bukshah are far too weak to travel as far as the coast," he said huskily. "They would perish on the journey."

"But they are dying now, one by one!" someone shouted. "If we leave them ..."

Rowan's stomach churned. "The bukshah will not be left alone," he said, very aware of Shaaran and Norris listening intently beside him. "I will be staying with them."

Shaaran gasped in horror, and looked around for Jiller, Rowan's mother. She expected Jiller to protest, to insist that her son escape from the village with them. But Jiller stood proudly silent at the front of the room, and Rowan's young sister, Annad, looked straight ahead without saying a word. Clearly they already knew of Rowan's decision, and had accepted it.

"Most will survive no longer than a week or two," Rowan went on quietly. "But if I can keep just a few of the younger, stronger beasts alive until the weather changes, there is a chance that the herd will grow again in years to come."

Only those who knew him best could hear the misery in his level voice. Only they knew what it cost him to speak of even *one* of his beloved bukshah dying.

"No, Rowan!" Shaaran cried. Ignoring her brother, who was tugging at her sleeve in embarrassment, urging her to be still, she looked wildly around at the tall, serious-faced people who surrounded her.

"Tell him!" she pleaded. "Tell him he must not stay!"

"Rowan is the keeper of the bukshah," Lann said harshly. "The beasts know and trust him. His presence will comfort them, and may help to keep them alive for a time even after their food is gone. You are a newcomer, girl, so perhaps you do not understand how important the bukshah are to Rin. Our whole way of life depends on them. Without them we would have no milk and cheese, no wool for clothing, no help in ploughing the fields. Rowan's decision is the right one."

Shaaran shook her head disbelievingly. "How can that be? How can it be right for Rowan to be left here to die alone?"

Lann raised her head. "He will not be alone," she said. Her lips curving in a grim smile, she gestured at her stick. "Plainly I cannot walk unaided to the coast, and I do not choose to be a burden on the rest of you. So I, too, will be remaining."

"And I!" said Bronden stubbornly.

The harsh lines on Lann's face seemed to relax. Suddenly she looked very tired and old.

"That is all there is to say, then," she said. "Go to your homes now, and prepare."

The people turned silently towards the door.

"Wait!" Solla's quavering voice rose in the silence. "What of Sheba?"

Nervous whispers filled the room. Yes. What of Sheba the Wise Woman, Sheba the witch, crouched, mumbling, over the fire in her hut behind the orchard? Sheba, whose evil temper had been made even fouler by the cold? Sheba, who for weeks had remained hidden away, spitting jeers and taunts at all who dared approach her door, even those brave souls who had struggled through the snow to bring her food?

Did Sheba know of the plan to abandon the village? Almost certainly she did. She had a fearful way of knowing such things without a word being spoken in her presence.

The brave people of Rin shifted uncomfortably at the thought. Sheba could no more walk to the coast than Lann could. Would she remain behind, shaking her fist as they left her, cursing them for deserting her?

Or would she insist on being carried? Many a strong man shuddered at the thought of Sheba's bony arms hooked around his neck, her greasy rat-tails of hair swinging as she clung to his back like a giant spider, hissing at him to move faster.

Jonn smiled grimly. "Sheba has not been forgotten," he said. "Jiller, Timon and I all tried to gain entrance to her hut this morning, to speak to her. All of us were refused in turn, and cursed for our pains. It seems there is only one person she wishes to see."

He looked towards Rowan.

Rowan's heart sank to his boots.

3 – Sheba

Rowan trudged through the orchard, following the trail of deep footprints left by Jonn, Jiller and Timon earlier in the day. He kept his head down. He did not want to look at the bare trees standing stark around him, their trunks smothered in whiteness, their twisted branches clawing at the grey sky like frozen skeleton fingers. He did not want to see Sheba's hut hunched ahead, half buried in snow, icicles fringing its low roof.

But he could not stop himself smelling the smoke of Sheba's fire, sour with ash and bitter herbs. He could not close his ears to the muffled sound of her voice, droning inside the hut and then stopping abruptly as he stepped into the flat, cleared space before her door.

It is foolish to feel this dread, he told himself, as slowly he crossed the icy, trampled ground. I am not the young, fearful boy I was when I faced Sheba for the first time. Nothing she can do to me will make things worse than they are. Nothing she can tell me will be more terrifying than my own imaginings.

But still he shuddered, because he had learned that for all Sheba's malicious teasing, for all her delight in watching her chosen victims squirm, she always told the truth. And if her purpose in asking for him was to snuff out the last small flame of hope that still burned in his heart, he could not bear it.

There was no sound from the hut now. All was silence, except for the sound of the snow crunching beneath Rowan's boots.

At the door he closed his eyes for a moment, forcing himself to be calm. He was determined that this time, at last, he would meet Sheba without fear, and that her tricks would not dismay him. He raised his hand to knock.

Before his knuckles touched it, the door flew open, slamming back against the inside wall of the hut with a thundering crash. Icicles cracked and fell, plunging like spears into the snow behind Rowan's back. A gust of hot, sour air hit him full in the face. Gasping and choking, he recoiled, heart pounding, eyes stinging.

"Why do you stand there with the door gaping?" Sheba shrieked from within. "All the good warm air is escaping! Cowering fool of a boy! Make haste!"

Rowan stumbled across the threshold and into the room. The door slammed shut behind him.

All was dark except for the fire, burning red with flashes of green. Slowly Rowan's watering eyes picked out the humped shape that was Sheba. She had slumped back into her chair, which had been drawn so close to the hearth that its feet were hidden by mounds of white ash.

"Come closer, Rowan of the Bukshah." The grating voice was deceptively gentle now. "Closer, but not too close. Your skin is cold, and my heat is precious."

Clumsily Rowan moved forward, feeling as though he was swimming through the thick, foul-smelling dimness. Then, with a cry, he leaped back as something huge and growling rose from the side of the room and lunged at him. Sheba's spiteful laughter rang in his ears as he fell sprawling onto the filthy floorboards and twisted wildly, trying to crawl to safety.

A burning, scaly nose nudged at his arm. Hot breath scorched his cheek. Flat yellow eyes stared down at him, and leathery wings thumped the floor, covering him with dust.

Rowan's blind panic vanished, to be replaced instantly by irritated shame. The attack had been no attack at all. He had merely been greeted by Sheba's companion, Unos the grach.

He crawled to his knees. The shock had left him weak. His hand was still shaking as he raised it to scratch Unos's shoulder. The scaly skin was not cool as he remembered, but burning hot. The grach hissed with pleasure.

"Had you forgotten Unos, boy?" cackled Sheba with malicious delight. "Why, for shame! Did she not carry you and your idiot friends all the way home from the land of the Zebak, only last summer?"

Rowan stood up, trying to ignore the pain in his bruised leg and shoulder.

"I had not forgotten Unos, Sheba," he said, as calmly as he could. "But I did not expect her to be in here with you."

And why should I expect it? he thought, as the grach's vast, mottled body swayed before him, radiating heat. Who would try to keep such a large creature indoors? Now that his eyes had adjusted to the light, he could see that there was no furniture in the room except for Sheba's chair. Everything had been cleared to make room for Unos.

"We have had work to do," Sheba said. She made a soft, twittering sound and Unos lumbered over to her, flopping down beside her chair. Sheba took a small stick from the bundle she held in her lap and tossed it into the fire.

The flames flickered green. The room seemed at once to become even hotter. The grach hissed contentedly and raised the spines on her back to their full height, the better to soak up the warmth.

Rowan wet his lips. "You wished to speak with me, Sheba?" he asked.

"Why would I wish to speak with *you*?" the old woman sneered. "Those fools in the village might think you are a great hero. *They* might think you have things of importance to say. But I know better. Oh, yes!" Her brown teeth gleamed in the firelight as she grinned.

Rowan said nothing. Sheba had done her best to shake him, and she had succeeded, but he was determined not to let her win this battle of nerves. The silence lengthened. The fire crackled. Rowan's head swam with the heat.

At last Sheba moved impatiently in her chair. "Do you dare play games with me, boy?" she rasped. "Do you not know by now that I could crack you like a nut if I chose?"

She snorted as Rowan kept silence. "Have you begun to believe the tales they tell of you?" she sneered. "You dreamer! Why, without me you would be nothing. Nothing! You have always been nothing but my instrument, following *my* instructions."

"I know that, Sheba," Rowan said hastily, even as it flashed into his mind that what she said was not quite true.

"Liar!" Sheba hissed, and Rowan's chest tightened as he realised that she had read his mind. As he began to stammer explanations, she spat viciously into the fire.

"Do you think I am a fool, that you try to flatter me, agreeing with me when you do not believe?" she demanded. "You are just like all the rest. Ungrateful and ignorant. Plotting and planning behind my back. Well, I will show you all!"

This sounded ominous. "Will ... will you be leaving here in the morning with the rest, Sheba?" Rowan ventured.

"No, I will not!" she sneered. "Am I baggage, to be carried by floundering oafs? Now, hold your chatter. I did not summon you here to speak *with* you, keeper of the bukshah, but to speak *to* you. Gather your poor wits and listen."

She leaned back in her chair, mumbling to herself, her claw-like hands clasped together at her throat. Slowly her eyelids drooped until her eyes were gleaming slits, shining first green, then white. Rowan's heart thudded painfully. The droning voice rose and fell, rose and fell, but he could not make out any words.

He took a step forward, but the heat—the heat of the fire, or of Sheba herself—was so intense that he gasped. Instinctively, he tried to stumble back, but could not move. The heat had caught and held him, like a web of invisible fire. He struggled in its embrace, feeling it burning his skin, heating his blood, scorching his bones.

Then Sheba's mouth opened, and she began to speak clearly. The words came to Rowan on waves of scarlet heat. It was as though he saw them, rather than heard them. They seemed to enter his eyes like burning brands, imprinting themselves on his brain.

> *"The beasts are wiser than we know*
> *And where they lead, four souls must go.*
> *One to weep and one to fight,*
> *One to dream and one for flight.*
> *Four must make their sacrifice.*
> *In the realm twixt fire and ice*
> *The hunger will not be denied,*
> *The hunger must be satisfied.*
> *And in that blast of fiery breath,*
> *The quest unites both life and death."*

The voice trailed away. Sheba's mouth closed. The terrible words ringing in his mind, Rowan found himself staggering backwards, out of the fiery haze.

Sheba's wrinkled eyelids slowly lifted. Her face was haggard with exhaustion.

"Well?" she mumbled.

"I—I do not understand," Rowan stammered.

"That is no business of mine," she snapped. "I have told you what I had to tell. The rest is your concern. I have another task to do, and do it I will, though I will have no thanks for it."

"Sheba, you must—" Rowan cried, but she waved him away irritably.

"Be still!" she ordered. "You are wasting my time, stealing my heat and draining my strength."

She took a deep, rasping breath. When she began to speak again, she spoke rapidly, and all trace of spite had left her voice. For the first time in Rowan's life, it was as if she was speaking to him as an equal.

"I cannot help you any further, Rowan of the Bukshah," she croaked. "All I know is that only you can do what must be done. All I can tell you is that everything you have learned until now has been preparation for this moment. All I can give you is ... this."

She clutched at her throat again, fumbling at something hidden under her ragged shawl. As she drew the object into the light, Rowan saw that it was the strange old medallion she had given him to take to the land of the Zebak. It was hanging around her scrawny neck, still threaded on its faded cord of plaited silk.

Rowan stared. He had forgotten all about the medallion. Certainly he did not remember giving it back to Sheba on his return to the village. But he must have done, for there it was, clutched between her long yellow nails that curved like claws over its dull surface.

She lifted the cord from her neck and held out the medallion.

"Take it!" she hissed. "Wear it. Learn what it is to be what I am."

Rowan hesitated. The last thing in the world he wanted to do was to obey. But his hand stretched out without his willing it, and before he could think the medallion was glowing warm between his fingers, and he was slipping the cord around his own neck. The medallion was heavy—far heavier than he remembered. It seemed to weigh him down.

Sheba slumped back into her chair, as if with relief.

"So—it is done," she muttered. "Go now. Unos and I must take in more heat yet. We must have all the fire has to give." She threw another stick into the fire. The flames crackled and burned green. Slowly she closed her eyes once more.

"But, Sheba, what am I to do?" asked Rowan desperately.

"Watch and wait," Sheba said, without opening her eyes. "When it is time, you will know it."

Green light flickered on her sunken cheeks. She began to breathe slowly and deeply. Rowan knew that she would not speak to him again.

He left the hut like one walking in a dream. As the door closed behind him, the freezing air rushed into his lungs like a knife, and white light dazzled his eyes. Dazedly, the medallion hanging heavy as a great stone around his neck, he stumbled along the line of his own footprints to the orchard. As he stepped among the buried trees, he heard Sheba's muffled, droning chant begin once more.

4 – One to Dream

Rowan knew that Jiller, Jonn and Annad would be waiting anxiously for him at home, but he deliberately slowed his steps as he left the orchard.

He was shaken and confused, but one thing was very clear in his mind. Whatever else he said of his time in Sheba's hut, the words of her terrible rhyme must remain his secret.

Four must make their sacrifice ...

If Jonn and Jiller heard those words, they would refuse to leave the village in the morning. It had been very difficult for Rowan to persuade them that they should join the march to the coast while he remained with the bukshah. Only when Lann had taken his side had they reluctantly agreed.

If they heard the rhyme, with its ominous talk of beasts and sacrifice, they would change their minds again.

And that must not happen, Rowan thought desperately. The one thing that will help me bear what is to come is knowing that those I love—the *people* I love, at least—are safe.

But as he left the orchard and began toiling past the snowy drifts that covered the vegetable gardens, even that comfort began to fail him. In the distance he could see many people gathered by the storehouse. Lann was passing out shares of the remaining food. The bundles people were carrying away looked pitifully small.

Rowan's heart sank as he pictured the group setting off on the morrow, ploughing towards the coast through deep, trackless snow, guided only by the sound of the buried stream.

The journey to Maris took at least a week at the best of times. How much longer would it take when every step was a battle? Three weeks? Four? Even longer? Slowly the food would run out, and cold, hunger, exhaustion and the wolves would take their toll.

Rowan felt a thrill of pure terror. Fighting it down, smothering the terrible imaginings that had caused it, he lowered his head and trudged on, hoping against hope that no one would turn and see him.

To his relief, he reached the first houses without being hailed. He moved on towards the village square. As he passed Bronden's workshop he heard the lonely sound of hammering. Bronden was working, stubbornly refusing to admit that soon there would be no one who needed her wares, trying to forget that soon only she, Lann and Rowan would be left.

One to weep and one to fight,
One to dream and one for flight.

Bronden is the fighter, Rowan thought. And I am the useless dreamer, if Sheba is to be believed. Lann might weep tears of rage at her helplessness. But who is the fourth soul? The one who will run away?

Unwillingly his eyes turned to the pottery. The door was closed, the windows were shuttered, and no sound came from within. If Neel was there, he was keeping to himself.

Like a shadow, Rowan slipped through the deserted square and moved on. He peered through the window of the house of books and saw that it, too, was empty. Only the silks stirred, gently billowing in the draught that blew beneath the door, so that the painted figures, trees and animals seemed moving and alive.

Rowan's eyes were drawn to one particular scene—the one that had always affected him most powerfully. It pictured the slave village in the land of the Zebak, just over three hundred years ago. It showed Zebak guards tearing the bravest and strongest of the slaves from their weeping loved ones and locking them in iron cages.

Perhaps the people in that painted scene already knew that the strong ones were to be chained to the oars of fighting ships and forced to row across the sea to fight in the Zebak cause. But no one could guess that in the new land the slaves would turn against their masters and gain their freedom. No one could know that in their new life, in the peaceful Rin valley, they would not remember their past, because the Zebak had destroyed their memories. And no one could predict that the gentle souls left behind in slavery would gradually dwindle until, three hundred years later, only Shaaran and Norris remained to represent them.

Or perhaps, Rowan thought, there was one who *had* seen the future. In the midst of the confusion, a bent old woman, who had been painted holding a bundle of herbs to show that she was a Wise Woman and a healer, was secretly passing a medallion to a younger woman in one of the cages.

Rowan raised his fingers to the medallion hanging heavy around his neck. His memory of it had come flooding back now. It did not just *look* the same as the medallion in the painting. It *was* the same. It had come to the Rin valley with that young woman. It had been passed down through the generations of wise men and women who had followed her, until it came into Sheba's hands.

And now Sheba has given it to me, Rowan thought. But not as she did before. In the land of the Zebak, she was with me in spirit. This time, it is different. I feel it.

There was a roaring in his ears as he remembered Sheba's words.

Take it. Wear it. Learn what it is to be what I am.

His breath was misting the window. He could no longer see the billowing silks. But he made no effort to wipe the glass clean. He did not want to see the grave, intent faces of the two women, young and old, as something rare and powerful was passed between them. He did not want to think of what Sheba's gift meant.

Learn what it is to be what I am ...

He turned from the window, made sure that the medallion and its cord were completely hidden under his clothing, and began walking rapidly away. Now he wanted to reach home as fast as he could. His face was burning, but his heart felt icy cold.

He covered the remaining distance quickly and soon was opening his own gate and hurrying down the cleared path to the house. Annad, who had plainly been watching for him, threw open the door before he reached it. She clasped his hand to draw him inside, then dropped it with a small shriek of surprise.

"Oh, you are hot!" she shrilled.

Rowan looked over her head to the anxious faces of Jonn and Jiller, who had left their packing and come to meet him.

"Sheba's fire was very warm," he said, pulling off his padded coat. "Far warmer than is natural. She has been weaving some sort of heat spell for herself and Unos, I think."

"No doubt we would be foolish to hope that she plans to share it with the rest of us," said Jiller dryly.

"I fear so," Rowan agreed. "She accused me of robbing her of heat, and it seems I did steal some, without knowing it."

He rubbed his hands together, only now realising that they had not felt cold since he left Sheba's hut.

"What did she tell you, Rowan?" Annad demanded.

Rowan shrugged. "She was angry. She said she would not be leaving in the morning. She said we were ignorant and ungrateful, and that she would show us all."

"*Show* us? What does she mean by that?" Jiller exclaimed.

"I do not know." Rowan slumped down at the table, which was cluttered with piles of folded blankets, food and other supplies to be packed. "She did say she had something to do for which she would get no thanks, but she would not explain what she meant."

"Perhaps she is going to try to stop us from leaving," Jonn said.

"Perhaps." Rowan bent to unlace his boots. He had done what he had set out to do. Without telling a single lie, he had turned his family's attention away from him, and towards Sheba's feelings about the forthcoming march to the coast.

It was a relief. But suddenly he felt very lonely, and terribly weary.

"I am sorry," he sighed. "I wish I could be of more help. But there is nothing more I can tell you."

* * *

That night it was colder than ever. No fresh snow fell, but by midnight the valley had filled with a strange, icy mist that chilled to the bone.

The people of Rin, packed and ready for the morrow, went silently to their rest, their minds and hearts numb with a dread few of them would admit, even to themselves. And in the darkness more than one remembered Neel's shrill voice rising in the crowded house of books.

The Cold Time ... when winter held the land in thrall, and ice creepers came down from the Mountain seeking warm flesh to devour ...

Rowan lay in his narrow bed, fully clothed, watching the shadows move sluggishly on the walls of his attic room as the candle burned low.

He no longer shared his room with Annad, who now slept in the small downstairs room Jonn and Jiller had built for her. Usually Rowan relished his privacy, and the extra space, but tonight the attic seemed very empty. He told himself that he should undress before the candle died. He told himself that he should try to sleep. But he could not find the energy to move.

The mist crawled at his window, white and smothering. He shuddered at the very sight of it, but at the same time he was glad of it, for it veiled his view of the brooding Mountain.

... the people of the Valley of Gold turned their backs on the Mountain and failed to honour it. And we—we have done the same!

Surely Neel had been speaking superstitious nonsense, as Lann had said. Surely ...

On the stool beside Rowan's bed stood the golden owl he had found in the ruins of the Valley of Gold, on the other side of the Mountain. The owl gleamed in the flickering candlelight. Its emerald eyes seemed to glow, as if they were trying to tell him something.

Rowan stretched out his hand to it. Its smooth surface seemed to warm under his fingertips.

The Valley of Gold was not destroyed by the Cold Time, he reminded himself. In the Travellers' tale, the people made their peace with the Mountain, and spring came again. The Valley did not meet its end until much later, centuries later, when it was overtaken by the killer trees of Unrin.

... the people made their peace with the Mountain ...

But how? How?

Four must make their sacrifice ...

Rowan's fingers tightened on the golden owl. Its green eyes seemed to flash.

The candle flickered, and went out.

* * *

Rowan opened his eyes in a place that was strange to him. It was cold and bleak. Snow covered the sloping ground, and the sky was dim but not yet dark. Cliffs towered above. He knew that he was on the Mountain.

Not far away, three cloaked and hooded figures were trudging through the snow in single file, following a well-trodden path that led upward. They were all carrying torches, the flames blowing and smoking in a bitter wind. The leader, tall and broad-shouldered, was limping, leaning on a long stick. The second figure was small and delicate. The third was slight, and of medium height.

This is the end ...

The last figure in line paused, turned his head and looked directly at Rowan. With a chill, Rowan recognised the face. It was the face he saw every time he looked into a mirror. The face stared at him, stared *through* him, as though he was invisible.

Rowan was outside himself. He was watching himself from a distance. But he could feel the emotions raging behind those glazed, unseeing eyes.

Fear. Anger. A terrible, aching grief.

I am dreaming, Rowan thought, and struggled to wake. But the dream was too real, too strong. It gripped him and held him helpless, forcing him to watch the scene before him, unable to move or speak.

The small middle figure stopped and turned. It was Shaaran. She was holding a long wooden box in her arms—the box of silks she had carried from the land of the Zebak.

"What is the matter?" the girl called in a low voice.

The Rowan figure shrugged. "I felt there was someone else here, watching us," he said.

The tall leader groaned impatiently, coming to a stop and easing his injured leg. "How could there be?" he growled. "We are the only ones left."

It was Norris, his handsome face tight with strain, his eyes haunted. "The only ones left," he repeated, and suddenly gave a bark of harsh laughter.

Shaaran glanced at him anxiously. "The light is failing," she said, clutching the box more tightly. "We must move on. We must follow the beasts."

Norris looked around and laughed again. "What is the point?" he said loudly. "What can it matter where we die?" Dropping the stick, he flung himself to the ground.

Shaaran ran to him, and Rowan saw himself move quickly to join her. Together they pulled at Norris's arms. Norris lay where he was, sprawled amid the churned mud and snow, his body racked again and again with gales of that terrible laughter.

"Get up," Rowan heard himself say, in a calm, determined voice he would not have recognised as his own. "We will not leave you. But if we stay here we will *all* die, to no purpose. And when the others return from the coast—"

"They will never return," Norris wheezed, between gasps of laughter that were more like sobs. "They are all dead by now, I am sure of it, and the Wise Woman with them. Do you not understand? We are finished. This is the end."

This is the end …

Shaaran opened her mouth as if to scream. But when the sound came it was very faint, as though Rowan was hearing it from far away. A mist was closing over his eyes …

He woke choking, his heart pounding. He was burning hot, bathed in sweat.

He tumbled out of bed. Shaaran's scream was still echoing in his mind as he stumbled to the window and flung it open. He leaned out into the night, taking deep, gasping breaths. The mist swirled around his head, thick and icy cold.

Learn what it is to be what I am …

No! Rowan told himself desperately, digging his fingers into the rough wood of the sill. It was nothing but a stupid dream! There was nothing real about it. How could I climb the Mountain with Shaaran and Norris? They are going to the coast with the rest, in the morning.

Then his heart gave a great thud, for suddenly the scream he had heard in his dream came again, muffled by the mist, but high and full of terror.

And this time there was no doubt that it was real.

5 – Shocks

owan pounded down the stairs. He pulled on his boots and coat, which had been left drying by the glowing embers of the fire, and hurtled out into the night. He heard Jonn, Jiller and Annad stirring and calling out. He shouted back to them, but did not stop.

There was no time. He was sure that the voice he had heard was Shaaran's, and Shaaran would not have screamed like that unless she was in dire need.

The mist was like a white blanket in front of his eyes. Arms outstretched before him, he felt his way to the garden gate and stumbled blindly on. For a few long moments there was utter silence. Then, from somewhere ahead, there was a crash, Shaaran's voice desperately crying for help, and another voice, high-pitched and gabbling.

And now he could see a flickering light—a flame—wavering faintly through the mist. Recklessly he began to run.

Other people had woken now. Rowan could hear voices raised in question and alarm, and the sounds of doors and windows opening. But he knew he was closer to the trouble than anyone else.

He could not understand a word of the frenzied gabbling that still mingled with Shaaran's cries, but its high-pitched tone was only too familiar, and the sight of the wavering flame gave him grim warning of what he was about to find.

Sure enough, when he reached the house of books, the door was gaping wide, and light and shadows leaped within. Shaaran, her fragile figure unmistakable even in the dimness, was struggling with a dark figure at the back of the room. And somewhere there was fire!

Shouting, Rowan flung himself through the doorway and nearly tripped over a body lying motionless on the floor. He staggered back. Flames threw dancing light on the unconscious face.

It was Norris. His head was pressed against the base of a tall shelf of books. His eyes were closed, his brow wet with blood. A flaming torch lay beside his hand, as if he had dropped it when he fell. The floorboards beneath the torch were smoking, and some of the books in the shelf were already alight, flames licking greedily upward, fanned by the draught from the door.

Rowan snatched up the torch and held it high. Now he could see Shaaran clearly. And he could see the struggling man she was clinging to with all her strength. It was Neel the potter, his pale face twisted with rage as he fought to free himself. Rowan took a step forward.

"No!" screamed Shaaran. "The fire, Rowan! Put out the—"

With a piercing squeal of rage, Neel made a final, violent effort, threw her aside and sprang at Rowan. Rowan caught a glimpse of his frenzied face, eyes wild, teeth bared, lips flecked with foam. Then Neel was upon him, wrestling him to the ground, trying to tear the torch from his hand.

"Let go!" Neel snarled. "Give it to me! The silks must burn! I must burn them, and save us all!"

"No!" Rowan panted, clutching the torch as Neel's strong fingers tried to break his grip. He knew he would not be able to hold on for much longer.

He twisted his head around until he could see the door, and made his eyes widen as if in surprise and relief.

"Jonn!" he shouted. "Help me!"

Neel's attention faltered, and his grip loosened as he, too, looked at the door. Only for an instant, but it was enough. Rowan tore his arm free and hurled the torch through the open doorway into the snow.

Neel gave a high wail and sprang after it. His head spinning, Rowan staggered to his feet and kicked the door closed. He tore off his coat and began using it to beat at the fire in the bookshelf. Many books were smouldering now. Small, hungry flames were running like insects along the rows. The room was full of smoke.

"Shaaran, get out!" he shouted.

Receiving no reply, he glanced around fearfully. Through a thick veil of smoke he saw, to his amazement, that Shaaran was standing on a table at the end of the room. She had her back to him, and was rapidly taking down the silks, rolling them up and piling them into their wooden box.

Rowan called again, but Shaaran did not turn. She was so intent on her task that he doubted she could even hear him. The smoke was growing thicker by the moment. As he watched, she began to cough and choke.

"Shaaran!" he bellowed.

The door crashed open behind him. He whirled around, terrified that Neel had returned, then a wave of relief flooded through him as he saw, wreathed in mist that mingled with the smoke, the shocked faces of Jonn, Jiller and Bronden, with a crowd of others behind them. Jonn was holding a glowing lantern.

"It was Neel!" Rowan gasped. "He tried to burn the silks. He has run away. Out there ..."

His face darkening with anger, Jonn turned and disappeared into the mist. Bronden ran after him. The others began calling for blankets and water.

Leaving them to see to the fire, and to Norris, Rowan wound his scarf around his mouth and nose and plunged into the thick smoke at the back of the room.

He found Shaaran a few steps from the table. The box of silks was clutched in her arms, but, overcome by the smoke at last, she had fallen to her knees. Rowan pulled her to her feet and began dragging her towards the door.

"I could not sleep," Shaaran choked, the words bursting from her in coughing, sobbing gasps. "I feared for the silks. So at last Norris and I came to take them, and ... and we saw a light, and it was Neel. We were ... just in time. He was about to ... Norris took the flame, and they fought, but then Neel pushed him, and he fell and hit his head ..."

"Be still now, Shaaran. Norris is safe," Rowan soothed her. "And the silks are safe also."

But a cold hand closed on his heart as they plunged at last into the swirling chill of the outside air and saw Norris, wrapped in a blanket, leaning heavily on Allun's shoulder. Norris's eyes were glazed, and he was sweating with pain as he tried to stand on a leg that clearly would not support him.

He had suffered more than a blow on the head. His leg had been injured when he fell. He would not now be leaving the village in the morning with the others. He could not possibly make the journey to the coast. And Shaaran would not leave her brother. Nothing was more certain.

This still does not mean the dream was a prophecy, Rowan told himself dazedly, as Shaaran broke away from him and stumbled to Norris's side. It does not!

He became aware that the bukshah were bellowing. They had been disturbed by the shouting and the smell of fire, no doubt. Or perhaps Neel had run towards them and startled them.

In their present restless state, this could be disastrous. Rowan knew that they could break down their fence again and bolt, if nothing was done to calm them. Pushing his way through the crowd, he began to walk swiftly towards the bukshah field.

To his relief, the strange mist had thinned, so he could see the familiar way well enough, even without a light. As he walked, he thought. And the more he thought, the more convinced he became that it was simply a coincidence that Norris and Shaaran would be staying in the village.

Those hooded cloaks we were wearing in my dream—why, they were old Rin warrior cloaks, made of bukshah skin, he told himself. There are no cloaks like that in Rin any more. And besides, in the dream Norris said that Sheba had gone to the coast. That will *certainly* not happen. Sheba told me so herself.

The bukshah were still calling, Star's distinctive low bellow louder than all the rest. Rowan quickened his pace. He was almost running by the time he reached the gate to the field.

Beside the gate was the shed where the herd's winter feed was stored. Rowan threw open the shed door, plunged into the sweet-smelling darkness inside and grabbed a half bale of hay from the edge of the sadly small stack remaining on the floor. He knew that a little food would calm the great animals more quickly than anything. Heaving the bale after him, he let himself into the field and called softly.

The bellowing ceased, but the bukshah did not come to him.

Puzzled, Rowan peered through the darkness and the mist that still rolled thickly over the frozen stream, and then he called again.

He could hear Star rumbling in reply, but still there was no movement. Rowan trudged towards the sound, moving upward, and at last saw humped grey shapes standing motionless against the fence that separated the field from the orchard. Here the mist was just a faint veil, and soon he could see the herd clearly.

The bukshah were crowded together in a tight group, the largest and strongest on the outside, the weaker ones in the centre. Even when they saw what Rowan was carrying, none of them moved except Star, who took a single step forward.

"Star, there is no need to fear," Rowan crooned, as he reached her and dropped the bale of hay at her feet. He patted her gently. "Neel would not harm you, and the fire is out. You are safe."

Star shook her head, rumbling deep in her throat. Her skin was twitching beneath the curled wool of her mane.

Rowan felt an unpleasant twinge of doubt. *Were* the bukshah safe? Star certainly did not seem to think so, and Rowan was uncomfortably aware that her instincts had proved more reliable than his in the past.

Rapidly he counted heads. Then, a cold feeling growing in his chest, he moved among the beasts, calling them by name. They all answered him but one. Pale grey Twilight, the oldest, shaggiest bukshah in the herd, Lann's favourite, was missing. And there could only be one reason for that.

Fighting despair, Rowan bent to tear the bale apart so that the herd could share it. "I am sorry, Star," he said. "I am sorry about Twilight. I did not realise she was—so weak. In the morning I will find her. For now—"

"Rowan! Is that you?"

Rowan jumped. It was Jonn's voice, sounding oddly strained, coming from the direction of the orchard.

Rowan peered over the fence. Dimly he saw the glow of a lantern. "Yes, Jonn!" he shouted.

"Rowan, come here!"

There was no mistaking the strangled tone in Jonn's voice now. What had happened? Was it something to do with Neel?

His heart in his mouth, Rowan gave Star a final pat, scrambled over the fence and waded through the snow towards the lantern's light.

He found Jonn waiting for him among the first of the half-buried trees. The big man looked distracted, but his eyes widened in shock as Rowan appeared from the darkness.

"Rowan!" he gasped. "Where is your coat? You must be frozen!"

Only then did Rowan realise that he had left his coat on the floor in the house of books. He had walked to the bukshah field with no protection other than his woollen jacket. And he had not even noticed.

He and Jonn gaped at one another for a long moment, then Jonn shook his head violently, as if to clear it.

"It is all part of the same thing!" he muttered to himself. Abruptly he beckoned to Rowan. "Come and see!" he ordered. "See what I found, when I was searching for Neel."

He turned and strode off through the trees. Wondering, Rowan followed. His stomach began to churn as he realised that Jonn was making for Sheba's hut.

At the edge of the orchard, Jonn stopped and held up his lantern. Ahead was the cleared space that lay before Sheba's door.

But it was not as it had been when Rowan saw it last. No flickering light shone from the hut. There was no smell of bitter smoke. No sound of chanting. And a broad, black path led away from the door, curving across the trampled snow and away to the hills beyond.

Rowan stared. "What is it?" he breathed.

Without a word, Jonn led him to the black path. As he stepped upon it, Rowan could feel heat rising from the ground, even through his thick, wet boots. He took a few steps, and with wonder saw steam rising where he trod.

"The path goes right through the hills," said Jonn, his usually calm voice taut with excitement. "I followed it, until I was sure. It meets the stream, then continues, towards the coast."

Rowan stared, unable to take it in. He swallowed painfully. "But Sheba told me—"

"Nothing but the truth!" Jonn broke in. "In her own spiteful, deceiving way she told you exactly what she planned. She said she would show us, and she *is* showing us! She said she would not be leaving the village with us and she will *not*. Because she has already gone! She is *leading* us!"

He gripped Rowan's arm. "Do you not see, Rowan? This is what the heat spell was intended to do. Sheba is going to blaze a path through the snow, all the way to the coast!"

"But ..." The word seemed to stick in Rowan's throat. He was choking with mingled astonishment, relief and fear. "But Sheba can barely walk, Jonn! Even if she could melt the snow, how could she ...?"

"She is not walking, but riding," said Jonn. He held his lantern low so that its light flooded the black ground. And there, unmistakable, were the heavy tracks of a huge, clawed beast.

The tracks of Unos, the grach.

6 – Grim Discoveries

And so it was that the people of Rin left their valley at dawn, not struggling through deep snow as they had expected, but tramping four abreast along the burned black trail that their Wise Woman had left for them to follow.

Rowan and Shaaran farewelled them at the place where the black trail met the stream, then stood watching as they marched away. The people's heads were high and their eyes were fixed on the horizon. Their hearts were full, but they did not weep, and only Allun, the half-Traveller, looked back.

"They do not care," murmured Shaaran. Her eyes were brimming with tears.

"They do," said Rowan. "But it is not their way to show it." He returned Allun's wave and then turned away so he could no longer see the long line travelling east, the only moving thing in a wilderness of white.

"Come," he said, putting his arm around Shaaran's shoulders. "We must get back to the others. Norris will be wondering where you are."

Shaaran bit her lip. "No, he will not," she said in a low voice. "He is very angry because I would not leave him. He says my weakness shames us both. But, except for our grandfather, Norris was my only companion in the land of the Zebak. I could not abandon him, Rowan. I could not!"

Rowan felt very sorry for her. He knew only too well how it felt to be the weakling, the different one, among the sturdy people of Rin. "You are not weak, Shaaran," he said, as they began to walk back towards the village. "You are very strong, in your own way. Look at how you struggled with Neel to protect the silks!"

Immediately he wished he had not spoken, for Shaaran winced at the sound of Neel's name. The potter had not been found the night before, despite a search that had lasted for hours.

"The fool has fallen into a hole and been frozen, you may count on it," Lann had said flatly.

But Rowan and Jonn had not been so sure. And Shaaran was haunted by the fear that Neel was lurking somewhere in the village, waiting his chance to strike at the silks again.

"I do not blame Neel," she said. "He only tried to do what he thought was right, and I hope with all my heart he is safe. But if only he could be found! Then we could talk to him, explain to him ..."

Rowan glanced at her. He hoped she would not repeat these forgiving words in front of Lann. The old warrior would greet them with withering contempt.

As they passed Sheba's hut and began tramping through the orchard, Rowan thought of something that might turn Shaaran's mind from her troubles.

"I must feed the bukshah," he said. "Will you come with me?"

Shaaran hesitated, a mixture of fear and the wish to please warring on her face. It had always amazed Rowan that she could fear the gentle bukshah, while Unos the grach, hideous and clawed, did not frighten her at all.

"Never mind," he said quickly. "I should report to Lann first, in any case, or she will fret. But the bukshah would never harm you, Shaaran. They are the gentlest of beasts."

"Their horns look very dangerous," Shaaran said in a small voice.

Rowan laughed. "I have told you—they never use their horns," he said. "Not even on each other."

"Why do they have horns at all, then?" Shaaran retorted.

Rowan could find no answer to that. He had often wondered the same thing himself.

The village was eerily silent when they entered it. They did not speak as they moved through the square, instinctively creeping on tiptoe past the barred and shuttered houses. Without people to give it life, the place seemed like a graveyard.

It was with relief that they reached the bakery, for there, at least, there was noise and movement. As Rowan and Shaaran entered the big kitchen, they heard Lann's voice barking instructions and the sound of furniture being moved around in the living room beyond.

It had been decided that to make the small supplies of wood and oil last as long as possible, the people remaining in Rin should move into one dwelling, so they could share food, light and warmth.

Lann had decided on the bakery because it was large and close to the village centre. Rowan was very glad. He loved the bakery, filled for him with pleasant memories of Allun's cheerful mother, Sara, and of Allun himself singing as he pulled trays of fragrant buns and rolls from the old black oven.

But when he and Shaaran walked into the cosy living room behind the kitchen, he realised that with Lann in charge life at the bakery would not be as friendly and comfortable as it had been with Sara as the home-maker.

The large room had been cleared of furniture. The only pieces remaining were one chair before the fire, where Norris sat, scowling furiously, and the stool on which his injured leg was propped.

Rugs brought from the bedchambers upstairs overlapped one another all over the floor to exclude draughts. The windows were closely shuttered. Bronden was blocking the staircase with furniture and old blankets to prevent warm air rising to waste.

Five sets of rolled bedding had been ranged neatly around the bare walls. Each person's bag of belongings had been placed beside his or her bedroll, and on the floor next to this were a tin mug, a plate, and a spoon.

It was like an army camp fitted out for a siege—a siege against the cold. Lann stood in the midst of it, hunched over her stick.

"So! Here you are at last!" she said as Rowan and Shaaran appeared. "See how much we have had to do while you two have been lolly-gagging in the hills? This is not a good way to begin!"

Her tone was harsh, her face a mass of frowning lines. Rowan felt Shaaran shrink back against him and sighed inwardly. He knew only too well that Lann was using work and anger to cover the misery she felt at the departure of her people. But to Shaaran the old woman seemed merely stern and frightening.

"Help Bronden with the stairs, Rowan of the Bukshah," snapped Lann. "You, girl, can fetch more wood for the fire."

"I can do that," Norris said, struggling to rise. "Shaaran is not strong enough to—"

"Stay where you are, Norris!" barked Lann. "If you do not rest your leg it will not heal. Your sister insisted on staying, and she must earn her keep."

Sulkily, Norris sank back into his chair.

"I cannot help Bronden just now, Lann," Rowan said. "I must tend the bukshah." He took a deep breath and forced himself to go on in the same level voice as before. "I may be a little longer than usual. Twilight died last night. I need to find her, and cover her for the sake of the others."

"Twilight?" The lines on Lann's face seemed to deepen, and for a moment something like despair darkened her faded eyes. But all she said was, "Cover her, then. But do not forget to shear her first. The wool must not be wasted."

* * *

The bukshah field was a silent wasteland of white, brown and grey. Behind it loomed the vast bulk of the Mountain, shrouded in mist.

The bukshah were still crowded together against the orchard fence. The snow around them was pocked with the holes they had dug to uncover grass roots, the only food still available to them in their field.

They did not come to Rowan when he called them, and even when he broke the ice on their pool with an iron spike, they did not stir. Only when he hurried to the shed and hauled out their daily ration of hay did they move towards him.

When they had all begun to eat, Rowan picked up the spade, the sack and the shears he had laid ready, and followed the tracks of stampeding hoofs down to a large, trampled patch of ground beside the snow-covered stream.

To his surprise there was no sign of Twilight's body anywhere.

The ice-bound stream gurgled secretly beneath his feet as he crossed the snow that covered it. The Mountain hulked before him, a shapeless wall of swirling white. Cold streamed from it, catching Rowan in the face like icy breath, making him gasp.

He recoiled in shock. Neel's shrill voice echoed in his memory.

It is a curse ... We have offended the Mountain, and now the Mountain has turned against us.

Then Rowan saw something that, in the past few, frantic days, he had not noticed before.

There were no bukshah tracks on this side of the stream. Long, smooth drifts of snow, rising one beside the other like waves on the sea of Maris, ran all the way to the mists of the Mountain. Even in their ceaseless quest for food, the bukshah had not crossed the stream since the last snowfall, three days ago.

Rowan jumped violently as a soft, grunting rumble sounded behind him. He whirled around and saw Star standing on the other side of the stream, watching him. As an experiment, he held out his hand, inviting her to come to him, but she tossed her heavy head and would not stir.

Dragging the spade behind him, Rowan crossed the stream again and moved to her side. He plunged his gloved hands into the thick wool of her mane, and felt her skin trembling beneath.

"Star, where did Twilight fall?" he whispered.

Star pawed the ground, her head lowered, the points of her great curved horns almost touching the snow.

"Twilight!" Rowan repeated, gripping her mane more tightly. "Show me, Star."

Star turned her head to look at him. Then, reluctantly, she began to move.

She led Rowan along the hidden stream until she reached the furthermost corner of the trampled space. There she stopped and pawed the ground again.

Rowan looked about him. There was nothing to see but a huge snowdrift which bridged the stream and ended in a tumbled pile at the edge of the space.

A horrible idea came to him. Perhaps Twilight had fallen to her knees, and the end of the drift had collapsed over her as she struggled to rise. His eyes burned at the thought. Dashing the tears away before they could fall and freeze on his cheeks, he took the spade and began digging in the pile of snow.

Star backed away, rumbling urgently.

"Do not fear, Star," Rowan said. Yet with every spadeful of snow he cast aside, his own fear grew greater. His hands were shaking.

What is the matter with me? he thought angrily. I have seen death before, many times. Gritting his teeth, he bent his back and shovelled more strongly, tunnelling into the mass of frozen white.

Then suddenly, with a cry of shock, he lurched forward, stumbling and almost falling. The spade had plunged into emptiness. Into a hollow beneath the snow.

Dropping to his knees, Rowan peered into the hollow. His skin crawled.

A long, narrow, blue-shadowed space. The loud gurgling of the stream, echoing from icy walls. Dead air, so chill that it stung his lips and eyes, so cold that the medallion around his neck seemed to burn.

Rowan gaped, hypnotised by the strangeness, frozen with dread. Star moaned, nudging him, urging him to rise. Her touch broke the spell. Slowly his eyes adjusted to the light, and his mind made sense of what he was seeing.

The tumbled snow had masked the entrance to a tunnel beneath the snowdrift. At the far end, jammed between frozen walls, lay something shaggy and grey.

Twilight.

A lump rose in Rowan's throat. He thought he could see what had happened. As he had feared, Twilight had fallen and been buried by collapsing snow. Somehow she must have dragged herself forward, creating a tunnel through the icy whiteness as she went. Then, at last, when she could go no further, she had simply laid down her head and died.

Trembling, he crawled to his feet. The thought of uncovering Twilight's pathetic remains and taking her wool filled him with revulsion. The thought of breaking into that icy, blue-shadowed tomb filled him with dread. He knew he could not do it.

He snatched up the spade and with a few strokes closed the mouth of the tunnel, sealing it once more.

Star nudged his arm roughly, anxious to be gone. Rowan took hold of her mane again and let her lead him away. Beneath her thick coat her skin still twitched, twitched.

The beasts are wiser than we know ...

Rowan's fingers tightened in the soft wool as a terrible knowledge pierced his mind like a shard of ice.

Star loved him, but she no longer trusted him to make decisions for her. She knew that the cold was coming from the Mountain. She had known it for days. She knew that all Rowan's care and comfort could only lead to a slower way for the herd to die.

As if she sensed Rowan's despair, the great bukshah stopped and lifted her head to look at him. She held his gaze, her small black eyes searching his. Rowan stared back helplessly. And at last Star looked away again, and plodded on.

* * *

The rest of the day passed like a dream—a strange, almost silent dream. The only sound was Bronden hammering, doggedly sealing one cottage after another against the weather.

Rowan said nothing of his discoveries in the bukshah field. He did not wish to speak of Twilight's strange and horrible death. Neither was he ready to speak of his terror when he felt the icy breath of the Mountain upon his face. If he told the others that the terrible cold that gripped the land was flowing from the Mountain, he would sound as hysterical and superstitious as Neel.

He spent the rest of the morning doing Lann's bidding, carrying food, fuel and other needs to the bakery, searching vainly for a misplaced lantern, which Lann insisted had been newly filled with oil and could not be spared. In the afternoon, after a meagre meal of bread and cheese, he worked in the bukshah field, checking the fences, breaking the ice on the pool again while the herd watched him listlessly.

As the light dimmed, the air grew colder. Colder than ever before. Rowan worked on. He kept his eyes lowered so that he would not have to look at the Mountain. But every nerve in his body was aware of it, looming above him, breathing cold, breathing death.

By the time the Dragon on the Mountain's peak roared at dusk, his hands were so numb that he could no longer hold his tools. Mist was thickening at the base of the Mountain, stealing across the snowdrifts towards the stream. He knew he had to seek the shelter of the bakery, and quickly. But he did not want to leave the bukshah, huddled together by the orchard fence. He dreaded what the night would bring.

7 – Night Terrors

Rowan crept through the shadowed, empty streets, past the shuttered houses, feeling like a ghost. But when finally he reached the bakery, and let himself into the warm, lighted kitchen, his spirits lifted a little.

A pot of soup, thin, but fragrant with herbs, was simmering on the stove. In the living room beyond, all was peace. Norris was showing Bronden how to knot rope in a way that was new to her. Lann was dozing by the fire. And Shaaran was standing before a piece of silk stretched on a frame, a fine brush in her hand.

"Lann said I should make a silk of this time—of the snow, and the people leaving the village," she explained to Rowan, as he joined her. "She said it was something of importance I could do. She said that I must carry on the work of my ancestors, painting the important events in our history, so that those who come after will not forget. I have nearly finished the outlines already."

Rowan looked with admiration at the clever sketch—the long, long line of people following a black road winding east, the bukshah in their field, the Mountain towering above all. Then he met Shaaran's eyes, no longer dull and despairing but filled with purpose, and blessed Lann for thinking of the one thing that might comfort her.

He went to his hard bed early that night. He did not want to talk. He had too much on his mind that he could not share. But though he was very weary, he fought against sleep.

He lay with his face to the wall while Shaaran painted and Lann, Bronden and Norris sat by the fire, speaking of the people who were gone, wondering how far they had travelled this day, and if they were safe.

Slowly the voices grew dim, until they were a soft buzzing

somewhere at the edge of his consciousness. He closed his eyes, and made himself relax.

You need not fear, he told himself. You will not dream this time. You will not dream ...

* * *

Rowan opened his eyes. He was in a cave. Mist swirled in the darkness beyond the narrow, ragged triangle of the cave's mouth. Beside him three figures wrapped in heavy cloaks huddled by a tiny fire. The flickering red light showed their faces only dimly, but Rowan saw enough to know who they were. Norris. Shaaran. Himself.

The three paid no attention to him. He knew they could not see him. This time, he knew at once that he was dreaming.

"The fire will keep us safe," Shaaran whispered. "Surely it will."

"It should," Norris said gruffly. "But the night will be long."

Rowan watched his mirror image glance at the girl. Her eyes were dark with fear. The box of silks was on her lap. She was clutching it so tightly that her fingers were white.

"Let us look at some of the silks," the Rowan figure suggested gently. "Let us think of old times. It will take our minds from the present, and remind us why we are here."

Norris snorted and turned away, but the girl nodded gratefully. She opened the box, revealing the familiar rolls of silk. She dug deep, pulled one out at random, then stood up and let it unroll. The Rowan figure caught his breath. Norris spun around. The girl looked down, saw what the picture was, and exclaimed in dismay, "Oh, what ill fortune! I did not mean ..."

Her voice trailed away as with trembling hands she began to roll the painting up again. But Rowan had seen enough to make the hair rise on the back of his neck.

The painting was all in white, black and shades of blue and grey. The shapes upon it were clear and precise, the creations of a skilful hand.

A long line of people trekking away through snow-covered hills, following a burned black path that wound towards a bleak horizon. Bukshah, the only dark objects in a white wasteland, clustered together beneath the Mountain, which loomed over all, wreathed in mist.

And writhing from the mist, in their hundreds, in their thousands, huge white snake-like things with no eyes. Things with gaping, blue-lined jaws and teeth like shards of ice. Things that slid and twisted out of the cold, things that tunnelled through the snow, seeking, seeking ...

Something gripped Rowan's arm. He jerked in shock, tried to shake it off. He tried to scream, but all he could manage was a strangled groan.

"Rowan!" The voice was loud in his ear. It was Bronden's voice, harshly whispering. "Wake! You are thrashing about and moaning in your sleep, disturbing all of us. Wake, or be still, for pity's sake!"

Rowan's eyes flew open. For a split second he lay still, panting, looking up at Bronden's puffy, irritated face. Then he sprang up, nearly knocking her off her feet.

"What is the matter with you?" she cried angrily.

Rowan's throat was tight with fear, his head spinning with the visions of the dream.

"The bukshah!" he choked, frantically pulling on his boots, snatching up his knife. "I have been wrong! So wrong! Star knew—they all knew ... ah, poor Twilight! She was the first. Seized and dragged under. Dragged ..."

Bronden gaped at him. In the dim light of the fire he could see Lann slowly sitting up, Norris and Shaaran staring.

The fire will keep us safe ...

Rowan ran to the other side of the room, pulled a torch from the pile and plunged it into the coals of the fire. It caught quickly.

"Rowan!" Lann barked, holding out an arm impatiently so that Bronden could haul her to her feet. "Report!"

"Bring torches!" Rowan shouted. "The bukshah field! Make haste, for pity's sake!"

Holding his flame high, he darted into the kitchen and out into the street where the freezing mist swirled like a living thing, catching at his clothes, rushing into his lungs, blinding him.

But he ran like the wind, heart pounding, chest aching with fear.

He could hear Bronden's heavy footfalls behind him. Lighter steps, too, behind Bronden. And Norris roaring to Shaaran to come back, to stay in safety. And Lann shouting fruitless orders after them all.

As he burst from among the houses and plunged down towards the silent bukshah field, Rowan glanced over his shoulder and saw the torches flickering through the mist. Four bobbing torches, strung out in a line.

One to weep and one to fight,
One to dream and one for flight ...

And suddenly, very near, there was an ear-splitting shriek.

Not Star. Nor any of the other bukshah. No beast had made that sound. That was a human voice, floating through the mist on waves of deathly cold.

The outline of the feed shed loomed ahead. Its door was gaping wide. Beside it a section of fence lay flattened, half buried in trampled snow. And very near, in the bukshah field, was a wildly moving light.

"Ah, no! No!" The sobbing scream rose, high and wailing.

Rowan stumbled forward, over the ruined fence. And through the mist he saw Neel the potter, slipping and staggering backwards in the snow.

Neel was screaming, scrambling back towards the feed shed, swinging a blazing lantern in great arcs in front of his body.

Wisps of hay stuck in his hair, on his clothes. The mist was swirling around him, above him, making writhing white shapes in the lantern light. His eyes were wide and staring, his twisted face turned upward, a gleaming mask of terror.

Neel is not dead, Rowan found himself thinking blankly, stupidly, as his mind grappled with what his eyes were seeing. It was Neel who took Lann's lantern. Neel has been hiding in the feed shed, behind the bales of hay, all this time. But what is he ... Why is he ...?

Neel shrieked, swinging the lantern high. Then Rowan, with a thrill of horror, saw at last what the potter could see. Saw what the shapes were that twisted and loomed just beyond the circle of light.

Surrounding Neel, towering over him, were huge, hideous, white, snake-like beasts, their blunt, eyeless heads jabbing downward, their gaping mouths like blue-shadowed holes in snow.

Neel screamed again, burning oil spilling from the lantern as he swung it above his head. Liquid fire spattered on his hands, fell sizzling on the snow. The lunging beasts hissed, and the icy cold of their breath seemed to freeze the very air so that it thickened and went white. Neel fell flat on his back, the sweat on his face frozen into a pale, cracked mask, the lantern still clutched in his hand.

Rowan shouted and leaped forward, the flaming torch held high above his head. He slithered down towards Neel, reaching for him desperately. But now Neel was screaming again, writhing on the icy ground. Rowan seized his arm, trying to drag him up. Wildly Neel clutched at him, pulling him to his knees.

"They have come for us!" Neel shrieked. "Now do you believe? Now do you see?"

"Get up!" shouted Rowan, struggling to regain his feet, to haul Neel up with him.

But mad with terror, crying and babbling as if gripped by a nightmare from which he could not wake, Neel clung to Rowan like a drowning man, holding him down.

And the terrible creatures struck downward, blue mouths yawning wider, wide enough to swallow a man, teeth gleaming like long ice needles, teeth that sloped backwards to strike deep, hold fast, drag into the freezing dark.

Ice creepers ...

The creatures hissed, and the sound was like a knife cutting through fresh snow, and freezing breath gusted from their open mouths.

"No!" screamed Neel, and threw the lantern wildly. It flew uselessly sideways and smashed into the wall of the shed. Flames leaped upwards.

Neel howled. His eyes rolled in panic. Then suddenly he was moving, flinging himself over Rowan's body, heedlessly crawling over it as though it was a log or a sack of grain, kicking back with his heavy boots, scrambling towards the fire.

The ice creepers turned their blunt, blind heads, following the movement.

And as Rowan crawled to his feet, one arm wrapped around his aching ribs, he saw only a white blur as one of the creatures struck down, and Neel was plucked, shrieking, into the air.

In seconds the beast had squirmed backwards into the mist, there was a soft sound of sliding snow, and Neel was gone. Gone, into icy darkness. The creepers that remained turned back to Rowan.

Frantically he swept the torch from side to side, backing away, forcing himself to go slowly, feeling his way on the treacherous, slippery ground. The beasts lunged, hissing, their breath cutting at him like cold knives.

Rowan's limbs seemed to freeze. He staggered. The flame wavered. Through the roaring in his ears he heard Shaaran screaming, Bronden cursing harshly, calling his name. Shaaran and Bronden had reached the fence. They had seen ...

"Stay back!" he heard himself shouting hoarsely. "Get away!"

But already there were heavy steps behind him, and the sounds of panting and sobbing. Rowan felt someone grabbing his arm. He caught a glimpse of Bronden's wild-eyed face as she thrust him roughly behind her.

Then Bronden was shielding him with her own body. Bronden was facing the beasts, a flaming torch held high, her sword gleaming in her other hand. And Shaaran, sobbing and shaking, was beside him, her frail arm around him, supporting him, her own torch lifted so that it flamed beside his.

"Back!" shouted Bronden. "Back!"

She took a giant step backwards, and Rowan and Shaaran stumbled back behind her. But the ice creepers were following, their jaws gaping, their heads striking down, down, down ...

8 – Facing the Truth

ut of the corner of his eye, Rowan could see fire flickering where the lantern had fallen against the feed shed. The old wood had caught, and flames were licking upward.

"The fire!" he shouted. "Bronden! Move towards the—"

Bronden heard, and began to edge towards the shed. Slowly, slowly ...

Then Norris, panting and cursing, came stumbling out of the mist, a flaming torch in one hand, Lann's sword in the other.

Bronden's eyes slid towards him. It was just a glance, a matter of a split second. But it was fatal. For as she looked, her torch tilted slightly to the left, and like lightning a creeper struck, its teeth fastening in her right side, just above her waist.

Bronden gave a groaning gasp. Her sword fell from her hand. Desperately she flailed in the creature's grip as it dragged her upward.

Rowan threw himself forward, catching her around the knees. Norris, shouting with horror, flung his torch aside and seized her left arm. But even their combined strength was not enough to pull Bronden back.

Wildly, Norris slashed at the beast's ghastly head with Lann's sword. The sword slid off the shining white hide with the sound of clanging metal. The beast seemed to shudder, but did not let go.

It would never let go. It had struck Bronden only a glancing blow, but its teeth were embedded in the padding of her coat, and had sunk into the flesh beneath.

Shaaran, white-faced, was sweeping her torch from side to side, protecting them from the other beasts that writhed around them.

"Shaaran!" Norris roared. "Leave us! Run!"

Shaaran made no answer.

"Bronden's coat!" Rowan gasped. "Norris! Get her coat—off! Then hold her legs! Hold her!"

Norris seized the back of Bronden's coat and heaved. There was a tearing sound as seams ripped and fastenings burst. Rowan waited an agonising moment while Norris took a firm grip on Bronden's legs. Then he thrust his torch straight at the beast's head.

The creeper jerked, hissing violently. Bronden gave a scream of anguish. And then the creeper was recoiling, the torn coat still flapping in its teeth, and Bronden was slumping to the ground, blood from her side sprinkling the snow.

The other ice creepers lunged forward in fury. Rowan, Shaaran and Norris clung together over Bronden's body, their torches held high in aching arms, the flames wavering and small, holding the terrible creatures back.

They all knew they could not last. The creepers knew it too. Their smooth, gleaming bodies arched and writhed. Their heads bobbed lower. They seemed to grin as their terrible mouths widened, hissing ...

Then Lann's defiant shout echoed through the mist, and the feed shed exploded in flames. Flames roared through the roof. Red-hot sparks and fragments of burning hay sprayed into the air. Waves of heat billowed over the snow.

The ice creepers reared back. There was a stealthy, slithering sound, like snow slipping from a roof. And the next moment—they were gone.

Hardly able to believe what had happened, that they were safe, Rowan, Shaaran and Norris dragged Bronden towards the fire, their heads lowered to protect themselves from the sparks falling all about them.

The blessed heat enfolded them as they reached the gap in the fence. The snow beneath their feet melted and steamed. Lann was waiting for them, her wrinkled face black with ash, her teeth bared in a ferocious grin.

"That gave the devils pause!" she rasped.

Except for her stick, she was empty-handed. She had given her sword to Norris. And Rowan knew that the torch she had carried to the field was in the burning shed. Lann, the most determined protector of the village stores, had thrown her torch into the precious hay. To speed the fire. To save their lives.

As if she felt his thoughts, Lann glanced at the inferno that the shed had become. Her grin of triumph faded, leaving her face grey and haggard. "There was no other way," she muttered.

"It does not matter now," Rowan replied. His voice sounded like the voice of a stranger, even to himself.

Lann looked at him searchingly for a moment. Then her lips tightened, and she bent to examine Bronden's side.

"Flesh has been torn away," she said, stripping off her own coat to lay it over Bronden. "A painful wound, but a strong woman like Bronden should not have been felled so completely by it. And there is too little blood for my liking. It is as though contact with the beast has chilled her to the bone. We must get her out of the cold without delay. Carry her between you. I will take the torches and lead the way."

Slowly, clumsily, Norris, Rowan and Shaaran lifted Bronden from the ground. Her body hung limp between them, a dead weight.

They had only taken a few steps when Shaaran suddenly halted. "Oh ... but what of the bukshah?" she cried. "We cannot leave them to—"

"Use your ears, girl!" Lann snapped. "Have you ever known the bukshah herd as silent as this? And use your eyes!"

She jabbed her stick at the ground. In the light of the fire still raging in the ruins of the shed, all could see the broad, trampled trail leading through the gap in the fence, and on into the mist and darkness.

"Star took the herd away long ago, Shaaran," Rowan said quietly, as they began to move once more. "She must have waited till I left, then done what she knew was right. So when the creepers came, the field was empty of prey. Except for Neel."

Lann and Norris looked around at him, startled. They had arrived too late to see what had happened to Neel.

"When Bronden and I reached the field, Neel—was there," Rowan said, his eyes fixed on the ground. "He had been hiding in the feed shed. For some reason he came out in the dead of night."

"To steal food from the storehouse, no doubt," said Lann grimly.

"Perhaps," Rowan said. He was reluctant to speak ill of Neel, though his bruised ribs still ached from the heedless kicks of the potter's boots. "In any case, he must have seen that the fence had been broken down while he slept. He went into the field to see if the bukshah had truly gone—"

"And found more than he bargained for," Norris finished grimly.

Shaaran gave a strangled sob.

"Neel was always too curious for his own good," Lann muttered. "Curious and weak-minded, like his father before him." She shook her head. "Yet his father died peacefully in his bed, and Neel should have done the same—*would* have, no doubt, if this disaster had not befallen us."

She hunched her shoulders, and pushed on through the snow. "It is unfortunate. Neel was never a merry soul, even as a child, but he could whistle to charm the birds from the trees. And his pots were as well crafted as anyone could wish."

The words were as plain and dry as Lann herself, but to Rowan they brought back vivid memories. The sound of whistling drifting from the pottery on sweet summer nights. The sight of Neel sitting at his potter's wheel, his wet, bony hands coaxing spinning lumps of clay into bowls, jugs and beakers.

Neel had not been the most likeable man in Rin. But he had been as much a part of it as the Teaching Tree or the house of books. Now he was gone.

A vision of Neel's face as he had last seen it—white with frozen sweat, mad with terror—rose before Rowan's eyes. He wondered if he would ever forget it.

The forlorn little group trudged on in silence.

"Neel was weak-minded, perhaps," Shaaran said in a low voice, as at last they reached the village streets and began labouring towards the bakery. "But he was right all along. He warned us that this was the Cold Time come again. He warned us of the ice creepers. He warned us, and we would not listen, and he died because of it."

"He died because of his own folly, girl!" snapped Lann.

"And what of the other things he said, Shaaran?" Norris demanded.

"Surely you do not believe that the Mountain is punishing the village because of us? Because of the silks?"

"I do not know what to believe," Shaaran whispered. "I only know that there must be a reason for all this. And if the reason is not what Neel claimed, what is it? When you and I came here, Norris, the village was full of life. Now it is all but dead. The people are gone. The bukshah are gone ..."

"*We* are still here, Shaaran of the Silks," said Lann stoutly. She stopped at the bakery door and threw it wide, so that Bronden could be carried inside.

Shaaran bit her lip. When she spoke again, her voice was unsteady. "We are here for now," she said. "But how long will it be before we, too, are gone? It grows colder every day. Monsters have come down from the Mountain, seeking prey. They have already invaded the fields. Perhaps, soon, they will be in the streets."

"Be still, Shaaran," growled Norris. "If they come we will defend ourselves. That is all."

They put Bronden down in front of the still-glowing fire.

"Bring blankets, Rowan!" Lann ordered, kneeling painfully beside the unconscious woman. "Also bandages, and healing balm. Norris, feed the fire. And you, girl, make yourself useful by putting water on to boil. We have work to do here."

Shaaran went towards the kitchen, but at the doorway she turned. Two spots of vivid colour burned high on her cheeks. She looked directly at Rowan.

"Lann refuses to discuss this," she said in a high voice. "And Norris turns away his head, pretending to be busy with the wood basket. But you know I am right, Rowan, and—and you know more than you are telling."

Her usually gentle eyes were snapping as the words tumbled out of her.

"What did Sheba say to you, Rowan? I know that it was more, far more, than you have admitted. I have seen it in your eyes all this long day. The time has come for you to tell the truth. And the time has come for us to face it, whatever it may be."

Rowan felt as though his heart was being gripped by an icy hand.

A suspicion had entered his mind the moment he saw the broken fence and the tracks of the bukshah leading away into the darkness. Now, suspicion had become a dread certainty.

When it is time, you will know it.

"Yes," he said huskily. He felt Lann's shocked, angry eyes upon him, heard Norris give a startled grunt.

"Sheba gave me a prophecy," he said. "The words were fearful, but I could not grasp their meaning. Perhaps I did not want to. Now, I think, I understand at least the first of them. As for the others ..."

The room was very still. The eyes of his companions were fixed on him. Rowan swallowed, stared into the fire, and slowly repeated the rhyme.

> *"The beasts are wiser than we know*
> *And where they lead, four souls must go.*
> *One to weep and one to fight,*
> *One to dream and one for flight.*
> *Four must make their sacrifice.*
> *In the realm twixt fire and ice*
> *The hunger will not be denied,*
> *The hunger must be satisfied.*
> *And in that blast of fiery breath*
> *The quest unites both life and death."*

The silence in the room was broken only by the crackling of the fire. Finally, Lann spoke.

"*Sacrifice?*" she breathed, her face stricken.

"The beasts ..." Norris said. "The creepers ...?"

Rowan shook his head. "Not the ice creepers. The bukshah. They have been straying from their field for weeks. Always, before, I have brought them back. This time I know that I should not do so. Their feed is burned. There is nothing for them here. But they will lead me—to where I must go."

"The rhyme says *four* souls must follow, not just one." Lann was scowling. "But Bronden is injured, and I—am not able-bodied."

Everyone in the room could see what this admission cost her. Her wrinkled face was set as though it was made of iron.

Norris drew himself up in his chair. "I will go with Rowan," he said.

Lann pursed her lips. "You cannot—"

"I can," Norris insisted. He turned to Rowan, who was shaking his head. "And do not think of creeping away alone, my friend," he said. "If you do, I will follow you. My place is beside you."

"And mine," Shaaran said, her voice trembling.

"No!" Rowan exclaimed sharply. "Norris, tell her—"

But Norris bent his head and kept silence.

Rowan stared at them hopelessly. He knew he could not fight this any more.

"But still," said Lann. "That will only be three."

Dream pictures were vivid in Rowan's mind, like painted silks stirred by the breeze.

Three figures trudging through the snow, a fourth figure watching from a distance. Three figures huddling in a cave, a fourth shadow close by.

One to dream …

Rowan's skin prickled. "Three will be enough," he said.

"How can you know that?" asked Norris, eyeing him curiously.

Rowan hesitated, wishing he had held his tongue.

Learn what it is to be what I am …

A vision of Sheba's grinning face loomed up at him. Sheba, hideous and cackling, brimming with spite, foam gathering at the corners of her mouth as she muttered over her evil-smelling fire. Sheba, feared and loathed by all.

The thought of her filled him with revulsion. The idea that people might think he was like her made his stomach churn. The gift of prophecy she had thrust on him was like an infection. He knew he had to hide it, keep the dreams secret. He would never admit to it and see Lann's lip curl, see Shaaran and Norris draw back from him in fascinated dread.

"Three—will *have* to be enough," he said at last.

"And where do you believe the beasts will lead you?" Lann demanded harshly.

Four must make their sacrifice.
In the realm twixt fire and ice ...

Rowan wet his lips. "To the Mountain," he said. "I think we must go—to the Mountain."

9 – The Carved Chest

reparations for the journey were quickly made. Food, fuel, torches, ropes and clothes were packed. Then there was nothing to do but wait. Even Rowan, worried that snow might fall and cover the bukshah tracks, knew that they could not set out until it was light.

Lann, keeping watch over the still unconscious Bronden, ordered them to sleep, but only Norris was able to obey her. With a calm Rowan envied, he flung himself down on his bed and was snoring in moments.

Shaaran moved to her own corner of the room, but when she was out of Lann's sight she quietly settled herself before the silk frame, and took up her brushes once more.

Rowan lay unsleeping, every now and then getting up to check for falling snow.

At last, the sky began to lighten. It had not snowed, but when Rowan slipped out of the kitchen door he realised that the air was not warming as dawn approached. It was freezing cold—even colder than it had been the morning before.

The door creaked behind him. He jumped slightly and looked around. Lann was standing in the doorway, a lantern in her hand. Her lined face was shadowed with weariness from her long night's watch.

"It will soon be time for you to leave," she said, her breath making clouds of mist in the freezing air. "I must fetch some items from my home before then, and I would be glad of your help."

Rowan nodded, swallowing hard as they began to walk. For the first time he allowed himself to face the fact that Lann and Bronden would be alone after this morning. An old woman and a gravely injured one, with little food, and less hope, to sustain them.

"How is Bronden?" he asked.

"She has not stirred," Lann said grimly. "She is still cold to the touch, though she is beside the fire, and wrapped in many blankets. The girl is watching her."

"Lann, I am sorry—" Rowan began. The old woman raised her hand to silence him.

"You are doing what you must do, Rowan of the Bukshah," she said. "And Bronden and I are also playing the hand fate has dealt us. There is no more to say."

They reached Lann's narrow cottage and she led the way inside. The house was sparsely furnished and scrupulously tidy. It smelled of well-worn leather and sandalwood.

Lann looked around, her face expressionless. Absently she touched the back of the chair which stood by the empty hearth. There, Rowan guessed, she had spent her evenings in peace. Before this. All this ...

"Because of Sheba's path, the people will reach the coast far sooner than we expected, Lann," he blurted out. "A rescue party will return with food and other supplies. Jonn promised."

"Indeed he did," Lann answered, still gazing about the room. "But as to what the rescue party will find when it arrives ..."

Abruptly she shook her head, and removed her hand from the chair. Rowan trailed after her as she hobbled to the tiny bedroom at the back of the house. She pointed with her stick at the iron bed.

"There is a wooden chest beneath the bed," she said. "Please pull it out."

Rowan bent to do her bidding. The chest was heavy, and he could feel rich carving beneath his fingers as he dragged it into the open. He supposed it contained more blankets, or perhaps bukshah skin rugs.

Lann lowered her lantern. Soft light glowed on the chest's lid, illuminating a carved pattern of birds, beasts and flowers.

"Why, it is beautiful!" Rowan exclaimed. Too late, he realised that Lann might be insulted by his obvious surprise. It was just that he had not expected her to own such a thing. Everything else in the house was so plain.

Lann did not seem annoyed, however. She herself was gazing at the chest with something like wonder.

"It is very fine," she agreed. "I have not seen it closely for a long time. For many years it has been too heavy for me to move into the light."

Stiffly she bent to touch the carving with the tips of her fingers. "It is fitting that you admire it, for it was made for me by Morgan, your father's father, as a wedding gift," she said.

This time, Rowan's gasp of surprise made her smile slightly.

"Ah, yes," she murmured. "We were betrothed at one time, your grandfather and I."

She sighed. "Morgan was a fine-looking man. Your father looked very like him. Family resemblances are often very strong in Rin. As your father grew to manhood, I used to look at him and think, You could have been my son, had things happened differently."

My father, who died saving me from a fire, Rowan thought, and looked at Lann with new eyes.

Throughout his childhood he had known that most of the villagers thought that a puny, sickly boy was a poor exchange for a strong and well-liked man. He now understood that Lann must have felt even more bitter than the rest. She had hidden it well. Why was she telling him now?

"The village thought it would be a fine match, for both Morgan and I were heroes of battles against the Zebak," Lann continued, without raising her eyes. "But ..." She shrugged. "But the marriage never took place."

"Why?" Rowan asked, then wondered how he could have dared ask such a question. He waited for Lann to rebuff him, but she did not. She answered, her voice halting as if the words were difficult to form.

"Morgan had a much younger brother, whose name was Joel," she said, staring down at the carved chest. "Joel had been born when his mother was long past the usual age of child-bearing. By the time he was ten years old, both his parents were dead, and Morgan was his only guardian."

Her worn fingers traced the graceful lines of the carving—birds in flight, lizards crouching by tufts of grass, flowers twining.

"Joel was a frail, dark-haired child—dreamy and shy, frightened of his own shadow. He was of little use in the fields. He could not fight. The other children mocked him. The people despaired of him."

Rowan felt his face grow hot. Lann could have been describing his own childhood. And he could tell by her voice and her lowered eyes that she knew it only too well.

"Was Joel, too, a keeper of the bukshah?" he asked in a low voice.

"Yes. It was work he could do," Lann said. "As you know, that task is always—*was* always—thought of as too easy for anyone but the very young or those who were in some way wanting."

Her lips tightened. She seemed to be forcing herself to go on.

"I despised Joel," she said. "I thought him weak and cowardly. The strengths Morgan saw in him—his gentleness with all animals, his loving nature—meant nothing to me. It shamed me to be seen in his company. But Morgan would not abandon him. Morgan said that Joel must live with us, until he was grown. We quarrelled over it. Quarrelled bitterly. Soon the whole village knew all was not well with us, and guessed the reason. I did little to conceal it."

She sighed, her fingers rubbing, rubbing at the carving as if somehow she could smooth away the past.

"I was young," she said. "Young and angry. Jealous, too, I think, of Morgan's loyalty to his brother. We all paid the price for my pride."

Rowan stared at her, speechless. Never had Lann spoken of her feelings to him—or to anyone else, as far as he knew.

"What happened?" he asked. The story had given him a dark, sinking feeling. He understood now why no one had ever told him of it before, and he did not want to hear its end. But he knew that the old woman wanted to tell it. For some reason, she felt compelled to tell it.

"Joel was killed," Lann said flatly. "He feared heights, but he climbed a tree to hide from some children who were taunting him because he had come between Morgan and me. His pursuers discovered him in the tree. They threw stones as he tried to climb higher. The next moment, he was falling. Perhaps a stone hit him. Perhaps he merely slipped. Or perhaps he just—let go ..."

Her voice trailed off, and the light seemed to dim, as though the shadows of the old tragedy had filled the little room. Rowan's eyes burned as he thought of the frail boy, shamed and desperate, hounded to his death because ...

Because he was like me, Rowan thought. A throwback to an older time, when our weak and our strong, our brave and our gentle, our artists and our warriors, lived together as one people. Before the Zebak separated us, and brought the strong, brave ones to this land, leaving the gentler ones behind. Whenever Lann looks at me, she sees Joel again. And she remembers …

"Joel fell from the great tree—the tree beneath which we of Rin marry and farewell our dead," Lann murmured. "It was a strange twist of fate that it should have been so, for when Joel died beneath that tree's shade, my hopes of marriage with Morgan died with him."

She was still staring at the chest, still smoothing its carving with her work-worn fingers.

"Morgan came to me that night and gave me this chest," she went on in a voice so low that Rowan had to strain to hear her. "He said Joel had drawn the pattern from which he had carved it. It was to have been their joint gift to me. He said no more, uttered no word of anger or blame, but I knew his feelings for me had changed. I could see it in his eyes. I released him from our betrothal."

Slowly she straightened and met Rowan's eyes. "Years later he wed Else, your grandmother. I was glad that he had found happiness at last. Or told myself so."

"And you …?" Rowan asked.

"I never found another to match Morgan, so I remained alone," Lann said, with some return of her old briskness. "No doubt it was for the best. I have always been too fond of my own way to share my life with another."

"I am sorry," Rowan mumbled, not knowing what to say.

"Ah well. It was all long, long ago," Lann said. "And what is done, is done."

For a moment she was silent, then she firmed her lips determinedly and fixed Rowan with her familiar steely gaze.

"Open the chest, if you please," she said.

The metal clasp was stiff, but at last Rowan managed to loosen it. Carefully he opened the lid.

Somehow he was disappointed to find what he had expected. The chest was filled with bukshah skin rugs, loosely rolled.

Lann gave a gasping sigh. She bent and gathered one of the rugs into her arms. Then she shook it out, and let it hang loose.

And Rowan saw that it was not a rug at all, but a long, hooded cloak. A bukshah skin cloak, made of whole hide, with the ragged wool on the outside and the leather, still amazingly soft and supple, within.

He had seen its kind before, in paintings and drawings in the house of books.

And he had seen it in his dream of the Mountain.

"I have four of these," Lann said. "They are Rin warrior cloaks—the last remaining in the village, for the young prefer woven garments now, it seems. One is mine, two belonged to my parents, and one was Morgan's, given to me by Else when he died. They have seen much. And they will warm you as nothing else will. You and your companions."

She pulled three more cloaks from the chest, shaking them out carefully, piling them into Rowan's arms.

Rowan could not speak. There was a roaring in his ears. But Lann was still speaking. He forced himself to attend to her.

"You and I have not always agreed, Rowan of the Bukshah," she said. "I have found fault with you, as once I found fault with Joel. You, no doubt, have thought me harsh and set in my ways. But over these past years, I have come to see that though we are very different, you and I, we are not unalike in all the ways that matter."

Seeing Rowan's stunned expression, she lifted her chin. Her weathered face warmed as she looked away from him.

"I do not pretend to understand this ... this thing that has been asked of you," she said stiffly. "If it is as it seems, it goes against all I have ever believed of our lives, and this land."

She paused. She was breathing deeply, as though she was struggling to control some deep emotion. Rowan waited.

"I am old, and my time in this world will soon be over," Lann said at last. "What I have to give my people has already been given. You are a different matter. It is very bitter to me that the weakness of my body prevents me from facing this ordeal in your place."

Rowan knew better than to insult her with useless thanks. He told her, instead, the truth.

"You could not have taken my place, Lann, even if you had the strength," he said bluntly. "You could only have accompanied me, as Shaaran and Norris seem fated to do. Sheba told me that only I could do what must be done."

Lann took a sharp breath. "Only you?" she rasped. "The one who climbed the Mountain and faced the Dragon to make the stream flow again? The one who has forged bonds of trust with the Maris and the Travellers? Who gave us knowledge of our past, and saved us from the attack of the Zebak?"

She turned away. "What evil would require our best as sacrifice?"

The hunger must be satisfied ...

Rowan felt a cold shuddering begin deep within him.

Without warning, in this narrow house filled with the homely objects and shadowed memories of an old woman's lifetime, the fear he had kept in check for so long escaped and threatened to overwhelm him.

His heart pounded. He was gripped with the urge to flee.

How easy it would be! To drop the cloaks on the floor and go back to the bakery. To snatch up the bag he had packed and run, along Sheba's clear, blackened path, through the hills and away.

In a day he could be far from here. The way would be hard and long, but at last he would reach the coast. If his own people would not take him in, if they turned from him in disgust, he could find a home with the Maris or the Travellers. On the coast, he could make a new life. He would be safe ...

The medallion hanging around his neck seemed to throb. He clutched it, intending to tear it from him.

But as his fingers touched the warm metal, the words of Sheba's rhyme began echoing, echoing in his mind. And with the words came a vision.

Rin, locked in a silent, frozen dream. Ice creepers twisting and sliding through the orchard trees and the still, white streets. The Mountain brooding above it, breathing cold malice over the land and into the sky. And the deadly chill spreading, spreading, never ceasing. Till the plains where the Travellers once roamed were deserts of misty white, and waves no longer crashed on the Maris shore, for the sea itself had frozen and grown still.

And Rowan knew that this was the future. The future if he ran. The future if he failed.

Rowan ...?

The voice of the Keeper of the Crystal whispered in Rowan's mind, soft as water. The vision was so strong, so clear and compelling, that the Keeper was sharing it. Deep in his rainbow cavern, far away in Maris, the Keeper, too, was gazing at those snowy wastes, that frozen sea.

"Rowan? Rowan!"

This voice was real. The hand shaking his arm was real also. Slowly Rowan turned to meet Lann's anxious eyes. He wondered how long he had been standing motionless, transfixed by something she could not see, listening to something she could not hear.

The frantic urge to flee had vanished, leaving sour shame in its place.

"Let us go back to the others," he said. "It is nearly time to go."

10 – Four Souls

Rowan, Shaaran and Norris left the village as the Dragon on the Mountain roared at dawn. Their path was clearly marked. The bukshah tracks lay on the snow like a broad, dappled ribbon, following the line of the buried stream and disappearing into the trees that clustered at the foot of the Mountain.

All three of the companions wore bukshah skin cloaks. As Lann had promised, the cloaks were very warm. They were surprisingly comfortable, too, though they almost brushed the ground. Lann had been forced to shorten two of them with her knife so that Rowan and Shaaran could walk without stumbling.

Norris carried Lann's sword and a long staff to lean on as he limped along. Shaaran carried the box of silks, which she had refused to leave behind.

"I am the keeper of the silks," she had said stubbornly, when Norris and Lann railed at her for her foolishness. "They must be with me. I feel it."

They passed the mill, standing tall and silent, its great wheel stuck fast in a bed of ice. On they went, and on, resting now and then but speaking little. Rowan knew that the sun must be climbing higher behind its thick veil of cloud, but the light did not brighten, and the air did not warm.

As they neared the Mountain, the trees grew more numerous and the bukshah path narrowed to wind between them. The trees stood like drooping sentinels, their dark branches bowed down with snow. The muffled stream gurgled eerily. The freezing air seemed hard to breathe. Ahead the Mountain loomed, huge and menacing.

Rowan fixed his eyes on the ground, trying to think of nothing. The medallion grew warm. Unwillingly he raised his hand to it.

Learn what it is to be what I am.

He heard the sound of splashing water and looked up. Through the trees he saw ... saw three figures in bukshah skin cloaks, kneeling beside a small pool at the foot of a sheer cliff. As he watched, one figure straightened, screwing the cap on a dripping water flask. Then it stilled and suddenly looked over its shoulder, straight at Rowan.

Like looking in a mirror. But the dark, anxious eyes were unfocused, searching ...

"Ah, this is where the stream begins!"

It was Norris's voice. Rowan blinked. The figures ahead shimmered and disappeared. Now only the cliff remained. Water gushed from a black hole near the cliff's base, splashing into a deep, round pool that was only partly iced over.

Norris pulled his water flask from his belt, and went to fill it. Rowan followed, but remained standing as Shaaran knelt beside her brother to fill her own flask.

"What is wrong, Rowan?" Norris demanded, staring up at him. "You look as if you have seen a ghost!"

It would be madness not to fill my flask, just to prove that the vision was not a picture of the future, Rowan thought. There is no fighting this. I was foolish to try.

Wearily he dropped to his knees and bent to let his flask fill to the brim. As he straightened he could not resist glancing back at the place where he had stood only minutes before. Of course he saw nothing—nothing but a mass of black trunks, dark, snow-laden branches and the tracks winding back towards the village.

Then his eye caught a flicker of colour in the sky above the trees—a flash of bright yellow, startling against the grey. The flash came again. Something was swooping towards them, moving fast. With a sharp cry of warning Rowan jumped up, reaching for his knife.

"What is it?" cried Shaaran in terror.

But already the vivid yellow shape was billowing above them. Then it was folding in on itself and sinking downward. And Rowan was gasping with astonishment to see, hanging beneath it, a lithe figure swathed in a bukshah skin cloak.

It was Zeel of the Travellers.

* * *

Rowan stared, stunned, as Zeel's soft boots hit the ground, her yellow silk kite collapsing behind her. Shaaran and Norris were exclaiming, but he could not speak.

"You are surprised to see me, Rowan!" Zeel laughed, gathering up the trailing silk and draping it over her shoulder. "Why, you gape like a Maris fish! But surely you knew I would come?"

Rowan found his voice at last. "No," he choked. "I never dreamed of it. Why—? How—?"

Zeel moved quickly to his side and clasped his hand. "The Travellers are camped just outside Maris," she said. "The Keeper of the Crystal summoned Ogden at dawn and told him of the vision he had shared with you. Ogden hastened back to our camp with the news and I left at once, to join you in your quest."

One for flight ...

The words seemed to flame in Rowan's mind. He had thought they meant that he, Shaaran or Norris would flee from danger at last. But he had been wrong, quite wrong—as he had been wrong to think that his dream-self was to be the fourth member of this ill-fated party.

The fourth member stood before him now. Ogden's adopted daughter Zeel, Rowan's friend, straight and strong, full of life.

What evil would demand our best as sacrifice? The memory of Lann's voice, shaking with anger, seemed to roar in Rowan's ears.

He felt Zeel's hand tighten on his.

"I flew over your people marching towards the coast along a strange black road, Rowan," she said. "I found your village deserted except for the old warrior Lann, and the woman Bronden deep in a frozen sleep. I learned that you, Shaaran and Norris had gone alone to the Mountain, following the tracks of the bukshah. Rowan, why did you not call me before this?"

"There is—great peril ..." Rowan began haltingly.

"I know that!" Zeel cried. "Why else am I here?"

"But I thought that Travellers could not survive the cold of the inland winter!" exclaimed Norris. "And I have heard that for Travellers the Mountain is forbidden!" His face was furrowed with anxiety. He knew Zeel from the adventure in the land of the Zebak, and very much admired her.

"That is true." Zeel grinned, her white teeth dazzling in her brown face. "But have you forgotten, Norris? I am not Traveller born. I was a Zebak infant—a foundling washed up on this land's shore and adopted by Ogden long ago. I can do what other Travellers cannot. I can climb the Mountain if I must. And I can survive bitter cold, though"—she shivered, drawing the cloak more closely about her— "though never have I felt such cold as this. I confess I am glad of the strange garment your old Lann gave me."

Thoughtfully she smoothed the shaggy fur. "Lann has changed very much. Once it would have enraged her to think that a Traveller— let alone a Zebak—might wear a Rin warrior cloak. But she made me take it. She said it had been waiting for me."

"That is because Sheba's rhyme said four souls would follow the beasts," Rowan muttered. "But Zeel, the rhyme speaks also of death, and sacrifice."

Zeel nodded, and the last traces of her smile disappeared. "I know," she said. "The rhyme passed from your mind to the Keeper's with the vision. As soon as I heard it, I knew that I was destined to join you and to share your fate, whatever it might be."

"No!" The word burst from Rowan's lips like a groan of pain.

Zeel drew herself up. "The land is under threat. Why should Rin alone make sacrifice, if sacrifice there must be? I am here of my own free will, with the Keeper's thanks and Ogden's blessing, to represent the Maris people and the Travellers. I rejoice that by an accident of birth I was the only choice that could be made. I rejoice that my kite could bring me to you quickly."

Her pale blue eyes swept across Shaaran's fearful face, and Norris's excited one, then returned to Rowan.

"We are four quarters of a whole," she said. "Each of us has a part to play in this. Each of us is needed. We do not yet understand how or why. But we will find out soon enough. And then … what will be, will be."

* * *

The bukshah tracks continued around the base of the Mountain until the cliffs of the eastern face gave way to tumbled masses of barren, snow-covered rocks on the southern side. And there the trail turned sharply inward and began to climb.

The companions halted and a great silence enfolded them. Nothing moved. Not a breath of wind stirred the freezing air. The Mountain brooded above them, waiting.

"At last!" exclaimed Norris, rubbing his hands with relish. "Here the real test begins!"

Rowan glanced at him, wondering. Norris's eyes held no trace of fear. His head was high, his strong shoulders thrown back. His mouth was set with grim determination.

So Lann must have looked, preparing to do battle with the Zebak, long ago, Rowan thought. Norris is a true child of Rin. Strong. Fearless. A warrior.

Then Rowan felt a movement beside him and looked around. Shaaran, too, was staring at the Mountain. But her delicate face was filled with dread. Desperately she clung to the box of silks, pressing it hard against her body to still her trembling hands.

Rowan thought of the pictures within the box—the paintings full of colour, life and movement. He thought of Shaaran's hand deftly moving the slim brush over silk, creating truth and beauty as her ancestors had done for centuries.

And with a jolt he remembered that Shaaran was also a true child of the people of Rin. Not the Rin people as they were now, but as they had been centuries ago, in the land of the Zebak, when artists and warriors lived side by side, and gentleness was valued as highly as strength. Before the strong ones were taken away.

And suddenly, in the terrible, waiting stillness, it was as though the parts of a puzzle fell into place.

Four souls ...

Four quarters of a whole ...

Shaaran and Norris, who were living proof of the story the silks told.

He, Rowan, who had brought them to the valley.

And Zeel, representing all those who had helped him do it.

We have offended the Mountain ...
An icy finger touched his heart.

* * *

The bukshah had picked their way between the rocks, making a narrow path that twisted and turned. With Rowan leading, Norris and Shaaran following him and Zeel bringing up the rear, the companions followed the trail.

It was hard and awkward work, especially for Shaaran, and for Norris, who was badly hampered by his injured leg. But neither of them asked for rest, and neither Rowan nor Zeel suggested it. The light was slowly fading, and all of them felt in their bones that this brutal maze was no place to be when dusk fell. So grimly they pushed on, always climbing, and always moving west.

Gradually the rocks grew larger, rising high above them, blocking their view of the way ahead. And at last the path was only a narrow, zig-zagging track lying deep between sheer black cliffs, and there was no way to go but forward or back.

They crept along in the gloom. The way grew narrower till the sky was just a slit of dull light far above them. The rocky walls that hemmed them in were marked by strange, long scratches at shoulder height. Rowan realised at last that these must have been made by the horns of the bukshah as the beasts pushed their way along the narrow path.

The medallion at his throat seemed to throb in time with his heart. His pack dragged at his shoulders, heavier by the moment.

"I do not like this." Zeel's voice echoed eerily. "What if we are being drawn into a trap? If something comes for us here there will be no escape."

Norris mumbled agreement. Shaaran's breath was sobbing in her throat. But Rowan barely heard them. He had turned a corner and suddenly his whole attention was riveted on something only he could see. Not far ahead, the passage ended in a rocky archway. Beyond the archway, strange blue light glowed. And within the light, something was moving.

Rowan froze, squinting at the wavering shape. Then his heart seemed to leap into his throat as he saw the swirl of first one long, heavy cloak, then another, and realised what the shape was.

Cloaked figures were walking ahead, walking in the blue light. They were one behind the other, heads bowed, pressed so closely together that at first they had seemed one creature. They were moving forward, very fast.

And they were afraid. Rowan could feel their fear as if it was his own.

Make haste! Stay close. Do not look ...

His skin prickling, hardly aware of what he was doing, Rowan opened his mouth to cry out. But before he could make a sound, the figures had vanished.

Rowan slumped against the cliff face on one side of the pathway, jamming his shoulder against the icy rock to keep himself upright. His knees were weak. His heart was still thudding with fear. The archway gaped ahead, blue light glowing. He could hear Shaaran, Norris and Zeel's exclamations as they caught up with him and they, too, saw the light. But he could not speak.

Clearly there was something fearful on the other side of the archway. He dug his gloved fingers into the hard rock to still their shaking.

"What is it?" Shaaran cried. "Rowan, what is that place? What must we do?"

And suddenly the medallion was scorching hot. Wincing with pain, Rowan clutched at it, trying to lift it away from his skin. But to his amazement it would not move. It seemed fastened where it lay, and the more he pulled at it, the more it clung to him, and the hotter it became.

He saw his companions turning to him in alarm as he cried out. He saw them reaching for him as he slid to his knees, tearing at his throat. But they could do nothing for him, nothing. For now it was as if the thing on his neck was sinking into his flesh. It was burning, burning, and his throat was filling with what felt like red-hot coals, filling to bursting till he was choking on fire.

He tried to scream, but as his dry lips gaped open there was no scream. Instead he felt the choking lumps of fire rise from his throat into his mouth and spill out into the freezing air. Even in his agony he was stunned to realise that they were not burning coals at all, but words—words that burst from him in a hoarse, grating voice he barely recognised as his own.

> *"Within this vale the blind are wise.*
> *Horrors lurk behind your eyes.*
> *The cure is water from a well*
> *Where hate and anger do not dwell."*

When the last word had been uttered, Rowan pitched forward into the snow, and knew no more.

11 – The Blind are Wise

Rowan came to himself slowly and painfully. His head was throbbing. He felt dizzy and sick. He could feel a soft hand patting his cheek, and could hear voices calling him, but he did not want to open his eyes. He wanted nothing more than to sleep, sleep forever. But the voices would not let him rest.

"Rowan, wake!" That was Zeel's voice, urgent and commanding. "We cannot stay here!"

"He is bewitched!" That was Norris, almost shouting. "Those words were not his! And that voice ... that was not—"

"Rowan, open your eyes." A gentler voice, Shaaran's voice, close to his ear. "Rowan, the bukshah need you. We must follow them. Remember?"

The bukshah ...

Memory swept through Rowan's mind and with a shuddering jolt he was wide awake. His eyes flew open. He clutched at his throat. Beneath his clothing the skin was smooth and undamaged, the medallion dangling harmlessly from its cord. He struggled to his feet, helped by six eager hands.

"What happened?" demanded Norris, clearly very shaken by what he had just seen and heard. "You began raving, words that had no meaning, Rowan, and your eyes rolled back—" He broke off with a shudder.

"The medallion ..." Rowan's voice was choked and husky. He cleared his throat and tried again. "Shaaran asked a question, and the medallion gave me the words to answer it. I cannot explain—"

"Do not try," Zeel said sharply. "We have our advice and our warning. There is danger beyond the archway. We know what we must do to protect ourselves against it. That is all that matters for now. We must move on, and quickly. The afternoon is waning."

Rowan nodded and, without saying anything more, began trudging unsteadily towards the glimmering blue light. Shaaran, her eyes dark with fear, crept after him.

Norris followed, continually glancing back at Zeel, searching her watchful face for answers to his confusion. At last, as the archway yawned ahead, filling their view, he could keep silence no longer.

"Why do you say we know what to do?" he burst out. "We know nothing!"

"Did you not listen, Norris?" Zeel snapped. "The rhyme told us that in the vale the blind are wise. Surely that means that what we do not see will not harm us."

"What?" Norris exclaimed. "Are we to walk into the unknown with our eyes closed?"

"We cannot do that," Rowan said, without turning around. "But we must make ourselves as blind as we can. Once we enter the blue light, we must put our heads down and follow the path, looking neither right nor left—at least until we reach this mysterious well that is a place of safety."

As he spoke, he was remembering the vision he had seen, remembering the cloaked figures walking quickly, close together, their bent heads hooded.

He shuddered as again he felt their fear.

Make haste! Stay close. Do not look ...

The archway was before him now. He stopped, steadying himself against the rock. The blue light seemed to swirl before his eyes like coloured mist. And now he could see the gleam of ice. The place beyond the arch was studded with great, twisted ice columns that rose from the earth like trees!

The ground was bare of snow. So the vale was covered. It was a cave—or perhaps a vast tunnel through the rock of the Mountain.

"It seems to me that only a fool would march through an evil place without keeping watch," Norris was muttering. "What if the rhyme is a snare?"

"It is not a snare!" Zeel flashed. "And *you* are a fool, Norris, to suggest it."

Norris flushed dark red and squared his heavy shoulders. "Perhaps

I *am* a fool," he mumbled. "My grandfather always thought I was, I know, because I had no talent for painting, and no ear for music, and because I relished fighting. But I saved his life in the land of the Zebak, many times, by being wary, by knowing an enemy when I saw one, and by being ready to fight, as he and Shaaran were not."

"That is true," Shaaran said in a low voice. "Without Norris we would never have survived."

Zeel frowned. "I beg your pardon, Norris," she said awkwardly. "I spoke without thinking. You are right to be wary. You have not had as much experience of these rhymes of prophecy as Rowan and I have had. But, believe me, they can be trusted."

Norris met her level gaze and nodded slowly. "Very well," he said. "But if we are to walk blind, let us at least stay close together so that we cannot be separated."

"That would be wise," Zeel agreed. She moved closer to him and put her hand on his shoulder. Blushing even more deeply, this time with satisfaction, Norris took hold of Shaaran's shoulder. Shaaran took hold of Rowan's.

"Heads down," Rowan said, and heard Zeel murmur a blessing. He took a deep breath and moved through the archway, his companions shuffling behind him.

The blue light closed in around them. And with it came the fear. Fear seeped into Rowan's mind like freezing water, chilling his blood, pooling in his heart. His skin prickled with awareness that they were not alone, that something here was aware of them, something filled with malice.

He felt Shaaran's hand tighten on his shoulder, heard her gasping breaths, and knew that she, too, was gripped by terror.

"Keep your head down," he whispered. But even as he forced the words from his dry lips, his urge to raise his own eyes was becoming almost overwhelming.

Spires of ice loomed at the edges of his vision like blue shadows. The bukshah's hoofs had made only faint marks on the hard ground, so that their narrow, winding trail was almost invisible. Many times Rowan was forced to hesitate before cautiously moving on.

Then the trail seemed to disappear altogether. A pillar of ice lay directly ahead, and Rowan could not tell if he should turn left or right.

He stood paralysed, desperately searching the misty ground. His forehead was beaded with freezing sweat. He was terrified of making the wrong decision. The thought of becoming lost, wandering aimlessly in this fearful icy maze, filled him with dread.

He felt Shaaran press against his back, as if she was being crowded from behind.

"I have lost sight of the trail," he called. "Wait—"

He broke off as Norris cursed ferociously and Zeel gave a long, drawn-out hiss.

Rowan felt a spurt of anger. Did they not know how hard this was? Let *them* try to lead, then.

"I am doing my best!" he shouted. "Be patient!"

There was a roar of baffled rage, then a weird, high cry, and suddenly Shaaran was pushed into Rowan's back so violently that he was almost thrown off his feet. Rowan shouted, staggering, fighting to stay upright as Shaaran clutched at him blindly.

Behind them someone fell heavily, crashing onto the hard ground. Rowan felt his cloak pulled and twisted, and groaned aloud as he realised that Shaaran had turned to look over her shoulder.

Shaaran screamed piercingly, screamed his name.

Within this vale the blind are wise ...

The words rang in Rowan's ears, but he could no longer listen.

He swung around, thrusting the shrieking girl aside and partly behind him.

And, in horror, he saw that they had walked into a trap. Two figures were grappling on the ground. They were fighting savagely, rolling between twisted columns of ice. Blue mist swirled about them, veiling them, so Rowan could not see whether it was Zeel or Norris who had been attacked. But he could see the bright blade of a dagger. He could see spatters of scarlet blood on the ice.

Fumbling for his own knife, he shrugged his pack from his shoulders and sprang forward, shouting. One of the struggling figures threw the other heavily aside and leaped up to face him.

The breath caught in Rowan's throat and he drew back, his heart pounding with shock. Snarling ferociously before him was a Zebak guard, her face smeared with blood, the tattooed black line which marked all her people running like a frowning furrow down the centre of her forehead.

The Zebak raised her dagger and sprang at him. Instinctively Rowan blocked her strike, seizing the wrist of her dagger hand, holding the weapon back. Her weight threw him back against an ice pillar, which shattered like glass. His own knife fell from his hand and spun away.

They rolled, shards of ice splintering beneath them. He could feel the Zebak's hot breath on his face. He could feel her hatred. Her dagger gleamed above him, its blood-smeared point aimed at his throat. His hands and wrists were strong from his work with bukshah—they were his only strength—but already they were trembling with the strain. For how long could he hold the dagger back? How long ...?

In the background, someone was screaming. Shaaran. Shaaran was screaming frantically for Zeel. Why did Zeel not answer? Why did she not come to help him?

And suddenly Rowan knew. Zeel did not come because she was dead. As, no doubt, was Norris, who had been the last in line. This fiend had killed them both.

And that had been the Zebak plan. To pick the four off one by one as they shuffled blindly through the mist. To ensure they would never reach their goal, never fulfil the prophecy.

And why? Rowan's mind was working like lightning. Why? Because the Zebak wanted this land, the land they had failed to conquer, to be doomed. They wanted its people punished for daring to defy them.

Scarlet rage blazed through him. His hands tightened on the Zebak's wrists and with a strength he had not known he possessed he heaved her away from him, smashing her dagger-hand against the jagged edge of the shattered pillar.

She shrieked with pain and rage. The dagger spun away. Rowan dived for it, seized it ...

And heard a strange sound.

He looked up and saw, rising directly in front of him, something dark and hideous. It was a squat, twisted tree. Its thick, stubby branches, tipped with clumps of dull purple leaves, were heaving and thrashing. Its fat white roots were already snaking hungrily towards him.

Rowan's blood ran cold. This was a tree of Unrin—a tree with a taste for human flesh, a tree like those which had long ago smothered the Valley of Gold.

Devil trees, Zeel had called them. She and Rowan had fought them together in the Pit of Unrin, had nearly died in their loathsome clutches. But the Mountain was the trees' natural habitat, and this one was here, reaching out for him, greedy for him ...

Shuddering with disgust, Rowan scrambled backwards, trying to keep his feet clear of those hungry, snake-like roots.

His cloak was tangling around his legs, hampering him as he tried to get up. He could hear Shaaran shrieking, sobbing wildly, and with a surge of panic he realised that she was running towards him. Her cries were growing louder. He could hear her steps, very near.

"No, Shaaran! Keep away!" he roared, slashing at the roots as they struck at him.

His mind was racing. By now the Zebak must be clambering to her feet, her rage fanned to white heat by the pain of her injuries.

She had lost her dagger, but she would attack with her bare hands if she had to, injured or not. And she was strong, very strong. She would do anything to complete the task she had been given. She would snap Shaaran's slender neck like a twig. She would wrest her dagger from Rowan at last, and kill him too.

But ... Rowan's heart gave a great leap. The devil tree! The Zebak would have no way of knowing how dangerous it was. If he could lure her into its clutches ...

He risked a glance behind him, to see if his way was clear. And his heart seemed to stop as he saw, rearing above him, a twisting white shape with gaping, blue-lined jaws and wicked, needle-sharp teeth.

12 – The Well

Dagger raised, Rowan stared up at the ice creeper, waiting for death. He was beyond terror now, beyond sorrow. His mind was wiped clean of every feeling but one: pure hatred. If he was to die, if all was lost, he would take as many of his enemies with him as he could.

He saw the Zebak crouched behind the beast, a shard of razor-sharp ice clutched in her bleeding hand. He felt a devil tree root seize his ankle, gripping it like an iron band.

So. Let them all fight over him, and kill one another in the battle.

He braced himself against the grip of the devil tree. He laughed at the Zebak, taunting her, daring her to come closer. Then he looked up at the ice creeper once more. Above the hideous jaws the creature's head was gleaming, as though some vile liquid was oozing from its skin. Rowan's face twisted with loathing.

The creature gave a strange, hissing gasp. It bent closer, its eyeless head nodding closer to him, closer …

Rowan tightened his grip on the dagger, preparing to strike. Then—astonishingly, he felt a splash of something warm on his upturned face.

And instantly the ice creeper coiled, shrank, vanished. In its place was Shaaran—Shaaran, bending over him, the box of silks clutched in her arms, tears streaming down her cheeks.

Rowan gaped at her, thunderstruck. The dagger fell from his hand. Then his heart seemed to leap into his throat as he saw a shadow rise behind the weeping girl—a shadow wielding a deadly blade of ice.

The Zebak!

"Beware!" he shouted. He grabbed Shaaran's arms and pulled her down, down and to one side. The plunging blade missed her by a hair, and her attacker pitched forward, stumbling over their rolling bodies and falling heavily to the ground.

And only then did Rowan see that the attacker was ... Zeel! He blinked, unbelieving. But there was no mistake.

There was no Zebak warrior. There never had been. It was Zeel who was crawling to her knees before him, one hand bleeding, the other fumbling on the ground for a weapon.

Stunned by shock, horror and joy, Rowan gave a choked cry. At the same moment Zeel's hand closed on his knife, which had been lying half hidden behind an ice column. She staggered to her feet. Her glazed eyes focused on him. Her face creased into lines of loathing.

"Die, ishkin!" she hissed, hurling herself forward.

"Zeel, no!" Rowan shouted. But even as the words left his lips, even as he jerked back and the knife slashed clumsily through the place where he had been, he understood.

Horrors lurk behind your eyes ...

Frantically he cursed himself for his stupidity, for not thinking more carefully about the words of the rhyme.

The line said *behind* your eyes, not before them! he raged at himself. And what is behind your eyes? Your mind, you fool! Your mind! *That* is the treachery of this place. It shows you the enemies that live in your memory. Zeel is not seeing you as you are! When she looks at you she sees an ishkin, a monster from the land of the Zebak. Just as you saw *her* as a Zebak guard, and Shaaran as an ice creeper. Enemies you hate as well as fear ...

With a start, he glanced down at his imprisoned ankle. Instead of a devil tree root, he now saw Norris's gloved hand holding him in an iron grip, Norris's arm outstretched stiffly, Norris lying face down on the ground, still as death.

"Rowan!" Shaaran screamed. Rowan looked up just in time to see her throw herself towards him as Zeel struck again.

And the next instant the knife aimed at his heart had plunged into the wooden box Shaaran held before him like a shield. The side of the box splintered. The precious rolls of silk began sliding out, spilling and rolling on the hard ground.

Shaaran gave an agonised cry. Zeel seized her and threw her violently to the ground.

"So, you would feed me to the ishkin, would you, guard?" she hissed at Shaaran. "You would like to see me skinned and dragged under the earth, like my friends? Well, no doubt you will have your wish. But you are coming with me, alive or dead!" Her bloodstained hands moved to Shaaran's neck, and tightened.

"No, Zeel, no!" Shaaran sobbed, clawing feebly at the strangling fingers.

Rowan struggled to pull Zeel back, to break her hold. It was useless. His mind was roaring with horror. Must he use Zeel's own dagger to save Shaaran? Was it to come to that?

"What—what is wrong with her?" Shaaran choked.

"She thinks you are a Zebak guard," Rowan said. "As I thought *she* was, until—"

He broke off.

Until what? What had broken the illusion? Why had he been cured so suddenly, so completely? What had ...?

The final words of the rhyme were suddenly ringing in his ears.

The cure is water from a well
Where hate and anger do not dwell.

Understanding struck him like a bolt of lightning. "Shaaran!" he shouted. "Wipe your eyes, then touch her face! Now! Make haste!"

It was typical of Shaaran that she did not question him, did not hesitate. She lifted her hands from her throat, smeared the tears from her eyes, then placed her fingers on Zeel's cheeks.

And instantly Zeel blinked and lurched back, her face showing her shock. Her hands fell from Shaaran's neck, and she stared at them as if they did not belong to her.

"Zeel!" shouted Rowan, filled with joy.

She turned to him blankly. Then, as memory flooded through her, she looked down at Shaaran lying gasping amid a tangle of silk.

"What ... have I done?" she breathed, aghast.

"Do not grieve," Shaaran managed to say, crawling to her knees. "It was not your fault, Zeel. Truly it was not."

"You did nothing that I did not do, Zeel," Rowan said. "And Norris. Shaaran was the only one of us who—"

A low groan made him turn in alarm.

Norris was waking. He lifted his head and opened his eyes. He looked full into Rowan's face. His eyes darkened, and he bared his teeth. His hand tightened on Rowan's ankle.

With a cry Shaaran began crawling painfully towards her brother.

Swiftly Rowan reached out, swept his fingers over the girl's wet cheeks, and smoothed the tears onto Norris's frowning brow. Norris shuddered all over. Then the frown lines vanished from his face, leaving it smooth, bewildered and almost childlike.

"I—I was dreaming," he mumbled. "Shaaran, you are alive! And Rowan! But I thought—"

Abruptly his face became alert, and he began struggling to rise, blood flowing freely from a terrible knife wound in his side.

"Norris, do not move!" Shaaran cried. But already Norris had gained his feet and was looking around wildly.

"There is a Zebak guard here!" he hissed. "She killed Zeel and took her place, somewhere on the trail. I blame myself. I heard nothing! I only knew when I turned to speak to Zeel, after we stopped. The fiend attacked me—we fought ..."

He tried to straighten, groaned, and clasped his side. "And there is a fighting grach here, too—huge! A killer! I had hold of it—trying to keep it back from you—but now I cannot see it! Rowan, Shaaran, get behind me. Where is my sword? My sword!"

Rowan saw the sword lying on the ground. He picked it up and thrust it into Norris's hand. "Here it is, but you do not need it, Norris," he said. "There is no one for you to fight. No guard, no grach." He sighed. "Just as there was no ice creeper, no devil tree ..."

"No ishkin," Zeel added soberly, limping over to join them. "They were illusions, Norris. We almost killed one another, fighting our memories."

Norris swayed, shaking his head in confusion.

"But I saw nothing!" Shaaran said huskily, one hand at her bruised throat. "I saw only you—all of you—attacking one another. And your faces ..." A shadow seemed to cross her own face, and she shuddered.

"You saw nothing because you have no enemies to see, Shaaran," Rowan said.

Shaaran almost laughed. "Why, that is ridiculous!" she cried. "I have more fears than all the rest of you put together!"

"You *fear* many things, but you *hate* nothing," Rowan said. "There is not a person or a creature you would willingly destroy, even to save yourself. Is that not true?"

Shaaran stared at him, her face colouring faintly as though, somehow, she was ashamed.

"Grandfather was the same," Norris mumbled. "And our mother and father too. Protecting them was an almost hopeless task."

"That I can well imagine," Zeel said fervently. "But it seems that this time the situation was reversed."

Norris looked bewildered.

He saw nothing of what happened, Rowan thought. He still does not understand.

"Shaaran saved us all," he told Norris. "Remember the last lines of the rhyme? The well free of hate and anger was not a real well at all, but Shaaran's overflowing heart. And the healing water was her tears."

"*One to weep,*" said Zeel.

Shaaran's blush deepened.

Norris scowled. "Then why did the rhyme not say so plainly?" he growled. "Why should we be tricked and puzzled by a riddle?"

"Perhaps because life itself is a riddle," said Zeel, "and as we journey through it we must all solve the puzzle for ourselves." She spoke lightly, but her eyes were thoughtful.

Shaaran had begun collecting the scattered rolls of silk. "I cannot see the bukshah tracks at all now," she said nervously. "I fear we are lost."

But Rowan could see his pack still lying where he had dropped it, not too far away.

"All is well!" he exclaimed, pointing. "That is where I left the path!"

"Thank the heavens," sighed Zeel. "Then let us bind our wounds, mend the box of silks somehow, and leave this accursed place as fast as we can. Its very air sickens me."

* * *

Within the hour the companions were slowly threading their way through the columns of ice once more, this time with Zeel in the lead. It had not taken long for her keen eyes to pick up the trail that Rowan had been unable to find.

All four of them were hurt, but Norris was in the worst state. His injured leg had been further damaged in the fight, and the wound in his side was deep and painful.

But was his suffering the only reason for his heavy silence? Rowan wondered. Or did the real trouble lie somewhere within?

For Norris's face was like thunder. He did not join in the chorus of feeble cheers that greeted the sight of another rocky archway ahead—an archway through which a blur of dull grey could be seen. He did not look up as the companions struggled at last out of the vale of horrors and into the open air.

This does not bode well, Rowan thought. And as he looked about him, and recognised the bleak, steep, snow-covered slope that lay beyond the archway, his heart sank.

A bitter wind swept around them. The light was very dim. The bukshah tracks showed dark on the snow, climbing upward until they were lost among tumbled rocks. Beyond the rocks was a wall of towering black cliffs. Above the cliffs there was nothing to be seen but swirling mist.

Three figures, trudging upward in single file ...

This was the place of his dream. The first dream of all.

But the dream will not come true, Rowan told himself. It *cannot* come true. Norris and Shaaran and I are not alone. Zeel is with us.

He realised that Zeel was speaking to him. "We must find shelter, and soon," she was murmuring. "A place where we can light a fire."

Three figures huddled in fear around a fire ...

"The cave ..." Rowan mumbled.

"Cave?" Zeel exclaimed. "What cave?"

Rowan shook his head to clear it. "I only meant—there—there must be a cave, surely, in those cliffs above," he stammered.

Zeel considered him with her head on one side. "Why are you so certain?" she asked.

Rowan hesitated. He could see that Zeel suspected he knew more than he was telling. In one way he longed to confide in her. But he had not admitted to his terrible dreams before, so how could he do so now, in this bleak place, with Shaaran and Norris hovering on the edge of despair?

Zeel shook her head impatiently. "Keep your secrets then!" she snapped. "But if you *know* there is a cave, Rowan, it is madness not to tell me. We are in danger! Where are we to go? How are we to hide?"

And instantly the medallion grew hot. In horror Rowan snatched at it, consumed by the memory of that burning pain, that terrifying feeling of being taken over by something other than himself.

"Oh, Rowan! I did not mean to ... oh, I am sorry!" Zeel's cry rang in his ears. "Rowan, do not fight it! Let it ..."

Her voice faded away.

Do not fight it.

Rowan resisted the urge to pull the burning medallion away from his skin. Instead he pressed it closer. The heat began deep in his throat, scorching and swelling, but he forced himself not to choke. And so the strange words flowed from him, not easily, but not agonisingly either, out into the icy air.

> *"Refuge waits on high ahead.*
> *Climb the ladder of the dead.*
> *Hide within the rocky walls.*
> *Be still while icy darkness falls."*

13 – The Climb

As the last word of the rhyme left his lips, Rowan fell to his knees in the snow, sick and dizzy. Slowly the world seemed to steady and he looked up. Norris was staring at him dully. Shaaran was staring too, her hand pressed to her mouth. And Zeel …

Zeel was unfolding her kite.

"No, Zeel!" Rowan cried in panic. He struggled to his feet, staggering as fresh waves of dizziness swept over him.

Zeel glanced at him. "I did not mean to put you through that pain, Rowan, but at least I can make it worthwhile," she said. "The rhyme spoke of 'rocky walls'. There must indeed be a cave up ahead. I will search for it from the air while you begin to climb."

"No!" Rowan argued desperately. "One of your hands is injured, Zeel. And it is too dangerous to fly here. If the wind changes you will be dashed against the cliffs!"

Zeel raised her head. "You forget," she said quietly. "I am a Travellers' Forerunner. My task in life is to fly ahead of the tribe in all weathers, seeking shelter, watching for danger. My skill can aid us now. I would not risk the extra weight of a passenger, but alone I can do it, one-handed if I must."

She lifted the kite so that the yellow silk billowed above her. "I will see you again, Rowan," she said.

Rowan recognised the words. They were used by Travellers farewelling one another in perilous times.

"I will see you again," he replied. Zeel grinned at him, turned her face to the wind, and was swept up and away.

For a moment Rowan watched the kite swooping above them, a splash of brightness against a background of white, black and grey. Then he turned back to Shaaran and Norris.

They were both still watching Zeel, Shaaran with fearful wonder,

Norris in despair. The young man was swaying where he stood, his face lined with strain, his shoulders bowed.

Rowan's heart sank. "We should light torches before we move on," he said. "We have a long climb ahead, and at any moment …" His voice trailed off as he met Shaaran's terrified eyes. He did not have to remind her of what might even now be sliding towards them beneath the snow.

Norris said nothing. Even when Rowan thrust a flaming torch into his hand, he did not speak, just turned and began to limp away, following the bukshah tracks.

Shaaran glanced at Rowan, her eyes filled now with anxiety.

"Let him go," Rowan said. "Just follow." Dread weighed him down. He knew what was going to happen next, but he was power-less to prevent it.

Learn what it is to be what I am.

In single file the three trudged upward. In Rowan's mind was a vivid picture of what they must look like. The tall, limping figure in the lead; the small, fragile figure next, clutching a long wooden box; he himself last of all …

Unable to resist the temptation, he turned and looked behind him. He saw nothing but snowy wastes, black rock and the archway, glimmering blue.

"Rowan, what is it?"

Shaaran had stopped, and was staring at him in alarm.

Rowan shrugged, determined to say nothing. He saw that Norris had also stopped and turned. Norris's eyes were haunted, but he did not speak.

This at least is not the same as it was in the dream, Rowan thought, with a flash of hope. By holding my tongue, I have changed things. Perhaps …

"Let us move on," Shaaran urged. "Soon it will be dark."

Norris's lips stretched into a ghastly smile. "What does that matter?" he said suddenly. "Whether we stop here or higher on the Mountain, whether it is night or day, we are doomed."

His stick and his torch fell from his hands and he crumpled to the ground.

Shaaran ran to him and began pulling his arms, calling his name. He merely turned his face away from her and burrowed deeper into the snow, like a child unwilling to rise from a cosy bed.

"Rowan, help me!" Shaaran screamed.

Rowan snatched up the fallen torch and forced himself to think.

I saw us all in the cave together, he reminded himself. I know that somehow Norris can survive this—that we can all survive it. But I also know that pleading with him and reasoning with him will not make him move. There must be another way.

But what other way? He and Shaaran did not have the strength to carry Norris, or even to drag him more than a short distance up this steep slope.

"Get up, Norris, oh, please!" Shaaran was crying. She was kneeling by her brother now, half-buried in snow herself.

"Let me sleep," Norris mumbled. "This is the end."

This is the end ...

Rowan saw Shaaran cover her mouth with her hand to muffle her cry of despair.

This was where his dream had ended. What now?

He threw himself down beside Norris. "It is not the end, unless you make it so, my friend," he said evenly.

Norris heaved a deep, shuddering sigh. Then he rolled onto his back, and looked up at Rowan.

"It *is* the end," he said. "We all had our part to play in this quest. One to weep, one to fight, one to dream, one for flight. Is that not so?"

Rowan nodded, and waited.

"Shaaran is the one to weep," Norris said, staring up at the darkening sky. "Her tears saved us all in the vale of horrors. You are the one to dream, Rowan, for you wear the medallion and say the rhymes. Zeel is the one for flight, as we have just seen. And I ..."

His voice broke, and he closed his eyes.

"Go on!" Rowan urged, fighting back the guilt that had flooded through him at the mention of dreaming. "And you ... you are the one to fight?"

"Of course!" Norris burst out, his eyes flying open. "I thought I was destined to be your protector. I was so sure of it that I did not even try to prevent Shaaran coming on this journey. I thought I was going to save you both."

Shaaran gave a choked sob. Norris's eyes slid in her direction, then immediately slid away.

"I was so proud of the part I was fated to play," he muttered. "I, who was always my grandfather's despair, was going to prove at last that I was a hero, not a fool."

He gave a snort of bitter laughter.

"Norris—" Rowan began. But Norris was not listening.

"When the time came for fighting, how joyfully I rushed into the attack!" he went on, his face twisted with pain and shame. "But then—then I found that I had not been fighting enemies at all, but the friends I had sworn to defend. I had been a heedless fool, yet again. And now I am nothing but a wounded, useless burden."

"Zeel and I also fell victim to the visions!" Rowan exclaimed. "You cannot blame yourself for what happened."

"I can, for I was the one who turned. I was the one who began it all, playing the great guard and protector," said Norris. "And now our quest is done. I realised it when I saw Zeel launch her kite. Weeping, fighting, dreaming and flight. All four parts have now been played."

Rowan's stomach turned over.

"And my part," Norris continued, his voice sinking lower, "my part, far from saving us, has been to leave us weak and helpless, easy prey for whatever fate the Mountain has in store. I have been nothing but a pawn in a wicked game."

His eyes were burning with bitter tears. "Leave me. I do not want to live through what is to come. The evil thing that brought us to this place has triumphed."

He turned back into the snow, covering his head with his arms and drawing up his knees to his chest.

"Norris!" shouted Rowan, shaking him. "Even if you are right—even if we have been led by some evil force into a trap—we cannot just lie down and die!"

But this time Norris did not stir.

There was a strange, high call from somewhere above. Zeel! Rowan clambered to his feet and looked up. The yellow kite was hovering near the cliff face, one side dipping slightly as though pointing to a place below.

He felt a stab of hope. Zeel had found the cave. All they needed to do was reach it, and there would be warmth, rest, some sort of safety.

But Norris lay like a log in the snow, binding them to this bleak and dangerous hillside. Norris, of all people! He who was so admired by all in Rin for his strength and courage.

Rowan felt anger rise within him. He knew it was unworthy and unfair, but for an instant he let it possess him. If Lann could see Norris now! Or Bronden! What would they do?

And suddenly he knew. Lann and Bronden would treat Norris as they would expect to be treated themselves. They would know by instinct what would pierce the shell of despair which had enclosed him, for he was like them.

Rowan took a deep breath, and steeled himself.

"Get up!" he said, and kicked Norris's shoulder contemptuously.

Shaaran shrieked.

Rowan ignored her, and kicked again.

Norris opened his eyes. "Leave me be," he groaned.

"Coward!" Rowan sneered. "You coward!"

"Rowan, how *could* you?" cried Shaaran. "He is in agony!"

But Norris's dull eyes had kindled, and his face had darkened with anger. "You call *me* a coward?" he growled.

Rowan turned away. No doubt it looked to Norris as if he was turning away in disgust. Norris could not see that his tormentor had his fingers crossed, and was holding his breath.

But Shaaran could. Her shocked eyes widened in understanding, and she fell silent.

Norris moved. Clumsily he felt for his stick. When he had it in his hand, he crawled painfully to his feet. Caked snow fell from his clothes in a heavy shower. He snatched his torch from Rowan's hand. "I will show you who is a coward," he snarled. "Keep up with me if you can!"

He staggered away, following the trail.

Shaaran and Rowan began toiling after him. No doubt he is cursing me, Rowan thought. But at least he is alive.

524   ROWAN OF THE BUKSHAH

Alive for now. Rowan pushed the unwelcome thought away, and doggedly pressed on.

The climb was long and hard. It grew colder and darker, and the wind was bitter, stinging their faces, blowing the smoke from their torches into their eyes. The way grew steeper and more winding as they neared the cliff face. Vast boulders hulked around them. The churned snow beneath their feet was icy, frozen hard into jagged lumps, and slippery as glass.

Zeel circled above their heads, watching for signs of danger— danger writhing beneath the snow, hidden in the mist that now swirled among the rocks.

At last the cliffs rose huge and dim before them. The bukshah tracks straggled off to their left, but Zeel swooped towards the right, and the three on the ground followed, floundering through deep snow. Soon the kite was hovering like a great yellow butterfly over a place where the top two-thirds of the cliff face bulged out over the rest, shadowing a dark, narrow opening in the rock.

Rowan at once recognised the opening as the cave of his dream, though without Zeel's help he would surely have passed it by. Seen from the outside, the narrow, ragged triangle seemed a mere crack in the rock. And it was not at the base of the cliff face as he had expected, but a third of the way up, just below the overhang.

Refuge waits on high ahead ...

The rhyme had spoken the literal truth. The cave was a high refuge indeed. How were they to reach it? The cliff face below it was straight and smooth, impossible to climb.

Rowan quickened his pace, passing Shaaran and Norris, almost running. When he was directly below the cave, he flattened himself against the cliff face and lifted his hand as high as he could. The tips of his fingers fell short of the opening by at least a body length.

Climb the ladder of the dead ...

"You must stand on my shoulders."

Startled, Rowan turned. Norris had come up beside him, his face drawn with pain and exhaustion.

"You first, Rowan, so that you can help Shaaran from above," Norris said. "Zeel can follow her."

"Norris, you are not fit—" Rowan began. But Norris shook his head.

"To reach the cave you must climb the ladder of the dead, so the rhyme said," he muttered. "And what am I but a dead man?"

Shaaran, still struggling towards them, heard his last words and exclaimed in horror. Norris did not turn to her. His eyes were fixed on Rowan.

"I cannot reach up to that gap, and the three of you together could not lift me," he said. "But I can be of service to you. And then perhaps—perhaps you, Zeel and Shaaran might have a chance of surviving this. It would mean so much to me to think it might be so. Rowan, I am begging you!"

Rowan could not deny him. Quickly he nodded, and with a muffled groan, Norris bent his back. Ignoring Shaaran's cry of distress, Rowan climbed onto the broad shoulders. Then, as Norris slowly straightened, he lifted his hands and grasped the base of the cave mouth.

His muscles strained as he hauled himself upward. His boots scrabbled uselessly on the smooth rock of the cliff face. But the thought of falling back onto the ground, of having caused Norris pain for nothing, gave strength to his arms. In a few moments he was sprawled, panting, on the cave floor.

The cave was gloomy but shallow. He could see well enough to tell that nothing lurked in its shadowy corners. Quickly he squirmed around so that he was facing outward again, and slid forward so that his head and shoulders protruded from the cave mouth.

Norris was bent double. Shaaran was crouched beside him, sobbing.

"Shaaran!" Rowan called, stretching out his arms to her.

But she was shaking her head. "He is in agony!" she cried. "I cannot do it!"

Rowan heard a sharp cry of warning from above. He looked up. The yellow kite was wheeling and plunging. Zeel was signalling wildly. He looked down again and his heart thudded as he saw that the thick snow further along the cliff face was moving, rising into a smooth, white drift.

Something was rushing towards Shaaran and Norris along the base of the cliff, snaking through the snow like an eel through water.

"Ice creeper!" Rowan yelled. "Shaaran! Norris! Beware!"

14 – The Cave

orris straightened. Gritting his teeth, he seized Shaaran around the waist and with a groan swung her up, up, with such tremendous force that Rowan was able to catch her around the shoulders and pull her into the cave.

They tumbled backwards onto the sandy floor. Shaaran was screaming. Rowan picked himself up and scrambled back to the entrance.

Zeel was nowhere to be seen. She must have flown up to the top of the cliff and landed there, Rowan thought dazedly. She must have feared that the ice creeper would snatch her out of the air. But Norris ...

Norris had his back to the cliff wall. The wound in his side had been torn open when he lifted Shaaran, and was again bleeding freely. He was holding all three torches before him like a shield.

"Norris!" Rowan shouted, pushing himself forward and stretching out his arms. "Take my hands!"

Norris did not even look up. "Get back!" he bellowed. "You cannot lift me. Protect yourselves. Light a fire at the cave mouth. Make haste! I will hold the thing back as long as I can, but—"

The snow at his feet bulged, then the icy surface burst open and a hideous blind head reared up, mouth agape. Norris did not flinch. He thrust the torches forward. The creeper hissed, recoiled, prepared to strike again.

Holding the screaming Shaaran back from the edge, Rowan tore new torches from his pack, and began trying to light them. His hands were shaking, and he cursed himself for his clumsiness.

Norris was shouting, jabbing with the torches. The beast was lashing in fury, its blue-shadowed maw gaping as it struck and struck again. Then it jerked as a yellow flash swept down from the cliff top and soared past its head in a flurry of heat and flame.

It was Zeel—Zeel, clinging to the kite with her good hand and brandishing a burning torch in the other. She had landed on the cliff top, certainly, but she had stayed there only long enough to coax the torch alight.

The ice creeper hissed and struck, catching the edge of the yellow silk in its teeth. The silk ripped with a high, terrible sound. The kite shuddered, tipped sideways, began slowly to flutter downward. The creeper reared and twisted towards it, ready to strike again.

Norris saw his chance, and took it. With a bellow he launched himself forward, pushing the three bunched torches straight into the beast's unprotected body.

There was a ghastly sizzling sound and a sour, hot smell. Dark blue mist gushed in a hissing roar from the beast's gaping mouth. For a moment the great body seemed to tremble in the air. Then, as Norris stumbled hurriedly out of its way, the creeper collapsed against the cliff face and lay still.

Norris stared with glazed eyes at the heap of flabby coils that reached almost to the cave mouth. He did not turn his head as Zeel came up beside him, the sad, torn fragments of her precious kite draped over her shoulder. But when she took his arm he did not argue, and he allowed her to support him as they approached the creature's body.

Zeel touched it with her foot. Its skin was already dulling and wrinkling slightly, and its flesh dented under her boot.

"You killed it," she said with respect.

"But it was only a small burn, on such a large body." Norris shook his head. "How could the creature die of it?"

"Heat must be like poison to it," said Zeel. "Like poison in its blood. Ah, how you went for it, Norris! Like a man possessed!"

"You gave me the chance I needed," he mumbled.

She shrugged. "I did what I could," she said. "But it was your strength that saved us all."

He made a small, choked sound and she glanced up at him. His eyes were strangely bright, and the taut muscles around his mouth had suddenly relaxed, leaving his face smooth and peaceful.

What did I say to make him look so? she thought. I only spoke the truth.

She puzzled over it briefly, then put it out of her mind, as she had put her grief for her kite aside, to concentrate on practical matters. Norris was staggering where he stood, and his clothes were soaked with blood. She took a firmer hold on his arm.

"Come," she said. "You have given us our ladder. Our ladder of the dead. Now we must climb it."

Together, with Rowan and Shaaran urging them on, the pair crawled upward, using the lifeless white thing as a ladder. The flabby coils slipped and oozed with every step. Zeel's jaw was set and her eyes were dark with horror. Norris was shaking all over.

In moments they had reached the cave, and were clambering inside.

As soon as he had clasped their hands in welcome, Rowan set about lighting a fire. He knew that Shaaran would care for Norris. He knew that Zeel would want to be left in peace, to mourn her kite in her own way. His task now was to make the cave safe—as safe as it could be—for the long night ahead.

* * *

As darkness deepened outside the cave, Rowan, Zeel and Shaaran boiled a little water for tea. Then they toasted bread, which they ate first with melted cheese and then with some of the honey and dried fruits Zeel had brought with her.

The fire and the warm food and drink brought comfort to their minds as well as to their bodies. Even Norris seemed to revive a little after a time, and was able to sit up, wrapped in blankets and leaning against the wall of the cave.

By unspoken agreement they did not speak of the past day, or of the future, though there was much to be said. Instead, they talked of small things—the sweet, fresh taste of the honey, past meals they had enjoyed.

Rowan talked of the salty, fishy food of the Maris. Shaaran and Norris spoke of the vegetables and fruits they had grown in the land of the Zebak. Zeel told of the Travellers' bees, carried from place to place as the tribe followed the blooming of flowers in season.

Then her voice trailed away, and Rowan suspected she was remembering that a time could be coming when there would be no more flowers, or bees, or even Travellers in the land. When there would be nothing but the cold, barren whiteness of an endless winter.

He moved restlessly, trying to put the thought from his own mind. "We had better try to sleep," he said. "I will keep the first watch."

"I will keep the second," said Zeel quickly, before Norris could speak. "Do not fail to wake me when it is time."

Soon all was quiet. The cave floor was hard, but Norris, Zeel and Shaaran were exhausted, and even their pain and fears could not keep them awake once they were curled up in their blankets.

Rowan kept watch as the long hours passed, sitting very upright by the fire, watching the dancing flames. Occasionally he added a stick to keep the fire bright, but every time he did so, he felt a pang of fear.

The bundle of sticks they carried with them was growing smaller by the hour. And if more creepers came ... if he, Zeel, Norris and Shaaran were besieged, trapped in the cave by dozens of the creatures ... what would happen?

They had food, and they had water. But these would not save them if they had no fuel.

The fire would go out. The last of the torches would burn away. Then there would be nothing to stop the ice creepers from plucking them out of the cave one by one, like lizards snatching baby birds from a nest.

Hide within the rocky walls.
Be still while icy darkness falls.

Icy darkness ...

Rowan shivered. Was this cave to be the end of the journey? Was this small hole in a freezing wall the place where they were all to die?

His heart was like a block of ice. His whole body felt numb. And then, in the silence, he heard faint sounds.

His skin crawled. He listened. The sounds came again, chilling and unmistakable. Something was writhing and scrabbling above him, on the overhang.

The sounds grew louder. Chunks of snow began to fall from the edge of the overhang, plunging past the cave entrance to the ground.

Zeel sat up, instantly alert. Norris and Shaaran stirred and their eyes flew open.

"It began not long ago," Rowan whispered. "There was only one at first, I think. But now there are many."

Zeel gritted her teeth. Shaaran began to tremble. Norris's face looked as if it had been carved out of stone. In all their minds, Rowan knew, was the terrifying picture of a twisting mass of white, snake-like bodies, blue-shadowed jaws, blind heads jabbing, jabbing at the rock, seeking entrance.

He added another stick to the fire. There was nothing else he could do.

"The fire will keep us safe," Zeel said. But she did not sound very sure.

Rowan searched for something to talk about—anything to mask the terrible sounds.

"Tell us of our people on Sheba's trail, Zeel," he said. "Were they well?"

"Well enough," said Zeel, following his lead determinedly. "I did not go down to them, for I was intent on reaching you and did not wish to risk losing the wind. But they were marching along at good speed, intent on their purpose and looking straight ahead, as Rin folk do."

Despite herself, she half smiled. "All but Allun, whose Traveller ways have still not quite deserted him," she added. "I think he may have seen me, for he raised his arm. But I had passed in an instant, and I am not certain."

"And what of Lann and Bronden?" asked Shaaran, rousing herself to keep the conversation going, though her lips were stiff with fear. "How do they fare?"

"Lann has things well in hand," Zeel said. "She has encircled the bakery with all the old, useless wood she can find. She plans to dash the wood with oil and light it if need be, to protect Bronden and herself from—"

She broke off, annoyed with herself for having reminded her companions of the danger that threatened them. For a moment they all became aware once more of the sounds above their heads.

The stealthy, rasping noises were louder now, and seemed closer. It was as if every moment more and more ice creepers were slithering through the snow that smothered the overhang. As if a squirming mass of cold, white bodies was scraping now on the rock itself.

Zeel's eyes fell on the box of silks Shaaran held in her lap. "Shaaran, let me see some of the silks again, I beg you," she said, raising her voice.

Rowan's heart lurched. So far, everything had been different from the scene in his dream. But it seemed there was no escape from what was to come. Zeel was asking the very question that he himself had sworn not to utter.

"Ogden has talked of little else but the silks ever since he first saw them in your village in the summer," Zeel went on. "And I believe he thinks of them even more often than he speaks. It is strange."

She leaned forward to feed the fire, not noticing the sudden still-ness of her companions. Rowan exchanged glances with Shaaran and Norris. He knew that they were sharing his thoughts.

Could it be that Ogden of the Travellers had sensed danger in the silks? Danger for the land? Now Rowan came to think of it, he had certainly studied the silks carefully, and left the village rather hastily thereafter.

He said nothing to me of any fears, but perhaps he wanted time to consider, Rowan thought. If so, he waited too long. But would we of Rin have listened to him, even if he had spoken? The people were so happy to learn a little of their past. They would not have welcomed a Traveller's warning.

He dragged his attention back to Zeel. She had warmed to her subject now and was speaking rapidly, staring into the fire. It was clear that Lann had said nothing to her of Neel the potter's fearful warning, or his attempt to burn the silks. Zeel had no idea that every word she spoke fuelled her companions' feeling of dread.

"It is puzzling," she said. "Over and over again Ogden has praised the skill with which the silks were made, and the timelessness of this way of keeping history. But there is no doubt that there is something about them he finds … disturbing. Once, speaking of them, he said, almost to himself, 'What should I do? Speak out, tell what I suspect, or leave well alone?' But when I asked him what he meant, he turned away, and would say no more."

She sighed. "It is a mystery. I resolved that when I had the chance, I would try to solve it. Could I see the silks?"

Breathing fast, unable to refuse, Shaaran fumbled with the clasp of the wooden box. The box looked very battered. Its splintered side had been roughly lined with part of a blanket to keep the silks inside secure. Carefully she opened the lid.

No, Shaaran, thought Rowan. But already the girl was pulling rolls of silk from the box. She loosened one roll and spread it out. Rowan felt a chill run down his spine. It was the silk she had painted in the bakery.

The colours were brighter than the colours of the silk in his dream, but otherwise the painting was very much the same, hideously the same. Rowan stared at the well-remembered shapes of black, white, blue and grey. He stared at the long line of people trekking away through snow-covered hills along a burned black path. He stared at the bukshah, neatly fenced in their snowy field.

Then he turned his eyes with dread to the Mountain. During that last long night before they set out, Shaaran had not only finished the painting, but added to it. Writhing from the mist of the Mountain were hundreds of hideous, snake-like shapes, with gaping, blue-lined jaws and teeth like shards of ice.

Zeel drew breath sharply and turned her face away. Norris gave a low groan.

"Oh, I am sorry!" Shaaran babbled, rolling up the silk with trembling hands. "I had to paint the truth. But I did not mean to show you this ..."

Then suddenly there was a deep, low growling from the rock, and it was as if the world fell in, with a crashing wave of sound. Rowan pitched forward, clapping his hands to his ears.

Dimly he heard Zeel shouting, Shaaran screaming, and Norris cursing.

The fire went out. Then all was cold, and blackness.

15 – Shadows

The bukshah were walking in single file up a narrow stairway cut into rock. They did not look as Rowan remembered them. Their heads were high. Their horns were sharp and white. Their thick coats seemed to glow. Their hoofs were gleaming gold in the sunlight.

Rowan was climbing the stairway after them, following the prints of the golden hoofs. He was filled with dread. His legs were aching, but he knew he could not stop. There was no choice now. There was no turning back.

We must follow the beasts …

Unwillingly Rowan raised his eyes. At the top of the stairs gaped a dark, steaming mouth, huge in the midst of rock that was seamed and pitted like an ancient face.

Hunger …

His eyes were blurred. The steps gleamed, dazzling, climbing up, up …

Dreaming. I am dreaming …

Rowan woke, his mouth dry, his heart pounding. He opened his eyes, but saw only blackness. For a single terrible moment he thought he had lost his sight. Then he heard Norris, Shaaran and Zeel calling to one another and to him. He remembered what he had felt and heard just before he lost consciousness. And the words of the rhyme echoed in his mind, taunting him.

Hide within the rocky walls.

Be still while icy darkness falls.

Frantically he cursed himself for a fool. The last words of the rhyme had told him what was going to happen—told him in plain words, though he had failed to understand.

The overhanging cliff top, that great shelf of rock burdened with snow and squirming with ice creepers, had broken away and fallen. Snow and rubble had piled up against the cliff face. The cave mouth was blocked.

Rowan felt sweat break out on his brow. They were trapped. Hidden within rocky walls indeed. Hidden forever. The dark seemed to press in upon him.

Blindly he felt for his flint, and pulled a torch from his pack. As the torch flared, he caught a glimpse of Shaaran huddled against a wall, Zeel kneeling with her head in her hands and Norris crouched by the cave mouth, holding his walking staff. The narrow triangle of the entrance gleamed white with snow.

Norris swung around, grimacing with pain as the movement pulled at his wound. "Put that out!" he roared. "The flame will eat the air we breathe, and there is little enough in here as it is!"

Hurriedly Rowan did as he was bid, shamed that in his panic he had not thought of this himself.

He heard Norris grunt with effort, and then the thrusting, crunching sound of the staff plunging into the snow. The sounds came twice more. Then, suddenly, Norris gave a shout of triumph and Rowan felt a small draught of cool air on his face.

"I am through!" Norris called. "We are in luck! The blockage is mainly snow, I think—and snow that is not even as thick as my staff is long."

He began jabbing at the snow again. Soon a patch of dim light glimmered in the inky darkness, and the draught of cold, fresh air grew stronger.

"The creepers," whispered Shaaran. "They will be waiting."

"I would rather face a hundred ice creepers than remain in this tomb," Zeel said. "But it is safe to light torches now, so please do so, Shaaran, while Rowan and I help Norris clear the way. Then at least we can make a fight of it."

But the torches Shaaran hastily lit were flickering low by the time Norris, Zeel and Rowan had made a gap wide enough to crawl through. And when at last the four cautiously squeezed one by one onto the great pile of rock and snow that now sloped down to the ground from the cave entrance, the only ice creepers to be seen were dead.

A sulky dawn was breaking, and dull red stained the sky. The companions stumbled down to ground level, slipping on heaped snow and treading upon the remains of dozens of creepers lying crushed and withered beneath huge, broken chunks of rock.

When they looked about them, they saw that it was not only the overhang above their cave that had collapsed, but a long portion of the black cliff face. The giant boulders that once had clustered at the foot of the cliff further towards the west were now invisible beneath a jumble of tumbled snow, rocks and dead trees. And everywhere were the partly covered bodies of ice creepers, mangled and grey.

So many ...

Rowan shook his head. It was as if someone had whispered in his ear. But that could not be so, for he could hear his companions talking to one another not far away.

"These dead creepers must be just a few of all those who were here. Think how many more must have escaped," Norris was muttering. "Why, there must have been hundreds of them moving in on us."

"How did so many know where to find us?" Shaaran asked.

"I think they must sense our warmth," Zeel said. "But whatever the case, it is fortunate that we did not camp in the shelter of one of those boulders, as I thought we might. We would have been killed, certainly, if not by the creepers, then by the collapse of the cliff. It was only because we were hiding inside the cave that we were spared."

... No one will be spared ... Nothing will survive ... Cold, so cold ... And there are so many ... so many ...

The words hissed through Rowan's mind. Then there was a flicker at the edge of his vision, and he saw that all around him there were shadows, wavering shadows with gaunt, starved faces and hollow eyes. And with horror he recognised, beneath the lines of suffering, features he knew. The features of Jonn, of Bronden, of Timon, of his mother ...

A deep shuddering began within him. He felt hot, then freezing cold. His mind seethed with whispers, hissing and echoing, twisting and mingling, sliding one upon the other.

So many ... too many ... What have we done?

Rowan pressed his hands to his ears, squeezed his burning eyes tightly shut. But it was no use. The shadows pressed about him. He could still hear the whispers, still see the familiar faces, hideously changed. His mother's hair was grey as ash. Her eyes were red with weeping.

We knew too much, and too little. We have been wrong ... so wrong ... Now the Mountain makes us pay ...

Someone touched his hand. "Rowan!" a soft voice called.

The shadows faded. The whispers died away. Rowan swayed.

"You are not well, Rowan," he heard Shaaran say. "You are faint." Her voice rose. "Norris! Zeel!"

Rowan heard exclamations, felt strong arms lower him gently to the ground. He sat with his head bowed and gradually the waves of sick dizziness grew less, and the world came back into focus. Zeel and Norris were on either side of him. Shaaran was kneeling in front of him, offering him water.

Gratefully he drank. His head was throbbing. The dim light hurt his eyes.

"I am sorry," he mumbled. "I could not help ..."

"Was it another rhyme? Tell us!" Norris urged.

"No—not a rhyme." Rowan swallowed. "I saw ..." He broke off with a shiver.

Zeel had been watching him keenly.

"I think there is something you must tell us, Rowan," she said. "I have thought so for some time. But this is not the time or place. We are too exposed to danger here. Can you walk?"

Rowan managed to nod, and she helped him to his feet.

"We will take it slowly," she said. "I will help you."

"But the bukshah tracks were covered when the cliff fell." Norris frowned, looking around him. "We have lost the trail."

Zeel shook her head. "I saw the trail from the air last night," she said. "It followed the cliff west, then entered a grove of trees. The herd might have stopped in the grove to feed, for the trees are very thick, and evergreen. At the very least, we will pick up the trail there."

They began to walk, staying close beside the cliff, picking their way over the mass of icy rubble. It was difficult, but all of them felt safer without deep snow around them.

At first Rowan leaned on Zeel's arm, as she had suggested, but quite soon he was able to walk alone, though he still felt weak. He was haunted by the fear that the shadows would return, but Zeel remained close beside him, speaking to him often as if she knew he needed distraction from his thoughts.

* * *

It was broad daylight by the time they reached the end of the rubble, at a place where the cliff face curved to the right. As they rounded the corner and stumbled gratefully down to the smoother ground, they found themselves standing amid a jumble of bukshah tracks.

"There! You see?" Zeel exclaimed, pointing. And sure enough, the tracks headed directly for a bright patch of green—a grove of trees nestled hard against the cliff face.

They all began moving towards the grove as fast as they were able. The living green, startling against the dead grey, black and white of the rest of the landscape, seemed to beckon them. But Rowan slowly realised that even if they had wished to turn aside from the grove, they could not have done so. The ground on their left had begun to fall away steeply. Soon the black wall of the cliff face rose on one side of them, and a chasm yawned on the other. Like the bukshah before them, they had no choice but to go forward.

And the trees stretched across the path, filling it from edge to edge.

Rowan's stomach began to flutter. The situation reminded him unpleasantly of the rock corridor before the vale of horrors. He could see that Zeel, Norris and Shaaran were also becoming uneasy. Their brisk pace was slowing little by little and their feet had begun to drag.

At last, as the trees loomed directly ahead, the four stopped. All instinctively raised their hands to their noses, for a strange, unpleasant smell, like the odour of bad eggs, hung in the air.

"I feel I have been herded to this place," Zeel said in a low voice. "I do not like it."

"Nor I," Norris agreed, peering into the trees. "Yet there seems no danger. The bukshah clearly entered without hesitation. You can see that by their tracks."

"The bukshah went through the vale of horrors, too," Shaaran reminded him. "Just because a place is safe for beasts, it does not mean it is safe for us."

"It may not even be safe for beasts," Zeel said, glancing at Rowan. "The bukshah entered the grove, but we do not know if they ever left it. That smell—"

"It is not the smell of death," Rowan broke in quickly. But a feeling of dread was growing within him. He was certain that the bukshah were very near. He sensed them. But the grove was utterly silent.

"Star!" he called.

The shout echoed dismally around the cliffs, and died away without response.

"They may have left the grove long ago, and be out of hearing," Shaaran whispered, plucking at his sleeve.

Rowan realised that she was trying to comfort him, but he could not answer her. He was tingling with the urge to plunge forward into the trees at once. But he knew his companions would follow. He could not drag them after him in a heedless rush into danger. He had to be cautious, find out all he could before going ahead, though it was agony to him to wait.

It was impossible to see very far into the grove. Many dead trees had fallen from the cliff top above, tangling with the branches of the living trees in the grove to form a low, thick canopy which shut out light from above.

The first few rows of trees were visible, however, and Rowan looked at them carefully. Certainly they did not look dangerous, and nothing like the devil trees of Unrin.

They were all of one type—sturdy though not very tall, with spreading branches and glossy, well-shaped leaves. The only difference between them was in their bark. The trees that grew at the outer edges of the grove had rough, shaggy grey bark. But the grey bark only appeared in patches on the trees further towards the centre, and the trunks and branches of the trees right in the middle, on either side of the bukshah trail, were quite smooth and white.

Perhaps the outer trees need more protection than the inner ones do, Rowan thought. Perhaps the grove makes its own heat. For he had noticed that the air was warmer here, and there was little snow on the trees or on the ground around them.

And this was very strange.

"We have been climbing steadily all morning," Zeel said, putting his thoughts into words. "We are higher on the Mountain now. It should be colder here, not warmer."

There was a short, anxious silence.

"What should we do?" exclaimed Norris.

And instantly Rowan felt the medallion grow hot as fire.

16 – The Grove

This time the rhyme came more easily. The burning, choking feeling was much less, and even the voice sounded more like Rowan's own. But somehow this made the experience even more horrible. Rowan's stomach heaved as helplessly he mouthed words that were as new and strange to him as they were to his companions:

"Make haste, your way is straight ahead.
Cast aside the fallen dead.
Life will ebb if you despair.
Sickness heals, and foul makes fair."

As the last word fell from his lips he braced himself, determined not to sink to the ground. But he need not have worried. Zeel, Norris and Shaaran had gathered around him, ready to support him.

"Sheba said, 'Learn what it is to be what I am,'" he murmured, looking around at them. "I know now, only too well. And I wish I did not."

"Anyone of sense would feel the same," Norris said bluntly. "I beg your pardon, Rowan. I should have watched my tongue. And it was all for nothing. That accursed riddle offered us little help and less hope."

Cast aside the fallen dead ...

Rowan shivered.

"The rhyme told us to move straight ahead, and to make haste, Norris," Zeel snapped. "It also told us not to despair. These things at least we can understand. For the rest, we will see."

She turned to Rowan. "Are you able to move on?"

For answer, he stepped forward, into the shadow of the trees. The others crowded after him.

They began to follow the bukshah tracks, the smooth white trunks of the trees rising on either side of them like guideposts. White boughs laced over their heads. They kept close together, their eyes and ears strained for any sudden sound or movement. But all was still, and as the trees closed in around them the silence and the shade grew deeper.

They said little to one another, and when they did speak, it was in whispers. Soon the tangled canopy had become so low that Norris had to limp along with his shoulders bowed and his head bent. A light mist hung in the dimness, mingling with the mist of their breath, and the evil smell they had noticed earlier was becoming stronger.

Then Rowan saw a glimmer of light ahead. His heart thudded. Had they reached the end of the grove already?

"Zeel!" he whispered.

"I see it," she hissed from behind him. "It is some sort of clearing, I think. And the smell is coming from there, I am sure of it."

Rowan had to force himself not to break into a run. His breath was coming fast. The skin of his chest and back had begun prickling and itching unbearably.

I am sweating, he thought. The cloak is too warm for this place. But he did not even consider pausing to take the cloak off.

Soon the clearing was very near, but still Rowan could see little detail because of the thick mist that hung within it. He could only see shapes and colours. The ground was not flat, but heaped with angular shapes of green and white. Amid the green and white there were patches of grey and one of black. There was no movement anywhere.

Rowan began moving faster.

"Take care," Zeel warned from behind him. "Rowan—"

Then Shaaran screamed.

Rowan and Zeel both swung around. Shaaran was clawing frantically at her shoulder, her face alive with horror. Norris was trying vainly to help her. "Get it off!" Shaaran was shrieking. "Help me!"

"What is it?" Zeel said sharply. "Shaaran, be still. Take your hands away. We cannot see—"

"They are on you too!" Shaaran cried, shuddering with revulsion. "Oh, they are everywhere! Oh, horrible!"

Rowan's skin crawled as he saw, beneath her clutching fingers, a grey, rough-skinned, star-shaped thing fastened to her shoulder. Flattened against the ragged wool of her cloak, it was perfectly disguised, almost invisible. But now he had seen it he could see others—one on her side, and yet another on her arm.

On Zeel's arm too. And on the back of her neck. And there, clinging to Norris's hood, were two more!

Where had they come from?

As the question raced through his mind, the tree branch above Shaaran's head seemed to move, and a flabby, star-shaped piece of bark peeled away and dropped quietly onto her back.

"The—the bark on the trees," Rowan stuttered. "It is not bark. It is—they are—"

His chest prickled. Filled with sudden, terrible suspicion, he looked down and shouted aloud in horrified disgust. His chest was covered in a mass of shaggy grey. Some of the creatures were still wriggling, still settling into place. Others were well fixed, and had clearly been so for some time, for they were swollen and plump.

Plump with his blood!

Frantically Rowan tried to pull the things away. Needle-sharp pains shot through his flesh as he tugged, but the grey things clung.

"Heat your knife in the torch flame, Rowan!" he heard Zeel shouting over Shaaran's screams. "Hot metal will surely make them break their grip."

As Rowan fumbled for his knife, an overhanging branch brushed his wrist and another of the creatures slid onto the back of his hand.

With a cry he flung out his arm. The creature flew spinning away. But as he looked after it he saw that the canopy was swarming with others. And hundreds more still were leaving the trunks of the trees beyond the pathway, climbing upward to join the crowd moving stealthily towards him and his companions.

"Run!" he gasped. "Out of the trees!"

They ran, stumbling clumsily towards the clearing, their heads down, their cloaks wrapped about them, shuddering and sobbing with horror.

And as they threw themselves out of the crawling green shade, onto a foul-smelling, steaming heap of dead trees tangled with vines, they saw the bukshah.

The beasts were lying near the centre of the litter, as still as stones. Their shaggy bodies were covered with star-shaped creatures so swollen, and fitted so closely together, that it was hard to tell where one ended and another began.

Star lay at the head of the herd. Her mighty horns were smeared with mud and wedged under a log. She was covered with feasting parasites.

With a cry of anguish Rowan dropped his torch and leaped forward, clambering over the fallen wood, careless of the thorny vines that tangled and tore at him. He reached Star and fell to his knees beside her, calling her name.

Her small black eyes opened. She rumbled softly, deep in her throat. A sound of love and trust.

Rowan's heart gave a great thud of disbelieving joy.

"She is alive!" he shouted, his voice cracking. "Star is still alive! The others—perhaps they too ... they too ..."

He swung around to the bukshah behind him. It was Treasure, the only black bukshah in the herd, born in Rin's last spring. Treasure's eyes were closed, and he made no sound as Rowan touched his nose. But he was warm. Still warm, and breathing!

If Treasure, so young and small, still lived, there was hope for all the others. Frantically, Rowan crawled between the still, grey bodies. He called the beasts by name, caressing them wherever he could put a hand. And at the sound of his voice and the touch of his fingers, warm skin twitched, eyelids fluttered, and the beasts groaned and sighed.

But it was almost too late. He knew it. He had seen it in Star's dull eyes, heard it in her feeble voice.

How long had it been since the bukshah walked through the grove, taking their time, stopping to eat the green leaves along their way? How long had it been since the star-shaped creatures clinging to the trees on either side of the track had slipped onto their backs, leaving the tree trunks in the centre of the grove smooth and white?

Rowan could guess how it had been. By the time the bukshah stumbled out of the trees, they were all covered with parasites, and weakening fast. Star had tried to lead them across the clearing, but one by one they had fallen. And they had lain here helpless ever since, slowly being drained of life.

He started up, looking wildly around him. He was dizzy, and for a moment his eyes would not focus. Where were Zeel, Shaaran and Norris? Why had they not come to help him?

He could not believe it when he saw they were still where he had left them. Shaaran was on her knees, her face white as chalk. Norris was bending over her, looking sick and panic-stricken. Zeel stood beside them.

"Help me, Zeel!" Rowan roared. "Bring the torch! Make haste!"

Zeel shook her head and beckoned. Inwardly raging at the delay, Rowan began clambering back towards them over the sea of fallen trees.

They came to meet him, moving slowly.

"You must help me!" he burst out as at last they came together. "The bukshah are dying! I need—"

"It is no use, Rowan," Zeel broke in quietly. "Do you think we have been standing idle? We have been trying to remove the vile things from our own bodies. And we cannot. It is as though they are made of stone. My dagger does not harm them, cold, warm or red hot."

He gaped at her. "But ... but surely ..."

She shook her head. "Even naked flame does no good. I have tried it." Ruefully she showed him her arm. Two hideous star-shaped creatures clung there, unmarked, in the centre of a great patch of charred cloth and raw, blistered skin.

"Zeel!" Rowan breathed.

Shaaran gave a choking sob and Norris grimaced. "She did it before we could stop her," he said grimly.

Zeel shrugged. "I had to try it," she said. "These things are sucking the life out of us."

"And it will not take long for them to finish the job, I fear," said Norris. "If they can fell the bukshah in a day, how much more easily will they finish us?"

Shaaran had slumped onto a log, her face shadowed with despair.

Life will ebb if you despair ...

"Wait!" Rowan exclaimed. "We have forgotten the rhyme!"

Shaaran looked up, her eyes startled. Slowly she repeated the words:

> *"Make haste, your way is straight ahead.*
> *Cast aside the fallen dead.*
> *Life will ebb if you despair.*
> *Sickness heals, and foul makes fair."*

"Truly, our lives, and the lives of the bukshah, will ebb away if we give up," Norris said. "That line at least I can understand. What of the rest? Do the first lines mean that we must leave the beasts to their fate and go forward, if we are to save ourselves?"

Rowan gnawed at his lip. That idea had occurred to him, but he did not want to believe it.

"If we go straight ahead, that only means that we cross the clearing and go on through the trees on the other side," Zeel said. "But the trees over there are thick with the star creatures. Every trunk is grey."

"Perhaps the creatures cannot live outside the grove," Shaaran suggested suddenly. "Perhaps, if we can leave it, we will be free of them."

Norris looked hopeful, but Zeel shook her head. "I think you will find they can live wherever there are trees to support them," she said. She pointed at the dead tree Shaaran was sitting on, and at the other trees lying about them. The white trunks were studded with faded, star-shaped marks.

"These trees have died and fallen from the cliff top," Zeel went on. "And clearly the star creatures once lived on them, just as they live on the trees here. They suck sap, perhaps," she added calmly, "until richer food comes their way."

Rowan saw Shaaran grow even paler. "Perhaps it is because the trees on the cliff top died that the trees in the grove are so heavily infested," he said quickly. "If the trees above died and fell ..."

And in a blinding flash he saw the answer.

"The fallen dead!" he said. "The *trees*! The dead trees lying here, in this clearing. *They* are what we must cast aside!"

"But why?" Zeel asked blankly.

"Because there is something *beneath* them!" Norris exclaimed. "Something that will help us! And—"

"But the clearing is *heaped* with dead trees!" Zeel objected. "We cannot possibly move them all. Not in time. Not—"

"We do not have to move them all," said Rowan. His heart swelling, he turned and looked towards the place where Star lay. He knew without a doubt that Star would have fought her weakness to the end. She would have tried to save the herd. And she had collapsed with her muddy horns still locked beneath a tree trunk.

"There!" He pointed. "There, where Star lies, and the mist and the smell are strongest. That is where we must clear the fallen dead. Whatever lies below them is the answer!"

17 – Foul Makes Fair

Rowan was desperate, Zeel was determined and Shaaran did not spare herself. But all of them were growing weaker by the moment, and the task would have been hopeless if it had not been for Norris.

Norris saw at once that they could not move the fallen trees by brute force. Instead he tied ropes to them, then found long, straight branches they could use as levers to prise the white trunks up while the ropes were pulled.

Zeel and Shaaran took charge of the ropes, Norris and Rowan the levers. Sweating and straining, the companions pushed and pulled to Norris's command till, with a creaking, cracking sound, each tree shifted little by little from the place where it had lain for so long.

For hours they laboured, as the light slowly dimmed in the sky above them. They moved aside one tree after another, uncovering nothing but more broken, tangled branches, more sad, uprooted trunks.

Norris's face was grey, set in deep lines of pain. The wound in his side had re-opened, his injured leg could hardly support him. But he would not rest, would not stop. Again he placed the levers, tied the ropes. Again he gave his orders and began limping to his place, ready to heave once more.

One to fight, Rowan thought distantly. But Norris will never recover from this. Perhaps none of us will. Perhaps this is how the story ends.

He could feel his mind clouding. He knew that the creatures that clung to him were draining his strength and his will. He watched unsurprised as without warning Norris stumbled, swayed, and then crumpled slowly to the ground between Star and Treasure. Shaaran's cries rang in his ears like distant bells as she ran to her brother and bent over him.

Rowan met Zeel's eyes.

"Once more," she said, and wound her rope around her hand.

He nodded dully, and moved to the place where Norris would have stood. He took hold of the long branch jammed beneath the tree trunk.

"Now!" he called. And summoning the last of his strength, the last of his hope and will, he pushed down.

For a long moment, nothing happened. Then the tree moved. Rowan heard Zeel's grunt of triumph, saw the rope straining. He pushed again, pushed with all his strength. But there was resistance. Something was holding the tree down. Something ...

"Shaaran!" he shouted. "Help us! Here!"

He did not really believe Shaaran would come. But she did. Tear-stained, pale as a ghost, she slipped in front of him and threw her tiny weight onto the branch.

And it was enough. There was a sucking, groaning sound. The tree rolled aside. And as it did, a great, solid mat of rotten wood, vines and dead leaves moved with it, and foul-smelling steam billowed from the place where it had lain.

Dizzy, staggering with weariness, Rowan, Zeel and Shaaran stared at the thing they had uncovered.

It was a pool of bubbling, steaming water. Star and Norris lay in the mud at its edge.

Shaaran sat down suddenly, her eyes wide with shock.

Cautiously Zeel leaned forward and tested the water with the tip of a finger.

"It is hot!" she said in awe. "Water bubbling hot from the ground! It is a miracle!" She sat back on her heels, wrinkling her nose. "But oh, it is foul. It stinks like a thousand eggs gone stale."

Sickness heals, and foul makes fair ...

Rowan was speechless, consumed with desperate hope. He knelt beside Star and cautiously dipped his cupped hands into the spring. He felt warmth and a mild tingling, but nothing more. He lifted his hands, brimming with cloudy water, and held them close to Star's nose.

"Star," he whispered. "Is this what you were seeking? Is this what will help you? Help us?"

Star's eyes opened. She saw the water dribbling through Rowan's fingers. She snuffled as its odour reached her nostrils. She began struggling to rise.

But she did not lick Rowan's hands, only rubbed her nose against them, so Rowan knew that the water was not to be drunk, but bathed in.

"Zeel!" he cried. "Your arm! Put it into the water!"

Zeel plunged her injured arm deep into the spring. She held it there for the count of three. And when she drew it out, the star creature had fallen away and was bobbing, curled and dead, amid the bubbles on the spring's surface

This Rowan had been hoping for. But what he had not been expecting, what made him gasp with wonder, and Shaaran cry aloud, was that Zeel's burned, blistered skin was whole and smooth again.

Zeel herself was looking down at her arm in amazement. "I—cannot believe it!" she stammered.

"It is like magic!" breathed Shaaran. "It is like the magic spring in the fairy land Grandfather used to tell me of, long ago." Hope leaped into her face, flaring there like a candle flame. She scrambled over the mud to her brother.

Zeel and Rowan ran to help her, and together they wrestled Norris's limp, heavy body into the spring.

Norris woke at the touch of the water. He flailed in panic, groaning and coughing. Then, suddenly, he grew still. His face changed. His eyes opened, free of pain, round with surprise.

Leaving him to Zeel and Shaaran, Rowan swung back to Star. She was still struggling to rise, with a bravery that nearly broke his heart. Tears sprang into his eyes as vainly he tried to help her.

Then Norris, Shaaran and Zeel were with him, all of them dripping wet, all of them free of parasites, their eyes clear and shining. As they, too, bent over Star, the water streaming from their hair and clothes ran over her body. And wherever the water fell, star creatures curled and dropped away.

Star groaned with relief, struggled again, and at last found her feet. She stood, thin and swaying, by the bubbling pool. But she did not move at once into the water. Instead she bellowed, calling the herd, commanding them to hear her.

The other bukshah stirred. Everywhere ears flickered feebly, dull eyes opened. Star bellowed again. Then suddenly she lunged forward, collapsing into the centre of the pool with a mighty splash, sinking beneath the surface.

Water rose in a great wave, surging over the muddy bank, drenching Treasure and a dozen other beasts, and spraying the clearing like warm, muddy rain. The surface of the spring seemed to boil as Star sank deeper, deeper ...

With a cry of fear Rowan plunged after her. The smell of the water burned in his nose, caught in his throat, making him choke and gag. Frantically he strained to see beneath the bubbling, leaf-fouled surface. He caught a glimpse of something pale far below him and dived, eyes screwed tightly shut, hands outstretched, feeling his way blindly.

He felt a sudden, stinging pain as the point of one of Star's horns pierced his palm. He slid his hand down, took a firmer grip and held on. He pulled with all his strength, but it was as though Star was a huge stone. He could not lift her. His lungs felt as though they were bursting.

He felt something dragging at his cloak. Someone was trying to pull him upward, but he was anchored by his own grip on Star, and he would not let go.

Then suddenly there was movement from below him and in a rush of bubbles he was propelled up, up into the light. His head broke through the surface and he gasped for air. His ears were ringing. As he opened his blurred eyes, the first thing he saw was Norris's sleek, drenched head bobbing beside him. Norris still had hold of his cloak. Norris was trying to drag him towards the bank, mouthing words he could not hear.

Then both of them were tumbled sideways as in a shower of spray Star's massive body surfaced almost directly below them. With a stab of joy Rowan saw the great bukshah lift her head clear of the water and begin swimming powerfully. Her eyes were bright, her horns were gleaming white, water streamed from her woolly mane. Rowan shouted, choked, and shouted again, but to his amazement, as he tried to reach out for her, Star nudged him vigorously aside, into the shallows.

He found his feet, then fell to his knees, dizzy with hurt and confusion. He felt Norris pulling him. He heard Star bellow. And finally his ringing ears made sense of Norris's shouts.

"Get out, Rowan!" Norris was bawling. "You will be crushed! Make way for them!"

Then Rowan saw that Star was not the only bukshah in the spring. Treasure was already up to his neck in water. Two other calves—Misty and Sprite—were splashing unsteadily after him. Three more followed. And behind them were the other members of the herd, thin, weak and staggering, star creatures covering them like hideous armour, except where they had been sprayed by Star's first mighty plunge into the water.

Frantically the huge ragged beasts pushed forward, deaf and blind to everything except the spring. Norris hauled Rowan out of their path, and an instant later hoofs were trampling the mud where the two had lain.

In threes and fours the bukshah sank into the deep water, moaning with relief as the parasites left them, then raising their heads and swimming to the opposite side of the spring, where Star now stood waiting for them.

And when all of them had made the crossing, when all were standing, steaming and dripping, on the other side of the spring, Rowan, Zeel, Shaaran and Norris collected their possessions, and followed them.

* * *

They stayed that night in the clearing, the bukshah all around them. Despite being soaked through, they were not cold, for the air beside the spring was as warm as a summer afternoon in Rin, though it did not smell as sweet.

They lit a fire, heated a little water for tea, and toasted bread to eat with cheese and honey. And as the sun set they lay down and slept well and deeply, for they knew that here at least the ice creepers could not come.

It was still very dark when Rowan woke. Star's nose was nudging his cheek. Her great curved horns, sharpened to knife points on the rock walls before the vale of horrors, loomed too close to his eyes for comfort.

"Star, why do you wake me so soon?" he mumbled, rolling over. "Dawn must be hours away."

Star rumbled to him and pawed the ground, then turned away. He sat up and saw that the other beasts were already standing, waiting. He watched as Star passed through them and began to lead the way into the trees.

The herd was on the move again. Quickly Rowan roused Norris, Shaaran and Zeel. Each of them took a hurried sip of water and a handful of dried berries. Then they lit torches, shouldered their packs and followed the bukshah, even Zeel still rubbing the sleep from her eyes.

The path through the trees beyond the spring was cluttered with dead wood, but the bukshah pushed through every obstacle, crushing it underfoot, clearing the way. The four strolled after them, revelling in the luxury of renewed strength and freedom from pain.

The torchlight flickered on the trees, flickered on star creatures thickly clustered on trunks and branches, but few of the parasites tried to settle on the humans or the beasts. Those that did paid instantly for their mistake, falling dead as they touched hair and garments still damp with the water of the spring.

Slowly the dampness disappeared in the forest warmth, and Rowan began to fear. But still the star creatures held back, and still the humans and the beasts walked in peace, as if the water had given them a protective coating.

It was like a walk in a dream, and it ended only too quickly. The sun was still far below the horizon when Rowan, Zeel, Shaaran and Norris stepped out of the trees, but they could see well enough the bleak and brutal place of icy rock to which they had come.

They were standing on the only level place in a landscape of sharp angles. Boulders cluttered the sloping ground ahead. To their right rose the cliffs, wreathed in mist, capped with dead trees and snow. The sheer black cliff walls were half hidden by the tumble of huge jagged rocks piled against them.

To the left all was darkness, but Rowan could see that the ground sloping away from the area where they stood was steep and barren. And, somehow, dreadfully familiar.

Zeel shivered. "We have reached the Mountain's western face," she said in a low voice. "Below is the Pit of Unrin."

18 – Before Dawn

haaran cowered a little closer to Norris. "What—what is the Pit of Unrin?" she stammered. She had heard many tales since arriving in Rin, but not this one. No one spoke willingly of the Pit of Unrin.

Rowan moistened his lips. "It is a place of doom—a dead valley filled with flesh-eating trees," he said. "Once it was the Valley of Gold. A great people lived there, ancient allies of the Travellers and the Maris."

"The Valley of Gold!" exclaimed Norris. "But that was the place Timon and Neel the potter spoke of at the meeting! The place of the people who turned their backs on the Mountain, and caused the first Cold Time."

The air seemed to darken. A small, cruel wind blew about them, nipping at their faces, tugging at the torch flames, tweaking the shaggy hair of the bukshah who were wandering among the rocks like lost souls, pawing the ground.

We have arrived, Rowan thought suddenly. This is the journey's end.

"The Cold Time happened in the land's earliest days," Zeel said slowly. "The people of the Valley of Gold lived on in peace and plenty long, long after it ended. Then, suddenly, they were no more. For centuries it was not known what had happened to them. Now we know that the devil trees overtook the Valley and killed them all. Ogden thinks that the tree roots then undermined this part of the Mountain, causing the cliffs above to crumble and partly fall."

"How could a whole people, rich and happy, just disappear?" murmured Shaaran, staring down at the blackness below. "Did they not call for aid? Did the Travellers not—"

"The Travellers were far away," Zeel said, her face sombre. "They had made camp on the coast near Maris for the cold season, as always.

The first winds of winter brought a Zebak invasion. The Travellers fought alongside the Maris people to defend the land, but the Zebak were many and the Maris were weak and divided, for their leader, the Keeper of the Crystal, was dying. Urgent word was sent to the Valley of Gold. The Valley people had never failed to answer a call to arms."

"But this time they did not come?" Norris was leaning forward, fascinated as he always was by tales of battle.

Zeel shook her head. "They did not come, and the Traveller messengers never returned. It is thought the messengers died of cold before reaching their goal. The snow was early and plentiful that year."

She turned away to look at the bukshah. Rowan did not prompt her. Zeel had no relish for tales of war. Though she pretended otherwise, the seemingly endless battle between her natural and her adopted peoples caused her much grief.

Norris had no such fine feelings. "So what happened then?" he demanded. "Go on, Zeel! The beasts are resting, it seems, or cannot decide which way to go. What else have we to do but talk?"

Zeel looked back at him and smiled wryly as she saw that he would give her no peace until the story had been completed.

"The city of Maris quickly fell to the enemy, and the Maris people were forced to flee into tunnels beneath the sea where their leader could still protect them," she said quietly. "The Zebak tried to take the Travellers as slaves, but the tribe slipped out of their clutches like shadows and escaped, going into hiding in the north."

She grimaced. "We can only guess what happened then, for neither Maris nor Travellers were there to see it. But when the Travellers returned to Maris in spring, they found that many of the Zebak ships had already been sent home—loaded with looted Maris goods, no doubt, for the city was stripped bare. The Zebak who remained thought that the war had been won."

She shook her head at their folly. "For the Travellers, of course, the struggle had only just begun. They sent fresh messengers to the Valley of Gold, and began to harry the enemy in any way they could. Ambushes and raids. Thefts of food and arms. Disturbances night after night ..."

She had all her companions' full attention now. Shaaran was listening to the story as intently as Rowan and Norris were.

"Starved of food and sleep, menaced by an enemy they could not see, the Zebak were soon jumping at shadows," Zeel went on. "Then what the Travellers had been waiting for took place. The old, weak Keeper died. A new Keeper took his place, and the magic Crystal of Maris flamed anew. The Maris people came up from the tunnels, united and filled with new hope. By this time the Zebak were no match for them. And so at last the enemy was defeated and driven away."

She frowned, looking down over the bleak slopes that disappeared into blackness. "But in the midst of the rejoicing, the new messengers returned from the centre, and triumph turned to sorrow as they told what they had found. Above the Valley of Gold, the face of the Mountain had changed to a mass of rubble, as if two giants had battled there. The Valley had gone. In its place was the horror later named the Pit of Unrin—a shadowed mass of hideous trees that seemed to breathe evil. And the people of the Valley had vanished from the earth."

Rowan gave a great sigh. He had heard the old story many times before, but never like this. Somehow, Zeel's flat, matter-of-fact voice had made the details of the tale stand out as Ogden's colourful and dramatic recounting never had.

Shaaran put his thoughts into words. "Chance truly played a fearful part in that history," she said. "If the Zebak had attacked a few weeks earlier ... if the snows had not come sooner than expected ... if the messengers had reached the Valley of Gold ... the Valley people would have gone to the coast to fight, and would not have been killed by the devil trees."

"They might have been killed by the Zebak instead," Norris said grimly. "Who knows? There is no point in 'ifs', Shaaran. But here is another one for you: if the people of the Valley of Gold had not died out, they could have told us what is in store for us. They could have told us how *they* made peace with the Mountain, and ended the first Cold Time."

Zeel sighed, her eyes drifting once again to the bukshah. "That knowledge is lost in the mists of time," she said. "The Valley people did not share it with their friends. Perhaps they were too proud. Or ashamed. Ogden knows many old secrets, but when I asked him of this one, he could not tell me anything."

Could not tell you, or *would* not? Rowan asked himself silently. A picture of Ogden's dark, hawk-like face floated into his mind— Ogden's face as it had been at their very first meeting, Ogden's black eyes intently searching his own.

Ogden the storyteller, leader of the Travellers, had been interested in Rowan from the beginning. Far more interested than might have been expected, by Rowan or anyone else.

Why? Why had Ogden probed his mind so deeply on that first meeting, wanting to know every trivial thing about Rowan's parents, the bukshah, and the life he led?

In his heart, Rowan knew the answer. He had known it ever since the night in the cave. Now he faced it squarely.

Ogden had sensed something. Sensed that, however unlikely it seemed, the puny, quaking boy before him was fated to play an important part in the story of the land they shared.

The storyteller had proved a firm ally. But always it had been as if he was holding something back—some secret knowledge or suspicion he could not bring himself to voice.

He had not been surprised when Rowan brought Shaaran and Norris from the land of the Zebak. He seemed to have been expecting it. Only when the silks were unrolled, and the people of Rin began exclaiming and wondering over them, had he seemed troubled, pressing his thin lips together and turning away.

Perhaps in that moment Ogden realised that what he had been waiting for, what he had feared, had already begun. That Rowan had unknowingly set in train a series of events that would end ...

End here, Rowan thought, looking around at his companions, gazing past them at the shadowy forms of the bukshah milling aimlessly among the rocks. End here, for good or ill.

"Dawn is not long away," Zeel said suddenly.

Rowan swung around to look at her. There had been something in her voice ...

"What is it?" he whispered.

Zeel was standing stiffly, her head up as though she was scenting the air. The torch she held threw yellow light on her high cheekbones, her strong, straight brows. "I do not know," she said, her lips barely moving.

What is happening? Rowan thought desperately. What must I do?

And he felt the medallion grow warm at his throat. His skin began to prickle, and the hideous, familiar sickness flooded through him.

No, he thought with dread. No!

But he knew it was no use. He had asked his question. The thing would happen whether he willed it or not.

He felt the torch drop from his numb fingers, heard Zeel's muffled exclamation as she turned to him. His mouth opened. His lips began to move, shaping the words.

"When earthbound thunder greets the day,
The breaking heart will clear the way.
And where the golden river flows,
The hidden stair its secret shows."

As he spoke the last line, memory flooded through him—memory of a dream, a terrifying dream that he had forgotten until this moment. He had been climbing a stone stairway towards a gaping mouth at the top, following the bukshah.

His head was spinning. He could not think.

When had he dreamed this? How could he have forgotten it? Was the memory true or false?

Wait, he told himself. Wait ...

Slowly the dizziness and sickness ebbed. His mind cleared. He became aware that he was sagging against Zeel, that her arm was around him and that Norris was supporting him from the other side. Gently he pushed them away to stand on his own feet.

He had remembered. The dream of the stone stairway had come to him in the cave. The fear of being trapped, the escape from the cave, and everything that had happened since, had driven it from his mind. But now the memory had come back, dark and fearful.

All the other dreams had come true, in every way that mattered. So this nightmare would come true also. And soon.

When earthbound thunder greets the day ...

When the Dragon of the Mountain roared at dawn?

Rowan's ears were buzzing. It was as though his head was full of bees. Dazedly he stared up at the misty cliff tops. Slowly his eyes moved downward.

And stopped.

Was it his imagination, or could he see a faint blur of lighter colour on the cliff face? He squinted, and became more and more sure that he was right. There was something—some mark or fault—just above the place where the steep slope of rocks began.

If he had not had the dream, he would have thought that the rocks were the stair of the rhyme. But he *had* had the dream, and he knew they were not. The bukshah could not climb those rocks.

The stair—the hidden stair—was here somewhere, masked by shadows.

The bukshah knew it. That was why they would not move from this place. That was why they were milling about among the rocks at the base of the pile, pawing the ground. The stairway was here, and they could not find it.

But at dawn the secret would be revealed. The rising sun would illuminate the rocks. The stairway, now hidden, would be bathed in a golden river of light.

It will happen, Rowan thought. I need do nothing but wait. He felt strangely calm.

"Why does he not answer?" The buzzing in his ears shaped itself suddenly into words, and he recognised Norris's voice, sharp with panic. He realised that his companions had been calling him for long minutes, trying to make him speak.

He turned towards the sound. Three anxious faces floated in the dimness. Zeel. Shaaran. Norris.

Slowly he realised that there *was* something he had to do. Before the dawn broke. Before the Dragon roared. Before the sun exposed the stairway and he began the last, long climb to meet his destiny.

It *will* happen, he told himself. But it need not happen to all of us. In the dream I saw no one on the stair but myself and the bukshah.

An immense loneliness descended upon him. His chest ached.

The breaking heart will clear the way ...

He had wondered what that meant. Now he knew.

He opened his dry lips. "It is time for you to leave me," he said, his voice sounding strange and croaking to his own ears. "What must be done now, I must do alone."

19 – Decisions

Shaaran, Norris and Zeel protested, as Rowan knew they would. The rhyme had shaken them, but it had not shaken their will or their loyalty.

He knew there was only one way to convince them. He had to tell them of his nightmare about the stone stairway and the steaming, gaping mouth at the top. He shrank from it, for if they were to believe that what he had dreamed would certainly come to pass, he would have to confess to the other dreams that had come true—the dreams he had kept secret all this time.

It will destroy their trust in me, he thought, the pain in his heart growing stronger. It will break our friendship. But ... but perhaps that is all to the good. Their love and loyalty bind them to me. If those ties are cut, they will be free to leave. The return to Rin will be perilous, but they will have water from the grove to aid them. And nothing is more perilous than remaining here.

"You do not understand," he said loudly, breaking in on their protests. "And that is because—because I have deceived you."

The babble of voices ceased abruptly. He saw three startled pairs of eyes staring at him, and bowed his head.

He took a deep breath to steady himself, and in a low voice confessed everything. He spoke rapidly, forcing himself to stick to the bare bones of the story. No one interrupted.

"I should have told you from the first, but did not, for my own selfish reasons," Rowan finished awkwardly, without raising his eyes. "I wanted our friendship to stay as it had always been. I did not want you to regard me with disgust or to fear me as people do Sheba. I have always felt a stranger among my people. Now I feel a freak. But that is no excuse. I am sorry."

There was silence. It lasted so long that Rowan half wondered whether the three had already moved silently away, leaving him alone. He forced himself to look up.

They were standing in front of him, exactly as they had been before he began his speech. Their faces were grave. Shaaran had tears in her eyes. At that moment Rowan almost wished they *had* gone without a word.

Then Shaaran flung herself into his arms.

"I cannot believe you have borne this burden alone, all this time, for our sake, Rowan," she cried. "Never could I have done it!"

"Nor I," said Norris, shaking his head and clasping Rowan's hand.

"Perhaps I could," said Zeel calmly. "But I thank the heavens that I did not have to try."

Stunned, Rowan stared at them. Their reaction was so different from the one he had expected that he was tongue-tied.

"I knew you were keeping something to yourself, Rowan, but I could not think what could be so fearful that you would need to hide it," Zeel said. "That is something I still do not quite understand, for why would anyone turn away from a good friend because he has an unexpected, and very useful, talent?"

"More a curse than a talent," Rowan managed to say.

"Curse or talent, it does not matter," said Shaaran, drawing back so she could look at him, but still keeping hold of his arm. "You cannot divide a true friend into parts and say, 'This part I like, but that part I will not accept'! You take the package as a whole."

"And speaking of that, if you think you can divide the whole we four have become, and send three-quarters of it home while you go on alone, you are very much mistaken," Norris growled.

Shaaran nodded agreement. "I will not say I am not afraid," she said. "I am very afraid. But this does not mean I wish to turn back."

"But—but did you not hear what I said?" stammered Rowan. "The dream of the stairway ... there was dread in it. And death. I felt it."

"And so?" Zeel asked coolly. "This is not your decision to take, Rowan of the Bukshah. Whether you saw us in your dream or not, Sheba's rhyme stated clearly that four souls must follow the beasts."

She looked from Norris to Shaaran, and then back to Rowan.

"And follow them we will," she added, "wherever the path may lead us. Not for love of you, but for love of this land, and everything we hold dear."

And, humbled, Rowan fell silent.

Norris cleared his throat. "Very well," he said briskly. "Now, let us think what we can do to help ourselves. Dream or no dream, I do not relish the idea of waiting here for dawn like a helpless victim who has no command at all over his fate."

"The stairway in Rowan's dream led to a gaping mouth," Zeel said. "The mouth, surely, must be the entrance to another cave."

"Must it?" Shaaran asked timidly. "But hot breath was steaming—"

"Dreams often show ordinary things in a strange way," Norris broke in. "The bukshah were also dreamlike—different from the way they really are. Is that not so, Rowan?"

Rowan hesitated. Norris was right, of course, but ...

Zeel was looking up, squinting through the dimness. "That patch of grey is the only sign of an entrance I can see in the cliff face. If we climb to it now, we may learn something that will aid us later."

Shaaran made a small sound of protest, but Norris agreed instantly. For him, a hard climb was far preferable to waiting help-lessly in the darkness. Rowan remained silent. He could see that Zeel's plan was sensible, but still he felt uneasy.

Perhaps I am just unsettled because matters have been taken out of my hands, he thought. Perhaps I have grown too used to being a leader.

The thought made him smile, despite his fears.

"I—I cannot possibly climb those rocks," Shaaran said in a small voice.

Norris snorted with laughter. "Of course not, Shaaran," he said. "No one expects you to. Zeel and I will see what is to be seen, then come back and report to you and Rowan."

Rowan felt a pang. This was all wrong. He knew it. But he could not forbid Zeel and Norris to try what they felt they must.

And neither can I wait here while they do it, he thought. I must see whatever is up there with my own eyes.

"If you are determined to do this, I will go with you," he said aloud. "I think I can manage the climb."

"But what of Shaaran?" exclaimed Norris. "She cannot stay here alone!"

"Of course I can!" Shaaran said with spirit. "I do not need a guard. I will stay here and keep watch. If any danger threatens, or the bukshah begin to stray, I will call you."

And so it was decided. In moments Zeel, Norris and Rowan were threading their way towards the rocks directly beneath their goal.

Star tossed her head and lumbered towards Rowan as he began climbing. It seemed to him that she would have tried to stop him if she could. But by the time she had reached the base of the rock pile, he was already too high for her to reach.

He looked down at her. She was pawing at the rocks as though she wanted to come after him. But she could not. The rock pile was much too steep for her. She stretched up her neck and bellowed dismally as he climbed higher.

Star does not like this any more than I do, Rowan thought uneasily. His foot slipped, and frantically he scrabbled for a hand hold, saving himself by a miracle.

"Pay attention, Rowan!" Zeel called from above him. "These rocks are treacherous, especially in the dark! You cannot climb with half your mind on something else."

Rowan knew she was right. He forced everything from his mind but the task at hand, and climbed on.

* * *

At last they reached the top of the rock pile. The air had suddenly become very much colder. Freezing mist swirled above them, and Rowan shivered as he looked at the patch of grey in the cliff face before him. It was not the place he had seen in his dream. He did not know if he was glad or sorry.

The grey area was far larger and lighter than it had appeared from below, and now they could all see that it was not a hole at all, but part of the cliff wall itself.

Part of the cliff, yet not part. It was quite unlike the dark rock that surrounded it.

Norris pulled off his glove, stretched forward and touched the grey material. A look of surprise crossed his face, and he snatched his hand away.

"I have never felt anything like it!" he exclaimed. "It is rough to touch, but far softer than rock. And it is not cold! It is only a little cooler than my fingers!"

"Norris, how could you be so foolhardy!" scolded Zeel. "It is probably some sort of fungus which has grown over the rock. You have no idea what damage it may do to you!"

Aghast, Norris began wiping his fingers vigorously on his cloak.

Zeel took out her dagger and stuck the point in the grey material. "If it is a fungus, it is very thick," she said, puzzled. She pushed the knife harder, and the shining blade slid forward, sinking to the hilt. Zeel jerked it back, twisting it, and a chunk of the grey material broke loose and fell onto her sleeve. She shook it off hurriedly.

"How strange," she murmured, her eyes alive with curiosity. Again she pushed the knife into the hole that now gaped in the grey, and began scraping energetically.

"Leave it, Zeel," Rowan said, without much hope that she would listen to him. He glanced down, over his shoulder, to where the bukshah milled anxiously, and Shaaran waited.

He could pick out Star among the herd. He could see Shaaran's pale, upturned face. His stomach turned over as he realised that the sky was lightening. Soon it would be dawn.

"Zeel!" he said, turning back towards the cliff. "Zeel, we had better—"

But Zeel was not listening. She had lifted herself up so that she was level with the grey material. Her eye was pressed against the hole she had made. As Rowan watched, she pushed herself back. Her face was expressionless.

"You had better look at this," she said evenly.

Rowan moved forward, but Norris was before him, eagerly

putting an eye to the hole. There was a moment's silence, then Norris, too, pushed himself back.

"What is it?" Rowan exclaimed.

Norris was very pale. His eyes were almost black. His mouth moved, as though he wanted to speak, but no sound came.

His heart thumping like a drum, Rowan flung himself forward and looked through the hole.

At first he could see nothing but a dull blue blur. The cold was so intense that it made his eye ache and water.

So much colder inside than out, he thought. *Yet the grey barrier is not cold in itself.*

It came to him slowly that the grey material was a seal. Like the bukshah skin cloak he wore, it was a powerful barrier against both heat and cold. It stopped one flowing into the other.

The grey material was filling a gap in the rock. It was being used to keep deathly cold in, and less freezing air out.

But why is it here? he thought confusedly. *Who made it?*

Then his eye adjusted to the strange blue light beyond the grey barrier, and he saw …

Saw a huge cavern, so large that the whole village of Rin could have fitted inside it four times over. Saw that the cavern's roof and walls were gleaming with the same white-blue fungus that he remembered from his journey within the Mountain years ago. Saw that the roof was studded with pale blobs that he slowly realised were the blunt, chewed ends of tree roots. Saw the entrances to other chambers, hundreds of other chambers, and tunnels leading upward, threading through the centre of the Mountain.

And saw, with a thrill of horror, ice creepers. Ice creepers in their tens of thousands. Ice creepers squirming through all of this vast space, coiling one on top of the other in a huge, moving mass of white. Ice creepers building, building relentlessly, sliding through the tunnels with working jaws, using the chewed material from their mouths to construct more and yet more of the grey cells that already lined the cavern's icy walls and rose in great towers to its roof.

The hollow core of the Mountain was a nest. A gigantic nest. In every finished cell lay a white worm—a tiny replica of the adults that tended it.

And then, in terror, Rowan saw the creatures nearest to him grow still, turn their blind heads towards him, open their jaws and hurl themselves, hissing, against the spyhole.

20 – Earthbound Thunder

Rowan jerked back with such force that he almost lost his grip and fell. His companions' cries of shock, and Shaaran's thin, echoing screams from below, rang in his ears as he clung by his fingertips to the sharp rock.

"Back!" he choked. "They sensed me! They felt the warmer air. They are——"

In horror he saw tiny cracks running like spiderwebs out from the spyhole. He saw the grey material begin to crumble as the hole grew larger, larger ...

Then he was scrambling downward with Zeel and Norris, scrambling backwards, the toes of his boots scrabbling for footholds, his hands aching, rock scraping rough and cold on his chest and legs.

But already the terrible head of an ice creeper was breaking through the grey barrier. Huge, ferocious, the creeper squirmed out onto the rocks and plunged after them. Freezing breath gushed from its mouth, filling the air before it with icy mist, coating the rocks with a film of white.

"Down!" Shaaran was screaming from below. "Get down!"

Down! Down! Down to where it was warmer. Where there were torches. Where the grove stood not far away.

Rowan slipped, recovered, slipped again. His breath was aching in his throat. Clutching desperately at the rock, he looked up.

The creeper was almost upon them, its blind head striking forward, its ghastly jaws gaping. It was so large that the tip of its tail still lashed the rocks at the top of the pile. And even in his terror Rowan marvelled that the grey barrier in the cliff already gleamed whole and smooth again. The moment the ice creeper had fully emerged, the hole had been sealed behind it.

So quickly. The thought tumbled through Rowan's dazed mind as at last his foot found a cleft that would support it and his perilous clamber downward began again. His stomach churned as he thought of ice creepers rushing to the hole, their blunt heads stabbing at it while their gaping mouths spewed out the sticky, grey material that would harden in moments, repairing the damage, sealing in the precious cold.

It would only take a few. A few among the tens of thousands of these hideous crawling things that infested the Mountain, tunnelling through the rock, chewing the roots of the trees. Building, building ...

Tens of thousands? Rowan heard himself groan aloud. *Hundreds* of thousands! And soon, hundreds of thousands more. The creepers' tunnels honeycombed the Mountain's freezing rock. The cells of their worm-like young packed the Mountain's ice-bound caverns.

In the bitter chill of the Cold Time they would breed unceasingly, and their young would spread outward from the Mountain in their millions. Till every tree in the land had fallen dead, and every living thing had been destroyed.

He slid down a sheet of rock, landing with a thud on a blessedly flat boulder at its base. He took a shuddering breath. It was not so cold here, he was sure of it. He had moved out of the freezing air at the top of the rock pile into the warmer air below.

He dared to glance up, and saw he was right. The ice creeper was slowing. It was swaying, hissing, clearly uncomfortable. But it was still coming. Rowan heard shouting, glanced around rapidly and saw Norris and Zeel just a little below him. They were both looking down, and calling. Norris was stretching out an arm to ... to where a flame bobbed far below them. A flame moving upward!

Rowan realised that Shaaran was climbing towards them, a flaring torch clutched awkwardly in her hand. The girl's pale, terrified face seemed to float in the dimness behind the flame. Below her loomed the bukshah. The beasts were gathered in a tight, unmoving knot at the foot of the rock pile. Shaaran must have had to press her way through them to begin her climb.

And she is so afraid of them! Rowan thought. Then he almost laughed. Afraid of the bukshah, when the rocks were hard, high and jagged, and an ice creeper hissed its rage above!

Yet he knew, none better, that small fears could be as terrifying as great ones. He knew that Shaaran had used all her strength in a desperate effort to take her companions what they needed to survive.

How easily she could slip and fall! In terror Rowan watched the wavering flame. He knew how difficult, how perilous, the climb up the rock slide was. And Shaaran, fragile and afraid, was doing it with one hand, hampered by the torch she was carrying.

"Rowan!" Zeel's sharp cry made him jump. Instinctively he looked up again, to where the ice creeper writhed in a cloud of icy breath. His eyes caught movement above it, and his blood ran cold. The cliff face was almost hidden by billowing white mist. And in the mist hundreds of blue-white shapes were coiling, slithering heavily down from the snow-capped cliff top.

Of course, Rowan thought numbly. How could I have thought that only one creature would defend the nest? The grey door had to be sealed, to keep the warmer air from entering the chamber. But higher up, where it is as cold outside as it is within, there would be no need for sealed doors. And through those openings more creepers are coming, coming in their hundreds ...

He began scrambling downward again. Fear gripped him, but he gritted his teeth, fighting it back. He had to keep his mind on what he was doing, think only of placing his feet surely, of using his hands well. If he slipped and cracked a bone—even twisted his ankle—he was finished.

A hissing sound filled his ears. A draught of freezing mist engulfed him. He gasped and choked, looked up and saw the first ice creeper rearing directly above him, its huge, snake-like body almost hidden in a white cloud.

Somehow it had gained the strength to brave the warmer air on the lower part of the rock pile.

And behind it—were others.

Rowan heard himself cry out in terror. The upper part of the rock pile was covered in billowing mist. The mist was crawling downward, and within it was a mass of hissing blue mouths, blue-white bodies writhing on rocks now gleaming with black ice.

They do not just thrive in the cold. They cause it! The more there are, the colder it grows … The thought pierced his mind like a dagger of ice. And terrible knowledge followed swiftly.

Nowhere is safe from them.

The ice creeper lunged blindly. Rowan jerked back with a yell, letting go of his handhold, slipping, sliding, all caution gone. His heels struck rock, skidded forward and down. The next moment he was trapped to his waist in a cleft between two boulders.

Terrified, struggling to haul himself free, he looked up. The creeper's mouth gaped wide above him. Its slanting teeth glistened as it struck down, reaching for him …

There was a ferocious shout, and Rowan, dazed with fear, saw a streak of fire blaze past his head and plunge straight into the yawning blue-lined jaws. The creeper reared back, the end of a torch still protruding from its mouth. Freezing dark blue mist gushed from its throat. Then it crumpled and fell.

Strong arms hauled Rowan out of the cleft, none too gently. "Make haste!" Norris roared in his ear.

The mass of white, coiling shapes on the rocks above them seemed to surge forward as Rowan and Norris half fell, half scrambled downward. When Rowan looked over his shoulder, he could see Shaaran and Zeel finishing their own panicky descent.

Do not fall! Do not fall! he kept thinking, speaking as much to them as to himself. It was with relief that he saw the two girls sliding down the last steep rock to land safely in the midst of the bukshah herd. Instinctively he and Norris aimed for the same place.

But when at last they reached the bottom they found that the bukshah had moved, and Shaaran and Zeel had moved with them. They were now at the far end of the pile of rocks—the end furthest away from the grove. Zeel and Shaaran were standing strangely still, the bukshah pressed closely around them.

Shouting, Norris and Rowan ran to the place. The bukshah moved aside to let them pass, closing in silently behind them.

"Why are you here?" Norris panted when he reached Shaaran's side. She did not answer, just stared at him with huge, frightened eyes.

He tugged at her arm. "Do you not see? Creepers are coming in their hundreds! We must get back to the grove. It is our only chance!"

But as he turned, dragging Shaaran with him, he found his way blocked by the bukshah. The beasts had moved to enclose the newcomers in their circle, and now stood shoulder to shoulder around them like a solid, shaggy wall. They snuffled and rumbled, nudging Rowan, Zeel and Norris gently with their noses as though eager to touch them. But they did not touch Shaaran, keeping back from her as if they knew she was afraid.

Norris called and pushed at them in vain.

"Rowan!" he shouted, looking wildly around him. "Make them shift!"

Rowan knew there was no hope of that. Star was in the centre of the group, right beside him. Her small black eyes were fixed upon him, and in those eyes he could see her determination. She would not let him pass.

The beasts are wiser than we know ...

Rowan felt the hair rise on the back of his neck.

"They will not move," Zeel said. "They pushed us here, and here they intend us to stay." Her voice was very low. Her light eyes were fixed and intent, as though she was listening to something no one else could hear.

"What is it, Zeel?" Rowan whispered.

"Listen!" she replied.

Rowan listened. And he heard ... nothing. Nothing but the beating of his own heart, Norris's heavy breathing, the slight scraping of the bukshah hoofs on the rocky ground.

The moaning wind had dropped. There was an eerie stillness, as though the Mountain was holding its breath. The silence seemed to press upon Rowan's ears and his eyes. His teeth began to ache. His skin prickled as though a million ants were scurrying among the hairs of his legs and arms.

He forced himself to look up. The creepers on the rock pile had halted. Amid the swirling mist, their blunt heads waved uncertainly.

"What—?" Norris began, and choked, as his voice dried in his throat.

The light had changed. The sullen sky was stained with red. It was dawn.

High, high above them, in its ice cave on the peak, the Dragon roared.

And there came, from deep within the Mountain, a long, low growl like the rumbling of thunder.

The air shimmered before Rowan's eyes. The earth seemed to tremble beneath him.

Then the rocks began to fall. Slowly, like a child's castle made of wooden blocks, a castle tipped by a careless finger, the rocks toppled, crashing down upon one another, and upon the ice creepers thrashing helplessly in their path.

Faster the rocks tumbled, as the Mountain quaked beneath them. Faster and faster they thundered down, crashing upon the place where only minutes ago the companions had stood, spinning over the edge of the drop into the Pit of Unrin, carrying the smashed and ruined bodies of the ice creepers with them.

Rowan fell to his knees, pressing his head against Star's shaggy side, hiding his eyes from the sight of the world coming apart around him, trying to shield his ears from the growling thunder.

But there was no escape from the sound. It was everywhere. Star's body was trembling with it. The earth was vibrating with it. It filled the air he breathed.

The sound! Rowan had never heard such a sound. Not from the Dragon of the Mountain. Not from the devil trees of Unrin. Not from the Great Serpent of Maris. The roar of the Mountain was loud and terrible, like a bellow of burning rage. And as Rowan cowered beneath it, it rose and rose until there was the shrieking, grating groan of splitting rock. Then a gale of hot breath swept over him, throwing him flat to the ground.

21 — The Stairway

owan's head was aching. His ears were ringing. Star's nose roughly nudged his cheek. Perhaps she had nudged it more gently many times before, trying to wake him. But now she could wait no longer. He could hear her rumbling anxiously, pawing the ground.

He opened his eyes. They watered and burned. Star loomed above him, a dark shape against the hazy sky. The terrible dawn had faded. It was daylight.

Slowly Rowan became aware of his surroundings.

Zeel, Norris and Shaaran were stirring beside him. The other bukshah still surrounded them all, still formed that vast, living grey wall that had shielded them from the worst of the Mountain's fury. But the wall was ragged and swaying now, and the air was filled with rumbling and snorting. The herd was impatient to be gone.

It is time, Rowan thought. He felt nothing. His mind was numb.

He clambered to his feet, trying to keep his swimming head steady, clinging to Star's mane for support. Her wool felt harsh under his fingers. Dimly he remembered that it had been so ever since it was soaked in the water of the grove spring. Then the thought drifted away.

Slowly, patiently, Star led him through the restless herd. He stumbled beside her, rubbing his streaming eyes. Dazed, he moved into the open, and saw what she had brought him to see.

The jagged stones that had been heaped against the cliff face were gone, tumbled away as if by a giant hand. Now Rowan could see that the cliff and the slope were not separate, but formed from one vast sheet of gleaming rock.

The stairway of his dream began where the rock started to rise steeply. He stared at it blankly through a haze of steam and tears. The stairway was shining, lit by a strange, yellow radiance that was not the sun.

He raised his eyes. Beside the stairway, from a great split in the rock about halfway up, flowed a river of gold.

The river of gold flowed slowly out of the rock. Steaming, rich and thick as treacle, it ran beside the stairway, down to the gentler slope where once the bukshah had milled and pawed the ground. And there it spread and moved on, in a broad, gleaming golden band, to ooze over the edge of the drop.

I am dreaming, Rowan told himself. But he knew he was not.

The breaking heart will clear the way ...

The heart of the Mountain had burst through its shell of rock, revealing its secret. And now the molten gold was running, running like blood, down the slope and into the Pit of Unrin.

Rowan became aware that Zeel, Norris and Shaaran were standing behind him, seeing what he was seeing. He could feel their presence. He could hear their rapid breathing. But none of them said a word.

He felt Star pull gently away from him, felt his hand fall to his side like a dead thing. He saw Star lumbering towards the stairway, over ground spattered with cooling splashes and puddles of gold, and the other bukshah following, one by one.

And as the beasts began to climb, Rowan's eyes cleared and he saw without surprise that they looked very much as they had looked in his dream, though far thinner and more wasted.

Their heads were held high. Their horns were white and razor sharp. Their shaggy coats were thick and gleaming. Their hoofs shone bright with gold, and where they trod they left golden prints behind them.

We must follow the beasts ...

Rowan moved towards the stair, and he also began to climb. He knew his companions were following, but he did not turn to look at them. He just moved up, one step at a time, while beside him liquid gold ran down, ran like steaming blood from the Mountain's heart, draining from the broken rock.

It was a dream that was not a dream. A dream of heat he could not feel. Of a plan he could not see. Of rags and wisps of memories his mind could not grasp. Of dread and suffering, yearning and regret, silence and death.

Only when he had passed the place where the golden river began did he look up. And there, not far below the patch of grey that marked the ice creepers' den, was the yawning mouth of his dream.

It was the entrance to a cavern, shadowed and ghastly, wreathed in billowing steam. A broad ledge of scarred rock jutted out below it, like a vast, deformed chin.

We climbed over it all unknowing, Rowan thought dimly. He looked from side to side, at the smooth, hard skin of the mountain-side. Beneath us now beats the Mountain's heart, he thought. Its heat, smothered beneath the rocks, slowed the ice creepers and saved us. Saved us ... for another purpose.

For this.

He turned his eyes upward again. He was nearly at the top of the stairway. Through the wafting steam he saw that the mouth in the rock was not quite the same as the bare, gaping maw of his dream. Three tall, jagged stones remained stuck in its base, jutting upward like crooked black teeth.

For the first time since he had set foot on the stairs, Rowan shuddered in dread.

Four must make their sacrifice ...

Rowan turned and looked behind him. Zeel met his eyes calmly. "So. We have arrived," she said.

Behind her, almost hidden by her broad shoulders, was Shaaran, breathless and wide-eyed, the battered box of silks in her arms.

And behind Shaaran towered Norris, his face steadfast.

High above them, snow heaped the cliff top and the grey patch sealed the cliff face, protecting the freezing cold within. Ahead, steam billowed from golden shadow.

In the realm twixt fire and ice ...

The bukshah were crowded on the pitted ledge. They were bellowing and pawing the ground. Some were pushing at the rocks.

They want to enter the cavern, but they cannot, Rowan thought. The spaces between the teeth—the rocks—are too narrow.

He felt his heart lift a little. Whatever was ahead, the bukshah, at least, were to be spared it. Their task was over.

The companions reached the ledge and began to push their way through the bukshah. Again the beasts snuffled and nudged eagerly at Rowan, Zeel and Norris, but let Shaaran pass by with nothing but a glance.

"They do not like me," Shaaran said.

"They sense your fear of them," Rowan answered absent-mindedly. Then he grimaced. If the smell of fear repelled the bukshah, why did they press so closely around him? His body was trembling with fear. His skin was prickling with it. He felt that terror must be radiating from him like heat.

He led the way to the opening. It was damp and gleaming. Steam drifted within it, faintly tinged with gold.

Star was in the centre of the line of beasts trying to force an entrance. She had set her shoulder against the middle rock, and was pushing, as she would push to flatten a fence. She had succeeded in moving it sideways a little. But thin as the bukshah were, the space created was still too narrow for them.

And never would she be able to push it inward. The cavern was a high step above the ledge. The rocks, all three of them, were jammed against the step.

"You cannot do it, Star," Rowan said quietly, putting his hand to her mane. "Save your strength."

Star raised her heavy head to look at him. Her eyes seemed filled with angry sadness.

"You and the herd have brought us here, and that is enough," Rowan told her, his throat tightening. "Now you must leave us to do—whatever must be done."

Star pawed the ground, made a deep, groaning sound and again turned to push fruitlessly at the rock.

"No! Go back, Star!" Rowan urged, tugging at her wool, desperate to make her understand. "Take the herd back to the grove now, and wait. There is a little food in the grove, and there is water, and safety from the cold and the creepers. And perhaps ... after a time ... the snows will melt and you can return to the valley."

If we do what we must, he thought. If we have the strength to do what we must.

He rubbed his cheek against Star's mane, feeling its unfamiliar roughness against his skin. Then he pushed gently past her, and slipped between the rocks.

The air was filled with shadowy golden mist. He could see little through the haze.

He raised his hand, found he could touch the roof with ease, and thought of the ice creepers coiling in their freezing nest not far above his head. Zeel, Shaaran and Norris came through the rock barrier behind him, crowding him, and he moved forward.

The bukshah had begun to bellow again, Star loudest of all. Their calls echoed weirdly, echoed on and on, till the hazy air seemed thick with mournful sound.

"It is lighter ahead," Zeel breathed behind him.

Rowan looked, and saw it was true. The cave entrance was well behind them now, but instead of becoming dimmer, the strange light was strengthening. They were walking towards a yellow glow that grew brighter with every step.

And the steam was growing less. It was only a thin veil now. The walls of the tunnel through which they moved were clearly visible. The roof hung low and glistening above their heads.

With a shock of recognition, Rowan saw cloaked figures walking not far ahead, walking in silence and in single file, walking in dread and despair while the distant bellows of the bukshah echoed faintly around them.

All is lost ... We are lost ... There is no escape ...

The figures shimmered and disappeared. Rowan felt his breath coming faster. The yellow glow was growing. Now he could see that where it began the tunnel broadened, opening into a much larger space. He knew that there they would find the source of the light, the end of the journey.

His legs were trembling. With part of his mind—that part that was still his own—he longed to stop, to throw himself against the glossy tunnel walls, to cling to them, hold himself back. But it was too late for that. He was being drawn onward by something more powerful than himself.

Instead of slowing, he found himself moving faster. And all at once dim golden light was all around him, and tremendous heat enfolded him, and he saw what he had come so far to see.

The roof of the cavern was low, and mottled black and grey. The black walls were veined with sparkling gold, lit, like the hazy air, by a radiance that streamed upward from a round hole in the centre of the smooth, gold-veined floor.

There was nothing else. Nothing but heat, and shadows in the corners, and the echoes of the bukshah mourning.

Like one in a trance, Rowan moved to the edge of the hole. Then he looked down—down into a pit so deep that his mind reeled. Down into the unimaginable heat, the terrible glare, of burning, molten gold.

Sick with dizziness, he gazed into the heart of the Mountain and could not look away. His head swam. He knew he had stopped breathing.

The hunger will not be denied,
The hunger must be satisfied ...

"Come away, Rowan. Come away from the edge."

Rowan heard Shaaran's voice, but he could not understand the words. Other voices were claiming his attention. Voices from his memory.

Neel's voice:

We have offended the Mountain, and now the Mountain has turned against us.

Norris's voice:

If the people of the Valley of Gold had not died out ... they could have told us how they made peace with the Mountain, and ended the first Cold Time.

Zeel's voice:

That knowledge is lost ... The Valley people did not share it ... Perhaps they were too proud. Or ashamed ...

"Ashamed," Rowan murmured. "Ashamed of what they had to do, to make amends. But our people will never know. Lann will not tell them, and I hope they will never guess."

The heart of the Mountain growled, waiting.

"And is this what must be done?" a steady voice asked. "If it is, I am ready."

22 – The Hunger

Rowan turned. Zeel was standing beside him at the edge of the drop. She took his hand and met his gaze proudly. He saw her strength and grace, Zebak and Traveller combined, and his heart seemed to break within him.

"I am ready," she said again.

Norris stepped forward, and took Zeel's other hand. "I, too," he said. "I have followed you this far, Rowan, and if I must follow you down into the depths, and into eternity, I will."

Rowan looked at him, saw his courage and his open, honest face, and again his heart twisted in pain.

Only Shaaran had not moved forward. Only Shaaran had not spoken. But now she did speak, and when she did, her voice was trembling, but firm.

"I do not believe it," Shaaran said.

"Shaaran—" Norris began. But Shaaran shook her head.

"The Mountain is a thing of rock and earth," she said. "It is mysterious. It guards many wonders. But it requires only that we respect it. It does not want our love, or loyalty, or fear—or sacrifice. It does not need them. It needs—it must need—something else."

Rowan lifted his head, as if waking from a dream. The medallion was throbbing at his throat. He turned. Shaaran was standing back from the drop. Tears were streaming down her cheeks.

One to weep ...

"You are afraid, Shaaran," Zeel said softly.

"Of course I am afraid," Shaaran flashed back. "Anyone of sense would be afraid! But that is not why I refuse to join you in this madness. I refuse because you are wrong! Wrong!"

They stared at her blankly.

She stamped her foot. "Do you not have minds as well as hearts?"

she demanded. "How can you think that throwing yourselves into the Mountain's boiling heart will cause one icicle to melt in Rin, or stop one ice creeper from being born, or make a single flower bloom?"

Rowan had turned around completely now. He took a step away from the pit.

A low growl came from deep below them. The rock trembled beneath their feet.

"We must not wait," Zeel said faintly. "The anger is growing. There is too much heat. Too much—"

"Rowan, the medallion!" Shaaran urged. "Use it!"

"Each of us has asked a question," Rowan said. "We have had four answers. I fear ... there will be no more."

But still he lifted his hand to the burning metal at his throat. It seemed to writhe under his fingers, as though it was alive. He felt words rising within him. He opened his dry lips, and spoke. The words came easily, and he heard them without surprise, for they were very familiar.

"The beasts are wiser than we know
And where they lead, four souls must go.
One to weep and one to fight,
One to dream and one for flight.
Four must make their sacrifice.
In the realm twixt fire and ice
The hunger will not be denied,
The hunger must be satisfied.
And in that blast of fiery breath
The quest unites both life and death."

He stood quietly as the words died away. He felt very tired, but that was all.

"So ..." Zeel murmured.

"Four must make their sacrifice," said Norris dully. "Here, in the realm between fire and ice. There can be no mistake."

But Rowan was listening again to a voice in his mind. Sheba's voice, saying the rhyme. He had just repeated it in exactly the same way. Every word, every pause. And ...

"The line that ends in 'sacrifice', and the line that ends in 'fire and ice' rhyme with one another, but there is a pause—a stop—between them," he said slowly. "They may be quite separate. I see it now, though I did not see it before. The line about sacrifice may be linked to the lines about the four souls that come before it. The line about fire and ice may be linked to the next lines, the lines about hunger. The rhyme reads quite differently then."

"Yes," Zeel said, after a moment's thought. "But it does not really change anything. The four sacrifices still have to be made."

"Do they?" Rowan said. "Or have they been made already? Shaaran abandoned the silks to save me in the vale of horrors. Norris gave himself up as lost, to save us from the ice creeper at the cave. You, Zeel, sacrificed your kite, and nearly your life, to save Norris. And I—" He smiled wryly. "I sacrificed the most precious thing I had—your friendship and trust—to try to make you leave me, and save yourselves."

"Yes," Shaaran breathed. "We all made sacrifices to reach this place. And now we are here. There is something we must do. Before—" She shuddered as the Mountain growled beneath their feet.

Before the rock bursts again, Rowan thought. Before the stairway falls, and the bukshah die. Before this cavern becomes our tomb.

"It is ... about the hunger," Norris mumbled. "The hunger ..."

The words hung heavy between them.

In the realm twixt fire and ice
The hunger cannot be denied,
The hunger must be satisfied ...

Something flickered at the edge of Rowan's vision. He turned his head and saw movement in a shadowy corner just behind Shaaran. He saw the stirring of a bukshah skin cloak on the floor, the feeble movement of a delicate hand as it curved protectively around a long wooden box. He saw another hand, a stronger hand, writing, and a bent head gleaming dark in the golden light. He felt the thoughts, the words scrawled upon the page ...

You must know how it was, when you return, and so I write these words ...

And he saw the picture the mind was remembering. A picture

painted on silk. A long line of people, trekking away over snow on a black, burned path. Ice creepers twisting from the mist of the Mountain. Bukshah standing together below, the only dark marks in an unbroken sweep of white.

The only dark marks ...

The beasts are wiser than we know ...

Rowan drew a sharp breath. The moving hand stilled, a face looked up.

It was his own face. And in it he read the end of hope, the end of fear, the acceptance of what must be. The eyes stared at him blankly for a moment, then the mouth seemed to curve in the shadow of a smile, and the head bent over the paper once more.

Rowan turned away quickly, his heart thudding in his chest, his mind grappling with the astounding idea that had come to him. He saw that his companions were looking at him in fascinated terror, their eyes filled with questions they feared to ask. He had always dreaded the day they would look at him like that. But it no longer seemed important.

"What did you see?" Norris blurted out, unable to contain himself. "You were staring—at nothing! Was it our future? Was it, Rowan?"

Rowan did not answer. He did not even hear. He was listening to the echoes. To the echoes of bellowing that had never stopped—the calls of the starving bukshah, still milling at the cavern entrance.

The bukshah.

The bukshah, who had lived and died in the shadow of the Mountain for as long as the Travellers had wandered the land, and longer. The great, wise beasts the companions had saved from death in the grove. The beasts who had led them to this place. The beasts who had snuffled and nudged eagerly at him, and at Zeel and Norris, but ignored Shaaran. The beasts with their newly sharpened horns, their gilded hoofs, their glossy coats hanging thick over thin, starved bodies ...

Hunger ...

Rowan looked around the cavern. Smooth black floor, veined with gold. Shadowed corners. Gold-veined black walls. Heat and light streaming upward from a well of fire to a low roof that was mottled black and grey.

Mottled grey ... though the walls and floor were black.

He lifted his hand, and touched the roof.

And in that blast of fiery breath ...

Rowan whirled around and grasped Norris's arm. "Help me!" he gasped.

And he ran, with Norris, Zeel and Shaaran pounding after him, their confused questions ringing in his ears.

Back through the mist they raced, the bellowing echoes growing louder, louder, white light taking the place of gold. Till there before them were the jagged rocks, the bukshah heaving vainly against them.

Star was still at the forefront of the herd. She raised her weary head.

"Back, Star! Back!" Rowan shouted.

Star saw him set his shoulder against the middle rock, with Norris beside him, and this time she obeyed. She backed away, and the other bukshah backed with her, till the path before the rock was clear.

Then Norris heaved, with all his great strength, and Rowan, Zeel and Shaaran added their weight to his. And the great rock, loosened by the bukshah long before, rocked on its base and rolled slowly away from the entrance.

The bukshah surged forward, Star at their head. The companions shrank back, flattening themselves against the side of the entrance. In frantic haste, the beasts pressed one by one through the gap in the rocks, half leaping up the shallow step into the tunnel, then breaking into a lumbering gallop.

The sound of their pounding hoofs was like thunder, the mist swirled like storm clouds. Rowan, Zeel, Norris and Shaaran ran after them as they galloped towards the cavern.

"What are we doing?" roared Norris.

"We are doing what we should have done in the first place," Rowan roared back. "We are following the beasts. All along, our part has been only to make sure they reached the cavern. It is *they* who are needed there, not us!"

"Why?" Shaaran shrieked. "What are they going to do?"

But Rowan did not have to answer her, for as she spoke they reached the cavern, and she saw it for herself.

She saw the great beasts tossing their heads, and their newly sharpened horns, the horns of which she had always been so afraid, doing what they were made to do. She saw the horns sinking deep into the pale patches that dotted the cavern roof, digging out great chunks of thick, stringy grey. She saw the bukshah gulping down the grey chunks ravenously, as if they were the sweetest food on earth, then raising their heads to tear out more.

The hunger must be satisfied ...

"This is the material the ice creepers use to seal their nest!" shouted Norris, staring panic-stricken at the crumbs of grey lying on the floor, and the shower of larger pieces falling like enormous hailstones from the roof. "The nest is directly above us—and the cavern roof is full of blocked holes! As full of holes as a sieve! Rowan, stop the beasts! They will dig straight through to the nest! They will be the death of us!"

"They will be our salvation," Rowan said.

But, sure as he was, even he held his breath as Star, with a mighty twist of her horns, ripped the last layer of grey from the huge hole above her head.

For an instant the hole was nothing but black rock encircling blue-white light. Then a hissing white horror was filling the gap from above, thrusting through it, needle-sharp teeth bared, blue throat gaping.

Shaaran screamed and screamed again. But the echo had not even begun when dark blue mist belched from the hissing mouth, the blue throat seemed to shrivel, and the ice creeper fell back, out of sight.

"It is the heat!" Rowan shouted over the noise of the bukshah and the echoes. "The creepers cannot bear it! It is death to them!"

And he turned back to watch as one by one more holes were cleared, and the heat of the Mountain's burning heart, no longer trapped within the cavern, gusted upward in a fiery blast to warm the hidden realms that the ice creepers had for so long, and with so much labour, made their own.

23 – Life and Death

In time the bukshah's frenzy slowed, and the process of digging out the strange food they knew would see them through the hardest winter settled into a steady, contented rhythm. Grey fragments littered the floor. Many holes were still blocked, but many others had been wholly or partly opened, and any ice creeper that had ventured near them had died in the hot air that gusted from below.

"So our quest has united life and death indeed," Norris said with satisfaction. "Death to the ice creepers, life to us."

"The ice creepers are not all dead," Zeel said, looking at him with amusement. "The great nest is destroyed, certainly, and the creepers who were marching downward, spreading the cold that was to their liking, are no more. But many others must still dwell in the high places of the Mountain, where the snow never melts."

She glanced up at the gaping holes in the cavern roof. "And as the heat continues to rise, and so grows less in here, they will be back, risking their lives to seal the holes again. It is in their nature to try to extend their territory."

The companions were sitting out of the way of the bukshah, against the entrance wall. Already it seemed cooler in the cavern, though they all knew by now that the heat was far greater than they could feel.

"I think the spring in the grove left a layer on our skin and clothes that protects us from the heat," Rowan said. "The bukshah's coats also."

"The passage to the vale of horrors sharpened their horns so that they would be ready to dig their food from the cavern roof." Shaaran shook her head in wonder. "And the water of the spring protected them from the heat that was to come. It is as though they were guided to follow the path they took."

"They *were* guided, I am sure of it," Rowan said. "Not by magic, but by ancient instinct. From the earliest days, the bukshah herd must have come to the cavern to feed in the winter. So every year the cavern roof was cleared, the ice creepers retreated, and the balance was kept."

"Then how did the first Cold Time come?" asked Norris. "Or was it just a legend after all?"

"Oh, no," said Rowan soberly. "It really happened, I am sure. I think that it happened because the people of the Valley of Gold decided to build fences, to keep the bukshah confined all year round."

"But why?" Zeel demanded. "Why would they do such a thing? They must have known what the bukshah did in the cavern! The Mountain was not forbidden to them, as it was to the Travellers."

Rowan sighed. "I suspect, though we can never be sure, that the people had discovered that the hotter the cavern became, and the more the pressure below increased, the more swiftly their secret river of gold flowed. They thought only of the beauty and power of the gold. They forgot that the Mountain had needs as well."

"And so the first Cold Time came," Zeel muttered. "The fools! At last they realised what they had done, and corrected it. But they would not tell the Travellers how. No wonder! No wonder they were ashamed."

Rowan sighed. "I am ashamed also, for not seeing that there must have been a reason why the bukshah have always tried to stray in winter. The bukshah are wise, not stupid. I knew that, yet I did not try to understand them. Instead, like all the keepers of the bukshah before me, I coaxed them back to their field with the food kept to feed them through the cold months. Often I wondered how they had survived before we came to the valley. Now I know."

Zeel frowned. "But when the Valley of Gold was destroyed at last, the stairway, and this cavern, were buried in the landslide caused by the devil trees. The bukshah could not have come here to feed after that."

"No," said Rowan. "Through all those years they must have turned away disappointed and returned home with only the leaves from the grove to fill their bellies. Then we came to the valley, built fences as the people of the Valley of Gold had once done, and began to feed the beasts in winter. So though their instinct to go to the Mountain remained, the urgent need for food was not there, and they were content to keep away."

"And all the while, little by little, the ice creepers' seals were growing thicker in the cavern roof, and the Mountain was becoming colder," said Zeel. "And the creepers bred more and more, creating more cold, and the winters grew longer and more terrible year by year."

Despite the heat, Shaaran drew her cloak more closely around her.

"So if the people of Rin had not settled in the valley and begun feeding the bukshah in winter, the herd would have died out!" exclaimed Norris.

"At last the whole land would have perished." Zeel's voice was sombre. "As it is, the bukshah survived, to lead us here, and show us what had to be done." She glanced at Rowan thoughtfully. "It was fortunate chance, it seems, that your people came, with their fences and crops and storehouses, and their ability to survive the cold in the centre."

Rowan wondered. Fortunate chance? Or something else?

"Rowan, what did you see, just before you ran to let the bukshah into the cavern?" Norris asked abruptly. "You would not tell us before. Will you tell us now? *Did* you see the future? Did you see—all this?" He waved his hand at the feeding bukshah.

Rowan shook his head, and slowly climbed to his feet. He knew it was time. Time to solve the last mystery. Time to share what he thought he knew. He had been unable to speak of it while urgent action was needed, and even after that he had kept silence, hugging the precious secret to himself, as if airing it might injure or destroy it.

If there is no proof, no trace, it will only be my word, he thought. The word of a dreamer, easily put aside and explained away. If there is nothing left, how can I bear it?

But with his companions following closely behind him, he began to thread his way through the bukshah, making his way to the shadowy corner where he had seen the last vision.

The corner lay in darkness, keeping its secrets.

He stopped a little way from it, and tried to light a torch, but his hands were trembling so much that he could not manage it. Glancing at him curiously, Zeel took the torch from him, and lit it herself.

The flame flared up. They approached the corner.

And there, in a nest of dusty bones, lay a long, wooden box.

"Why, Shaaran!" exclaimed Norris. "You have left the silks ..."

But his voice trailed off as he saw that Shaaran still clutched in her arms the box she had carried all the way from Rin.

Rowan knelt before the tangled bones, and put his hands upon the box. The wood was iron-hard, preserved by the steady, dry heat of the cavern. The catch fell away from the lid as he opened it.

What he saw inside the box made his heart pound. It was a shallow tray holding a clutter of tiny glass jars, in every colour of the rainbow. And, lying on top of the jars, a scrap of parchment.

He lifted the parchment out. It was covered in weak, straggling writing.

He read the words aloud.

My Friends,

You must know how it was, when you return, and so I write these words. Fliss is too weak to do more.

Bron escaped the Zebak attack, and ran back to warn us. He arrived in two days, despite his injuries. Following the plan, Bron, Fliss and I took the treasure, left plentiful food for the horses, and followed the beasts on their secret way from the Valley of the Bukshah into Mountain Heart. Once we were safe here, we kept good watch. Every day we expected you to return, either driven by Zebak whips or blessedly free, but you did not come ...

Rowan's voice faltered.

"What is this?" breathed Norris hoarsely. "I do not understand. Who—?"

"Be still, Norris!" Zeel hissed, her face intent.

Rowan swallowed the lump in his throat, and read on.

At the end of winter the bukshah left Mountain Heart, but we remained. From afar we saw the new crop bloom in our valley, and sorrowed that we alone could see its beauty.

Again Rowan stopped. This was almost too much for him to bear. He could guess what that "new crop" was—sweet-smelling bushes loaded with fruit, bushes grown from berries brought down from the Mountain. The unknown writer had little realised what evil was disguised in that beauty, had not known that from the pretty little bushes foul, flesh-eating trees would grow.

His companions were waiting, breathless. He forced himself to continue.

A little time afterwards we saw that some dread illness had befallen the horses and the birds, for they lay still in the streets. Fearing a Zebak plot to tempt us out of hiding, we retreated into the cavern. A few nights later there was a fearful thundering. The ground shook, and when we arose, we found that the gate was dark and sealed by rock.

"They were in here when the devil trees erupted from the earth and caused the landslide," Zeel said grimly. "They were trapped." She looked down at the pathetic pile of bones, and her fists clenched.

Rowan took a deep breath, and read on.

Many weeks have passed since then. Bron has laboured mightily to free us, but even his great strength cannot move the barrier. Our food and water are long gone. We are dying. But the treasure is safe, and we are together. This comforts us.

We grieve for you, our friends, but our hearts tell us that some day you will find a way to return, for the land will call to you and you will hear. And when you return you will open Mountain Heart once more so that the bukshah can enter as they must. Then you will find us, and lay us at last in the good earth, beneath the open sky, where we long to be.

We leave with you our blessings.

Evan of the Bukshah

"Evan of the Bukshah," Zeel breathed. She had tears in her eyes. The first tears that Rowan had ever seen her shed.

He put down the parchment. Then he put his hand back into the box and took out the tray that held the tiny jars, laying it carefully aside. There was a deep cavity beneath the tray. It was filled with rolls of silk.

With a cry, Shaaran threw herself down and with trembling hands reached into the box and took out the roll that lay at the top. Tenderly she unrolled it.

Blue, white and grey. A long line of people trekking across white snow, following a burned black path ...

"It is the same!" Norris whispered, his face filled with fear. "It is the silk *you* painted, Shaaran."

"No," said Shaaran quietly. "It is far, far older than that. See the faded colours? And ..."

Her slender finger pointed to the bukshah standing in the snow. "See, Norris? My painting showed the bukshah fenced. But the people of the Valley of Gold had torn down their fences long before this was painted, leaving the bukshah free to roam. The keeper of the silks—Fliss—painted only the truth, as we are bound to do. Ah ... the work is beyond compare!"

And as Norris, Zeel and Rowan watched in awe, Shaaran unrolled another silk, and another, and another. The silks were frail as gossamer, but the colours still lived, and the shapes still spoke.

The Wise Woman leading her people through the early snows to battle on the coast. The Zebak army attacking on the plains, fierce and unexpected. One injured man, eerily resembling Norris, escaping and staggering away. The same man, leaning on a long stick, telling the news to two figures in a valley paradise where paths were paved with gems, miniature horses wandered, and a golden owl with emerald eyes watched beside every door. Three figures, wearing furred cloaks, following a bukshah herd up steep stone steps towards the mouth of a great cavern ...

"The people of the Valley of Gold *did* receive the Travellers' call for help," Zeel said in wonder. "They set out for the coast with the messengers, leaving only the keeper of the bukshah and the keeper of the silks behind. But on the journey they were attacked by the Zebak."

"They were captured, marched to the coast, loaded into ships and taken away into slavery across the sea," Rowan murmured.

Zeel shook her head. "And the Maris and the Travellers were in hiding, and never knew. No one knew. Until now."

"But—" Norris's eyes were very wide. "But that means that— that—"

"It means that the people of the Valley of Gold were our ancestors," Shaaran whispered, unable to take her eyes from the silks. "It means that this land is not new to us at all. It is our place. It has been all along."

"A rich, varied people, big and small, strong and gentle, disappeared," said Zeel, trying to take it in. "Centuries later a band of tall, sober warrior slaves with no memory of their past arrived on the Maris shore. How could anyone think they were one and the same?"

"I think Ogden does," said Rowan. "Or suspects, at least. He knows more tales of the Valley of Gold than anyone alive. I would say that one of the things he knows is that history there was kept on painted strips of silk."

And as Zeel and Norris and Shaaran bent once more over the ancient treasures Shaaran was unrolling one by one, Rowan picked up the scrap of parchment and touched the scrawled words gently.

"We have returned, Evan of the Bukshah," he said softly. "We found a way. Just as you knew we would."

24 – Meetings

And so it was that Rowan, Zeel, Shaaran and Norris left the bukshah to their feast and came down from the Mountain, carrying far more than they had carried when they began their journey.

They carried two boxes of silks instead of one. They carried a knowledge that filled their hearts to bursting. And they carried the bones of the three who had perished in the cavern—Bron the warrior, Fliss the keeper of the silks, and Evan, keeper of the bukshah.

"They looked so like us, our ancestors?" Shaaran asked Rowan quietly, as they walked together.

"Very like," he said. "So like, that I thought I was seeing our future. But we were only treading in their footsteps."

"And what of the shadow people? The starving ones you saw outside the cave? Were they ...?"

Rowan shivered under the sunlight. "I think they were far, far older," he said reluctantly. "I think they were some of our people who lived through the first Cold Time." Again he shivered. The memory of those familiar, tortured faces haunted him still.

Shaaran bit her lip, and for a long time they walked in silence. Then, at last, she spoke again. "Rowan, Sheba told you that only you could lead the quest. Have you thought why that was?"

Rowan nodded. "Because I am the keeper of the bukshah, and love and trust the beasts as they love and trust me. Because I am a dreamer, and the medallion would accept me. Because I have had— much practice in thinking of new ways to solve problems ..."

He swallowed. "And because ... because you, Norris and Zeel were my friends, and would follow me," he added in a low voice. "For you were all needed too, if the quest was to succeed."

Shaaran bowed her head. "I was wondering," she said, "if part of the reason Norris and I were called was that we were like the other two. The two long ago. Just as you were like Evan."

"Yes." Rowan hesitated. "And perhaps it was also because you and Norris represented the two halves of the people of Rin. And I—was the bridge between you."

"And I?" asked Zeel dryly, moving up beside them. "What was my part?"

"You stood for the Travellers, the Maris and perhaps the Zebak too," said Rowan. "You were the witness."

* * *

The way was long, and full of hardship, but the companions were filled with happiness. For all around them the snow was melting and the land was awakening after the long, cold winter.

And as they reached the place where the water flowed down to Rin from the Mountain top, they came upon three figures kneeling to fill their flasks at the pool.

Jonn. Jiller. Allun.

Rowan stared at them in disbelief.

The three at the pool looked up, and their faces broke into smiles of pure joy. With a cry, Jiller flew into Rowan's arms. Allun and Jonn followed quickly, and soon the four companions were all part of a joyous circle.

"How can you be here?" Rowan exclaimed. "How could you know that it was safe to return?"

"We did not," said Allun cheerfully. "Quite the reverse. We thought we were tramping into the jaws of death, in fact."

"When Allun told us he had seen Zeel overhead, speeding to Rin, we feared something new and very grave had happened," Jonn said. "We could not go on. We had to return."

"Marlie and Annad too," Jiller said. "They are fretting back at the village, with Lann and Bronden. We came to try to find you—to help if we could. Though now it seems there is no need."

"Lann? Bronden?" asked Rowan eagerly. "Are they—?"

"Both are well," Allun said. "Bronden is still very weak, but recovering—though when she finds out that Lann made bonfires with the village's whole supply of furniture, she may have a relapse. There is a busy time for her ahead."

Rowan glanced at Zeel. "Old, useless wood?" he murmured. Zeel shrugged. Tables and chairs meant nothing to her.

"And by the way, Rowan," Allun went on. "Sheba says to tell you that the medallion she gave you may look like base metal, but it is made of pure gold, and she expects it back the moment she returns. She says that you could not take her place in a thousand years, whatever you may think."

"I am glad to hear it," Rowan said with feeling.

"How can you waste time with nonsense about furniture and Sheba, Allun!" scolded Jiller. "The Cold Time is ending! We can see the proof all around us! Somehow these brave young ones have saved us all. But how? How?"

She turned to Rowan, her tear-stained cheeks flushed with happiness and pride. "Tell us!" she begged. "What happened on the Mountain? What did you discover that has changed so much, so quickly? Where are the bukshah?"

Rowan's heart was too full for him to speak. And, in any case, he hardly knew where to begin.

"They will tell us all in their own time, no doubt," Jonn said calmly, putting his hand on Rowan's shoulder. "We already know the most important things. These four souls are safe. The long winter has ended. And the people can come home."

Rowan exchanged glances with Norris, Shaaran and Zeel. He thought of all they had to tell. He thought of the sad, small bundle he carried, and of the place where he would bury it, with honour, under the great tree in Rin. He thought of the suffering, grief, mistakes and waste of centuries.

Then he thought of the future, and he smiled.

"Yes," he said. "At last, the people truly can come home."